DEADLY LOVE

Two floors above the parlor, on the top floor of the inn, in an ancient, upholstered rocking chair, he sits and rocks and waits.

Sighing, he flips to the first page of the photo album in his lap. It's a special album, one that only has room for a single eight-by-ten picture on each page.

A wedding album, actually—bound in white leather, its cover stamped in gold with the words, "Our Wedding Memories."

This first page belongs to Sandy. There's an empty slot, waiting for the photograph he'll place there.

He has already labeled the oval opening with an ivory place card that has a raised rectangular border, the kind of card you find on the tables at a wedding reception.

On it, he has meticulously lettered her name in calligraphy, using a special pen.

And his own blood.

It's really quite lovely, he decides, studying the lettering on the card below the empty photo slot. Over the past few months, the blood has faded to a soft, brownish-maroon color that complements the rich ivory surface of the place card. Very elegant.

But this card isn't permanent, of course.

He'll replace it, very soon, with an exact replica.

Except that this time, the blood he'll use to letter Sandy Cavelli's name will be her own . . .

Books by Wendy Corsi Staub

DEARLY BELOVED

FADE TO BLACK

ALL THE WAY HOME

THE LAST TO KNOW

IN THE BLINK OF AN EYE

SHE LOVES ME NOT

Published by Pinnacle Books

WENDY CORSI STAUB

DEARLY BELOVED

PINNACLE BOOKS
Kensington Publishing Corp.
http://www.kensingtonbooks.com

For my terrific editor, John Scognamiglio
with love and gratitude

And for my own dearly beloved:
My husband Mark
and our newborn son, Morgan James
(whose unexpected arrival interrupted
the writing of this book . . .
and who often slept on my lap as I finished it!)

Prologue

Sandy Cavelli glances at her watch as she hurries up the icy steps of the red-brick post office. Four-fifty-nine. She has exactly one minute to retrieve today's mail before the place closes for the day.

She hurries over to the wall that is a grid of rectangular metal doors and eagerly turns her round key in the lock of post office box 129. Jammed, as it always is on Mondays. *Connecticut Singles* magazine comes out on Friday mornings, and Sandy is beginning to believe that every guy in the greater Hartford area who doesn't have a weekend date spends Friday and Saturday flipping through the classifieds in the back of the magazine, answering ads.

She removes the bundle of letters from the box and does a quick mental count. Nine—no, ten. Ten eligible single men have responded to her ad this week. So far. If everything goes according to the pattern that has established itself over the past month, only two or three more letters will trickle in over the next few days. Then, if she chooses to run the ad again—she has to decide by six o'clock Wednesday—there will be a new stack of letters waiting in the box next Monday.

Renting a post office box was definitely a good idea, Sandy reminds herself, even if it has set her back over thirty dollars. This way, she doesn't have to deal with the questions her parents would undoubtedly have if she'd suddenly started getting a blizzard of mail at home every week. They would never go for the idea of their daughter's placing an ad to meet a man through the classifieds. Christ, they still wait up if she stays out past midnight!

Sandy walks slowly toward the double front doors, flipping through the envelopes as she goes. As usual, a few of them don't have return addresses; the ones that do are mostly from Hartford or the immediate area. . . .

But look at this one, from a post office box on Tide Island!

Intrigued, Sandy shoves the other letters into her oversized black shoulder bag, then slides a manicured nail under the flap of the envelope.

"Miss? We're closing," a uniformed postman says. He's jangling a ring of keys and waiting expectantly by the front door.

Sandy looks up. "Oh, sorry."

"No problem." He smiles. His teeth are white and straight, and his eyes crinkle pleasantly. "Pretty cold out there, huh?"

"Yup. It's supposed to snow again overnight."

She doesn't recognize him. He must be new. Almost every face in Greenbury is familiar; she has lived here all her life.

She isn't usually drawn to redheads. Still, he has a nice, strong jawline. And his hair is a burnished-auburn shade, and she likes the way it is cut—short on the sides, up over his ears, and slightly stubbly on top.

"More snow? Where was all this white stuff a few weeks ago, for Christmas?" he asks good-naturedly, reaching out to open the door for her.

"You got me." Sandy shrugs and glances automatically at the fourth finger of his left hand.

Married.

Oh, well.

"Thanks. Have a good night," she says, walking quickly through the door.

She pauses on the slippery top cement step to finish opening the letter she is still clutching.

A brisk wind whips along High Street, sending a chill through Sandy as she slits the envelope open the rest of the way. Her teeth are starting to chatter. It's too cold to read this letter out here, no matter how intrigued she is. She tucks it and the others into her purse and fumbles in her pockets for her gloves. Swiftly she puts them on and clings to the ice-coated metal railing as she picks her way down the four steps to the sidewalk.

Then she gingerly goes, slipping and sliding every few steps in her black-suede flats, along the nearly empty street to her car in the Greenbury municipal lot around the corner. Her footsteps sound lonely and hollow on the brittle frozen pavement.

Just a month ago, in the height of the holiday season, downtown Greenbury was strung with twinkling white lights and festive red bows bedecked the old-fashioned lampposts. Carols were piped into the frosty air from speakers at the red-brick town hall, and High Street bustled well past five o'clock on week nights.

The picturesque, historic village is only fifteen miles outside of Hartford. Even the lifelong residents are aware of the postcard beauty in its white-steepled churches, window-paned storefronts, and broad common dotted with statues and fountains. And as one of the few small towns in central Connecticut that still has a thriving downtown commerce area, Greenbury performs a feat that's becoming nearly impossible in America. It actually draws shoppers away from the malls and superstores that dot the suburban Hartford area.

But now that Christmas is over, the businesses along High close early and downtown is almost deserted in the frigid January twilight.

Sandy's car is one of few left in the parking lot, which is really just a rutted, grassy area behind the town hall. She hurries toward the Chevy, stepping around patches of snow and absently noting the dirty chunks of ice that cling to the underside of the car just behind each wheel.

She doesn't bother kicking it off. The car is ugly enough anyway, with rust spots all over the body and a sheet of thick plastic covering the triangular opening in the back where a window is missing. She's come to loathe the old clunker; it belonged to her father, and she's long past being grateful to him for handing it down to her without making her buy it.

She's been saving for a new car—a new *used* car, of course—ever since she started working at the Greenbury Gal Boutique last spring. She blew a good chunk of her savings on community college tuition in August, and the spring semester bill will be due next week when she registers for classes. But that will still leave nearly four thousand dollars in her account. She socked away over five hundred dollars in December alone, when her commission checks were considerably higher than usual. Of course, that won't keep up. The store was dead all day today, and her hours have already been cut way back.

Sandy settles into the front seat, her breath puffing out in little white clouds. She whispers "brrr" and turns the key in the ignition. After a few tries, the engine turns over, and she adjusts the heat control to high. A blast of cold wind hits her in the face and she closes the black plastic vents. She'll probably be home before the hissing air actually becomes warm, but she leaves it on high anyway.

Eagerly, she reaches into her purse and retrieves the letter with the Tide Island return address. She takes out the single sheet of paper inside and notices that it's real stationery, creamy and heavy.

That's a first, she thinks, pulling off her right glove with her teeth and leaving it clamped in her mouth.

Most of the men who have responded to her ad so far

have written on either yellow legal paper or their company letterhead.

The interior light of her car burned out long ago. Sandy tilts the paper so she can see better in the filtered glow from the streetlamp a few feet away.

Dear Sandra:

I saw your ad in Connecticut Singles *and was struck by how similar our interests are. You sound like the kind of woman I've been waiting for my whole life. Like you, I never thought I'd resort to personal ads to meet someone; but since I'm a medical doctor with a thriving practice, my hectic lifestyle makes it hard to meet anyone the traditional way. I've enclosed a photograph of myself. . . .*

Photograph? Sandy frowns and checks the envelope. Yes, she missed it. There's a picture tucked inside. She grabs it and holds it up in the light.

He's gorgeous! is her immediate reaction.

He has rugged, outdoorsy good looks—and what a bod! He's shirtless in the photograph, which was taken on a sailboat as he hauled the sheet in, or whatever people do on sailboats. Even in the shadows, Sandy can make out his bronzed, hairless chest and bulging arm muscles. He's grinning into the camera, revealing a face that she instantly decides is honest, intelligent, and friendly.

She anxiously turns back to the letter.

. . . so that you'll recognize me when we meet— which, I'm hoping, will be soon. However, I'm on call at the hospital every weekend until mid-February. I've taken the liberty of assuming you'll agree to spend a romantic weekend with me on Tide Island, where I have a weekend house. Since I realize you may be hesitant about staying with a stranger, I've arranged

*accommodations for you at the Bramble Rose Inn.
Your expenses will, of course, be paid entirely by me.
I'm a romantic at heart, and hope you'll agree that
prolonging our meeting until Valentine's Day weekend
will add to the enchantment of what may become a
lasting relationship. The innkeeper of the Bramble
Rose, Jasper Hammel, has agreed to act as our liai-
son. You can call him at (508) 555-1493, to accept
this invitation. I'll look forward to our meeting, Sandra.*

> *Fondly,*
> *Ethan Thoreau*

Ethan Thoreau?

Sandy shakes her head and tosses the letter onto the passenger's seat beside her.

This has to be a fake . . . some nut who gets his jollies
by answering ads and propositioning strange women.

Grimly, she puts on her seat belt and shifts the car into
Drive. As she pulls out onto the street and turns toward
home, she mentally runs through his letter again.

He sounds too good to be true, a gorgeous MD with a
name like Ethan Thoreau. Like a character in one of those
category romance novels Sandy likes to read.

A romantic Valentine's Day weekend on an island.

Yeah, right.

Bramble Rose Inn—the place probably doesn't even exist.

Call the innkeeper.

Sure. And find out that this whole thing is a stupid trick.

Well, she should have known that sooner or later, some
nut case was going to answer her ad. Her friend Theresa,
a veteran of the singles classifieds, warned her that would
happen.

Still, what if there's a chance that this guy is for real?
After all, he did send a picture. . . .

A doctor.

A gorgeous, muscular doctor.

A gorgeous, muscular doctor with a thriving practice and a weekend house on Tide Island.

Sandy chews her lower lip thoughtfully as she rounds the corner from High onto Webster Street.

Well, what if he is for real?

Things like this happen, don't they? Sure they do. She recalls reading, a few years back, about some lonely bachelor who had rented a billboard, advertised for a wife, and proposed to one of the women who responded before they ever met in person.

This guy—this Ethan Thoreau—didn't propose. All he'd done was invite Sandy to meet him. He doesn't even expect her to stay with him.

The Bramble Rose Inn. Jasper Hammel.

Hmm.

Sandy slows the car as she approaches the two-story raised cape where she lives with her parents. The house is pale green, the color of iceberg lettuce, and it desperately needs a paint job.

A grime-covered, white panel truck bearing the name *Cavelli & Sons, Plumbing and Heating Contractors* sits in the short driveway. Sandy parks the Chevy behind it, inwardly groaning. Now that she's on break from college, she likes to beat her father home at night so that she doesn't have to get up early to move her car out of the way when he leaves in the mornings.

She grabs her purse from the seat beside her. Then she thoughtfully picks up Ethan Thoreau's letter and photograph.

"So what's the deal?" she asks, and sighs, her breath coming out in a milky puff of frost. "Are you real, or not?"

Sighing, she puts the letter into her purse with the rest of them. Then she steps out onto the slippery driveway and makes her way along the frozen walk to the house.

In the kitchen, Angie Cavelli is stirring a pot of sauce on the stove. The front of her yellow sweatshirt is splashed with greasy tomato-colored dots.

"Hi, Ma," Sandy says, closing the door behind her and stamping her feet on the faded welcome mat by the door.

"You're late," her mother observes, then takes a taste from the spoon. "I thought you got off at four-thirty."

"I did. I had to run an errand afterward." Sandy shrugs out of her coat and walks across the worn linoleum.

"Your father's already at the table. He wants to eat."

Sandy fights back the urge to say, *then let him eat.*

After twenty-five years of living in this house, she should know better than to consider questioning her father's rule. If you're living in his house, when it's five o'clock, you sit down at the dining room table and you eat. Everyone. Together.

Sandy walks toward the hallway off the kitchen, carrying her purse.

"Ah-ah-ah—where are you going?" her mother calls.

"I just want to change my clothes. I'll be right back down for supper, Ma. Two minutes."

"Two minutes," her mother echoes in a warning voice. She's already at the sink, dumping a steaming kettle of cooked pasta into the battered stainless steel strainer.

In her room, Sandy kicks off her shoes and takes the letter out of her purse again.

She stares at it.

If she doesn't call this Bramble Rose Inn place, she'll probably always wonder whether she passed up the chance to meet a handsome, wealthy doctor.

If she calls, she might find out that he actually has made paid reservations for her. That he really does exist.

Sandy pauses for another minute, thinking it over.

Then she takes the letter across the hall to her parents' room. Unlike the rest of the house—including her own room—which holds an accumulation of several decades of clutter, Angie and Tony's bedroom is spare. The walls are empty except for the crucifix hanging over the bed, and the only other furniture is a dresser and the wobbly bedside table. On that sits the upstairs telephone extension.

Sandy perches carefully on the edge of the old white chenille spread, lifts the receiver, and starts dialing.

Liza Danning hates Monday nights.

Especially rainy, slushy Monday nights in early January, when you can't get a cab and the only way of getting from the office on West Fortieth Street to your apartment on the Upper East Side is the subway. That, or a bus . . . and the glass shelters at the stops are so jammed that waiting for a bus that isn't overcrowded to finally roll by would mean standing in the rain. Which wouldn't be so bad if she had an umbrella.

And she doesn't.

She'd left for work this morning from Alex's place, where she'd spent the night. And since the sun had been shining brightly when they rolled out of bed, borrowing an umbrella from him, just in case, hadn't occurred to her. Besides, she'd been too busy dodging his efforts to pin her down for next weekend.

"I don't know, Alex," she'd said, avoiding his searching gaze as she slipped into her navy Burberry trench—a gift from Lawrence, an old lover—and tied the belt snugly around her waist. She'd checked her reflection in the floor-to-ceiling mirror in his foyer and tucked a few stray strands of silky blond hair back into the chignon at the back of her neck. "I think I have plans."

"What plans?"

She'd shrugged. "I'm not sure."

"You think you have plans, but you're not sure what they are," he'd said flatly.

So she'd told him. She'd had no choice. "Look—" She

bent to pick up her burgundy Coach briefcase. "I like you. Last night was great. So was Saturday. And Friday. But I'm not ready for an every-weekend thing, okay?"

He'd stared at her, the blue eyes she'd found so captivating on Friday night now icy and hard. "Fine," he'd said, picking up his own Coach briefcase—black leather—and Burberry trench, also black.

Then they'd walked to the elevator, ridden the fifty-three stories down to the lobby in silence, and stepped out into the brisk Manhattan morning. Alex had asked the doorman to hail them separate cabs, even though his law office was just two blocks from the publishing house where she was an editor.

The doorman had blown his whistle and immediately flagged a passing cab. Alex stuffed some bills into his hand, then leaned over to again narrow that ice-blue gaze at Liza as she settled into the back seat.

"West Fortieth at Sixth," she'd said to the driver. Then, to Alex, "Call me."

"Right," he'd replied, and she knew he wouldn't.

She'd shrugged as the cab pulled away from the curb. So he'd expected more out of their little tryst than she had. He'd get over it.

She hesitates on the street in front of her office building, trying to talk herself into taking the subway. But it will mean walking the two and a half blocks to the station near the library on Forty-second Street. Then she'll have to take the Seven train one stop to Grand Central and wait for the uptown local. That will take forever.

She shakes her head decisively and checks the Movado on her left wrist. Six-fifteen. If she goes back upstairs and works until seven-thirty, she can take a company car home. The publishing house pays her peanuts and doesn't offer many perks besides free car service for employees who work late. But it's the least they can do. After all, most of the editors are females, and Manhattan's streets are increasingly dangerous after dark.

Liza walks briskly back into the lobby.

Carmine, the night guard, looks her over appreciatively, as he always does. At least this time, he doesn't tell her how much she resembles Sharon Stone, or ask her if she's ever considered becoming an actress.

"Forget something?" he asks, his eyes on her breasts even though she is bundled into her trench coat.

"Yes," she replies shortly, walking past him toward the elevator bank, conscious of the hollow, tapping noise her heels make on the tile floor.

An elevator is just arriving, and she steps aside to let the full load of passengers step off.

"Liza, what's up? I thought you'd left," says a petite brunette, emerging from the crowd.

Liza vaguely recognizes her as one of the new editorial assistants who started right before Christmas. The girl is one of those bubbly, fresh-from-the-ivy-league types. The kind who can afford to take an entry level job in publishing because her rich daddy pays the rent on her Upper East Side studio.

"I have to go back up. I forgot something," Liza tells her briefly.

"Oh, well, have a good night. See you tomorrow," the girl says cheerfully, fastening the top button of her soft wool coat.

Liza recognizes the expensive lines, rich coral color, and ornate gold buttons. She'd reached for that coat in Saks a few months ago. The price tag was over a thousand dollars.

She'd put it back.

"See you," she echoes, and strides onto the elevator. She rides alone up to the sixth floor and steps into the deserted reception area of Xavier House, Ltd.

She fishes in her pocket for her card key and flashes it in front of the electronic panel beside the double glass doors behind the receptionist's desk. There is a click, and she pushes the door open.

Liza walks swiftly down the dimly lit hall, past a janitor's cart parked in front of one of the offices. She can hear a cleaning lady running a vacuum in another part of the floor. She turns a corner and heads down the short corridor toward her own office. The other editors who share this area are either long gone or behind closed doors, probably catching up on manuscript reading after taking the holidays off.

Liza unlocks the door marked LIZA DANNING and steps inside. She slips her coat over the hanger waiting on a hook behind the door, then smooths her cashmere sweater and sighs. She isn't in the mood for reading, although she *should* try to make a dent in the pile of manuscripts that sit waiting on her credenza.

You could open the mail, she tells herself, glancing at the stack in her IN box. She hadn't gotten to it today. Or Friday either, for that matter.

She sits at her desk and reaches for the first manila envelope, slitting the flap with the jewel-handled letter opener that had been a gift from Douglas. Or was it Reed? She can't remember anymore. And it doesn't matter, anyway. He's long gone, whoever he was. Like the others.

She removes a sheaf of papers from the envelope and scans the top sheet. It's a painstaking cover letter, composed on an ancient typewriter whose vowels are filled in with smudges. Some anxious would-be writer, a midwestern housewife, describes the enclosed first chapter and outline of a historical romance novel about a pirate hero and an Indian princess heroine. The woman has spelled desire *d-e-z-i-r-e.*

Liza tosses the letter into the wastepaper basket and reaches into her top drawer for the packet of pre-printed rejections letters she keeps there. She removes one and slips it under the paper clip holding the partial manuscript together. She tucks the whole stack into the self-addressed, stamped envelope the woman has included, seals it, and tosses it into her OUT basket. Then she reaches for the next envelope.

Fifteen minutes later, the stack in her IN box has dwindled and her OUT basket is overflowing. She has worked her way through all the large packages and is now starting on the letters in their white legal-sized envelopes.

She glances idly at the return address on this first one. What she sees makes her sit up and do a double take.

D.M. Yates, P.O. Box 57, Tide Island MA.

P.M. Yates—David Mitchell Yates, reclusive best-selling author? She recalls that the man has a home on some New England coastal island.

Liza grabs the letter opener and hurriedly slits the envelope open. She unfolds the single sheet of creamy white stationery and notices that a train ticket is attached to the top with a paper clip. Amtrak. Penn Station to Westwood, Rhode Island. First Class.

Intrigued, she skips past the formal heading to the body of the letter.

Dear Ms. Danning:

As you may or may not be aware, I am the author of several best-selling spy novels released by Best & Rawson, a New York City publishing house, over the past ten years. Since my editor, Henry Malcolm, retired last month, I have been searching for a new home for my novels. Would you be interested in meeting with me to discuss the possibilities of a deal with Xavier House, Ltd.? I have enclosed a round-trip train ticket to Westwood, Rhode Island, for the second weekend in February. You will be met by a limousine that will transport you to the dock in Crosswinds Bay, where you will board the ferry to Tide Island. I have arranged for you to stay at the Bramble Rose Inn. I will, of course, pay all expenses for your journey. I

*will be traveling abroad for the next several weeks.
To confirm, please contact the innkeeper, Jasper Hammel, at (508) 555-1493. It is imperative that you keep
this meeting confidential. I'll look forward to meeting
with you.*

> *Sincerely,*
> *David Michael Yates*

Liza is electrified.

David Michael Yates.

The man is gold.

He's also an eccentric recluse whose face has reportedly never been seen by the world at large. The jackets of his books bear no photograph; not even a biography. Over the years, it has been rumored that David Michael Yates is actually a pseudonym for a high-ranking government official; that he's really a woman; that he had his face blown off in Vietnam.

Just last week, the cover story in *Publisher's Weekly* chronicled the retirement of Yates's longtime editor and the bitter contract battle that resulted in the severed deal between the author and Best & Rawson. According to the article, Yates was about to depart for Europe to research his newest novel and hadn't yet decided upon a publisher, although several of the most prestigious houses were courting him.

How on earth did he decide to approach me, of all people? Liza wonders.

True, she's been getting some PW press herself lately. She recently put together a well-publicized nonfiction deal with an elusive, scandal-ridden senator for a tell-all book. Of course, the powers-that-be at Xavier aren't aware of just how Liza had managed to persuade the man.

And she'll never tell.

Eagerly, she reaches for the phone and begins to dial the number for the Bramble Rose Inn.

* * *

Jennie Towne hears blasting music—an old Springsteen song—the moment she steps into the first-floor vestibule of the restored Back Bay town house. She rolls her eyes and hurries toward the closed white-painted door ahead, which bears a nailed-on, dark green 1.

She transfers the stack of mail from her right hand to her left, then fits her key into the lock and turns it. It sticks a little, as always, and she tugs.

Finally the door opens, and she steps into the apartment. She stomps her snowy boots on the rug and deposits the mail on the small piecrust table that once sat beside her grandparents' front door in the old house in Quincy.

"Laura?" she calls, walking straight to the stereo on the wall unit across the living room. She lowers the volume to practically nothing and promptly hears a disgruntled "Hey!" from the other room.

"It was too loud," she tells her sister, who appears in the doorway within seconds.

"Oh, please." Laura tosses her head. Her ultra-short cap of glossy black hair doesn't even stir.

"Come on, Laura, do you want Mrs. Willensky down here again, threatening to call the landlord?"

Laura shrugs. She says, "Keegan called."

"What did he want?" Jennie looks up from tugging off her boots.

"What do you think? To talk to you. He said he'd tried you at the shop but you'd already left. He wants you to call him. He's on the overnight shift and he's leaving for the precinct at six-thirty."

Jennie just nods.

"You going to call him back?"

"No."

"Oh, come on, Jen, cut the guy a break. He sounded so

pathetic. I mean, he didn't *say* anything specific, but I could tell the guy's going crazy without you."

She tries to ignore the pang that jabs into her at the thought of Keegan hurting. "Laura, I can't. I have to make a clean break. Otherwise we'll keep going back and forth forever."

"I see what you mean," her sister says dryly, folding her arms and fixing Jennie with a steady look. "You love him; he loves you; you both love kids and dogs and the Red Sox and antiques and the ocean. . . . It'll never work."

"Laura—"

"I mean, Jen, I know what your problem is, and you have to get over it. It's been three years since—"

"I don't want to talk about that," Jennie effectively cuts her off, fixing her with a resolute stare.

Laura sighs and transfers her gaze to the stack of mail Jennie dumped on the table by the door. "Anything good come for me?" she asks hopefully. "Like an airmail letter?"

Her new boyfriend, Shawn, is spending a month in Japan on business. She's been moping ever since he left right after New Year's.

Jennie shrugs. "I didn't look."

She unbuttons her winter coat and hangs it in the closet while Laura flips through the stack of mail.

Bill, bill, bill, b—hey, what's this?" she hears her sister say.

She glances up. Laura's holding an oblong white envelope.

"A letter from Shawn?" Jennie asks, running a hand over her own shiny black hair, exactly the same shade and texture as Laura's, except that hers hangs well past her shoulders. And right now, it's full of static, annoying her.

I should just get it chopped off, like Laura did, she tells herself, even as she hears Keegan's voice echoing inside her head. *I love your hair long, Jen. Don't ever cut it.*

"No, this isn't from Shawn. The return address is a post office box on Tide Island," Laura is saying with a frown. "I don't know anyone there."

"Well, open it."

"I'm afraid to."

Jennie knows what she's thinking. Laura's ex-husband, Brian, pursued her relentlessly after their marriage ended last spring. Her sister had finally been forced to get a restraining order against him. He'd dropped out of sight right after that, presumably returning to Cape Cod, where his parents still live.

Jennie's aware that her sister is still afraid he'll resurface and start bothering her again. Brian is a deceptively mild-mannered guy; but when he's drunk, he's a monster. Jennie witnessed his violent, alcohol-induced temper on more than one occasion and had suspected he was abusing Laura long before her sister ever admitted it.

"Don't worry," she tells Laura now, watching her carefully. "It's probably just some travel brochure, or a charity asking for money. And if it's not—if it *is* from Brian—you can take it straight to the police."

"I know." Laura, her face taut, opens the envelope carefully and withdraws a sheet of white paper.

Jennie watches her sister's features, identical to her own except for a small scar by her left eye—courtesy of her ex-husband—gradually relax over the next few seconds.

"What? What is it?" she asks, hurrying across the room and peering over Laura's shoulder at the letter.

"I can't believe it. I mean, I never win anything," Laura says, handing her the letter. "Read this."

Jennie takes it, noticing that the stationery is heavy and expensive. There is a delicate pen-and-ink drawing of a charming house on the top. The imprint on the stationery reads *Bramble Rose Inn, Box 57, Tide Island MA*. Jennie scans the bold type.

Dear Ms. Towne:

    It is our pleasure to inform you that you have won the grand prize in the annual New England Children's

Leukemia Society fund-raising sweepstakes. You are hereby entitled to an all-expenses-paid solo visit to Tide Island on the second weekend in February. The prize includes three-nights, four-days deluxe accommodations at the Bramble Rose Inn, all meals, and round-trip transportation on the Crosswinds Bay ferry. Please confirm with me at (508) 555-1493, upon receipt of this letter.

> *Sincerely,*
> *Jasper Hammel*
> *Innkeeper*

Jennie lowers the letter and looks at Laura. "This sounds pretty good," she says cautiously.

"It *would* be, if it were any other weekend. Shawn's coming home that Saturday in time for Valentine's Day. I already arranged my hours at work so that I could take off and be with him. I can't go."

"Maybe you can switch to another weekend," Jennie suggests. "Then you and Shawn can both go."

Laura shakes her head. "See that small print on the bottom? It says this offer is only good for that particular weekend. And I remember buying the sweepstakes ticket right before Christmas. The man who sold it to me said the prize was for *one* person, no guests. Sort of a pamper-yourself, get-away-from-it-all thing."

"I never heard of the New England Children's Leukemia Society," Jennie comments, scanning the small print.

"Neither did I. But he told me it's been around for a while. Actually, I think I've seen him before—he looked familiar. He's probably been collecting for charity before, and I'll bet I ducked him. If I hadn't just gotten paid and been feeling rich that day, I probably wouldn't even have bought the ticket from him. Although, I may have if I knew what it was for," she adds soberly.

Of course Laura would never refuse to contribute to that

particular charity. Jennie wouldn't either. Their younger sister, Melanie, had died of leukemia fifteen years ago.

Jennie glances again at the letter. "Where'd you buy the sweepstakes ticket, Laura?"

"In the parking lot at Stop and Shop. Don't worry, Jen. It was legit."

"I didn't say it wasn't," Jenny says.

"But you're thinking that Brian might have something to do with this, aren't you? That it's some sort of set-up to lure me to this island so that he could convince me to give him another chance. Right?"

Jennie meets her sister's lilac-colored eyes guiltily. "The thought did cross my mind."

"Trust me. Brian's not this clever. Can you see him going through all the effort of making up a fake charity, hiring some stranger to persuade me to buy a ticket, and then somehow getting his hands on the stationery for this Bramble Rose place and forging a letter from an innkeeper?"

Jennie grins. "You're right. He couldn't do that in a million years." She glances down at the drawing of the inn again. "Too bad you can't go. It looks really cozy."

"Why don't *you* go instead, Jen?" Laura asks suddenly.

"Didn't you read the rest of the small print? It says the prize can't be transferred."

"So? We're identical twins. When was the last time we switched places?" Laura asks with a grin.

Jennie smiles. "I thought we agreed never to do that again after that time in high school."

Her sister's boyfriend hadn't been very appreciative to discover that Laura had sent Jennie on a date with him while she went out with someone else. Of course, he probably wouldn't have figured it out if Jennie hadn't done such an unconvincing job of faking a sudden stomachache so she wouldn't have to have sex with him.

Laura had neglected to mention to her sister that they'd

been sleeping together for over a year and he might expect it.

"Jen," Laura says, "this isn't high school. Take my driver's license as ID and go to the island. You can spend some time drawing and painting, or whatever. The place is really artsy. You know, that's they call it Tie-Dye Land."

"Huh?"

"Tide Island—Tie-Dye Land. That's what everyone calls the place. Didn't you ever hear that before?"

"Nope."

"Figures. Sometimes, Jen, you're in a total fog," Laura says, shaking her head. "Anyway, a lot of artists hang out there in the summers. You know—long-haired types who wear grungy tie-dye outfits and sit around painting the scenery all day."

Hmm. The idea of bringing her art supplies to a picturesque island is tempting to Jennie. She's been too busy lately to spend any time on her hobby. Still . . .

"You have short hair in the picture on your license. Mine's long," she points out to Laura.

"So? I got it renewed over a year ago. I could have grown my hair out. Go ahead, Jen. You need to get away after all this craziness with Keegan."

Keegan. She winces.

Oh, God. Will she ever be able to hear his name and not react this way?

Jennie glances again at the drawing of the inn. It shows an old-fashioned, scallop-shingled house complete with plenty of gables and a picket fence with a kitten perched demurely on the gatepost. It appears to be a dreamy, quaint little place where you can curl up with a sketch pad and a mug of tea and forget about the painful end of a relationship.

"Maybe you're right," she tells Laura slowly.

"I *am* right." Her sister bounces the few short steps to the telephone on a nearby table. She picks up the receiver and dangles it from her fingers, looking expectantly at Jennie.

"Read off the phone number on the letter. I'll dial. And don't forget—you're Laura."

Jennie sighs. "Right. I'm Laura." She looks down at the letter and starts reading the number aloud.

One

The ferry isn't yet a far-off speck on the dusky horizon, but he knows it's there, cutting toward Tide Island through the choppy gray waters off the New England coast. Complete darkness will fall well before it docks at the landing down the road to release its load of weekend passengers.

In summer, the Friday-night ferry is always crowded with commuting husbands and vacationing families, college students who work as weekend waiters or lifeguards, couples in love, sticky-faced children.

But now, in the shortest month of the year, when winter is at its bleakest and the island offers nothing but silent, chilly isolation, there won't be many people on board. Just the few hardy nature-loving souls willing to brave the elements; perhaps some island-dwellers returning with groceries from the mainland; maybe a handful of summer house owners coming out to inspect the damage December's Nor'easter inflicted upon their property.

That's about it.

Except for *them*.

He knows they're on board—all three of them. Still strangers to each other, but not to him.

He has been watching them for so long now.

Waiting.

A quiver of anticipation passes over him and he cautions himself to relax. He has to maintain control at all times.

He can't afford to take any risks at this point, just when it's all coming together at last.

After all these years . . .

Soon enough, he assures himself. *It won't be long now.*

He casts his gaze back out over the water, giddy with excitement. He'd heard on the radio a little while ago that there's a growing likelihood this weekend might be stormy.

Wouldn't that be perfect?

Even at this moment, they're probably enjoying the brisk twilight ride. He pictures them scattered in different corners of the deck or cabin, lost in their own thoughts, thinking about the weekend ahead, filled with excited expectations.

They aren't the only ones who are looking forward to it.

His features twist with mirth, and he stifles a giggle.

Very, very soon.

He lets the filmy lace curtain drop back into place and turns away from the window.

He still has a lot to do before they arrive.

As the ferry leaves Crosswinds Bay and heads out into the open Atlantic, Jennie turns her face into the cold, salty wind and smiles.

What a relief to be leaving everything behind, if only for a few days. Already, she can feel the chronic tension starting to loosen its grip on her body. She takes a deep breath of the sea air and lets it out on a satisfying sigh.

By the time she reached the ferry terminal twenty minutes ago, her jaw ached from clenching and her neck and back muscles had been a jumble of stress knots.

Knowing Friday night traffic out of Boston was always bad, she'd left at three o'clock to beat it. Unfortunately, a jackknifed tractor-trailer had rammed into a car on I-95 and brought her to a standstill by three-fifteen. And she'd lost an hour by the time she'd managed to creep by the accident scene, ducking her head after a fleeting glimpse of the emergency vehicles with their flashing red lights.

Spinning domed lights—and sirens—always bring her back to that awful day three years ago.

So does the sight of blood, no matter how scant. Just two days ago, she'd cut her finger on a paring knife and found herself still trembling uncontrollably a half hour later.

Today, she had struggled to shake the disturbing memories from her mind and concentrate on the road. She really had to step on it to make the five o'clock ferry from Crosswinds Bay on Rhode Island's southwestern coast.

As a rule, she hardly ever went more than five miles above the speed limit, but she didn't really have a choice if she wanted to get away for the weekend. And she was determined to do that.

The cozy Bramble Rose Inn seemed to beckon silently from miles away, promising refuge. She couldn't miss the ferry—it was the last one tonight. She was willing to risk a speeding ticket to catch it.

Besides, everyone else on the road seemed to be flying by at eighty miles an hour anyway. Jennie had slid her small red Hyundai out into the passing lane and let the speedometer climb to seventy.

Just past Providence, she was stopped by a humorless trooper who promptly slapped her with a speeding ticket.

Now, shaking her head at the thought of having to part with a precious fifty dollars to pay the fine, she pulls her black leather gloves out of the bag at her feet and slips them over her winter-chapped hands. It's freezing on the deck, but she doesn't want to go inside yet.

There's something cleansing about standing out here with the fresh, fishy air whipping through her hair and stinging her cheeks so that they feel swollen. A bell clangs on the bridge somewhere above her, bidding a hollow farewell to the shore they are rapidly leaving behind.

"Excuse me, do you know what time it is?"

Jennie turns toward the voice. A young woman stands behind her, clutching the railing with one hand to keep her balance as the boat rolls over the waves. She's so bundled in a parka and scarf that all that's visible is a pair of pretty brown eyes and a snub nose that looks bright red from the frosty air.

Jennie pushes her glove up her wrist and peeks at her watch. "It's almost a quarter after six." She practically has to shout to be heard over the wind and crashing waves.

"Thanks. Do you know when the ferry is supposed to get in?"

"I think at around seven-thirty. At least, that's what the schedule said."

"Good. I'm starving."

"Me, too." Jennie remembers that she hasn't eaten since the half a blueberry muffin from Dunkin' Donuts that she'd gulped down this morning in the car on the way to work. She'd been too busy trying to wrap things up and make an early getaway to even think about lunch.

The other woman reaches into her pocket and produces a fat-free granola bar in one fuzzy-mittened hand. "Want half? It'll tide you over."

Jennie hesitates. "Oh, that's all right, you don't have to—"

Abruptly, the woman snaps the bar in two and hands one piece to Jennie with a grin. "Here. I'd feel guilty gobbling the whole thing down myself. Besides, I'm on a diet."

"Thanks," Jenny says.

"Don't look so grateful. It's fat free and it tastes like cardboard, so I'm not being as generous as you think."

Jennie smiles back at her and clumsily pushes the bar up through the torn wrapper with gloved fingers before taking a bite.

For a moment, they stand side by side, crunching and staring out at the water.

Then the other woman says brightly, "I'm Sandy Cavelli."

"Nice to meet you. I'm . . . Laura. Laura Towne." Might as well get into the habit now so she won't be as likely to slip and say Jennie when she gets to the inn.

For another long moment, they both lean on the railing and stare out at the darkening sky and sea, munching the granola.

"Have you ever been to Tide Island before?" Sandy asks, popping the last bite into her mouth. She crumples the empty wrapper and shoves it into her pocket.

"No. Have you?"

"Once when I was younger, with my parents and brothers. I don't remember much about it, except that we came across some people skinny dipping one day when we were trying to have a picnic on the beach. My parents freaked out."

Jennie smiles. "I bet."

"They didn't like the island much, anyway. They thought it was overrun with hippies. That's what my father kept saying."

"Tie-Dye Land," Jennie says, remembering. "That's what people call the island, according to my sister."

"Exactly."

"Well, the place is beautiful, from what I've heard."

"Yeah, and deserted at this time of year." Sandy shakes her head. "I wasn't even going to tell my parents where I was going for the weekend, but my mother overheard me talking about it on the phone with my best friend. And she asked me about it, and then she told my father, and he blew up, as usual. But they can't stop me, you know? Even though I live under their roof, I'm an adult." She lifts her double chin stubbornly. "You know what I mean?"

Jennie nods, thinking she doesn't seem so sure of that as she wants to be. She looks and sounds almost like a rebellious teenager.

Abruptly, Sandy changes the subject. "So how come you're coming here, and not jetting off to St. Thomas or something? I mean, isn't that what people do when they go on vacation in the dead of winter?"

Jennie shrugs. "I don't know. The Caribbean is probably so crowded when it's winter in the northeast."

Probably. Why'd you say that? You know it is.

But she doesn't want to remember her November trip to Jamaica with Keegan.

"True." Sandy grins. "But I'll bet it's crowded with lots of eligible guys."

"You're single?"

"Unfortunately, yes. I was engaged once, but it didn't work out. How about you?"

Jennie nods. She's on the verge of saying, "I just broke up with someone," but catches herself. It isn't at all like her to spill the details of her life to a complete stranger. And of course, she would never tell this Sandy Cavelli her *whole* painful, horrible story. The people she works with don't even know about that.

"It's so hard to meet anyone halfway decent. I haven't even had a date in two months," Sandy says wistfully. "How about you?"

Something about this woman is making Jennie uncharacteristically tempted to confide in her, but again she holds back. "Not really," she says simply.

"I'm meeting someone on the island," Sandy informs her.

Jennie assumes she just means that she's determined to find a nice guy this weekend until Sandy goes on, "It's kind of a blind date."

"That's nice."

"Yeah. This was his idea. He has a house out here. He's a doctor."

"A doctor—wow," Jennie comments because she knows Sandy expects it.

"Wow is right."

"Where does he practice? On the island?"

"No, this is just where his weekend house is," Sandy

says a bit smugly. Then her expression grows a little embarrassed. "I, uh, I'm not sure where his practice is. Like
I said, this is a blind date. I don't know much about him."

"Huh," Jennie says, nodding. "Sounds romantic."

"You're telling me. And it doesn't matter where he works,
because wherever it is, I'd move out there in a minute if
we hit it off. It would be a pleasure never to set foot in
Hartford again . . . unless he happens to live there, too."

"That's where you're from?"

"Yeah. Actually, not Hartford. Near it, though . . . a little
town called Greenbury." At Jennie's blank look, she nods.
"Never heard of it, huh? I'm not surprised. How about
you?"

"I live in Boston."

"What do you do?"

"I'm an antique dealer," Jennie says, before she remembers that she's supposed to be Laura, and Laura is a sales-
clerk at the Gap. Well, it's too late to take it back now.

Her expression must have revealed something, because
Sandy says, "Not all it's cracked up to be, huh?"

"No, it's not that, it's just . . ."

*It's just that every damn thing in my life reminds me of
Keegan, that's what.*

"What don't you like about it?"

"Oh, I like it." Jennie tilts her face upward. "Did you
just feel a drop?"

"No, but I'm so bundled up a baseball-sized hailstone
wouldn't make me flinch. Is it raining?"

"Maybe it was just spray. But I think I'm going to go
inside anyway. My feet are starting to get numb."

"Okay. I'll stick around out here for a while longer. Maybe
I'll get windburn on my face. I look a lot better when I have
some color."

"Thanks for the granola."

"Anytime."

"See you later." Jennie lets go of the railing and moves toward the door on unsteady feet.

A blast of warm air rushes at her as she steps into the cabin. The silence there is pronounced after the roar of the wind outside. Jennie loosens the top button of her coat and heads toward a vacant spot on the bench against the wall.

As she sits down, she notices that the striking blond woman beside her is clutching her stomach, looking wan. Still feeling the effects of Sandy's outgoing friendliness, Jennie reaches into her pocket for the Tums she put there earlier, just in case.

"Excuse me, but would you like one of these?" she asks the stranger, holding out the roll.

The woman barely shakes her head, then closes her green eyes abruptly, effectively shutting Jennie out.

I guess I wouldn't be very friendly if I felt seasick, either, Jennie tells herself, slipping the Tums back into her pocket and reaching into her bag for a magazine.

She settles back to read as the last streaks of pink fade from the sky and the ferry chugs swiftly through the darkness toward Tide Island.

Liza steps from the gangplank onto the old wooden pier and looks around. There's nothing to see. Blackness is everywhere—the water, the sky, the buildings a few hundred feet away. The only light is on the boat deck behind her, and even that casts a murky glow that only makes the place seem eerier.

She doesn't know what she'd expected. She'd known the island wouldn't be hopping in the off-season, that there wouldn't be many shops or restaurants open.

But this . . . this is like a ghost town.

Across from the landing, through the wisps of fog that hang in the air, she can make out the main street. She recognizes it from a brochure she'd picked up at a travel agency in her neighborhood. She'd been enchanted by the street in the photograph, with its row of grand Victorian hotels and quaint shops.

Now their mansard roofs and gables loom in spooky silhouettes against the night sky. They're obviously deserted, the windows boarded with plywood against winter's harsh weather.

Liza hesitates as other passengers disembark and scurry toward a nearby parking lot. She can hear a few shouted greetings; apparently some people are being met at the landing by friends or relatives.

She glances around, wondering what happened to the woman on the boat who had offered her the Tums. Apparently, she'd thought Liza was seasick. She wasn't.

She had been thinking about Robert, a man she'd been dating lately. He'd left at least twenty-five messages on her home answering machine this week. Couldn't he take a hint?

When the other woman had approached her on the boat, Liza hadn't been in the mood for company. But those friendly lilac-colored eyes would be beyond welcome right about now.

There's no sign of her.

Feeling suddenly alone, Liza reaches for her gloves again. She sets her Vuitton bag on the rough planks at her feet, slips her hands into the cozy cashmere lining, and feels instantly better.

She tries to figure out which direction she has to walk in to find the inn.

When she'd made her reservation, Jasper Hammel had said to bear right along Main Street and it would be a quarter-mile up the road. "You can't miss it," he'd assured her.

Somehow, Liza can't seem to force herself to move away from the landing and into the deserted street. She can hear car engines starting in the parking lot. Several pairs of sweeping headlights swing in the opposite direction, turning down the deserted main street and fading away.

Behind her, a few passengers are still trickling off the ferry. In another moment, they—and the boat itself—will be gone. She'll be completely abandoned in this desolate place.

Liza takes a deep breath, picks up her bag, and heads for the street.

She makes her way along the empty boardwalk, her boot heels making a hollow, lonely sound that triggers her heart to beat faster. There are no streetlights, no passing cars—nothing.

The wind whistles mournfully as it blows in off the water. Over it, Liza hears the grinding of the ferry engines as the boat turns around in the harbor.

She peers ahead through the darkness. Never before has she been in such a desolate place. Never before has she experienced such utter and complete darkness. There's no moon to illuminate her path. No reassuring neon signs, or even lamplit homes, to tell her that there are people nearby.

Fighting back a growing sense of panic, she steps down off the boardwalk at the end of the row of buildings and into the wide, sandy road. It curves away from the water now, heading slightly uphill.

Liza hesitates, uncertain whether or not to keep following it. She can always turn back, and—

Above her head, a shutter bangs suddenly.

Liza jumps and cries out before she realizes what it was.

Clutching her trembling hands in fists against her mouth, she acknowledges that her nerves are shattered.

This is ludicrous. What is she doing out here, fumbling in the dark all alone? In New York, she never walks down a deserted street by herself at night. Any idiot knows better than that. A woman alone, in the dark—it's just asking for trouble.

She has to go back.

Forget D.M. Yates.

All she wants to do is be back in familiar Manhattan.

The ferry bell clangs just then, telling her that the boat is heading back out toward the mainland.

Wait, she wants to scream. *Take me with you! Don't leave me here alone!*

But it's too late. She'll never catch the boat, even if she runs all the way back to the landing.

So she hurries on, clutching her bag so tightly her nails dig into her palms even through the gloves.

The fog seems to grow more dense by the minute, rolling in off the water, carried by the ever-present wind.

There are a few low buildings at the side of the road here; but they, like everything else, look deserted. Their signs—bearing cheery names like "Sun 'n Fun Surf Shop" and "Buddy's Beachfront Bike Rentals"—seem ridiculously out of place in this somber setting.

Gradually, Liza becomes aware of a pebble working its way down into her boot. After trying to walk several steps on it, she finally stops to get it out. She sets her bag down and balances on one foot while she removes her boot and dumps the little stone out onto the frozen concrete.

As she laces her boot again, she wonders how far she's come. Surely it's been a quarter of a mile by now.

Suddenly, the skin just above the hairline on the back of her neck begins to prickle and an unmistakable feeling steals over her.

The feeling that she's being watched.

Leaving her boot half-unlaced, Liza grabs her bag and begins walking again.

The eerie awareness mounts.

She doesn't know who's peering at her through the night, or even where they're hiding; she's only acutely conscious of invisible eyes boring into her from somewhere nearby.

She quickens her pace.

Then she hears it, even over the incessant howling and the crashing sea.

Footsteps.

They're coming from somewhere behind her. Not *right* behind her, but they're there.

Someone is following her.

She doesn't take the time to turn her head and find out who it is.

She doesn't care.

Breaking into a run, she heads up the dark, sloping road. Her eyes frantically scan the brush lining the sides.

On a low rise overlooking the water ahead, she thinks she glimpses a light.

Please, God . . .

There! That has to be the inn. As she rounds a bend, she sees that it is, indeed, a house. And a weathered sign by the foot of the steep drive bears the name Bramble Rose Inn.

Liza's heart thumps painfully, threatening to shatter her rib cage as she quickly makes her way up the winding path. Glancing up at the house, she half-expects to see someone in a window, looking out into the night.

But there's no one, and she tells herself to stop being ridiculous.

He steps back from the window.

Had she seen him?

She'd looked up just before the evergreen branches below enveloped her, screening her from his sight. But he'd glimpsed enough of her to see which one she is.

Liza Danning.

She's still startlingly pretty, with enormous seafoam-green eyes.

Wary eyes.

And she still doesn't even know what lies in store for her.

He waits, tapping a pen against his palm impatiently. The antique mantel clock ticks a steady rhythm behind him.

Within moments, the shrill ring of the old-fashioned door buzzer shatters the silent house.

Realizing he'd been holding his breath, he exhales now. Carefully, he puts the pen into the holder on his desk and walks out of the room toward the stairs.

The first guest has arrived.

The others will soon follow.

And soon it will begin.

Jennie is just about to ring the bell a second time when the heavy wooden door is flung open before her.

"Well, hello! I was beginning to wonder if you had gotten lost." The man who stands there is of medium height, with a somewhat stocky build. He has a neatly trimmed mustache that is the same auburn shade of his hair. His friendly smile is like a beacon, reaching out into the chilly night air and enveloping Jennie.

"Hi," she says breathlessly. "I was beginning to think I *was* lost. It's really dark out there."

"It is, isn't it? Cold, too. Come on in." He steps back and motions her through a short entry hall and into the brightly lit foyer, then closes the door behind her, shutting out the incessant wind at last.

Jennie sets her bag on the wide-planked wooden floor and breathes an audible sigh. She's made it. What a relief.

The foyer is cozy and pleasant, with lots of plants in wicker baskets, a few wing-backed chairs, and globed lamps on low antique tables. Beyond the tall reception desk, a narrow wooden staircase leads to a landing, then turns sharply. The cinnamon-berry scent of potpourri wafts invitingly in the air, and classical music plays softly in the background.

Her host has walked briskly around to the back of the desk and is scanning a registry book. "Let's see now. Ms. Danning has already checked in, so you must be . . ."

"I'm Laura Towne." Jennie assumes the blonde she'd followed over from the boat was Ms. Danning.

She might have tried harder to catch up to her if the woman had been friendlier on the boat . . . and if she hadn't been walking so fast. Jennie had thought she looked spooked. Actually, she doesn't blame her. The place *is* pretty creepy in the dark, although it'll probably be perfectly delightful tomorrow morning.

"Ah, yes, Laura Towne," the man behind the desk is saying.

"That's me." She feels a twinge of guilt at the lie.

"You're our sweepstakes winner. We spoke on the phone a few weeks back, didn't we? I have you down right here. You're staying for three nights."

Jennie notices that there's something effeminate about his movements, and his voice is slightly high-pitched.

"That's right." She runs a hand through her long, dark hair, trying to tame the flyaways.

"Well, then, you're all set." He looks up and smiles again. "Have you ever been to Tide Island before?"

"No."

"Well, let me be the first to welcome you. I'm Jasper Hammel, and I'm here to make your stay as pleasant as possible. If you have any questions, or if there's any way I can—"

The doorbell cuts him off. He holds up a finger, motioning to Jennie that he'll be right back. Then he hurries toward the entry hall.

Jennie sees a copy of *Country Living* magazine in a basket on the desk and starts flipping idly through it.

Cold air blows into the room as soon as the door opens

behind her, and the blustery howl drowns out Jasper Hammel's voice as he greets someone there.

It isn't until he's closed the door again and is leading the new guest into the foyer that Jennie recognizes a voice.

Spinning, she sees Sandy from the ferry.

"Hey, long time no see" is the first thing she says when she sees Jennie. With a grunt, she deposits her oversized suitcase unceremoniously on the floor in front of the desk.

"You're staying here, too?" Jennie asks.

She doesn't know if she's pleased or disappointed. It might be nice to have some pleasant company over the weekend. But on the other hand, she isn't really in the mood for this woman's brand of cheerful chitchat. She's counting on some solitary time to draw and paint . . . and sort things out.

Still, Sandy did mention that she's meeting some man here. She'll probably be busy with him.

"I see that you two have met already?" Jasper asks, returning to stand behind the desk.

"Uh huh. We ran into each other on the ferry," Sandy says distractedly. "Um, listen, I'm meeting someone here—Ethan? Ethan Thoreau? I thought he'd be waiting for me down at the landing, but he wasn't."

Must be her blind date, Jennie thinks, noting the breathless way she says his name. Her round face is flushed, probably from excitement as much as from the cold.

"That's right, you're Mr. Thoreau's guest this weekend," Jasper says, smiling and nodding. "He called an hour ago. He said to tell you that he was still at the hospital—some sort of surgical emergency—but he'll be here as soon as possible."

Sandy's face falls. "But I thought we just took the last ferry in tonight."

"That was the last ferry, but the airport is still open, of course."

"He's flying in?" Sandy asks.

"I didn't think the airlines served this island," Jennie comments. She'd checked, wanting to avoid the long ferry ride if at all possible.

"They don't," Jasper says. "Mr. Thoreau will be arriving on his private plane."

Sandy perks right up at that news. "Private plane," she murmurs, turning to Jennie. "Figures. I mean, a rich doctor—surgeon?" she adds, glancing at Jasper Hammel for confirmation. At his nod, she goes on, "Of course a rich surgeon would have his own plane."

"Of course," Jennie agrees, wondering how someone like Sandy had managed to hook up with this guy in the first place. Oh, she's nice and friendly, and even pretty despite her chubbiness. But she doesn't seem like the type who would appeal to a wealthy surgeon.

For Sandy's sake, Jennie hopes the guy didn't suddenly draw the same conclusion and stand her up.

Jasper Hammel clears his throat. "I'll just get the two of you settled into your rooms now. I'm sure you're anxious to relax and warm up."

A floorboard creaks above, and Jennie looks expectantly at the stairs behind the desk, waiting to hear footsteps descending.

But there's no other sound. It's as if someone is poised there, listening to what's going on below.

Jasper, busy writing in the registry, doesn't appear to have noticed it. But Sandy catches Jennie's eye, knitting her brow slightly. Apparently she heard the sound, too.

Jennie remembers the figure she'd seen at the window upstairs, at the very top of the house, as she'd approached the inn. She decides that the silhouette couldn't have belonged to Jasper. The outline of the man in the window had been longer, narrower, than the innkeeper's short, round frame.

Someone else had been watching her from the window.

So? Jennie tells herself. *Big deal. Probably a bored guest.*

But is that same person now standing someplace above, eavesdropping?

And if so . . . why?

As soon as Jasper Hammel's footsteps retreat down the hall, Sandy turns the latch on her door, locking it.

Then she surveys the room.

Raspberry-colored floral wallpaper. White-painted woodwork. Lace curtains. Rose-sprigged bedspread with flounces that reveal a matching dust ruffle. Framed pastel watercolors. Dried rosebuds in a white wicker basket on the table by the bed.

She peers into a delicate pink-and-white china bowl on the mantel and discovers the source of the lavender scent that fills the air: potpourri.

This room must be reserved for female guests, she decides. No way would a man be comfortable here.

She turns and opens her suitcase, which Jasper Hammel deposited on the stand near the door. The first thing she removes is the new outfit she bought for her date with Ethan Thoreau. She bought it at Greenbury Gal, and it was outrageously expensive even with her employee discount. But it was worth it.

Her friend Theresa had assured her that the long, navy-blue knit skirt concealed her saddlebag thighs and that the cream-colored angora sweater accentuated what Theresa kindly called her "hourglass figure."

Sandy would gladly sacrifice her forty-double-D boobs if she could get rid of her forty-six-inch hips as well. But nature—and a weakness for junk food—has padded her generously, and she's resigned to the fact that she's never going to be thin.

Not like Laura, whom Jasper showed to a room at the other end of the hall before depositing Sandy in here. Laura has one of those cute, petite shapes that Sandy has always envied. Sandy hadn't missed the way several men on the ferry had checked Laura out, even though she was bundled into a winter coat.

Well, not all men like stick figures, she reminds herself. *Some men like women who have some meat on their bones.*

Oh, God. Now you sound like Ma.

Angie Cavelli, roly-poly in her own right, is always telling Sandy that there's no reason she shouldn't be able to find a husband. Besides, she always adds, at twenty-five, Sandy has no time to waste. After all, as Angie likes to point out, by the time she herself was twenty-five, Tony Junior was in kindergarten, Frankie was potty trained, Danny was on solids, and she was pregnant with Sandy.

Good for you, Ma, Sandy always wants to add.

But she doesn't. She was taught to respect her parents. No matter what they say or how they make her feel.

So she doesn't say anything to her mother, and she doesn't say anything to her father, either, when he tells her—only when her mother's out of earshot, of course—that if Sandy would just lose some weight, she could find a husband. After all, "no man wants a fat wife."

She knows that her father is thinking of Joe, assuming that he broke the engagement because of her being overweight. She knows neither of her parents believe that *she's* the one who called it off and that they both think the best she could ever get out of life is to become Mrs. Joseph Marconi with a houseful of kids.

Sighing, Sandy carefully hangs her new outfit in the tiny closet, which is empty except for several wire coat hangers bearing paper sleeves that read "Sampson Bros.— 42 Years as Tide Island's Premier Dry Cleaners."

As she turns away from the closet, she hears a floorboard creak overhead.

Nothing unusual about that. The inn has three floors. She noticed the narrower staircase that leads upstairs when Jasper Hammel led her and Jennie along the hallway on the way to their rooms.

But Sandy thinks of how the floorboard had creaked on the second floor when she and Jennie were checking in awhile ago and how she had almost felt as though someone might be lurking there, eavesdropping.

Why anyone would want to do such a thing is beyond her, but the notion that they might definitely gave her the creeps then and does again now.

You're just not used to big old houses, she tells herself, shaking her head. *Besides, you're afraid of your own shadow.*

If she weren't such a baby, she would have moved out of her parents' house years ago. But she can't stand the thought of living alone.

Not that she'd admit that to anyone, not even Theresa. She tells her friends that she doesn't move out because she can't afford to. Luckily, her parents don't think a woman should leave home until she gets married, so they don't charge her rent.

Going back over to her suitcase, she removes the rest of her clothes—a few oversized sweaters, turtlenecks, and pairs of leggings—and stacks them neatly in the drawers of an antique bureau. She catches sight of herself in the mirror above it and leans closer to examine her reflection.

You have such a pretty face. . . . How many times has she heard that?

She knows it's true—her eyes are big and brown and fringed with thick lashes, and her lips are full and red, and she has dimples in her cheeks when she smiles.

Will Ethan Thoreau think she has a pretty face, too?

She takes her quilted pink makeup bag out of her suitcase and unzips it. She opens a compact and begins meticulously applying blusher, tracing the contours of her cheekbones the way the girl at the Clinique counter showed her.

She wonders what time Ethan will arrive on his private

plane and whether she should change into her new skirt and sweater just in case he decides to pop in at the inn without calling her first.

She decides against it. Why waste her best clothes on a chance? She looks fine in the chocolate-colored stretch pants and matching oversized tunic she has on. Not only does the outfit camouflage her bulges pretty well, but it exactly matches the shade of her eyes. At least, that's what Danny told her when she wore it on Christmas.

Sandy smiles when she thinks of him. She can always count on her favorite brother to compliment her.

She can't seem to help feeling a little wistful ever since he married Cheryl, his college sweetheart, and moved out of the house last summer. Of course, they only live a few blocks away and Danny still goes out of his way to be nice to Sandy, but things aren't the same between them.

Not that Sandy resents Cheryl.

It's just that she wishes she had someone, too.

Maybe things will work out with Ethan.

Maybe he and Sandy can buy the cute little split level down the street from her parents. She's always loved that house, and just the other day, she noticed a For Sale sign on the snowy lawn. It would be a perfect starter home, and it already has a swing set and sand box in the backyard.

Sandy reaches for her eyeliner and smiles as she imagines the children that she will have with Ethan Thoreau.

And when the floorboard creaks above again, she doesn't even notice.

Two

Liza is starving.

If it weren't for that—and the irresistible savory aroma wafting up to the second floor—she wouldn't be on her way down to the dining room for dinner. She certainly isn't in the mood to mingle with the other guests—small talk isn't her forte, and there's no point in wasting an effort on people she'll never see again, anyway.

But she can't ignore her rumbling stomach.

And anyway, it's not as though she has anything else to do tonight.

D.M. Yates isn't going to contact her until tomorrow. The innkeeper, Jasper Hammel, had handed her a pink telephone message slip when she checked in. All it said was that Yates had called and would be in touch again in the morning.

When Liza questioned Jasper Hammel about the message, he'd shrugged and told her he wasn't the one who had taken it—must have been the hired girl, but she had already left for the weekend.

And when Liza asked Jasper Hammel what he knew about the famous author, he'd shrugged again. Yes, Yates had a house on the island. No, Hammel had never met him. Didn't Liza know he was a recluse?

"Of course I know that," Liza had snapped, biting her tongue to leave off the *you idiot* that would have followed naturally.

Jasper Hammel hadn't seemed fazed by her tone. He'd

regarded her calmly from behind his wire-framed glasses, then said, "You will be joining us for dinner in the dining room, won't you? Eight-thirty sharp."

"No, thanks," Liza had muttered.

And now here she is, hurrying down the stairs to the main floor, lured by the rich, mouth-watering scent that fills the air.

She hesitates in the entryway for only a moment before following her nose through the archway to her left, passing through a cozy parlor and into the dining room.

Though she hasn't seen or heard any of the other guests until now, for some reason, she's expecting to find a crowd gathered for dinner.

Instead, only two other people are seated at the enormous, polished wooden table, tucked away at the far end, across from each other. Classical music plays softly in the background, and it's especially fitting in a room like this, with its old-fashioned furnishings and decor.

Candles glow on the ornately carved sideboard and in the center of the table. Heavy burgundy-colored drapes are drawn over the two windows, and the elaborate crystal chandelier gives off only a dim glow.

It takes a moment for Liza's eyes to adjust to the lighting. When they do, she's startled to recognize the woman from the ferry—the one with the kind, lilac-colored eyes and the straight dark hair. The other person seated at the table is a pudgy, round-faced woman who's wearing too much makeup and yammering away to the brunette, who's obviously trying to seem interested.

At first, neither of them sees Liza.

Then the chatterbox turns around and spots her.

"Hi!" she says brightly, waving.

Liza clears her throat and wishes she'd stayed upstairs. But it's not too late to go back. She mumbles a reluctant "hello," but before she can take a step backward, Jasper Hammel sweeps into the room carrying a huge platter. On it is an elaborate presentation of lobsters and shellfish and what looks like heaps of wild rice and vegetables.

"Oh, good, Liza, you've decided to join us," he says, spotting her in the doorway. "I was counting on you."

He motions to the head of the table, where a third place setting waits.

Liza moves toward it and slips into the chair, aware that both of the other women are regarding her curiously. She focuses on the table, taking in the hunter-green brocade place mat, the delicate china with its ivory background and gold trim, and the silver that's obviously been lovingly polished. An etched crystal goblet sits in front of her place, and it's already filled with amber liquid.

"The wine is great," Sandy says, and Liza looks up to see that she's watching her with wide, friendly brown eyes. "Not too dry. I hate dry wine."

"Really? I like dry wine." Liza reaches for the glass, taking a sip. Not as fine as the bottle of chardonnay she'd shared last night on her first date with Albert, a stockbroker, at Le Cirque on the Upper East Side. But not bad, either.

"Liza Danning, this is Sandy Cavelli," Jasper says, sweeping a hand to indicate the chubby woman, then motioning toward the brunette, "and Laura Towne. I'll be right back." He disappears into the kitchen again.

"Nice to meet you," Sandy says cheerfully, turning back to Liza.

"You, too." Liza glances at Laura, including her.

The woman seems subdued, merely nodding over her own wineglass.

Liza recalls the way she snubbed her on the ferry. Well, how was she to know she'd be sitting at a dinner table with her later?

Nothing like an awkward beginning, though.

"So you're staying here alone, too, huh?" Sandy asks Liza, breaking the strained silence.

"Yes." Liza frowns slightly, realizing that no other

places are set at the table. The other guests must have gone out to eat—even though it's raining steadily outside now. And where could they have gone? She hadn't noticed a single open restaurant, or even a sign of life, on the boardwalk.

Come to think of it, she hasn't seen any signs of other guests, either. . . .

"What a coincidence," Sandy comments.

Liza catches her hungrily eyeing the platter full of food on the table.

"What's a coincidence?" Laura speaks for the first time, putting down her glass.

"You know, that three girls would all come to a place like this, alone."

Liza arches a brow at Sandy's reference to them as *girls*. She's about to open her mouth, but Laura says, "I don't usually travel alone. My—I won this trip, and it was only for one person."

"You won it? How? I never win anything," Sandy tells her wistfully.

"It was one of those charity sweepstakes things."

"What charity?"

"I can't remember," Laura says simply and reaches for her wineglass again. She doesn't sip it, just spins the stem in her fingers, and Liza decides she's looking for something to do with her hands. For some reason, she looks uneasy.

"How about you, Liza? What are you doing here alone?"

Doesn't she ever mind her own business? Liza wonders, studying Sandy's eager, curious expression.

"I'm here on business," she informs her tersely, and waits for the inevitable.

Sure enough . . .

"What kind of business?"

"Publishing."

"Wow. Are you an editor?"

Liza nods.

"Where?"

"New York."

"What publisher?"

"Xavier House."

"Wow."

Liza can't tell if Sandy's ever heard of them or if she simply says *wow* to everything.

Sandy clears her throat and says, "I don't usually travel alone, either."

Liza nods. She can tell Sandy wants her to ask what she's doing on the island this weekend. But she doesn't really care. And she isn't in the mood to be polite.

After a pause, Sandy looks at the platter of shellfish and rice and licks her lips.

Liza glances at Laura again and sees that she's staring off into space, still fiddling with her glass.

After a few more moments of silence, during which the strains of classical music and the pattering of raindrops against the windows seem to grow steadily louder, the door leading to the kitchen suddenly swings open.

Jasper Hammel breezes back into the room, carrying a cloth-covered basket that gives off the unmistakable yeasty aroma of hot bread.

"Here we are," he says, setting it on the table and reaching for a silver serving spoon near the platter of hot food. "I'll serve. Sandy, why don't you lift your plate for me?"

"Sure. Um, what is it?"

"Steamed fresh shellfish on a bed of wild rice with grilled spring vegetables. I prepared it myself, and I'm sure you'll find it tasty."

"Steamed and grilled . . . that's great. Low fat." Sandy lowers her heaping plate and smiles at Liza and Laura. "I'm on a diet."

They nod.

As Jasper fills Laura's plate next, Sandy goes on, "I'm

meeting a guy here this weekend. A surgeon. He's totally great-looking. And he's flying in on his private plane."

Liza arches a brow. Either Sandy's lying or the great-looking surgeon is pretty hard up. Why else would he date such a dumpy, unsophisticated chatterbox?

She finds herself asking, despite her vow not to make conversation, "Where did you meet him?"

"Oh, we haven't met yet. It's a blind date." She hesitates. "He . . . uh, he answered an ad I placed in the personals."

That explains it.

Liza lifts her plate for Jasper, who dumps a heaping serving of rice on it, then scoops up some oysters and mussels.

The food is delicious, which isn't surprising. Liza would expect to find excellent shellfish on Tide Island, and Jasper Hammel strikes her as the kind of man who would enjoy cooking.

As they eat, he hovers, pouring wine and urging them to have more rice, another piece of bread. He makes conversation about the island as he bustles about, telling them that it's a lovely place, particularly in the winter, when there aren't many tourists around "to spoil it."

"We're tourists," Liza can't resist pointing out.

The man actually blushes, and his mouth quivers nervously beneath his trimmed brown mustache. "Oh, but I didn't mean *you*," he says quickly. "I meant all the people who have no regard for the wild, natural beauty of the place. They litter and they stomp all over the dunes and they make a dreadful racket with their blasting radios and screaming children." He shudders. "It's not pleasant."

"How long have you been running the inn?" Sandy asks.

"Not long. Oh, I almost forgot—the dessert! It's in the oven, and I can't let it burn. If you'll excuse me . . ." He darts into the kitchen again.

Sandy looks at Liza and Laura, then whispers, "He's kind of strange, isn't he? Do you think he's gay?"

Laura's lilac eyes widen.

Amused, Liza asks, "What makes you say that?"

"My father said there are a lot of homosexuals on this island. That's part of the reason he doesn't like it. He's not very—you know, liberal."

And you are? Liza wants to ask, but she doesn't. She just spears a chunk of eggplant with her fork and pops it into her mouth.

"So what do you think?" Sandy asks again.

"I have no idea," Laura says. "Does it matter?"

"Of course not. I was just wondering."

Sandy turns her attention back to wrestling with the lobster claw on her plate.

By the time Jasper Hammel reappears five minutes later, they've all finished eating and Sandy has initiated a new conversation, mostly one-sided, about whether a person should count calories or just fat grams when trying to lose weight.

"Why don't we have coffee and dessert in the parlor?" he suggests, starting to clear the table.

"I'll pass," Liza says, rising and tossing her green-brocade napkin onto the table.

"Oh, but you can't!"

Startled, she looks at the man, who offers a nervous little smile. "It's a tradition here at the Bramble Rose for *all* of our guests to adjourn to the parlor for dessert."

"Well, what about the other guests?" Liza asks.

"They'll join us. . . . Won't you?" Jasper asks Laura and Sandy.

Laura offers a reluctant nod, and Sandy says cheerfully, "Sure we will. I can never pass up dessert. What is it?"

"Chocolate raspberry torte with real whipped cream," Jasper tells her. "And we have wonderful fresh berries to serve over—"

"Not these two guests," Liza interrupts him. "I'm talking about everyone else who's staying here at the inn."

"There's no one else staying here, besides me," Jasper informs her. "You three are the only guests."

There's no one else staying here.

Jennie can't get Jasper Hammel's words out of her mind—nor can she shake the memory of that floorboard creaking above when she and Sandy were checking in earlier.

If there's no one else here at the inn, then it must have been Liza lurking on the floor above. But why?

Jennie isn't crazy about the sleek, snobby blond. But she certainly doesn't seem like . . .

Well, like she's up to something.

And ever since she's arrived at the inn, Jennie's been feeling uneasy. As though things aren't what they seem. As though something odd is going on.

If Liza wasn't the one who was eavesdropping at the top of the stairs, then Jasper Hammel is lying about there not being anyone else at the inn.

That wouldn't be hard to believe. The man seems distinctly nervous. It could just be his personality type, but Jennie can't help wondering whether there's more to it than that.

On the other hand, why would there be something sinister going on at a quaint island inn?

You must be imagining things Jennie tells herself again. And it wouldn't be the first time she's done that since that horrible day three years ago.

Sometimes, she would be standing in line at Stop and Shop with a cartful of groceries and manage to convince herself that the person behind her had a gun.

And once, when she had been driving on the Mass Pike, she'd been so certain that she was being followed that she'd had to pull off at the rest area, so shaky that it was over an hour before she could calm down enough to keep driving.

Lately, those episodes were fewer and farther between. But she knows she still isn't entirely okay—that sometimes, her mind plays tricks on her, sending her into near-panic over imaginary threats.

And that's all it is this time, Jennie assures herself as she settles into a Victorian rosewood parlor chair and looks around.

This is a cozy room, cast in a warm glow from a fringe-shaded Victorian floor lamp and the small blaze that crackles in the hearth. The lace curtains and floral-patterned wallpaper are similar to the decor in Jennie's room upstairs; and the parlor, too, is filled with antiques.

Jennie's skilled eye notes that all of the furniture and bric-a-brac appear to be authentic period pieces—and expensive. She bought a nineteenth century coatrack like the one in the corner at an auction in Marblehead just last week and paid a fortune for it.

She glances at Liza, who is perched on the edge of the matching parlor chair on the other side of the fireplace. The woman runs a manicured hand over her smooth blond hair, looking bored.

Sandy flops her heavy body onto the sofa beneath the only window. "Hey, did you notice there's no TV?" she asks, looking around. "There's not one in my room, either. Do you guys have them in yours?"

Liza ignores her, concentrating instead on adjusting the belt buckle on her trim black slacks.

Feeling sorry for Sandy, who's obviously trying hard to make conversation, Jennie says, "A lot of inns don't have television sets in the rooms, and some don't have them in the public areas, either."

"Why not?"

Jennie shrugs. "Probably to maintain authenticity, in this case. After all, television didn't exist a hundred and twenty years ago, and that's probably when this place was built."

"Oh, yeah, that's right—you're an antique dealer, aren't

you?" Sandy asks. "You must love this place. Everything looks really old."

"It is." Jennie runs her fingertips over the curved arm of her chair, noting the worn spot in the nubby raspberry-colored fabric.

"My room looks like it popped out of a Laura Ashley catalogue," Sandy tells her. "I love it. But I don't think my brothers would be crazy about it. I guess not all the rooms are so frilly."

"Probably not," Jennie agrees, though her room has lilac-sprigged wallpaper and a lace-covered canopy bed.

Liza, who hadn't even appeared to be listening, comments, "I don't know about that. My room looks like it was decorated for a ten-year-old girl. The wallpaper's covered in pink roses, and the bedspread has eyelet trim. Definitely not up my alley."

"Well, I think my room's beautiful," Sandy says, almost defiantly. "How about you, Laura?"

Jennie nods.

"I'll bet you have all kinds of antiques in your house in Boston, too," Sandy says. "What kind of place do you live in?"

"It's an apartment, actually." Jennie shifts on her chair.

"Do you live alone?"

"No." Then, because she knows Sandy is waiting for her to elaborate, she adds, "I live with my sister."

"What does she do?"

"She works at the Gap. Liza," Jennie said, turning away from Sandy in an effort to change the subject, "what part of New York do you live in?"

"Manhattan. The Upper East Side."

Jennie nods, because there isn't much to say to that. Suddenly, she wants nothing more than to be up in her room, alone, where no one is prying into her personal life and where she doesn't have to make forced conversation with strangers.

Or, better yet, she wishes she were back in her familiar town house in Boston, even with Laura blasting Pearl Jam from the stereo and spilling something or other on the carpet or upholstery. And it's a Friday night, so right about now, Keegan would probably be on his way over with a pizza. . . .

No, she corrects mentally. *He wouldn't be. Not anymore.*

It's so hard to believe she'll never spend another night with Keegan—cuddled on the couch under the antique wedding-ring quilt she'd bought at her first auction, watching a video and eating pizza and wearing matching thick gray cotton socks with red-banded tops, the kind that are toasty warm but tend to unravel in the laundry, leaving red threads all over everything.

Jennie thinks about how Keegan always likes to have his feet sticking out of the bottom of the quilt—he can't sleep with them covered, either. He has huge feet, and so does she—he always teased her that when they had kids, they would have to order special custom-made giant baby shoes.

When they had kids—not *if.*

Keegan was always so certain of their relationship, right from the start. But then, he's like that about almost everything—casually confident, breezing through life with an easygoing, happy-go-lucky assurance that things will go his way.

Jennie pictures the stark pain that took over his handsome features when she told him it was over. Pain, and surprise, as though he couldn't believe she would do this to him— that she would abandon him.

She feels a stab of sorrow in the vicinity of her heart—a distinct physical sensation that nearly takes her breath away.

This must be what people mean when they talk about heartache, she realizes.

"Laura?" Sandy says loudly.

Jennie blinks. "Yeah?"

"You're on another planet, aren't you? I was talking to you and you were looking right through me."

"Oh, I, uh—I'm sorry." Jennie is about to stand up and excuse herself when Jasper Hammel suddenly shows up carrying a cherrywood tray. He has a way of doing that—appearing with no warning.

"All right, ladies, here we are. Coffee and a rich dessert—just the thing for a blustery February night."

"I think I'll pass," Liza says, rising. "I'm pretty exhausted."

But her sharp green eyes don't look sleepy. She seems edgy—as edgy as Jennie feels.

"Oh, come on, now. . . . You have to taste my torte," Jasper informs Liza firmly, putting a porcelain pedestal mug into her hand and motioning for her to sit down again.

She does; and once again, her eyes collide with Jennie's. Her expression is wary. Jennie instinctively realizes that Liza, too, is uneasy about this place and this man.

Sandy, on the other hand, seems oblivious. She happily accepts a mug and a plate and tells Jasper that the torte looks "yummy."

Liza catches Jennie's gaze again when Sandy says it, and this time, she rolls her eyes.

Jennie quickly looks away. Sandy might be a little on the immature side, but she's a nice person.

Liza, on the other hand, is something of a bitch, and Jennie isn't particularly eager to align herself with her.

Again, she wishes she were back at home in Boston. She would give anything to have Keegan's arms around her right now.

Because Keegan has always made her feel safe.

And right now, for some reason she can't pinpoint, even as she sits in this quaint, quiet parlor, she feels vaguely threatened.

By what, she doesn't know.

But it's *real;* something dark and terrible—as dark and

terrible as the nightmare that changed her life forever on that bloody day three years ago.

Two floors above the parlor, on the top floor of the inn, in an ancient, upholstered rocking chair, he sits and rocks and waits.

At one time, the attic room must have been servants' quarters for the inn's summer help. A deep, stained white porcelain sink and an ancient gas stove are tucked into an alcove. In another corner, behind a warped wooden door, there's a tiny bathroom with a steep, sloping ceiling. There's no shower, only a chipped clawfoot bathtub. And the toilet no longer flushes on its own; he has to lift the tank, reach into the clammy water, and pull the chain.

He thinks of the enormous master bedroom suite back at his estate on Long Island's north shore. It has a king-sized bed, a fireplace, and an adjoining Jacuzzi in a glass solarium with a sweeping view of the sound. It also has his-and-hers dressing rooms, each with its own private attached bathroom.

His dressing room and bathroom are cluttered with his belongings.

The other one—the one he'd intended for his bride—is empty.

It always has been.

Sighing, he flips to the first page of the photo album in his lap. It's a special album, one that only has room for a single eight-by-ten picture on each page.

A wedding album, actually—bound in white leather, its cover stamped in gold with the words, "Our Wedding Memories."

This first page belongs to Sandy. There's an empty slot, waiting for the photograph he'll place there.

He has already labeled the oval opening with an ivory

place card that has a raised rectangular border, the kind of card you find on the tables at a wedding reception.

On it, he has meticulously lettered her name in calligraphy, using a special pen.

He remembers the day he went to the art supply store to buy that pen.

The clerk, a pretty blond in her teens, had smiled pleasantly at him and said, "Will that be all, sir? You don't need a bottle of ink to go with it?"

He'd smiled back and said, "No, thank you. I have plenty of ink at home."

It was a lie, of course.

He wasn't planning on using ink at all.

Instead, he'd used his own blood.

It's really quite lovely, he decides, studying the lettering on the card below the empty photo slot. Over the past few months, the blood has faded to a soft, brownish-maroon color that complements the rich ivory surface of the place card. Very elegant.

But this card isn't permanent, of course.

He'll replace it, very soon, with an exact replica.

Except that this time, the blood he'll use to letter Sandy Cavelli's name will be her own.

"Sandy?" Jasper Hammel asks. "Would you like another slice of the torte?"

"I really shouldn't," she says. After all, both Liza and Laura refused, and neither of them has even finished their first servings.

But she can't help glancing at the rich chocolate concoction that's still left on the doily-covered plate Jasper is offering.

"Oh, go ahead," the man says, stepping closer to her and practically holding the torte under her nose. "Just a sliver?"

"All right," she relents, because she's never been able to resist anything chocolate.

I'll do fifty sit-ups before bed tonight, she promises herself as she holds up her dish to let Jasper serve her.

He spoons on the fresh raspberries and a generous dollop of whipped cream.

A hundred sit-ups, Sandy amends, then stifles a yawn behind her hand. *If I can stay awake long enough.*

Suddenly, she can't wait to crawl into bed. Must be all this fresh sea air.

As Jasper discreetly heads back toward the kitchen with the torte, Sandy picks up her fork again and tries to return her attention to the conversation she and Laura had been having. Actually, she had been doing most of the talking, but she suddenly can't remember what about.

Oh, yes. She had been telling Laura about her brothers.

"Anyway," she says, cutting off a piece of the torte and raising it to her lips, "Danny is my youngest brother. He's the only one who's not in the plumbing and heating business with my dad. He's a gym teacher at St. Agnes High."

Laura nods.

Sandy swallows the bite of torte, then yawns again. "Oh, gosh, excuse me," she says. "I'm really tired."

"So am I." Liza stands and places her mug and the delicate plate containing her half-eaten cake on a polished table beside her chair. "I'm going up to bed. Good night."

"Night," Laura murmurs.

"Good night. See you tomorrow," Sandy calls after Liza, who doesn't even turn around.

"She's not very nice, is she?" Sandy whispers to Laura when she's sure Liza is out of earshot.

Laura shrugs and looks uncomfortable.

"I mean, it's not that I don't like her," Sandy lies. "It's just that she doesn't seem very friendly. But then, maybe she's just shy," she adds hastily. After all, it isn't right to talk about someone behind her back—especially when the person you're talking about, and the person you're talking to, are both virtual strangers.

"Maybe she is shy," Laura agrees. She stretches and glances at the watch on her wrist. "I should get to bed, too. It's getting late."

"How late is it?"

"Almost ten-thirty."

"Uh-oh." Sandy remembers something.

"What's the matter?"

"I forgot to call my parents. They would have gotten home at a quarter to ten—they work bingo at the church hall every Friday night—and I promised I'd call and let them know I'd arrived safely. Jasper?" she calls, hearing the man's footsteps approaching from the kitchen again.

"Yes?" He appears in the doorway.

"Is there a telephone I can use?" When he seems to hesitate, she adds, "I'll call collect."

"Of course," he says. "There's a phone in the hall, behind the check-in desk."

Sandy gulps down the rest of her dessert in a single bite and stands up, brushing the crumbs off her lap. "Thanks. I'll just—"

"I'll show you where it is," Jasper says, moving toward the hall. "Right this way."

Both Sandy and Laura follow him out of the parlor.

In the front hall, Laura yawns and says, "I'm going up to bed. Good night."

"Good night," Sandy and Jasper answer in unison.

Sandy makes a move toward the desk and the telephone, but suddenly Jasper is standing over it, lifting the receiver and asking her what the number is.

"I can dial it," she says. "I'll call collect."

"That's fine." He makes no move to hand her the phone or step aside so that she can walk behind the desk.

Sandy shrugs and recites her parents' telephone number,

wondering if it's her imagination or if Jasper suddenly seems even more nervous than usual.

He must think I'm not really going to call collect, she decides. Maybe other guests at the inn have used the phone and rung up major long distance phone bills.

"All set, here you are." Jasper hands the receiver to Sandy.

As she speaks to the operator, he steps away, but remains behind the desk, straightening an already neatly stacked pile of papers.

He hovers there the entire minute or so that she talks to her mother, making her feel self-conscious. Actually, it seems somewhat rude, the way the man doesn't allow her to have a private conversation.

Maybe he just doesn't know any better.

"Make sure that you're careful, Sandy," her mother says, before they hang up.

"Careful of what?"

"Everything. After all, you never know."

Sandy sighs. "I'm always careful, Ma. You worry too much," she adds, watching Jasper Hammel carefully flick a nonexistent speck of dust off the polished surface of the desk.

He doesn't venture out of the attic room until well after midnight, when the house is silent.

Outside, the wind has picked up, blowing in off the water to rattle the windows. The rain has turned to sleet, and he wonders, as he creeps down the stairs, whether the storm will become a full-blown nor'easter.

That would be perfect.

Tide Island is practically deserted at this time of year anyway, but nasty weather would virtually guarantee that no one will disturb him as he carries out his plans.

He stops at the bottom of the stairs. Behind this first

door, he knows, is Laura Towne. She will have locked herself in from the other side, no doubt feeling secure.

He licks his lips.

All he has to do is use his master key to slip into the room.

He pictures her the way he last saw her and wonders whether time has altered her beauty.

Is she asleep now, on the other side of this wall?

Of course she is, he reminds himself. Thanks to the sedative she'd unknowingly ingested, masked by the strong flavors of chocolate and raspberries.

He wants desperately to open the door and see her. It's been so very long, and there have been many nights when he has ached for her. The knowledge that she's here, that she's once again under his roof, fills him with tantalizing urges.

But this time, he's the one in control.

Of himself.

And, though she doesn't know it, in control of Laura.

And the others, as well.

Liza Danning.

Sandy Cavelli.

He sighs. Then he reaches into his pocket, removing a single key. Carefully, he slips it into the top lock, the one that only works from the outside.

He turns it and listens for the click that means Laura Towne is locked into the beautiful room with the lilac-sprigged wallpaper that exactly matches the shade of her eyes.

I'll be back, he promises her silently. *But not tonight.*

The next stop along the hallway is Liza Danning's room, where he swiftly but stealthily locks her door, too, from the outside, then moves on.

Anticipation is building within him now.

In front of the last door, he again brandishes the key. But

instead of putting it into the top lock, he inserts it into the bottom one—the one that works from both sides.

And instead of locking Sandy Cavelli into her room, he ever so quietly turns the key, opens the door, and slips over the threshold.

He pauses just inside the shadowy room until he hears the slow, rhythmic sound of her breathing.

Closing the door quietly behind him, he tucks the key back into his pocket and moves cautiously across the wooden floor until he's standing over the bed.

She's lying on her side, her brown hair tousled on the white linen pillowcase. Her mouth is slightly open, and he fights the urge to run a gentle finger over those full lips. She should be sound asleep, thanks to the torte, but he doesn't want to take any chances.

So he simply looks at her.

And as he looks, his fingers slip down his belly to the top button of his trousers. He unfastens it, then slowly begins to edge the zipper down.

Her face, he notes, is much rounder than it used to be. And though she's wearing a long-sleeved flannel nightgown, he can tell that the arm that's thrown over her head is chubby.

It doesn't matter to him.

Struggling to remain in control, he gingerly extends his left hand and tentatively pulls the bedspread and sheet away from Sandy's body. He lowers them to her waist, then pauses to make sure she isn't stirring. When he's satisfied that she's still deeply asleep, he continues pulling the bedding down until her legs, too, are exposed.

The nightgown is bunched around her hips, revealing white thighs that are full and dimpled. Holding his breath, he moves his left hand to grasp the flannel hem and raise it, past her high-waisted white cotton underwear and the soft rolls of her belly to her heavy, bare breasts that sag almost to her navel.

Still, she doesn't move, and he desperately longs to touch her.

But he can't.

Not yet.

Not tonight.

His left hand curls into a tight fist and he forces it to fall at his side.

The fingers of his right hand probe past his open fly and fumble in the layers of his Brooks Brothers boxer shorts until they close over his own hot, hard flesh.

Staring at Sandy Cavelli's near-naked body in the bed, he strokes himself, lightly at first so that his skin tingles all over.

His movements become more rapid, more urgent as he nears release, and he bites his lower lip to keep from moaning.

He closes his eyes.

Images flash in his mind.

Past, present, future . . .

Sandy as she had looked at thirteen, when he had known her—all sweet and awkward and willing to please . . .

Sandy as she is now, sleeping before him, blissfully unaware of his presence . . .

And Sandy as she will be tomorrow—her big brown eyes wide with terror, her full lips quivering as she begs him to let her go, her plump body clad in the pure white wedding dress he's had custom-made for her . . .

The dress that, after tomorrow, will be stained with her blood.

Three

Overcome by stark, black terror, Jennie runs for her life.

Someone is chasing her through the Colonial Mall in Boston—someone she can't see or hear, yet she knows he's there, closing in behind her. The wide corridors are eerily dark and deserted, silent except for the echo of her pounding footsteps and desperate panting.

She's looking for someplace to hide, for an open shop where she can duck behind the clothing racks or underneath the cashier's counter. But every store she passes is closed, the security gates lowered and padlocked.

Panicked, Jennie pushes on, dogged by the knowledge that her time is running out.

He's going to get me, she tells herself frantically. *There's no escape.*

Suddenly, just as she feels him looming behind her, just as clammy fingers grab her throat, the air is pierced by a shrill ringing sound.

Jennie sits straight up in bed, gasping and looking around. She instinctively reaches for her travel alarm clock on the nightstand and pushes the button on top to still the jangling bell.

Where am I?

She blinks and gazes from the lilac-sprigged wallpaper to the red-brick fireplace to the lace-curtained window that reveals only rain-splattered glass and a patch of gray sky.

Tide Island. The inn.

She takes a deep breath and releases it, then runs a hand through her tangled hair. Groggily, she struggles to clear the fog in her brain and take hold of her senses.

I'm safe. It was only a dream.

Not a dream, she amends—*a nightmare.*

And this isn't the first time she's had it. For three years, the same familiar, terrible images have haunted her sleep.

Never, in the past, has her invisible predator caught her.

This time, though, is different. This time, she felt his evil touch.

She shivers at the memory of his cold skin against hers, even as she reminds herself that it wasn't real.

He can't get you. He's dead.

Always before, that awareness has comforted her.

This time, even though she knows it was just a nightmare and she knows the person who triggered it can no longer harm her, Jennie finds herself feeling distinctly uneasy . . .

And uncertain.

This time, she can't help but wonder about the person who was chasing her through the Colonial Mall.

You know who it was. It's always him.

Or is it?

In her whole life, with all its hardship, only one person has ever put her in mortal danger. Only one person, in a few chilling, mercifully fleeting moments, ever held the power to shatter her world—and did.

But he's gone. She saw him take his own life in a blast from the same gun that had demolished everything Jennie held dear. She saw his crumpled, lifeless body with her own eyes.

So why can't Jennie shake the feeling that she's suddenly in danger again? And that this time, the threat is more ominous, more deadly, than before?

Shuddering, Jennie abruptly throws the covers back and swings her bare feet to the cold wooden floor. As she stands, she finds herself swaying unsteadily, almost sinking back down to the mattress.

What's with you? she asks herself, frowning and clinging to the headboard for support. She feels woozy and a little queasy, almost as though she's got a hangover. But of course, that's impossible. She only had that one glass of wine last night.

Maybe it was the rich chocolate dessert. Jennie isn't usually much of a sweet-eater. It's Laura who loves stuff like that. And Keegan.

Unbidden, an image enters her brain—Keegan sitting at the kitchen table in her apartment, eating gooey brownies she's just taken out of the oven. She can hear his voice telling her how delicious they are, can taste the warm chocolate on his lips as he kisses her. . . .

She cringes and shuts out the memory.

She grabs her robe from the bedpost and wraps it around herself, then crosses on slightly wobbly legs to the window.

Last night when she checked in, it was too dark to see the view.

This morning, although the weather is gloomy, she can make out the sloping terrain below—the rocks and sand and long brown grass that cover the landscape, and beyond that, the sea. The water, foaming with whitecaps, is the same murky color as the sky so that there's no distinguishing line at the horizon.

Suddenly, Jennie longs to be down there on the narrow strip of beach, with the roar of the water and wind in her ears and cold salt air filling her lungs.

That's what I need. A walk by the ocean would wake me up and maybe even snap me out of this weird, paranoid mood.

She grabs the small blue case that contains her toiletry items and walks across the room, hoping that no one is already using the shared bathroom across the hall. She flips the latch that unlocks the door, then turns the knob and pulls.

Nothing happens.

Overtaken by an intense, sudden stab of claustrophobia, Jennie tugs the door again. This time, it budges. Relieved, she quickly steps out into the empty hallway.

It probably just sticks in damp weather, she tells herself. That happens a lot in old houses like this.

You really need to calm down, Jen. . . . You're completely on edge and there's absolutely no reason. Relax.

A half hour later, freshly showered, her hair still damp and caught back in a black headband, Jennie is feeling much better, though not totally relaxed.

For some reason, she can't seem to let go of a nagging sense that something isn't quite right.

A walk on the beach will probably help clear her mind, though.

She pulls on her heavy down jacket as she walks down the stairs. She's dressed for the damp, chilly New England morning: her oldest, softest, most faded jeans; rubber L.L. Bean boots; a thick navy cable knit sweater.

"Good morning, Laura," a voice says as she rounds the landing.

Startled, Jennie glances down to see Jasper Hammel standing in the front hall. He's holding a feather duster, which looks out of sync with his clothing: an expensive-looking black turtleneck and pleated dark-gray corduroy slacks.

"Oh . . . good morning." Jennie walks down the last few steps, fumbling with the zipper on her jacket.

"There's a continental breakfast set up on the sideboard in the dining room," Jasper informs her, flicking the duster over the carved newel post at the bottom of the stairs. "Nothing elaborate . . . just coffee and danishes. Feel free to help yourself."

"Um, no thank you." Jennie hesitates. "I was just going to go for a walk on the beach."

"I'm afraid it's not a very nice day for that," he says, glancing toward the window. "According to this morning's radio forecast, there might be a storm on the way. Quite a nasty one, for that matter . . . but don't be alarmed," he adds quickly, catching sight of her expression. "The weather on Tide Island is always unpredictable. For all we know, the nor'easter will pass us by and blow right out to sea."

"I hope so," Jennie murmurs, tugging the zipper on her jacket up to her chin.

"Just the same, I wouldn't advise you to wander too far, Laura. The island may seem small and easy to maneuver, but there are some remote patches, and you wouldn't want to get lost."

"I won't," Jennie assures him, and heads for the door.

As she steps out into the windy, rainy morning, she tries to ignore the little voice inside her head . . .

The one that's warning her to leave the island—before the storm rolls in and strands her here.

Before it's too late, the voice adds.

And though she tries not to acknowledge it, telling herself it's just paranoia again, Jennie can't help wondering . . .

Too late for what?

"Damn, damn, damn."

Liza jerks the black silk stocking back down her leg and tosses it across the room, scowling.

How can she have been careless enough to give herself a run when she only brought one pair with her?

Just to be sure, she gets up and walks over to the bureau drawer where she put her clothes when she unpacked last night. She digs through the neatly folded stacks carelessly. Nothing but two pairs of black knee-highs and one pair of tan pantyhose.

Now what's she going to do?

Feeling frazzled, she stands in the middle of the room and contemplates the situation.

It's no wonder she ran her stocking, after the way things have been going this morning.

She's been feeling out of sorts ever since she forced herself to get out of bed an hour ago. Her head is pounding and she can't seem to wake up. She got out of the shower and was drying off when she remembered that she'd forgotten to shampoo her hair, which meant she had to get back in and wait again for the ancient plumbing to groan into action. And she'd dropped her favorite compact on the floor of her room, cracking the mirror and breaking the pressed powder into crumbly chunks.

I hope this isn't an omen for how my meeting with D.M. Yates is going to go.

Liza glances at her reflection in the full-length mirror on the back of the door. She smooths the soft cashmere fabric of her well-cut black suit, with its three gold buttons on the jacket and the skirt that's just long enough to be professional, but short enough to show off her long, firm legs.

Legs that, right now, are mismatched—one clad in the un-run black stocking she'd put on first, the other bare and winter-white.

Rolling her eyes, Liza unhooks the good stocking from the garter hooks and unrolls it, then tosses it onto the still-rumpled bed.

She takes off her suit, careful not to muss her hair. It took her fifteen minutes longer than usual to get it into a perfect French twist at the back of her head. The first few tries, it either came out too severe or too tumble-down sexy.

Now her hair is just right—swept back to reveal her high cheekbones and expertly made-up eyes, with a few soft tendrils escaping around her ears.

This is the same suit and same hairstyle that she'd worn last fall when she'd met Senator Albert Norwood that first time for dinner at the Japanese restaurant in the Waldorf-Astoria. She remembers how he'd commented, over sushi, about how silky and "touchable" her hair looked and how his fat fingers had slowly climbed up her silk-covered leg beneath the table and how shocked he'd looked when he'd discovered that beneath her proper suit she was wearing a garter belt . . . and nothing else.

She has imagined treating D.M. Yates to a similar experience, and it simply won't work if she has to wear pantyhose.

Sighing, Liza buttons a plain black cardigan over her champagne-colored Christian Dior lace chemise and yanks on a pair of slim-fitting black leggings. She pulls on her warmest wool socks and flat black lace-up boots that probably aren't practical for the miserable weather outside, but who cares?

If the fine Italian leather gets ruined, she can always have Albie buy her another pair.

Liza grabs her down-filled Nautica ski jacket, which she hasn't worn since her Christmas trip to Aspen, and leaves her room.

Hopefully, D.M. Yates won't call her until she gets back. But just in case, she'll let that scrawny fruitcake Jasper Hammel know where she is.

Conveniently, he's right at the bottom of the stairs when she gets to the first floor. He looks up from watering the large parlor palm with a bright-yellow enamel watering can that looks like something out of a nursery rhyme.

"Good morning, Liza," he chirps.

"Morning." She finds herself irritated at his cheery tone and broad smile beneath that squirrely mustache of his. "If Mr. Yates calls—"

"Mr. Yates *already* called you . . . bright and early."

She blinks. "He *what?*"

"He called you, bright—"

"Why didn't you let me know he was on the phone?"

"No need," he says simply, reaching up to tip the long-necked spout into a hanging pot of ivy beside the front door.

"What do you mean, 'no need'?" Liza asks evenly, glaring at him.

"He merely called to tell you that he's been detained by unexpected business and won't be able to meet with you until tomorrow."

"Tomorrow?" Liza stares at Jasper Hammel in disbelief. "He's putting me off until tomorrow . . . and you didn't even have the decency to let me speak with the man?"

Jasper shrugs and says, in his clipped, formal manner, "I didn't want to wake you at such an early hour after your long trip on the ferry last night. But," he adds quickly, "apparently, I made the wrong decision. I'm sorry I didn't alert you to the call."

"So am I," Liza snaps.

Suddenly, she longs for Manhattan, where people are sharp and mind their own business, not taking it upon themselves to make important decisions for total strangers.

Liza strides toward the door.

"There's a continental breakfast set up in the dining room," Jasper tells her, stepping out of her way and looking unruffled by the black look she sends him.

"All I need," she says in a clipped tone, "is directions to a store that can sell me a pair of good stockings."

"I'm fairly certain that Hartigan's General Store on the boardwalk carries pantyhose."

"Not pantyhose. Stockings."

Jasper eyes her levelly. "I'm afraid you'd probably need a women's clothing store for that. And they're all closed off-season."

"It figures."

Liza opens the front door, steps out into the raw February morning, and lets the door bang shut behind her. Then she starts trudging down the steep driveway toward the deserted road, cursing Jasper Hammel, D.M. Yates, and this whole stupid godforsaken island.

The first thing Sandy sees when she arrives on the first floor of the inn is Jasper Hammel. The little man is polishing a carved wooden table near the front door, a thick yellow rag in one hand and a can of Pledge in the other.

The second thing Sandy sees is the enormous vase of red roses sitting on the front desk by the telephone she used last night.

"Good morning, Sandy," Jasper says with a smile. "Did you sleep well?"

"Like a rock, actually." She yawns. "I thought maybe the sound of the ocean would keep me awake since I'm not used to it, but I was out cold. What beautiful flowers on the desk, there."

"I'm glad you like them, because they're yours."

Sandy gasps. "You don't have to . . ."

"I'm not. They were delivered here for you from the Island Breeze Florist Shop this morning."

"I can't believe it." Sandy hurries over and plucks the small rectangular card off the tall plastic fork that's nestled among the buds. She knows, even before she opens the envelope, who sent the flowers.

Sure enough . . .

Sandra,
   I'm sorry I didn't make it in last night. I stayed on the mainland, but will be there tonight. Dinner at eight? We'll dine at my home. I'll pick you up at the inn.

                                            Yours,
                                            Ethan

She closes her eyes and leans over the vase, breathing the fresh, sweet floral scent deeply into her lungs.

"Mmmm," she murmurs, opening her eyes and glancing at Jasper. "I love roses."

"And they're certainly appropriate—aren't they?—for a guest at this inn . . . the Bramble Rose."

"You know, I hadn't even thought of that." Sandy does a quick count and realizes that there are two dozen buds in the vase. This must have cost Ethan Thoreau a fortune.

But then, he's rich. He probably sends women flowers all the time.

Sandy has never received flowers in her life, unless you counted the corsage from her prom date, Frankie DeRusso, her senior year, and the daisies her brother Danny picked and brought her when she had her tonsils out as a kid.

What would it be like to date—no, to *marry*—a man who would send roses for every occasion, and sometimes, maybe, for no occasion at all?

Joe had never even remembered to send her a card on Valentine's Day or her birthday, Sandy thinks wistfully. And when they got engaged, he used a ring he'd bought at a pawn shop, one that had someone else's initials engraved in the band. "You can have that buffed off," he'd told her.

She'd never bothered, knowing, even as she first slipped that ring over the fourth finger of her left hand, that she wasn't going to marry him. She'd stayed engaged to him for three months, long enough to work up her nerve to tell him that she didn't want to get married.

Who would have guessed that he would have reacted the way he had? Sobbing hysterically—a man, crying!—begging her not to leave him, telling her that she was the only woman he'd ever loved. He hadn't taken no for an answer. Even now, after almost a year, he still drove by her house every now and then, and he always called Sandy when he drank, incoherently asking for another chance. . . .

"Are you hungry?" Jasper Hammel is asking her, snapping her out of her reverie.

"Starving . . . as usual," she admits ruefully.

"There's coffee and danish in the dining room, on the sideboard. Please help yourself."

"Thank you." Sandy glances toward her roses again.

"You can leave those here until after breakfast, if you'd like," Jasper tells her. "I'll keep an eye on them."

"Oh . . . okay. Thanks."

Hating to turn her back on the beautiful blooms even for a short time, Sandy heads toward the dining room.

Then she pauses and thinks of something. "Jasper?" she asks over her shoulder.

"Yes?"

"Do you know where Ethan Thoreau's house is? I thought I might go for a walk, and . . . you know." She feels her cheeks growing warm, wondering what he thinks of a woman who would pull a junior high stunt like checking out someone's house.

"You know, I haven't been here on the island very long," he tells her, not looking fazed by her question. "I don't really know where Mr. Thoreau lives . . . somewhere on the other side of the island, I would imagine. That's where all the wealthier people have their private homes."

"Okay. Thanks."

Still feeling embarrassed, Sandy walks into the dining room.

She seats herself at the long, empty table with a cup of coffee and a plate containing two cheese danishes, wondering where Laura and Liza are. Maybe one of them will want to do something this afternoon.

On the other hand, Sandy doubts that. Liza doesn't seem to have any intention of being friendly, which is just as well, since Sandy knows she probably has nothing in common with the woman anyway.

And Laura, though she's a lot nicer and warmer, seems lost in her own little world.

Besides, neither of them is around, anyway.

It looks like Sandy's on her own.

As she shoves the last bite of the second danish into her mouth, she decides she might as well do some exploring since there's really nothing else to occupy her until tonight.

And she might as well start with the other side of the island.

Hartigan's General Store is a two-story wooden building in the center of the boardwalk, nestled in a row of other businesses, all of them boarded up for the winter. There's a huge orange "Open" sign hanging in the glass front door of the store.

Jennie sees it from the beach and heads toward it, hurrying across the wet sand. Though it's stopped raining for the moment, the icy wind is picking up again, and suddenly, she can't stop shivering. Hopefully, the store will have hot coffee, and maybe something she can gobble down for breakfast.

Jennie opens the door and finds herself wrestling with it as a sudden gust kicks up, struggling to keep it from blowing backward and slamming into the side of the building. Finally, she pulls it closed, shutting out the roaring cold.

"Gettin' pretty nasty out there, isn't it?"

Jennie glances around and sees an elderly man standing behind a cash register to her right. He has a shock of thick white hair, a ruddy complexion, and eyes that twinkle from his handsome face.

"It's freezing out," Jennie tells him, stomping her numb feet on the mat in front of the door.

The store is surprisingly roomy, with several aisles of groceries near the back and what looks like a soda fountain and a few booths off to the side in an alcove. Jennie sees that only a handful of people are here, a few browsing for food and a few others seated in the alcove.

"We're in for a bad one, this time," the man says, gesturing toward an old-fashioned radio on the shelf behind him. Jennie can faintly hear the staticky sound of big band music coming from the speaker. "Been listening all morning, and the announcer keeps saying that it's looking like a full-blown nor'easter's on the way. Rain, cold, high winds—supposedly worse than what hit the Cape a few years ago on Halloween. We get these storms every once in awhile," the man tells her. "You're not from here, are ya?"

"Nope."

"Where you staying?"

"The Bramble Rose."

The man nods, then asks, in a friendly but somewhat nosy way, "Where you from?"

"I live in Boston," Jennie says, "so I know all about nor'easters, actually."

She knows enough to realize that she's not going anywhere for a few days—not if this storm is worse than the Halloween nor'easter. She and Laura had been visiting a friend of theirs out in Chatham that week, and Jennie remembered how the furious, foaming waves had attacked the coast and carried away houses and cars and trees.

"You're from Boston? What part?"

"Back Bay."

"Nice there, isn't it? I grew up in Quincy."

So did I, Jennie almost tells him, but she stops herself. No reason to get into a conversation with a stranger, nice and friendly as he seems.

She casts a glance at the soda fountain. "Do you serve coffee there?"

"Are you kidding? Of course. Go on over and Shirley will fix you up. She's my wife, and anyone can tell you that she brews the best coffee on the island."

Probably the only coffee on the island, Jennie thought,

heading toward the alcove. This place wasn't exactly hopping.

The beach had been deserted the whole time she'd spent walking—well over an hour. First she'd gone north, away from the inn, where the strip of sand gradually became wider and the landscape along the coast rougher and more desolate. A few houses dotted the shore here and there, but all of them were deserted.

It was hard to imagine what those places must be like in summer, when the windows and doors would be open and flowers would be blooming in windowboxes and people would be sitting around on decks.

It was hard to imagine the beach itself in another season, too—when children would be building sandcastles, teenagers listening to radios and gossiping, and people jogging and swimming and tossing frisbees.

Now, in winter, the shore was a gray, wild, lonely place—so like the coast in England. Jennie unexpectedly found herself with memories of the semester she'd spent there. With Harry.

Harry of the wide grin and twinkling eyes and surprisingly gentle touch . . .

She'd walked and thought about him until the beach gave way to a rocky cliff that loomed ahead, rising straight up and jutting out into the water. On top of the cliff was an enormous, sprawling house with turrets and peaks and porches, looking like something out of a gothic novel.

With a shiver—mostly cold, but partly a response to the creepy-looking house—Jennie had turned away and headed back toward the inn. She'd planned on going in, but when she reached it, she realized she wasn't ready. She wanted to be alone awhile longer, with the ocean and her memories of Harry.

"Hi, sweetie. What can I get you?" asks the angular, gray-haired woman behind the counter in the alcove.

"Just a cup of coffee, please—with milk, instead of

cream, if you have it," Jennie tells her, then spots a glass bakery case. "And a croissant, too," she adds, and suddenly her mouth is watering and her stomach feels completely empty.

"Coming right up, sweetie. You can go ahead and have a seat."

Jennie nods and turns toward the booths. Out of five, only two are occupied. In one, an artsy-looking couple—he with long dreadlocks, she with a crew cut and an earring in her nose—sits having an animated conversation.

In the other booth, Jennie sees, is a blond woman who looks an awful lot like . . .

"Hello—Laura, isn't it?"

Reluctantly, Jennie nods and approaches the booth where Liza Danning is waving to her. She doesn't look particularly friendly, but her tone is civil enough.

"Mind if I join you?" Jennie asks, because it would be awkward not to.

"No, go ahead." Liza gestures at the empty seat across from her, and Jennie can't tell whether or not she's pleased to have company. Her expression is cool and her manner detached.

Maybe that's just her way, Jennie thinks. It's what Gran would have said. She always wanted to give people the benefit of the doubt, and she'd taught her granddaughters to do the same.

Laura is so like Gran—optimistic and trusting, even with strangers. Unlike Jennie.

But I'm trying, Jennie silently tells her grandmother and her sister. *See?*

She puts on a smile and asks Liza Danning how she is.

"Lousy," the woman says, taking a sip of her black coffee, then shaking her head. "I've had the worst day already, and it's barely even started."

"What's wrong?" Jennie knows she'll be sorry she asked, but what else can she do?

"I ran my only pair of stockings when I was getting dressed, for starters. I have an important business meeting here and now I don't know what I'm going to wear."

"Doesn't this store sell pantyhose?" Jennie looks over her shoulder, thinking that even though the place is small, its crowded shelves look like they must hold a pretty good variety of items.

"Sure, they sell *pantyhose,* but I need silk stockings," Liza says, a pout curling her pink lips.

Jennie frowns. She doesn't know anyone who wears real silk stockings, the kind you attach to a garter belt—although Laura did buy some when she was shopping for honeymoon lingerie a few years back. She'd gleefully reported that Brian had actually ripped them off of her on their wedding night. Back then, Jennie had thought that sounded passionate. But that was before Brian had shown his true colors.

"Well, what are you going to do?" Jennie asks Liza.

"I have no idea. Probably buy pantyhose. But of course, this rinky-dink place doesn't have any black ones."

She says it loudly, and Jennie realizes it's so that Shirley, the waitress, will hear. She's walking toward them with Jennie's coffee and croissant, and her expression doesn't look nearly as friendly as it did before. Obviously, Liza has already registered a complaint or two.

"Here you go," Shirley says brusquely, plunking Jennie's order down in front of her and walking away.

Great, Jennie thinks. *I'm making enemies by association.*

Hanging around with Liza obviously isn't a good idea, especially on such a small island. Jennie decides to steer clear of the blonde after this.

"And on top of this whole wardrobe fiasco," Liza goes on, as though there has been no interruption, "that twit at the inn, Jasper Hammel, didn't call me to the phone when the person I'm meeting tried to get in touch with me."

Jennie murmurs, "That's too bad," and stirs her coffee.

"Oh, well," Liza says with a sigh. "Too late to do anything about it now. So how's your day? Better, I hope."

"So far, it's fine." Jennie marvels at the way Liza can seem like a self-absorbed bitch one moment and turn on the charm the next. Maybe she's an actress in her spare time.

"You didn't opt to have breakfast at the inn either, I see," Liza comments, motioning at Jennie's coffee and croissant.

"Uh, no, I—"

"Couldn't wait to get out of there?" Liza supplies. "It's creepy, don't you think?"

Jennie isn't sure what to say. "I guess it is a little. . . . I don't know. . . ."

"Creepy. Like I said. Not my kind of place at all," Liza tells her. "But business is business, and it's not like I *chose* to come here."

Jennie recalls what Liza had told Sandy last night. "You said you were in publishing?"

Liza nods. "I'm an editor."

"Must be exciting."

"It is. What do you do?"

Jennie's pretty sure the woman was around when Sandy was asking about her job last night, but obviously Liza hadn't cared enough to remember. She probably doesn't care now, either, but Jennie tells her, "I'm an antique dealer."

"Really? I'm not crazy about antiques."

"Oh . . ." Jennie has no idea what to say to that.

"I like modern things. Although someone once gave me an exquisite antique gold locket that I really loved."

"That's nice."

"Yeah, it was. I sold it for a lot of money."

Again, Jennie's at a loss for words, so she just repeats, "That's nice."

* * *

Liza decides she likes Laura Towne. She's nice to talk to, and she doesn't ask too many questions—not like that chubby chatterbox back at the inn. Personally, she herself isn't much of a conversationalist when it comes to talking to strangers, but she finds herself curious about the woman sitting across from her. There's a haunted look in her lilac eyes that's been there since last night, and Liza wonders what she's hiding.

She takes another sip of her coffee, which by this time has grown cold. She looks around, considering asking that old lady behind the counter for a refill. But then again, it's not even that good. Liza usually drinks only gourmet latte from Starbucks.

She sets down her cup and looks at Laura. "Where are you from?" she asks directly.

Laura looks a little taken aback, but says, "Boston."

Figures. She looks like the preppy New England type. "Perfect place for an antique dealer." Liza wrinkles her nose. "After all, Boston's full of old buildings and churches and museums and that sort of thing, right?"

"Right. Just like New York."

Liza grins. She knows Laura's making a point, and she decides she respects her. In Liza's opinion, there's nothing worse than someone who shrinks from her sharp tongue.

"Yeah, I guess New York's just as historic as Boston," she concedes. "And some of those older landmarks in Manhattan are actually halfway decent."

Laura raises an eyebrow.

"Although personally," Liza goes on, just to bust her chops, "if I had the choice of an apartment in the Dakota or in Trump Tower, I'd go for the Trump. You can't beat being right upstairs from Tiffany's."

"I don't know," Laura says, "I'd rather be in the Dakota, with Central Park across the street."

"You know New York?"

"Yeah." Laura looks down and stiffly stirs her coffee.

"How? Did you go to school in the city or something?"
There's a pause.

"I had a . . . friend who liked to spend time there," Laura says softly.

Liza watches her. Then she says, *"Had?"*

Laura looks up and meets her gaze. "Yeah. He died."

"Oh. Sorry."

"It's okay. It was awhile ago."

There's an awkward moment of silence, and Liza wants to ask the details, but somehow, she can't bring herself to do it. Instead, finally, she asks, "Do you have family in Boston?"

"Just my sister."

"Older or younger?"

Again, Laura hesitates, then says, "Actually, she's my twin."

"Interesting."

"Yeah."

"Is that your only family, then?"

"Uh huh." Laura bites her lip, then adds, "I had a younger sister, too—Melanie—but she died when I was seventeen. And my dad died when Melanie was just a baby. He was a cop, and he was killed in a robbery. My mom was devastated. We moved in with her parents after it happened, because Mom couldn't cope alone. She missed him so much that I heard her crying in her room every night for years. I did a lot of crying, myself."

"That's rough." Liza thinks of her own father, who raised her single-handedly. It would have been much better, she decides, if Chet Danning had been a hero and died when she was little, instead of being a hopeless alcoholic and still living in the same shabby Brooklyn apartment after all these years.

"How about you?" Laura asks. "Where are you from?"

"New York."

"Manhattan?"

Liza never tells anyone the truth, and she isn't about to start now, so she nods.

"What about your family?" Laura nibbles her croissant.

"What about them?" She's sorry as soon as the sharp retort leaves her mouth and tries to make up for it by saying, "I don't have much family. Just my dad. I lost my mother when I was young."

"I'm sorry. I know how it is."

Liza nods.

She doesn't tell Laura that she didn't lose her mother to a tragic accident or illness, but instead to a rich Arab businessman who carried her off to Kuwait to live happily ever after—without her husband and daughter.

During the Gulf War, Liza had wondered often about her mother, whether she was still alive and whether she was sorry about leaving. But she never heard from Diane Danning again. And now that the war is a dim memory, now that Liza has escaped that miserable Flatbush apartment, she no longer cares.

"Are you close to your father?" Laura asks.

"Not really. Are you close to your mother?"

"No . . ." Laura looks like she wants to say more, and Liza waits. Finally, Laura says, "My mother died, too. After we lost Melanie, she kind of fell apart. It was like it was too much for her, after losing my dad and everything, and she slowly faded away. They said it was cancer; but I know that if my dad and my sister were still here, she would be, too."

Liza nods. No wonder Laura Towne's beautiful eyes always seem so sad. She's been through a lot. Liza wonders who the "friend" was—the one who died, too—but she can't bring herself to ask.

She looks toward the plate-glass window up at the front of the store. It's raining again—pouring, actually. She wiggles her damp toes inside her thin, leaky leather boots.

"It's going to be fun walking back to the inn, huh?"

Liza looks up at Laura and sees that she, too, is staring out the window.

"I don't suppose they have taxis on Tide Island," she says wistfully.

"I doubt it." Laura sighs and slides her empty plate and cup away. "Guess we'll have to make a run for it."

"Or," Liza says impulsively, "we can just order more coffee—even though it does taste like mud—and stay here until it lets up."

Laura looks surprised, then smiles and says, "That's fine with me."

And Liza realizes, as she smiles back, that she doesn't have any real friends anymore—that maybe she never has.

Not that she wants or needs them.

She's better off living a solitary existence. She has plenty of work—and plenty of men—to keep her company when she needs it.

But, Liza decides, if she *did* ever decide to make a new friend, Laura Towne is the kind of person she would choose.

He slips silently into the room with the lilac-sprigged wallpaper, knowing that Laura's safely out of the house, but still somehow feeling the need to be cautious.

He locks the door behind him, of course, just in case.

Then he hurries over to the suitcase that's lying open on the luggage stand beneath the lace-curtained window.

His breath comes more quickly in anticipation as he reaches in and carefully pushes aside the neatly folded stack of jeans and tee-shirts and sweaters. Beneath them, he finds what he's looking for.

Lovingly, he takes out a pair of panties and a bra.

Then he frowns.

These simple white cotton garments aren't at all what he was expecting . . . what he remembers.

No, Laura always went for the daring lingerie—wisps of black lace, sheer teddies, push-up bras . . .

He checks the suitcase again to see if she's hidden the good stuff, but there are only a few more pairs of plain white underwear.

And something else isn't right . . .

He leans forward, burying his face in the sweater on top of the pile of clothing in the suitcase.

That scent that clings to the cotton knit . . . it's not right either.

Too light and . . . floral.

Laura always wore a heavier, musky fragrance. He remembers how it used to drive him crazy, how he would burrow into the soft skin at her throat and breathe her essence until he felt intoxicated with the mere scent of her.

He remembers what it was like to slide his hands beneath her clothes to stroke her warm skin, what it was like to undress her, sometimes gently, other times roughly in his impatience to consume and possess her . . .

How she used to throw her head back and moan his name and pull him to her with the same urgency he felt . . .

That was before she started pushing him away whenever he came near her.

Before she cast him aside carelessly, telling him she no longer needed him, that she never really wanted him in the first place . . .

He squeezes his eyes shut against a stab of pain that's as sudden and fresh as if he's just lost her all over again.

And when it subsides, he reminds himself that it was a long time ago. That Laura Towne will never hurt him again.

No one will ever hurt him again.

Not Laura.

Not Liza.

Not Sandy.

And not Lorraine.

The thought of Lorraine, and what he'd finally done to her, makes him giddy with excitement.

Soon, he promises himself, he'll have that delicious sensation again . . . power and control . . .

He hears a tearing sound and, startled, looks down to see a pair of Laura's panties, ripped in his hands.

For a moment, he feels panic rising in his throat, threatening to gag him . . .

What have I done? She'll know I've been here. She'll figure out what's going on, and she'll escape before I can carry out my plan . . .

Then he gets hold of his senses.

Calmly, he tucks the torn panties into his back pocket and replaces everything else in the suitcase, just as it was when he found it.

She'll never know. Even if she notices the panties are missing and gets suspicious, she would never, ever suspect that you're here.

And even if, somehow, she happens to catch sight of you before it's time, she still won't know.

As he walks toward the door he glimpses his reflection in the mirror nailed to the back and he pauses to examine himself, pleased with what he sees.

Hair that's permed so that it looks wavy, and that's dyed a natural-looking shade of brown.

Eyes whose true shade is hidden behind light-blue-colored contact lenses—cornflower blue, the lady in the optical shop had called them.

And a chiseled, handsome face—the face that he picked out of a catalogue in his plastic surgeon's office three years ago.

Sandy huddles under the overhang of rock that juts over the beach like an awning. Here, her body flattened up against the steep, rocky incline that rises from the sand toward the road above, she's partly sheltered from the driving cold rain and the wind that roars in off the water.

And from here, she can see most of the magnificent houses that sit atop the crescent-shaped, windswept shoreline. One of them, she's certain, belongs to Ethan Thoreau. She's half in love with him already.

As she waits for the rain to let up, she dreams about tonight . . . about what it will be like with Ethan. And the goosebumps that cover her flesh have nothing to do with the chill wind or her drenched clothes.

Sandy knows that she'll make love with Ethan tonight. There's no question of waiting, like she had with Frankie, and with Joe. There's no need, this time.

After all, with Frankie, her high school boyfriend, it was different because she was a virgin. They both were, actually, and though Frankie had pressured her for the first year they dated, she had suspected that he was secretly just as terrified as she was. And when they finally made love, rather than being a wonderful experience that was worth waiting for, Sandy couldn't believe what a letdown it was.

She'd continued to date Frankie anyway, until graduation, when he'd enlisted in the navy. He was married now and stationed in Washington State, the last she'd heard. His wife was someone he'd met in Florida during training. Theresa had met her when Frankie brought her home to Greenbury one Christmas. She had told Sandy that Mrs. Frankie, as they called her, was cute and petite even though she was seven months pregnant and that she had a thick southern drawl.

When Sandy had told Theresa she was happy for Frankie, Theresa had just patted her arm, as if to say, *Sure you are.* Sandy knew Theresa was thinking that she was jealous of Mrs. Frankie. The truth was, Sandy had never wanted to marry him. She just missed sleeping with him . . . not because the sex was terrific, but because she missed having sex, period.

She'd been celibate for two years after he left for the navy, until she'd started dating Joe. She still remembered how attracted she'd been to him, that first time she'd seen him at the Knights of Columbus Mardi Gras Night. He'd been wearing a v-necked sweater and tight jeans that emphasized his beefy build, and she'd thought the tattoo on his forearm was sexy.

She'd poked Theresa and pointed him out. Theresa, of course, had zipped over to some guys she knew and found out that the stranger was Joe Marconi, a twenty-five-year-old beer-truck driver from Hartford, and that he was single.

When Sandy met him a few minutes later, she'd seen that Joe wasn't quite as perfect up close. He had a beer belly that wasn't quite camouflaged by the dark sweater, and his teeth were stained yellow, probably from the cigarettes he chain-smoked. But still, there was something about him that drew Sandy; and when he'd asked her out, she'd eagerly said yes.

And when, after their first date—dinner at Pizza Hut and a Jim Carrey movie that had Joe laughing uproariously, to Sandy's embarrassment—he had taken her back to his apartment, she'd eagerly slept with him.

If sex with Frankie had been disappointing, sex with Joe was even less satisfying. He was purely selfish in bed, and he insisted on the missionary position, lights out, every time. Sandy, who was ashamed of her lumpy body anyway, didn't mind the dark, but she did mind the routine lovemaking and the fact that Joe never even bothered to kiss her anymore, or hold her afterward. It was a wonder that he'd been so traumatized when she'd broken the engagement—he'd never acted as though he were in love with her, especially when they had sex.

I bet Ethan Thoreau is fantastic in bed, she thinks now,

gazing up at the huge houses overlooking the beach. And as she stares dreamily into space, thinking about her date tonight, it gradually dawns on her that the rain has stopped. The sky still looks ominous, though, as if it could open up again any second.

Sandy scrambles out from beneath the overhang and picks her way up the craggy slope from the beach to the winding road that follows the shore. The wind is in her face and she keeps her head bent as she heads back toward the inn.

She doesn't see the middle-aged woman who's walking a black Lab along the side of the road until she nearly bumps into them.

"Hi," the woman, who's wearing a yellow rain slicker and matching hat, greets Sandy with a smile as her dog lifts its leg and urinates on a bush.

"Hi." Sandy points to the dog. "He's beautiful. What's his name?"

"He's a she, actually. Lady."

"I used to have a yellow Lab." Now that the dog is finished with her business, Sandy bends over to pat her sleek head. "Hello, there, Lady. Hi, girl. You're just beautiful. Yes, you are. Yes, you are."

"You're not from the island, are you?" the woman asks, winding another length of leash around her hand.

"No, I'm not. . . . How'd you guess?"

"You don't look the type. Most of the young people who come to Tide Island are hippie types. They call it Tie-Dye Land."

"I've heard that." Sandy straightens and asks, "Do you live here year round?"

The woman nods and points to a large house with weathered gray shingles that's set back from the road. "My great-grandfather built that over a hundred years ago. I grew up here. Now my husband and I are about to move to Boca Raton, and my son and his wife are going to move out here.

They're both investment bankers in New York, and they're taking an early retirement."

"That's nice." Sandy smiles politely. The woman seems to be the chatty type, so she adds cautiously, "Um, I was looking for a friend of mine who lives around here someplace. Maybe you know him . . ."

"If he lives around here, I'm sure I do."

"His name is Thoreau . . . Ethan Thoreau?"

At the woman's blank look, Sandy says, "He's a surgeon in Connecticut, so he wouldn't be a year-round resident, but . . ."

"I've never heard of him," the woman informs her decisively. She glances down at her dog, who's nosing along the weeds at the edge of the road. "You must have the name wrong."

"I don't think so . . ."

"Then he doesn't live around here. Maybe on the other side of the island, where there are some newer, smaller houses. A lot of those are rentals, and—"

"I doubt he'd live in a small rental," Sandy cuts in. "He has a private plane and he's very wealthy." She wishes she could take the last few words back. They make her sound so . . . pathetic.

The woman purses her lips and yanks the dog's leash. "Come on, Lady, get out of there." To Sandy, she says, "If your friend lives in this area, then I'm afraid I somehow haven't met him."

"Maybe he's new to the island."

"Most of these homes stay within families for generations, like mine. If one had been sold recently, I'd know about it."

Sandy shrugs and watches as the woman tugs Lady onto the concrete and starts back toward the huge gray house.

"Thanks anyway," Sandy calls, and the woman dismisses her with a brief wave.

These island people sure are strange, Sandy decides.

She glances back at the majestic row of waterfront homes, again wondering which one belongs to Ethan.

Then, as she feels icy raindrops on her face, she turns and hurries in the opposite direction, toward the inn.

Four

Liza sweeps into the foyer of the inn on a gust of wind and rain and slams the door shut behind her with a curse.

Thanks to this lousy weather, she's drenched and chilled to the bone. She and Laura had waited as long as they could in the general store for the rain to let up, but finally, Liza's patience wore thin and she decided to make a run for it.

Laura had stayed back at the store, saying she wanted to browse around a bit.

"In *here?*" Liza had asked incredulously, looking around at the meager inventory.

"I need some art supplies, and there's a whole section of them over there," Laura had pointed out.

"It figures. No stockings, but this place sells all the paintbrushes and canvases anyone could want."

"A lot of artists come to Tide Island," Laura said quietly.

"And you're one of them, obviously."

"Not professional. I just like to paint."

"Well, knock yourself out," Liza had said, heading for the door.

Even as she'd walked out onto the stormy boardwalk, she'd regretted being so snippy with Laura. Why did she always find herself doing that . . . jeopardizing the few potential friendships that ever came along by displaying a generous dose of attitude problem?

It wasn't that she had disdain for Laura's painting hobby, or even for the outdated excuse for a store. It was just that

Liza couldn't help herself sometimes. The hurt little girl she'd once been seemed to surface when she least expected it, lashing out at anyone who happened to be around.

Like poor Laura Towne, who, to her credit, hadn't seemed all that thrown by Liza's bitchiness.

I'll make it up to her later, Liza thinks, squishing across the foyer floor in her ruined Italian leather boots.

There's no sign of Jasper Hammel.

She reaches for the small silver bell on the counter and rings it impatiently. She wants to ask Hammel whether D.M. Yates has called for her again, but there's no response to the bell.

Frowning, Liza rings it again. When there's still no response, she walks toward the back of the first floor, checking first the parlor, then the dining room and a small library off the hall. They're all deserted and the whole house seems eerily silent except for the ticking grandfather clock in the hallway.

Liza pokes her head into the kitchen. It's a large room with an old-fashioned black cookstove and double white porcelain sink. Built-in glass-paned cupboards display several different sets of dishes and glassware. A cozy nook off to one side holds a small table covered in a blue-and-white-checked cloth and surrounded by four chairs.

It occurs to Liza that this is the kind of kitchen that belongs in a quaint country farmhouse inhabited by a happy, messy family—not in this remote New England inn. It's almost too perfect—every dish and glass in perfect order, the counter-tops and stove sparkling, the dishtowel hanging over the sink folded just so. It doesn't look *lived* in—and neither does the rest of the inn.

No, it's hard to believe that, even in season, the Bramble Rose is ever overrun by tourists with the accompanying noise and disorder a houseful of people would bring.

Liza's brows knit thoughtfully as she steps back out of the kitchen and returns to the front of the house. There's still no sign of Jasper Hammel. After a moment, she starts up the stairs.

She pauses in front of the door to her room, struck by a sudden impulse to keep snooping around.

What do you think you're going to find? asks a little voice inside her head.

Nothing in particular . . . I'm just curious.

Well, maybe more than curious. Maybe a little suspicious, she admits to herself. There's just something strange about this inn, something she can't put her finger on.

The other doors on the second floor are closed, with the exception of the one to the bathroom. Liza quickly and gingerly uses the ancient facilities, wrinkling her nose as she reaches out to pull the old-fashioned chain on the toilet. The pipes creak as she turns on the faucet in the sink, and she's reminded of the uncomfortable shower she took in the battered clawfoot tub this morning. The water kept going cold and waning to a trickle, and she had shivered her way through, cursing D.M. Yates the whole time.

Now she hurries out of the bathroom and hesitates in the hallway, staring at the steps leading to the third floor.

There's no reason why I shouldn't just go up and have a look around, she tells herself. *After all, what else is there to do?*

On the third floor, she finds herself in a long hallway identical to the one below. There are several closed doors in roughly the same locations as on the second floor.

Liza tries the one that corresponds with the room she's in, and is surprised to find that it swings open.

The room is the identical shape and size as hers, with a similar fireplace and windows in the same spots. But the decor here is drastically different: the furniture is merely functional, the bedspread and tightly drawn curtains an austere white cotton. The floors are wooden and lack the high polish and pretty area rugs of the room below, and the walls are painted a pale yellow that, Liza concedes, might glow warmly on a sunny summer afternoon, but looks drab in the gray cast of winter.

It's clear that no one is occupying this room at the moment. The open closet door reveals empty hangers, and a musty smell permeates the air, as though it's been a long time since the curtains were opened and the windows raised.

Liza makes her way down the hall, peeking into the other rooms, and sees that they're similarly devoid of embellishment and are obviously deserted. In the third-floor bathroom, the small sink is dry and the white towel on the rack is precisely folded in thirds and lacks even the slightest wrinkle or smudge.

At the end of the hall, Liza reaches for the knob on the last door, assuming that it must lead to the top floor and cupola, which she'd noticed from outside the house.

Funny . . . the door won't budge.

And it can't be locked, because there's no keyhole . . . Unless it's bolted from the other side.

And if that's the case, Liza realizes, then someone must be up there, someone who has locked himself in.

She leans forward and presses her ear against the cool wooden door. Sure enough, she hears the faint sound of classical music coming from above.

Rattling the knob, Liza calls, "Jasper?"

"What are you doing?"

Gasping, she turns to see that the little man is standing behind her in the third-floor hallway.

His voice is calm, but his eyes are narrowed and his mustache twitches nervously.

"I . . . uh, I was just looking for you," Liza tells him, stepping back from the door and dropping her hand to her side. "I thought you might be up there."

"I'm right here."

"Obviously." Liza quickly regains her composure. "Who's upstairs?"

"Nobody. It's used for storage."

"I heard music coming from there," she informs him. "And the door's locked from the other side."

Is it her imagination or does Jasper Hammel look panicky for a moment before a look of cool detachment settles over his features once again?

"Nonsense," he says, stepping closer to the door and cocking his head. "I don't hear anything."

"But I just . . ." Liza presses up close to the door and frowns. Nothing but silence. "Well, I heard it," she tells Jasper. "And the door's locked."

"It can't be. There's no keyhole, as you can see."

"It's locked from the other side."

"That's impossible. But I can explain why you couldn't open it. In damp weather, some of the doors in this place stick. Very common in old houses."

"But—"

"Anyway, I'm glad I found you, Ms. Danning, although I'm afraid it's too late. David Yates just stopped by the inn a few minutes ago, looking for you."

"He *what?*"

"He was sorry he missed you."

"Why didn't you—"

"I went up to your room, hoping you'd returned from town, but there was no reply to my knock."

Flabbergasted, Liza simply stares at him.

"I told him you'd gone into town," Jasper Hammel continues, "and that I wasn't sure when you'd be back."

"Where did he go?" Liza demands, hurrying toward the stairs. "I'll catch up to him."

"I have no idea. He was quite perturbed at your absence and said he's a busy man and doesn't have time to waste. But he did say he'll contact you later this afternoon."

"I don't believe this," Liza mutters, striding down the stairs to the second floor, Jasper Hammel dogging her heels like a nervous puppy. "At this rate, I'm never going to hook

up with D.M. Yates. It's like fate's playing a cruel joke on
me."

"Yes, it almost does seem that way, doesn't it?" Jasper
agrees as Liza heads off to her room in a huff.

The man listening on the other side of the bolted attic
door loosens his hold on the knife handle as he hears both
sets of footsteps retreat.

He'd grabbed the knife and crept down the attic stairs
when he'd heard the doorknob rattling. When he'd recognized Liza Danning's voice calling for Jasper, he'd formu-
lated an instant plan.

She'd been scheduled to die second, after Sandy Cavelli,
but it had occurred to him that there was no reason he
couldn't switch the order on a whim. After all, *he* was the
one in charge, here . . .

This time.

Yes, everything was up to him, and a feeling of power
had surged through him as he clenched his sweaty fingers
around the handle of the knife.

He was just about to open the attic door and clamp his
hand over Liza Danning's startled mouth when he'd heard
Jasper's voice in the hallway.

Oh, well.

Liza's turn would come soon enough anyway.

Stealing back up the stairs, he sighs and decides to stick
with the original plan.

Sandy first.

Liza second.

Laura last.

When he'd first come up with his plan, he'd considered
luring them out here to the island one by one to prolong
his pleasure. But then he'd thought better of it. Prolonging
the pleasure would also prolong his chances of being
caught.

He'd decided he'd better take care of all of them in a single weekend.

And what could be more fitting than the one before Valentine's Day?

Come Monday, it will all be over.

Sandy, Liza, and Laura will have joined Lorraine in a place where no one will ever find them.

And *he'll* be on the way to a place where no one will ever find him. . . .

Jennie slips out of the inn with the blue canvas bag containing her art supplies tucked under her arm.

There . . . I made it, she thinks as she heads around to the path leading down to the beach. She'd successfully avoided an encounter back at the inn; no one had seen her come back from town.

As she hurried down the stairs just now, she had heard Jasper's voice humming along to classical music somewhere toward the back of the house. But he hadn't come out to talk to her. She's grateful for that. The little man is pleasant enough, but something about him makes her distinctly uncomfortable.

And it's not just him. It's this whole place. She knows Tide Island is beautiful and idyllic and quaint—and so is the Bramble Rose Inn—but Jennie doesn't want to be here.

Maybe it would be different, she tells herself, if she weren't here by herself. And if it were summer.

But even being here in winter wouldn't be so bad, she thought, if she had some company. Maybe if she and Keegan had come here together . . .

No! Stop it! Keegan's out of your life.

With a sigh she picks her way around a tangle of wet sea grass and vines, continuing toward the water.

The weather can't seem to make up its mind. One minute it's windy and raining furiously; the next—like right now—

it's curiously calm, though the air is still misty and the sky remains threatening.

As Jennie scoots down the last few feet of the sloped path behind the inn to reach the beach, she scans the horizon and sees that it looks dark. There's no doubt that a storm is on the way—she can sense it.

She wonders, not for the first time since this morning, whether she should just leave—pack her things and hurry to catch the ferry to the mainland while she still can.

She's tempted, so tempted that her legs feel jittery and she has to fight the urge to run back to the inn. She can't get past the feeling that she's in danger here, that something evil is lurking nearby.

But you know why you feel that way; and after three years, it's time to get over it. You can't spend the rest of your life being terrified of everything . . . of nothing.

Besides, if you leave, what are you going to tell Laura? She'll want to know what you're doing back home two days early. And she'll talk you into going back to that psychiatrist.

Dr. Bonner.

Jennie scowls at the mere thought of the man, remembering his thoughtful, bearded face and piercing black eyes. She'd seen him several times in the months after the . . . incident. One of the social workers she'd met during the police investigation had referred her to his office, telling her he specialized in post traumatic stress disorder.

Unfortunately, Laura had been right there with her when the social worker said it, and Jennie had agreed to see Dr. Bonner at her sister's insistence.

She'd disliked him instantly, but had returned to his office a few times because it was easier than arguing with Laura. She knew her sister was just worried about her and wanted to help; but Laura couldn't know that it was pure torture for Jennie to talk about what had happened, that she relived the horror every second of every day in her mind, and that nothing anyone said was going to help her.

Not that Dr. Bonner had said much, anyway. Just fixed her with his level stare and told her to tell him what she was feeling.

What the hell did he think she was feeling after what she'd been through?

No, Jennie can't bear the thought of going back to his office again, or of facing Laura's well-meaning concern. There's nothing to do but stay on this island for the weekend, the way she's supposed to, and try to ignore the irrational feelings of panic that keep creeping over her.

Jennie sets her jaw resolutely, and, for the second time today, makes her way across the wet sand. She finds the wide, flat rock she'd noticed this morning and climbs onto it, carefully pulling her coat down in back to sit on it so that her jeans won't get soaked.

There. This isn't so bad, she decides, looking out over the churning water again and taking a deep breath, drinking in the cold, salty air.

She reaches for her blue bag and removes her sketch pad and pencils. It's too damp to paint, but she's not in the mood anyway. She feels like working with charcoal, has an urge to fill page after page of creamy paper with bold, dark strokes.

Her hand poised over the sketchbook, she looks up and sees a lone gull swooping over the water. To her left, for about a mile, the beach curves out toward the horizon in a crescent shape, and through the gray mist, she can barely make out a scattering of enormous houses sitting above the rocky shoreline.

It looks just like England, she realizes, remembering the remote seaside homes along the shore on the other side of the Atlantic. She gazes out over the ocean and thinks how strange it is that it's still out there, hundreds of miles away—that isolated patch of beach where she had sat, sketching and feeling homesick, the day she'd met Harry.

She still remembers how startled she'd been to hear a voice behind her—a voice with an American accent, no less.

"If it's any good, I'll buy it," he'd said, and she'd looked up to see a lanky, sandy-haired guy standing there grinning at her.

"Excuse me?" was all she could say in response, and he'd gestured at the sketch pad in her lap.

"Your drawing. Can I see it? If it's good, I'll buy it and frame it and hang it on the wall of my room. I love this spot. It reminds me of the beach back home. In fact," and he'd held up the camera in his hand, "I was just about to take a picture of it so I can keep it with me forever."

She'd known what he meant. There was something special about this lonely stretch of shore where the waves foamed over jutting rocks to crash against the crescent of sand. The tiny beach was only about a half-a-mile wide, separated from the rest of the coast by rocky cliffs that jutted out into the water, topped by magnificent homes.

Jennie had discovered the spot soon after arriving the month before to spend the semester at nearby Hillshire University, and she went there often to be alone with her thoughts.

Her mother had already been dead for two years at that point, while Gran was growing weak from the heart disease that had always plagued her and Gramps was terribly concerned over her. Jennie had felt guilty leaving Laura alone with their failing grandparents in Quincy while she went off to England, but Laura had insisted that she go.

"After all, one of us has to go to college and see the world, and it's not going to be me," her twin had pointed out cheerfully. Laura had only lasted a semester at a community college in southern Massachusetts before dropping out to become a bartender in Cambridge, much to their grandparents' dismay.

It was while Jennie was overseas, in fact, that Laura had started dating Brian. Jennie has always thought that if she had been around, her sister never would have fallen for him. She would have glimpsed his dark side and could have talked Laura out of it. By the time she'd returned to the states, Laura was engaged and it was too late for Jennie to do much but paste on a smile and tell her sister she was happy for her.

But even though her absence had, in her opinion, resulted in a disastrous relationship for her twin, Jennie wouldn't have traded England for anything. If she hadn't gone, she would never have met Harry.

Then again, she thinks wistfully now, *if you hadn't met Harry, he would still probably be alive . . .*

Jennie had found England quaint but so foreign that she couldn't seem to shake her homesickness during those early days. Maybe that was why she had latched so eagerly onto Harry from the start. It wasn't like her to flirt with a stranger; but when he'd told her that he thought her sketch was terrific, she'd ripped it out of her pad and handed it to him.

"Hey, thanks! How much do I owe you?"

She'd shrugged. "How about just a cup of coffee?"

That easy grin had spread over his handsome face and he'd said, "Sure. Come on. Only it'll probably have to be tea. You know . . . when in Rome."

It turned out that Harry was also spending the semester at Hillshire. He was from a small town on the Oregon coast, and he, too, was homesick. Even that first day, as he'd enthusiastically told Jennie about his hometown, and how he couldn't wait to go back, she'd found herself feeling oddly regretful.

After all, Oregon was on the opposite side of the country from Boston. Jennie had no intention of leaving the northeast, not with Gran and Gramps doing so poorly. And the way he was talking about his friends and family back home, Harry didn't seem like the type who'd relocate, either.

Looking back, Jennie never ceases to be amazed that even in those first moments she'd spent with Harry, she'd had hopes of a permanent relationship.

They'd been inseparable during that semester in England. And when it was over, they'd prolonged their time together, spending the summer traveling through Europe together. Too soon, it was August and time to head back to the States. Harry had spent several days with Jennie in Boston before flying back to the west coast to finish his senior year.

She hadn't seen him until Christmas break, when she'd flown out to visit him. There, she had seen how truly connected Harry was to the scenic Oregon town and to his large, warm family that included five brothers and sisters. And there, Jennie had realized that she was deeply in love with him and couldn't bear to be without him.

Harry had proposed to her on Christmas Eve, and she had fiercely wanted to accept. But she thought of Laura, who was planning a spring wedding to Brian—they had already moved into an apartment on the Cape together. And she thought of her grandparents, both of them old and feeble and Gran so sick. They couldn't be left alone. And Jennie had already had her taste of freedom. It was Laura's turn, now.

So she'd told Harry she couldn't marry him. She couldn't leave Boston, and she didn't expect him to leave his home, either.

The rest of her visit was subdued. There wasn't much for them to say to each other. Jennie had managed to fight back the tears until she boarded the plane back to Boston. Then, knowing she would probably never see Harry again, she had spent the entire five-hour flight sobbing miserably.

When she'd walked heavily into the familiar old house in Quincy, though, her grandfather had said, "Harry called and he wants you to call him the moment you get in."

Reluctantly Jennie had dialed the familiar number, not wanting to hear his voice, unable to bear the thought that it was over between them.

"Jen?" he'd said breathlessly when he'd answered the phone. "I need you to do me a huge favor."

"What is it?" she'd asked dully.

"Find me an apartment for June first. One that's cheap and close to your grandparents' house."

"You want to spend the summer here?" she'd asked slowly. She forced herself to get past the tingle of excitement at the thought of seeing him again, to be realistic. Prolonging the inevitable would only be more painful in the end. "But Harry, I don't think that's a good idea. We both know you'd just have to leave again in the fall, to go back to law school in Oregon."

"What, there aren't any law schools in Massachusetts?"

Her heart had instantly jump-started as she realized what he was saying. "Harry, you can't mean you're moving to Boston," she'd protested weakly.

"I can't? Why not? Don't you want to marry me?"

The lump that rose in her throat was so enormous she couldn't speak for a moment. Then, in a strangled voice, she'd said, "I want to marry you more than I've ever wanted anything in my life. But I can't—"

"What? You can't marry me?"

"I can't leave Gran and Gramps," she'd said in a whisper, casting a glance over her shoulder toward the living room, where her grandparents were watching 'Wheel of Fortune.' "I already told you. They took care of us when we had no one else. Now it's my turn to be there for them."

"Well, I'll be there for them, too. Okay?"

She'd paused, letting it sink in. Then she'd said, in disbelief, "You'd actually leave your family and friends and your hometown for me?"

"I love you, Jen. And yes, I can leave my family and friends and my hometown. It's you I can't leave."

"Do you promise?" she'd asked, her voice choked with tears. All her life, she'd been abandoned by the people she loved. First her father. Then Melanie. Then her mother. Now even Laura had left, caught up in a new life.

"I promise, Jen," Harry had said. "I'll never leave you. Never."

Now, as she stares out over the gray Atlantic, his words echoing in her mind, she feels something wet on her cheeks.

Raindrops . . .

And tears.

Lying flat on her stomach, Laura reaches under the couch to retrieve the can of furniture polish that had rolled when she'd dropped it.

Her fingers find something small and round, and she pulls out a dust-covered silver hoop earring she'd lost awhile back. She'd accused Jennie of borrowing it without asking, actually . . . not that she can imagine her twin wearing jewelry this flashy, come to think of it.

No, Jennie only wears the small gold-and-diamond studs that Harry had once given her, when she bothers to wear earrings at all.

Laura sets the silver hoop on the coffee table, which is half-coated in a white film of lemon-scented polish, and reaches under the couch again.

The doorbell rings just as her hand closes around the can of Pledge.

Frowning, Laura pulls it out, scrambles to her feet, and heads for the door, wondering who can be dropping by in the middle of a rainy Saturday afternoon.

"Hi, Laura."

"Keegan!" she says, surprised to see him standing in the hall. "What's up?"

He shrugs. "I just wondered—"

"Jennie's not here," she tells him, wondering how her

sister can possibly resist him. His shoulders are incredibly broad beneath that worn jean jacket and gray sweatshirt he's wearing, and his face is so handsome, with a generous mouth and sculpted bone structure that might look *too* pretty on someone else but that's masculine on Keegan.

"She's not here? Where is she?" He doesn't look like he believes her, and Laura can't blame him. After all, every time he's called lately—which has been often—Jennie has made her lie and say she's out.

"She's away for the weekend."

"Oh, yeah? Where'd she go?" Keegan's sharp eyes are looking over Laura's shoulder, as if he's searching for clues that Jennie really is here.

"I'm telling the truth, Keegan," Laura says. "She really is away."

Disappointment settles over his features. "Oh. Where'd she go?" he repeats.

"To Tide Island."

"Tide Island? What's she doing out there?"

"I won a free weekend at some inn there, but I can't go because Shawn—he's the guy I'm seeing—is coming home from Japan this weekend. In fact," she checks her watch, "I have to leave for the airport in about twenty minutes to pick him up and I need to finish cleaning the apartment first, so . . ."

"You're cleaning?" He looks suspiciously at her. "Are you sure you're not Jennie?"

She rolls her eyes. "Very funny."

"No offense, Laura, but you're not exactly the world's best housekeeper."

"Well, Shawn's pretty whipped on me, and I don't want to scare him away, you know?" She brandishes her can of Pledge. "Now, if you'll excuse me . . ."

"Wait. What about this free trip to Tide Island?"

"What about it?"

"How'd you win it?"

"I bought a sweepstakes ticket at Stop and Shop. It was for a good cause. The New England Children's Leukemia Society."

"Never heard of it." Keegan frowns. "You wouldn't still have that ticket around, would you?"

"Are you kidding? I'm lucky if I manage to hang onto my purse. You know me—hey, wait, you know what? I do have the ticket!"

"You do?"

"Yeah . . . I wrote Shawn's flight number on the back of it. I remember because the day he called to tell me he was coming home was the same day I found out I won the sweepstakes and I had to pull out the ticket to confirm the number. It's stuck to the fridge with a magnet so I wouldn't lose it." She's halfway to the kitchen, followed by Keegan, before she turns to look back at him, puzzled. "Why do you want it?"

"Because I've never heard of the New England Children's Leukemia Society, that's why. And a friend of mine at work—do you remember Buddy?" At her nod, he continues, "Well, he's working on a task force to uncover a ring of bogus charity collectors that's operating in the area."

"What, you think the sweepstakes was a scam?"

"I didn't say that."

"Well, it's definitely real because they awarded the prize." Laura continues to the kitchen, plucks the ticket from beneath a "Cheers" magnet on the refrigerator door, and hands it to Keegan.

"That doesn't mean the sweepstakes was legitimate, Laura. They probably collected thousands of dollars selling tickets. A free weekend at an inn—particularly on Tide Island in the middle of winter—only costs a few hundred at most. How do you know the rest of the money really went to charity?"

"I don't." She shrugs, then says, "Hey, what are you doing with that?" as Keegan starts to tuck the ticket into his jacket pocket.

"I'm giving it to Buddy. He'll probably want to check it out."

"Well, at least let me copy Shawn's flight information off the back." She grabs a pen from the table and writes the information on a napkin, then hands the ticket back to Keegan. "Here, it's all yours now."

"Thanks. So, how's Jennie doing?"

"She's all right. You know . . ."

"No, I don't. I haven't talked to her in weeks."

"Well, she thinks it's better that way."

"Oh, really? And why is that?"

"Because if she talks to you, she might not be able to stay away from you."

His face clouds over. "Well, what I want to know is why she thinks she has to stay away in the first place."

"Come on, Keegan," Laura says, even though she's wondering the same thing. "You guys are broken up. Forget about her."

"I can't," he says, and she's startled by the raw pain in his voice. "I keep trying, but . . . I don't know, maybe if I could understand why . . ."

Laura hesitates. She wants, more than anything, to tell Keegan what had happened to Jennie three years ago. In her opinion, her sister should have at least explained it to him—that because of her ordeal, she doesn't want to love a cop. That she's afraid of losing him to violent death. Just like she'd lost her father . . .

And just like she'd lost Harry . . .

But Laura clamps her mouth shut. It's not up to her to tell Keegan why Jennie left him. She'd promised her sister that she wouldn't . . .

And besides, she realizes, glancing at her watch—there's no time to get into it now.

She wants to be there when Shawn walks off the plane, and Saturday traffic is always heavy around Logan.

So she just shrugs and tells him, "Look, Keegan, I'm very sorry about you and Jen, but that's really between the two of you. I don't like to get involved in her personal life."

He gives her a look that says *since when?* But he simply nods and starts back toward the front door.

He pauses, his hand on the knob, and turns back to Laura.

"Just for the record," he says quietly, "I really love her. And I'm not going to give up. Will you tell her that for me?"

Laura nods.

But even as the door closes behind him, she fights the urge to run after him, to tell him the truth about Jennie.

And if she weren't running so late, she would do it.

But I will, she promises herself. *Next time I get the opportunity, I'll tell him, no matter what Jennie says. It's for her own good.*

She tucks the napkin containing Shawn's flight information into the back pocket of her jeans and thinks again about that sweepstakes ticket.

Now that Keegan has planted the idea that the charity might have been a fraud, she finds herself going back over what happened that afternoon in the Stop and Shop parking lot.

She remembers being frazzled as she rushed toward the double glass doors of the store. It was a blustery December day and she had lost her gloves, as usual—as well as the grocery list Jennie had jotted for her. She'd been trying to recall what her sister needed for the gingerbread cookies she wanted to bake when a voice had interrupted her thoughts.

"Hey, miss . . . want to take a chance in a sweepstakes? You might win a free vacation, and it's for a good cause."

She'd turned to see a man standing there with a roll of tickets. He was wearing a button that said New England

Children's Leukemia Society. Instantly, she'd thought of Melanie and had smiled and said sure.

He'd waited patiently while she dug a dollar out of the bottom of her purse—she'd lost her wallet before Thanksgiving and hadn't gotten around to replacing it yet.

Frowning, Laura searches her memory and pictures the man. He'd been bundled up against the cold, with a bulky down coat, a ski hat, and a thick scarf wrapped around the lower half of his face. His voice had been muffled, and he hadn't spoken much except to thank her after he'd handed her the ticket.

But now, as she thinks back over the incident, she recalls vaguely thinking, at the time, that he sounded familiar. But she didn't recognize him.

No, she'd decided then that he was a stranger.

And she's still positive of that now.

After all, scatterbrained as she sometimes is, Laura never forgets a face.

Especially someone whose eyes are the same striking, light shade of blue as those colored contact lenses Shawn wears.

Cornflower blue.

Five

Sandy wraps her robe more tightly around her wet body and hurries across the deserted second-floor hallway back to her room.

She'd planned on taking a leisurely bubble bath to get into a romantic frame of mind for her date with Ethan. But after only a minute or so of running the water into the ancient clawfoot tub in the inn bathroom, it had gone from lukewarm to chilly. And even if it had been steaming, it was only a trickle when the faucet was on full blast, so it would have taken hours to fill the tub.

Sandy had settled for taking a shower that was icy enough to set her teeth chattering and body shivering.

Back in her room, she locks the door and goes over to the window.

Dusk falls early during New England winters. It's only late afternoon, but already the stormy sky is rapidly darkening. The wind has picked up again, rattling the windowpanes and moaning around the drafty old house, and raindrops splatter furiously against the glass.

Sandy imagines how romantic it will be to snuggle before a roaring fire with Ethan Thoreau as the weather rages outside. Maybe, if this actually turns into a full-blown nor'easter as threatened, she'll be stranded here on the island with him for a few days.

And a lot can happen in a few days, Sandy tells herself,

turning away from the window and flicking on the floor lamp near the bed.

Who knows? Maybe I'll go back home engaged. And it won't be like it was with Joe. This time, I'll definitely go through with the wedding.

Dreamily, she closes her eyes and imagines what her wedding day will be like.

A long, frilly white gown, definitely. Sandy has always dreamed of being an old-fashioned bride. She can just picture the dress . . .

Of course, she has quite a few pounds to lose between now and the day she gets married.

Her eyes snap open and she strips off the robe. Standing naked in front of the full-length mirror, she examines herself from head to toe.

Hair . . . fine, once you've used some mousse and blown it dry.

Face . . . not bad at all, once you get some makeup on.

Boobs . . . well, they certainly are big. Too big—considering that your nipples sag to your bellybutton—although maybe Ethan Thoreau won't think so. Maybe he likes women with giant breasts. Most men do, don't they?

Stomach . . . definitely flabby. Look at those rolls. Yuck.

Hips . . . much too wide, and so is your butt.

Thighs . . . well, at least the new skirt will hide your saddlebags.

Legs . . . not bad—but uh-oh! They're bleeding in a few spots from where you nicked them shaving over goosebumps in that freezing cold shower.

Sandy grabs some Kleenex from the packet in her cosmetics bag and cleans the blood off her legs, making a face when she sees the red smears on the clean white tissues.

She's always been squeamish at the sight of blood.

* * *

Liza restlessly tosses aside the manuscript page she's been trying to read for the last five minutes and glances at her watch.

It's after four. Why hasn't D.M. Yates called back?

Is he trying to punish her for not being here earlier?

Or . . .

Liza stands and paces across the room, not wanting to even think that this whole thing might be an elaborate hoax.

But how can she help but be suspicious? After all, it's not as though she were born yesterday. It's not as though she actually believes that famous, elusive writers routinely go around giving breaks to relatively unknown female editors.

The more time she spends on Tide Island, stewing and waiting for D.M. Yates to show up, the more she wonders whether she's been had. Only . . .

Who would go to the trouble to play such a nasty trick on her?

Albie.

His name is the first to enter her mind. Only, would a high-powered man like Senator Albert Norwood actually have the time and energy to pull something like this off?

He might, Liza realizes. He might, if he were angry enough at her.

And there's no question that he's not exactly thrilled with her these days.

After all, he hasn't taken kindly to being blackmailed.

But it's his own fault, Liza tells herself. *Married men who have a lot to lose politically shouldn't go around sleeping with women like me.*

It certainly hadn't been very hard to seduce Albie.

She cringes slightly at the memory of his naked body—a white, quivering mass of Jello—hovering over hers and of his hot, garlicky breath in her face as he'd pounced on her, forcing himself into her with no foreplay other than roughly squeezing her bare breasts once or twice.

It certainly hadn't been difficult to hide the video camera in her bedroom, either. Albie was always so hot for her that he probably wouldn't have noticed if a film crew had stood at the foot of the bed.

Once Liza had the incriminating evidence on tape, all she'd had to do was send him a copy and threaten to give the original to Cathy, his wife of thirty-seven years. Albie had been furious, at first. Then he'd tried acting like the whole thing was just a big joke.

But when he'd realized that Liza meant business, his demeanor had changed and he'd become desperate to do whatever she asked. "Just don't show Cathy the tape," he kept begging.

And Liza hadn't . . .

Yet.

At first, she'd used it to get Albie to write his autobiography for Xavier House. Every publisher in New York had been after him for years, trying to make a deal, thanks to his famous, scandal-ridden background.

His father was Tyson Norwood, the oldest son in a family that had been America's premier political force before the Kennedys arrived on the scene. And his mother was Lexie Jones, who had been one of the most famous Hollywood starlets of the thirties. Albie was their only child—the lone heir to the Norwood legacy since Ty's brother Miles was unable to have children and his brother Wendell had been killed in the D-Day invasion without ever marrying.

Ty, a charismatic congressman, was a notorious ladies' man who was rumored, at one point, to be sleeping with the First Lady right under the President's nose. As a result of his philandering, Lexie had killed herself when Albie was a teenager, jumping off the Empire State Building at high noon on their twenty-fifth wedding anniversary. Ty had promptly made headlines by turning around and marrying a beautiful, recently divorced English duchess only a few months later. During the mid-sixties, the two of them were gunned down on the sidewalk in front of their Manhattan brownstone by someone who had never been caught. There were rumors that the murder was connected to Ty's gambling debts or that he had been caught sleeping with a famous Brooklyn mobster's wife, but no one was ever arrested for the crime.

Despite his family's high-profile activities, Albie had managed to lead a fairly quiet life. But that didn't stop the press from hounding him everywhere he went, or from speculating about his family's colorful past.

Now, thanks to Liza, the world was going to learn the darkest secrets of the Norwood family, via Albie's soon-to-be-published autobiography.

And thanks to that book, Liza had earned a fat bonus at work, not to mention a promotion and that write-up in *Publisher's Weekly*.

The last time she had seen Albie, for dinner a few weeks ago, he had seemed resigned to the fact that she had a degree of power over him. He hadn't seemed bent on revenge . . .

But then, if his idea of revenge is sending Liza on this wild-goose chase to a rattletrap inn on an out-of-the-way island in the dead of winter; she should probably be relieved.

After all, she isn't exactly a stranger to using men to get what she wants.

In fact, it's a wonder no one has tried to get even with her before now.

If this D.M. Yates thing turns out to be a hoax, she'll be pissed as hell. But, she supposes, there are worse things someone could do to her . . .

The rain beating on the roof above the attic drowns out the sound of the classical music coming from the small portable CD player, so he shuts it off.

It's almost time to go, anyway.

He notes a tremor of anticipation in the pit of his stomach and wonders if Sandy's feeling the same way. Is she jittery with excitement over the prospect of a date with Ethan Thoreau? Is she primping for him, right this very moment, behind the door to her room two floors below?

He pictures her round face and thinks about how different she looked back when he first met her.

Of course, she'd been much younger then.

She wasn't quite thirteen, her body already curvy and womanly, but not yet overweight.

And he, at fifteen, had been a poor little rich kid: acne-ridden, clumsy, painfully shy—and that wasn't all. He had a hideous, horribly ugly face. His features were elongated and thrust forward, as though a giant suction cup had forced them out. The doctors had told his parents that something must have happened to his face as he passed through the birth canal, and that it would probably look better as he grew older. But it hadn't.

Once, when he was about seven, he'd overheard his mother telling one of her friends that it was as though God had played a horrible trick on her and his father. After all, they were both beautiful people.

He closes his eyes and thinks back to that long-ago, hot June day. After spending the morning aimlessly wandering along the water behind his parents' summer home on the Connecticut shore, he'd walked in the back door, and there she was. Sandy Cavelli. Sitting at the kitchen table, looking bored, while a fat, dark-haired woman spoke with his mother.

He'd quickly realized that the woman, Angie, was interviewing for a part-time maid's position. The house already had a staff of four—a full-time housekeeper, a cook, a gardener, and a handyman who doubled as a chauffeur. But lately, his mother had been complaining that the housekeeper, Tess, couldn't keep up with all the entertaining they did on weekends. His father, barely looking up from his *New York Times,* had told her to go ahead and hire part-time help then.

"And what about your daughter?" his mother had asked Angie, casting a glance of displeasure in Sandy's direction.

"She'll have to come with me when I work," Mrs. Cavelli had said. "Her father and brothers are busy working on weekends. My husband's a plumbing and heating contractor, and my sons are all involved in the business."

He still remembers the look of pride on the woman's face as she said it, and the look of disdain on his mother's.

"Well, if you have to bring her, she'll have to help," she'd said in her clipped tone.

"That's fine. Sandy's always a big help."

And she was. She regularly dusted and vacuumed and made up the guest rooms, which were always occupied on weekends by his parents' friends from the city. And she often helped the cook in the kitchen, making wonderful canapes for his parents' Friday and Saturday night cocktail parties.

It took him several days to work up the courage to say hello to Sandy. Until he did, he spent a lot of time watching her—peeking through the doorways of guest rooms as she bent over to make up the beds or watching her through the kitchen window as she worked over the stove, pausing every now and then to wipe trickles of sweat off her neck before it could drip down between her breasts.

As far as he knew, she never realized he was there.

When he'd finally been brave enough to talk to her, she'd responded with a broad, cheerful grin and a bright, "Hi! It must be great living in a house like this, huh?"

How could he tell her that most of the time, it was a nightmare? That his father was never there emotionally, even on the rare times that he was there physically. And that his mother . . . well, he couldn't tell anyone about his mother. About what she did to him. About what she made him do.

He'd never told another soul about that.

So, in response to Sandy's question, he'd smiled and shrugged and said, "Sure, it's great."

And from that day on, they'd been friends.

Though to him, it was always more than that. He'd thought it was more to her, too. He'd been wrong.

But how was I to know? he wonders fiercely, clenching his grown-up fists in his attic room. *She acted like she cared about me . . . like she loved me. She was the first person who ever treated me as though my looks didn't matter.*

But obviously, they had mattered.

Because in the end, she'd abandoned him.

Just like the others would, in years to come.

With a sigh, he opens his eyes and his gaze falls on the portable stereo.

Oh, yes. He mustn't forget to bring the music.

He hurries over to remove the round silver CD he'd been playing, presses it into the plastic case, and puts it away in alphabetical order.

Then he reaches for a cassette tape from the stack on the table. It took him several days of combing record stores to find all the right songs to record on this tape.

He checks the neat lettering on the inside sleeve of the plastic cassette case to make sure he has the right one.

Yes, this is it.

The one that begins with "One Hand, One Heart" and ends with Mendelssohn's wedding march.

"I'm telling you, it isn't right," Tony Cavelli repeats, this time thumping the table with his fist so hard that the ladle topples out of the bowl of sauce, sending tomato-colored splatters all over the plastic tablecloth.

Danny and his wife Cheryl, who is seated to his right, exchange a glance.

Cheryl raises her eyebrows slightly, as if to say, *Aren't you going to stick up for your sister?*

Danny sighs inwardly. Cheryl's right. But he hates to get into this whole thing about Sandy and some weekend trip she's apparently taken.

He and his father don't get along very well as it is. Never have. Pop doesn't understand why he'd insisted on going to college or why he hadn't gone into the family business. Or why he'd married a girl who wasn't Italian when he could have settled down with Donna Aglieri, his high school sweetheart.

It isn't that Tony Cavelli doesn't like Cheryl. Who can help but like her? She's sweet and kind and pretty with dark blond hair and big blue eyes and the kind of smile that lights up her whole face.

No, Pop is crazy about Cheryl. But that doesn't mean he doesn't think Danny should have stuck with his own kind and married Donna.

After all, both Tony Junior and Frankie managed to find Italian wives. You wouldn't find a happier family man than Tony Junior, as Pop points out every chance he gets. Maryanne is pregnant again—with their fourth child; they're trying for a son—Tony the third, of course—to add to their brood of daughters, all of them under seven.

Meanwhile, Frankie and Sue have been separated more than a year now, but Pop refuses to acknowledge that one of his sons might end up divorced—or that it might be Frankie's fault. Everyone in Greenbury knows about Frankie and Char, the new beautician down at Hair and Now. Of course, no one in the Cavelli family ever brings it up. No one ever asks Frankie about Sue, either.

Danny clears his throat. "You know, Pop, a lot of women travel on their own these days. It's not like when you were young. It doesn't mean Sandy's a . . . well, you know."

A *putana* is what his father had called her. Italian for whore. Well, Pop hadn't exactly said his sister is one, just that when single girls go away alone, people talk. People, according to Tony Cavelli, would say that Sandy is out looking for men.

And even though Danny suspects people would be right, he isn't about to tell his father that. What his sister does is her own business. Still, these days, you can't be too careful.

"I know it's not like when I was young," Tony says, wiping an orange smear of sauce from his mustache before spearing another gnocchi on his fork. "You don't have to tell me. I just expect my daughter, my own flesh and blood, to behave like a young lady. Not like a—"

"Frankie, what's the matter with you?" Angie interrupts, jabbing her middle son in the arm. "Don't tell me that's all you're gonna eat."

"Ma, I had a huge plateful." Frankie pushes back his chair and stifles a burp.

"Where are you going?" Tony Junior asks, resting an elbow on the back of Maryanne's empty chair. She's in the kitchen, making sure the kids are eating.

"What do you mean where am I going? It's Saturday night. Bowling, where else?"

"Well, before you go, you have to come over and help me move that dresser out of the baby's room. You said you would."

"Oh, geez, I forgot. Come on, Tony, I'm late already," Frankie says, checking his watch. "I'll help you do it tomorrow."

"Can't. We have Maryanne's mother's birthday party right after church."

"Danny will help you," Angie says, looking at him. "Right?"

This time, Danny sighs out loud. "I'll help you," he tells his oldest brother. "But we have to make it fast. Cheryl and I are going to the movies at eight-thirty."

Maryanne, just coming back into the dining room, says, "The movies! God, Tony, remember when we used to go to the movies on Saturday nights?"

"We still go to the movies sometimes."

"Yeah, Disney matinees." Maryanne looks at Cheryl. "Enjoy it while you can. As soon as you have kids, you two will never get away by yourselves again."

Cheryl catches Danny's eye.

He knows what she's thinking. *If only we had kids.* They've been trying since their wedding night, with no luck. For a while, Cheryl had been pestering him to let her see a specialist, a doctor who's had a pretty good success rate with patients who have difficulty conceiving. Danny has resisted, not wanting to get into that.

A friend of his at work has been through the whole gamut. Tests. Fertility drugs. *In vitro* fertilization. He and his wife drained their bank accounts, took out a second mortgage on their house, endured years of stress and prayers, and nothing worked. Now they're trying borrow money to adopt.

Danny supposes that as a last resort, he and Cheryl can go that route, but he can't help wanting to hold out longer, to see what happens. And Cheryl seems to have started to see things his way lately. At least, she hasn't pestered him about that doctor for the last month or so.

There's a sudden sound of breaking glass in the kitchen, followed instantly by the sound of one of Danny's little nieces wailing and another one saying, "I told you not to touch that."

"Ashley? What happened?" Maryanne is in there like a shot.

Angie jumps up and follows her, saying, "Eye-yi-yi, I hope that wasn't my new water pitcher."

A moment later, the crying has escalated, and Danny's oldest niece, Caitlin, appears in the doorway, her dark eyes solemn. "Daddy? Ashley cut herself on some glass and she's bleeding."

Tony Junior gets up. "Where?"

"Over by the stove."

"No, I mean, where on her body? Never mind, I'll come." He, too, disappears into the kitchen.

Frankie pulls on his leather jacket, says a quick "later," and heads out the side door.

"Crazy," Tony Cavelli says, throwing his hands up in the air, then picking up his fork again.

"What's crazy, Pop?"

"This family, what else?" He shovels some gnocchi into his mouth, then says around it, "Three girls. Your brother better hope this new baby isn't another one. He has his hands full already. Raising a daughter isn't easy."

"Oh, come on, Pop, Sandy never gave you any trouble growing up."

"Then, no. Now . . ." He shakes his head.

"What's she done now?"

"She won't lose weight. She won't get married. She's off alone on some crazy island. . . ."

"What island?" Cheryl asks brightly.

"That's the worst part. Tide Island. I took you kids there when you were little, remember?" Tony asks Danny, who nods. "Crazy place. All kinds of hippies there. Not the kind of place where a young lady should go alone."

Danny pushes his chair back abruptly. "Come on, Cheryl. Let's go make sure Ashley's okay."

As they head into the kitchen, leaving his father alone at the table, Danny wonders if the day is ever going to come when he can stop coming to Sandy's rescue.

Sandy's heart has been pounding for the last half hour or so as the time for her big date drew near.

Now, when she peeks through the glass in the front door

of the inn and sees the shiny black sedan outside, her heart starts pumping so violently that it almost hurts.

Relax, she tells herself as she reaches for the knob. *Act as though you've seen it all before . . . done it all before . . .*

"Ah, Sandy, your date must be here."

She jumps and turns to see Jasper Hammel behind her. "I guess that's him."

"May I help you with your coat?"

"Oh . . ." She has it slung over her arm.

She'd pictured Ethan Thoreau coming up to the door to greet her, had imagined how his hands would brush against the bare skin at her neck as he gallantly helped her into her coat.

Now, it's Jasper Hammel who takes it from her and holds it open so she can slip her arms into the sleeves. Disappointed, she glances out the window again with a frown.

"Um, are you sure that's Ethan?" she asks Jasper.

"Ethan? Oh, no, that's not Mr. Thoreau. It's his driver, of course."

"Of course." Though startled, Sandy can't help but feel relieved. Her mother had taught her, back when she was in high school, that if a date didn't come up to the door, she shouldn't go out with him again.

But chauffeurs don't count, Sandy thinks gleefully now as Jasper holds the door open for her and she walks out into the rainy night.

The driver's side door opens and a tall, dark figure puts up an umbrella in one quick movement. He comes to the bottom of the steps and tips his hat at Sandy. "Good evening, Miss Cavelli."

"Good evening," she says coolly, practicing for later. She wants Ethan Thoreau to think that she's sophisticated.

Like Liza.

An image of the woman flits into Sandy's brain, and she frowns. She has nothing in common with Liza Danning.

But it probably wouldn't hurt to imitate her haughty attitude, under the circumstances.

The chauffeur holds the umbrella over her head as they walk back to the car. He opens the door and helps her into the back seat, grasping her arm firmly with a black leather glove. He's wearing tinted aviator-framed glasses and a long, dark wool overcoat.

As they pull away from the Bramble Rose, Sandy settles back against the leather upholstery and takes a deep breath, then exhales slowly.

This is it, she thinks. *I'm off to meet the man of my dreams.*

Then she feels a sudden prickle of panic.

What is it? What's wrong with you?

She knits her brows, confused.

There's something. . . .

Something triggered a completely negative sensation inside her just now. She has no idea what it was, but it was there, as real as anything she's ever felt in her life.

In the dark back seat of the car, she starts to chew her lower lip, then stops when she realizes that she'll ruin her lipstick, which she applied so carefully for Ethan's benefit.

What's bothering her? She stares vacantly at the back of the chauffeur's head, trying to put her finger on whatever it was that made her uneasy.

Was, because she no longer feels an acute sense of something unpleasant. Still, though the anxiety is fading, she can't shake it entirely.

In the depths of her consciousness, something has stirred. Something disturbing.

She blinks and looks over the front seat, through the rain-splattered windshield. The road ahead, the one she walked along earlier this afternoon, is rain-slicked and deserted. The headlights cast a murky glow in the rain. Outside, the steadily howling wind mingles with the rhythmic crashing of the ocean and the squeaking of the windshield wipers.

"Is the house far from here?" Sandy's voice is strained even to her own ears.

"No," the chauffeur says simply, not turning his head.

She looks at his black-gloved hands, notes the way they clench the steering wheel. His posture is stiff and he focuses intently on the road.

He must be nervous about driving in such nasty weather, Sandy tells herself. It certainly is getting worse. The rain is streaming over the windshield despite the furiously moving wipers, and she can feel the car being buffeted by the gale.

Is that why I'm so edgy? she asks herself. *It must be the storm.*

That makes sense. After all, who would want to be out in weather like this, in a strange, out-of-the-way place? Anyone might feel a little nervous about it. Anyone might confuse that feeling for something else.

Déjà vu.

That's what Sandy thought she was feeling a moment ago. It was as though she'd done this before, somehow. But . . .

A romantic weekend on a beautiful island, a chauffeur, a date with a wealthy, gorgeous man . . .

Nope, you've never done anything like this before, she tells herself wryly. *But if you're lucky, maybe this is only the beginning. . . .*

Liza lies on her bed, trying to read the manuscript she'd started this afternoon. Normally, her experienced editor's eye can whiz through three-hundred-and-fifty pages in a matter of hours. But it's taken her ten minutes to read two paragraphs, and she finally shoves the white pages aside again in frustration.

D.M. Yates still hasn't called back again, and Liza is more and more certain that she's been had.

The only thing that's keeping her from being entirely sure is Jasper Hammel.

If he'd merely spoken to Yates on the telephone, it would be one thing. Someone could have called the inn pretending to be the reclusive writer.

But Jasper said Yates was actually here, in the inn, looking for her.

Would Albie—or whoever is behind this scam—actually come all the way out to this island and pose as Yates? Or, even more farfetched, would he go to the trouble of hiring an impostor?

Somehow, Liza can't picture it. After all, Albie—he's the only one she really suspects—is an incredibly busy man. If she's not mistaken, he's in Washington until the end of the month anyway.

So what's going on here, then?

If it's not a wild-goose chase, there's only one other solution. D.M. Yates actually did summon Liza to this island, and he really did come looking for her.

And if that's the case, then sooner or later, he's going to show up again.

When—*if*—he does, Liza plans to be ready for him.

The way she was ready for Albie, and all the others before him.

Men.

If there's one thing Liza knows how to handle, it's a man.

She learned young. As a teenager, she realized she could wrap her father around her little finger. All she had to do was make him feel special. The disgusting, slobbering drunk actually believed her when she told him she loved him, that she thought he was the best daddy in the world.

She wonders what he thinks now. . . .

Now that she hasn't seen him in over ten years.

She walked out of that Brooklyn apartment on the morning after her high school graduation, and she never looked back. Never made an effort to contact him, to let him know where she was or why she had left. Never bothered to find out, in all these years, whether he was dead or alive.

She doesn't care.

At least, that's what she tells herself.

Leaving wasn't something she'd planned to do. Not until she'd marched into the auditorium in her cap and gown and looked toward the spot where her father should have been sitting. It was empty.

And he'd promised. He'd *promised* he'd be there for her, that afterward, he'd take her to White Castle and let her have as many greasy little hamburgers as she could eat.

She had known where he was instead that day, where he always was when she needed him. At the run-down bar a few blocks from their building.

How many times had Liza, as a child, gone in there looking for him?

How many times had she found him, with bloodshot eyes and reeking of liquor, slumped on a stool in the corner of the bar? How many times had he already been passed out when she arrived so that the bartender would have to round up two volunteers to carry him home as little Liza led the way through the seedy neighborhood to their dilapidated building?

Well, she was through. She wasn't going to show up at the bar in her cap and gown, demanding to know why he hadn't shown up to watch her receive her diploma, why he'd allowed her to be the only person in her class who had no one in the audience. Who had no one, period.

Even now, ten years later, Liza feels tears welling up at the memory of that horrible day.

But the next day—the day she left—well, that was the best day of her life. Because that was the first time she'd realized she didn't need that lousy excuse for a father.

That was the day she'd marched into realtor George Vlapos's office clutching the classified section of the *Times* in one hand and her imitation Chanel purse in the other.

Inside the purse was the several hundred dollars she'd just received from a pawnbroker. She'd sold him her mother's wedding and engagement rings.

She'd always known where her father kept them—in the small wooden box on his dresser, along with a lock of his own dead mother's hair and a faded photo of his former wife holding newborn Liza.

Through all the bad times, all the times when there was no food on the table and no heat in the tiny apartment, all the times when her father was desperate for a drink but couldn't even afford cheap wine, those rings had been in that wooden box. Liza had often wondered why he didn't just take them out and sell them.

Deep down, though, she really knew why.

Maybe she felt the same—that as long as the rings were there, a part of her mother remained. A part of the family they had once been.

The pawnbroker was a shifty-eyed slob who had terrible b.o. and leered at Liza over the counter of his shop. He'd snatched the rings in his grubby hand and held them up to the light, then offered a fraction of what Liza knew they were worth. But she didn't care. She needed money, and she needed it fast. Money, and an apartment.

But George Vlapos didn't want to let her rent one of his apartments without references and a security deposit of a month's rent. Unless . . .

Unless what? eighteen-year-old Liza had asked eagerly, sensing a loophole.

There was a loophole, all right. All she had to do was go out to dinner with the swarthy, leering realtor. And, over dinner, she understood the rest of it.

All she had to do was sleep with George Vlapos, and she'd have her apartment.

It was surprisingly easy.

She hadn't let herself think of it as losing her virginity. She hadn't let herself think about it at all, once it was over.

Once she had her own apartment—a shabby studio in Hell's Kitchen, but it was *hers*—she hadn't ever looked back.

And she hadn't dealt with George Vlapos again . . . at least, not until he tried to raise the rent. When he did, she slept with him again, and her rent remained the same.

Men, Liza thinks now, stretching and getting off the bed. *They're all the same. And I know exactly how to handle them.*

D.M. Yates will be no different.

If D.M. Yates is really the one who had summoned her here.

And if not . . .

If Albie, or one of the others, thinks he can get back at her this way . . .

Well, Liza will show him that he can't get the best of her.

Just as she had shown her father.

The shiny black sedan pulls to a stop in front of the last house on the seaside road—a massive Victorian that sits at the tip of the rocky ledge that juts into the ocean.

Sandy stares up at it through the rain-spattered window as the driver turns off the engine and gets out. The house has a classic scallop-shingled mansard roof crowned by an iron-railed widow's walk. Its shuttered double windows are tall and narrow with curved tops. The lamplit ones on the third floor are dormered and the shades are partly lowered, giving the eerie appearance, Sandy thinks, of lidded eyes glowing from beneath a dark hood.

There's a somber air about the place, and Sandy shudders inwardly as she stares up at its silhouette against the stormy night sky.

This isn't what she pictured when she imagined Ethan Thoreau's home. A mansion, yes—this creepy gothic monstrosity, no.

The chauffeur puts up his black umbrella, opens the back door, and offers a gloved hand to help her out.

Sandy wavers for only an instant before placing her fingers in his leather grip.

He holds the umbrella over her head as they hurry through the driving rain up the wooden steps of the porch that runs the length of the house. He turns the knob on one of the double doors and pushes it open. Sandy steps inside, vaguely wondering why it isn't locked, then realizing that there probably isn't much crime on the island. And what burglar would want to come out in this weather?

The door closes behind her, abruptly shutting out the roar of the storm. She turns and sees that maybe she was wrong about crime on the island. Looking out of place on the old-fashioned door panel is a shiny silver deadbolt, the kind that, once it's locked from the inside, requires a key to open it again.

Her father wanted to put one of those locks on their front door back in Greenbury after someone broke into one of their neighbor's homes.

But Angie had talked him out of it, saying it would be a fire hazard.

"What are you talking about?" Tony had asked. "We'll just leave the key in the lock all the time so that if there's a fire, we can get out."

"If the key's in the lock, the burglar can just break the window, reach in, and unlock it anyway," Angie had argued.

They'd settled for a sturdy chain instead.

But in Ethan Thoreau's house, Sandy notices, the double doors don't have windows and the key is sitting in the inside lock.

She wipes her feet on the mat beneath her feet and looks around. She's standing in a dimly lit entrance hall that rises two stories with a sweeping wooden staircase that leads to a second-floor hallway lined with closed doors. The decor is formal and old-fashioned with dark, heavy drapes over the windows and a tapestry-style carpet on the floor. The dark woodwork is elaborately carved, and the wallpaper is a deep maroon brocade that's illuminated in patches where gaslight sconces dot the walls.

"Wait in there," the chauffeur says, and Sandy turns to see him pointing at a room that's through an archway to the right.

She nods and heads in that direction, again feeling an elusive pin prick of *déjà vu*.

Frowning, she steps into the room and sees that it's a parlor filled with heavy, old-fashioned furniture along with more dark brocade wallpaper, more sconces, more dark woodwork.

She spots a gilt-framed painting hanging over the fireplace and is moving closer to inspect it when she hears a telltale *click* from the foyer.

She knows what it is even before she peeks over her shoulder and sees the chauffeur moving away from the double front doors.

The key that had been in the shiny silver lock is gone.

And Sandy realizes, with a pounding heart, that she's locked in.

Six

Jennie looks up from the magazine she's been trying to read, startled by a knock on the door of her room.

Must be Jasper Hammel.

She'd told the man, when she'd returned from the beach, that she wasn't interested in coming down for dinner.

Oh, but you must, he'd said, his mustache twitching. *I'm making my special rock cornish game hens.*

She'd insisted that she had a stomachache and wasn't hungry, but he'd just smiled and said she'd probably feel better later. *I'll see you in the dining room at eight-thirty,* he'd said.

It's eight-twenty now, according to the travel alarm on the nightstand.

Sighing, Jennie rises from the wingback chair by the fireplace and goes to answer the door, prepared to be rude if she has to be. After all, the whole point of this weekend was to relax, not to be bullied into joining strangers for dinner and conversation.

Throwing the door open, Jennie opens her mouth to speak, then clamps it shut again when she sees who's standing there.

"Hi, Laura." Liza Danning tosses her blond hair over her shoulder. She's taken it out of the French twist, and it falls past her shoulders in straight, silky strands.

"Hi." Jennie wonders what she could possibly want.

"What are you doing?" Liza peers over Jennie's shoulder into the room.

"Reading."

"What?"

"I'm reading." Jennie idly notices that Liza's black sweater is cashmere with velvet trim and part of an expensive fall designer collection. Laura has one just like it, and she splurged more than a week's pay to buy it. Of course, then she couldn't come up with her half of the rent and Jennie had to cover her, as usual. And though that was a few months ago, Laura still hasn't paid her back—as usual.

"No—I meant, what are you reading?" Liza asks.

"Oh . . . just a magazine. *Country Living.*"

"Oh." Liza wrinkles her nose. "I'm not really big on this country stuff. In fact, I'm going nuts out here. There's absolutely nothing to do."

"What about your business meeting?"

"Oh. That."

"What's wrong?"

Liza shrugs. "I just haven't heard from the guy I'm supposed to meet yet, that's all."

"Well, the weather isn't that great." Jennie glances toward the window, which is rattling from the fury of wind and rain outside. "Maybe he couldn't get here."

"You mean to the island? He lives here . . . supposedly."

Jennie frowns. "What? You don't think he really does?"

"I'm not sure. Who knows?" Liza throws her hands up and shakes her head. "But anyway, I wondered if you wanted to come down to dinner with me."

"I wasn't going to—"

"I know, I wasn't either." Liza lowers her voice. "He's a little too weird for me."

Jennie doesn't ask whom she's talking about. Obviously, she isn't the only one who's put off by Jasper Hammel.

"But," Liza continues, "I'm starving. And I refuse to go down there alone. I bumped into that other person who's staying here, Sandy something-or-other, going into the bathroom a few hours ago, and she was getting ready to go out for the night."

"Well, as I said, I—"

"You've got to eat. And you have to admit, whatever he's making smells pretty good. Come on."

Jennie hesitates. On the one hand, she isn't crazy about Liza's tone, which isn't so much cajoling as it is commanding. On the other, she isn't thrilled by the thought of spending the entire evening alone with her magazine—and her memories.

"Okay, I'll come down with you," she tells Liza, who promptly looks relieved and flashes a smile that actually seems genuine.

"Thanks, Laura. I appreciate it."

"No problem." Jennie gestures at the room behind her. "I'll just comb my hair and meet you—"

"That's okay. I'll wait here for you."

Liza's already past her, walking into the room and glancing around. "It's so frilly," she says with a look of distaste. "Like the one they stuck me in. Only mine's done in pink, not purple."

"Uh huh," Jennie says, watching Liza pick up a gold-rimmed porcelain bud vase, examine it briefly, and plunk it back down on the piecrust table by the bed.

"You know," Liza gestures at the lilac-printed wallpaper, "this light color purple is the exact same shade as your eyes."

"I guess."

"That's kind of a coincidence, don't you think?"

"I guess," Jennie says again.

Liza turns to meet her gaze directly, her own eyes sharp and narrowed. "Does this place give you the creeps?"

"You asked me that before, when we were in town."

"I know. I'm asking you again. Because it seems even

creepier now that it's dark out and the storm is going full force."

"It doesn't bother me," Jennie lies.

"Well, it bothers me. I can't wait to get off this island and back to civilization."

Not knowing what, if anything, to say to that, Jennie goes to the dresser and runs a brush through her hair, conscious of Liza watching her. She sets the brush down and picks up a cherry-flavored Chapstick, running it over her dry lips.

"Don't you wear makeup?" Liza asks.

"Not really."

"Mmm."

Jennie knows what she's thinking. It's what Laura always says to her, too—*you'd be so much prettier, Jen, if you'd just take some time to fix yourself up. Wear makeup. Change your hairstyle . . .*

There was a time when Jennie used to take the time to make herself attractive. Back when she and Harry were together . . .

But once Harry was gone, she hadn't bothered. It seemed so unimportant, so frivolous, somehow, after what had happened.

Laura had told her, after she lost Harry, that she should get right back out there and make an effort to find someone new. As if they were in eighth grade again and a boyfriend of the week had dumped her.

At least put on some mascara and use some gel in your hair. You'll never find a man if you don't at least try and look sexy, Jen.

But she'd proved Laura wrong without intending to.

It was almost a year ago that Keegan had materialized in her antique shop one Saturday afternoon in early May, wanting to look through the Haviland china she had on hand. It was for a Mother's Day gift, he'd told Jennie, looking a little sheepish—his mom collected the stuff.

It wasn't until their third date that he'd told Jennie the

truth—*he* was the one who collected antiques, including china. Most women, Keegan had added, thought that was a strange hobby for a man to have. *But you seem different, Jennie. . . . You're special. I don't know you that well, but I want to. And I want you to know me, too.*

Jennie fell in love with him on the spot.

But, she reminds herself now, Keegan—like Harry—is history.

Jennie puts down the Chapstick, looks in the mirror again, and sees a reflection of Liza, behind her, zeroing in on the sketch-pad she'd carelessly left open on the bed. She's standing over it before Jennie can divert her.

"Is this what you drew today?" she asks, picking the pad up and looking at the sketch.

"Yeah." Feeling invaded, Jennie turns away from the bureau and is about to tell Liza she's changed her mind about dinner.

But Liza's expression has softened. She smiles at Jennie and says, "This is good, Laura. *Really* good. I mean, I'm not usually crazy about drawings of scenery—I usually like modern art, abstract stuff, better—but I think this is wonderful."

"It's the beach behind the inn."

"Yeah, I recognize it. It's got such a lonely aura. Sad. Not the place itself, but . . . your drawing. Is it your interpretation of what you see out there?"

"I guess it is." Jennie thinks that she obviously revealed too much in her sketch. She doesn't want Liza prying into her private world, asking questions about her past, so she changes the subject. "Why don't we go down to eat? I'm ready."

"Good." Liza takes another look at the sketch, then puts it carefully back on the bed, exactly the way she found it.

Jennie picks up her room key from the dresser and tucks it into the pocket of her jeans. It's probably not necessary to lock the door, but she can't help feeling that she should.

Just in case . . .

In case what? she asks herself, and realizes she doesn't know the answer.

Somehow, she just can't shake the feeling that this inn might not be as idyllic and charming as it seems. That her belongings aren't safe unless the door is locked securely . . .

And that maybe *she* isn't, either.

He hums to himself as he buttons his pristine-white pleated shirt, standing in front of a full-length mirror in the large master bedroom that overlooks the dark, storm-churned sea.

So far, it's been so easy . . . so wonderfully easy that he can't help but worry that something might go wrong.

Relax. . . . What can go wrong now? Everything is in order. Sandy Cavelli is downstairs waiting for you.

He wonders what she's doing right this moment, what she's thinking, whether she's frightened. Probably not. Not yet.

But it won't be long before she's terrified.

Before she's suffering, just as she made him suffer all those years ago.

Just as Lorraine suffered.

He smiles at the thought of her . . .

Lorraine LaCroix.

He will never forget the first moment he laid eyes on her, in the lobby of the American Embassy in France. She was the most beautiful woman he'd ever seen, with that milky skin and deep red hair and eyes the color of emeralds. Her clothes were so impeccable, so stylish that he'd thought she had to be French. No, considering her last name, she'd apparently had French ancestors, she'd told him, but she was an American, working at the embassy as a translator.

He will never forget how sophisticated she was, how she

treated him with cool detachment until she found out who he was—rather, who his family was.

Then, those emerald eyes had twinkled at him and her voice had warmed to him. She'd allowed him to take her out to dinner at the finest restaurant in Paris and to make love to her that night in his suite in the finest hotel in all of France.

As dawn filtered through the plate-glass windows on that morning, he'd whispered that he loved her. She hadn't looked horrified or shrunk away from his touch. She had simply smiled the mysterious, close-lipped smile that he would grow to know so well, and she had slipped down beneath the sheets to do incredible things to him. Things no one had ever done to him, not Sandy . . . not Liza . . . not Laura . . .

No one but his mother.

And he wouldn't allow himself to think about that—not then, and he won't now.

He reaches for the bow tie that waits on the dresser and slips it around his neck, tucking it beneath the pointed collar on his shirt. With fluid, expert movements, he ties it, still humming to himself, watching his reflection in the mirror and remembering the last time he wore this tuxedo.

That morning, his hands had been trembling, and he certainly hadn't been humming.

But then, as now, he was fantasizing about the woman who waited for him, and hoping that nothing would go wrong.

Now, the woman is Sandy Cavelli.

Then, it was Lorraine LaCroix—his bride.

It had been her idea to plan a large wedding and to have it in his Manhattan brownstone. She said she wanted everyone they knew to bear witness when she became his wife. She said she wanted the most perfect wedding anyone could imagine, the kind of wedding she had only dreamed of when she was growing up in a bona-fide orphanage where she had been forced to live an austere, loveless existence.

He remembered the intricate details that had gone into

planning the affair, the details Lorraine had embraced with her usual fervor.

Nothing but the finest for his fiancée. Waterford crystal toasting glasses for all of the guests and imported champagne and caviar. A silk wedding gown created especially for her by the most famous designer in Paris. A guest list that included not only their friends and her family, but New York's social elite, as well as European royalty. Two tickets for a honeymoon trip that would take them around the globe, with reservations for the most exclusive hotels and resorts on every continent.

And, of course, red roses. Hundreds of dozens of them. Roses for the brownstone, for her hair, for her bouquet, for his lapel. They were her favorite flower, and their fragrant aroma would forever remind him of her.

He had sent one-hundred-and-two red roses—one for every day they'd been together—to her suite at the Waldorf-Astoria on the morning of the wedding, along with a carefully composed note that told her how happy he was that she was going to marry him . . .

And how sorry he was for what had happened the night before.

After the rehearsal dinner, he had gone up to her suite with her, assuming he would spend a few hours there, if not the entire night.

Lorraine had told him she didn't want him to come in, that she didn't want to make love to him that night. She had gone on to tell him something about how she wanted their next time to be after they were married.

He hadn't been able to focus on what she was saying.

Stung, he had only stared at her, seeing only rejection on her face, hearing it in her voice . . .

Once again, seeing and hearing Sandy Cavelli . . .

Liza Danning . . .

Laura Towne . . .

And now Lorraine, too.

Suddenly, he had gone into a frenzy, grabbing his startled fiancée and throwing her down on the bed. As she protested, then screamed, and finally cried hysterically, he had forced himself on her, violently invading her body with his mouth and fingers and ultimately with his penis, mercilessly thrusting into her over and over again until he at last was able to release several years worth of pent-up fury.

Only when he had rolled off of her and seen her tear-stained, scratched and bleeding face, her torn dress, her terror-filled eyes, had he realized what he'd done.

Too stunned to react, he had simply gotten dressed and left the suite, leaving Lorraine still whimpering and huddled on the bed.

He hadn't slept that night.

He had lain in his own king-sized bed in the brownstone, listening to the traffic going down Fifth Avenue and wondering how he could have lost control that way.

He was sorry, truly sorry.

And Lorraine, he knew, would forgive him.

Because Lorraine loved him. She wanted to marry him. She wanted to spend every moment, the rest of her life, with him.

Lorraine was his, would always be his.

At exactly noon, dressed in his tuxedo with a white rosebud carefully pinned on his lapel, he had taken his place in the drawing room on the first floor of his brownstone. There—in front of the twenty rows of rented white folding chairs, in front of the two hundred people who at first smiled and chattered quietly, then began to shift uncomfortably on their seats and check their watches—he waited.

And waited . . .

And waited . . .

Sandy sits on the edge of an uncomfortable antique sofa, her clammy hands clasped tightly in her lap so that they won't tremble so much. Beneath her long navy skirt, the one she chose so carefully for her date tonight, her right leg is bouncing rapidly up and down from nerves.

But not the kind of nerves she'd expected to have now as she is about to meet the man who summoned her here.

She's not breathless with romantic anticipation.

No, she's breathless with fright.

For the last twenty minutes, as she's sat here in the parlor waiting for Ethan Thoreau to appear, she's repeatedly told herself that she needs to calm down. That there's absolutely no reason to feel panicky. That she's certainly not in any kind of danger.

Even though this house looks like something out of a gothic horror movie.

Even though the chauffeur locked her inside, then vanished up the stairs.

If she were a different kind of person, Sandy thinks for the umpteenth time, she would get off this sofa and leave this room and look around the house, making sure there's another way out.

Just in case.

But, being spineless Sandy Cavelli, she just sits here in the parlor, looking helplessly back at the archway leading out into the hall and at the French doors on an interior wall at the other end of the room, their glass windows made opaque by heavy draperies on the other side.

And she grows more and more agitated, wondering. And listening . . .

For something. Anything.

Outside, the wind grows more and more ferocious, sweeping in from the sea to batter the house.

Inside, the minutes tick by on the old grandfather clock in the corner of the parlor.

The parlor is lit only by the fire on the hearth and the white votive candles that glow from tables and shelves around the room. The effect might be cozy or even romantic somewhere else, Sandy thinks; but here, the flickering light only seems eerie.

Finally, she hears a creaking from the hall; someone is descending the stairs.

One step at a time.

No longer caring about her lipstick, Sandy bites down, hard, on her bottom lip and clenches her hands even more tightly, holding her breath and listening.

Finally, the footsteps reach the bottom.

Sandy braces herself for whatever is going to happen. She turns and looks expectantly toward the archway leading to the hall.

But instead of coming into the parlor, whoever is out there—can it really be Ethan?—passes by, still moving in that same methodic manner, fleetingly casting a tall shadow on the wall opposite the sofa where Sandy waits.

This is too strange. . . .

There's something wrong. . . .

I have to get out of here. . . .

Sandy's eyes dart wildly around the room. She looks at the two sets of narrow double windows which stretch almost from floor to ceiling. Can she open one and climb out?

No. Instinctively, she knows that they, too, will be locked. And they're paned, so she can't break one and escape that way, either.

Escape.

Are you crazy? You've been waiting for weeks to meet Ethan Thoreau. And now you want to break a window and escape from him? What are you thinking? What will this man think if he hears shattering glass and sees you fleeing into the night? You've definitely lost it. You have to—

Suddenly, she hears a faint sound coming from behind the French doors.

Music.

Wide-eyed, she turns in that direction and strains to listen. She knows this melody. . . .

It's from *West Side Story,* she realizes abruptly. She's seen the movie countless times. This is the song Maria and Tony sing when they pretend to get married.

"One Hand, One Heart."

The lyrics become audible as the song grows louder in the next room, as though someone has turned up the volume. The familiar tune is reassuring, and Sandy feels her body relax slightly.

He's setting the mood for seduction, she tells herself. *This is classic. Soft music, candlelight . . .*

Everything is going to be all right.

For a long time, she sits there, listening to the song and waiting for something to happen.

"One Hand, One Heart" ends and a new song begins.

Sandy recognizes this one, too. "Color My World." Her cousin Maria sang it at Danny and Cheryl's wedding.

She hears the footsteps again, this time approaching the French doors. There's a click; and then, as she watches, the knobs turn and both doors swing slowly open.

A man is standing there, his face lost in the shadows, but his tall, broad-shouldered frame clearly silhouetted in the doorway.

"Sandra Cavelli . . . you're here with me at last." His voice is low and soft, so soft that she has to strain to hear him above the music.

She clears her throat and stands, subconsciously wiping her sweaty palms on her skirt. "Hello . . . Ethan?"

He doesn't respond, just stands there. She can't see his eyes in the dim light, but she can feel him watching her. She fights the urge to squirm under his gaze.

When he doesn't move or say anything else, she takes a few tentative steps toward him. As she draws closer, she sees that he's wearing a tuxedo.

A tuxedo! For a date in his own house!

She takes a deep breath and notices that the air suddenly

seems filled with a heady floral scent, like potpourri or perfume . . .

"You look lovely, Sandra," he says quietly.

This time, something strikes her about his voice. She's heard it someplace before . . .

The chauffeur!

An involuntary shiver shoots through Sandy. She nearly gasps out loud as she realizes that the man standing in the doorway is the chauffeur who drove her from the inn.

But why? Why would he do it—pretend to be someone else?

She struggles to maintain her composure, telling herself that he's probably just eccentric; lots of rich people are that way, aren't they?

Hysteria mounts inside her; yet outwardly, she forces a smile and says, "It's so nice to meet you at last, Mr. Thoreau."

She expects him to say *call me Ethan.*

But he doesn't. He says, "Oh, we've met before, Sandra."

Should she admit that she realizes what he's done?

"Do you recognize me?"

He steps closer to her, and she peers at him through the flickering light. "Actually, I do recognize you," she says, deciding to play his game and thrusting lightness into her voice. "You're the chauffeur who picked me up at the inn, aren't you?"

He laughs, a surprisingly robust sound that catches Sandy off-guard . . .

A sound that again triggers that feeling of *déjà vu* she experienced in the car.

I know him, she realizes uneasily. *Not just because he drove me here earlier. I know him . . . from a long time ago.*

But who is he?

"Who am I, Sandra?" he asks as though he's invaded her

thoughts. "I *am* the chauffeur, but who am I, really?" There's a smirk in his voice.

A prickle of panic shoots through her again. Her mind races, searching for the answer.

Who is he?

Who *is* he?

It becomes a refrain that screams inside her brain as she stares at him, trying to remember.

"You don't know, do you?" he asks, the smirk fading into a sinister chill. "Damn you. I knew I didn't matter to you. But I didn't think you cared so little that you'd forget me entirely. Admit it, Sandy. Admit it!"

"Admit what?" she asks in a small, strangled-sounding voice.

"Admit that you don't even know me!" He takes another step closer to her. Suddenly, his face is illuminated in the path of a candle on the grand piano.

Sandy freezes, then claps a hand over her mouth.

"Say it, Sandy. Say it, damn it!" His voice is hoarse with vehemence. "Say you don't know who I am!"

But she can't.

Because suddenly, she does know exactly who he is.

And she's paralyzed by stark terror.

Rain is pouring from the black night sky as Danny Cavelli slams the car door and walks up the driveway to the back door of the house he and Cheryl bought right before they were married. He notices, as he stomps heavily up the back steps, that another piece of wood has crumbled away from the edge of the tiny back porch.

He turns to Cheryl, who's hurrying through the rain a few steps behind him, and gestures at the splintered floor. "Look at that. This whole place is falling apart. But I'll never get around to fixing it because I spend all my time helping my family fix things around their houses."

They climb onto the porch, where the leaky roof keeps some of the rain out.

Cheryl sighs. "Danny—"

"I mean, Tony says he needs help moving a freakin' piece of furniture, and I get over there, and what does he have me doing? Cleaning the gutters on his house. In the pouring rain. In the dark."

"Danny," Cheryl says again as he jabs the key into the lock, "you know he didn't plan on having you do it. He just noticed that tree branch had fallen into the gutter, and he can't climb because of his knee, and he—"

"Yeah, the knee he hurt running away the day he and Frankie left me alone in the woods when I was six years old, Cheryl. Nice guy, huh?"

Muttering to himself, Danny opens the door and steps into the kitchen. He flips on a light and tosses his keys on the counter.

"Danny, come on, don't ruin our night," Cheryl says, following him in and locking the door behind her.

"I'm not the one who's ruining it," Danny tells her. "My brother ruined it. Thanks to him, we missed the movie."

"I told you that if we hurried, we could have gotten there only a few minutes late."

"Who wants to miss the first few minutes? You really have to pay attention in those John Grisham movies. We wouldn't know what was going on."

"They never start them on time at the Cineplex anyway," Cheryl points out. "They have coming attractions."

"Yeah, well, whatever." Danny goes over to the refrigerator and pulls out a can of beer. "You want one, babe?"

Cheryl shrugs. "Why not? I'll make some popcorn and we'll watch TV."

"Nothing good on—not on a Saturday night."

"Well, then we'll think of something else to do," Cheryl says, shooting a meaningful smile in her husband's direction.

"Yeah," Danny says, meeting her gaze as he pops open one beer, then the other. "Maybe we will. Hey, maybe Tony didn't ruin my night after all, huh?"

"Laura! I'm so glad you decided to join us after all!" Jasper Hammel looks up from the tapered candles he's lighting in the middle of the dining-room table.

"Oh, um, yes . . . I'm feeling better." Jennie smiles faintly and glances back at Liza, who's two steps behind her.

"Did you hear from D.M. Yates again?" Liza asks Jasper abruptly in a no-nonsense voice.

"No, of course I didn't," he replies in his unruffled way. "If he had called or come by again, I would have come up to get you."

"Are you sure about that?" Liza scowls and plunks herself into a seat at the table.

Jasper seems to be ignoring her as he bustles over to the sideboard and uncorks a bottle of wine with a flourish.

Only two places are set at the long oval table tonight.

"Where's Sandy?" Jennie asks, settling into the chair across from Liza's.

"I'm afraid she had a change of plans."

"What do you mean?"

Jasper sniffs the open wine bottle, his eyes closed. "Mmm, an exquisite bouquet. Yes, well, Sandy decided, earlier, to go back to the mainland."

Liza, who had been fiddling with her silverware, looks up sharply.

Jennie frowns and glances toward the window. "In this weather?"

"I'm afraid so."

"But what about her hot date?" Liza asks. "I thought she was meeting some guy here tonight."

"Apparently, she changed her mind. She was driven to the ferry dock a little while ago."

"But I thought the last ferry of the day left this afternoon," Jennie says.

Jasper looks up from the wine decanter he's tilting over her glass. He clears his throat, and his mustache twitches. "Oh, it normally does leave early. But not today. Because of the, er, holiday weekend, there are extra ferries scheduled for today. Sandy caught the last one."

"Oh." Jennie toys with the blue cloth napkin she was about to spread in her lap.

"I'll be right back with some rolls," Jasper says and hurries through the door into the kitchen.

As soon as he's gone, Liza leans toward Jennie. "Did you hear that?" she asks in a low voice.

"Hear what?"

"What he said about Sandy and the ferry?"

"What about it?"

"He was lying."

Jennie tries to ignore the jittery feeling in the pit of her stomach. "Why would he lie?"

"Who knows? I told you he was strange. But trust me, Sandy wouldn't change her mind about going out with that guy."

"How do you know? You barely know her."

Liza rolls her eyes. "Oh, come on, Laura. I know enough to be sure that a chub like her wouldn't turn down a chance to date some good-looking guy who has a lot of bucks."

Turned off by Liza's attitude, Jennie just shrugs and says, "Whatever." But inwardly, her heart is pounding. It didn't take Liza to tell her that Jasper Hammel wasn't telling the truth. She sensed it herself.

"Laura, I'm telling you," Liza whispers loudly, "something's up." Her green eyes are wide.

Looking at her, Jennie senses that Liza has a vulnerable side.

And that perhaps her own nerves about this place aren't merely due to her post-traumatic stress disorder after all.

But if Jasper Hammel really is lying . . .

Why?

And if Sandy didn't really leave the island . . .

Where is she?

"What's wrong, Laura?" Shawn asks, leaning across the small table in the crowded Newbury Street restaurant.

"Nothing," she says brightly, snapping out of her reverie and stabbing a large piece of shrimp tempura with her fork. She pops it into her mouth.

"You look preoccupied."

"I was just thinking about how glad I am that you're back. . . . I really missed you." That last part is the truth, although it wasn't what she'd been thinking about.

"I missed you, too." Shawn smiles at her and reaches across the table to pat her hand before picking up his chopsticks again.

Laura looks at him, wondering how long it'll be before she screws up this relationship, as she has all the others. Somehow, she can never keep a man. Well, not any man she'd want, anyway.

The only ones who ever get hooked on her for the long term are the losers. And her ex-husband, Brian, was the biggest loser of all.

A dangerous loser at that.

Laura still has the scar on her cheek, just beneath her left eye, where he burned her with his cigarette the night he accused her of sleeping around on him. She'd hysterically tried to explain that she hadn't come home because she'd been at the emergency room with her grandfather, waiting for the prognosis on her grandmother, who'd had another heart attack.

But Brian, crazed with jealousy and booze, had only

reached out to burn her again. That time, at least, the red tip of his cigarette had missed her face, instead landing on the couch cushion after she'd ducked. She'd let him keep the couch when she left; had let him keep everything, in fact, except the few mementos she had of her parents and the antique set of china that Jennie had given them as a shower gift.

She still has the china, in a box under her bed in the town house. Since she and Brian never actually used it, she figures she won't mind keeping it for when she's married again. *If* she's married again . . ."

She sighs inwardly and looks at Shawn, whose dark, boyish good looks have attracted quite a few appreciative glances from the other women in the restaurant.

"Don't you like your tempura?" he asks.

"Sure, it's good." She eats another piece of shrimp. "I can't believe you wanted Japanese food after spending a month in Tokyo."

"I got used to it." Shawn shrugs and grips a glistening red slab of raw tuna with his chopsticks.

Laura wrinkles her nose, watching as he dunks it into the small porcelain bowl that contains a mixture of soy sauce and some disgusting green goop—wasabi, he calls it.

"You know, Shawn," she says as he reaches for another slimy piece of fish, "sushi isn't good for you. It's full of worms—you know, parasites."

"Oh well."

"Jennie doesn't care, either. She loves that stuff," Laura says, shaking her head and having another bite of her shrimp with its light, deep-fried breading.

"How *is* your sister?"

"She's okay. I guess."

"What's wrong?"

Laura looks at him. "I don't know. I mean, I keep thinking about her tonight. It's like I'm worried about her, or something. Not that there's any reason to be. But Keegan—"

"He's her boyfriend, right? The cop."

*"Ex-*boyfriend now. He stopped over right before I left to pick you up at the airport, and I guess he started me thinking about my sister. She's out on Tide Island for the weekend, staying at some inn."

"Alone?"

Laura nods and quickly fills him in about the charity sweepstakes and how she'd won and given the trip to Jennie, who is posing as her.

Shawn rolls his eyes. "I thought you said you guys never pull that twin stuff anymore."

"I said I would never switch places with Jennie to fool you," Laura says with a grin.

"Don't worry. . . . You couldn't fool me. Even if your hair was long like Jennie's, I'd know you from your sister the second we got into bed."

"Shawn!"

"Laura!" He grins at her, and his cornflower-blue eyes look her up and down. "You're about a hundred thousand times more uninhibited than Jennie."

"Oh? And how do you know?"

"Be serious. Your sister's a little . . . straitlaced."

"And what am I?"

He bobs his eyebrows suggestively. "I'll tell you later."

Laura smiles, puts her fork down, and wipes her mouth with her napkin. "Why wait until later? Leave the rest of that stuff you're eating here—it'll probably swim away on its own—and let's get out of here. Unless you're still hungry."

"You know, I'm suddenly feeling full." Shawn puts down his chopsticks and motions for the check. Then he turns back to Laura. "Forgive the cliché, but—your place or mine?"

"You're joking, right? You have three roommates. My sister's away for the weekend."

"Right. But I do have to stop home first."

She groans.

"Come on, Laura, I haven't been there in a month. I just want to check my mail and messages and find something unrumpled to wear. It'll take two minutes."

"Shawn, with you, two minutes is usually two hours."

"I'll be fast. I promise."

"Fine." She pushes her chair back as the waiter drops the check on the table. "But then we go straight back to my place."

"Definitely." He lowers his voice and leans forward. "Believe me, Laura, I want you as much as you want me. It's been a helluva long time to go without it."

She murmurs her agreement.

But she can't help thinking that eagerness to be alone with Shawn isn't the only reason she wants to get back to the town house she shares with her sister.

For some reason, she feels compelled to make sure Jennie's all right, that she hasn't called from the island, or perhaps come back early.

Of course she's all right. Laura tells herself as she follows Shawn out onto the street. *What could be wrong?*

Nothing.

Jennie is probably having a wonderful time.

But Laura can't seem to shake her concern for her twin. And the last time she felt this way—the *only* other time she was ever plagued by this nagging anxiety about her sister's well-being—was the fateful day three years ago when disaster struck and shattered Jennie's life.

"Stephen? Stephen Gilbrooke?" Sandy finally manages to utter his name and sees him stiffen at the sound of it.

"You remember."

"I . . . yes." Sandy clamps her mouth shut and stares at him through frightened eyes.

"How did you recognize me? I had the best plastic surgeon in Europe make me into a new person. I don't look anything like my old self."

Sandy isn't sure what to say. A moment ago, he was disturbed that she didn't know who he was. Now, he seems disturbed that she does.

He's waiting for an answer, standing absolutely still and watching her.

"It's your eyes, actually," she tells him. "They look familiar."

"But I'm wearing colored contacts. Blue. My eyes are usually brown, like yours."

"I know," Sandy says around the lump of fear in her throat. She can't tell him that it isn't the eyes themselves that triggered the memory. . . . It's the expression in them.

An expression that fills her with dread now, just as it did so long ago.

Though she hasn't thought of it in years, that day has suddenly come back to her with crystal clarity.

The day she told Stephen Gilbrooke to get lost.

It was early September, the last Friday before Labor Day weekend. Sandy had spent so many days that summer at Stephen's parents' estate on the Long Island Sound. . . .

It was the year her father had twisted his back crawling out from under a sink and couldn't work for several months. Her mother had been forced to take a part-time job as a maid for Andrew Gilbrooke, who owned a thriving import-export business, and his wife, Aurelia.

Their only child was Stephen, who was about thirteen that summer. Sandy had felt sorry for him from the moment she first saw him hovering outside the kitchen door, shyly kicking the manicured grass with the toes of his immaculate white sneakers.

He was ugly . . . pitifully ugly.

His hair was black and kinky and stuck out awkwardly around his teacup-handle ears. Acne covered his face, and his features were misshapen. "Funnel Face," the other summer kids called him. At least, that was what he'd told Sandy.

She'd been kind to him, because her mother had told her to be and because she felt sorry for him. She knew how cruel other kids could be. The boys at school had taken to calling her Thunder Thighs that spring.

Sandy had accompanied her mother to the Gilbrookes' estate many times that summer, and she and Stephen had become friends. Sandy had taught him how to fish, just as Danny had taught her a few years earlier. He'd shown her where wild raspberries grew in the woods, and the two of them had eaten the sun-warmed berries until their fingertips and tongues were stained red.

Toward the end of the summer, Sandy had started feeling uneasy when she was with Stephen. There was something unnerving about the way he looked at her and the way he spoke to her.

Almost as though he worshipped her, or something.

No one—especially no *boy*—had ever treated Sandy that way. She'd always thought it would be wonderful if someone would.

Maybe if it were someone else . . .

But something about Stephen made her want to squirm. It wasn't his homely looks that bothered her, or his painful shyness.

It was more the quiet intensity that radiated from him, the sense that though he said little, a lot was happening in his mind. Things Sandy might rather not know . . . particularly when it pertained to the kids who called him Funnel Face.

Or to his mother.

She had seen Stephen's back stiffen and his jaw clench at the sound of his mother's voice, and she had seen something dark glinting in his eyes whenever he mentioned her.

Stephen frightened her.

It seemed that the more uncomfortable she grew around him, the more attached he became to her.

Angie Cavelli wouldn't let Sandy stay home alone while she was working and her father and brothers were all busy with the business, so she had no choice but to go to the Gilbrookes' estate with her mother through the end of the season.

It was about a week before Labor Day that Stephen tried to kiss her.

They'd been walking up the lane from the pond where they fished, and Sandy had been lost in thoughts of school's starting in a few days. With no warning, Stephen had suddenly grabbed her and planted his lips over hers.

Astonished, Sandy had shoved him away and shrieked, "What are you doing?"

He'd looked even more startled than she was. "I'm . . . I'm so sorry. I mean . . . God, I'm sorry." He'd blushed so quickly and completely that Sandy found herself feeling sorry for him.

"It's okay," she'd said, even though it wasn't. "We'll forget it happened."

Thank God, she was thinking, that there were only a few more days left of seeing him.

He had been more subdued than usual for the remainder of that week. Then, on that Friday, the last day Sandy would be at the estate, he had grabbed her and tried to kiss her again.

That time, she had reacted by slapping his pock-marked face, hard.

His jaw had dropped in shock, and she had seen fury in his eyes before he grabbed her and forced his lips over hers again. This time, he held her head firmly beneath his, his fingertips digging painfully into her scalp as he ground his wet, open mouth against hers.

Only when she'd let out a strangled sob did he release her.

"What do you think you're doing?" she'd screamed, her voice echoing through the quiet woods around the pond.

"Kissing you," he'd said calmly.

"Well, I don't want to kiss you." She'd wiped her mouth furiously with the back of her hand. "I don't even like you."

"What do you mean, you don't like me? You've been hanging around with me all summer."

"I wouldn't be here if it weren't for my mother's job," Sandy had heard herself saying. "She makes me be nice to you because she wants to suck up to your mother. Thank God today's the last day I'll have to hang around with an ugly freak like you. Because I can't stand you."

For a moment, he'd just looked at her, and the pain in his expression was raw enough to cut to Sandy's heart.

But before she could take her cruel words back, he changed. As though something had snapped inside of him, his eyes had hardened and his mouth was set grimly.

"Get away from me," he'd said in an ominously quiet voice.

"But Stephen, I—"

"Get the hell away from me. And don't ever come back here again. Because if you do, I'll . . . I'll kill you."

How many times had her two oldest brothers told her exactly that?

I'm going to kill you, Tony Junior or Frankie would say when she'd threatened to tell their parents about something or other or when she'd teased about a girl from school or when she was simply being a bratty little sister.

I'm going to kill you.

She'd heard it so many times before.

But never in her life had the words struck her with such icy force as when Stephen Gilbrooke uttered them on that long ago, sunny summer day. Though she'd been shaken at first, she'd eventually forgotten all about that, had forgotten him, too, until now.

And now, as Sandy looks into those same hard, cold eyes, the threat echoes back at her over the years.

I'm going to kill you.

Seven

Liza sets her dessert plate on the low table in front of the sofa and glances at Laura, who's still picking at the pastry on her plate.

"Don't you like strudel?" she asks lightly, reaching for her teacup, which is nearly empty.

"What?" Laura looks up at her, then shakes her head. "It's not that. I'm just . . . I guess I'm not very hungry."

"Are you okay?"

"I'm fine."

Liza shrugs and drains her cup. Laura Towne isn't fine. For the last fifteen minutes, as they've sat here in the parlor in silence, the woman has worn a haunted, faraway look in her lilac-colored eyes. She hasn't touched her tea, and she's barely eaten the pastry Jasper Hammel painstakingly arranged on her plate.

At least, Liza thinks, he hasn't been buzzing around them as much tonight. Earlier, she heard the sound of water running and pots clattering in the kitchen, which meant he must be doing the dishes. And now there's only silence at the back of the house.

Liza is about to reach for the porcelain teapot on the serving table beside her when she hears a faint knocking.

Laura, too, looks up sharply at the sound.

"What was that?" Liza asks.

Laura shrugs.

They both sit absolutely still, listening.

At first, there's only the ever-present wind and the staccato spattering of raindrops against the windows.

Then the knocking sound again.

"That's coming from the front of the house," Laura says, and Liza nods.

"I think someone's at the door," she tells Laura.

"But why would someone knock? Isn't the door kept unlocked at this hour?"

"Who knows?" Liza hears the knocking again, this time more persistent. "Maybe that fruitcake in the kitchen can't hear it."

"I'll get him." Laura stands and goes over to the door, poking her head into the hallway. "Mr. Hammel?"

Liza watches as she moved down the hall and opens the kitchen door, repeating, "Mr. Hammel?"

After a moment, Laura returns and says, "He's not around."

"He's not? Where could he be?"

"I have no idea. There's a back stairway in there—maybe he's upstairs."

"Well, we'd better answer the door." Liza is already halfway there.

In the foyer, she sees a tall figure standing on the other side of the glass door. Sure enough, the bolt is turned, and Liza hurries to open it.

Maybe this is D.M. Yates at last, she thinks, as a tall man steps inside, his face obscured by the hood of a bulky black storm coat.

He shakes the water off like a wet dog, then lowers the hood and pulls the door closed behind him.

Liza stares. He's a large man, not handsome exactly, though his red-hair, freckled complexion, and wide, easy grin are appealing.

"Hi," he says cheerfully, wiping the rain off his ruddy cheeks. "How are you ladies tonight?"

Ladies? Liza turns and sees Laura standing behind her beside the front desk.

"I'm Pat Gerkin," the guy continues. "You two must be staying here at the inn."

"We are," Liza tells him.

"Is the manager around?"

"He's here someplace, but we're not sure where. Why?"

"I wanted to let him know that if this storm gets any worse, the homes along the coast are going to be evacuated. You can all take shelter at the Congregational church. It's pretty much in the center of the island."

"Do you think that'll happen?" Laura asks, sounding concerned.

"What? The storm getting worse? Maybe. It's a nor'easter, and right now, it's blowing right for us. Hurricane-force winds, and maybe even some snow, too. Of course, it might still veer off and miss the island; but as of the last weather report, we're in for trouble."

"You seem pretty happy about it," Liza observes, noting the guy's perpetually twinkling blue eyes.

He shrugs. "I've been through a lot of these storms. I'm a fisherman on the island year-round. And in the summer, I work part time on the local police force. These things are rough while they last; but eventually, they blow by and we clean up the damage. Hopefully, this one won't be too bad."

"How do we know if we should evacuate?" Laura asks.

"Someone will come around and let you know. Have some things packed to take with you, just in case." Pat looks around. "The manager didn't go out in this weather and leave you here, did he?"

"Who knows?" Liza shrugs. "Do you know him well?"

"Who?"

"Jasper Hammel."

"Oh, that's his name? The little guy with the mustache, right?"

She nods.

"Yeah, I've seen him around here and there, but we've never met. He's not the friendly type. And he's new on the island."

Liza frowns. "How new?"

"Only been here a few weeks. And this is the first weekend the inn's in operation again since it was sold to the new owner at the end of last summer."

Liza and Laura exchange a glance.

"Who's the new owner?" Laura asks.

Pat Gerkin shrugs. "I have no idea. Some businessman from the mainland. He hasn't been out here since he bought it, but he's kept the people who live here pretty busy with renovation work."

"Let me ask you something," Liza says, frowning. "Have you ever heard of D.M. Yates?"

"The writer?"

"You know him?" she asks, relieved at the expression of recognition that crosses the guy's features.

"Sure."

"Then he does live out here, after all," Liza says. "Thank God. I was really starting to think this was just a wild-goose—"

"Who lives out here?" Pat interrupts. "Yates?"

"Doesn't he?"

"Live on Tide Island? Nope."

"What do you mean? I thought you said you knew him."

"I know his work. Just finished *Before a Fall* last week, as a matter of fact." Pat leans against the wall and folds his arms across his chest. "It was hard to get through those first few chapters; but once you got into it, it was a good story."

"When you said you knew him, I thought . . ."

"You thought the man himself, not his books. No, I read a lot. Hey, don't look so surprised. I may be a fisherman now, but I was an English major in college. Used to write poetry and everything."

"I'm not surprised about that," Liza murmurs, glancing over her shoulder at Laura, who looks a little paler than usual. "It's just that I was supposed to meet Yates out here, and I've been waiting for him to show."

"Well, I guarantee you that he doesn't live here. I'm on this island year-round and have been all my life. I know everyone here, except for the tourists. And even if Yates is on his way out here to meet you, you're going to have a long wait. The ferry schedule has been suspended until the storm passes by. Water's too rough."

"You mean we can't leave?" Laura asks, her voice sounding slightly high-pitched. "The last ferry tonight was the last one, period?"

"There was no ferry tonight," Pat Gerkin says, looking puzzled. "There never is on Saturday nights."

"Not even on holiday weekends?" Liza asks, her heart flip-flopping erratically in her chest.

"Nope," Pat Gerkin says. "The last Saturday ferry left this afternoon."

Slowly, Liza turns to look at Laura again. She knows what Laura's thinking. It's the same thing that Liza is thinking.

That Jasper Hammel really did lie about Sandy.

That she didn't leave the island on the late ferry, because there was no late ferry.

That somewhere on this island, right this very moment, Sandy Cavelli might be in serious trouble.

Keegan McCullough is sitting in front of the television on the verge of biting into the enormous ham-and-cheese sandwich he just bought at Subway, when the phone rings.

He reaches for it with his left hand, still holding the sandwich with his right. "Hello?" he says, then bites into the sandwich.

"Hey, Keegan, it's me."

"Buddy?" he asks around a mouthful. He hurriedly chews and swallows.

"Yeah. What are you doing?"

"Watching the tail end of 'Cops' and eating dinner. Why? What's up?"

"You know that sweepstakes ticket you gave me?"

Keegan lowers the sandwich. "What about it?"

"That charity is bogus."

"No way." The food he just swallowed churns in Keegan's stomach. "Are you sure?"

"Yup. I'm telling you, these crooks are all over the city."

"Bud, Jennie's out on Tide Island for the weekend, courtesy of that bogus charity."

"Yeah, you told me that before. At least whoever put this scam together awarded the prize. They usually don't."

"Why would they?" Keegan asks, trying to ignore the chill that's creeping through him.

"I don't know—probably to keep people from being suspicious. You know, they probably figure that whoever wins will tell people about it, which means those people will be more likely to buy tickets for that same so-called charity the next time around."

"I guess . . ."

"Listen, Keegan, do you know the name of the place where Jennie's staying on the island? I'm going to call the management there and see what they can tell me about whoever made the arrangements."

"I don't know the name of the inn, but I'll find out for you. Her sister Laura will know."

"Good. Give me a call back when you get it."

"I will." Keegan puts the sandwich aside, rewrapping it, then shoving it back into the Subway bag. He no longer has an appetite. "Hopefully, Laura will be home now. If not, I'll keep trying tonight until I get her."

"No big rush."

Maybe not for you, Keegan thinks, saying goodbye to

Buddy and hanging up. But he can't help feeling a sense of urgency. The sooner he tracks Jennie down, the better.

With swift but fumbling fingers, he begins dialing the familiar number of the Back Bay town house.

Trembling from head to toe, Sandy tears her eyes away from Stephen Gilbrooke's strangely expressionless face.

For the first time, she looks into the room behind him, the one beyond the French doors. What she sees there is puzzling, so puzzling that she glances at him again, wondering if this is some kind of joke.

"What do you think, Sandy?" he asks in a low, crooning voice. "Isn't it lovely?"

She stammers that it is, then takes an involuntary step backward when he reaches for her arm.

"What's the matter?" he barks. "You don't want me to touch you? You don't want me near you? Just like before?"

"I'm sorry," she says helplessly, forcing herself to remain still as his fingers close over her wrist.

"Come with me, Sandy."

He propels her through the doors, then stops and sweeps a hand through the air. "This is for you. I did all of this for you."

She nods, afraid that if she tries to speak, she'll sob.

The room is enormous, with a delicate crystal chandelier hanging in the center. It must have been a ballroom once, Sandy thinks vaguely as she takes in the scene before her.

The music wafting from the portable stereo on a table— "Sunrise, Sunset" from *Fiddler on the Roof.*

The rows of white folding chairs.

The white runner stretched along the center aisle.

The vases of red roses that are everywhere, filling the air with a floral scent so overpowering that Sandy feels dizzy.

Stephen lets go of Sandy's arm, and she glances wildly about, looking for a place to run.

But then he's grabbing onto her again with one hand and waving something at her with the other.

Puzzled, she can only gape.

It's a hanger . . .

On it is a white dress . . .

A wedding dress.

"I had this made for you," Stephen is saying.

His words aren't sinking in.

Sandy stares at the dress, her mind racing.

He's crazy. I have to get out of here.

"I *said,* put it on," Stephen shouts, pinching her arm painfully.

"I'm sorry. . . . I didn't hear you." Sandy winces as he thrusts the dress at her with a rustle of silk. Her fingers automatically close around the fabric.

"Good. Now wear it."

"But—"

"Now." Stephen steps back and folds his arms, watching her. "It should fit perfectly."

"But how . . ."

"I had it made just for you. It wasn't hard to do. All I had to do was find out your size, and that was easy. Your co-worker at Greenbury Gal was very cooperative."

Greenbury Gal. The store where Sandy bought the outfit she has on right now, the special outfit for her date with Ethan Thoreau . . . who doesn't even exist.

"Andrea told you what size I wear?" Sandy asks incredulously, staring at Stephen Gilbrooke's smirking face. "Why would she do that?"

"Why does anyone do anything? Money. And I've got plenty of it. But then, Sandy, you already know that, don't you?"

"What do you mean?"

"Just put the dress on. And the veil."

Sandy glances down and sees the layer of illusion netting that's fastened to a headpiece looped around the top of the hanger.

Then she looks up at Stephen again.

"I don't want to wear this," she says resolutely, hoping he'll back down. He always was a wimp.

For a long moment, he just stares back at her and she fights not to let herself break the eye contact.

Then he reaches into the inside pocket of his black tuxedo coat and pulls something out.

It's a butcher knife.

"If I were you, Sandy," he says in a quiet, lethal tone, "I'd put on the wedding gown."

Laura sits on Shawn's rumpled twin bed, bouncing impatiently as he unpacks his luggage, tossing nearly everything into the blue plastic laundry basket on the floor.

"I can't believe you went away for over a month and didn't make your bed before you left," she says, leaning back against the pillow.

"Well, not everyone is as good a housekeeper as you are." Shawn holds a folded T-shirt up to his nose, sniffs the sleeve, makes a face, and tosses it into the basket.

"I just like to keep things in order," Laura lies, toying with the frayed edge of his beige comforter.

What would Shawn say if he knew she's a bigger slob than he is? So far, she's managed to fool him, cleaning her room every time she knows he's coming over. The rest of the place always looks fine . . . as long as Jennie's around.

At the thought of her sister, Laura sits up again and checks her watch.

"In a rush to get someplace?" Shawn asks, glancing up at her.

She pins on a sexy smile and purrs, "Yeah. Home. With you."

"In that case . . ." He crosses over to the bed and leans down to give her a long, lingering kiss. "Why bother going back to your place?"

"For one thing, I have a double bed."

"The smaller the cozier," Shawn says, patting the mattress.

"And you have three roommates. Not to mention paper-thin walls."

"So? Eddie's over at Lisa's apartment, and Craig and J.C.never hang around at home on Saturday nights. They're probably getting ready to go out as we speak."

"In this weather?" She looks toward the rain-spattered window. "It's crappy out there."

"Right. All the more reason for you and me to stay here."

"But—"

Shawn silences her with another kiss. This time, his expert hands slide down over her shoulders and up under her shirt. The moment his warm fingers encounter her bare skin, Laura moans and leans back helplessly.

"I kinda thought you'd change your mind," Shawn murmurs, trailing hot kisses along her neck.

Jennie looks around the rose-papered room and tells Liza, "It's nice."

"Get serious. It looks like it was decorated for someone's Sweet Sixteen."

Jennie sighs. "Some people, including me, like antiques and floral prints."

"And some people, including me, like grown-up stuff. . . . Oh, God, Laura, I'm sorry."

Jennie raises an eyebrow at Liza, who sinks onto the edge of the bed and rakes her manicured nails through her hair. She looks exhausted all of a sudden.

"I'm just stressed," Liza says, "and when I'm stressed, I get bitchy."

Jennie nods, thinking that Liza's pretty bitchy all the time. But right now, she's all Jennie has, and sitting here with Liza is better than sitting in her own room, alone.

She suddenly hears a creaking sound above and looks at the ceiling, wondering if Jasper Hammel is on the third floor. There has been no sign of him since dinner.

Liza, too, glances up, then at Jennie. "We probably should have just gotten out of here—gone with that guy."

"Who?"

"Patrick Gerkin—who else?"

Jennie shrugs. "It's too late now." The man had left after telling them again where the Congregational church was and that, if they were evacuated, they should bring blankets and pillows with them.

"He seemed normal, at least. Although anyone who lives on Tide Island year-round can't be all that normal."

"Some people say the same thing about people who live on *Manhattan* Island," Jennie quietly points out.

"True," Liza says, and to Jennie's surprise, she grins. "You know, Laura, I'm really glad you're here. I'd hate to be stuck alone . . . or with Sandy. She'd drive me nuts with all her chattering."

Just when I thought she was being nice, Jennie thinks.

"I wonder where she is?" Liza asks then, sobering. "You think she's in some kind of trouble?"

"I have no idea."

"If she is in trouble, Jasper Hammel must have something to do with it."

"Unless Sandy lied to him about leaving," Jennie points out.

"Why would she do that? And anyway, we know *he* lied. About the ferry schedule."

"Maybe he was just telling us what Sandy told him." Jennie wants desperately to believe that.

Liza shakes her head. "Wouldn't you think he'd know

there's no late Saturday ferry? After all, he's been on this island for a while."

"Not that long. Maybe he doesn't know."

"You want to believe that he's not up to anything."

Jennie hesitates, then nods. "I guess I do."

"Well, so do I. But, Laura . . ." She pauses to yawn, then continues, "I'm positive something's going on. And, to tell you the truth, I'm a little rattled. I thought it just had something to do with me, but—"

"What do you mean?"

Liza pauses, then exhales heavily and says, "When I kept missing Yates, I started to think someone got me out here to this crazy place as some kind of practical joke."

"Who would do that?"

"I have no idea," Liza says quickly. Too quickly. "But anyway, now that something's up with Sandy, I wonder if maybe . . ."

She trails off, and after a few moments of silence, Jennie says, "You wonder if what's going on with Sandy—if anything is going on—has anything to do with you?"

"Something like that."

"But she's a total stranger, isn't she?"

"Of course she is."

"Well then . . ."

Liza throws up her hands. "I don't know. I don't know. I just have a bad feeling. . . ."

You're not the only one, Jennie thinks.

"Laura, what should we do?" Liza asks, looking frightened and vulnerable—not Liza-like at all.

"What *can* we do?" She shrugs. "I mean, there's no way to leave the island now—and anyway," she adds, catching herself, "why *would* we? Nothing has really happened."

Maybe if I keep saying that, I'll start believing that there's nothing strange about this place. That it's just my own stupid paranoia getting the best of me . . . again.

"You're right," Liza says abruptly, standing and stifling another yawn. "I'm really tired . . ."

There's nothing for Jennie to do but stand and say, "Me, too. I'm going back to my room."

Even though she isn't tired.

Even though she knows she won't sleep a wink tonight.

"Okay. G'night," Liza says, stretching. Her eyelids already seem droopy.

"Night." Jennie pauses with her hand on the doorknob. "If you . . . you know, want to talk or anything, you can knock on my door."

"Thanks. You, too."

Jennie nods and slips out into the hall, then freezes when she hears another creak from above. She glances at the stairway that leads to the third floor, wondering what's up there. For a moment, she contemplates finding out.

The wind suddenly picks up outside, slamming into the house with a high-pitched howl, and Jennie shivers.

No, there's no way she's going to go sneaking around this place, taking a chance of bumping into Jasper Hammel . . . or someone else.

Instead, she hurries down the hall to her room.

She locks the door firmly behind her.

There. You're perfectly safe now.

But somehow, she can't quite convince herself of that.

"It fits perfectly, doesn't it?" Stephen croons, staring at Sandy as though he's mesmerized.

She's trembling uncontrollably as she stands before him in the white wedding dress, the veil perched precariously on her head so that a layer of illusion falls over her face.

She hopes that he can't see how frightened she is, can't see the tears that keep rolling down her cheeks to land on the white silk gown.

"It's not too tight in the waist, is it, Sandy?"

She shakes her head mutely.

"Is it?" he bites out, and she cringes.

"No," she says in a small voice, trying to keep her teeth from chattering.

"Good. Because you're fat, and I'd hate to have that pot belly of yours bursting through the dress. I paid a lot of money to have it made just for you."

"Th-thank you."

"I have shoes for you, too. Here you go." He holds up a pair of rhinestone-encrusted, white-satin slippers. "Aren't they beautiful?"

She nods.

"Just like Cinderella," he says, crouching before her and helping her slide her stockinged feet into the shoes. The heels are impossibly high. "A perfect fit. Just like Cinderella," he repeats, standing again and looking at her, "and I'm your prince."

"Yes, you are."

Just keep talking to him, she tells herself, trying to ward off the panic that threatens to overtake her. *Just act as though this is normal.*

As though you aren't the least bit alarmed at having been kidnapped by a psycho from your past.

As though you didn't mind undressing while he stood there leering at you.

As though you don't think he's out of his mind, forcing you to put on this wedding gown and veil.

As though you aren't terrified of what he's going to do next.

"This," Stephen says gallantly, presenting a bouquet with a sweep of his arm, "is for you. I know how you love roses. Red roses . . . the color of blood," he adds in a faraway voice.

"Th-thank you," she whispers raggedly, taking the flowers in her trembling hands.

"Now it's time, Sandy," he says, taking her arm firmly

and leading her to the end of the white runner on wobbling ankles, her skirt rustling along the floor as she moves. "I'm going to walk to the front of the room and wait, and I want you to come down the aisle when your music starts."

Bile rises in her throat, gagging her, and she forces it back, unable to speak.

"You know which music I mean, Sandy, don't you?"

She shakes her head, her mind whirling.

I have to get away. I have to get out of here before he . . . Before he hurts me.

Or worse.

"The wedding march, of course. You know . . . *Here comes the bride . . . dum dum da dum,"* he sings cheerfully. "You'll recognize it. It's coming up next. Now," he adds, letting go of her arm and giving it a pat, "don't start walking until your music starts."

"I won't," she promises, and braces herself.

It's now or never, she thinks as he turns his back and starts walking up the aisle, careful to step on the floor at the edge of the runner.

When Stephen is almost at the first row of seats, Sandy tosses the bouquet aside, kicks off the satin pumps, grabs her skirt, and runs.

Back through the French doors and into the parlor, then the foyer, and then, because she knows the front door is locked, up the stairs.

Up the stairs? What are you doing? she screams at herself frantically as she reaches the second-floor hall. *How are you supposed to escape now? There's no way out!*

She hears him cursing and chasing after her, approaching the bottom of the stairs. After a split-second pause, she turns and runs down the long hall. She has to hide someplace . . .

In one of the bedrooms.

And then what?

He'll find you! her mind shrieks. *It's only a matter of time before he'll find you!*

Blindly, she throws a door open at the end of the hall and finds herself in a study. She closes the door behind her, then flattens her back against it and tries to catch her breath without making a sound.

His running footsteps have come to an abrupt halt, and she hears him coming down the hall. "Lorraine? Where are you?"

Lorraine? Whom is he talking to?

"Come on out, sweetheart. I won't hurt you," he says plaintively. "I'll never hurt you again. Why did you run away? You were going to be my bride, Lorraine. We were going to get married and live happily ever after. Come out, Lorraine. Please."

He's sobbing now, and Sandy holds her breath, praying that he'll just go away.

But Sandy hears him opening doors along the hallway, looking into the rooms, trying to find her.

He thinks I'm someone else . . .

"Please don't leave me, Lorraine. I'll give you anything. . . . I'll give you everything. Everything you want. Please stay. Don't leave like the others . . ."

He's insane.

Sandy closes her eyes briefly, then opens them again. Though the room is shadowy, she can make out the silhouettes of familiar objects. A chair . . . a desk . . .

Her gaze falls on something that's sitting on top of the desk. Swiftly and silently, she moves across the room to it.

Picking up the telephone receiver, she prays for a dial tone.

Yes!

She forces her fingers to stop shaking as she punches out 9-1-1 and waits for the emergency operator to answer.

But there's nothing but a tone, and then a recording that begins, "We're sorry. There is no 9-1-1 emergency service in this location. To reach your local police or fire officials, dial—"

Sandy depresses the button on the phone. Her mind races.

Outside the door, she hears the footsteps stop. The doorknob jiggles.

"Lorraine, I know you're in there. But I'm going to get you out."

Panicking, Sandy clutches the receiver and stares, wide-eyed, at the door. She hears a dull thump, as though Stephen has thrown his shoulder against it.

"Lorraine, open this door. Right now. I mean it. If you open it, everything will be fine. If you don't . . . I'll get it open myself. And trust me, Lorraine, you'll wish you had done as I asked."

There's another thump, and a grunt.

And then another thump.

Sobbing now, Sandy starts dialing the phone again, automatically punching in the first number that comes to mind, knowing there's nothing anyone can do to help her . . .

But praying for a miracle anyway.

"Oh, terrific." Danny Cavelli groans and looks down at his wife, who's lying beneath him on the bed. "Why does that damn thing always have to ring when we're right in the middle of something?"

"Better get it," Cheryl says, untangling her fingers from his hair. "It could be important."

"It's probably Tony, telling me another branch fell into his gutter. Or Pop, wanting me to come over and jump start his truck for the fiftieth time this week. We never should have bought a house this close to my family."

The phone rings shrilly again.

"Danny . . ." Cheryl lifts her head from the pillow to look at it on the nightstand. Her eyes are wide, fearful. "It might be my mother. What if Daddy's . . ."

She trails off, and Danny nods. Cheryl's father has been

in the hospital for over a month now, suffering terribly from
the last stages of lung cancer.

"Okay, I'll get it, babe," Danny says, rolling off her and
reaching for the receiver. "Hello?"

For a moment, he doesn't hear anything, just heavy
breathing.

Scowling, he turns to Cheryl and is about to tell her it's
just an obscene phone call when he hears a voice.

"Danny . . ."

It's nothing more than a faint whisper, but he recognizes
it, and his blood runs cold.

"Sandy?" He clutches the receiver. "Where are you?
What's going on?"

"Danny, help . . ."

"Sandy, I can barely hear you. Speak up."

"I can't . . . oh my God, Danny . . ." Her voice trails
off.

"Jesus . . . Sandy? Sandy, where are you?"

Behind him on the bed, Cheryl sits up and leans toward
him, brushing his wrist with her fingers. "Danny, what's
wrong?"

There's a sudden crashing sound on the other end of the
line, the sound of a male voice, ranting something that
sounds like "Open the door!"

Sandy lets out a blood-curdling scream.

"Sandy?" Danny shouts. "Sandy!"

But the line has already gone dead.

Eight

"How dare you?" Holding the butcher knife high above his head in his left hand, he throws the phone against the wall with his right. It crashes to the floor with a jangling thud. "Did you try to make a *phone call?*"

"I tried, but I couldn't—"

"Speak up when you talk to me!" he thunders.

"Please . . ." she whimpers, shrinking back, then trying to scurry across the floor like a cockroach.

"You're pathetic." He reaches down and closes his fingers over her ankle, then pulls her toward him. Her heavy body slides across the polished wooden floor with a rustle of silk even as she claws the air with her arms, trying to take hold of something.

He grabs her arm and turns her toward him, then leans down and lifts her chin roughly, forcing her to look up at him.

"I told you, Lorraine . . ." He trails off, gaping. "You're not Lorraine."

"No . . . please, Stephen, don't hurt me."

Befuddled, he stares into her round face. "Where is she?"

"I-I don't know."

"Lorraine . . ." Confused, he closes his eyes and tries to remember. What happened to Lorraine?

Images flash in his memory—a red-and-white blur.

Roses and baby's breath . . .

Full lips and ivory skin . . .

Blood on silk . . .

Lorraine's blood, spilling over the wedding dress she wears as she lies crumpled on the floor of her suite.

Now it's coming back to him. Leaving the brownstone through the back door in a frenzy while two hundred guests and the minister mill around wondering what happened to his bride and speculating on where he's going.

When he reached the door of her suite, she had opened it quickly, saying, "You can take the bags that are—"

Then she'd seen that it was he. "Stephen," she'd said, growing pale. "I thought you were the bellman. . . ."

"Where the hell are you going?" he'd asked, taking in her jeans and jacket, the luggage stacked by the door, including the trunk he'd bought her for their honeymoon. It was empty, he knew. She was planning to fill it with the lovely things he would buy for her as they traveled around the world.

You'll have the finest Scottish wool, Lorraine, and silks from the Orient and the latest dresses from Paris . . .

He remembered, as he faced her in the hotel suite, how his promises had made her clap her hands together in glee, like a child getting excited about the prospect of an ice-cream cone on a sweltering August day.

"Lorraine," he'd said, softening, "you're not going anywhere without me, are you? We're going together, remember? Just as soon as we're married, we're leaving for Europe. Tonight, Lorraine. Just a few more hours. Now come on, let's go back home. The minister is waiting, and all of our guests, and—"

"No, Stephen, I can't. I just can't marry you. I changed my—"

"Stop it! Don't say it, Lorraine! You love me. You told me that you love me. You said you want to marry me. Now do it!"

"I can't. . . . I-I have to go, Stephen," she'd told him,

sounding as though she were on the verge of tears. "Please . . ."

"Please . . ." sobs the woman who cowers at his feet now. "Let me go."

"Shut up!" he barks, squeezing his eyes closed, seeing only Lorraine.

Lorraine had backed away from him as he stood there in the doorway, as though she couldn't stand to be near him. She'd averted her eyes, as though she couldn't stand looking at him.

And he'd snapped.

Stepped into the hotel room and slammed the door closed behind him, sliding the bolt and fastening the chain. The first thing he saw was the white-silk confection of a dress that hung in the corner of the room, perfectly pressed and hooded in clear plastic. A wedding dress, waiting for the bride to step into it.

"Why aren't you wearing that?" he had demanded.

"Because I'm not going to marry you," Lorraine had replied, lifting her chin, suddenly defiant.

"Yes, you are."

"No, I'm not, Stephen. I'm leaving town. Going back home to Chicago for a while, until I figure out—"

He'd slapped her then, hard, across the face, leaving a harsh red handprint on her white cheek.

"You're not going anywhere," he'd told her. "You're going to put that gown on, and you're going to marry me."

"No . . ." She looked less certain now, taking another step backward and watching him with frightened green eyes.

"Yes, dammit! Today is our wedding day. And we're going to get married. Now put . . . on . . . the . . . dress." He'd said it in a deadly quiet tone, locking his eyes on hers.

When she didn't respond, he reached into his jacket and removed the thing he had brought with him for some reason . . . the ice pick he'd swiped from the caterer's cart that had been set up in his kitchen. He held it up at her and raised his eyebrows, as if to ask whether she wanted him to do something he'd regret.

She had come to her senses then and, with trembling hands, reached for the dress. As she fumbled to release it from its plastic shroud, he had leaned back against the wall to watch her, his arms folded and his jaw set resolutely, his hand still clutching the ice pick.

She tossed the jacket, sweatshirt, and jeans aside and stood there for a moment wearing only her white-lace bra and matching panties and a look of dread.

"Put it on," he'd urged her, his eyes fastened on the swell of her breasts in the delicate lace cups, on her flat belly and her long, firm legs. Even in February, her body was tan, thanks to Christmas in Hawaii and their January trip to St. Bart's.

Lorraine had pulled the dress over her head, and it settled around her with a soft *swoosh*. She hesitated for a moment, glancing up at him, and then began to fumble with the row of buttons at her back.

There was a knock at the door then, and she froze, her eyes widening as she glanced in that direction. She opened her mouth; but before she could speak, he was beside her, covering her lips with his hand and muffling the sound of her voice.

Another knock and then he heard the bellman's voice calling, "Miss LaCroix?"

After a few moments of silent waiting, the footsteps faded down the hall outside the suite.

"Now, Lorraine," he had said in a reasonable tone, his hand still clamped over her mouth, "I'm going to let go of you and you're not going to make a peep. If you do, you'll be sorry. Do you understand?"

She'd nodded, her eyes big and round above his fingers.

"Good." He'd let go, and she'd instantly opened her mouth to scream.

"Damn you!" he'd hollered, grabbing her and throwing her onto the floor. "I told you to be quiet!"

"I'm sorry. . . . Please, Stephen, I'm sorry. I'll be quiet. Please, no," she'd begged as he advanced on her, brandishing the ice pick. "Please, don't hurt me. Oh, God . . ."

"Don't hurt me," the woman at his feet is whimpering now as he stands over her, holding the butcher knife. "Please, don't hurt me."

"Shut your mouth!"

She obliges, staring up at him with frightened eyes, just as Lorraine had.

"Sandy," he says softly, suddenly remembering.

She only stares at him, waiting.

"You don't love me. You don't want to marry me, either. You ran away, just like Lorraine did."

"No . . ."

"Yes! I bought you this dress, and I made everything beautiful for you downstairs. I got roses . . ." He drifts off, wondering if she likes roses, as Lorraine did.

"Stephen, I'm not Lorraine," she says, looking somewhat calm though her voice bears a telltale high pitch. "I never said I would marry you."

"Why not?" he asks abruptly, his eyes snapping back to her.

"Don't get upset again, Stephen. I didn't say I would marry you because I was just a kid when I knew you."

"But you're not a kid now."

"No . . ."

"And you're going to marry me now!"

"Okay, okay, I'll marry you now." Her voice is shaky. "I will. Whatever you want."

"Before we get married, though . . ." He leans over her and, in one swift movement, shoves her so that she goes sprawling onto her back.

"No, please . . ." she says, clearly realizing exactly what his intentions are.

"No?" he asks, hesitating, watching her. His fingers clench around the knife-handle.

She's shaking. "I just meant . . . not . . . not like this, Stephen."

"Yes, just like this." Still holding the knife, he fumbles with the fly on his black tuxedo pants.

"Oh, God, no . . ."

He looks down at her and sees that she's squeezing her eyes closed.

"Look at me!" he commands her.

She doesn't move, just lets out a little sob.

"I said . . ." He bends over her so that his face is only inches from hers. "Look at me!"

She opens her eyes. They're rimmed with smudged mascara and eyeliner, and tears are streaming down her cheeks.

Disgusted, Stephen yanks her dress up around her hips and rips off her panties and stockings, exposing her abundant, ripply white thighs and hips and droopy lower belly.

"Look at you," he says, shaking his head. "You're fat."

She looks up at him hopefully, as though he might have changed his mind now that he sees her.

But he steps calmly out of his pants, then his boxer shorts, and, still holding the knife, sinks to his knees, his mighty erection throbbing as he imagines sinking into all that quivering flesh.

"Stephen, please . . . no!" Her voice explodes into a shrill scream as he forces her legs apart and rips into her.

He pounds away, trying desperately to sate himself. But he can't . . . not even with his powerful climax, not even as he imagines that he's pumping her full of himself, possessing her completely.

He collapses on top of her, panting and shuddering all over, but still filled with pent-up urges that have nothing to do with sex.

As soon as he catches his breath, he rolls off her and sees that she's lying still, eyes closed. The only thing that's moving is her mouth, and it takes a moment before he realizes what she's doing.

She's praying, her voice a mere whisper.

"Stop it," he orders her, and slaps her face.

She does. Still her eyes are closed.

As he pulls his underwear back on, he calmly says, "Open your eyes."

She does. Her expression is one of panic. And hate.

She hates me, he thinks, stepping into his trousers again, and the knowledge doesn't bother him. Not anymore.

Lorraine hated him, and he took care of her.

Now he'll take care of Sandy.

He sips his pants, then says, "Get up," raising the knife in warning.

When she doesn't move fast enough, he grabs her arm and pulls her to her feet, the white wedding dress falling around her again to hide the blood that's streaked between her chubby thighs.

She sways as though she's going to faint, then seems to get hold of herself. She even meets his gaze and lifts her chin.

"I wouldn't look so defiant if I were you, Sandy," he says softly, "because I'm the one who's in control here. And I have a sneaking suspicion that you're not going to like what I have planned for you next."

With that, he starts to laugh, a wild, frenzied sound that releases more of his pent-up frustration. . . .

But not nearly enough.

There's only one way to rid himself of it, only one way to satisfy the intense craving that fills him to the very core.

Clutching the butcher knife, he leads Sandy out of the room and down the dark hall.

"Hello, Laura, are you there? Laura? Okay, this is Keegan again. Please call me as soon as you get in. 555-4107, just in case you didn't get the number when I left it before. I'll be home all night. . . . Make sure you call, Laura. Thanks. Bye."

Frustrated at having reached the answering machine yet again, he hangs up the phone and taps his fingertips against the arm of the couch in a jittery staccato beat. For all he knows, Laura isn't planning on coming home at all tonight.

In fact, he'd almost bet that she won't be back until tomorrow. After all, she's been known to spend the night with guys on first dates, and this Shawn is someone she's been seeing since before Keegan and Jennie broke up.

Correction—before Jennie dumped you. No warning, no excuses. She just dumped you, buddy, like a beat-up piece of trash.

Keegan sighs and gets up, moving restlessly into the small kitchen of his one-bedroom apartment. He grabs a Molson from the refrigerator and pops the cap off, tossing it in the general direction of the trash container in the corner. He misses. The cap skitters across the linoleum and disappears into the gap between the refrigerator and the stove.

Normally Keegan, who hates disorder of any kind, would grab a yardstick and fish it out, but tonight he merely shrugs. He's too distracted to care about anything but Jennie.

Jennie . . .

Forget about her, he tells himself yet again as he takes a gulp of beer, then stifles a burp.

She doesn't care about you—why should you worry about her?

But he is worried. So worried that he can't seem to focus on anything else. For over an hour now, he's been pacing around the apartment, wondering if Jennie's okay. There's no reason, really, to think that she wouldn't be . . .

Except that the damn sweepstakes was a scam.

Still, that doesn't necessarily mean Jennie's in danger.

But Keegan can't shake the feeling that she is. He's been a cop for too long, seen too much not to listen to his instinct, especially when it's this strong.

Listen to it, yeah. Make a fool out of yourself over it, no.

He takes another gulp of beer and walks back into the living room, imagining what Laura will think when she gets home and finds that he's left three messages. And the last one sounded almost frantic.

And over what?

Nothing at all.

He sighs and stares blankly at the television screen, where an episode of "America's Most Wanted" is drawing to a close with a recap parade of mugshots.

Maybe, he tells himself, *your anxiety over Jennie is coming from the break-up, and not from anything that has to do with that bogus sweepstakes or her trip to Tide Island.*

For a month now, he's been trying to get to her, but she hasn't returned his calls. All he wants is an explanation—for her to tell him why she left him like she did.

He'll never forget the way she did it. They'd been taking a walk on the frozen, deserted beach at Scituate, just the two of them. He had been thinking about how lucky he was to have her, toying with the notion that next year at this time, they might be married, or at least engaged. After all, he'd known from the start that Jennie was the woman for him. It was only a matter of time, as far as he was concerned, before they made a formal commitment.

So there he was, daydreaming about what Jennie would look like in a wedding gown—antique, no doubt, with rich ivory lace and a train—when she'd suddenly pulled her gloved hand from his and stopped walking.

Startled, he'd turned to ask her if something was wrong. And the moment he saw the look on her face, he knew. He hadn't been expecting it. In fact, if anyone had asked him mere seconds before whether Jennie would ever break up with him, he would have laughed and said, "Don't be ridiculous."

But there it was. A somber, distant look in her lilac eyes that said it all even before she did.

Not that she said much.

Just that she had done some thinking and she couldn't see him anymore.

He'd asked questions, but she'd refused to answer them, only repeating what she'd already said, as though the lines were from a script she'd over-rehearsed. So he'd protested, then argued—or at least, tried to. Jennie hadn't argued back, had only closed her mouth resolutely and stared straight ahead.

So that was it. They were through.

And it had happened on New Year's Day, no less, as though she'd re-evaluated her life and made a resolution to get him out of it.

Why, Jennie? he'd asked her countless times that day, has asked himself countless times since.

Why did you leave? he wonders again now, peeling the label off the beer bottle and discarding the shreds of sticky paper on the hardwood floor without thinking.

All I want is an explanation.

But that's not true, he realizes a moment later. He wants much more than that.

He wants Jennie back.

And I'm not going to give up, he vows, finishing his beer in one long swallow, *until she's mine again.*

More than anything, Danny Cavelli wants Theresa Benedetti to be home tonight. As he dials her phone number, conscious of Cheryl's frightened eyes on him, he prays for Theresa to be there. But it's not likely. Not on a Saturday night. She usually hangs out at the Knights of Columbus on weekends. And tonight they're having their annual pre-Ash Wednesday Mardi Gras Night.

"It's ringing," Danny informs Cheryl, who nods and pats his shoulder. He's perched on the edge of their bed again, just where he was when Sandy called.

It's been over a half hour since then. He kept waiting for her to call back, not wanting to tie up the line in case she tried. But the phone has been silent, and he finally decided he can't wait anymore. He has to try and find her.

Please God, let Theresa be home. Please God, let Theresa be home. Please God, let—

"Hello?"

"Theresa?"

"Yeah," she says in a scratchy voice that doesn't even sound like her. "Who's this?"

"It's Danny, and I've got to—"

"Danny who?"

"Cavelli. Sandy's brother. I've—"

"Oh, hi, Danny. What's up? She's not sick, is she? Because I just found out I've got strep—"

"Theresa," he interrupts, "listen to me. Do you know the name of the inn where my sister's staying on Tide Island?"

There's a pause. "Sandy told you she went to Tide Island?"

"Yeah," he says impatiently. "And I need—"

"I thought she wasn't going to tell anyone. She said your father would freak out."

"He did. Theresa, I mean it, you've got to listen to me. I need the name of the place where she's staying. You've got to tell me."

"Why?" she asks suspiciously. Theresa and Sandy have been best friends since they were toddlers, and Danny realizes that she knows Tony Cavelli too well. Well enough to instinctively want to protect Sandy.

"It's a long story. Just tell me, please."

"I don't want to get Sandy into trouble. She—"

"Theresa, she's already *in* trouble!" Danny explodes. "For God's sake, tell me where she is!"

"Why? What happened?"

Danny shakes his head, and his eyes meet Cheryl's. Then he glances at the clock on the nightstand behind her. Too much time has passed since Sandy called. He has to find her, before it's too late . . .

"Theresa, she called me, and she sounded terrified. Like some guy was doing something to her," he says desperately. "She didn't say what."

"Some guy was *doing* something to her?"

"And then she screamed, and I heard someone yelling at her."

"What?"

"Tell me where she is, Theresa. You've got to." His voice breaks, and he runs a hand raggedly through his hair. Every muscle in his body is tensed, and his fingers ache from being coiled into tight fists.

"It's the ivy . . . no, the rose," Theresa says, "the Rose-something Inn. No, I think it's the Something-rose Inn. It's something that makes me think of a fairy tale. . . ."

"Oh, Jesus Christ," Danny mutters, then automatically clamps his hand over his mouth. Angie Cavelli would faint if she heard that.

"The Thorn-rose!" Theresa shouts triumphantly, despite her hoarse throat.

"Is that it?"

"I don't know." She sounds hesitant. "Something like that . . . The Bramble Rose?"

"The Bramble Rose?"

"That's it. I'm positive. Danny, you really think she's in trouble? Because there's something else you should know."

"What is it?"

"She was placing personal ads in a magazine. You know, to meet guys."

"Sandy did a sleazy thing like that?"

"And that's why she went to Tide Island," Theresa continues. "To meet someone."

"Who?"

"Some guy. I can't remember his name, but he's rich, and he's a lawyer—no, a doctor. She got this great letter from him, inviting her to the island."

Danny is too stunned to reply to that. How could his sister be so stupid? How could she go away for a weekend with a total stranger?

Beside him on the bed, Cheryl watches him, asking, "What? What is it?"

He looks at her and shakes his head, fresh worry coursing through him. He's going to find out who lured his sister out to Tide Island; and if the guy so much as laid a hand on her, Danny's going to beat the crap out of him.

"He'd better not hurt her," he tells Cheryl, and Theresa, clenching his hands into fists.

"But if she called you, Danny, she was probably afraid of him," Theresa points out.

"Yeah, well, a lot of times when Sandy calls me to bail her out of something, it turns out to be a false alarm," Danny says, even though he knows in his heart that this time, his sister is really in serious trouble. The memory of her terrified voice, and the way the call was abruptly cut off, makes his blood run cold.

"You're right," Theresa says optimistically. "She was probably just over-reacting to something when she called you."

"Yeah. Thanks for helping me out, though," Danny says.

"Let me know what happens, okay, Danny?"

He hesitates, then says, "Sure. I'll have Sandy call you. Bye." He hangs up the phone and turns to Cheryl, struggling to ignore the fist of fear that's clenching his gut. "I'm going to call the inn on Tide Island and find out what's up."

"Everything's probably fine, Danny. Don't worry until you have to," Cheryl says, patting his arm reassuringly.

But Danny can hear the anxiety in her voice. And as he dials the number for directory information, he can't help bleakly wondering if there's anything he can do even if everything *isn't* fine.

After all Tide Island is miles away, out in the ocean, and there's a wicked storm brewing. If Sandy really is in some kind of trouble, she's on her own.

The satin pumps are scuffed from her struggle with Stephen, Sandy notices vaguely as she stands with the toes exactly lined up at the edge of the white runner. She clutches the bouquet of roses he forced into her hands and tries to convince herself that everything will be fine if she just keeps doing what he tells her to.

"Okay, ready?" he calls from the front of the room where he's fiddling with the tape player.

She nods; and when he looks up sharply, as though to make sure she's acknowledging him, she calls weakly, "Ready."

"Good." He presses the *play* button, then takes his place at the head of the runner. "Now, wait for my cue," he says, as if he's a high school drama teacher directing a musical revue.

Sandy knows better than to try to run this time, even if she had the strength. She's weak and her legs feel bruised, particularly between her thighs. The thought of what he did to her upstairs fills her with revulsion, and she forces the memory out of her mind.

She takes a deep breath as she stands there waiting, telling herself to calm down. If she panics, she's dead.

Maybe literally.

The thought immediately overwhelms her with a renewed sense of alarm that chokes her throat with bile and makes her want to pass out. She forces it back, clutching the bouquet in trembling hands and watching Stephen from behind the layer of illusion veil he arranged over her face.

Just pretend you're playing bride, the way you and Theresa used to do when you were little. Just pretend it's a game. . . . Pretend he doesn't have that knife tucked into his tuxedo pocket.

He's insane—that much is clear. But Sandy has no idea why he's making her go through this grotesque charade.

Why me? she wonders desperately again. *Why after all these years?*

She'd almost forgotten Stephen Gilbrooke, having resigned him to some distant corner of her mind reserved for storing the memories of particularly unpleasant adolescent experiences. It had been a shock to recognize him here, to realize that he hadn't forgotten her . . .

Far from it.

Apparently, her rejection had a major impact on him. Major enough to make him want revenge.

Sandy feels sick again, and it's all she can do to remain standing as the first strains of music waft from the portable stereo across the room.

"All right," Stephen says, holding up his index finger, then pointing it at her, "Now."

Sandy gingerly takes the first slow step forward with her right foot, then glides to meet it with her left and pauses. It's the walk she first learned when she was a junior bridesmaid at her brother Tony's wedding, the walk Stephen showed her just before he went to start the music. He had been fairly bouncing along the white runner when he demonstrated it, saying, "This is how you're going to come to me, okay, Lorraine?"

She hadn't corrected him. He kept mistaking her for someone else, someone who had obviously rejected him, just as she had.

Sandy wonders now, as she makes her way fearfully down

the aisle, who Lorraine is, where she is now, and whether Stephen freaked out on her, too.

Did he force himself on her?

Is he going to rape me again when I get to the end of the runner?

She watches him fearfully from behind her veil and she keeps walking because if she doesn't, he'll hurt her. She knows that he will. Even though he's acted relatively calm, even gleeful, ever since he brought her back downstairs, she's glimpsed the deranged expression in his eyes, and it terrifies her.

"Come on, Sandy," he calls above the rhythmic strains of the wedding march. "Pick up the pace."

She does, although everything inside her is screaming for her to back away, to run away. If there were any possible way to escape, she would try it.

But there's not.

And the thought of Stephen chasing her again, and catching her and violating her, makes her physically ill. Anything would be better than that.

She's almost reached him now. She is close enough to see that his mouth is set grimly, that his eyes look glazed as he stares at her, as though he's seeing someone else.

Lorraine—who is she? Sandy wonders again, taking another deep breath, trying desperately to stay calm as she forces herself to draw nearer.

The moment she's within arm's length, Stephen reaches out and hooks his elbow around hers.

Startled, Sandy bites her lip to keep from crying out. He walks a few more steps alongside her until they reach the edge of the runner. Then, as the music ends, he lets go of her arm, turning her to face him.

"Lorraine," he says softly, reaching for the wisp of veil covering her face. "I've been waiting for this moment for so long."

Sandy stays absolutely still and silent despite the violent thudding of her heart in her ears.

"I love you," he says and lifts the veil, leaning toward her as though he's going to kiss her. His eyelids start to drift closed, then open again abruptly as he zeroes in on Sandy's face.

"You're not Lorraine!"

Sandy numbly shakes her head.

"Where is she?"

"I . . . I don't know, Stephen," she says in a small voice, wanting to beg him not to hurt her again, but knowing, from the crazed look in his eyes, that he wants to.

"Where's Lorraine?" he asks again, dropping the veil back over her eyes.

"I don't know," Sandy repeats, hearing the hysteria creep into her voice.

Stephen's right hand is moving toward his pocket . . . the pocket that has the knife.

Sandy's head is filled with a buzzing sound and she sways as though she's going to faint. Struggling to stay alert, she watches him reaching into the pocket, sees him produce the deadly blade.

He runs his fingertips over the handle almost lovingly, then looks up at her again.

"Lorraine, I don't want to do this," he says in a near-whisper. "But you've left me with no choice."

"Stephen, no!" Sandy protests, reaching for the veil so that she can show him, again, that she's not Lorraine.

But it's too late. Horrified, she sees the silver blade slashing at her, feels the sudden stinging pain as it slashes her on the forearm.

She screams when she looks down and sees her own red blood spilling over the sleeve of the dress, dripping down onto the skirt.

"Shut up!" Stephen hollers and raises the knife again.

"No!" Sandy howls, reaching blindly forward to stop him.

But the blade descends rapidly again, and again, even after she's collapsed in a heap on the floor, vaguely aware of what's happening to her.

He's killing me, she thinks incredulously. *I'm dying.*

The last thing she's aware of before blackness descends over her is the brilliant flash of a camera and Stephen's gleeful voice saying, "Smile for your wedding portrait, Sandy!"

Nine

The rain stings Jasper's face as he hurries toward the back door of the inn, relieved that his grim task is over. He's disposed of Sandy Cavelli's belongings just as Stephen told him to—buried her suitcase in the deep pit he'd dug earlier in the dunes behind the inn, concealed by the tangle of beach grasses.

It took longer than he thought because of the weather—his hands were numb and clumsy because of the cold, and the wind made it difficult to work efficiently.

But the weather is a blessing, too, Jasper thinks as he nears the inn. Because of it, the wave-battered beach is deserted.

No one in their right mind would venture outside tonight, Jasper thinks, then realizes he's outside himself. His lips curve into a tight smile at the irony.

But, anything for Stephen, he tells himself, quickening his pace over the rough, muddy ground.

He owes everything to Stephen Gilbrooke, his only friend in the world for as long as he can remember.

They'd met back when Jasper was still going by his real name, Arnold Wentworth—one of *the* Wentworths of Philadelphia. He'd been miserable at prep school until Stephen came along. The other boys constantly made fun of "Arnie," as they insisted on calling him—tripping him in the halls and teasing him in falsetto voices, telling him that everyone knew he was "queer," so he might as well admit it.

But Arnold refused to—wouldn't even admit it to himself, back then. Even though he'd had those strange, unacceptable feelings since childhood. It had started out as mere admiration for other boys, usually the strongest, smartest, most popular ones in his class at the private school near his parents' mansion. But it rapidly progressed into a series of crushes, and then full-fledged obsessions, where Arnold could think of nothing but what it would be like to kiss the object of his affections on the lips, to touch him in places that made Arnold blush with mingling pleasure and shame at the mere thought.

His father, Grayson Wentworth, had been a football star at Princeton in his youth, and he was horrified that his only child was not only uncoordinated and clumsy, but a "sissy," as he called Arnold. He had long since given up on trying to make a "man" out of his son, but regarded him only with disgust from the time Arnold was five years old.

Meanwhile, Arnold's mother, who spent her days at home drinking gimlets and her nights on the town drinking straight vodka, could have cared less about her husband or her son.

It was a blessing for Arnold when the Wentworths decided to send him away to school in New England, having virtually washed their hands of him.

One day, during his first semester there, Arnold found himself taking a shower in the dormitory bathroom, right next to his current obsession, Gregory Sloane. He'd struggled not to stare at Gregory's naked body so tantalizingly close to his own, but he couldn't resist stealing glances.

The next thing he knew, as he was furtively stroking his hard, soap-slicked penis while he stared at Gregory, the other boy had suddenly turned and caught him in the act.

"Oh, my God," Gregory had shouted, pointing at Arnold's pulsating erection. "He's getting off on me!"

Instantly, the steamy stall seemed to have been filled with Gregory's friends, who had first ridiculed the humiliated Arnold, then manhandled him out into the dressing room, where they forced him to lie, naked, on a hard bench. Some-one produced a tube of Ben-Gay, and they started smearing it all over Arnold, coating his bare flesh with the stinging stuff as they jeered him.

He didn't know which was more excruciating—the harsh, true words the boys flung at him, or the physical pain.

They left him there, at last, sobbing and writhing on the floor where they'd shoved him.

And it was Stephen Gilbrooke who had found him. One of the new students, he was a virtual stranger to Arnold; but for some reason, he decided to become his savior.

Stephen had helped him up and wiped the Ben-Gay off with warm, wet towels, talking to Arnold in a soothing voice. Arnold had never remembered what he said, only that he was kind. Kinder than anyone had ever been to him before.

And he'd fallen in love with Stephen Gilbrooke on the spot. He didn't look like Arnold's usual crushes. Stephen was blatantly ugly, with a face that had earned him the nickname "Elephant Guy" among the other boys. But Arnold swiftly came to overlook Stephen's appearance.

All he cared about was that Stephen was nice to him. And he seemed to understand how it felt to be an outcast—and how it felt to have parents who didn't care at all.

The two boys had become inseparable by Christmas, and they were the only ones in the dormitory who didn't go home over holiday break.

One night, as they lay on Stephen's bed in the deserted dorm, playing chess, Arnold had impulsively leaned over and kissed Stephen square and hard on the lips.

It was something he'd wanted to do for months, but as soon as he pulled back, he chastised himself. How could he have been so stupid? Now he would lose his one and only friend.

But to his surprise, Stephen hadn't recoiled in horror or

even surprise. He had simply said quietly, "I know how you feel about me, Arnold. And it's okay."

"It is?" Arnold had been utterly shocked.

"Sure." Stephen had laid a hand on his thigh then, sending quivers of pleasure through Arnold's whole body.

It hadn't gone any further that night, or for a long time afterward. But Arnold had thrilled to the secret knowledge that Stephen loved him back.

And he had ignored the irritating voice in his mind that sometimes told him to be careful . . . that Stephen was too good to be true. That maybe Stephen wasn't who he seemed to be.

The voice seemed to surface whenever Arnold found himself doing a favor for Stephen. Like the time he stole the answers to the math test out of the teacher's locked drawer. Stephen was failing the course and he needed a passing grade or, as he said, his father would beat the hell out of him.

And on several occasions, Arnold had agreed to meet Stephen's dealer in the city to pick up a bag of marijuana or a little vial of cocaine or whatever it was that Stephen was in the mood for.

He didn't mind doing favors for Stephen, even when there were risks involved, because he got so much back in return. Stephen let Arnold hold his hand—when no one was around, of course—and a few times, when Arnold tentatively kissed him, he opened his mouth and kissed back.

Arnold sensed that Stephen wasn't getting as much pleasure out of it as he was, but that was probably because Stephen was more reserved, more uptight about things like that. He just needed to learn to relax and enjoy himself, Arnold decided, and there was plenty of time for that. After all, they were going to be together forever. He was sure of it.

And here we are, together still, he thinks now as he reaches into his pocket and produces the key to the back door of the inn. *And I'll still do anything for Stephen. Anything at all. That's the way it should be when you're in love. . . .*

He pauses just inside the door, listening. Oh, Lord, that's the phone ringing. If it's Stephen, he'll be so upset that Jasper didn't answer on the first ring.

Tossing the keys on the counter, he scurries toward the front of the house. He's rushing down the hall toward the foyer when the phone abruptly stops ringing.

"Hello?" he hears a female voice saying. "Yes, it is . . ."

Panicked, Jasper dashes around the corner and sees Liza Danning standing in a slinky black-lace nightgown behind the desk, speaking into the receiver.

"I'll take that," he says, grabbing the phone out of her hand and glaring at her. Stephen's going to be furious.

"I was coming out of the bathroom, and I heard it ringing," she says, yawning. "So I thought I'd better get it."

"Thank you," he tells her curtly, clearing his throat. Into the phone, he says pleasantly, "Hello?"

"Uh, I need to speak to one of your guests," says an unfamiliar male voice. "Sandy Cavelli."

A chill runs through Jasper's veins. He's conscious of Liza watching him, though, and forces himself to seem unruffled. He's gotten very good at that these past few days.

"Can you excuse me for a moment?" he says into the phone, then covers the receiver and turns to Liza. "Thank you for your assistance," he says shortly. "I'll take care of this."

She narrows her eyes suspiciously at him. "It's not D.M. Yates, is it?"

"Of course it isn't."

"I didn't think so," she says, wearing an odd, calculating expression in her otherwise sleepy green eyes as she stares back at him.

But Jasper's too preoccupied to worry about Liza right now. He waits until she starts up the stairs, then turns his back and quietly says into the phone, "Sandy Cavelli? I'm afraid she's already checked out."

"She checked *out?* When?"

"Who is this, please?" he asks crisply.

"It's her brother, and I need to know where she went."

"I'm afraid I have no idea. She said she was leaving the island on the late afternoon ferry."

"But she called me just a little while ago . . ."

Jasper's ears prick up. Sandy had called her brother? From where? How had she gotten to a phone? Where was Stephen?

"What did she say when she called?" he asks carefully.

"She sounded like she was—nothing. Never mind," the man says abruptly, as though he has changed his mind about offering any information.

Jasper frowns and wonders if Stephen knows Sandy made the call. He should tell him.

"Thank you for your time," the man is saying into the phone.

"Of course. I'm sorry I couldn't offer more information." He replaces the receiver in its cradle and rubs his chin, wondering if Stephen—

"Who was that?" a voice asks, and Jasper gasps, then turns to see Liza standing on the landing.

"Who was that?" Jasper echoes awkwardly, grasping for something to tell her. He impulsively opts for the truth. "It was Sandy's brother, wanting to speak with her."

"Why?"

"Because of the storm . . . he heard there was a terrible storm and he was worried about her," Jasper says smoothly, looking Liza in the eye.

"Oh." She shrugs, still wearing the same shrewd expression as she watches him.

Frantic inside, Jasper tries to recall what he said on his end of the conversation. Was there anything that might have made her suspicious? No. No, he doesn't think so.

He dismisses Liza with a wave of his hand. "Good night, Miss Danning. Have pleasant dreams."

"Yeah, right," she says bluntly and turns to climb the stairs.

He watches until she reaches the top, then listens until he hears her shut and lock the door to her room.

"Good riddance," he whispers in her direction before turning to the matter at hand.

He hurries down the hall toward the back of the house again, stopping in front of a closed door just beyond the parlor. With a key from his pocket, he unlocks it and slips inside.

It was once a storage room, he knows, and it's too small, really, for a bedroom. Yet this is where Stephen wants him to sleep, on an old, narrow bed with a lumpy mattress.

Jasper knows it's only temporary, though.

Soon, he'll be sharing Stephen's king-sized bed, for good. Stephen promised.

Urgently, he reaches for the cellular phone Stephen gave him and dials the number he's supposed to use only in an emergency.

The fact that Sandy Cavelli called her brother qualifies. It means that everything isn't going exactly according to Stephen's plan.

If anything goes wrong with the plan, Stephen might decide that Jasper is somehow to blame. Then, Jasper's dreams of a glorious future alone with Stephen will be ruined.

And Jasper can't let that happen. No matter what. He's so close, so tantalizingly close, to winning Stephen forever . . .

Nothing is going to stand in his way.

Nothing.

Sherm Crandall has been the chief of police on Tide Island since the early seventies. Back then, his biggest problem was keeping a rein on the flocks of hippie artists who tended to smoke a lot of marijuana and skinny dip on public beaches, which wasn't exactly good for tourism—at least, not the family trade that frequented other New England coastal islands.

These days, while hippies and grass and nudity aren't unheard of on the island, Sherm doesn't get so uptight about them. He's gotten older, yes, but a lot less conservative than he was in his youth. The horror stories he hears about crime in big cities and even suburbs on the mainland make him a lot more tolerant of Tide Island's few problems.

At least here, there are no car-jackings—few people even bother to have vehicles on the island—and no teenage gangs, unless you count the four boys who formed a rock band and pierced their noses, to the horror of some of the island's old-timers.

In fact, during the off-season, Sherm's the *only* cop on duty for Tide Island. About the most pressing issue he ever has to deal with is a storm.

And the way things look tonight, they're in for a doozy.

Sitting at his desk in the small, gray-shingled cottage that serves as Tide Island's municipal building, Sherm looks up as the door opens and someone blows into the room on a gust of wind.

"Pat, is that you?" he asks, recognizing the shock of red hair that's sticking out from under the hood of the big storm coat.

"Sure is," he says, his voice muffled until he unwinds the scarf from around his face. "It's nasty out there, Sherm."

"The kind of night your father would have called 'fit for the devil,' huh, Pat?" Sherm asks, with a fond grin. Robert Gerkin was one of his boyhood buddies here on the island. In fact, they'd been best man at each other's weddings, and Sherm is Patrick's godfather.

It's hard to believe that Robert's been gone almost a year

now. Damn cancer moved so fast no one had a chance to say a proper goodbye.

"Dad loved a good nor'easter," Patrick says, sitting in the chair by Sherm's desk. "As long as there wasn't serious damage."

"Well, I hope that's the case this time, son. But it looks like this one's pretty powerful. I just talked to Joe Dominski at the weather station on the mainland and he says it hasn't diminished any. If anything, it's getting stronger and the rain is becoming snow as the temperature drops."

"We haven't had snow all winter."

"Nope." Sherm shrugs. "And it's a little late for 'Jingle Bells' and chestnuts roasting over an open fire and all that stuff, huh? But who knows? Maybe it won't be that bad."

"Well, I made the rounds of the evacuation route, anyway," Pat says.

"Anyone give you any trouble?"

"Just Old Man Mooney."

Sherm chuckles, thinking of the eccentric octogenarian who lives in one of the old houses on the north shore. "As usual. Did he threaten you with that toy shotgun of his?"

"Yeah, and the thing looks real, Sherm. If I didn't know better, I'd think he really was going to blow me away with it. Anyway, he says he's not going to budge, no matter what the weather does. Says he's been here on Tide Island too many years to worry about some little storm."

Sherm shakes his head. "Someday that old fool's gonna find himself floating in the Atlantic in his rocking chair. But there's nothing you can do. Everybody else knows to go to the church, right? Including the weekenders staying at the Seawind Hotel and Millers' Guest House? Those are the only two places open for tourists during the off-season."

"And don't forget the Bramble Rose," Pat adds.

"Oh, right. Almost didn't remember that place is open for business now, huh?"

"I guess. There were two women staying there, and I

don't know who else. I didn't get to talk to the owner, but I told them to let him know that they might be evacuated."

"Good." Sherm pauses, then remembers something else. "What about the old Gilbrooke place?"

Pat frowns. "What about it?"

"I saw a light on inside when I drove by on patrol earlier. Looks like someone might be there."

"I thought the Gilbrookes haven't used the place in years. Didn't they used to spend their summers at that fancy estate in Connecticut instead?"

"They sure did." Sherm shakes his head, thinking of the beautiful old oceanfront mansion that's gone to waste ever since Andrew Gilbrooke married that Greenwich snob who decided Tide Island's summer crowd wasn't high-society enough for her.

"So you think they sold the place or something?"

"Not that I know of. Someone might be back—probably the son."

"Well, it can't be the old man. He's in a loony bin, isn't he?"

Sherm thinks of pathetic old Andrew Gilbrooke, who had been a summer playmate of his when they were kids. He'd been rich as hell, but the most spineless son of a gun Sherm had ever known, ruled first by his overbearing mother, then by his tyrannical wife, Aurelia.

He looks at Pat, nodding sadly. "Yup, I heard Andrew went off the deep end after his wife killed herself. But the kid's still floating around someplace. He was a real mess, too—mentally and physically. I had only met him a few times, when he came out here with his father to check on the property. Poor kid had the ugliest face you ever saw. Last I heard, he had taken over the family import-export business a few years back. Maybe he's back here on the island for a while, though, to get away from the rat race or something."

"Maybe." Pat puts his hood up again. "You want me to go out there and check?"

"Would you?"

"No problem, Sherm. Then I'll come back and help you board up those windows."

"I'd appreciate it. After that, I'm going to head on home and take care of things there."

Pat hesitates in the doorway. "Any word from Carly?"

"Nope." Sherm shrugs, as though it doesn't matter that his wife of thirty years hasn't called or written in months.

"Any idea where she is?"

"Nope. But I can tell you one thing. She sure as hell isn't on an island," he says on a bitter laugh.

She never liked it out here in the first place, even though she'd grown up a Tide Islander just as he had. She hated the island as much as he loved it and had married him despite knowing he never wanted to leave. Then she'd complained and pestered him about it for the next three decades.

Finally, last fall, she'd left with the last of the tourists, telling Sherm she wanted out for a while. "I'll be back," she'd promised as he'd stood with her on the ferry dock that rainy September morning.

"For good?" he'd asked hopefully. "Or just to pick up the rest of your stuff?"

"I'm not sure."

Carly is nothing if not honest. Brutally so, sometimes. He still vividly remembers the day she told him that the doctor had called with results of the tests they had both undergone after trying unsuccessfully to have a baby.

"I'm fine. It's you. You're sterile," she'd said flatly, as though informing him that he had ketchup on his chin. No beating around the bush, ever—not with Carly.

"So Sherm, I'll see you in a little while, okay?" Pat asks from the doorway now.

"No problem." He watches Pat head out into the storm again. The room seems quieter than ever when the door closes behind him, shutting out the howling wind.

Sherm leans back in his seat, stretches, and reaches for

the paperback detective novel that's opened face-down on the desk. He tries to get back into the story, but he can't seem to concentrate.

He's read the same sentence five times without comprehending it when the sudden shrill ringing of the telephone shatters the silence.

Sherm grabs for it immediately. "Tide Island Police."

Maybe it's Carly, he tells himself, feeling a flutter of excitement in the vicinity of his heart.

He thinks that every time a phone rings anywhere. And it's never her.

"Uh, yes. I, uh, have a missing person to report."

"Excuse me?" Sherm puts down his novel and sits up straighter in his chair.

"At least, I *think* she's missing."

"Who is she?"

"My sister. She's spending the weekend on the island, and she supposedly left on the late afternoon ferry; but I just called the ferry office in Crosswind Bay, and according to the schedule on the recording I heard, there's no late ferry on Saturdays."

"No, there isn't." Sherm picks up a pen and grabs the pad he uses to take notes in situations like this—which, on Tide Island, occur once in a blue moon. Usually, when someone calls the police department out here, it's to report a missing dog or cat.

"She's in trouble," says the man on the phone. "She called me a little while ago, and someone was doing something to her—some guy. She screamed, and—"

"Whoa, hang on," Sherm cuts in. "I need you to backtrack and start at the beginning. What's your name?"

The caller sighs. "Danny Cavelli. And my sister's name is Sandy. She was staying at the Bramble Rose Inn."

There's a coincidence, Sherm thinks, writing it down. *That's the second time in five minutes that someone's mentioned the place.*

"And you don't know where she is now?"

"Missing!" Danny Cavelli practically shouts into the phone. "Aren't you listening to what I'm saying? I can't find my sister. Do you know what it's like to have no idea where to find someone you care about?"

Sherm's eyes fall on the framed photograph of Carly that sits on his desk.

You bet I do, he thinks grimly.

Aloud, he says only, "Please go on with your story, Mr. Cavelli."

Stephen is methodically washing his hands with strong, anti-bacterial soap, watching Sandy's blood mix with water in the kitchen drain, when a sudden, shrill, ringing sound shatters the silence.

His eyebrows shoot up and he turns to look at the old-fashioned black telephone on the desk by the window. Only one person has the number here: Jasper. Well, that's not entirely true. Father has it, of course—but considering where Andrew Gilbrooke is, he's not likely to be making phone calls.

Frowning, Stephen hurriedly turns off the faucet and dries his hands on a paper towel instead of the dish towel, just in case there are still telltale remnants of blood on his fingers. Then he picks up the phone.

"Yes?" he asks cautiously.

"Stephen, it's me."

"Jasper, what the hell are you doing, calling me out here? I told you only in an emergency—"

"I know, and I'm sorry—" Stephen curls his lip in distaste at the near sob in the fool's voice. "—but this *is* an emergency."

"What do you mean?" Stephen's stomach churns slightly, and he looks back in the direction of the drawing room, where Sandy Cavelli's bloodied body lies in a heap on the floor.

"She called her brother," Jasper says in a near-whisper.

"Who called her brother? What are you talking about?"

"That Cavelli girl. She got to a phone and called her brother, Stephen, and now he's worried about her."

Stephen frowns, thinking back to when he cornered Sandy in the upstairs study. Everything was a blur. . . . But she *had* been holding the telephone, he realizes now, his heart dropping with a sickening thud. At the time, he'd been too frenzied to realize that she might have actually made a call.

"How do you know this?" he asks Jasper urgently.

"Her brother called here looking for her a few minutes ago."

"What did you tell him?"

"Just what I've been telling the other two guests . . . that she left the island on the late ferry."

"You idiot! There *is* no late ferry today."

"I know, Stephen, but I got so confused and I didn't know what else to say . . ."

"You were supposed to say that she checked out early and you saw her leaving with her date!" Stephen rakes his fingers through his hair, trying to think straight.

"I know, I . . . I forgot." Please don't be mad at me, Stephen. I'm sorry. I just got nervous, and—"

"Shut up so I can figure this out!" he barks into the phone and is met by instant silence.

After a moment, he asks, "Did you get rid of her stuff, like I told you?"

"Yes, I buried it out in the dunes, just where you said," Jasper replies quickly.

"And what about the other two? Where are they?"

"Upstairs. When I went out to get rid of Sandy's bags, they were having dessert and tea in the parlor; and when I came back, they were already up in their rooms."

"Thanks to the sleeping pills you tucked into their dessert . . . right?"

Is it his imagination or does Jasper hesitate slightly before answering, "Of course, Stephen."

"Are you sure?"

"Yes, I'm sure. Everything is under control. Don't worry about anything."

"Then don't give me any reason to."

Stephen hangs up and examines his short fingernails for traces of blood. Nothing. Good.

Reaching into a kitchen drawer, he pulls out a pair of gardening gloves and slips them on. Then he returns to the drawing room and stands over Sandy's body, clad in the red-stained white wedding gown.

Just like Lorraine, he thinks, pleased, remembering that day in the suite at the Waldorf-Astoria.

Getting rid of her had been surprisingly simple, though, thanks to that fancy brass-trimmed steamer trunk he'd bought her for their honeymoon.

A smile curls his lips as he remembers how he'd tipped the eager-to-please bellhop fifty dollars to bring the pile of luggage to the lobby for him.

At first, the guy had looked perplexed when Stephen had opened the door of the suite. "I was just up here a little while ago," he'd said. "Miss LaCroix called the concierge and asked for someone to bring her bags down. But no one answered the door when I knocked."

Stephen had thought rapidly and pasted a sly smile on his face. "Oh, well, we, uh . . . you know, we're about to be married, and we, uh . . ."

"Gotcha," the bellhop had said with a wink. "Say no more, sir."

With that, he had carted the bags, including the trunk and its macabre cargo, down to the lobby. Stephen had met him there and stood by as the luggage was loaded into the trunk of a yellow cab. He'd instructed the driver to take him to the Connecticut estate that had been deserted ever since his father had been committed to a mental hospital a few years before.

That night, by the light of a full February moon, Stephen had buried his unfortunate bride deep in the barren, sandy soil of what had once been his mother's herb garden . . . a few feet from the decaying corpse that had once been his mother.

Now, he sighs and eyes Sandy. Too bad he can't just bury her on the cliff behind the house and have it over with. But what with the erosion that plagues the coast of the island, he can't take any chances. Especially since this time, he's going to have three bodies to worry about.

No, he'll have to go along with his original plan. That means stowing her body on board his yacht, which is moored in the water behind the house. Then, when he's left Tide Island for good, he'll simply toss Sandy Cavelli—and Liza Danning, and Laura Towne—overboard and let the shark-infested waters of the Atlantic destroy the evidence.

A gust of wind slams into the house as Stephen bends over Sandy's body, and he remembers the storm that's raging outside. No, he can't bring her out to the boat now. He'll have to find someplace inside to keep her until the weather dies down.

He's dragging her across the floor when a sudden ringing sound makes him stop short.

He mentally curses Jasper again.

Then he realizes, with a chill, that it isn't the phone after all.

It's the doorbell.

Ten

Sherm Crandall waits until nearly midnight for Pat to return to the police station.

Finally, yawning and closing the still-unfinished detective novel, he stands and goes over to look out the window. From here, across the wide main street, he can see the waves slamming fiercely into the deserted ferry dock. The storm is gaining momentum, and if he doesn't start boarding up windows now, it might be too late.

Reluctantly, he reaches for his coat on the hook behind his desk.

He wonders idly whether Danny Cavelli's sister Sandy is out somewhere in this weather, maybe lost or disoriented . . . or worse.

But there's not much he can do at this point. He's already called the Bramble Rose and spoken to Jasper Hammel, the manager. The man confirmed what Cavelli said—that the sister had checked out earlier.

"Do you know where she was going?" Sherm had asked, his pen poised over the pad on his desk.

"She said she was leaving on the late ferry, but of course, there is no late ferry on Saturdays," Hammel had told him. "I didn't let on that I knew that, though, because I assumed there was a reason she was lying to me. I seem to remember that she had earlier said something about meeting a date here on the island . . . a blind date. Maybe—and this is indelicate, I know—but I got the impression that she didn't want me to suspect she might plan on spending the, er, *evening* with the man."

"I see. Is there anything else you think might be helpful?"

"No. There was no reason for me to think anything unusual was going on, so I didn't pay much attention to Miss Cavelli while she was here. Do you . . . you don't think something happened to her, do you?"

"I hope not," Sherm had said, thinking not just of her worried brother but of the negative publicity it would bring to Tide Island—and its police department.

"It would be a shame . . . such a nice, cheerful girl. If I think of anything else, Lieutenant Crandall, should I call you?"

"Please."

After Sherm hung up, he'd made a mental note to stop by the Bramble Rose as soon as he got a chance, to check it out. It was probably less expensive than the other island hotels that were open during the off-season. His sister Michelle and her husband had wanted to come out and visit him over Easter, and Sherm didn't have room to put them up at his place.

No, it's not that you don't have room. . . . It's that you've let the place go to hell every since Carly left. Cleaning, cooking, laundry . . . that was all her department. Now it's barely fit for you, let alone company.

With a sigh, Sherm glances again at the pad where he jotted down the notes about the Cavelli girl. Since she hasn't been missing for twenty-four hours yet, his hands are tied—something her brother failed to understand.

"But what about that phone call?" he kept asking Sherm, a note of desperation in his voice. "She sounded so scared . . ."

"It could have been a joke," Sherm had told him, hating himself for the cold efficiency in his own voice. But it was his job to handle this by the book. It wouldn't be the first time that some young girl had taken off with a guy and made her family crazy with worry.

"And even if it weren't a joke," he'd added, "I have no way of finding your sister without a trail to follow."

"Can't you just go out and *look* for her?"

"Where do you suggest I start?"

"I don't know. . . . Isn't it a small island?"

"Everything's relative, Mr. Cavelli. We're in the middle of a nasty storm out here; and anyway, I can't just go driving around aimlessly, looking for your sister. At least, not at this stage." With exaggerated patience, he repeated, "She's not officially a missing person until she's been gone—"

"Yeah, yeah, I know. Twenty-four hours." Danny Cavelli's voice had an edge, and he said curtly, "I'll be in touch again before that, believe me."

And with that, he had hung up with a sharp click.

Now, zipping his coat up to his throat and pulling the hood snugly over what's left of his graying hair, Sherm puts Cavelli and his sister out of his head.

As he heads for the door, his thoughts return to Pat. It isn't like him to say he'll do something and then not do it. But then again, the poor kid's not even supposed to be on duty in the off-season, and here he is, going out of his way to make sure everyone on the island knows where to go if they need to evacuate.

Pat lives in a small, weathered cape on the north coast of the island, not far from the old Gilbrooke place. Sherm decides that he probably headed home for a while to change out of his wet clothes or grab something to eat.

After pulling on his thick, insulated gloves, Sherm starts to gather the hammer and other supplies he'd gotten ready earlier, then pauses.

Something's making him uneasy, and it isn't just the fury of the storm, or the run-in with Cavelli.

After a moment, he goes back to his desk and takes off his right glove. He checks the number in his Rolodex, then punches out the buttons on the phone and waits for Pat to pick up.

After four rings, the answering machine clicks on.

"Hey, you've reached Pat Gerkin. You know what to do. Later."

At the tone, Sherm says, "Pat, this is Sherm. . . . I waited for you at the station, but it's almost midnight and I'm heading out now. I'll be home if you need me, and I'll call you if we have to start evacuating. If not, have a good night, and thanks for helping out."

He hangs up the phone, frowning.

If Pat isn't home, where is he?

Don't drive yourself crazy. . . . The kid has a lot of friends on the island. Probably stopped off for a beer or a hand of cards somewhere, Sherm tells himself, and pulls his glove on again.

But as he heads out into the roaring wind to board up the station windows, he can't shake the feeling that something isn't quite right on the island tonight.

And after so many years of police work, Sherm's instincts are usually on target.

Danny Cavelli paces the bedroom, as he's been doing ever since he hung up with the Tide Island police station over an hour ago.

"If she would just call again," he tells Cheryl, glancing at the silent phone on the nightstand. "I mean, I just want to know that she's okay."

"I know you do. I still think you should call the local police. And your parents."

"Oh, jeez Cheryl, we've been through this. What are the Greenbury cops gonna do if the Tide Island police don't even give a shit about Sandy and she disappeared out there? And I'm not dragging my parents into this unless I have to. Maybe nothing's wrong . . ."

"Maybe not."

Danny stops pacing and looks at his wife. "No. No, she's in trouble. I know she's in trouble. The way she sounded . . . she would never play a joke like that on me."

"I know."

"Some guy was doing something to her, dammit!"

"Even if he were, Danny . . ." Cheryl gets off the bed and walks over to where he's standing by the dresser. She puts a hand on his wrist. "Even if some guy *date-raped* her . . ."

He winces at the words.

". . . *if* that's what was going on—she's going to be okay, Danny," Cheryl finishes. "She'll have a hard time getting over it, but she'll be okay."

"And if that's what happened, I'm going to kill the son of a bitch with my bare hands," Danny says, shaking his head and narrowing his eyes. "I swear to God, Cheryl. I'll find him and kill him."

"Okay, Danny, calm down. It's not helping Sandy if you get carried away . . ."

"And it's not helping Sandy if I just hang around here waiting for something to happen, either," Danny announces suddenly, slapping his palm on the dresser-top so hard that the framed wedding photograph of him and Cheryl topples onto the floor.

"What are you going to do?" she asks, bending to retrieve it.

"Go out to Tide Island."

"Danny, don't be—"

"Cheryl, I can't just sit here. I've got to find my sister; and if the cops don't want to help, that's fine. I'll do it on my own."

"No, you won't," she says quietly, and he spins angrily to face her. But as he opens his mouth to lash out, Cheryl adds, "You won't do it on your own, because we'll do it together."

His jaw closes; and wordlessly, he gathers her into his arms and gives her a grateful squeeze.

In the attic of the Bramble Rose, Stephen carefully removes his blood-soaked tuxedo from the plastic bag he used to transport it back from the house by the water. He had so wanted to wear the same suit again for Liza, and for Laura, but he had forgotten about the blood.

It splattered him from head to toe as he stabbed Sandy, something he hadn't taken into consideration earlier.

And that bothers him. He'd trusted himself to think of everything—how could he have overlooked such an important detail?

It's not a good sign.

That—coupled with Jasper's phone call about Sandy Cavelli's brother, not to mention the unexpected visit from that redheaded kid—is making him nervous.

Somehow, his careful plan suddenly seems in danger of derailing.

No, it won't, he tells himself as he feels along the sloping wall for the familiar loose board. *Everything is fine. There's no problem, not really. Just a few complications.*

He finds the loose board, pulls it away from the wall, and shoves the tux into the space behind it. He'll deal with it later. Then he removes the wedding album he'd stashed there and replaces the board.

Sitting in his rocker with the album on his lap, he closes his eyes momentarily and takes a deep, cleansing breath, then exhales.

Better . . . much better.

He begins to rock, gently so as not to creak the floorboards and wake anyone below . . . not that Liza and Laura are likely to stir, considering the strong doses of Seconal Jasper was supposed to give them in their dessert.

Flipping the album open to Sandy's page, he replaces the

old name card with the new one . . . the one written in her blood. Squatting beside her body in the drawing room, he'd taken the time to painstakingly letter her name in calligraphy, dipping an old-fashioned pen again and again into the pool of red on the floor as he worked.

Now he holds the wedding album away from his face a bit to admire his handiwork, then glances over at the camera he put on the table by the door. Such a pity he can't go ahead and develop the photographs he'd taken of her as she lay dying at his feet.

Now, thanks to an unexpected interruption, he might as well wait for the others. He'll do them all at once, in the makeshift darkroom back at the waterfront house.

Again, he thinks of how messy things got.

Why did that damn kid have to come along and ruin everything?

He hadn't opened the door, not even when the kid rang the bell persistently and kept calling, "Anybody home?"

Then, just when he'd thought the intruder had left, two things had happened simultaneously.

He'd remembered that he'd left the car parked in front of the door and the porch light on so that Sandy wouldn't get suspicious when he'd brought her here earlier. . . .

And he'd glanced up to see the kid's face pressed against the window of the drawing room as he stood on the porch, peering in.

The horror in those eyes as they took in Stephen and the bloodied body of Sandy Cavelli was clear even through the rain-spattered glass.

He'd leapt into action, dashing for the door and collaring the kid as he tried to get away. If the intruder hadn't been so shaken by what he'd just seen, Stephen had no doubt that he would have escaped. After all, he had an athletic build and he was strong. But as it was, his shock and fear had undoubtedly slowed him down and it took little effort for Stephen to restrain him long enough to pull out the knife he'd used to kill Sandy.

As soon as the kid saw the blade, he'd started begging for his life.

Stephen had only debated for a brief moment before realizing what he had to do. The kid had seen too much. There was no way he was going to let him go now.

So he'd done it swiftly and effortlessly, slashing the jugular in the kid's strong young neck and feeling warm, sticky blood gush over his just-washed hands.

He'd wondered, as he dragged the kid's body into the first-floor closet under the stairs, who he was and why he was here. Not that it mattered, really.

He'd gone back to the drawing room for Sandy, hurriedly dragging her, too, into the closet, dumping her heavy body on top of the other one. He had a lot of cleaning up to do after that, and it had taken him well over an hour to wash the blood carefully away from the front porch and hardwood foyer and drawing room floors. He'd congratulated himself for not getting any blood on the white satin runner, at least. That, he would need again . . . for Liza, and then for Laura.

With a contented sigh, he closes the wedding album and stands. The night isn't getting any younger, and he's been looking forward to paying Liza a visit.

Stealthily, he moves across the attic floor to the steps. Then, pocketing the ring containing the special keys to the doors of the guest rooms, he slips down the stairs.

Jennie is running through the deserted shopping mall again, desperately trying to get away, when all of a sudden a freight train slams into the side of the building.

She cries out as everything shudders around her, flinching and waiting for the inevitable. . . .

Then, suddenly, she's awake, staring into her pitch-black room at the Bramble Rose Inn.

It was just the same old nightmare, she realizes, sitting up and turning on the light on the bedside table.

But the noise of the freight train was real—apparently caused by a sudden blast of wind off the ocean. It continues to batter the old house now, rattling the windows and howling like a mournful ghost.

Still trembling and breathless from her dream, Jennie swings her feet over the edge of the bed and gets up to go to the bathroom for a drink of water. After pulling on her robe, she pads across the chilly floor in her bare feet and reaches for the doorknob.

It's stuck again, she realizes as she tugs on it.

She remembers what Jasper said about the old wood swelling in damp weather and pulls more forcefully. It refuses to budge.

Then, feeling an edge of panic rising within her, Jennie puts both hands on the knob and tries, with all her might, to open the door.

It's not stuck, she realizes with a stab of fear. *It's locked . . . from the other side!*

"Help!" she screams spontaneously, hoping to wake Liza, whose room is just down the hall. She bangs on the door. "Help! Someone get me out of here!"

Then she realizes that whoever locked the door is possibly nearby and the last thing she should be doing is attracting attention.

She clamps her mouth shut and backs away from the door, her heart pounding furiously as she hears footsteps pounding up the stairs and down the hall toward her room.

There's a long pause, and then Jasper Hammel's voice reaches her ears above the incessant sound of the wind. "Laura . . . Miss Towne, it's me. Are you all right?"

"I'm locked in," she says in a small voice, shrinking into the shadows at the far end of the room and staring at the door.

"I know, I'm sorry, I . . ." There's a jangling noise, and

then the sound of the locks clicking. The door swings open, and Jasper is standing there, wearing a pair of striped blue-cotton pajamas.

"I must have locked it by accident," he says, stepping into Jennie's room, wearing an apologetic expression. In his hand is an oversized key ring. "I was, uh, cleaning in the empty guest rooms earlier, and I somehow must have locked yours instead of one of those."

Jennie only stares uneasily at him for a moment, then nods. "Don't worry about it. It's all right."

"I'm so sorry," Jasper says again, sliding the ring over his wrist and rubbing his hands nervously. "You must have been so startled . . ."

"It's all right," she says again. "Really."

With a final apology, he steps back out into the hall and shuts the door behind him.

Jennie waits until she's heard his footsteps retreat back down the stairs to the first floor. Then she goes over and locks the inside bolt again . . . unsettled by the thought that it doesn't matter—not really.

Jasper, of course, can unlock it any time he feels like it. He just did.

And as for what he said about mistaking her room for one of the empty guest rooms . . .

She's well aware that the doors to the empty rooms are kept open and unlocked. Isn't that what Liza told her earlier?

Liza.

Strange that she didn't hear Jennie screaming.

Biting her lip, Jennie unlocks her door again and slips quietly out into the dark hallway. It's deserted, and she knows Jasper is back downstairs because she heard him go, but she still can't get past the strange but distinct feeling that someone is lurking nearby.

Don't be paranoid, she commands herself. *Who on earth would be doing a thing like that? And why?*

But as much as she knows it doesn't make sense, she can't seem to shake her anxiety.

Wrapping her robe more tightly around herself, she hurries to Liza's door and knocks quietly. When there's no response, she knocks again, calling, "Liza?" in a hushed voice.

No reply.

She hesitates there, considering knocking or speaking more loudly. But that might bring Jasper Hammel up the stairs again.

Shaking her head, she tells herself that Liza is probably just a deep sleeper, like Laura. Her twin sleeps through blasting alarm clocks, ringing telephones and doorbells, everything.

And anyway, there's the noise of the storm, Jennie remembers, as she becomes aware, once again, of the pounding rain and ceaseless wind howling outside the old inn. It probably drowned out the sound of her screams earlier, and the knocking now.

Slowly, Jennie retreats down the hall to her room and locks her door again. Then, feeling slightly ridiculous, she quietly pulls a straight-backed chair from the desk across the floor and wedges it under the doorknob.

Trembling, Jennie stares at it for a moment, wondering what she's trying to protect herself from. The only person who might ever want to hurt her is dead.

But you're not supposed to be Jennie right now. . . . You're supposed to be Laura.

And who knows how many enemies flighty, irresponsible Laura has made?

Trying not to think about the most obvious one—her sister's ex-husband, Brian—Jennie goes back over to the bed. She slips beneath the blankets again, leaning her back against the headboard. Bringing her knees up to her chest, she wraps her arms tightly around them and stares at the lilac-patterned wallpaper, vowing not to let herself fall asleep again tonight.

* * *

Stephen is trapped in Liza's room, afraid to move, afraid to breathe.

He stands with his back flat against the closed door, listening for another sound from the hallway. A few moments before, he heard Laura Towne go back to her room and close the door, but he can't help thinking it was a close call.

What if her knocking had woken Liza?

Not likely, thanks to the Seconal, but there's always a chance. . . .

Stephen presses his fingertips against his throbbing temples and tries to calm himself, glancing toward the bed for reassurance that his sleeping beauty is still sleeping.

Even in the darkness, he can see the blond hair on the pillow, the pale, creamy skin of her bare arms against the eyelet bedspread.

He had barely been in her room for a few minutes when that Towne woman had started screaming for help. Stricken, he'd realized that she'd found herself locked in.

Thank heaven for Jasper, who had come rushing up the stairs just as Stephen opened Liza's door and peered out into the hall. He'd wordlessly handed the key ring to Jasper, who had nodded his understanding and hurried toward Laura's room, which had grown curiously silent.

There was nothing for Stephen to do but close Liza's door again and wait as Jasper went to Laura's aid. He'd listened with relief as he'd heard Jasper's spur-of-the-moment explanation, followed by his retreat back to the first floor.

Then, just as Stephen was about to give up on Liza for tonight and slip out of her room, he'd heard Laura's door open, and then her knocking and whispering.

Clearly, the woman is suspicious . . . or, at the very least, concerned enough to want to discuss it with the other guest.

You should just get it over with, Stephen tells himself,

clenching his fists and setting his jaw grimly. *It's getting too dangerous.*

But then he turns to look again at Liza on the bed. And he exhales raggedly, struck by how innocent and unsuspecting she looks as she sleeps just a few feet from her worst enemy.

He makes up his mind. This isn't something to be done in a rush. It's something that needs to be savored.

He'll stick with the plan.

Sighing softly in pleasure, Stephen stealthily moves across the floor to stand beside Liza's bed, reaching with one hand for the edge of the eyelet bedspread, and with the other for the already taut fly of his trousers.

Keegan wakes from a nightmare in a cold sweat and looks around, disoriented.

He realizes that he's on the living room couch, sprawled in an uncomfortable position, still holding the television remote control in his hand. The last thing he remembers is thinking about Jennie and wishing Laura would call him back, but knowing that if she hadn't yet, she probably wouldn't until tomorrow.

Keegan sits up and rubs his eyes, then glances at the television, where a real estate infomercial is blaring away at ear-shattering volume. He points the remote control at it, hits the power button, and zaps the screen into dark silence.

There.

Now, at least, he can think.

Jennie . . .

In his dream, he had been struggling to reach her as she screamed for help, balancing precariously on a narrow raft in the middle of the storm-tossed ocean.

Hold on, Jennie, he kept calling to her. *I'm coming. I'll get you. Just hold on!*

The dream was so incredibly real that Keegan can still hear the roar of the waves—and Jennie's piercing screams.

"Dammit, Jen," he says aloud into the empty room. "Where the hell are you? Why do I have this feeling that you're not okay?"

Keegan checks his watch. Just past three A.M. He debates for a moment, then reaches for the phone. If Laura's pissed that he's calling her at this hour, he'll be pissed right back at her for not calling him the moment she got home.

And if she's still not home . . .

Well, he'll have to figure out what to do next. Because he definitely has to do *something*.

After dialing the familiar number, Keegan listens to the phone ringing and then, just as he'd anticipated, the answering machine picking up again.

"Damn," he says, and slams down the receiver.

For a few minutes, he sits there, staring off into space and trying to figure out what to do.

Then, his mind made up, he stands abruptly and heads for the bathroom to take a quick shower before setting out.

In his first-floor bedroom, Jasper rolls over noisily on the narrow, lumpy mattress and punches the pillow beneath his head.

He wonders what Stephen is doing upstairs in Liza's room.

No, you don't wonder. You know. He's looking at her, probably touching her . . .

Jealousy bubbles up inside of Jasper as he squeezes his eyes shut against the image of Stephen with a woman . . . Stephen with someone else.

Oh, Jasper's no fool. He knows Stephen has been with women since he came along. And even though he believes Stephen when he promises that they mean nothing . . .

He's still troubled by the knowledge and haunted by unbidden images that fill his thoughts, especially at night.

At least now, Jasper tells himself, Stephen is taking steps to rid himself of those women for good.

He still remembers his own excitement when Stephen had first revealed his plan nearly a year ago. It seemed too good to be true . . . just like what had happened to Lorraine.

Jasper thinks back to that horrible February day—Valentine's Day, wasn't it?—when Stephen was all set to marry Lorraine. He'd actually asked Jasper to be his best man, promising him, secretly, that things between them wouldn't change.

I just need a wife to keep up appearances, he'd told Jasper. *You know, for the sake of the business. You understand how it is.*

Jasper had acted like he did, because he didn't want to disappoint Stephen. He didn't see any point in reminding Stephen that *he,* Jasper, hadn't bothered to keep up appearances in his own life. No, he'd gone straight to his parents as soon as he realized he was in love with Stephen and he'd told them the truth.

Of course, his parents had disowned him on the spot. His father had told him to get his "pansy ass" out of the house and never come back.

Jasper hadn't.

Had never wanted to, or needed to.

His home, from that day on, had been with Stephen. Stephen, who'd been generous enough to put Jasper on his payroll as an assistant. Jasper had been only too happy to be at Stephen's beck and call.

He was the one who had made the funeral arrangements for Stephen's mother, handling all the messy details since there was no body to bury.

Aurelia Gilbrooke had unexpectedly jumped off the Tappan Zee Bridge in the wee hours of the morning, leaving her Mercedes idling in the breakdown lane and a suicide note tucked under the floor mat.

Or so everyone thought.

Only Stephen and Jasper knew the truth. It was Jasper who, roused out of bed after midnight by a distraught Stephen, had helped him dispose of his mother's bloodied body in the garden. And Jasper who had come up with the suicide story. And Jasper who had donned Aurelia Gilbrooke's favorite blond wig and fur coat with the hood—just in case anyone happened to glance into the Mercedes as he drove it from the Connecticut estate to the bridge, with Stephen trailing along behind in his own car.

Luck had been with them that night, and no one had seen Jasper abandon the car on the bridge, then hop into Stephen's Cadillac for the trip back to Connecticut. And since Aurelia had been such an unstable, miserable woman, no one had ever suspected what had really happened, either.

No one except Stephen's father.

But Andrew Gilbrooke had gone completely off the deep end when he'd figured it out, first flying into hysteria and then slipping into a catatonic state from which he had never recovered. Now he spent his days in a mental institution, staring off into space with a trickle of drool spilling from his slack lips.

Everyone thought poor Andrew, who had always been emotionally frail, couldn't handle the loss of his wife. No one ever realized that what he couldn't handle was the knowledge that his only child had killed his own mother.

Jasper, of course, understood why Stephen had done what he had, although they'd never discussed it, not before Aurelia's death and not after. But he had always speculated that the mother-son relationship was twisted. Apparently, Stephen had finally just snapped.

And, luckily for Jasper, the same thing had happened with Lorraine.

As he waited in Stephen's rose-laden brownstone that

February day, he'd outwardly wondered, along with the minister and wedding guests, where the groom had gone and why the bride hadn't shown.

But inside, Jasper had been hoping, praying, that Stephen would do to Lorraine what he had done to his mother.

And that was exactly what had happened.

Again, Jasper had helped Stephen come up with a story. Lorraine, they had told people, had simply gotten cold feet. That much, of course, was the truth.

She had taken Stephen's car, they said, and all her luggage and left the city for an unknown destination. They didn't report her disappearance to the authorities, of course. And by the time the car was located, months later, in long-term parking at LaGuardia, most everyone had forgotten about the curtailed Gilbrooke-LaCroix nuptials.

Everyone, except Jasper.

He has long since forgiven Stephen for feeling like he needed a woman to keep up appearances, for not wanting the world to know that he, Jasper, was his one true love.

But he has never forgotten.

In the back of his mind, he occasionally wonders, with a sharp little pang, whether Stephen really meant it when he promised that the two of them will sail away together for good, just as long as Jasper helps him with his plan.

Of course he means it, he tells himself now, flipping restlessly again on his bed.

But he can't help wondering why, if he's the only one Stephen really cares about, he's going to so much painstaking trouble with these three women. And why Stephen insisted that Jasper drug them with their dessert so that he would be able to creep into their rooms unnoticed after they've gone to bed.

After the way Stephen had hollered at him when he'd called the mansion earlier, Jasper hadn't dared to tell Stephen that Laura Towne had barely touched her dessert. Which meant that she wasn't drugged.

Which was obviously why she had unexpectedly awakened to find herself locked into her room.

Stephen is going to be so angry when I tell him that she didn't eat her dessert and that I kept it from him earlier, Jasper thinks, staring into the darkness.

So then don't tell him, a voice says reasonably inside his mind.

But I don't like to have secrets from Stephen. I've always told him everything.

And do you think, the voice scoffs, *that he tells you everything in return?*

Not wanting to answer that, Jasper flips over and pulls the pillow over his head tightly to drown out the annoying voices in his head.

Eleven

Sunday morning dawns raw and stormy in Boston.

Laura opens her eyes to find herself entangled in the twin sheet on Shawn's bed as he slumbers peacefully beside her. It amazes her how he can sleep that way—naked and uncovered. For all her own brazen sexuality, Laura always makes sure to slip her own nude body under the covers when she falls asleep.

Jennie, she thinks idly, *probably doesn't even sleep naked when she's with someone.*

She can easily imagine her prudish sister climbing out of bed after Keegan's asleep and pulling one of her warm flannel nightgowns over her head.

Then again, it's surprising that Jennie is sleeping with Keegan in the first place . . .

Was, Laura corrects, remembering that Keegan is history.

Then she remembers something else.

Last night, she'd been worried about her sister for some reason . . .

For no reason, she tells herself, recalling her inexplicable uneasiness over Jennie's trip to the island.

She'd managed to put it out of her head last night, thanks to Shawn's expert hands and lips and—well, everything. But now the memory of her worry comes back to Laura full force and she sits up and frowns.

"Laura?" Shawn asks groggily, stirring beside her on the mattress.

"Yeah. I have to go home."

"Huh?"

"I have to leave," she says, already on her feet and reaching for his robe to wear for a quick trip to the bathroom down the hall.

"But it's lousy outside," he says, sitting up and looking toward the window. "And you don't have to work today. Stay here with me . . ."

"I can't," she says, feeling a distinct sense of urgency taking over. "I have to get home and check on my sister."

"I thought she's away for the weekend."

"She is, but I have this feeling that she might have tried to call. I'm worried that something's wrong with her."

Shawn frowns, apparently about to say something but thinking better of it. Instead, he asks, "Can't you access your answering machine from here?"

"Uh-uh. I've never been able to figure out how to do that. Jennie's the one who knows how, but . . ." She shrugs. "Anyway, I have to go."

"I'll go with you," Shawn says, getting out of bed and stretching, his naked body magnificent in the gray morning light.

Surprised, Laura asks, "How come?"

"Because I want to be with you," he says simply.

A small smile plays over her lips. "Good" is all she says.

But she's thinking that she's found Mr. Right at last.

Jennie wakes with a start.

Oh, God, you've been sleeping. . . . How could you fall asleep? she scolds herself, looking around the room. She's still sitting up with her knees up against her chest, and the bedside lamp is still on. She looks toward the window and sees dim light filtering through. It's morning, and the storm is still ranting outside.

Harry, Jennie remembers suddenly.

She'd been dreaming of him. The details are fuzzy, but she recalls his face and the fact that he was telling her something, over and over.

"What was it?" she whispers to the silent room. She closes her eyes, trying to bring the dream back.

It's the strangest thing. She can see Harry's familiar face wearing an uncharacteristically serious expression as he speaks to her, and she can hear the urgent tone of his voice. . . .

But she can't seem to grasp the words themselves.

Jennie gives up, for now, and checks her watch. It's nearly nine o'clock.

She grabs the small nylon bag containing her bathroom stuff, then pulls on her robe and heads for the door. She moves the chair she'd wedged under the knob and reaches out to open the door, wondering, with a sudden stab of trepidation, whether she'll find it locked again.

No. Though it sticks slightly, it opens, and Jennie steps out into the hall, relieved. She glances toward Liza's door, wondering if she should check in with her.

Later, she tells herself and continues across the hall.

The bathroom pipes groan loudly in protest as she turns on the faucets, and the water that comes out of the ancient overhead spout is a mere lukewarm trickle.

I'll be glad to take a real shower when I get home, she thinks as she steps into the ancient tub and pulls the curtain closed around her.

Home . . .

That's it.

In her dream, Harry was telling her to go home. To leave the island . . .

"You're in danger, Jennie," he kept saying. "Trust me. You have to leave. Get out of the inn and off the island. Hurry, Jennie, before it's too late . . ."

* * *

Keegan pulls his red Toyota into the ferry parking lot at Crosswinds Bay, turns off the motor, and gives a sigh of relief.

You made it, he tells himself. *Barely.*

I-95 from Boston to Rhode Island is never a pleasant road to travel, but today it was more treacherous than ever. Visibility was terrible because of the storm, which grew steadily worse as daybreak fell and he drew closer to the coast. The rain had turned to sleet, then to heavy, wet snow that coated the already-slick surface of the highway and made it impossible to go faster than thirty miles an hour. Just outside of Providence, there had been a three-car pile-up that slowed traffic to a standstill for over an hour.

Seeing the red flashing lights of rescue vehicles and police cars, Keegan had debated stopping to see if he could help, then guiltily decided against it. He had to get to Jennie, and there was no time to waste.

In the few seconds since he turned off the car, the windshield has been covered over with sloppy snow, making it impossible for Keegan to clearly see the ferry terminal building just ahead of his parking space. He turns on the wipers again and sees that there's a sign on the door.

"Uh-oh," he says quietly and zips up his jacket. He opens the door and is met by a gust of wet, blowing snow. Slamming the door behind him, he hurries across the narrow stretch of parking lot to the door and tries the knob without reading the sign.

It's locked.

"Damn," Keegan says over the wind and glances at the bold black magic-marker scrawl.

All Tide Island Ferries Canceled Until Further Notice Due to Storm.

"Damn!" he says again and turns to go back to the car just as a battered dark-green Buick with Connecticut plates pulls up next to him.

"Hey, what does that sign say?" the driver, a handsome,

dark-haired man who appears to be in his late twenties, calls to Keegan after rolling down his window and poking his head out.

"It says the ferry's canceled," Keegan shouts over the wind.

"What?"

"It's canceled!"

The driver shrugs, motioning that he can't hear him, and Keegan goes over to the car. "Are you looking for the Tide Island ferry?" he asks the guy, noticing that he has deep purplish circles under brown eyes that look distinctly troubled.

"Yeah . . . we have to get out there."

For the first time, Keegan notices that there's a passenger in the car—a pretty, petite woman with long, dark-blond hair poking out from beneath the hood of a bright-pink ski jacket.

"Sorry," Keegan tells them, "but the ferries to the island are canceled because of the storm."

"Shit!" The guy bangs the steering wheel and looks at the woman. "We've got to get to her."

Keegan frowns. "What was that?" he asks, knowing it's none of his business.

"It's my sister," the guy says, turning back to him. "She's out there on the island, and she's in trouble. We have to get out there and find her."

Keegan hesitates only a moment before saying, "My girlfriend's out there, too. I feel the same way."

"Yeah?" The guy reaches over his shoulder and unlocks the back door. "Why don't you get in out of the snow for a few minutes? Maybe we can figure something out. I'm Danny Cavelli, and this is my wife, Cheryl."

It's past ten o'clock when Liza finally hurries down to the first floor of the inn. She doesn't know what's wrong with her—she never sleeps in on weekends at home. But this morning, she woke late, feeling groggy and unable to keep her eyes open, even after a shower.

The tub was already wet when she got in, and she figured Laura must already be up and about. When Liza knocked on her door on her way out of the bathroom, there was no answer.

Now, as she arrives in the quiet foyer, she smells coffee and wonders if Laura's in the dining room having breakfast.

"Good morning, Miss Danning," Jasper Hammel's voice says as she heads in that direction, and she turns to see him standing behind the front desk.

"Oh . . . good morning. I didn't see you there." She rubs her temples, still feeling out of it.

"Sleep well?" he asks, his mustache twitching.

"I guess. Have you seen Laura?"

"No, I haven't," he says, frowning slightly. "In fact, I was just going to ask you the same thing."

"Oh. Well, I haven't seen her. And I don't suppose D.M. Yates has called looking for me, hmmm?"

"No, I'm afraid not."

"I didn't think so." Liza shoots him a level gaze through her bleary eyes, wondering if he knows that there *is* no D.M. Yates on the island . . . and whether he's in on this nasty little practical joke someone's obviously playing on her.

"Listen, Jasper," she says pointedly, trying to stifle an uncontrollable urge to yawn, "I was wondering if you happen to have a ferry schedule handy there."

His eyebrows shoot up beneath his neatly trimmed auburn hair. "A ferry schedule?" he echoes. "I . . . I'm not sure. Why?"

"Because I'm going to leave on the first ferry this morning, that's why," she says firmly. "And if you don't have a schedule, I'll borrow your phone and call the dock."

"No, don't do that. . . . I'll look for it. I'm sure I have

one here someplace," he says, rummaging through some papers on top of the desk. "It'll take me a moment to find it, though. Why don't you go into the dining room and help yourself to some breakfast and coffee?"

Liza is about to say she's just fine and she'll wait right here, when she feels yet another yawn stealing over her.

On second thought, coffee *would* be a good idea. She can't seem to shake her drowsiness this morning. Must be the weather.

She mumbles a thanks to Jasper and goes down the hall to the dining room where she helps herself to a mug of steaming hot coffee. She sits at the table to drink it and is halfway through when she hears the unmistakable sound of footsteps going up the stairs.

It has to be Jasper.

Annoyed, Liza debates following him up and demanding to know why he hasn't produced the ferry schedule yet.

But for some reason, the thought of going all the way back to the foyer and up the stairs seems daunting. She's so numb with exhaustion this morning that her limbs feel weak and useless.

Hopefully, the coffee will help, she thinks again and reaches for the carafe on the table to refill her mug.

Sherm Crandall wakes, as he has every morning for the past thirty years, in the master bedroom of the gray-shingled cape on the west side of Tide Island. The house sits on a little rise more than half-a-mile from the beach; but even from here, the first sound that reaches Sherm's ears is that of waves crashing over the rocky shore.

Sherm stretches and sits up to look out the window, which is on his side of the bed.

My side . . . as if Carly still has a side, he thinks, glancing at the empty pillow beside him.

Even after all these months, he still sleeps on the right,

never crossing the imaginary line into the territory that had always belonged to his wife. And it's funny, because he'd always felt that their double bed was too small for both of them. He'd wanted to buy a queen-sized mattress and box spring for the longest time so they'd have more room, but Carly always said they couldn't afford it. Since she was the one who kept the checkbook and paid all the bills, Sherm had always let her decide what they needed and what was a luxury.

Now, he wonders what she's living on—and where she's living. She might be waitressing somewhere—she'd spent a few summers working part-time in island restaurants when they were first married—or maybe she's doing secretarial work. She always was a good typist . . .

Stop thinking about her, Sherm commands himself, looking away from the empty pillow, back to the window. It's one of the few he left uncovered last night, figuring he had to be able to see out.

The bedroom's on the west side of the house, so the morning light is never good in here. But even from the bed, without his glasses, Sherm can see that the storm hasn't let up at all. Looks like it's snowing out now, and the sky is ominously dark.

With a sigh, Sherm swings his legs over the edge of the bed, wincing as his bare feet hit the cold wooden floor. Damn place is so drafty. Most of the old houses on the island are. The bedroom doesn't even have a radiator, and Sherm hasn't bothered with the portable electric heater since Carly left. She's the one who was always cold . . .

"Warm me up, Sherm," she used to say on cold winter mornings, snuggling up to him beneath the worn blue-and-red patchwork quilt her grandmother had made them for a wedding present.

And he would, gladly.

Sighing again, he pulls on his robe and pads quietly

through the silent, lonely house to the kitchen, where he stands at the sink and fills the glass coffee carafe.

And as he does, he remembers Pat.

He'd never stopped by or called last night, and Sherm had been up into the wee hours, nailing plywood over most of the windows of his house.

Frowning, Sherm dumps the water into the old Mr. Coffee machine on the counter, measures some grounds into the filter, and presses the button. Then he goes over to the wall phone and dials Pat's number.

After one ring, the answering machine picks up.

The beep is pretty long, suggesting that Pat never played the message Sherm left for him last night.

He leaves another one, then hangs up and rubs the razor stubble on his chin.

Maybe Pat is seeing someone and spent the night at her place. But whom? The number of eligible females who live year-round on the island is practically zero. . . . And besides, Sherm would have heard if Pat were seeing someone, even if Pat didn't tell him himself. Tide Island is a gossipy kind of place.

Okay, so if Pat never made it home, why hadn't he?

What if that clunker Chevy of his broke down somewhere and he was stranded out in the storm all night?

I should have gone out looking for him last night, Sherm tells himself, shaking his head. *He was going to the old Gilbrooke place. That's way the hell at the end of the north peninsula, and most of the other houses out there are closed for the winter.*

He pictures Pat, shivering, in a broken-down car in the middle of nowhere.

Some godfather you are, Sherm scolds himself.

When Pat's father, Robert, had found out he was dying, what had he asked Sherm to do?

"Look out for the kid, okay, Sherm? Make sure he's all right, will you?"

"Sure, I will," he'd promised.

And that's just what he's going to do now.

Turning abruptly, Sherm heads for the bedroom. He'll get dressed, then grab a quick cup of coffee and head out toward the Gilbrooke place to see if he can't find Pat.

Her head still bent against the biting wind and driving snow, Jennie sets down her bag and reaches out to open the door of the ferry terminal.

It's locked, she realizes with a stab of panic. She walked all the way here, rushing so she wouldn't miss the eleven o'clock boat, and the door is locked. The ramshackle wooden building looks deserted, too.

That can only mean one thing . . .

Sure enough, Jennie sees a sign taped to the glass window beside the door.

Sunday Ferry Canceled.

"No," she cries out softly, shaking her head.

She has to get off the island.

She *has* to . . .

But how?

There's no way. You have to go back to the inn, she tells herself, trying to be reasonable. But returning to the Bramble Rose is the last thing she wants to do.

She had felt so relieved as she slipped out the door earlier, her hair still damp from the shower. It had taken her all of ten minutes to pack and get dressed once she'd made up her mind to leave. And she hadn't even had to deal with Jasper, who had been nowhere in sight when she'd come down the stairs.

She supposed it wasn't very responsible of her to simply leave, but since her room was paid for, there was no reason to go through the formality of checking out and providing the innkeeper with an explanation.

She *had* felt guilty just leaving Liza. But she hadn't wanted to take the time to stop and say goodbye to her.

With Harry's dream-warning still echoing in her ears, she'd left in a rush.

And now, for all her urgency to get away, she's stranded on the island.

It'll be all right, she tells herself as she stands on the dock, buffeted by wind and snow, the fine, grainy kind that stings like blowing sand.

But I'm afraid. . . . I have to get off this island, she whimpers mentally, desperately looking back at the window and hoping that the cancellation sign will have miraculously vanished.

But it's still there, of course, and there's nothing for Jennie to do but start trudging back through the storm toward the inn.

Jasper finds Liza sitting in the dining room, staring moodily into space. She looks up when he pokes his head in the doorway, and says, "Well?"

"There's an eleven o'clock ferry," he says smoothly, "and I've called to arrange for a car service to bring you to the dock."

She frowns and sets her mug down on the table. "You did? Why?"

"Surely you don't think I'm going to let you walk all the way to the ferry, with your luggage, in this weather." He gestures toward the window behind her, where the snow is falling steadily.

"Well, I appreciate it," she says after a pause, during which she had seemed to be trying to decide whether to accept his offer. She pushes back her chair and gets up. "I'll go up and get my bags. When is this car service supposed to show?"

"In about twenty minutes," Jasper tells her and moves

over to the sideboard to flick a speck of dust from the gleaming wooden surface.

"Okay. I'll be ready. You didn't see Laura while you were upstairs, did you?"

She heard him go upstairs? He keeps his expression carefully neutral as he says, "No, I merely went up to find the schedule, which I correctly thought I had left in one of the guest rooms."

"Mmm." The blonde is staring at him with a calculating look, and Jasper nervously wonders what she's thinking.

Well, it doesn't matter now, does it? In twenty minutes, she'll be leaving the inn for good. And he'll never have to worry about her again.

Two down, one to go, he thinks, humming softly to himself as he leaves the room.

"Come on, Keegan, pick up," Laura says, listening to the phone ring for the tenth time.

"He's not there?" Shawn, standing at her side, asks. "Doesn't he have an answering machine?"

"No, and it used to drive Jen crazy when they were dating."

Her sister was going to get him one for Christmas, Laura remembers, but then she had decided it was too impersonal. She'd bought him a pair of antique cufflinks instead . . . then dumped him a week later. Go figure.

"You might as well give up, Laura," Shawn says, as she continues to let Keegan's line ring.

"I guess you're right." She plunks the receiver into its cradle and looks at him. "Where do you think he went?"

Shawn shrugs. "He was pretty anxious to talk to you. Maybe he's on his way over here."

She contemplates that, then shakes her head. "He left the last message in the middle of the night. It's—" She checks the stove clock. "—past ten-thirty now. He would have called back this morning before coming all the way over, don't you think?"

"I guess." Shawn shoves his hands into the front pockets of his faded jeans and leans against the counter. "Now what?"

"I have no—oh, yes, I do. I'm going to call the inn where my sister's staying and make sure she's all right."

"Good idea."

"But first," she says, looking around with a puzzled expression, "I have to figure out where she is."

"You don't know?"

"I can't remember. But I got a letter when the sweepstakes people told me that I'd won, and I'm pretty sure it mentioned the name of the inn."

"Did you keep the letter?"

"I think so," she tells Shawn, jerking open a drawer and starting to shuffle through the papers inside. "I'm just not sure where. But it shouldn't take me long to find it . . ."

Liar, she scolds herself, closing the drawer and opening another one. *It's going to take forever. And Shawn—Mr. Right—is going to find out that you're a pack rat and a slob.*

The sign on the diner near the ferry parking lot at Crosswinds Bay says *We Never Close.*

"Isn't *that* the truth," Danny mutters as he and Cheryl follow Keegan McCullough inside.

After all, the weather can't get much worse than it is on this dismal Sunday morning, but the place is lit up and there are even a few people inside.

They take one of the empty booths along the wall, and a waitress instantly appears to pour steaming coffee into the cups that are already on the table.

"You want menus?" she asks, tossing a handful of sugar and creamer packets onto the chipped formica surface.

"No thanks," Cheryl says, and Danny and Keegan shake their heads.

As soon as the waitress leaves, Danny takes a sip of the hot coffee, not bothering to add anything, though he usually takes it light and sweet. Then he says, "Now what?"

For a moment, Keegan says nothing. He's the quiet type, Danny has noticed in the brief times since they met. Hasn't said much, except to tell him and Cheryl that he's worried about his girlfriend, who's out on the island.

When Cheryl had asked him why he was worried, he'd just said, "Because of the weather."

Danny suspects it's more than that, but he wasn't about to push it. He had told Keegan, briefly, that his sister had gone out to the island to meet some blind date, then made the phone call that had alarmed him and Cheryl. The guy had asked a few questions, acting concerned, which Danny thought was pretty nice, considering that he seemed to have problems of his own.

Now, Keegan shrugs and tells Danny and Cheryl, "We obviously need a boat. I thought we might find some fisherman types in here."

Danny glances at the counter where two men, one elderly, the other barely out of his teens, sit on adjoining stools, having a cheerful, loud argument about something.

"What about them?" Danny asks, pointing.

Keegan nods. "I'll go talk to them." He gets up and ambles over to the counter.

Cheryl looks at Danny. "You okay?"

"Fine," he lies.

"You look beat."

"Yeah, well, it wasn't exactly a pleasant drive down here," he reminds her, and gulps more of the bitter, hot coffee. Then he turns to look at Keegan, who's having a conversation with the two men.

From here, it's impossible to hear what's being said, but

the fact that the men are shaking their heads doesn't seem to be a good sign.

As Danny watches, Keegan reaches into his pocket and pulls something out, showing it to them.

Whatever it is seems to have a big impact, because now the men are nodding reluctantly and getting to their feet.

Cheryl and Danny exchange a puzzled look.

"What do you think he's up to?" she asks.

"Beats the hell outa me." Grimly, Danny swallows more coffee, burning his throat and not caring.

Keegan comes back over to the table and says, "We're all set."

"What do you mean?"

"The older guy's retired, but the younger one's still a lobster man. Has a boat. He doesn't want to take it out on the water in this weather, but he'll let us borrow it."

"Yeah?" Danny raises his eyebrows. "How'd you talk him into that?"

"Showed him my badge."

"You're a *cop?*"

"Yeah."

Relief courses over Danny. "Thank God. I know you need to find your girlfriend, but maybe you can help me with my sister . . ."

"I'll try." Keegan tosses a couple of dollar bills onto the table. "You guys ready?"

"You bet," Danny says and takes Cheryl's hand as they get to their feet.

"So you know how to drive the kind of boat this guy has, right?" she asks Keegan as the three of them approach the two men at the counter again.

From the look on his face, Danny knows what's coming.

"Actually, I don't," Keegan tells her slowly. "I've never driven a boat in my life. How about you two?"

"I know how to row," Danny says feebly as Cheryl turns white and shakes her head.

"What about the weather?" she asks, glancing toward the plate-glass window of the diner. Outside, the churning Atlantic is clearly visible several yards away, the same brackish color as the sky.

"You two can stay here if you want," Keegan says, following her gaze. "But I have to go. I have to get to Jennie."

"I'll go," Danny tells him resolutely, thinking of his sister, hearing her panicked voice again. He turns to his wife and squeezes her clammy fingers. "But, Cheryl, you stay here."

"No way," she says, shaking her head. "If you go, I go."

Danny is about to protest, but knows, from the gleam in her blue eyes, that she's not going to waver now that she's made up her mind.

He turns to Keegan. "We're with you. Let's go."

Twelve

Liza is standing in the foyer of the inn, looking out the window, when a big black car glides to a stop at the foot of the driveway.

"That must be the car service," she says, turning to Jasper Hammel, who's at the desk behind her.

He looks up from the paperwork he's been doing and comes over to look through the window. "That's it," he says.

"Do I need a voucher or anything to give the driver?"

"A voucher? Oh, no. It's all taken care of. The inn has a contract with the driver."

"Okay." She picks up her bag and reaches for the doorknob.

He gets to it first. "Allow me, Miss Danning." He opens the door with a sweeping gesture. "It's been a pleasure having you as our guest. Please come back to stay with us again."

Not on your life, she thinks, but merely nods as she steps out into the icy wind.

Then, remembering something, she turns and looks back at him. "Do me a favor. . . . Tell Laura Towne to look me up if she's ever in New York." She reaches into her purse and pulls out one of her business cards.

Jasper Hammel takes it and smiles. "I certainly will."

Liza hurries through the wet snow toward the car, thinking, *Good riddance, you little creep.*

The driver steps out and opens the trunk so that she can

put her bag in, holding an umbrella over her head. He's a tall man; and though Liza keeps her head bent against the stinging snow, she notices, in surprise, that he's wearing a long dark coat and a cap with a visor.

Who would expect a formal car service on such a podunk island? *This is more like it,* Liza thinks to herself.

Pleased, she smiles and thanks him as he holds the back door open so that she can get into the car.

He nods, and she sees that he's wearing tinted aviator glasses—the kind that went out of style years ago.

Oh, well, she thinks, *I guess upscale service and high fashion would be too much to ask out here. And it could be worse. He could be wearing a leisure suit or something . . .*

Amused with her thoughts, she settles back against the upholstery—real leather, at least, she notes, running her fingers over the seat.

The driver gets behind the wheel again and shifts the car into Drive. Its engine purring, the car pulls away from the shoulder of the road.

Liza is so busy thinking about how thrilled she is to be leaving that, for a few seconds, she isn't paying attention to where they're going.

Then, with a start, she glances out the window and says, "I'm supposed to be taken to the ferry dock."

The driver merely nods.

Uneasy, Liza looks out the window again, then back over her shoulder at the winding road.

"Isn't the dock back that way?" she asks.

The driver doesn't reply, just keeps looking straight ahead through the windshield, his black-gloved hands expertly maneuvering the steering wheel as the car speeds along the winding seaside road.

Liza frowns and tries to ignore the edge of panic that's working its way through her. "Excuse me," she says frostily, trying to keep the shakiness out of her voice. "I asked you a question. Isn't the ferry dock back in town?"

He nods.

"And aren't we heading *away* from town?" Her voice sounds shrill to her own ears as she stares out the window at the remote landscape, then looks at him again.

His only response is to step on the gas so that the car picks up speed, barreling in the wrong direction.

She sees him watching her in the rear-view mirror; and though she can't see his eyes behind the tinted lenses, there's no mistaking the cunning smile that plays over his lips.

Liza looks wildly about, terrified. For a moment, all she can do is wonder who this man is, why he's doing this to her—and *what* he's doing to her. Abducting her? For what? Money? Revenge?

Revenge.

Her mind fills with rapid-fire images of her past, of the things she's done, the men she's used. . . .

Somewhere along the way, she realizes, she crossed the wrong person.

Now someone wants to make her pay for her sins.

She can't bear to consider what he has in mind, and she has no intention of finding out.

So she does the only thing she can think of to do.

Her heart beating a frenzied staccato, Liza waits until he slows the car slightly to go around the curb.

Then, in one swift motion, she reaches for the door handle, opens it, and—silently offering the first prayer she's said in years—hurls herself out of the moving car.

Jennie finds Jasper Hammel in the foyer, behind the desk, when she comes in.

He glances up and says pleasantly, "Good morning, Laura."

Then a tiny frown darts over his face as he catches sight of the traveling bag over her shoulder.

"I, uh, was planning to take the ferry home this morning," she says, because she feels that she should.

"Oh?" He raises his eyebrows and seems to be waiting for more of an explanation.

"I wasn't feeling well, so I thought . . ." She shrugs.

"But you changed your mind?"

She wants to say yes, but decides against lying. "No. Actually, the ferry was canceled."

"I see. Because of the storm, no doubt."

She nods and starts for the stairs, then remembers something. "Is Liza around?" she asks Jasper over her shoulder.

"Liza?" He looks blankly at her.

"The other guest? Liza Danning?"

"Oh, of course," he says, nodding. "She . . . I haven't seen her yet today, no."

"I saw a car pulling away from the inn as I was coming around the curve in the road, and I thought maybe she was leaving for that meeting she was planning to have with that author." Jennie watches him carefully.

But he only says, "I don't think she left. I've been right here for the last half hour."

Jennie nods. She wants to ask him who was in the car, but decides it's really none of her business. Instead, she nods toward the stairs and comments, "I guess Liza must still be in her room."

He looks as though he's about to say something, then apparently changes his mind. "She must be," he agrees.

Jennie heads up to the second floor with her bag, conscious of Jasper Hammel watching her until she rounds the landing.

He's definitely an odd man.

But is he dangerous? she wonders, going toward her room. *Is all of this my imagination or am I really in trouble here?*

Not wanting to dwell on her fear again, she unlocks her door, deposits her bag on the floor just inside, and then goes back down the hall to Liza's room.

The door is closed, and there's no answer to her knock.

Puzzled, Jennie calls, "Liza?" and jiggles the knob.

No reply.

Maybe she's still sleeping, she thinks. *Or she might be listening to a walkman or something and can't hear me.*

But as she stands there in the hallway, staring at the closed door, Jennie senses that there's no one behind it.

If Liza really is gone, she thinks, suddenly feeling a case of the jitters descend over her again, *then where can she be?*

Even if Liza had decided to take the ferry, not realizing it was canceled, Jennie would have seen her down at the dock or on the road between here and there.

Maybe she did leave to have her meeting with that author, Jennie thinks hopefully before she remembers what Pat Gerkin told them about D.M. Yates last night.

I guarantee you that he doesn't live here.

But the fact that the man doesn't live on the island doesn't mean he wouldn't come out here to meet with Liza. On the other hand, why would he? And Liza herself had seemed to have doubts about it.

Her mind jumbled with disconcerting thoughts, Jennie turns away from Liza's locked door and slowly makes her way back to her room.

Sherm drives slowly up the narrow lane leading to the old Gilbrooke place at the northern tip of the crescent-shaped stretch of coast. There's been no sign of Pat's Chevy so far, but maybe he got stuck at the house itself.

In winter, when the trees are bare, the Victorian mansion is visible from the road that winds by it and then away from the coast. In summer, when the Gilbrookes used to use the place, it's shrouded from view by dense trees and shrubbery that border the edge of the property. The Gilbrookes liked it that way, Sherm recalls. They were an odd bunch, even before Aurelia came along.

Andrew's father, Andrew Senior, had made a fortune in his Manhattan-based import-export business in the early part of the century. He and his wife, Helena, used to throw lavish parties on the island when they spent summers here.

Of course, back then, Tide Island had been a fashionable resort for the social elite of Boston and New York. It was even dubbed "Little Newport" in the roaring twenties, when the enormous homes on the northern coast of the island were filled with wealthy urbanites every June, July, and August.

But then, with the depression years and then the war, the summer crowd had gradually dwindled. Many of the rich had sold their lavish oceanfront homes.

The Gilbrookes never did, though. In fact, they seemed to like the island better when it became less populated. They had always been big on privacy, keeping themselves carefully apart from the rest of the island's inhabitants.

Andrew Senior and Helena had spent their summers here well into the fifties, usually with their son Andrew, who had been Sherm's playmate when they were both children. His parents probably hadn't been crazy about their son's mingling with the locals; but then, they might have been grateful he had any friends at all.

These days, Sherm thinks, *kids would call old Andrew a wimp. Back then, he was a sissy.*

But a sissy who has money, Sherm had learned, is more attractive to women than a virile kid who doesn't. When they were in their teens and met vacationing girls on the island, it was Andrew they were always drawn to, once they found out who he was.

And you didn't care when they bypassed you, Sherm reminds himself. *You always had Carly.*

His mouth set grimly at the thought of his wife, Sherm steers around a huge pothole in the lane, then turns his thoughts back to the Gilbrookes.

As Andrew Junior grew older and was being groomed to take over his father's business, he had spent less time on the island. Then his parents died within months of each other and he met Aurelia, and that was it.

The big old house has been virtually abandoned ever since.

But maybe the son is back, Sherm thinks, maneuvering the last sharp bend in the lane. Stephen, his name was. Rumor had it that Andrew hadn't named his son after himself and his father because of what he referred to as the boy's "hideous facial deformity."

Supposedly, he'd wanted his wife to bear him another son, one worthy of being a namesake. But Aurelia, according to the island gossips, had wanted no part of pregnancy and childbirth, having already experienced the "torture" once.

Sherm had only met Andrew Junior's wife once or twice. Though she was an attractive woman, her disposition made her unpleasant to look at. Her mouth was permanently turned down at the corners, as if in distaste, and her black eyes had perennially borne a sharp, beady gleam.

She had undoubtedly married poor Andrew for his money as she clearly had no patience for him, or anyone else. And as for Andrew—Sherm supposed he had married Aurelia because she told him to. He was that kind of man.

He pulls up in front of the Gilbrookes' sprawling old Victorian and sees fairly recent tire tracks in the snow. Is Stephen Gilbrooke back on the island?

Or did the tracks come from Pat's car . . .

And if so, where is it now?

Sherm had driven by Pat's small house on the way out here, but there was no sign of anyone there. The few inches of wet snow on the driveway and walk had been undisturbed.

Sherm had considered stopping by Rosalee Gerkin's place to see if she'd heard from her son, but had decided against it. Ever since she lost her husband, Rosalee has been a nervous wreck. No need to worry her if Sherm doesn't have to.

Frowning, Sherm puts the police car into Park and leaves it running as he gets out and picks his way across the messy drive to the front steps. They're snow-covered, but he can make out indentations where someone walked up and down at some point recently. Probably Pat, checking on things.

Clinging to the icy railing and wincing against the stinging wind and snow that are whirling off the ocean, Sherm climbs the steps and knocks on the door.

He waits, then knocks again, and calls, "Anyone home?"

He doesn't expect an answer. The wind would probably have drowned out his voice, and anyway, there doesn't seem to be anyone here.

With a sigh, Sherm goes back to his car and gratefully slips into the heated interior.

"Where the heck are you, Pat?" he says aloud as he shifts into reverse and backs carefully away from the house.

"You okay?" Keegan calls, looking over his shoulder at Danny Cavelli and his wife Cheryl. They're huddled on the bench behind him, clinging to the sides of the boat as it rocks violently in the foaming water.

"Fine," Danny shouts above the roar of the engine and the wind.

Cheryl doesn't reply. She looks green.

Keegan sees Danny glance at her in concern, saying something in her ear.

She nods and offers him a valiant smile, clinging to his hand.

She must really love the guy, Keegan thinks, turning to look ahead again at the surging gray-black water. *She's doing this for him—risking her life on this damn boat in a storm, with an inexperienced idiot at the helm.*

And Keegan, the inexperienced idiot, is risking his life for Jennie.

And why? he wonders bleakly.

She doesn't even care about you. And you don't even know that she's definitely in trouble. . . . You just think she might be.

What's wrong with you? Are you crazy?

No, he tells himself, he's not crazy. He's doing it for Jennie because he really loves her. And he can't make himself stop, no matter what she's done to him.

And she loves you, too, he thinks, then narrows his brows in surprise.

She does. If you didn't believe that, you wouldn't be hanging on after almost two months.

Keegan ponders the notion that Jennie loves him and feels hope surging within him at the realization that it's true. Somehow, he just knows that it is.

She loves you, but she can't be with you for some reason. There's definitely something she's not telling you.

But, Keegan promises himself, when he reaches the island and finds her, he'll make her see that no matter what her reason is, it isn't good enough to justify leaving him.

He pictures her lilac eyes and wonders why he never asked her about the haunted expression that sometimes filled them. He'd always sensed that she was keeping something from him, but he'd figured that she'd tell him when she was ready.

Never had he imagined that there wouldn't be plenty of time for that.

And even after she'd unceremoniously broken up with him, he hadn't quite grasped that she meant it. Reeling from shock, he kept thinking that she would come to her senses eventually . . . that if he could just talk to her, she'd realize that they belonged together.

Never had he expected her to refuse to answer his calls or see him.

But this time, Jennie Towne, he tells her silently, *I'm not going to let you get away with it.*

As soon as I get to you—

A monstrous wave breaks over the front of the boat then, and Keegan grips the steering wheel with all his might to keep control, remembering the few pointers the fisherman had given him back at the dock.

If I get to you, Keegan amends, wiping the stinging saltwater from his eyes with his shoulder as he clings to the wheel, *I'm going to grab you and hold you and I'm never going to let go again.*

Stephen drives as fast as he dares along the slippery coastal road, still jittery from the shock of seeing Liza jump out of the car.

He hears a thump and a muffled groan from the trunk and grits his teeth. His knuckles are white as he grips the wheel, clenching it as much out of necessity as out of fury.

What the hell did she think she was doing? he asks himself, his eyes narrowed into angry slits behind the tinted aviator lenses.

Then again, it shouldn't surprise him that Liza would figure out what he was up to and try to escape. She'd always been the perceptive type, he remembers, even when he first met her.

He remembers the way her green eyes had sized him up that first day . . .

He'd been browsing through a stack of imported woolen socks in the large Brooks Brothers store on Madison when he'd felt someone watching him. Glancing up, he'd seen a gorgeous, slender blonde standing a few feet away. She had a scarf in her hands, and she was running her fingers lovingly, absently, over the fine cashmere as she looked directly at him.

He'd found himself mesmerized, first by the sensuous way her fingertips stroked the scarf, then by how she slowly and oh-so-tantalizingly slipped her tongue from her mouth and ran it over her full lips.

Then she'd smiled and raised her eyebrows slightly at him, as if in silent invitation.

Stephen had glanced over his shoulder to be sure it was he she wanted, and not someone else. But he was the only one in the vicinity, and Liza had tilted her head coyly at him, appearing amused at his uncertainty.

He'd moved to stand beside her in a matter of seconds.

"Hello, there," she'd said in that wonderfully throaty voice of hers. "I'm Liza Danning."

"Stephen Gilbrooke," he'd responded, holding out his hand and taking the manicured fingers she offered. Her grip was warm and confident, and she'd let her fingertips play over his knuckles before he released them.

Then she'd let her green eyes wander down the length of him, and Stephen had felt as though he were standing there stark naked and absolutely alone with her.

When she raised her gaze to meet his again, she had grinned suggestively.

"Married?" was all she said.

Stephen blinked and shook his head.

"Good."

With that, Liza had slipped her arm through his and leaned up to whisper in his ear, her cloying perfume swirling around him in an enticing, heady cloud. "Take me to dinner tonight."

Of course, he had. It wasn't every day that a beautiful woman threw herself at him. Oh, Stephen was used to gold diggers, of course—he'd always encountered his share. They were easy to pinpoint, because they wanted nothing to do with someone who looked like him . . . until they found out who he was.

"You're one of *the* Gilbrookes?" they would ask, their eyes growing suddenly interested.

But Liza was different, at first. She seemed interested in him right from the start, before she even knew his name. It wasn't until later that night, over dinner at Le Cirque, when he'd caught the calculating way she looked at his Rolex, that Stephen realized she was a gold digger like the rest of them.

But by then he didn't care, because her hand was doing astonishing things in his lap beneath the tablecloth and he thought he would die from sheer pleasure.

He had taken her back to his brownstone that night and watched her absorb the authentic antique French furnishings, the Impressionist collection started by his grandfather, the Persian carpets, and the rest of the trappings that trumpeted his vast wealth. He told himself it didn't matter that she was obviously fascinated by his money, that all that mattered was the fact that she was there, that she was going to let him make love to her.

But she hadn't . . .

Not that first night.

No, *she* had made passionate love to *him,* pleasuring him repeatedly, beyond his wildest dreams, leaving him sated and exhausted and mad with the need to see her again and again and again.

He had showered her with gifts over the next several weeks, not caring that she hinted for the lavishly expensive things she wanted or that she barely bothered to hide her greed as she accepted them from him. All that mattered to Stephen was that she did incredible things to his body with hers.

And then one night, out of the blue, Liza had seemed moody and cold over dinner at Lutèce. Stephen had tried to draw her out, plying her with fine French food and champagne and outrageous compliments in his flawlessly accented French.

But he had sensed, when she turned those bored green eyes on him as he'd helped her into the mink he'd bought her, that she was about to bring their affair to a close. She had gotten everything she needed from him.

Simmering with rage, Stephen had driven her back to his place, not bothering to ask whether she wanted to be there. She'd gone along with it, probably planning to play him for a fool one last time and see what he would give her in return for her sexual services.

But the moment Stephen had closed and locked his bedroom door behind them, he had been the one in control for a change.

Instead of letting Liza tease him by undressing bit by bit, he had ripped her clothes off her. Instead of lying back, naked, and letting her hands and mouth and hair trail over his body, he had thrown her onto the bed, face down. And instead of turning her over, he had entered her, roughly and swiftly, from behind, eliciting a scream of fury and pain from those pouty lips of hers.

When he was finished, he had roughly flipped her over onto her back, expecting to see her sobbing, or at least weakened and ashamed.

Yet to his utter astonishment and dismay, those hard green eyes of hers had betrayed nothing but disgust for him.

"Are you finished?" she'd asked coldly, sitting up, then standing. "Because I'm going home now. I'm through prostituting myself to a cretin like you, although it was definitely worth it. Even this last little tantrum of yours."

Stunned into silence, he had merely watched as she pulled her dress over her head.

"And Stephen? If it weren't for your money, I never would have given you the time of day in the first place. I was hanging around Brooks Brothers that afternoon just waiting for a rich sucker like you to come along."

Laughing, she had grabbed her coat and purse and left the room, leaving him lying on the bed, reeling from her cruel words . . . even though he had known the truth all along.

Now, as Stephen slows the car to make the turn into the lane leading to his family's old summer house, he thinks, *We'll see who gets the last laugh now, Liza.*

He's chuckling to himself when he stops short, spotting a car coming toward him down the lane . . .

A police car.

Stephen's blood runs cold as he slows and pulls over to the side. What else can he do? There's no room on the narrow lane for the cars to pass each other, and anyway, it would seem suspicious for him to try to keep going.

Panic screams through his mind as the other car stops alongside him. The uniformed man behind the wheel is rolling down the window and leaning out, despite the nasty weather.

Stay calm, Stephen commands himself, pasting an artificial grin on his mouth and raising his right hand in greeting after rolling the window down with his left. *The wind will muffle any sounds coming from the trunk. And no one can possibly recognize you or the car.*

After all, he hasn't been to the island in years, and the last time was before he had the plastic surgery. And there's nothing flashy about the American-made black sedan he's driving. He left his own silver Mercedes and cherry-colored Porsche back in Manhattan. He won't need them where he's going after this.

"Hello there," the man in the cop car calls, waving back. "I'm Sherm Crandall, chief of police on the island."

Stephen nods, still grinning, and says over the roar of the wind, "Nice to meet you. My name's . . ." He hesitates for the merest second before uttering the first thing that pops into his head. "LaCroix. John LaCroix."

"Oh, yeah? I was half-expecting one of the Gilbrookes."

"You were?" Stephen wonders if the cop can tell that he's barely managing to keep himself together. Hopefully the blowing wet snow is obscuring his face somewhat. "Who are the Gilbrookes?"

"The family that owns this place."

Play dumb, and he won't get suspicious.

"What place?" he asks, making his eyebrows furl as though he's confused.

The officer gestures with his head at the house behind him, just out of sight, Stephen knows, around the bend.

"There's a big old mansion back here," Crandall tells him, his breath coming out in white puffs in the frigid wind. "Thought that was where you were headed."

"If I am, it's not on purpose." Does he sound too edgy? He shrugs, trying desperately to appear casual. "Just wanted to turn around . . . looks like I'm lost."

"You a tourist?"

"You bet."

"Where are you trying to go?"

"Back to the inn where I'm staying," Stephen says, thinking quickly.

"Which one is that?"

Is the cop just making conversation or is he suspicious? It's impossible to tell. It *feels* like an interrogation, but it might just be Stephen's own guilt.

"Where are you staying?" the cop asks again.

"The Bramble Rose," Stephen says quickly.

"Oh, yeah? How is that place?"

"Very nice. I like it."

"Good. I might have relatives coming to visit soon, and I thought they might like to stay there. The place is new, so I haven't heard much about it."

"Uh huh." Why won't the guy just move on? Stephen wonders, agitated. He realizes that he's jiggling his leg impatiently on the brake pedal and stops abruptly. He makes a big show of shivering, as though it's the cold that's making him antsy.

Sherm Crandall doesn't seem to have noticed. But he's not moving on, either.

"Say," he says, as though he's just thought of something, "you wouldn't have happened to run across a young girl named Cindy staying at the Bramble Rose this weekend, would you? No, wait—not Cindy. Sandy. Italian last name . . . Cavelli. That's it."

Fighting to maintain his composure, Stephen shakes his head and blandly responds, "Nope. Didn't see her."

"Huh." The cop rubs his chin thoughtfully, then shrugs. "Well, if you do, you let me know, okay? You can call me down at the police station."

"I sure will." He hesitates, wanting badly to ask, knowing he should just leave it be, but ultimately unable to stop himself. "What's up with this girl, Officer? Is she in some kind of trouble?"

Is it Stephen's imagination or is Sherm Crandall suddenly eyeing him more closely?

You shouldn't have asked, Stephen scolds himself. *Now look what you've done.*

"No, she's not in any trouble that I know of," the cop says. "I just want to talk to her, is all."

"Okay. Well, I'll let you know if I see her." Stephen gives a cheerful wave and shifts in his seat to let the cop know their conversation is over.

"You have a good day now," Sherm says with a wave and rolls up his window.

Stephen does the same, pulling the car ahead, then turning it around on the narrow road, because he knows the cop is probably watching him through his rear-view mirror as he drives away.

Stephen slowly drives away from the house, following the police car back out onto the highway. It turns left, toward town, and Stephen watches until it disappears around a bend in the road.

He waits a long time after that, parked at the edge of the lane, hoping the cop won't decide to get nosy again and turn around and come back to check on him.

Finally, after a good ten minutes, Stephen turns the car around once again and heads back toward the house.

And as he drives, he wonders if Liza Danning is unconscious in the trunk. He hasn't heard a sound from her in awhile, for which he *was* grateful. . . . But now he dearly wants her to be awake. He can't wait around for her to regain consciousness now that that cop is snooping around, asking questions about Sandy Cavelli.

No, he'll have to get Liza over with quickly, and then it will be Laura's turn.

Filled with regret that he won't have the luxury of savoring their reactions, making them suffer for a while before he kills them, Stephen sighs and pulls the black sedan around to the back of the house.

He drives into the ancient carriage house and parks beside the clunker of a Chevy that nosy kid had been driving.

By the time anyone finds it, Stephen will be long gone.

Thirteen

"I've got it!" Laura exclaims, backing out of her closet and waving the letter at Shawn, who's sitting on her bed.

"Where was it?"

"In this plastic milk crate where I toss things I need to put somewhere but I'm not sure where . . . never mind," she finishes hastily, not wanting to make herself come across as any more sloppy and disorganized than she already must seem to him.

He nods and asks, "So, where is this place?"

Laura sits back on her heels and skims the letter. "The Bramble Rose Inn—I've got to call there right away. The number's right here."

She starts for the kitchen with Shawn right behind her.

"You still feel that Jennie's in trouble?" he asks as she hurries toward the phone.

"More than ever. I know it sounds strange, but it's just this . . . this *twin* thing, I guess." She pauses to dial the inn's number, then adds to Shawn, "The last time I felt this way about my sister, she was in real trouble. It was—hello?" She interrupts herself as someone picks up the line on the first ring.

"Yes, may I help you?" It's a polite, male voice, and Laura can barely make it out because of static.

"I'd like to speak to my sister—she's staying at the inn. Her name is Jennie Towne."

There's a pause, and for a moment, Laura thinks the connection has been broken.

Then the voice slowly repeats, *"Jennie* Towne? Are you sure that's—"

"Oops, I'm sorry, wrong sister," Laura interrupts him quickly, chastising herself for being a total idiot. "Her name is *Laura.* Laura Towne."

"Oh, Laura . . . yes, she's . . . I don't believe she's—Oh, Miss Towne," he says suddenly, to someone on the other end. "I didn't realize you were right there. Someone wishes to speak to you. It's your sister."

Laura hears Jennie's voice murmuring something, then she's on the line saying a cautious "Hello?"

"J—Laura, it's me," Laura says, realizing that whoever answered might still be within earshot.

"Oh, hi," her sister says, sounding glad to hear from her. "How's it going?"

"Fine, here, but are you okay?"

Jennie hesitates just long enough to tell Laura two things—one, that the man who answered is hovering nearby and she doesn't want to say anything in front of him; and two, that she's not all right.

Laura's heart does an anxious flip-flop and she frowns as her sister's hollow voice says, "Sure, I'm great. This place is beautiful."

"Jen," Laura lowers her voice to a whisper, "you're not okay, are you?"

The line dissolves into static then, and Laura turns to Shawn. "I don't know what—hello?"

"Can you hear me?" Jennie's voice is saying as the static dissipates.

"Now I can. What's going on out there? Are you having bad weather?"

"Yes, there's a storm."

"Jennie, I'm worried about you. Are you okay? Tell me the truth."

"I . . . I'm not sure."

Laura glances at Shawn, who's watching her. He raises his brows, and she shakes her head.

"Listen, Jen," she says hastily, keeping her voice down, "something's up with that sweepstakes I entered. I talked to Keegan, and he said it's not—"

Suddenly, the line explodes into static again. Laura jerks the phone away from her ear at the loud noise, then puts it back and calls, "Jen? Jen?"

"What happened?" Shawn asks.

"I don't know. . . . I think the line went dead."

"I think the line went dead," Jennie tells Jasper, who's looking curiously at her.

"It's the storm." He glances toward the window.

Jennie knows he's right. She saw an enormous bolt of lightning moments before she lost contact with her sister.

But if Jasper hadn't been standing here the whole time she was talking to Laura, she would almost think he somehow . . .

No. It was the storm.

Despite that knowledge, Jennie is suddenly looking at the man through different eyes. Suddenly, he seems almost sinister.

If she hadn't happened to come downstairs just as the phone was ringing, would he have let her speak to Laura?

She'd heard him starting to tell her sister that she wasn't available—at least, that's what it had sounded like.

Was he just being lazy about tracking her down?

Or was there another reason?

"Are you all right?" he asks now, watching her carefully from where he's standing behind the desk.

"I'm fine." She hands him the receiver and he replaces it in the cradle.

What was Laura about to tell her? Something about the

sweepstakes . . . and Keegan? What does Keegan have to do with anything?

"Miss Towne?" Jasper says it loudly, as though he's repeating it.

She blinks. "Yes?"

"I asked if you'd like me to fix you something for lunch? I realize that with the weather so horrid, you won't be able to leave the inn."

You won't be able to leave the inn.

The words send a shudder through her.

"I'm . . . it's okay; I'm not hungry," Jennie tells him. "Thank you anyway."

"Are you sure? There's no telling how long this weather will last, and it's going to get worse before it gets better."

"I'm sure, thanks. I had just come downstairs to see if you had heard anything from Liza yet. I just knocked on her door again, and there's no reply."

"Oh?" He looks surprised . . . or does he? "That's strange. I haven't seen her all morning."

"Maybe she's having that meeting with D.M. Yates, the author she was supposed to meet," Jennie suggests, and waits for his reaction, just to see . . .

"Yates?" He shrugs. "As I told you earlier, I really have no idea where she is."

"Mmm. Well, if you do see her, will you have her come and find me?"

"Of course."

Jennie turns back toward the stairs, hoping he doesn't sense how nervous she is. She can feel his eyes on her as she walks back up toward the landing.

Sherm Crandall sits at his desk in the police station, still trying to get through his detective novel and nibbling on half a ham hero that's left over from yesterday afternoon.

It isn't very good, but he's so hungry he'll eat anything at this point. He'd stored the sandwich in the tiny dorm-sized refrigerator behind his desk, and the bread has, unfortunately, absorbed the strong food-smells from two weeks' worth of leftovers.

Sherm isn't exactly vigilant about getting rid of things, either here or at home. In fact, he wouldn't be surprised if the fridge at home still contains stuff from before Carly left.

He takes another bite of the sandwich and wrinkles his nose, then washes it down with a swing of Pepsi from the can on his desk.

The door opens just as he's swallowing, and he glances up expectantly, hoping to see Pat.

But it's Ned Hartigan who steps into the room and pulls the door closed behind him. His normally ruddy complexion is redder than ever from the biting wind and snow, and he shakes white flakes out of his whiter hair before saying, "Hi, Sherm."

"Hey there, Ned." He sets the sandwich down and stands, brushing the crumbs off his uniform pants. "What's going on?"

"Not much. Just wondering if we're going to evacuate. Pat Gerkin was by last night and told Shirley he'd let us know."

"So far, we're okay. I'm keeping a close eye on things, though."

"Well, I figured I'd better check in with you in person since the phones are down."

Sherm looks at him in surprise, echoing, "The phones are down?"

"Yep, went out a little while ago. Shirley was on with Myra Tallman when the line went dead on her."

"Great." Sherm reaches for the phone on his desk and picks it up. No dial tone. "I've been waiting for Pat to check in with me. . . . Maybe that's why I haven't heard from him. You haven't seen him today, have you?"

"Not since early last night, around supper time. Why?"

"I'm just a little worried, is all," Sherm tells Ned, rubbing his chin. "I sent him out to the old Gilbrooke place to make sure there was no one staying there, and he was supposed to come back here right afterward. Never showed, and I don't think he was home all night, either."

Ned's normally twinkly eyes look concerned. "You don't think something's happened to him?"

"Naw." Sherm tries to sound upbeat. "He's probably just over visiting one of his friends or something."

"Probably. So, you don't know if there was anyone out at the Gilbrooke place?"

"Didn't look that way. At least, no one answered my knock. I did see some footprints that were blown over by the time I got there. They were probably Pat's."

Ned nods.

"You know, I bumped into someone as I was pulling out of the lane onto Salt Marsh Road," Sherm goes on. "A tourist. The guy was lost, trying to find his way back to the Bramble Rose Inn. There was something familiar about him, but I'm pretty sure I never met him before. I never forget a name, and he said his was LaCroix."

"LaCroix?" Ned repeats thoughtfully. "Wasn't that the name of the woman that young Gilbrooke kid was supposed to marry a few years back?"

"Was it?"

"I'm pretty sure. The reason I remember is that we get the *New York Times* in on Sundays; and in the winter when business is slow, Shirley likes to read it. She always looks at the wedding announcements—you know, women like that kind of thing. Reads every darn word, and I can't understand why she cares. 'Shirley,' I tell her, 'why do you care? These people are strangers.' And she says, 'But they're so interesting.' And then one day, she runs across a familiar name—Gilbrooke. What a coincidence, huh? And I remember her saying something about the kid being engaged to someone named LaCroix."

Sherm is frowning. "Are you sure about that name?"

"I'm positive. Shirley commented on it, because she has a cousin who married a woman named LaCrosse right around the same time, and I remember her saying, 'Isn't that funny, Ned? LaCroix and LaCrosse—they're almost just the same.'"

"And you're sure it was the Gilbrooke kid who was marrying this woman?"

"Positive. That's what caught Shirley's eye. She dated poor old Andrew Gilbrooke back when he used to spend summers here on the island, you know. Told me the guy was so afraid of women that he could barely work up the nerve to kiss her. That was when I was serving overseas, you know? I'll tell you, it seems like only yesterday . . ."

Sherm nods, tuning Ned out and thinking back to his encounter with the man in the black sedan. There was something odd about him—something that's been bothering Sherm, though he hasn't been able to put his finger on it. It isn't just that the guy seems familiar. . . .

No, more than that, he seemed edgy. He didn't look Sherm in the eye when they spoke. And the way he'd given his name—it was almost as though he were making it up on the spot.

Abruptly, Sherm says, "If you'll excuse me, Ned, I have to go out and check on something."

He realizes, from the expression on Ned's face, that he must have interrupted him, and he quickly says, "Sorry. But something just occurred to me and I need to check it out."

"What's that, Sherm?"

"I just want to go over to the inn where that LaCroix fella was staying. We had a missing person's report about a young woman who's a guest there over the weekend, and he did seem a little nervous when I talked to him, now that I think of it."

"A missing person's report? Not that sweet young girl from Boston?"

"No, she's from Connecticut. You didn't meet her, did you? Name's Sandy Cavelli?"

"Tall, thin, blond hair?"

"No. The description her brother gave me says she's on the short side and overweight, with brown hair."

"Didn't see anyone who looks like that."

"Who's the tall, thin blonde? You say she's from Boston?"

"No, the one from Boston has dark hair, too, and the prettiest eyes you ever saw. Light purple, like Liz Taylor's."

Trying to mask his impatience, Sherm asks again, "So who's the blonde?"

"I don't know, but she's staying at the Bramble Rose, too. She was rude to Shirley when she came in for coffee, and she gave me hell because I don't carry black silk stockings. Wanted *real* stockings, the kind you wear with a garter belt. I said, 'What do you think this is, Filene's?' And she was real snippy with me. If you ask me, she—"

Sherm cuts him off because if you let Ned get started, he'll talk all day. "I really have to get on over to that inn now, Ned. But you tell Shirley I said hello, will you?"

"I sure will. Say, you haven't heard anything from Carly, have you?"

"Nope," he says shortly, grabbing his key ring from the desk and shoving it into his pocket.

"Too bad."

"Yep."

The trouble with living on an island as small as this one is that everyone knows everyone else's business. Which really helps when Sherm is conducting an investigation, but irks him when it comes to his own private life.

"Listen, Ned," he says, grabbing his storm coat and walking with the other man toward the door, "do me a favor. If you see Pat around anywhere, let me know."

"Will do."

"You opening the store today?"

"In this weather?" Ned shakes his head. "I'm going home and build a fire in the old woodstove. Put my feet up, listen to some Benny Goodman. If you want to swing by later, Shirley's making her chowder for Sunday dinner. I know it's probably been awhile since you had some good home-cooking."

"Yeah, it has," Sherm says, glancing down at the discarded sandwich and trying not to let the wistful note creep into his voice.

Carly used to make chowder on Sundays, too, creamy and rich, with succulent bits of shellfish and potato. Chowder or a big pot of beef stew or spaghetti sauce . . .

Together, he and Ned step out into the blustery world of swirling snow.

"See you, Sherm," Ned calls, lifting a hand. "You swing by later if you're hungry."

"Maybe I will," Sherm calls back, watching Ned with envy as he goes trudging off toward the cozy old captain's house he shares with Shirley.

Feeling lonelier than ever, he gets into his car to drive over to the Bramble Rose Inn.

Someone has glued Liza's eyelids shut.

At least, that's what it feels like. She can't seem to lift them.

Dazed, she wonders where she is, why her body feels battered and raw . . .

Then, as consciousness overtakes her again, she remembers, with a start, what happened.

She was in the back seat of the car . . .

And the driver was watching her in the mirror with that sinister smile . . .

And she'd thrown herself out onto the road.

That was the last thing she knew before now.

Please, God, let me be in the hospital, she prays fervently and, concentrating with all her might, forces her eyes to open.

For a moment, everything is blurry . . . and white.

Am I in heaven?

No, because there can't be pain in heaven, and I'm in agony.

She blinks and tries to focus again, but still, all she can see is filmy white.

Biting down on her inner lip to keep from crying out, she lifts her head slightly . . . and realizes that something is draped over her face. Some kind of white netting . . .

And she seems to be wearing white, too—a hospital gown?

No . . .

Numb with horror, Liza stares down at herself through the mask of illusion veiling that covers her eyes.

It's not a hospital gown; it's a wedding gown.

Someone has dressed her in a wedding gown!

Liza opens her mouth to scream, then clamps it shut again as a face appears, hovering a few feet above her.

"Hello, sleeping beauty," a masculine voice says, and chuckles. "I'm so glad you're back among the living . . . although, it's a pity it won't be a permanent stay."

It's the chauffeur from the car, Liza realizes, only he's changed his clothes, too. His face is rimmed by a white collar and a black bow tie. . . . Good Lord, is the man really wearing a tuxedo?

Nothing makes sense. It's like some grotesque dream—

Liza groans as she feels him lifting her shoulders, then forcing her to sit up. She squeezes her eyes closed for a moment to fight the anguish that wracks her body, then opens them to see that she's in a vast, empty room.

Empty, that is, of people, except for the nut case in the tux.

But there appear to be rows and rows of chairs . . .

And flowers everywhere, red roses . . .

And—oh, God—there's a white-satin runner stretching ahead in front of Liza.

"Get up," barks the chauffeur's voice from somewhere above. "We're already late getting started."

"Started with what?" she murmurs, feeling her body sway. It's so tempting to let herself sink back down to the floor again, to give in to the gauzy darkness that keeps trying to edge its way back to her.

"Started with what? The wedding, of course! What did you think?" His voice floats above her somewhere.

"Do you like the dress?" he goes on. "I had it made especially for you—remembered that you're a perfect size five. I should remember. . . . I bought you so many lovely clothes. Do you remember?"

She's vaguely aware of being lifted further. "Stand, damn it. Stand up. I can't just hang around here and hold you, you know."

It's as if some other part of Liza takes over, and her aching legs automatically lock into place so that she finds herself standing on her own.

Still, she can't grasp what's going on.

Suddenly, she hears the sound of music playing. It fills her ears, some old love song that seems faintly familiar . . .

What the hell is going on, here?

She turns her head and sees him beside her, his face only inches from hers.

"What are you doing? And—who *are* you?" she whispers, searching her memory for his face and coming up with a blank.

He looks pleased. "You don't recognize me, do you?"

"No, I . . ." Her voice trails off as she feels herself sway-ing, about to go down. But somehow, she manages to fight the impulse, wins another few moments—she hopes—of consciousness.

"It's me," he announces gleefully, his face twisted into a distorted grin. "Stephen!"

"Stephen?" she repeats fuzzily, trying to remember.

"Stephen Gilbrooke," he elaborates.

"Stephen Gilbrooke . . ."

He waits.

She searches her memory desperately.

Stephen Gilbrooke?

There have been so many men. No way she can remember all of them, the ones she used and then casually discarded like used Kleenex . . .

Oh, why hadn't she been more careful? Why hadn't she realized that it would catch up to her someday?

"Stephen Gilbrooke," he says again, this time more harshly. "You do remember me, Liza . . ."

She shakes her head faintly, still trying to recall the name, the face . . .

Suddenly, he's grabbing her shoulders roughly, shaking her so that her body screams in pain.

"Stephen Gilbrooke," he keeps repeating.

"I remember you," she blurts finally, trying desperately to remain alert, though she's fading fast.

"You do?"

"Of course . . ."

It's a lie. She has no idea who he is. She's never been good with names, and the face is totally unfamiliar. . . .

So many men, she thinks vaguely again. *Too many men. . . . Which one is he?*

"Who am I, then?"

A shred of panic rises in her weary, tormented body, a fearful response to something ominous in his sharp com-mand.

"You're . . . Stephen."

"Where did we meet?"

"New York," she guesses weakly, watching him through heavy-lidded eyes.

For a split-second, he seems appeased. Then his gaze narrows and he says, "Where?"

"Manhattan . . ."

"But *where*? Tell me, Liza. Right now. If you really know who I am, tell me where we met!"

"I—I don't know!" Her voice is a whimper.

He slaps her, hard, across the face, and she starts to crumple; but he's grabbing her, forcing her to keep standing.

"You don't know me! After everything I gave you, everything we did together, you don't know me?"

She can only shake her head mutely, too frightened to lie to him again.

The stranger's face is contorted by rage now, his grip on her shoulders a deadly vise from which she can't escape.

"You never cared for me at all, did you? You never loved me, after all I did for you. I gave you everything your heart desired, but you never loved me, Lorraine."

Lorraine? Who's Lorraine?

Oh, Christ, who is this lunatic? What is he going to do?

"I'm not Lorraine," she protests weakly as he releases his right hand from her shoulder.

For a moment, she believes he's going to let her go.

But then, paralyzed with terror, Liza watches as he reaches inside his coat, his movements slow and almost mechanical. His blue eyes are still focused on her veiled face, but they suddenly seem void of recognition.

"You don't want to marry me, do you?" he says in a faraway voice, and it isn't really a question.

"Yes," Liza says anyway, hoping desperately to divert him. "Yes, I want to marry you . . . Stephen."

"Why?" He's removing something from his jacket.

She sees that it's a butcher knife.

He looks at it intently, strokes the handle almost lovingly.

Trembling all over, she battles to keep the sob out of her voice as she answers, "Because I love you, Stephen. I've always loved you. I always will. Marry me, Stephen."

For a moment, he looks soothed by her words.

But when he raises his gaze to her again, he frowns and looks startled.

"No!" he barks abruptly, brandishing the knife. "You're not Lorraine, and you don't want to marry me. You don't even remember me, Liza."

"Yes I do," she cries plaintively. "I remember you, Stephen. And I love you. Please don't—"

Even though she sees the knife slashing through the air toward her, she's stunned to hear her own voice suddenly dissolve into a bloody gurgle as the unmercifully sharp blade slices into her throat.

"Don't lie to me," he shouts as he brings the knife up, then jabs it into her again, this time catching her across her wrist as she brings her hand up to shield her face. Blood spurts like a fountain as her vein is severed; and she falls, bewildered, to the floor.

As the frenzied stranger continues to stab her, Liza's mind screams *Why? Why? Why?* in a chilling refrain until black silence swoops over her like a shroud.

Fourteen

Jasper paces the tiny first-floor bedroom, wishing Stephen would hurry up and get back here so that he can tell him what happened.

He can't risk calling the emergency phone number again.

Not after what happened last time.

Not when Stephen is right in the middle of . . .

Well, taking care of Liza Danning.

And the blond bitch deserves everything she gets, Jasper tells himself, remembering how she had spoken to him, how she had looked at him as though he were a mere speck of dirt.

It was all he could do, the entire time Liza Danning was staying here, to treat her as a guest . . .

To keep from informing her that *he*, Arnold—no, Jasper Hammel—is the person Stephen Gilbrooke has chosen to spend the rest of his life with. *Not* Liza . . .

Or Sandy.

Or Laura.

Or Lorraine.

Frowning, Jasper runs his hands over his neatly trimmed hair and tells himself that everything will work out fine.

Despite the fact that the plan isn't going as smoothly as he and Stephen had expected.

He thinks again about the phone call for Laura Towne. He isn't sure what, exactly, her sister had started to tell her, but it doesn't matter, not really.

A bolt of lightning had miraculously intercepted the call.

And if that isn't a sign that everything will be all right, Jasper tells himself reassuringly, *I don't know what is.*

All he has to do now is keep an eye on Laura to make sure she doesn't get any ideas about leaving again . . .

And wait.

Wait for Stephen to come back to the inn.

Then wait for him to leave again, with Laura.

Then wait for him to come back a final time, for Jasper . . .

And then we'll sail away together, Jasper tells himself contentedly. *Just as Stephen promised—just the two of us, forever and ever.*

But somehow, his image of bliss is marred by an elusive, but nonetheless disconcerting sensation that keeps flitting through his mind . . .

The nebulous notion that maybe everything isn't as it should be.

That maybe things are about to go horribly irrevocably, wrong.

And when the doorbell rings suddenly and shrilly a moment later, the thought lands with a dull thud.

His fury spent once again, Stephen stoops down and slowly pulls the knife out of the heap of red-stained, white-covered flesh at his feet.

Liza Danning will never look at me again with that superior smile and smug green gaze of hers.

The knowledge should leave him with some degree of satisfaction, but Stephen feels oddly unsettled.

She didn't remember you, he thinks incredulously and gives the bloodied corpse a frustrated kick with the toe of his black wing-tip shoe.

How could she have forgotten?

Had he meant that little to her?

Of course he had. He had known all along that she'd never cared about him, only about his money and the things that it could buy for her.

But never had he imagined that she would forget he had ever existed. That to her, he wasn't even worthy of a tiny, distant corner of her memory. He had been invisible to her even when they were together; and after their affair had ended, she had simply wiped her mind clean of any remnants of Stephen Gilbrooke.

"Bitch," he mutters, and kicks her again, noticing the pool of blood that's seeping at his feet.

He ought to get Jasper over here and make him clean up the mess, he thinks, distastefully eyeing the gore he's created. After all, he might as well put the simpering pain in the ass to some good use, instead of letting him sit back at the inn, twiddling his thumbs.

But no, that would be impossible. There isn't time. Not when there's a chance that that dolt of a police officer might get suspicious and come back snooping around here.

Stephen would rather not have to raise the body count even higher. It would be so . . . messy.

And besides, when he's made a plan, he likes to stick to it.

It's bad enough that he can't wait until tomorrow to take care of Laura Towne, as he had originally intended.

Oh, well.

Reaching into his pocket again, he thoughtfully takes out the blank rectangular place card and black-handled pen he'd brought along with him. He crouches beside Liza's lifeless body and dips the tip carefully into the thick pool of blood, then begins to letter her name in swirling calligraphy.

He's almost free . . . almost to the point where he can banish, forever, the demons that have been tormenting him for so long.

Just a few more things to take care of, and he'll be home free . . .

Sailing off into the proverbial sunset toward a glorious future . . . alone.

Sherm rings the doorbell again, thinking that it seems strange that the door of an inn would be locked, when suddenly, a face appears in the glass, startling him.

Even through the ice-encrusted window, he recognizes the man, having seen him around the island lately. Must be Jasper Hammel, he thinks as the door swings open.

Sherm doffs his hat and pastes an affable smile on his face. "Good afternoon," he says pleasantly above the roar of the wind. "You the fellow who runs the place?"

"I'm Jasper Hammel, yes," the man says, offering his hand, but making no move to gesture him inside.

"Sherm Crandall—I'm chief of police here on the island. We spoke earlier." Sherm grasps the man's fingers in a firm handshake and notes that they're clammy.

Well, it's a raw, chilly day. That could be all it is.

On the other hand . . .

"Just thought I'd drop by," Sherm goes on, stepping past the innkeeper into the foyer of the inn, "to check things out."

He turns and glimpses a startled expression in Hammel's eyes; but it vanishes quickly, and the man seems composed as he smiles and says, "Of course. Please come in."

"I'm already in," Sherm notes.

"Yes, you are, aren't you?" Hammel closes the door, shutting out the blasting storm, and turns to Sherm expectantly.

"Nice," he comments, looking around the foyer, his sharp eyes taking in the fussy antique furniture and globed lamps. On the check-in desk is a basket of magazines, a telephone, a tall vase filled with dried flowers, and a bowl of pink shredded things that look and smell like potpourri. Carly always loved that stuff.

"Is there anything in particular that I can help you with?" Hammel asks in a clipped tone, watching Sherm cautiously sniff the cinnamony contents of the bowl. "As I said earlier, I'm afraid I've told you everything I know about that woman . . . Sandy, isn't it?"

"Yep, it is." Sherm wonders if it's his imagination or if Hammel seems edgy as he moves across the small room and takes up a post behind the desk.

"I wish I could tell you something more . . ."

"That's all right. I'm actually not here on business," Sherm lies. "Thought I'd check the place out, see what it's like. I've got some relatives coming to the island soon, and I need to find someplace for them to stay."

"Oh, we'd love to have them."

Is that relief spreading over the man's face above his neatly trimmed mustache, or merely a cordial response to a business deal?

"Are you pretty booked for the upcoming months?" Sherm asks.

"Oh, no, we have plenty of availability."

"How about this weekend?"

"This weekend? I thought they weren't coming until—"

"No, I mean how booked are you this weekend?"

"Why do you ask?" This time, there's no mistaking the look in Hammel's eyes. He's definitely on guard.

"Just curious," Sherm says casually, yet focusing intently on the man's face. "How many guests do you have staying here?"

"This weekend? Well, I don't know off the top of my head . . ."

Sherm raises an eyebrow.

The place isn't *that* enormous. He doesn't say it, but the pointed look on his face gets the message across to Hammel, who smiles nervously back.

"I guess . . . Let's see, there's Sandy Cavelli, but she left, as you know. And . . . oh, yes, there's Miss Laura Towne . . ."

The Boston brunette with the Liz Taylor eyes, Sherm wonders, or the blond bitch?

"And," Jasper finishes, "that's about it."

"That's it?" Sherm keeps his expression carefully neutral, though his mind is racing.

That can't be it.

Even if Ned Hartigan was mistaken about the blonde staying here, what about that LaCroix fellow Sherm had spoken to out at the old Gilbrooke place?

Jasper Hammel is thrumming his fingertips on the desktop.

Somebody's lying, Sherm thinks, *but who?*

Judging by the innkeeper's actions, he's hiding something. *But why?*

Sandy Cavelli's disappearance is looking more suspicious by the second.

"Officer . . ." Hammel says after another moment of silence.

"Oh, sorry—I wonder if I could look at a few of the rooms? Just to see if it's what I have in mind for my sister. She's pretty fussy. You know women," he throws in, adopting a good-old-boy attitude.

Hammel does his best to rise to it, nodding and agreeing, "Certainly. I know women."

I'll just bet you do.

"So how about it?"

"The rooms?"

Sherm nods, thinking that the guy can't possibly worm out of this one. He just finished saying that there are only two guests at the inn this weekend, and one of them has already checked out.

"I . . . of course. I'd be happy to show you," the man says abruptly, as though he's just reached a decision. "Just let me find the keys . . ."

"No problem."

Just as Hammel starts digging through a drawer, there's a distinct creaking noise above. Footsteps.

Sherm turns to look toward the stairs, wondering if the woman from Boston is about to make an appearance.

He'd like to ask her—

The thought is cut short by a swift and sudden blow to the back of his head.

Stunned, Sherm sinks to his knees and looks up to see a blurry image of Jasper Hammel holding the heavy crystal vase of dried flowers.

As the police chief opens his mouth weakly in futile protest, Hammel brings it down again, obliterating Sherm's senses with the brutal impact.

Jennie pauses with her hand on the doorknob, frowning.

She just heard a thud from the foyer downstairs, as though something heavy has toppled onto the floor.

She stays absolutely still, listening for the voices to resume their conversation, but there's only silence.

Oh, God . . . something happened to the police officer. What did Hammel do to him?

She had been napping on her bed when she'd awakened to hear muffled voices floating up from below. She couldn't hear what they were saying. Though one voice was a deep, unfamiliar rumble, she easily recognized that the other belonged to Jasper Hammel.

After trying to make out the conversation, she had gotten up and looked out the window that faced the front of the inn. A police car was parked there.

Jennie had been both elated and frightened.

If the cops were here, did it mean Jasper really was up to something? And if so, had something terrible happened to Sandy and Liza?

She was about to go downstairs and see what was going on when the thud had stopped her cold.

Now, she wonders, with a sinking feeling, what's going on down there. She hears a faint groan—Jasper again—and then the sound of something being dragged across the floor toward the back of the house.

He's killed the cop, and now he's taking the body away.

What should I do?

Run for it?

Jennie considers that option, and discards it.

The inn is virtually in the middle of nowhere, and there's a storm raging outside. Even if Hammel didn't hear her leaving, where would she go?

She could take the chance that she'd find someone in one of the few houses between here and the boardwalk, but what would she tell them?

She has no proof of anything. She's not even sure what's going on here. If she goes running to a total stranger and starts raving about something strange happening at the inn and there turns out to be nothing wrong, it'll mean she really is crazy.

She'll have to start seeing Dr. Bonner again, with his unforgiving dark gaze, and he'll make her talk about Harry and relive the terror of what happened to him again and again and again . . .

And she can't do that.

You're not crazy, she tells herself fiercely. *You didn't hear anything downstairs. And nothing strange is happening here.*

But then where are Sandy and Liza?

And what was Laura trying to tell you when she called? And what about Harry, in the dream?

Stop it! Everything is fine. It's just your imagination again, and you have to stop letting it take over. You have to prove you're not crazy!

You're not crazy!

Shaken, Jennie slowly removes her hand from the door-knob and returns to her bed.

She curls up into a ball on her side, hugging her knees against her chest. She closes her eyes tightly and rocks back and forth, trying desperately to shut out the memories that are trying to force their way into her consciousness.

"There it is!" Danny shouts, pointing off to the port side of the boat.

"What?" Keegan shouts back over the roaring wind and water, his hands wrestling with the wheel.

"I just saw a speck of land over there. . . . It has to be the island!" Clenching his teeth to keep them from chattering, Danny squints against the driving mist of seawater and snow, trying to find it again.

But the boat is rocking violently on the enormous waves; and every time he thinks he might just be able to see it, they tilt crazily away in the opposite direction.

He glances back to make sure Cheryl's okay. She's still sitting on the bench behind him, clinging to the rail and looking frightfully pale with fear and nausea. She's already thrown up twice, miserably choking and gagging as Danny held her head and tried to keep her steady despite the wildly pitching boat.

"We're almost there, babe," he calls to her now, and she looks up and offers a weak, trembling smile.

At least, I hope we're almost there, Danny thinks, grab-bing the rail and pulling himself cautiously forward along the deck until he reaches Keegan's side.

"What do you think?" the man asks, turning to Danny. He, like Danny and Cheryl, is drenched and shivering vio-lently.

"I saw it. . . . I'm almost positive. Out there." He points to the left.

"That's where it should be," Keegan hollers back. "And

I'm trying to steer toward it, but it's impossible to fight this wind. We might be way off course."

Danny's stomach turns over. "You mean we could be lost on the open sea?"

"What?" Keegan yells, shaking his head to indicate that he can't hear.

Danny doesn't repeat it. He doesn't want to risk letting Cheryl hear that. She'll be terrified.

Grimly, he wipes at his eyes, which are stinging from the salt spray and grainy snow, and peels them on the distant horizon again.

Nothing.

Oh, Jesus . . . we're going to die trying to reach you, Sandy.

The thought of his sister in trouble eats away at him, and he tries to put it out of his mind. Tries not to think of how upset and scared she had sounded when she called him.

Tries not to wonder where she is now . . .

Whether she's all right.

The deck lurches suddenly as they ride over an enormous breaker, and Danny grips the rail with all his might.

He turns again to make sure Cheryl is all right, and for a moment, panic seizes him when he can't find her.

But no, there she is, crumpled on the floor of the boat as a gush of water pours over the tilting rail directly onto her face.

Danny bellows, "Babe, are you all right?"

She doesn't reply.

"Babe?"

"Is she all right?" Keegan shouts.

"I don't know . . ." Petrified, Danny makes his way along the rail and crouches at Cheryl's side.

She opens her eyes, looking dazed, as soon as he cups her face in his icy hands.

"Cheryl?"

"That wave knocked me off the bench. . . . I guess I hit

my head and passed out for a second . . ." She draws her brows together in a confused furrow.

Danny pulls her into his arms, cradling her. "This is insane. . . . We've got to go back. . . . I can't put you through this . . ."

He turns toward Keegan and raises his voice. "Hey, McCullough! McCullough, we've got to go back!"

"There it is!" Keegan hollers simultaneously, pointing off to the horizon on the port side. "I see the island! It's right there! We made it!"

Jasper can't seem to stop shaking.

What have you done? he asks himself over and over as he stares at the unconscious Sherm Crandall, whom he's managed to drag into the small storage room off the kitchen.

You need to kill him, Jasper thinks, *before he comes to.*

He fingers the meat cleaver he'd taken from a drawer in the kitchen and imagines plunging it into the man's soft belly.

What would it feel like? Would there be sinewy resistance or would the tip of the blade sink into flesh like a sharpened stick into a marshmallow? Would blood spurt out or would it ooze slowly from the wound?

Jasper doesn't want to know.

It was difficult enough to hit the police officer over the head with the lead-crystal vase. He'd done it impulsively when the man turned his back, realizing he'd heard Laura Towne's footsteps. In another few moments, Jasper had thought desperately, Crandall would be questioning her. She would tell him about Liza, and he'd find out that Jasper had lied.

And he'd done such a clumsy job of it, too, he thinks, wincing at the memory of his lame cover-up.

Stephen would be furious if he knew.

But you couldn't help it! The damn cop caught you off

guard! He made you flustered, made you so nervous you couldn't think straight!

Jasper shakes his head, thinking none of that would make a difference to Stephen. He never gets nervous under pressure. Even when he'd snapped and bludgeoned his own mother to death, he hadn't seemed all that flustered.

Jasper still recalls the matter-of-fact way in which Stephen had revealed what he'd done—"I killed Mother."

As if he were informing Jasper of something as mundane as "I had tuna for lunch."

Back then, and again with Lorraine, Jasper had come through for Stephen, helping him to hide the evidence of his gory crime.

He's counting on you again, Jasper reminds himself. *And you've let him down.*

No, you haven't. Not yet. Everything is still under control. No one knows what happened.

He'd been half-expecting Laura Towne to come bounding down the stairs after Crandall hit the floor, but there had been only silence from above.

Maybe that isn't such a good sign, Jasper thinks reluctantly.

He can't risk making her suspicious. She's the only thing standing between Jasper and his future with Stephen. If she somehow figures out that she's in danger, if she somehow escapes, he's in big trouble.

No, he has to make sure she's here and unaware when Stephen comes back for her.

And he has to get rid of Crandall, too.

Again, he fingers the handle of the cleaver in his hand. It would be so easy . . .

All he has to do is lower the blade until it sinks into Crandall's heart.

Jasper swallows hard and closes his eyes for a moment. *I'm not capable of murder.*

That fact makes itself known as suddenly and as plainly

as another, long-ago revelation had—when he had realized, with sudden clarity, that he was a homosexual.

He acknowledges this new self-discovery with the same, frank acceptance as he had the old. He can't change it, can't force himself to be something other than what he is.

No, he's not going to kill Sherm Crandall.

If Stephen wants to do that when he returns, he can.

For now, Jasper will simply lock the door to the storage room and then do something about the police car parked in front of the inn. Thanks to the storm, there's not much chance that anyone would be out and about and have noticed the car there, but he can't let it stay indefinitely.

Gingerly, he bends and rolls Sherm Crandall over, retrieving a key ring from his coat pocket.

"First, I'll move the car," he says softly to the unconscious man, "and then, I'll take care of Miss Towne."

"Well?" Shawn asks expectantly as Laura comes back into the living room, where he's sprawled on the couch.

"No luck," she says, shaking her head. "The phones are still out of service there. I keep getting a recording."

"Did you try the police station again?"

"On Tide Island? Yes. Same recording." She plops heavily into a chair and looks at the gray, blustery world outside the window.

"She's probably fine, Laura."

"Probably," she agrees hollowly.

"After all, you were just going on a hunch when you decided something was wrong."

"What about the bogus sweepstakes?" she points out. "And Keegan? He was obviously worried when he kept calling me and leaving messages."

"Did you try him again?"

"No answer. I don't know where he could be. I tried the precinct, too, and they said he called in sick this morning.

I know he's not sick because I saw him yesterday. And Keegan's not the type who would play hooky without a good reason."

"Well, there's nothing you can do but wait, Laura."

"I know." She looks at him bleakly. "And maybe everything really is fine. But I keep thinking about . . ."

"What?" Shawn prods her.

"It's Brian. My ex. He's a nut case, Shawn. *I* was the one who was supposed to be out there this weekend, not Jennie. What if Brian—" She cuts herself off abruptly, shaking her head.

"Did you try calling him?"

"I have no idea where he's even living now. And his parents moved to Florida months ago, and I have no idea where."

"How about finding him through one of his friends?"

"Those creeps?" She makes a face. "They'd never tell me where he is. They all think I'm a cold bitch. That's what he told them. And you know what? I *can* be a cold bitch, when someone treats me the way Brian did."

She stares off into space, remembering her ex-husband's cruel mind games and violent temper. She can still feel the sting of his hand smacking her face, the agonizing pain of his cigarette butt searing into her skin.

"Do you honestly think Brian is up to something?" Shawn asks her, and she shrugs.

"I don't know. There *was* something familiar about the man who sold me the ticket. . . . I told you that. But I can't seem to place him. Every time I feel like I'm about to remember who he is, it flits right out of my mind. It's driving me crazy, Shawn."

"Well, do you think he has something to do with Brian?"

"No." She frowns. "That's the strange part. I don't think he does. But for the life of me, I can't figure out who else it can be."

"Was there anyone else you dated . . . or knew . . . who might have something against you?"

Laura hesitates, not wanting to get into her past with Shawn. He's the first normal guy who's come along—she doesn't want to scare him away by telling him anything that might make her seem promiscuous . . . or hard up.

Then again, it's helping to think aloud and she has to do whatever she can to jog her memory. For Jennie's sake.

"Let me see," she says slowly, looking off into space. "I went out with this real asshole for a while after I dropped out of college. But he's definitely not the one who sold me the ticket."

"How do you know?"

"The guy I dated was Hispanic. The one who sold me the ticket was definitely white, and he had these bright blue eyes—you know, the kind you wouldn't forget. Like yours."

"Mine are contacts."

"I know, but . . ."

"Maybe his are, too."

"Maybe, but even so, I'd recognize the face. And it wasn't Orlando."

"Okay, so who else did you know who was a real jerk?"

"There *was* someone," she goes on thoughtfully, remembering, "about a year ago. A real S.O.B., it turned out, but he seemed totally normal—had a lot of money. I met him when I was working at the Four Seasons last spring to make extra cash to pay off my Visa bill . . ." She catches herself before she spills the rest of it—that the Visa account had been delinquent and a collection agency had come after her. No reason to tell him *that*.

"And . . ." he prompts.

She shrugs. "He was in Boston on business for the month, staying at the hotel. We went out a few times. He wined and dined me. Then he turned into a creep."

"What happened?"

She hesitates, not wanting to tell him that, either. How

the guy had been pissed off because she wouldn't sleep with him one night. She just wasn't in the mood.

But things had gotten ugly. Who would have guessed that such a supposedly mild-mannered businessman would have a nasty temper? Well, with everything you heard about date-rape these days, maybe she should have been more careful.

But she had been truly shocked when he had turned into a ranting lunatic, ripping off her clothes and forcing her to have sex with him.

And not just the regular way.

No, he'd gotten out the handcuffs, the leather S&M gear, the vibrator—all the little toys she'd introduced him to, which he kept stashed in the drawer next to his bed in his hotel suite.

Suddenly, that awful night, the props that Laura had used as innocent, pleasure-enhancing gadgets were transformed into terrifying instruments of torture. She still remembers how helpless she had felt when he'd cuffed her to the bed and had his way with her body, poking and prodding her endlessly, laughing when she sobbed and begged him to stop.

If the guest in the next room hadn't called the management to complain about the noise, who knew what would have happened?

"Laura . . ." Shawn asks, still waiting.

What would he say if he knew what she had done? Would he feel that she had gotten what she'd deserved?

Of course he'd think that. Laura thought it herself. How many times, since that dreadful night, had she chastised herself for being habitually promiscuous? She was lucky she hadn't run into trouble before the Four Seasons guy and that she'd gotten away from him relatively unharmed.

The experience had made her vow never to sleep with a virtual stranger again, never to use toys or play kinky sex games again.

She'd kept that promise, too. Oh, she and Shawn *were*

sleeping together and she still had a healthy appetite for lovemaking. But when she'd met him, she'd played hard to get for the first time in her life. She hadn't slept with him until their fourth date. And he'd been pleasantly surprised, he told her, to discover that she wasn't a prude after all. She'd gotten a private kick out of *that*—imagine, someone thinking *she* might be a prude!

"What about this guy?" Shawn asks again.

Laura snaps out of her reverie. "Oh, right. Well, he was a major creep. But he definitely wasn't the guy who sold me the ticket that day in the parking lot."

"Are you sure?"

"Positive. And anyway, he comes from big bucks, like I said. His family's pretty famous."

"For what?"

She shrugs. "Just being rich, I guess. The other clerk at the hotel recognized his name right away the first time he checked in."

"Really? What is it?"

Laura frowns, trying to remember.

Then she nods and says, "Oh, yeah, that's right. It was Gilbrooke. Stephen Gilbrooke."

Jennie is still huddled on her bed in a fetal position when the noise of the storm ebbs momentarily and she hears footsteps approaching her door.

Her entire body grows tense as she listens and waits.

It has to be Jasper Hammel.

A short time ago, she had heard the front door slam, and then a car engine starting up.

By the time she had reached the window to see what was going on, the police car that had been parked out front was no longer there.

Either the cop had left . . .

Or Hammel had moved the car.

Jennie wanted desperately to believe the latter was just another example of her imagination carrying her away. But minutes after the car had vanished, she had heard the front door open and close again.

Which meant Hammel could have parked the car someplace nearby, but out of the way, and now he was back.

In the half hour or so that had passed since then, all had been still downstairs.

Not that Jennie could have heard much of anything, anyway. The storm had grown steadily more powerful, and now the wind was fairly screeching around the house and the wild sea was leaping at the rocky coast like a rabid dog straining on its leash.

Now she waits, wondering if she really did just hear footsteps or if it were—

No, there they are again.

Frightened, Jennie turns to look expectantly at the door, as though any moment, Jasper Hammel is going to splinter it and burst into her room, a raving madman.

The thought should seem ludicrous, but it isn't. Not entirely.

There's a knock at the door, a brief, staccato rapping that causes Jennie to shrink back into the pillows in wide-eyed fear.

"Miss Towne?"

It's Jasper Hammel, all right. But he sounds like his usual self—formal and pleasant.

Still, Jennie can't seem to find her voice.

"Miss Towne?" he calls again with another knock. "Are you in there?"

"Yes," she finally manages, realizing that he would have the key so there's no point in trying to hide.

"Oh, good. There's a call for you."

For a moment, she's too startled to reply.

"Do you want to take it?" Hammel asks through the door.

"I . . . I thought the phones were knocked out," she says thinly.

"They were, but they've made repairs."

She doesn't say anything, wondering whether to believe him.

"In fact," Hammel goes on, "when one of the island police officers stopped by awhile ago to see that we were all right, he promised me that the local phone company was working on the lines. And a short time later . . . *voilà!* The phone rang."

She ponders that, still hugging her knees tightly to her chest. She didn't hear the phone ringing. But then, the noise of the storm would probably have drowned it out anyway.

"Who is it?" she asks Hammel after another moment's hesitation. "On the phone for me, I mean."

"It's your sister. She says it's important or I wouldn't have disturbed you."

It's Laura again.

Jennie debates only another split-second before getting off the bed and going over to the door.

"I'll take it," she says, opening it.

Too late, she realizes that she's made a big mistake.

Jasper Hammel instantly reaches out, grabs her, and clamps a damp handkerchief that reeks of something acrid over her mouth and nose.

"Breathe deeply now, Laura," he says in his proper, clipped way. "That's the girl. You're going to take a nice nap, and when you wake up—"

The rest of his words are lost on her as she collapses in his arms.

Fifteen

The big black sedan skids on the icy gravel drive as Stephen pulls around to the back of the inn. He steers into the skid, regains control, and parks beside the gardening shed, thinking that if it keeps snowing like this, he won't be able to get back out to the house. And what about leaving the island on the boat? It's going to be terribly treacherous in this weather.

He sits with his hand poised on the door handle, wondering whether he should go back to the original plan and wait until tomorrow to deal with Laura Towne.

If he does, there's a greater risk of being caught—especially if that cop he met earlier actually is suspicious.

But if he goes ahead and takes care of everything today and leaves by nightfall, what about the nor'easter? He's an accomplished yachtsman, thanks to all those years at prep school; but skill, he knows, can become moot when Mother Nature is venting her fury.

No, he probably shouldn't chance it. The thought of drowning in the Atlantic isn't exactly a pleasant one. And besides, if the cop comes snooping around again, he can be easily taken care of . . . just like the red-haired kid.

Stephen makes up his mind to wait. He'll stay here, in his attic room, for the night, he decides, and then he'll be able to sneak down and sneak a peek at Laura once she's safely asleep later.

Just the way he did with Sandy. And Liza.

It's like a tantalizing little appetizer before the main course, he thinks, his lips curving into a smile as he thinks of those stolen moments in the wee hours of the morning, when he'd fondled the unsuspecting women as they slept.

And Laura . . .

Well, when he had dated her last year, she had been a regular tigress. Stephen writhes slightly on the leather car seat just thinking about the things she had done to him in that suite at the Four Seasons.

He's in for a real treat once again, he thinks, feeling slightly breathless.

In fact, too bad he can't keep her around—let her come with him when he leaves the island.

But then he remembers how she had turned on him, just as the others had.

He thinks back to that night in the hotel suite, when she had tried to resist his advances. At first, he'd thought she secretly wanted him—that her cold fish routine was just an act, to tease him, get him all worked up. He'd gone along with it, forcing her—cuffing her to the bed, using those devices of hers, working himself into a frenzy.

Then she'd started crying and calling for help, and the hotel management had come knocking on the door, wanting to know if everything was all right. What a mess. He'd played the role of a sheepish guest, apologizing to the night manager if he and his "girlfriend" had gotten a little out of hand.

When he'd closed the door and gone back over to the bed, Laura had looked at him darkly through her mascara-smudged lilac-colored eyes and ordered him to unlock the handcuffs. "If you don't," she'd threatened, "I'll scream so loudly that the management will be back here in two seconds flat."

For a wild moment, he'd considered killing her right then and there, as he had Lorraine. But then he realized that there had already been a complaint, that the manager knew who he was, and that he would never get away with it.

So he'd let her go.

The next afternoon, he'd come back from his meeting to find her working at the desk, dressed in her deceptively prim, high-collared, navy-plaid dress with her hair coiled at the back of her neck in a schoolmarm's bun.

He'd gone over to her and whispered suggestively that if she came upstairs to his suite when her shift ended, he'd pretend to be a naughty schoolboy and let her spank him.

"You pig," she'd said in a low voice that barely contained her palpable wrath. "If you don't get out of here right this second and leave me alone, I'll go to the police and tell them what you did to me last night."

Shocked, he'd protested, "What did I do?"

"You raped me."

"I did not! You wanted it. You loved it. You know you did."

"You actually think I *wanted* to sleep with an ugly son of a bitch like you? What are you, nuts? I never wanted you, not from the start. The only way I could get off with you was to use those toys . . . and close my eyes and pretend you were someone else. Someone who looked *human*."

Stung, Stephen had simply closed his mouth and walked away. By the next day, when he had decided he had to do to her what he had done to Lorraine, it was too late. The girl behind the desk told him that Laura had quit abruptly after her shift ended the day before. And no, she wasn't at liberty to give out Laura's home address or number.

At first, he had planned to track her down immediately and make her pay for what she had said.

Then he had thought again of Lorraine . . .

Of how incredibly satisfying it had been to see her vivid red blood spill over the white-silk wedding gown.

And he had thought of Liza Danning . . .

And Sandy Cavelli . . .

And how they, too, had hurt him.

That was when he came up with the plan.

It had taken awhile to put it into motion.

First, he'd had to arrange a leave of absence from his father's company. He'd been running it—and better than meek Andrew ever had—ever since his father had gone off the deep end. When Stephen had made arrangements for a year off, he'd explained that he was simply burnt out from all the international travel the business required. No one questioned him—or suspected that he had no intention of ever coming back.

Then there had been the plastic surgery, which he'd always intended to do. He'd gone to Europe, where he had plenty of connections—and where privacy was ensured. And now, thanks to one of the world's most prominent surgeons, he bore no resemblance to the "Elephant Guy" who had been taunted all through school, scorned even by his own parents.

Finally, of course, he'd had to buy the inn and get it ready. He'd chosen Tide Island because his mother had always complained about how remote and sparsely populated it was. She'd said repeatedly over the years that she didn't know why Andrew insisted on keeping that Victorian albatross, which was so far off the beaten path that it made the rest of the island seem positively urban.

What better place, Stephen had decided, to carry out his plan?

And now, his long hours of meticulous preparation have paid off.

Sandy Cavelli is dead.

Liza Danning is dead.

Only Laura Towne remains.

The pain she caused him is the freshest. Torturing her will be sweeter, even, than it had been to torture Sandy and Liza.

He imagines Laura in the white wedding gown he'd bought for her.

It's more daring than the others were. Sexier. It has a plunging neckline and skin-tight skirt. When he'd bought it, he'd pictured her in that daring lingerie she was always wearing.

Now, he frowns slightly, thinking of the plain white-cotton underwear he'd found in her suitcase yesterday. It isn't at all like her to be so modest and . . . boring. Obviously her tastes have changed over the past year.

Oh, well.

Stephen opens the car door and steps out into the storm, hurrying across the frozen drive to the back door of the inn.

He's no sooner closed it behind him and shaken the snow out of his hair than Jasper is standing in front of him, looking agitated.

"I've been waiting for you, Stephen . . ."

Irritated, he rolls his eyes. "Why?"

"I . . . here, come in and I'll show you."

Stephen steps into the kitchen, then follows Jasper through the dining room and into the parlor, saying, "I hope this doesn't take long. I have to change out of this tuxedo. It's covered with—"

He stops short when he sees her.

Laura Towne.

She's lying flat on her back on the old rose-colored sofa beneath the window, her hands folded over her stomach. She appears to be sleeping peacefully.

Stephen looks at Jasper, who blurts, "I had to do it, Stephen! She tried to get away."

"What the hell did you do?" he asks hoarsely. "You didn't—"

"No, I only knocked her out with chloroform. She'll come to in a little while," Jasper says nervously. "And that's not the only thing . . ."

Stephen scowls, bracing himself.

"An Officer Crandall came here, wanting to know about the inn, asking all kinds of questions . . ."

That nosy cop I met on the road. I should have guessed.

"You didn't tell him anything, did you?" Stephen asks Jasper. "You didn't—"

"Of course not. But you'd be proud of me, Stephen. I knocked him out with that vase from the desk, and then I locked him into the storage room off the kitchen. And his car is parked out back, near the dunes. I left the keys in it so that—"

"I want you to finish him off," Stephen interrupts tersely, jabbing a finger at Jasper, "and then I want you to meet me out at the summer house."

The little twerp gulps visibly. "But how will I get there?"

"Take my car," Stephen says, tossing him the keys to the sedan.

Jasper misses, of course, and they go clattering onto the carpet.

"But then how will you get—"

"I'll take the cop car, you idiot," Stephen bites out in disgust. "What else can I do? Who knows how long it'll be before someone else comes snooping around here?"

"But I took care of the cop, and—"

"And now he's missing, too. Who knows how many people he told about Sandy Cavelli? He was looking for her. I bumped into him on the road earlier. He seemed suspicious. But never mind, it doesn't matter now. Just take care of him. Can I trust you to do it, or are you going to screw up on this, too?"

"I'll do it," Jasper says firmly, raising his chin. "You know I'd do anything for you, Stephen."

He lays a tentative hand on Stephen's arm, and he fights the urge to recoil. He can't risk putting Hammel off now. He still needs him.

He forces himself to soften his gaze as he looks at Jasper,

to say soothingly, "I know you'll do anything for me. And I appreciate it."

"You do?"

"Of course I do."

Jasper smiles happily. "Thank God. I was a little worried that you might not want me to come with you, the way you promised. I thought maybe you'd change your mind . . ."

"Why would I do that?"

Jasper hesitates, then says, "You wouldn't. I know you wouldn't. You promised. It's going to be you and me forever, just like you said."

Though his words are decisive, there's a note of uncertainty in his voice, and Stephen wonders if little old Arnie is more perceptive than he gives him credit for being.

"Sure. You and me forever, Arnie," he says to reassure him.

The man's mouth quivers beneath his mustache. "You haven't called me that in years."

"And I didn't mean to now. It was a slip of the tongue. You're Jasper. . . . Don't forget that."

"I won't."

"Good."

"I love you, Stephen."

"I love you, too."

Stephen sighs inwardly. There are times when he thinks he's lucky to have this eager-to-please flunky on his side. But other times, he worries that he's making a big mistake trusting someone who's one sandwich short of a picnic.

Still, it won't matter after a few more hours, he reminds himself.

Like Laura Towne, Jasper Hammel—a.k.a. Arnold Wentworth—will be history.

Keegan looks back over his shoulder at the boat that bobs furiously in the water where he docked it.

"You think it's going to hold?" Danny asks him.

"I don't know. The rope's pretty strong, but with this storm . . ." Keegan trails off and shakes his head.

"Should we go back and see if we can make it sturdier?" Cheryl asks, clinging to her husband's arm and ducking her head against the driving wind and snow.

"We can't worry about it now," Keegan replies, looking toward the cluster of weathered buildings near the boardwalk straight ahead. "We've got to find out about your sister, and my—and Jennie."

Walking as swiftly as they can despite the powerful wind and icy pavement, they make their way toward the nearest building.

"It's the police station!" Danny calls as they draw closer to it, pointing to a sign above the door.

"Yeah, but it looks deserted," Keegan points out, shaking his head.

"The windows are probably just boarded up because of the storm," Danny argues.

"Probably, but it doesn't look like anyone's there," Keegan tells him.

They approach it anyway and find the door locked.

The three of them huddle in the doorway beneath the shingled overhang that barely offers protection from the nasty weather.

"Now what?" Cheryl asks, shivering and stamping her feet on the concrete step, a note of despair in her voice.

"We go to the Bramble Rose Inn," Danny says decisively, turning to Keegan. "Right?"

"Right. First we have to find someone who knows where it is, though." Keegan looks around and spots a big white house with a widow's walk at the top right on the water near the boardwalk.

"There's a light on in the window of that old house," he tells the Cavellis, pointing. "Let's go see if someone there can help."

The three of them set out again, and it feels like hours before they finally reach the house, though it's probably only a matter of minutes. Keegan can no longer feel his feet, and his face is so stiff from the cold that it feels as though it's going to crack open every time he speaks.

Please let someone answer the door, he begs silently as he, Danny, and Cheryl stomp up onto the porch of the old house. *If I don't get out of the wind and cold for a few minutes, I'm going to collapse.*

He glances at Cheryl and instantly feels ashamed of himself. If he's overcome, she must be barely hanging on. Her face looks wan and she seems weak and shaky, as if she'd wilt and drop to the ground if she weren't hanging onto Danny for dear life.

Keegan reaches out and, with numb fingers, pushes the old-fashioned buzzer beside the door.

Moments later, it's thrown open and a ruddy-faced man is there wearing a welcoming smile.

"Oh," he says, and the pure-white brows that match his hair furrow at the sight of three bedraggled strangers standing on his porch. "Thought you were going to be Sherm Crandall."

"Crandall? The police chief?" Danny asks.

"That's right. You know him?"

"I talked to him last night, about my sister. She's missing."

The man looks taken aback. "Did you say your sister is missing?"

"Yeah, why? You know something about it?"

"Sherm mentioned something about it—a girl from Connecticut, right?"

"Right. You don't know if he found her, do you?" Danny asks excitedly.

"He hadn't—least not when I saw him around lunchtime. He was on his way over to the inn where she was staying—wanted to have a look-see, I suppose."

"Ned?" calls a female voice from the back of the house. "What are you doing with that door open? You're letting all the heat out!"

"That's the missus—Shirley. And I'm Ned Hartigan," he explains, and steps back, gesturing for the three of them to step inside.

They do, and Keegan gratefully unzips the top of his jacket, lifting his chin away from the soaked fabric at last. The house is like an oven, and a savory aroma fills the warm air. The white walls of the hall they're standing in are covered in wood-framed photographs, and two bright rag rugs are scattered on the honey-colored plank floor.

Ned closes the door firmly behind them just as a lanky gray-haired woman comes into the hall, wiping her hands on a dish towel. Her thin eyebrows shoot up at the sight of three strangers dripping on the doormat.

"Thought Sherm might be here for dinner," is all she says, glancing at her husband and then back at the visitors.

"So did I, but this is the fella whose sister is missing from the inn—remember I told you what Sherm—Say," he interrupts himself, "how did you folks get here, anyway? There's no ferry service today."

"We borrowed a boat," Keegan says simply.

"Pretty brave of you to come across the water in this storm, I'd say."

"Would you like some hot coffee?" Shirley asks, looking with concern at Cheryl, who's still trembling from head to toe.

"My Shirley brews the best coffee on the island. Ask anyone, and they'll tell you," Ned says proudly.

Danny and Keegan exchange a glance. "We really don't have time," Keegan says reluctantly, thinking about how heavenly it would be to stay in the warm house and sip something hot.

But there's no time to waste.

Not when Jennie might be in trouble.

"But if you wouldn't mind, why don't you let my wife stay here for a little while and warm up," Danny puts in.

Cheryl starts to protest, but Shirley swoops right in like a mother bird and puts her arm around Cheryl's shoulders. "Don't you be silly," she says. "You look like you're about to faint. Now you come right back into the kitchen and sit by the fire and have some chowder."

"Go ahead, babe," Danny urges his wife, who looks at him questioningly.

"But what about Sandy?"

"We'll go see what we can find out," he assures her, and she nods.

"Can you tell us where the Bramble Rose Inn is?" Keegan asks, turning to Ned. "Is it within walking distance?"

"It would be if it weren't snowing and blowing like the dickens. But come on. We'll take my pickup . . . if it starts."

It does . . . after several tries.

As Ned Hartigan pulls out onto the ice-covered road that leads back toward town, Keegan peels off his wet wool gloves and blows on his numb fingers.

"Frostbite?" Hartigan asks, glancing at him.

"Hope not."

"My feet are starting to sting like crazy," Danny says.

"That's a good sign. Circulation's coming back."

Keegan tries not to think about his own feet. He can't feel them at all.

"So did you see my sister at all this weekend?" Danny asks. "She's a little chubby, but pretty, and the sweetest girl you'd ever want to meet."

"Well, the gal I saw who was staying at the inn was anything but sweet," Ned says with disdain as the truck creeps along the road. "Blond, and acted like she was the Queen of England."

Definitely not Jennie, Keegan thinks. Glancing out the

window at the slowly passing buildings along the board-walk, he asks, "I don't suppose you came across the woman I'm trying to find. She was staying at the inn, too."

"From Boston?"

"Yeah!" Keegan turns excitedly to Ned. "Jennie Towne. You met her?"

"Does she have the prettiest light-purple eyes—like Liz Taylor's?"

"That's her! Where'd you see her?"

"Came into my store—that's it over there, by the way," Ned says, pointing to a building on the boardwalk that's fronted by a painted Victorian-style sign that reads "Harti-gan's." "Anyway, she came in yesterday and was nice as can be. Then she sat down and had coffee with the nasty blonde, which surprised me because I didn't think the two of them could be friends. Although my wife, Shirley, is a good woman and she has some friends who are downright obnoxious, I'll tell you. This one gal, Myra's her name, Myra Tallman, well she—"

Keegan, sensing that Ned Hartigan is the kind of man who can easily lose track of a conversation, interrupts. "Excuse me, Mr. Hartigan, but how did the woman from Boston seem?"

"How did she *seem?*" he repeats, not missing a beat, which tells Keegan that he must be used to being inter-rupted. "What do you mean?"

"Was she . . . I don't know. Nervous?"

"Not really. Just a little stand-offish, maybe. But real nice. You could tell. She was probably just shy. Didn't want to open up much about herself, not like some of the tourists who stop by."

That's Jennie, all right, Keegan thinks as Danny says, "My sister doesn't have a shy bone in her body. You'd know if you met her. She's a real chatterbox."

"Wish I could say I'd seen her, son," Ned replies.

They all fall silent as the pickup truck plods along the

road that has started curving away from the boardwalk. Keegan stares vacantly out the window at the boarded-up shops and hotels, some bearing signs that read, "See you in June!"

Dusk is falling rapidly and the snow is coming down harder than ever. The truck's windshield wipers beat a bleak rhythm that seems to be echoing the refrain in Keegan's head—*Find Jennie. Find Jennie. Find Jennie . . .*

"There's the inn, up ahead," Ned Hartigan says suddenly, pointing. "On that little rise, to the right."

Danny and Keegan lean forward, peering through the stormy twilight outside the truck.

Keegan's shoulder and arm are against Danny's, and he can feel the guy's apprehension as Hartigan slows the truck even more and starts to pull off the road.

"Say," Ned Hartigan leans forward over the wheel, "isn't that . . ."

Keegan catches sight of what he's looking at. A car is just pulling out onto the road from the other side of the inn, its headlights cutting an arc through the blustery shadows.

"Is it a cop car?" Danny asks just as Keegan catches a glimpse of the official insignia on the door and the round dome on the roof.

"Sure is . . . only one on the island. That's Sherm Crandall," Ned says. "Must be headed back to his house. Lives up toward the center of the island."

"Shouldn't we follow him and see if he knows anything about Sandy?" Danny asks urgently.

Keegan's heart sinks. He knows Danny's desperate to find his sister; but now that they've arrived at the inn, he can't bear the thought of not getting to Jennie right away.

"Can we just—Look, I just want to stop here," he says, "to see if Jennie's inside. You two can go on and catch up to the police officer."

"Yeah, but look at Sherm go," Ned comments with a low whistle. "Looks like he's on someone's trail."

"I'll come in with you," Danny says, turning to Keegan. "Just to see if the innkeeper knows what's going on."

As Ned pulls up in front of the inn, Keegan watches the police car driving rapidly away in the opposite direction, the red taillights visible for only a few seconds before disappearing around a curve.

Jennie stirs, then opens her eyes, wondering why her bed is shaking violently. Can it be an earthquake?

Not in Boston, she thinks groggily.

But you're not in Boston, she remembers, trying to think straight. Why is it so cold? She must have kicked the covers off . . .

Boston?

No! You're on the island . . .

And you're not in your bed, she realizes as she gradually regains her senses. *It's pitch black, and you're lying on some kind of rough carpet, and . . . and . . . you're moving.*

That's it . . .

It's not your bed that's shaking . . .

You're going over bumps in a road . . .

Thoroughly confused, she squints into the darkness and tries to remember what happened.

Then it comes rushing back to her.

Jasper Hammel standing in her doorway and the cloth he'd clamped over her nostrils and that overpowering smell . . .

He knocked you out!

The knowledge fills Jennie with a chill more intense than the one caused by the frigid temperature.

He knocked you out, and now you're . . . you must be in the trunk of a car, and he's driving you somewhere . . .

Oh, God.

Oh, God!

Panicking, Jennie squirms, then kicks her legs, only to find that they're bound together at the ankles of her jeans.

And her wrists, too, are bound, behind her back so that she can't move, can only lie helplessly on her side as the car whisks her closer to . . .

Where?

Where is he taking me?

Calm down! She orders herself fiercely, taking a deep breath, and then another. At least there's no gag in her mouth . . .

She can scream for help as soon as—

No. She can't. If Jasper Hammel—or whoever's driving this car—thought there was a chance of anyone hearing her, he would have made sure she couldn't make a sound. Wherever he's taking her, it must be someplace where no one will ever hear her. Where no one will ever find her.

Squeezing her eyes tightly shut again, Jennie whimpers softly to herself, feeling tears slipping down her cheeks.

Why? she keeps asking herself.

Is Jasper Hammel some psycho who abducts unsuspecting women?

And who then . . .

What?

Rapes them?

Tortures them?

Murders them?

She pictures the odd little man with his formal, clipped way of speaking and shudders. Is he a psychopath in disguise?

You knew something was wrong all along, she tells herself. *Why didn't you listen to your instincts?*

Because you thought it was just your imagination acting up again, she responds flatly to the plaintive inner voice.

Ironic, isn't it, she thinks, that after all the times when she's panicked for no reason, she really is in danger again?

Just like the time with Harry—

And Harry, she recalls, had come to her in a dream to warn her.

Tears trickle down her cheeks as she thinks of the man she had loved, of how he had given his life for her.

That day three years ago had started out as one of the happiest Jennie had ever known.

She had woken in Harry's arms in his small apartment and glanced out the window beside the bed to see that it was snowing. Big, downy flakes, the kind that would turn Boston into a winter wonderland.

And it was a Saturday, which meant that she and Harry would be together every minute for another forty-eight hours; and Christmas was right around the corner; and Harry's engagement ring was sparkling on the fourth finger of Jennie's left hand. . . .

She had actually shivered with joy.

"Wake up, you big lug," she'd said playfully. "It's going to be a wonderful day."

"Why?" he'd asked groggily.

"Because it's snowing and I love you and we're going to go shopping."

He'd raised one eyelid. "What was that last thing?"

"Come on, Harry, we have to go to the mall. I haven't gotten any of my shopping done, and Christmas is this week."

"That place will be insane on a Saturday."

"So? It'll be fun. Get you into the spirit."

"It'll get me *out* of the spirit, Jen. You know I hate to shop."

But she'd gotten her way, of course. Harry always gave in when she wanted something. And besides, he had shopping of his own to do. He wasn't going home to Portland for the first time ever, having decided to spend the holidays with Jennie, and that meant he had a lot of gifts to ship to his family.

After a leisurely breakfast of waffles and freshly-ground hazelnut coffee, they had taken the T over to the Colonial Mall so they wouldn't have to fight for a parking space. The fake-cobblestone corridors had been jammed with people, just as Harry had predicted.

For several hours, they had traipsed from store to store, buying gifts for their families, and even a few for each other. Harry kept trying to peek into the sporting goods store bag Jennie was carrying, knowing she'd stashed something for him inside, along with the in-line skates she'd bought for Laura.

Finally, they had everything they needed. Harry wanted to beat a hasty exit, but Jennie had persuaded him to stop at the food court for hot cocoa. "My feet are killing me," she'd said when he protested, "and you know we're going to have to stand on the T all the way home."

He'd given in, of course.

Jennie has wondered, so many times a day, every day of the past three years, what her life would be like now if Harry had said no to that cocoa. Or if they'd driven to the mall instead of taking the T. Or even if they'd arrived at the food court a few minutes earlier, or a few minutes later.

And even though she knew it was useless to torture herself with idle speculation, she couldn't seem to help it.

If things had been just slightly different that day, Harry would still be alive.

It was while Jennie and Harry were seated at one of the small wrought-iron tables in the skylighted food court, sipping their hot whipped-cream-laced cocoa, that the first shots had rung out.

"What was that?" Jennie had asked, frowning and looking over her shoulder.

"Sounded like—Oh, Jesus."

"What?"

Baffled, Jennie had seen a throng of people pushing frantically toward them.

Someone screamed, "He's got a gun! He's got a gun!"

There were more shouts and shrieks, more staccato blasts—sounds that would later haunt Jennie's nightmares.

She had seen the man with the gun coming at them, firing haphazardly to the left and right. He was so nondescript, she would tell the police later, still dazed. He looked like a balding, middle-aged English teacher or salesman, wearing glasses and jeans and a down jacket like so many other people at the mall that day.

Her eyes had locked with his as he happened to turn his head toward the table where she was sitting with Harry. She had seen him swing the gun again and point it in their direction, right at her.

"Oh, Christ, Jennie, duck!"

Harry had stood and leaned over the table, plastering his gigantic palm over the top of her head and shoving her down, throwing his big body over hers just as another shot rang out.

Jennie heard someone holler "Grab him" and turned her head to look up, bewildered, past Harry's arm that was thrown across her face, toward the commotion above.

That was when she had seen the man with the gun, with swift efficiency, placing the barrel into his own mouth. He pulled the trigger without hesitation, and blood and bone and brains had exploded from his head instantly.

Repulsed and panic-stricken, Jennie had screamed, "Oh, God, Harry, he just—"

And then she had seen him.

Harry.

The man she loved, the man whose engagement ring sparkled on her hand, the man who only moments before had been smiling at her across the table . . .

The left side of his face was oddly intact, the eye open and fixed vacantly on Jennie . . .

But the right side . . .

The entire right side of Harry's face was gone.

Later, much later, she would find out that the man who had done this—who had killed seven innocent people in a matter of moments—was married and had five children and had been laid off from his factory job the week before. He was despondent over mounting bills, his wife said, and wondering how they were going to heat their rented house this winter and get food on the table, let alone provide Christmas presents for their kids.

"I guess he just snapped," the grief-stricken woman was quoted as saying in an article in the *Globe*.

He just snapped. . . .

The words had stayed with Jennie.

A stranger had snapped, and her entire world had instantly fallen apart.

It wasn't fair.

For a long time after that, she hadn't cared whether she lived or died.

Then she'd met Keegan and fallen in love before she'd realized what was happening.

It wasn't until Christmas approached, bringing with it memories of what had happened to Harry—memories she had fought so hard to shut out—that Jennie had realized what she had to do.

She could never live with loving a cop—a man whose entire job was about danger and violence, a man who laid his life on the line every day.

She could never live with the constant fear of losing Keegan the way she had lost Harry, in the split second it takes for someone to pull the trigger of a gun.

And now, Jennie thinks in despair, futilely kicking her bound legs against the side of the car trunk, *I'm the one who's going to die.*

Sixteen

Jasper Hammel has just stepped into the storage room where officer Sherm Crandall's big body lies unconscious on the floor, when the sound of the doorbell pierces the air.

He freezes, his heart erupting into a rapid pounding as he waits and listens, wondering frantically what to do.

It rings again, more insistently this time.

It can't be Stephen. He wouldn't come to the front door, and besides, he has a key.

Jasper hesitates only another moment before tossing the meat cleaver onto the floor. It clatters across the scarred wood and stops just short of the cop's big belly.

Turning, Jasper flees the storeroom, stopping only long enough to lock the door so that the man can't get out if he comes to.

I'll be back to take care of you later, Jasper promises him, even though he knows it's a lie.

He wouldn't have been able to do it. He knew that even as he had stood over the man, clutching the knife, seconds earlier.

He's half-grateful to whoever rang the doorbell and saved him from having to attempt murder and half-furious that the unwelcome visitor is forcing him to take flight like a frightened gull.

He scoops the keys to Stephen's car off the kitchen counter, then slips out the back door as the bell rings again.

Racing across the frozen yard through the driving snow,

Jasper wonders who can be at the door. He knows Crandall is the only cop on the island in winter. Who else would be stopping by in the middle of a storm?

Does it matter? he asks himself as he reaches the car and jerks open the door. *All that matters is that you get out of here.*

He gets behind the wheel, jabs the key into the ignition, and starts the engine. As he drives around to the front of the big old inn, he thinks wistfully of his packed suitcase waiting in the little room on the first floor.

He would have to leave it behind now. All the mementos he had collected through the years—a lock of Stephen's hair, a photograph of the two of them at prep school graduation—not to mention the new wardrobe he had bought to take with him.

Stephen had said they would be living on a tiny island in the West Indies—an island he had bought with cash. He had paid off a lot of people to erase the trail of paperwork that might lead the authorities to connect him to the island.

"No one will ever find me, Jasper," he'd said gleefully.

"You mean *us*," Jasper had said. "Don't you?"

"Of course I do. No one will ever find *us*."

Jasper remembers how much fun he'd had shopping for the clothes he'll need on the island—splashy tropical-print shirts and Bermuda shorts and sandals. Now he'll never get to wear them. . . .

But you'll get new things, he promises himself. *Stephen will buy you anything you want, when you get to the island.*

He pulls carefully out onto the highway heading north, looking back at the inn through the rear-view mirror. Before the snow obliterates the view, he makes out a battered-looking pickup truck parked in front of the Bramble Rose.

"Farewell forever, whoever you are," he calls softly as he heads up the coast toward the old Gilbrooke mansion.

* * *

"Did you see that?" Danny asks Keegan and Ned, watching the big black sedan disappear up the highway in the same direction the police car had taken.

"Something's up," Keegan says, nodding and pounding on the door of the inn. "Anyone here?" he calls.

"No way anyone could hear you from inside," Ned advises. "Not with this wind."

"Who do you think just left in that car?" Danny asks.

Ned shrugs. "Never saw it before. Not many cars on the island, either, in the off-season. I'd know most of 'em. Must be a tourist."

"We've got to follow them," Danny tells him and Keegan, stepping away from the door. "This is useless. There's no one here."

"Might be," Ned says thoughtfully, "that the evacuation is in effect."

"What evacuation?" Keegan asks as Danny pauses impatiently at the top of the steps.

"Because of the storm, Sherm said we might have to evacuate along the shore. Bet that's it. That'll mean Shirley and me have to clear out of our place, too. I best be getting back—"

"No!" Danny cuts him off abruptly, unable to contain himself any longer. "Look, my sister is out here somewhere and I've got to find her. Please, can't we just drive up that road a little ways to see if something's happening?"

"It's not a bad idea," Keegan agrees, looking from Danny to Ned. "That police officer was going like a bat out of hell. It seemed like he was rushing to get someplace."

"Well, I suppose we can check it out," Ned says after a long moment, with a sigh. "Sherm *did* mention something about the old Gilbrooke mansion, and it's up in that direction."

"The Gilbrooke mansion?" Danny and Keegan echo, practically in unison.

"What's that?" Danny asks. "Does it have something to do with my sister?"

"Probably not, but something might be going on out there. I'll tell you what I know in the truck," Ned says, starting down the steps toward the pickup. "Come on, let's head out there."

Stephen opens the trunk and peers inside, expecting to see Laura still slumped and unconscious.

Instead, she's looking directly up at him, her startled gaze visible even in the shadows of dusk.

"Who . . . who *are* you?" she asks as he bends and gathers her into his arms.

"I'll tell you when we get inside," he promises, inhaling the scent of her silky hair as it brushes against his face. It's not the musky fragrance he remembers her wearing, he thinks, frowning slightly. No, it simply smells . . . clean.

He reaches down to close the trunk, then trudges up the steps and balances her carefully over his shoulder as he unlocks the door.

"Home, sweet home," he says lightly, carrying her over the threshold. Just like a bride, he thinks, and smiles to himself.

He deposits her on the sofa in the parlor, then steps back to look at her. "Well?" he asks. "Do you remember?"

"Remember what?" She looks frightened, but oddly under control—as though she's resigned herself to the fact that she's helpless here.

"Oh, come on, Laura," he croons, starting to take off his coat, then thinking better of it. There hadn't been time for him to change out of the blood-stained tuxedo. No need to have her start panicking so soon.

He smiles and says, "You can't have forgotten me so quickly." He reaches down and trails a finger lightly down her cheek.

She opens her mouth as if to say something, then clamps it closed again.

"What is it?" he prods. "Do I seem familiar?"

She shakes her head, watching him, and he can feel her trembling as he moves his finger under her chin and tilts her face up toward him.

Strange, he thinks as he studies her, *she seems . . . different, somehow. Softer, even though she's trying to be defiant. And not quite as . . . overtly alluring. Her beauty seems more subtle now.*

"Here," he says, stepping away, opening a closet door and taking out the plastic-wrapped wedding dress he had made for her. "I had to guess the size because I didn't have time to find out exactly, but . . . are you a seven?"

She nods, looking bewildered.

"Then put it on. Oh," he remembers, reaching for the rope that binds her wrists. "Guess I'll have to untie you first. Don't you dare try anything funny, though. If you do, I'll have to do to you what I did to Sandy."

"Sandy?" she echoes in a whisper, and her eyes take on a sudden look of stark fear.

"Don't worry," he says, moving down to untie her feet. "If you're a good girl, you'll be fine."

She's visibly shaking as he hands her the dress.

"Go ahead," he orders, sitting on the edge of the sofa and folding his arms across his chest. "I want to watch. You always did like to strip for me, remember? You wore those lacy black underpants . . ." He moans slightly at the memory of her teasing him as she removed them, slowly and tantalizingly, in his hotel suite.

Now she studies him for a moment, then fumbles awkwardly with her sweater. She raises it over her head, and he sees that she's wearing a plain white bra underneath. He considers asking her to remove it, too, so that he can see her wonderfully firm breasts bare one last time, but realizes that it might cause him to get carried away and there probably isn't time for that.

So he simply watches, and squirms on the uncomfortable sofa, as she lowers her jeans to reveal white-cotton panties, the high-waisted kind that hide even her belly button.

He can't help feeling another prickle of disappointment. What happened to daring, provocative Laura and her seductive lingerie?

She steps shakily into the dress and pulls it up over her shoulders. It hugs her curves just as he'd thought it would, but he can't help feeling that maybe it wasn't the right choice. Suddenly, it seems as though a traditional, lacy gown might have suited her better after all.

Oh, well. At least the dress fits perfectly. He stands and says, "I'll do the zipper for you."

She nods mutely, and he rises and moves behind her.

He can feel her shaking as he tugs the zipper pull up along her bare back, can sense her acute fear.

But for some reason, it isn't making him feel quite as satisfied as it had when he'd seen Sandy and Liza shaking in terror. Something's different . . . but he can't put his finger on what it is.

He moves around to stand in front of her again.

"Well?" he asks, watching her watch him. "Do you recognize me?"

"No," she says simply, "I don't."

"I don't look the same," he tells her. "I've changed in the *four seasons* since we were together. That's a hint," he adds, delighted with his own clever pun.

"Laura worked at the . . ." She trails off abruptly.

"You worked there, yes," he says, thinking vaguely that it's peculiar that she'd refer to herself in the third person. "And we met there . . . and made love there."

He waits.

Nothing.

She's fastened those lilac eyes blankly on him, as though she has no idea what he's talking about.

"Oh, come on, Laura," he says, feeling anger surging up inside of him. "Did you sleep with *every* businessman who came through that hotel?"

Maybe she had, he realizes. Maybe he was only one of many.

And maybe, like Liza, she has completely forgotten that he ever existed.

Furious at the prospect, he grabs her arm and jerks her to her feet, holding her steady.

"I'm not," she begins, then stops.

"You're not what?" he bites out, glaring at her. "You're not a slut who can't even remember someone who took such good care of her?"

He slaps her, hard, across the face.

"I'm not Laura."

He stops short, poised with his hand raised to slap her again. "What are you talking about?"

"I'm not Laura Towne."

He brings his flattened palm down on her face again, sees her bite her lip against the pain. "What do you think I am, a fool?" he lashes at her. "I know you're Laura Towne."

"No, I'm her twin sister. Jennie."

"She doesn't have a twin," he says, frowning. *Or does she?* He would have no way of knowing.

But Laura always was the cunning type. He wouldn't put it past her to come up with a story like this, anything to save her skin.

"She does have a twin," the woman in front of him protests. "I swear, I'm her sister. Look at—my face."

"What about it?"

"Look at my cheek. Laura has a scar under her eye. If you really know her, you've seen it. And I don't have one."

He peers at her, remembering the scar, remembering the

way he had kissed it tenderly the first night they were together in his hotel suite. She'd winced when he touched it and refused to tell him how it got there. He remembered suspecting that it wasn't the result of some innocent childhood accident, that someone had hurt her.

Now, all he can see on her cheek is an angry red smear where he slapped her.

The scar is gone.

Bewildered, he meets her eyes again, not wanting to believe that his plan is actually about to fall apart—that he's abducted the wrong girl.

"I'm Jennie," she says again, the only hint of her fear a slightly high-pitched tone in her voice.

"You're Jennie," he repeats, stunned. "You're not Laura?" Just to make sure . . .

"I'm not Laura."

She's telling the truth. He knows it, without a doubt. It would explain why she's wearing different underwear, why she smells different, why he feels different this time. . . .

He shakes his head, closes his eyes, tries to figure out what to do next.

"You'll have to be punished," he concludes after a few moments thought. "As long as you're here in your sister's place, you'll have to die in her place. It's that simple."

"You really should eat something," Shawn says with a full mouth, looking up at Laura over the sandwich he's just bitten into. "You haven't had anything all day."

"I'm not hungry." She stands across the table from him, both hands resting on the back of a chair, and shakes her head. "I feel sick."

"What's the matter?"

"I can't explain it . . . I just—my stomach. It's messed up. And my head is killing me, too. I feel awful."

"Do you think you're coming down with something?" he

asks, putting the sandwich down and coming to stand beside her. He puts a hand on her forehead.

"No, not that kind of sick," she says, pushing him away. "It's Jen. I just know she's in trouble. I feel it so strongly that it's like . . . taking over my body. And there's nothing I can do to help."

"You really do think it has something to do with that guy, Stephen What's-his-name?"

"Gilbrooke. I don't know. It doesn't make sense. The man who sold me the ticket looked nothing like him, but there was something about him, I guess, that *could* remind me of him. . . . But what does it matter? It's not helping Jennie for me to sit here and think about some creep I used to date."

"Laura," Shawn says quietly, "right now, there *is* no way for you to help Jennie."

"I know," she says, and buries her face in his shoulder, sobbing.

You'll have to die.

The stranger's words ring through Jennie's brain, and she simply stands there and stares at him.

Then something snaps inside her. Something that causes her to stiffen her spine, narrow her gaze, and say resolutely, "You don't want to kill me."

He looks taken aback.

"What do you mean?" he asks suspiciously. "Of course I want to kill you."

"Why?" She forces herself to take a step closer to him, to run her finger along his cheek, just as he had done to her moments before. "Why would you want to kill me when you haven't even gotten to know me yet?"

"I—" He shuts his mouth, looks puzzled.

She moves her finger down, trailing it along his neck to his chest. He's wearing a thick wool overcoat, and she glimpses a bow tie and white shirt beneath it. The shirt is smeared with something . . .

Oh, Lord, Jennie realizes in horror, *it's blood.*

She swallows hard and bites her lower lip to keep from screaming. She doesn't speak for a moment, waiting until she's certain her voice won't dissolve into a frightened sob.

Then, she says seductively, "Laura may have slept with everyone she met, but I haven't. And I don't want . . . anyone but you."

His eyebrows shoot up beneath his dark hair, and his cornflower-blue eyes widen. "You want me?" he says hoarsely, then shakes his head abruptly. "You do not. You're just saying it. Like the rest of them."

"I am not." She knows what she has to do, and the thought of it sends repulsion coursing through her, threatening to gag her.

She fights back the bile and stands on her tiptoes, clamping her mouth firmly over his. She moves her lips over his cold, rubbery lips, hears him groan in surprise and passion deep in his throat, feels his lips opening against hers, his wet, invasive tongue slipping through to probe hers.

It's all she can do not to retch as she pulls back and exhales shakily—as though she's carried away by passion, not overcome with revulsion.

"I want you," she whispers again, watching him, praying fervently that it will work.

"You want me," he repeats, and sighs. A slow smile slips over his features, and he nods. "You do. You're not like the others."

"I'm not," she agrees, her mind screaming, *What about them? Sandy? And Liza?*

She keeps her eyes focused on his face, not letting them wander lower, where the blood-stained shirt is still visible inside his coat.

"I'll take you with me," he says just as the front door opens.

Jennie spins and looks through the archway leading to the hall, half-expecting to see that someone's come to save her.

But the man stepping into the hall and stomping the snow off his feet is distressingly familiar.

"Miss Towne . . . fancy meeting you here," Jasper Hammel says with a wave.

"Can't you go any faster?" Keegan asks, finding himself jabbing at the floor of the pickup truck with his unfeeling right foot as though he's stepping on an imaginary gas pedal.

Ned shakes his head and frowns. "Not unless you want me to get us all killed. The tires are really bad on this truck, and the roads are a mess. We're lucky we haven't skidded into a ditch yet. In fact, we should just—"

"No!" Danny says forcefully. "We can't go back. Not yet. We have to get to that place."

Keegan nods.

Ned Hartigan sighs and keeps driving, inching the truck along the perilous stretch of highway that follows the coast.

Keegan thinks of what Hartigan told them. How Sherm had run into a suspicious character out here, a man who seemed to be using an alias—and claimed to be staying at the Bramble Rose. How Sandy Cavelli isn't the only person who's missing on the island this weekend. One of the part-time cops is gone as well, and the last place he was known to have headed was the old Gilbrooke mansion.

Oh, Jennie, Keegan asks silently, *are you somehow involved in this? Where are you?*

Beside him, Danny Cavelli beats a staccato rhythm on the dashboard with nervous fingertips. "How much farther to the house?" he presses as Ned slows the truck to creep around a sharp curve.

"Another mile or so, I'd say."

Keegan groans inwardly. At the rate they're going, and with the storm showing no sign of letting up, it's going to take ages for them to get there.

And by then . . .

What if it's too late?

"What are you doing here?" Stephen asks, frowning.

Jasper crosses the floor to the parlor, saying, "I know you told me to wait, but I had to come right away, Stephen. Someone showed up at the house just after you left."

"Who was it?"

"I have no idea," Jasper tells him, moving to sit on the edge of the sofa. "I didn't answer the door. I just left as fast as I could."

"And what about that fat cop?"

Jasper hesitates only a mere second before deciding to lie. Stephen will never know. Not after they've left this island for good. "I took care of him first, just the way you said to," he tells Stephen, sinking with relief onto the sofa cushion.

Everything's going to be all right now.

He made it here, having driven dangerously fast over that treacherous highway. There were a few times when the sedan started to skid and he thought . . .

"What do you think you're doing?"

"Excuse me?" Jasper looks up at Stephen, puzzled.

"Get up!" he barks and grabs Jasper's arm, pulling him to his feet. "Can't you see that I'm not finished here?"

"Oh, of course. I'm sorry." Jasper looks from Stephen to Laura, who stands, looking pale, in a white, ridiculously low-cut wedding gown. He smiles at the thought of what Stephen's going to do to her and can't resist taunting her a little.

"It's too bad you're going to ruin that lovely dress with all that blood," he says, grinning.

"Shut up, you idiot!" Stephen shouts and takes a menacing step toward Jasper. "Shut up!"

"But Stephen, I—"

"She's not going to die like the rest. She's coming with me."

"What do you mean?" Feeling a tide of paranoia rising in his gut, Jasper looks at Stephen's arm, which actually seems protective of the woman whose shoulder it rests upon. "You hate her, Stephen," Jasper babbles, "remember?"

"I hate her *sister*, Laura. This is Jennie, her identical twin."

In a flash, Jasper thinks back to the phone call—the woman who'd asked to speak to *Jennie* Towne. He should have realized then that the woman at the inn was an impostor, he thinks frantically. If he had, he might have been able to prevent this from happening . . .

He turns his troubled gaze back on Stephen. "But—" he begins.

Stephen cuts him off. "Let's go out to the boat," he says. "I need you to help me drag the others along."

"The others?" The woman in the wedding dress speaks for the first time since Jasper arrived. "What others?"

"Nothing for you to worry your pretty little head about, darling," Stephen says, looping his elbow around hers. "Come along. Jasper will get them."

"Where are they?" Jasper asks, fighting back the urge to burst into frustrated tears.

"In the closet under the stairs. Now, make it quick," Stephen says, and leads Jennie Towne toward the back of the house.

Jasper stands there, watching them go.

This isn't how it was supposed to happen!

It was supposed to be just the two of them, he fumes, shaking his head. Not he and Stephen and some *woman*.

Clenching his jaw, Jasper moves toward the closet and opens the door.

Inside, lying in a heap on the floor, are the three gory corpses, one belonging to the nosy kid Stephen had told him about, and the other two—Sandy Cavelli and Liza Danning—clad in blood-stained wedding gowns.

With a sigh, Jasper starts lugging the first corpse out of the closet and down the hall toward the back door.

Stephen glances again at Jennie, who's sitting on the narrow bed in the hold of his yacht, the *Aurelia*. The sea is churning from the storm, which causes the boat to rock wildly.

That, Stephen tells himself, is why Jennie looks pale. She must be getting seasick. He feels a little queasy himself.

"Don't worry. . . . We'll sail right out of this atrocious weather," he promises, admiring the way she looks wrapped in his overcoat, which he'd insisted on giving her. After all, she can't go around in this weather wearing only that skimpy dress.

He had seen the way she'd looked at his clothes when he'd taken off the coat. "It's a shame I ruined my tuxedo with so much blood," he had said. "But I won't need it where we're going."

She had nodded and offered him a smile, and his heart had swelled with love for her.

She isn't like the rest. She really does care about me.

In all his life, no woman had ever looked at him with anything other than repulsion in her eyes.

Laura.

Liza.

Sandy.

Lorraine.

And, worst of all, his own mother, Aurelia.

All of them had used him to get what they wanted—even his mother. But for her, the attraction hadn't been money. It had been far more unsettling than that.

Stephen still shudders every time he thinks of the first time she'd ever called down the hall to him from her bedroom. "Stevie?" she had said as he passed by on his way to his room. "Can you come in here for a moment?"

He must have been all of ten years old at the time; but even then, he had somehow sensed, by the tone of her voice, the unspeakable thing that was about to happen.

Aurelia had been propped against her goose-down pillows, wearing a filmy pink negligee that plainly revealed her round, pointed nipples and the dark triangle at the base of her flat torso.

"Sit down," she had said in a soft voice she had never used on him before.

Stephen sat, and tried to keep his eyes averted. "Where's Father?" he had asked in a small voice.

"Who cares?" Aurelia dismissed Andrew with a wave of her hand. "I have no use for a man like that. He doesn't give me the time of day—always has his head buried in that stupid paperwork. And he certainly doesn't have the first idea how to satisfy a woman. Stevie . . ." she had added. "Do you want to touch me?"

"No, Mother."

"You can admit it," she said, sounding breathless. "Go on. You can touch me here . . ." And she had slid her fingers over his, bringing his hand up and resting it against her left breast. "You can touch me everywhere."

"You'd better do it, Stevie," she'd added when he'd sat there, frozen, his heart pounding so hard he thought it would burst through his rib cage. "This is your only chance to touch a woman. No one else is going to let someone who looks like you near her."

There's a thumping sound on the boat deck overhead, and Stephen snaps out of his reverie.

"That's Jasper again," he tells Jennie, standing and glancing toward the steps that lead out of the hold. "I'll be right back. I just want to go see where he's . . . never mind." He decides it's probably best not to say the rest—*Where he's putting the bodies.* Just in case Jennie Towne is the squeamish type.

He bends and plants a light kiss on her dark hair. "I'll be right back, my darling. I love you."

"I love you, too," she says.

Her voice is trembling slightly, and he decides that she must be as overwhelmed with emotion as he is. Dear, sweet Jennie . . . he'll make her his bride just as soon as they reach their destination.

Humming the wedding march to himself, Stephen climbs up to the deck and sees that Jasper is just depositing the third body—Sandy Cavelli's—on the rocking deck.

He looks up at Stephen. "That's it," he calls with a grunt, straightening and wiping the mix of snow and sweat from his brow. "They're all out."

"Good." Stephen is about to order him to go back to the house and clean up any telltale spots of blood when he catches sight of the distressed look on the man's face. "What's wrong, Jasper?"

"It's just . . ." The little man pauses, then takes a deep breath and says, over the howling wind, "I must admit, Stephen, that I'm somewhat upset at this most recent turn of events."

"What are you talking about?"

"Her," is the shouted one-word reply, accompanied with a gesture toward the hold, where Jennie waits.

"Do you mean Jennie?"

"Yes. I thought it was going to be just you and me, Stephen."

"You didn't really," Stephen calls, amused at the disillusionment on the man's face.

Jasper hesitates, knits his brows. "I didn't really . . . what?"

"You didn't really think I was going to take you with me?" Stephen reaches inside his jacket and pulls out the pistol he'd tucked into his pocket earlier. He had been going to save it for later, when they were safely at sea, but . . .

Suddenly wild-eyed, Jasper looks in disbelief from the gun to Stephen's face. "What are you going to do with that?" he asks, his voice reduced to a pitiful high-pitched whimper.

"Sorry, old boy," Stephen shouts, cocking it and aiming squarely at Jasper's head. "But I've run out of uses for you."

With that, he pulls the trigger.

The shot pierces the violent roar of the storm, and Stephen's lips curl into a satisfied smile as Jasper Hammel topples backward over the rail into the foaming water.

Seventeen

"The house is right around this next bend . . . there!" Ned says, pointing triumphantly.

Keegan leans forward, peering at the gothic monster rising in front of them. There are two vehicles parked in front, he realizes—both the police car and the black sedan they'd seen leaving the inn.

Danny Cavelli is out of the truck like a shot the moment Ned stops at the foot of the porch steps.

"Wait!" Keegan calls, hurrying after him and grabbing his shoulder to pull him back.

"Let go of me! My sister—"

"I know, but you can't go rushing in there!" Keegan says as Ned comes slipping and sliding around the truck on the icy gravel. "You don't know what's going on inside. It could be dangerous. I'll go first, and if it's all right, I'll wave you ahead."

Danny starts to protest, but Ned interrupts. "Better listen to him, son. He's right about not rushing in there. But maybe," he adds, turning to Keegan, "it's too dangerous for us to fool around here at all. Maybe we should just leave and—"

"I'm a cop," Keegan says resolutely. "I'm trained in this kind of thing. But you two need to step back."

"Fine," Ned says, shrugging. "In fact, I'll wait in the truck."

"Good idea." Keegan looks at Danny. "And you should—"

"Forget it. I'll be right behind you."

Realizing it's not worth it to waste time arguing, Keegan gives a curt nod and says, "Fine."

With Danny Cavelli right at his heels, he steps carefully up onto the porch and peers through the windows. His instincts tell him that the place is deserted, but the cars parked out front mean that at least two people are around here . . . someplace.

Reaching for the knob, Keegan is surprised to see that the door isn't locked. He slowly pushes it open and steps inside just as Ned hollers something from the pickup truck.

Startled, Keegan turns to see what's going on.

Danny is already hurrying down the steps.

"What is it?" Keegan calls above the roaring wind.

"He says there's someone out in back of the house by the boat dock!" Danny is already running awkwardly across the icy gravel toward the lawn that sweeps down to the water.

"Wait!" Keegan hurries after him, hearing Ned's bellowed, "Be careful!" coming from the direction of the truck.

Running on the snowy grass is far easier than it was to make his way across the driveway, and Keegan quickly overtakes Danny, grabbing his shoulder and forcing him to the snow-covered ground in front of a low shrub.

"Get your hands off of me!" he says, jerking under Keegan's sturdy grasp.

"Just wait," Keegan says, lying on his stomach beside Danny and pointing in the direction of the water. "We're sitting ducks up here if anyone sees us. I just want to see what's going on. Stay still and stay down, dammit."

The younger man suddenly obeys, and Keegan can hear Danny's heavy panting mingling with his own and with the roaring wind as he cautiously raises himself to peer over the top of the bush.

The lawn descends to a short dock that juts out into the

water, and moored at the piling is a large luxury yacht. From here, despite the snow and darkness, he can make out the figure of a man standing on the deck. As he watches, whoever it is descends into the hold.

This whole thing could be entirely innocent, Keegan tells himself.

But his sharply honed police officer's instincts tell him that something sinister is going on.

And he can only pray that, somehow, Jennie is still safe.

"Is everything all right?" Jennie asks, looking up to see Stephen framed in the doorway of the hold again.

"Everything's fine," he says with a beatific smile. "I just had to take care of something."

"What?"

"Nothing for you to worry about."

She nods, struggling to remain calm. He just killed Jasper Hammel. She's certain of it. The sound of gunfire was as vivid as it had been that long-ago day at the Colonial Shopping Mall; and the moment she had heard it, Jennie had found herself on the verge of hysteria.

Only the thought of Keegan had allowed her to regain control.

I can't lose it, because if I do, he'll kill me. And I'm not ready to die. I have to get back to Keegan. I have to tell him that I really do love him. I have to explain why I left him.

And if she manages to get out of this and get back to him, she vows, she will never, ever, let him go again.

Desperation threatens to edge into her voice as she asks Stephen, "Are we going to leave now?"

"Do you want to?"

"I don't know. . . . Maybe we should stay here," she tells him, trying to sound casual, despite the terror building within her. "Just for tonight. Because of the storm."

"Well . . ."

He appears to be considering that, then shakes his head. "Too risky," he tells her.

"Oh, Stephen, come on. You're such a strong, brave man. Don't tell me you're afraid to take a risk."

Please! she screams at him inside her brain. *Please don't try to take the boat out now.*

He has to be insane to even consider it.

She doesn't know which prospect is more chilling—meeting her death at his hands or in the violent storm-tossed sea.

"All right," he says after a moment, with a nod. "We can wait—if not until morning, at least until the weather lets up. It can't stay like this forever. Come on."

He reaches out and offers her a hand, pulling her to her feet.

It's nearly impossible for her to walk in the skintight gown with the boat beneath her feet rocking and rolling over the waves.

"I'll carry you," he says, turning and seeing her moving awkwardly across the floor.

Before she can protest, he's lifting her into his arms, holding her in a powerful grip against his blood-spattered clothing. "There . . . isn't that better?"

Feeling trapped, Jennie can only nod as he starts up the steep steps. The rancid smell of drying blood, mingled with the overpowering scent of dying roses that had filled the house, assaults her nostrils, and it's all she can do to keep from vomiting. A blast of wind and snow hits her as soon as they step out onto the deck, mercifully eradicating the scent of blood and roses.

Jennie squints against the driving snow, turning her head down toward the deck to see if there's any sign of Jasper.

The sight that greets her there causes her to gasp in utter shock and horror.

"What is it?" Stephen asks, stopping and looking down at her.

Speechless, she can only stare at the heap of corpses on the deck.

Oh, Sandy . . . She shakes her head, gazing at the unmistakable chubby figure encased in white satin that's streaked with rust-colored blotches.

And Liza . . . She sees the matted, blood-soaked blond hair and shakes her head in despair.

And . . .

The third body is face up, unlike the others, the face coated with snow, the eyes open and staring at the stormy night sky. It takes a moment for Jennie to realize where she's seen him before . . .

Patrick Gerkin.

"Jennie?"

It's Stephen, his blue eyes probing her face.

"You . . . you killed them! Oh, God! You're a murderer!" The words spill out of her before she can stop them, a harsh, unforgiving accusation.

For a moment, he merely looks surprised, and Jennie tells herself that it's okay . . . she can take it back, convince him that she didn't mean to react that way . . .

But then, before she can open her mouth again, his eyes harden into icy daggers and his grip on her tightens so that she can barely breathe.

He says nothing, only stalks across the deck toward the ladder leading to the dock.

Jennie's heart sinks as she realizes what he's going to do.

Take her into the house . . . and kill her there.

Like the others.

"Please," she says on a sob. "Please don't hurt me. I love—"

"Shut up!" he hollers at her. "You don't love me. You never did. It was a lie. You're like the others, just as I thought. But I almost believed you! How could I believe you? How could I think you were different?"

He's talking more to himself than to her, shaking her, ranting, and squeezing her tighter with every sentence so that she feels as though her ribs are going to shatter. She can no longer speak, can't inhale . . .

She's going to die like this, she realizes in horror, gasping for air . . .

He's going to squeeze the life right out of her.

Oh, God, Keegan . . . I'll never—

"Let her go!"

The words reach her ears on a gale, and Jennie thinks that it's only the wind. It can't be . . .

But that voice . . .

No, it can't be. It's just your imagination again. It's because he's on your mind, because you're so terrified, because you know that you're about to . . .

"I mean it. . . . Put her down!"

This time, Jennie realizes that the voice is real—and familiar.

It's coming from the dock above the boat, and Jennie looks up just in time to see a dark figure leaping through the air, landing on the deck a few feet away.

Stephen is so startled that he drops her as Keegan McCullough scrambles to his feet and faces him.

"You son of a bitch!" he bellows above the roaring wind and sea, as Jennie stares in disbelief.

Keegan . . .

But how . . .

Why . . .

"You son of a bitch!" Keegan repeats, advancing on Stephen.

But Stephen has regained his control and is standing his ground before Keegan, a bemused smile on his face.

"And who are you?" he asks, his hand slipping into his jacket pocket.

"Keegan, no!" Jennie finds her voice and screams as he makes a move to tackle Stephen. "He's got a gun! No!"

But Keegan is already upon Stephen, hurtling at him with a guttural cry of fury. The two men topple onto the pitching deck.

Horrified, Jennie struggles to get up. Her right leg is seared by an agonizing pain. It had twisted beneath her when she landed, and now she can only claw at the deck helplessly with her hands, unable to put any weight on her leg.

She hears another shout from the dock above. In despair, she looks up to see a second man, a stranger, standing there. He's poised as though he's about to jump onto the boat and help Keegan when, suddenly, his gaze drops to the battered corpses on the deck.

"Oh, Sweet Jesus, no!" His strangled cry pierces the noise of the storm. "Oh, God, not Sandy. No . . . please, not Sandy!"

Her brother? The one who called . . .

In numb horror, Jennie looks from the grief-crazed man on the dock back at the tumbling blur of arms and legs on the wildly pitching boat deck.

Then she sees a flash of the gun in Stephen's hand.

She opens her mouth to warn Keegan when, with a sudden, swift movement, he knocks the weapon out of Stephen's grasp, sending it skittering across the icy boat deck.

Sobbing in desperation, Jennie strains to pull herself toward the spot where it lies near the railing as the two men scuffle in the opposite direction. She's about to close her fingers over the barrel when a hand moves in and grabs it away.

Stunned, Jennie looks up to see Jasper Hammel standing over her, clutching the gun against his chest and looking dazed.

Water streams from his hair and over his body, and there's

blood trickling from his temple. The bullet Stephen fired only grazed it, Jennie realizes, knocking him overboard and he must have pulled himself back on board the boat somehow without Stephen's realizing it.

"You bastard!" The voice belongs to Keegan, yet it sounds far off and muffled.

Jennie jerks her head around to see that only Keegan's lower legs are visible as Stephen dangles the rest of him backward over the rail of the boat, holding onto his ankles.

"Are you ready to die, Mr. Hero?" Stephen shouts, wearing a deranged grin.

"No!" Jennie screams, looking desperately toward the man on the dock to do something, to help Keegan somehow.

But he's gone—running across the snow-covered lawn toward the house, shaking his head blindly as if to shut out the sight of Sandy's body.

Jennie turns her head back to look at the two men by the rail just as a shot rings out.

She hears a blood-chilling shriek, not realizing for a moment that it's coming from her.

It becomes a high-pitched wail as she squeezes her eyes shut to block out the horror, knowing that when she opens them, Keegan will be gone, just as Harry was . . .

But then she hears his voice saying, "Drop the gun."

Astounded, Jennie opens her eyes and sees Keegan scrambling back up over the rail and onto the deck . . . where Stephen lies writhing from a bullet wound in his side.

Relief courses through her and she gasps his name on a nearly hysterical half-sob, half-laugh.

"Drop the gun," Keegan repeats.

Jennie turns to see that Jasper Hammel is still holding the pistol straight in front of him in both hands, arms rigid, trembling all over.

"What are you doing, Arnie?" Stephen gasps, clutching

his side and looking up at Hammel in bewilderment. "What are you doing? Don't do anything foolish, Arnie. It's me, Stephen . . ."

"I know it's you." Hammel's voice is a bitter sob. "You lying bastard. You lying . . . You never planned to bring me with you when you left. You . . . I loved you. . . . I was the only one who stood by you. And you . . . you tried to kill me."

"No, Arnie . . ."

Stephen starts to say something more, but Hammel closes his eyes tightly and fires again, this time hitting Stephen square in the throat. His words die instantly in a gurgle of blood.

"Drop it," Keegan says again, taking a step closer to Hammel.

For a brief, terrifying instant, Jennie believes that Jasper Hammel is going to fire again, this time at Keegan. But then, with a shudder, he drops the weapon at his feet and opens his eyes.

At the sight of Stephen's bloody body, he sobs. "Oh, look at you. . . . Look at what I've done to you. . . . I loved you, you lying bastard."

Keegan moves forward and grabs him, pulling his arms behind his back. Hammel doesn't resist, but, as if in a stupor, allows his wrists and ankles be tied with two lengths of rope Keegan finds in the compartment where the life jackets are stored.

Only when Jasper Hammel is restrained and lying on his stomach on the deck, weeping bitterly about Stephen, does Keegan turn to Jennie.

"Are you all right?" he asks gently, bending over her and touching her cheek.

"My leg hurts, but . . . I'm going to be fine," she assures him, meeting his gaze. "Now that you're here."

"Oh, Jennie . . ." He gathers her into his arms. "Thank

God you're all right. Don't you even think of leaving me, not ever again."

"I won't," she promises. "I'll never leave you again, Keegan."

Epilogue

The sun shines brightly on New Year's Day, glistening on the drifts of snow that blanketed Boston overnight.

"Be careful now, Jen," Laura, wearing her black-velvet matron-of-honor dress, warns as her sister's white-satin pumps hover over the sidewalk in front of the church. "It's probably icy."

"I'm all right." Jennie gathers the voluminous ivory skirt of her antique wedding gown over her arm and steps down from the horse-drawn carriage.

Laura is right behind her, carrying her bouquet and Jennie's.

They're not roses—Jennie had told her sister she'd carry anything but roses.

She has no idea how Laura got her hands on lilacs in January, but her sister had come through for her.

"Are you ready?" Shawn is waiting on the sidewalk, handsome in a dark suit and tie.

Jennie nods at her brother-in-law. He'd been so happy when she'd asked him to give her away. "I'd be honored," he'd said, and Laura had positively beamed at his side.

It is hard to believe that six months have passed since their June wedding—that it has been almost a year since Jennie's ordeal on Tide Island.

But she pushes the thought of that out of her mind. This is the happiest day of her life. There's no room today to let unpleasant memories haunt her. . . . There never will be again.

Jennie takes Shawn's arm and they walk toward the church with Laura right behind them, fussing with the back of her sister's antique-lace veil.

The church is hushed and filled with waiting friends and family.

Jennie stops at the edge of the satin runner and takes a deep breath.

"Nervous?" Shawn whispers.

She smiles serenely and shakes her head.

The organist begins playing Pachelbel's "Canon in D."

It's time.

Laura leans toward her sister and plants a kiss on her cheek. "I love you, Jennie."

"I love you, too," she says, and watches as her sister starts down the aisle, each step a saucy little sashay typical of Laura.

Then it's Jennie's turn. She and Shawn step onto the white-satin runner, and she looks up. The congregation has stood, blocking her view of the groom.

It's all right. . . . I'll see him soon enough, she thinks, and begins to move forward.

Familiar faces beam at her from the pews.

Midway toward the front, she sees Danny and Cheryl Cavelli. In Danny's arms is their three-month-old baby girl, Sandra. Cheryl had been pregnant on that icy February day on Tide Island. She had been keeping it a secret, planning to tell her husband on Valentine's Day.

Jennie nods slightly at them as she passes and is rewarded with two slightly wistful, but happy smiles—and one drooly one from the baby.

Then she's nearing the altar . . .

And there he is, waiting for her, tall and dashing in his charcoal morning coat and striped ascot.

Keegan, the man she's going to spend the rest of her life with.

He steps forward as she arrives in front of him, taking her arm from Shawn, looking down at her face with teary eyes so full of love that a lump rises in Jennie's throat.

Together, they take the final few steps to stand in front of the priest.

Looking down on the bride and groom with a benevolent smile, he begins. "Dearly beloved . . ."

Please turn the page for an exciting sneak peek of
Wendy Corsi Staub's newest thriller
coming in June 2004
from Pinnacle Books!

Prologue

Her thoughts, that Tuesday night as she walks along the edge of the road, are mainly occupied by the first day of school tomorrow.

What she'll wear, who she'll have for homeroom, and whether she'll get third or fourth lunch. Seniors always get one or the other of the later lunch periods. That'll be a nice switch. Last year, she had first period; who wants sloppy joes or egg salad at ten-twenty in the morning?

The pothole pocked pavement of Cuttington Road shines in the murky glow of streetlights; the strip of ground that borders it is still muddy from this morning's hard rain.

Ma always reminds her to walk in the gutter, not the road, on her way home from her job at the fast-food place out on the highway. But she can't walk in the mud; she's wearing sandals.

And anyway, it's less than half a mile, and there isn't a lot of traffic on this old, winding back road leading to their apartment complex at this time of night. A year or two ago, there wasn't any through traffic at all; the only thing out here in the woods was Orchard Arms, a cluster of boxy stucco two-story buildings with rectangular wrought iron balconies cluttered with potted impatiens, tricycles and hibachis.

Then bulldozers rolled in and created a development where the woods used to be. They call it Orchard Hollow, probably because of all the apple trees they tore down to make way for the houses. Now, farther down the road, just past Orchard Arms, cul de sacs branch off from Cuttington Road like jeweled fingers on a work-roughened hand.

Two- and three-story houses with two- and-three-car garages sprang up where there used to be only trees and brambles. In the garages are shiny cars and SUVs; in the homes are people who complain about the ruts and poor lighting along the old road that leads to Orchard Hollow. It's always been bad but until now, nobody other than the apartment complex's residents ever cared. The construction equipment has torn up the pavement worse than ever, but they're still building back there.

The new houses have broad decks and brick terraces instead of wrought iron balconies. They have real yards with raised beds of roses, wide gas grills and elaborate wooden swing sets. Some of them even have in-ground pools.

On the hottest days of this summer, as she sat out on the balcony, she could sometimes hear the sound of splashing and gleeful shouts in the distance.

She often wondered what it would be like to make friends with one of the girls who ride her bus. Then she might be invited over to one of their pools to swim.

But so far, that hasn't happened. The girls from the development stick together, and she, as the only kid her age living in Orchard Arms, keeps to herself on the bus. Sometimes she eavesdrops on the other girls' conversations, when they talk about things that interest her. Things like boys at Woodsbridge High and sales at Abercrombie and Fitch over at the Galleria. But when they discuss things to which she can't relate—like curfews and overly strict fathers and nosy mothers who are always home, always asking questions—well, then she tunes them out.

She sticks to the very edge of the pavement as she walks, doing her best to pick her way around the puddles that fill the potholes. Her toes are getting wet and dirty anyway.

Tomorrow, she'll have to put on regular shoes again for the first time in two months, she thinks with a tinge of regret. Regular shoes, and regular clothes. In western New York, the days of sandals and shorts and tank tops are too fleeting as it is—you'd think Woodsbridge High would allow students to wear them through the warm days of early September, but nope.

What a waste of a pedicure, she thinks, remembering how painstakingly she polished her toenails pearly pink just this morning while she was sitting on the balcony watching the rain.

She hears a car splashing toward her from behind and steps farther off the road to let it pass.

It doesn't pass.

Gravel crunches beneath the tires as it slows; the headlights illuminate the road before her, casting an eerily long, distorted shadow of herself.

She wonders, as she turns toward the blinding lights, whether it's somebody she knows from Orchard Arms, stopping to give her a ride.

Her next thought, a belated thought, is that Ma always tells her to walk facing traffic, not with it, so that she can see what's coming toward her.

And her last coherent thought, as the car door opens and she is dragged roughly inside, is that she never, ever would have seen this coming.

One

"Mrs. Carmody?"

Startled, Kathleen glances up at the orthodontist's pudgy, bleached blond receptionist.

"Yes?"

"We need your insurance card again."

With a sigh, Kathleen puts aside an issue of *Rosie* magazine—a relic of a bygone era when there actually *was* a *Rosie* magazine—takes her purse from the back of her uncomfortable chair, and crosses the crowded waiting room. Her nine-year-old son, Curran, absorbed in his Gameboy, is the only one who doesn't look up.

Kathleen fishes for the card in her wallet, hands it to the woman, and waits while she examines it, frowns, photocopies it, and frowns again.

"Is this new insurance?" the receptionist asks.

"Not since we started coming here in May." She wonders if the receptionist is new. She's never seen her here before.

"Not a new group number?"

"Nope." Kathleen sighs inwardly. What is it with insurance? It's been six months since Matt switched jobs and they moved to western New York, but every doctor, dentist and orthodontist appointment brings another round of complications.

The woman spins her chair toward a computer, taps a few keys with her right hand while holding the insurance card in her left. The computer whirs, and she glances up. "It'll be a few seconds; I just have to check something, Mrs. . . . *Katie?*"

Katie.

A name from the past. Which means that the unfamiliar receptionist is also a name, a voice, a face from the past.

It's Kathleen's turn to frown, in that vague, polite, *have we met?* manner she's perfected since the move.

"You're Katie Gallagher, right?"

Not anymore, thank God.

"I used to be." Kathleen forces a pleasant smile. "It's Kathleen Carmody now."

"I'm Deb. Deb Duffy, I used to be, but now I'm Deb Mahalski."

The name doesn't ring a bell. Not that it would. Kathleen did her best to block out just about everyone she used to know. It's easier that way.

"I thought you moved away years ago," the woman chatters on.

Kathleen wants nothing more than to grab Curran and his Gameboy and bolt, but that's out of the question. This isn't the first time she's run into somebody who used to know her. And anyway, the receptionist is still holding the insurance card hostage.

"I'm . . . I did, but I'm back," Kathleen murmurs, absently noting Deb Mahalski's impossibly long, curved crimson fingernails and wondering how she manages the keyboard.

"Where are you living now?"

"Woodsbridge."

Kathleen watches the woman glance down at her file on the desk; sees her overly plucked and penciled-in eyebrows rise. "Orchard Hollow? You've moved up in the world since the old days at Saint Brigid's."

So that's it. We were Catholic schoolgirls together in another lifetime.

"Did you hear they tore down the church a few years ago to build a new Wegman's?"

"I heard."

"That's your son?" Deb asks, with a nod at Curran.

"Yes . . ."

"I have two girls, three and five." She gestures her poufy pile of hair, caught back in a plastic butterfly clip, toward a framed photo on the desk. "Do you have other kids?"

"A younger son. And a daughter. She's . . . older."

"And you're married?"

"Mmm hmm."

It's not as though she can dodge the questions. After all, a few taps of the computer keys would reveal everything anyone would want to know about her life.

Not everything.

Nobody knows everything. Not even Matt. Nor the children.

And they never will, Kathleen assures herself, clenching her trembling hands into fists within the deep pockets of her corduroy barn coat.

"I'm home! Sorry I'm late, Jen!" Stella Gattinski calls as she simultaneously steps from the attached garage into her kitchen and out of the brown leather pumps that have tortured her feet all afternoon.

"It's okay, Mrs. Gattinski."

Jen Carmody, the "bestest and most beautifulest babysitter in the whole wide world," according to Stella's two-year-old twin daughters, smiles up from the floor of the family room, where a stuffed animal tea party is in progress.

The April day the Carmody family moved to Woodsbridge from the Midwest was one lucky day for Stella. Wholesome Jen is terrific with Mackenzie and Michaela, and she's at the perfect age: about thirteen. Old enough to be responsible for two small children, and too young for dating, driving, and most extra-curricular school activities.

She comes every Wednesday to meet the twins when the day care bus drops them off. Wednesdays are Stella's late day at school; she's the French club advisor and that's the afternoon they meet.

"Mommy, Jen doesn't have to leave now, does she?"

"Yeah, Mommy, she said we can play Candyland again after this," Michaela promptly joins Mackenzie's whining. "I want you to go back to work."

Stella grins. "Sorry, kiddo. You're stuck with me. Did anyone call, Jen?"

"Just Mr. Gattinski." Jen doesn't seem to mind Mackenzie's hands attempting to braid her long blond hair. "He said to tell you he's got a late meeting and to eat without him."

Stella's grin fades. Another late meeting. That's the second time this week, and it's only half over.

"Kenz, get your hands out of Jen's hair," she says absently, wondering who Kurt's meeting with tonight.

His promotion to vice president at Lakeside Savings and Loan seemed like a blessing, coming at the tail end of Stella's extended maternity leave. But that was almost two years ago, when money was scarce and family togetherness was not. Their household had just doubled in size, sweeping a dazed Stella from busy middle school teacher to invalid on bedrest to stay-at-home mom. Quite honestly, Kurt—with his banker's hours—was underfoot and on her nerves at that point, anyway.

Now she's back to work; he's a vice president; they've got a savings account, a Volvo station wagon, a weekly housekeeper, and this newly built center hall Colonial in Orchard Hollow.

Not to mention the most adorable little girls on the planet.

Life couldn't be better.

Really.

After checking the clock on the microwave—
five-twenty-six already?—Stella fumbles in her wallet for
a twenty and a ten. Jen's been here since three, and her
hourly rate is only eight dollars, but Stella gives her ten an
hour and always rounds up. The twins are a handful. Plus,
it's only one afternoon a week.

"Girls, get off Jen's lap so she can stand up," Stella says.

Her daughters ignore her.

Jen giggles as Michaela throws her arms around her and
gives her a bear hug.

Depositing her purse on the breakfast bar, Stella strides
across the toy-strewn carpet, money in hand. She deftly
plucks a wriggling Mackenzie off of Jen and pries
Michaela's arms from around Jen's neck.

"I know you guys love Jen, but she has to go home. Her
mommy is probably wondering where she is." *And your
mommy is wondering where your Daddy is.* "Please tell
your mom I'm sorry it's so late, Jen."

"Actually, my mom's not home. She had to take Curran
to the orthodontist in Amherst at four, and they never get
out of there for hours."

That's true. Kathleen Carmody was complaining about
it just the other day when Stella ran into her at the super-
market. She mentioned that her older son has had three
appointments with Doctor Deare so far and he's always
running behind—and that his waiting room magazines are
more than a year old.

"Maybe I should take up cross-stitch or knitting," Kathleen said, rolling her green eyes. "I've got years of this
ahead of me. Our dentist is already positive that Riley"—
the youngest Carmody— "is going to need braces, too."

But not Jen. Stella finds herself admiring the teenager's
perfectly even white smile. Add that to her wide-set brown
eyes, fine bone structure and willowy build, and she looks
like a fresh-faced fashion model. She even has a quirky
characteristic on a par with Cindy Crawford's mole and
Lauren Hutton's widely spaced front teeth: a thin streak of

white hair running through the golden hair of her left eyebrow.

Next to her teenaged sitter, Stella feels frumpier than ever. Her own unruly dark blond hair is pulled back into a black velvet headband—the kind that went out of style more than a decade ago for all but New England finishing school students. The last twenty pounds of maternity weight still cling stubbornly to her hips and stomach, yet Stella refuses to acknowledge that they might be here to stay. That's why she's still wearing skirts and tops she bought a few months into the pregnancy, instead of something more streamlined and fashionable. She refuses to buy new clothes in size fourteen.

She notes with envy Jen's slender figure in jeans and a simple tucked-in tee shirt. Oh, to be young and skinny again . . .

"Do you still need me on Saturday night, Mrs. Gattinski?" Jen brushes off her jeans and casually tosses her silky hair back over her shoulders as she stands.

"Saturday night . . . yes! We've got that Chamber of Commerce dinner. I almost forgot. Mr. Gattinski will pick you up at seven."

"I can walk over," Jen protests, and murmurs her thanks as Stella hands her the thirty dollars.

"You're welcome. And no, you can't walk over; it'll be dark by seven. In fact . . . " Stella glances over Michaela's red hair at the sliding glass doors that lead out to the deck and fenced yard. "It's almost dark now. Come on, I'll drive you home. Girls, where are your coats?"

"That's okay, don't do that, Mrs. Gattinski. By the time you get them bundled up and into the car seats, I'll be home."

"I don't know . . ." Stella looks again at the darkness falling. The thought of packing the kids into the car *is* exhausting, but—

"I'll be fine. I'll see you two on Saturday, okay?" Jen

plants a kiss on each twin's cheek and heads for the front door.

As it closes behind her, Stella cuddles her daughters close on her lap and smooths their hair, the same shade and texture as her own. She sighs in contentment. Another long day has drawn to a close. All she wants to do is throw on sweats—even better, pajamas—and collapse on the couch.

"I miss Jen," Mackenzie laments.

"Me, too," chimes the inevitable echo.

You should have insisted on driving Jen home, Stella chides herself, glancing again at the shadows beyond the sliding glass door. *It isn't a good idea for a teenaged girl to be out alone after dark.*

Not that this neighborhood isn't the safest around. It isn't like their old street in Cheektowaga, where there were three car break-ins in the month before they moved. But still . . .

April Lukoviak.

The name flits into Stella's thoughts, sending a ripple of uneasiness through her.

April Lukoviak, who lived with her mother up the road at Orchard Arms, has been missing for weeks now—since right around Labor Day. There were fliers up all over the development back when school started. They were cheap, photocopied fliers made by the people who lived in the apartment complex, featuring a poorly reproduced black-and-white image of a pretty teenaged girl with long, straight blond hair like Jen's.

At first, the other mothers at the bus stop were disconcerted by the fliers. They kept a wary eye even on their teenaged children, especially the girls. Then people started talking about how April didn't get along with her mother, who supported the two of them with food stamps, welfare checks, and by tending bar. People said that April was always threatening to run off to California, where her father reportedly last lived. The police seemed to think that was what happened to her, and that, everyone concluded, made perfect sense.

After awhile, September rains blurred the typed descriptions of April. Fierce autumn winds blew in off the Great Lakes to tear the fliers from the development's lamp posts and slender young trees, blowing them away altogether.

But every once in awhile, when Stella passes Orchard Arms or goes through the drive-through at the fast-food restaurant where April worked, she finds herself thinking of her. She wonders what ever happened to her; wonders if she really did run away.

If anything ever happened to Jen, you'd be responsible. Next time, you'll insist on driving her home. After all, bad things can happen in safe neighborhoods, too.

Jen has always liked the sound of leaves crunching beneath her feet. So much that she goes out of her way to step in the piles that line the edge of the pavement along the cul de sac. There are no sidewalks here in Orchard Hollow, and the houses are bigger, farther apart, and newer than they were back in Indiana, where centuries-old trees scattered abundant drifts of leaves in October.

Here, there are leaves, too, but not many. There's only a scattering of old trees that weren't bulldozed when the houses were built, and the slender new maples and oaks that are still supported by stakes and wires barely have branches.

"I don't like it here," Riley announced on sunny moving-in day last April. "There's no shade. I want to go home."

He had been whining in an annoying singsong voice already for six hours in the over-packed Chevy Tahoe, making Jen long to be riding in the U-haul behind them with Dad and Curran. But this time, Jen secretly agreed with her little brother's sentiment. She desperately missed Indiana already. Even the trees. *Especially* the trees.

"There will be shade when the leaves pop out," Mom promised, as she put the car into PARK and turned off the engine, sealing their fate. Nine Sarah Crescent—a two-story white Colonial with red shutters and stickers still on the windows—was officially Home.

The house—and Woodsbridge—really *do* feel more like home now, six months later. Especially now that school and soccer are underway and the strangely cool, mostly cloudy western New York summer has given way to the more familiar and comforting chill of autumn.

Realizing she's starved, Jen quickens her pace. Rounding the corner onto Cuttington Road, she walks along the edge where tangled vines, bushes, and trees border the still vacant lots. From here she can see the cluster of homes, including the Carmodys', that make up Sarah Crescent just ahead.

Jen inhales the sweet, smoky scent of leaves and somebody's fireplace, wondering what Mom has planned for dinner. Maybe she's got stew or chili in the crock pot. And some of those brown-and-serve rolls that taste like the kind you get in a bread basket at a nice restaurant.

Back in Indiana, Dad worked late every night, and they ate a lot of grilled cheese and frozen pizza. But Mom's been on a cooking kick ever since they moved east, planning and preparing nightly family dinners like she's trying to transform herself into Martha Stewart or something. Over the summer, she was the queen of marinating and grilling; now she's into the crock—

Jen jumps, hearing a noise behind her.

Probably a dog in the bushes, she thinks, scanning the seemingly empty road. Or maybe some kind of animal. What if . . .

Are there bears here?

Oh, please, she scoffs, even as her heart quickens its

pace. *This is suburban Buffalo. Not the mountain wilderness.*

She starts walking again, quickly, toward home.

Her eyes are trained on the loop of well-lit houses ahead; her ears on the thatch of bushes to her left.

Is something rustling in there? Another set of footsteps crunching in the leaves?

Feeling foolish, yet frightened, Jen starts to run, and she doesn't stop until she's safely barricaded in the empty house.

"Way to go, Jen! *Woo hoo!*" Blinking into the October morning sunlight, Kathleen waves a victorious fist in the general direction of her daughter on the soccer field.

"Mom!" Curran, sprawled on the ground before her nylon folding spectator chair, is clearly mortified. "Can't you keep it down? Geez!"

"Your sister scored again. I'm proud of her." Green eyes glinting with mischief, Kathleen shouts another *"Woo hoo!"* for good measure, and grins when Curran cringes. He moves a few feet forward to a new patch of grass and resumes pretending he doesn't know her.

Seated beside Kathleen in an identical folding chair, Maeve Hudson laughs. She pushes her designer sunglasses up to rest above her dark bangs and leans closer. "What are you going to do when he's starting quarterback on the high school football team? Show up with pom-poms and a bull-horn so you can really embarrass him?"

"Football? Curran?" Kathleen shakes her head, her auburn ponytail brushing against her fleece collar. She jerks it away, feeling it crackle. Static. Ugh. Static gives her chills. So does the ragged fingernail that's just snagged a strand of hair.

Her nails need filing; her hair needs trimming. Kathleen sighs inwardly. Some days, she's tempted to have it cut short, the way she wore it as a teenager. Short hair would be so much easier.

But Matt likes it long on her. On Jen, too.

Her daughter's blond hair was neatly bound into a single braid when they left the house an hour ago. Now, long strands have worked their way loose, streaming behind Jen as she runs, falling into her wide-set brown eyes when she stops, causing her to distractedly shove impatient fingers through the deviant tresses.

Amazing how Jen can be such a tomboy on the field, then turn around and spend an hour in the bathroom putting on makeup and primping when people—namely her mother—are waiting to take showers.

Not only that, but Kathleen is fairly certain Jen has been going through her drawers again after several warnings not to borrow her mother's clothes without asking. Kathleen noticed a faint ketchup stain on the collar of her favorite yellow sweater when she took it out to wear it this morning.

"Matt played football, right?" Maeve is asking.

Kathleen's gaze shifts from her daughter to her strapping husband, jogging down the field after the girls and the ball with a coach's whistle in his mouth.

Yes, Matt played football. Baseball and basketball, too. He's got two cartons full of trophies in the basement to prove it. They lined the family room shelves in the old house, but so far, Kathleen hasn't found a place for them here.

The way things look now, wiry Curran doesn't have a chance of approaching his father's six-foot-three height or broad-shouldered build. Kathleen shudders just imagining her elfin son collapsing beneath a heap of brawny athletes.

"Matt played football," she tells Maeve, "but Curran takes after my side of the family. He's built like a Gallagher."

"So I guess Jen and Riley got his share of Carmody blood."

Avoiding the question, Kathleen focuses on her younger
son, rolling pell-mell down a low hill several yards away.
"Look at that kid. He's going to be covered with grass
stains and I'm all out of Oxy-clean again. And if he sur-
vives childhood without broken bones, he's the one who's
going to be the star athlete of the family."

"He looks just like Matt," Maeve says. "Acts like him,
too."

Yes, Riley, with his dark curls and full throttle personality, is certainly the image of his father. And Jen . . .

Well, Jen doesn't look a bit like Matt. But she's the
apple of his eye, nonetheless.

"So was that Jen's second goal this game?" asks Maeve,
who arrived late, having made her ritualistic Saturday
morning detour to Starbucks.

"Her third."

"Her third? Geez, what are you feeding her for breakfast?"

Kathleen can't quite keep from beaming as she turns her
attention back to the field, where the pack of long-legged
girls, knees bared above their soccer socks, race down the
green field beneath a piercing blue sky. There's a hint of
wood smoke in the air, mingling with the sweet musk of
damp earth and fallen leaves.

That's odd, Kathleen thinks, staring out across the field
into the late morning glare.

Somebody is watching the game from the opposite end
of the field, far from the rest of the spectators. Standing on
the very edge of the clearing against a backdrop of peak
foliage, he looks as though he might have just stepped out
of the thatch of woods that border the park.

Or is he a *she?* The figure is draped in a long garment
of some sort, making it impossible to discern gender from
this distance.

There's a chill autumn wind blowing off the eastern
Great Lakes, but an overcoat would be out of place in this

crowd of fleece and down-jacketed, jean-clad families. Then again, so would a dress or skirt.

Her skin prickling with inexplicable apprehension, Kathleen squints into the sun, wishing she hadn't left her sunglasses on the dashboard of the Explorer in the parking lot.

The fact that somebody is standing on the "wrong" end of the field—and wearing a long coat or dress—is no reason to be suspicious.

"Way to go, Jen!" Maeve hollers as Kathleen's daughter barrels down the field toward them, expertly kicking the ball in front of her.

"All right, Jen!" Momentarily forgetting the oddly dressed stranger, Kathleen shrieks as her daughter approaches the goal again. She puts two fingers between her lips and whistles. "Come on, Jen!"

Curran flashes a glare over his shoulder. She ignores him, watching her long-legged daughter jab the ball with her right cleat. It sails into the air . . . only to be stopped by the other team's goalie.

"Almost." Maeve sighs. "I wish Erin were as into the game as Jen is. Look at her. It's like she can't wait for it to be over so that she can go home and crawl back into bed."

Kathleen watches Maeve's brunette daughter trying to conceal a yawn behind a manicured hand. "She takes after her mom," she says with a laugh.

"Yeah, without the caffeine habit," Maeve agrees, lowering her sunglasses again. "Although I was tempted to give her a shot of espresso this morning to get her out of bed. You'd have thought I was torturing her. She's the one who insisted on playing soccer, but you'd think it was my idea for us to be out here in the cold at this god-awful hour on the only morning of the week I can sleep past nine."

Kathleen nods, but the hour is hardly god-awful, and she has little genuine sympathy for Maeve, whose existence is as stress-free as a single mom's life can possibly be.

Maeve's ex is a dentist; her two-year-old four-bedroom

Colonial and two-year-old Lexus are entirely paid for; she doesn't have to work, thanks to her hefty alimony and the child support she gets for Erin.

The girls take off down the field again, chasing the ball toward the opposite goal.

With an uneasy twinge, Kathleen glances back toward the trees, about to point out the lone spectator to Maeve.

The spot by the woods is empty.

Startled, she scans the perimeter of the field, expecting to see someone striding away, coat or dress flapping about their legs in the gusting wind.

But there is no sign anywhere of the person she saw earlier. It's as though he—or she—has been swallowed by the dense woods once again.

A chill slithers down Kathleen's spine, and this time it has nothing to do with static electricity or ragged fingernails.

Naturally, the moment Lucy stops pacing the floor to perch on the edge of a hard-backed kitchen chair, the phone rings.

Heart pounding wildly, she leaps to her feet again and hurries across the worn linoleum, snatching up the receiver before it can ring again. Henry's working the night shift this week, asleep in the bedroom down the hall.

Lifting the receiver, she utters a hurried, hushed "Hello?" and holds her breath, waiting.

The male voice is familiar, uttering a mere two words. But they're the two words she was half-hoping, half-dreading, to hear.

"It's her."

ISAAC ASIMOV

ROBOT VISIONS

ILLUSTRATIONS BY

Ralph McQuarrie

A BYRON PREISS VISUAL
PUBLICATIONS, INC., BOOK

A ROC BOOK

ROC
Published by New American Library, a division of
Penguin Group (USA) Inc., 375 Hudson Street,
New York, New York 10014, USA
Penguin Group (Canada), 90 Eglinton Avenue East, Suite 700, Toronto,
Ontario M4P 2Y3, Canada (a division of Pearson Penguin Canada Inc.)
Penguin Books Ltd., 80 Strand, London WC2R 0RL, England
Penguin Ireland, 25 St. Stephen's Green, Dublin 2,
Ireland (a division of Penguin Books Ltd.)
Penguin Group (Australia), 250 Camberwell Road, Camberwell, Victoria 3124,
Australia (a division of Pearson Australia Group Pty. Ltd.)
Penguin Books India Pvt. Ltd., 11 Community Centre, Panchsheel Park,
New Delhi - 110 017, India
Penguin Group (NZ), 67 Apollo Drive, Mairangi Bay,
Auckland 1311, New Zealand (a division of Pearson New Zealand Ltd.)
Penguin Books (South Africa) (Pty.) Ltd., 24 Sturdee Avenue,
Rosebank, Johannesburg 2196, South Africa

Penguin Books Ltd., Registered Offices:
80 Strand, London WC2R 0RL, England

Published by Roc, an imprint of New American Library, a division of Penguin Group
(USA) Inc. Previously published in a Roc hardcover edition.

First Roc Mass Market Printing, March 1991
40 39 38 37 36 35 34 33 32

RoC REGISTERED TRADEMARK—MARCA REGISTRADA

Printed in the United States of America

Acknowledgments

"Too Bad!" copyright © Nightfall, Inc. First appeared in *The Microverse*, November
1989.
"Robbie," copyright Fictioneers, Inc., 1940. Copyright renewed © Isaac Asimov, 1967.
First appeared under the title "Strange Playfellow" in *Super Science Stories*, September 1940.
"Reason," copyright Street & Smith Publications, Inc., 1941. Copyright renewed ©
Isaac Asimov, 1968. First appeared in *Astounding Science Fiction*, April 1941.
"Liar!" copyright Street & Smith Publications, Inc., 1941. Copyright renewed © Isaac
Asimov, 1968. First appeared in *Astounding Science Fiction*, May 1941.
"Runaround," copyright Street & Smith Publications, Inc., 1942. Copyright renewed
© Isaac Asimov, 1968. First appeared in *Astounding Science Fiction*, April 1941.
"Evidence," copyright Street & Smith Publications, Inc., 1946. Copyright renewed ©
Isaac Asimov, 1973. First appeared in *Astounding Science Fiction*, March 1947.
"The Evitable Conflict," copyright Street & Smith Publications, Inc., 1950. Copyright renewed © Isaac Asimov, 1977. First appeared in *Astounding Science Fiction*, June 1950.
"Feminine Intuition," copyright © Mercury Press, Inc., 1969. First appeared in *The
Magazine of Fantasy and Science Fiction*, October 1969.
"The Bicentennial Man," copyright © Random House, Inc., 1976. First appeared in
Stellar #2.
"Someday," copyright © Royal Publications, Inc., 1956. First appeared in *Infinity
Science Fiction*, August 1956.
"Think!" copyright © Davis Publication, Inc., 1977. First appeared in *Isaac Asimov's
Science Fiction Magazine*, Spring 1977.

To Gardner Dozois and Stan Schmidt,
colleagues and friends

CONTENTS

■

CONTENTS

ESSAYS

ISAAC ASIMOV
ROBOT VISIONS

· INTRODUCTION: ·
THE ROBOT
CHRONICLES

·

What is a robot? We might define it most briefly and comprehensively as "an artificial object that resembles a human being."

When we think of resemblance, we think of it, first, in terms of appearance. A robot *looks* like a human being.

It could, for instance, be covered with a soft material that resembles human skin. It could have hair, and eyes, and a voice, and all the features and appurtenances of a human being, so that it would, as far as outward appearance is concerned, be indistinguishable from a human being.

This, however, is not really essential. In fact, the robot, as it appears in science fiction, is almost always constructed of metal, and has only a stylized resemblance to a human being.

Suppose, then, we forget about appearance and consider only what it can do. We think of robots as capable of performing tasks more rapidly or more efficiently than human beings. But in that case *any* machine is a robot. A sewing machine can sew faster than a human being, a pneumatic drill can penetrate a hard surface faster than an unaided human being can, a television set can detect and organize radio waves as we cannot, and so on.

We must apply the term robot, then, to a machine that is more specialized than an ordinary device. A robot is a *computerized* machine that is capable of performing tasks of a kind that are too complex for any living mind other than that of a man, and of a kind that no non-computerized machine is capable of performing.

In other words to put it as briefly as possible:

robot = machine + computer

Clearly, then, a true robot was impossible before the invention of the computer in the 1940s, and was not practical (in the sense of being compact enough and cheap enough to be put to everyday use) until the invention of the microchip in the 1970s.

Nevertheless, the *concept* of the robot—an artificial device that mimics the actions and, possibly, the appearance of a human being—is old, probably as old as the human imagination.

The ancients, lacking computers, had to think of some other way of instilling quasi-human abilities into artificial objects, and they made use of vague supernatural forces and depended on god-like abilities beyond the reach of mere men.

Thus, in the eighteenth book of Homer's *Iliad*, Hephaistos, the Greek god of the forge, is described as having for helpers, "a couple of maids . . . made of gold exactly like living girls; they have sense in their heads, they can speak and use their muscles, they can spin and weave and do their work. . . ." Surely, these are robots.

Again, the island of Crete, at the time of its greatest power, was supposed to possess a bronze giant named Talos that ceaselessly patrolled its shores to fight off the approach of any enemy.

Throughout ancient and medieval times, learned men were supposed to have created artificially living things through the secret arts they had learned or uncovered—arts by which they made use of the powers of the divine or the demonic.

The medieval robot-story that is most familiar to us today is that of Rabbi Loew of sixteenth-century Prague. He is supposed to have formed an artificial human being—a robot—out of clay, just as God had formed Adam out of clay. A clay object, however much it might resemble a human being, is "an unformed substance" (the Hebrew word for it is "golem"), since it lacks the attributes of life. Rabbi Loew, however, gave his golem the attributes of life by making use of the sacred name of God, and set the robot to work protecting the lives of Jews against their persecutors.

There was, however, always a certain nervousness about human beings involving themselves with knowledge that properly belongs to gods or demons. There was the feeling that this was dangerous, that the forces might escape human control. This attitude is most familiar to us in the legend of the "sorcerer's apprentice," the young fellow who knew enough magic to start a process going but not enough to stop it when it had outlived its usefulness.

The ancients were intelligent enough to see this possibility and be frightened by it. In the Hebrew myth of Adam and Eve, the sin they commit is that of gaining knowledge (eating of the fruit of the tree of knowledge of good and evil; i.e., knowledge of everything) and for that they were ejected from Eden and, according to Christian theologians, infected all of humanity with that "original sin."

In the Greek myths, it was the Titan, or Prometheus, who supplied fire (and therefore technology) to human beings and for that he was dreadfully punished by the infuriated Zeus, who was the chief god.

In early modern times, mechanical clocks were perfected, and the small mechanisms that ran them ("clockwork")—the springs, gears, escapements, ratchets, and so on—could also be used to run other devices.

The 1700s was the golden age of "automatons." These were devices that could, given a source of power such as a wound spring or compressed air, carry out a complicated series of activities. Toy soldiers were built that would march;

toy ducks that would quack, bathe, drink water, eat grain and void it; toy boys that could dip a pen into ink and write a letter (always the same letter, of course). Such automata were put on display and proved extremely popular (and, sometimes, profitable to the owners).

It was a dead-end sort of thing, of course, but it kept alive the thought of mechanical devices that might do more than clockwork tricks, that might be more nearly alive.

What's more, science was advancing rapidly, and in 1798, the Italian anatomist, Luigi Galvani, found that under the influence of an electric spark, dead muscles could be made to twitch and contract as though they were alive. Was it possible that electricity was the secret of life?

The thought naturally arose that artificial life could be brought into being by strictly scientific principles rather than by reliance on gods or demons. This thought led to a book that some people consider the first piece of modern science fiction—*Frankenstein* by Mary Shelley, published in 1818.

In this book, Victor Frankenstein, an anatomist, collects fragments of freshly dead bodies and, by the use of new scientific discoveries (not specified in the book), brings the whole to life, creating something that is referred to only as the "Monster" in the book. (In the movie, the life principle was electricity.)

However, the switch from the supernatural to science did not eliminate the fear of the danger inherent in knowledge. In the medieval legend of Rabbi Loew's golem, that monster went out of control and the rabbi had to withdraw the divine name and destroy him. In the modern tale of Frankenstein, the hero was not so lucky. He abandoned the Monster in fear, and the Monster, with an anger that the book all but justifies, in revenge killed those Frankenstein loved and, eventually, Frankenstein himself.

This proved a central theme in the science fiction stories that have appeared since *Frankenstein*. The creation of robots was looked upon as the prime example of the overweening arrogance of humanity, of its attempt to take on, through misdirected science, the mantle of the divine. The creation of human life, with a soul, was the sole prerogative of God. For a human being to attempt such a creation was to produce a soulless travesty that inevitably became as dangerous as the golem and as the Monster. The fashioning of a robot was, therefore, its own eventual punishment, and the lesson, "there are some things that humanity is not meant to know," was preached over and over again.

No one used the word "robot," however, until 1920 (the year, coincidentally, in which I was born). In that year, a Czech playwright, Karel Čapek, wrote the play *R.U.R.*, about an Englishman, Rossum, who manufactured artificial human beings in quantity. These were intended to do the arduous labor of the world so that real human beings could live lives of leisure and comfort.

Čapek called these artificial human beings "robots," which is a Czech word for "forced workers," or "slaves." In fact, the title of the play stands for "Rossum's Universal Robots," the name of the hero's firm.

In this play, however, what I call "the Frankenstein complex" was made several notches more intense. Where Mary Shelley's Monster destroyed only Frankenstein and his family, Čapek's robots were presented as gaining emotion and then, resenting their slavery, wiping out the human species.

The play was produced in 1921 and was sufficiently popular (though when I read it, my purely personal opinion was that it was dreadful) to force the word "robot" into universal use. The name for an artificial human being is now "robot" in every language, as far as I know.

Through the 1920s and 1930s, *R.U.R.* helped reinforce the Frankenstein complex, and (with some notable exceptions such as Lester del Rey's "Helen O'Loy" and Eando Binder's "Adam Link" series) the hordes of clanking, murderous robots continued to be reproduced in story after story.

I was an ardent science fiction reader in the 1930s and I became tired of the ever-repeated robot plot. I didn't see robots that way. I saw them as machines—advanced machines

—but machines. They might be dangerous but surely safety factors would be built in. The safety factors might be faulty or inadequate or might fail under unexpected types of stresses, but such failures could always yield experience that could be used to improve the models.

After all, all devices have their dangers. The discovery of speech introduced communication—and lies. The discovery of fire introduced cooking—and arson. The discovery of the compass improved navigation—and destroyed civilizations in Mexico and Peru. The automobile is marvelously useful—and kills Americans by the tens of thousands each year. Medical advances have saved lives by the millions—and intensified the population explosion.

In every case, the dangers and misuses could be used to demonstrate that "there are some things humanity was not meant to know," but surely we cannot be expected to divest ourselves of all knowledge and return to the status of the australopithecines. Even from the theological standpoint, one might argue that God would never have given human beings brains to reason with if He hadn't intended those brains to be used to devise new things, to make wise use of them, to install safety factors to prevent unwise use—and to do the best we can within the limitations of our imperfections.

So, in 1939, at the age of nineteen, I determined to write a robot story about a robot that was wisely used, that was not dangerous, and that did the job it was supposed to do. Since I needed a power source I introduced the "positronic brain." This was just gobbledygook but it represented some unknown power source that was useful, versatile, speedy, and compact—like the as-yet uninvented computer.

The story was eventually named "Robbie," and it did not appear immediately, but I proceeded to write other stories along the same line—in consultation with my editor, John W. Campbell, Jr., who was much taken with this idea of mine—and eventually, they were all printed.

Campbell urged me to make my ideas as to the robot safeguards explicit rather than implicit, and I did this in my fourth robot story, "Runaround," which appeared in the

March 1942 issue of *Astounding Science Fiction*. In that issue, on page 100, in the first column, about one-third of the way down (I just happen to remember) one of my characters says to another, "Now, look, let's start with the Three Fundamental Rules of Robotics."

This, as it turned out, was the very first known use of the word "robotics" in print, a word that is the now-accepted and widely used term for the science and technology of the construction, maintenance, and use of robots. The Oxford English Dictionary, in the 3rd Supplementary Volume, gives me credit for the invention of the word.

I did not know I was inventing the word, of course. In my youthful innocence, I thought that *was* the word and hadn't the faintest notion it had never been used before.

"The three fundamental Rules of Robotics" mentioned at this point eventually became known as "Asimov's Three Laws of Robotics," and here they are:

1. A robot may not injure a human being, or, through inaction, allow a human being to come to harm.

2. A robot must obey the orders given it by human beings except where such orders would conflict with the First Law.

3. A robot must protect its own existence as long as such protection does not conflict with the First or Second Law.

Those laws, as it turned out (and as I could not possibly have foreseen), proved to be the most famous, the most frequently quoted, and the most influential sentences I ever wrote. (And I did it when I was twenty-one, which makes me wonder if I've done anything since to continue to justify my existence.)

My robot stories turned out to have a great effect on science fiction. I dealt with robots unemotionally—they were produced by engineers, they presented engineering problems that required solutions, and the solutions were found. The stories were rather convincing portrayals of a future technology and were not moral lessons. The robots were machines and not metaphors.

As a result, the old-fashioned robot story was virtually killed in all science fiction stories above the comic-strip level. Robots began to be viewed as machines rather than metaphors by other writers, too. They grew to be commonly seen as benevolent and useful except when something went wrong, and then as capable of correction and improvement. Other writers did not quote the Three Laws—they tended to be reserved for me—but they *assumed* them, and so did the readers.

Astonishingly enough, my robot stories also had an important effect on the world outside.

It is well known that the early rocket-experimenters were strongly influenced by the science fiction stories of H. G. Wells. In the same way, early robot-experimenters were strongly influenced by my robot stories, nine of which were collected in 1950 to make up a book called *I, Robot*. It was my second published book and it has remained in print in the four decades since.

Joseph F. Engelberger, studying at Columbia University in the 1950s, came across *I, Robot* and was sufficiently attracted by what he read to determine that he was going to devote his life to robots. About that time, he met George C. Devol, Jr., at a cocktail party. Devol was an inventor who was also interested in robots.

Together, they founded the firm of Unimation and set about working out schemes for making robots work. They patented many devices, and by the mid-1970s, they had worked out all kinds of practical robots. The trouble was that they needed computers that were compact and cheap—but once the microchip came in, they had it. From that moment on, Unimation became the foremost robot firm in the world and Engelberger grew rich beyond anything he could have dreamed of.

He has always been kind enough to give me much of the credit. I have met other roboticists such as Marvin Minsky and Shimon Y. Nof, who also admitted, cheerfully, the value of their early reading of my robot stories. Nof, who is an Israeli, had first read *I, Robot* in a Hebrew translation.

The roboticists take the Three Laws of Robotics seriously and they keep them as an ideal for robot safety. As yet, the types of industrial robots in use are so simple, essentially, that safety devices have to be built in externally. However, robots may confidently be expected to grow more versatile and capable and the Three Laws, or their equivalent, will surely be built in to their programming eventually.

I myself have never actually worked with robots, never even as much as seen one, but I have never stopped thinking about them. I have to date written at least thirty-five short stories and five novels that involve robots, and I dare say that if I am spared, I will write more.

My robot stories and novels seem to have become classics in their own right and, with the advent of the "Robot City" series of novels, have become the wider literary universe of other writers as well. Under those circumstances, it might be useful to go over my robot stories and describe some of those which I think are particularly significant and to explain why I think they are.

1. "Robbie:" This is the first robot story I wrote. I turned it out between May 10 and May 22 of 1939, when I was nineteen years old and was just about to graduate from college. I had a little trouble placing it, for John Campbell rejected it and so did *Amazing Stories*. However, Fred Pohl accepted it on March 25, 1940, and it appeared in the September 1940 issue of *Super Science Stories*, which he edited. Fred Pohl, being Fred Pohl, changed the title to "Strange Playfellow," but I changed it back when I included it in my book *I, Robot* and it has appeared as "Robbie" in every subsequent incarnation.

Aside from being my first robot story, "Robbie" is significant because in it, George Weston says to his wife in defense of a robot that is fulfilling the role of nursemaid, "He just can't help being faithful and loving and kind. He's a machine—*made so*." This is the first indication, in my first story, of what eventually became the "First Law of Robotics," and of the basic fact that robots were made with built-in safety rules.

2. "Reason:" "Robbie" would have meant nothing in itself if I had written no more robot stories, particularly

since it appeared in one of the minor magazines. However, I wrote a second robot story, "Reason," and that one John Campbell liked. After a bit of revision, it appeared in the April 1941 issue of *Astounding Science Fiction*, and there it attracted notice. Readers became aware that there was such a thing as the "positronic robots," and so did Campbell. That made everything afterward possible.

3. "Liar!:" In the very next issue of *Astounding*, that of May 1941, my third robot story, "Liar!" appeared: The importance of this story was that it introduced Susan Calvin, who became the central character in my early robot stories. This story was originally rather clumsily done, largely because it dealt with the relationship between the sexes at a time when I had not yet had my first date with a young lady. Fortunately, I'm a quick learner, and it is one story in which I made significant changes before allowing it to appear in *I, Robot*.

4. "Runaround:" The next important robot story appeared in the March 1942 issue of *Astounding*. It was the first story in which I listed the Three Laws of Robotics explicitly instead of making them implicit. In it, I have one character, Gregory Powell, say to another, Michael Donovan, "Now, look, let's start with the Three Fundamental Rules of Robotics—the three rules that are built most deeply into a robot's positronic brain." He then recites them.

Later on, I called them the Laws of Robotics, and their importance to me was threefold:

a) They guided me in forming my plots and made it possible to write many short stories, as well as several novels, based on robots. In these, I constantly studied the consequences of the Three Laws.

b) It was by all odds my most famous literary invention, quoted in season and out by others. If all I have written is someday to be forgotten, the Three Laws of Robotics will surely be the last to go.

c) The passage in "Runaround" quoted above happens to be the very first time the word "robotics" was used in print in the English language. I am therefore credited, as I have said, with the invention of that word (as well as of "robotic," "positronic," and "psychohistory") by the Oxford English Dictionary, which takes the trouble—and the space—to quote the Three Laws. (All these things were created by my twenty-second birthday and I seem to have created nothing since, which gives rise to grievous thoughts within me.)

5. "Evidence:" This was the one and only story I wrote while I spent eight months and twenty-six days in the Army. At one point I persuaded a kindly librarian to let me remain in the locked library over lunch so that I could work on the story. It is the first story in which I made use of a humanoid robot. Stephen Byerley, the humanoid robot in question (though in the story I don't make it absolutely clear whether he is a robot or not), represents my first approach toward R. Daneel Olivaw, the humaniform robot who appears in a number of my novels. "Evidence" appeared in the September 1946 issue of *Astounding Science Fiction*.

6. "Little Lost Robot:" My robots tend to be benign entities. In fact, as the stories progressed, they gradually gained in moral and ethical qualities until they far surpassed human beings and, in the case of Daneel, approached the god-like. Nevertheless, I had no intention of limiting myself to robots as saviors. I followed wherever the wild winds of my imagination led me, and I was quite capable of seeing the uncomfortable sides of the robot phenomena.

It was only a few weeks ago (as I write this) that I received a letter from a reader who scolded me because, in a robot story of mine that had just been published, I showed the dangerous side of robots. He accused me of a failure of nerve.

That he was wrong is shown by "Little Lost Robot" in which a robot is the villain, even though it appeared nearly half a century ago. The seamy side of robots is *not* the result of a failure in nerve that comes of my advancing age and decrepitude. It has been a constant concern of mine all through my career.

7. "The Evitable Conflict:" This was a sequel to "Evi-

dence" and appeared in the June 1950 issue of *Astounding*. It was the first story I wrote that dealt primarily with computers (I called them "Machines" in the story) rather than with robots per se. The difference is not a great one. You might define a robot as a "computerized machine" or as a "mobile computer." You might consider a computer as an "immobile robot." In any case, I clearly did not distinguish between the two, and although the Machines, which don't make an actual physical appearance in the story, are clearly computers, I included the story, without hesitation, in my robot collection, *I, Robot*, and neither the publisher nor the readers objected. To be sure, Stephen Byerley is in the story, but the question of his roboticity plays no role.

8. "Franchise:" This was the first story in which I dealt with computers *as computers*, and I had no thought in mind of their being robots. It appeared in the August 1955 issue of *If: Worlds of Science Fiction*, and by that time I had grown familiar with the existence of computers. My computer is "Multivac," designed as an obviously larger and more complex version of the actually existing "Univac." In this story, and in some others of the period that dealt with Multivac, I described it as an enormously large machine, missing the chance of predicting the miniaturization and etherealization of computers.

9. "The Last Question:" My imagination didn't betray me for long, however. In "The Last Question," which appeared first in the November 1956 issue of *Science Fiction Quarterly*, I discussed the miniaturization and etherealization of computers and followed it through a trillion years of evolution (of both computer and man) to a logical conclusion that you will have to read the story to discover. It is, beyond question, my favorite among all the stories I have written in my career.

10. "The Feeling of Power:" The miniaturization of computers played a small role as a side issue in this story. It appeared in the February 1958 issue of *If* and is also one of my favorites. In this story I dealt with pocket computers, which were not to make their appearance in the market-

place until ten to fifteen years after the story appeared. Moreover, it was one of the stories in which I foresaw accurately a social implication of technological advance rather than the technological advance itself.

The story deals with the possible loss of ability to do simple arithmetic through the perpetual use of computers. I wrote it as a satire that combined humor with passages of bitter irony, but I wrote more truly than I knew. These days I have a pocket computer and I begrudge the time and effort it would take me to subtract 182 from 854. I use the darned computer. "The Feeling of Power" is one of the most frequently anthologized of my stories.

In a way, this story shows the negative side of computers, and in this period I also wrote stories that showed the possible vengeful reactions of computers or robots that are mistreated. For computers, there is "Someday," which appeared in the August 1956 issue of *Infinity Science Fiction*, and for robots (in automobile form) see "Sally," which appeared in the May–June 1953 issue of *Fantastic*.

11. "Feminine Intuition:" My robots are almost always masculine, though not necessarily in an actual sense of gender. After all, I give them masculine names and refer to them as "he." At the suggestion of a female editor, Judy-Lynn del Rey, I wrote "Feminine Intuition," which appeared in the October 1969 issue of *The Magazine of Fantasy and Science Fiction*. It showed, for one thing, that I could do a feminine robot, too. She was still metal, but she had a narrower waistline than my usual robots and had a feminine voice, too. Later on, in my book *Robots and Empire*, there was a chapter in which a humanoid female robot made her appearance. She played a villainous role, which might surprise those who know of my frequently displayed admiration of the female half of humanity.

12. "The Bicentennial Man:" This story, which first appeared in 1976 in a paperback anthology of original science fiction, *Stellar #2*, edited by Judy-Lynn del Rey, was my most thoughtful exposition of the development of robots. It followed them in an entirely different direction from that in

"The Last Question." What it dealt with was the desire of a robot to become a man and the way in which he carried out that desire, step by step. Again, I carried the plot all the way to its logical conclusion. I had no intention of writing this story when I started it. It wrote itself, and turned and twisted in the typewriter. It ended as the third favorite of mine among all my stories. Ahead of it come only "The Last Question," mentioned above, and "The Ugly Little Boy," which is not a robot story.

13. "The Caves of Steel:" Meanwhile, at the suggestion of Horace L. Gold, editor of *Galaxy*, I had written a robot novel. I had resisted doing so at first for I felt that my robot ideas only fit the short story length. Gold, however, suggested I write a murder mystery dealing with a robot detective. I followed the suggestion partway. My detective was a thoroughly human Elijah Baley (perhaps the most attractive character I ever invented, in my opinion), but he had a robot sidekick, R. Daneel Olivaw. The book, I felt, was the perfect fusion of mystery and science fiction. It appeared as a three-part serial in the October, November, and December 1953 issues of *Galaxy*, and Doubleday published it as a novel in 1954.

What surprised me about the book was the reaction of the readers. While they approved of Lije Baley, their obvious interest was entirely with Daneel, whom I had viewed as a mere subsidiary character. The approval was particularly intense in the case of the women who wrote to me. (Thirteen years after I had invented Daneel, the television series *Star Trek* came out, with Mr. Spock resembling Daneel quite closely in character—something which did not bother me—and I noticed that women viewers were particularly interested in him, too. I won't pretend to analyze this.)

14. "The Naked Sun:" The popularity of Lije and Daneel led me to write a sequel, *The Naked Sun*, which appeared as a three-part serial in the October, November, and December 1956 issues of *Astounding* and was published as a novel by Doubleday in 1957. Naturally, the repetition of the success made a third novel seem the logical thing to do. I even

started writing it in 1958, but things got in the way and, what with one thing and another, it didn't get written till 1983.

15. "The Robots of Dawn:" This, the third novel of the Lije Baley/R. Daneel series, was published by Doubleday in 1983. In it, I introduced a second robot, R. Giskard Reventlov, and this time I was not surprised when he turned out to be as popular as Daneel.

16. "Robots and Empire:" When it was necessary to allow Lije Baley to die (of old age), I felt I would have no problem in doing a fourth book in the series, provided I allowed Daneel to live. The fourth book, *Robots and Empire*, was published by Doubleday in 1985. Lije's death brought some reaction, but nothing at all compared to the storm of regretful letters I received when the exigencies of the plot made it necessary for R. Giskard to die.

Of the short stories I have listed as "notable" you may have noticed that three—"Franchise," "The Last Question," and "The Feeling of Power"—are not included in the collection you are now holding. This is not an oversight, nor is it any indication that they are not suitable for collection. The fact is that each of the three is to be found in an earlier collection, *Robot Dreams*, that is a companion piece for this one. It wouldn't be fair to the reader to have these stories in both collections.

To make up for that, I have included in *Robot Visions* nine robot stories that are not listed above as "notable." This in no way implies that these nine stories are inferior, merely that they broke no new ground.

Of these nine stories, "Galley Slave" is one of my favorites, not only because of the word-play in the title, but because it deals with a job I earnestly wish a robot would take off my hands. Not many people have gone through more sets of galleys than I have.

"Lenny" shows a human side of Susan Calvin that appears in no other story, while "Someday" is my foray into pathos. "Christmas Without Rodney" is a a humorous robot story, while "Think!" is a rather grim one. "Mirror Image" is the only short story I ever wrote that involves R. Daneel Olivaw, the co-hero of my robot novels. "Too Bad!" and "Segregationist" are both robot stories based on medical themes. And, finally, "Robot Visions" is written specifically for this collection.

So it turns out that my robot stories have been almost as successful as my Foundation books, and if you want to know the truth (in a whisper, of course, and please keep this confidential) I like my robot stories better.

Finally, a word about the essays in this book. The first essay was written in 1956. All the others have appeared in 1974 and thereafter. Why the eighteen-year gap?

Easy. I wrote my first robot story when I was nineteen, and I wrote them, on and off, for over thirty years without really believing that robots would ever come into existence in any real sense—at least not in my lifetime. The result was that I never once wrote a serious essay on robotics. I might as well expect myself to have written serious essays on Galactic empires and psychohistory. In fact, my 1956 piece is not a serious discussion of robotics but merely a consideration of the use of robots in science fiction.

It was not till the mid-1970s, with the development of the microchip, that computers grew small enough, versatile enough, and cheap enough to allow computerized machinery to become practical for industrial use. Thus, the industrial robot arrived—extremely simple compared to my imaginary robots, but clearly en route.

And, as it happened, in 1974, just as robots were becoming real, I began to write essays on current developments in science, first for *American Way* magazine and then for the Los Angeles Times Syndicate. It became natural to write an occasional piece on real robotics. In addition, Byron Preiss Visual Publications, Inc., began to put out a remarkable series of books under the general title of *Isaac Asimov's Robot City*, and I was asked to do essays on robotics for each of them. So it came about that before 1974, I wrote virtually no essays on robotics, and after 1974 quite a few. It's not my fault, after all, if science finally catches up to my simpler notions.*

---

* You are now ready to plunge into the book itself. Please remember that the stories, written at different times over a period of half a century, may be mutually inconsistent here and there. As for the concluding essays—written at different times for different outlets—they are repetitious here and there. Please forgive me in each case.

ROBOT VISIONS

■

I suppose I should start by telling you who I am. I am a very junior member of the Temporal Group. The Temporalists (for those of you who have been too busy trying to survive in this harsh world of 2030 to pay much attention to the advance of technology) are the aristocrats of physics these days.

They deal with that most intractable of problems—that of moving through time at a speed different from the steady temporal progress of the Universe. In short, they are trying to develop time-travel.

And what am I doing with these people, when I myself am not even a physicist, but merely a—? Well, merely a *merely*.

Despite my lack of qualification, it was actually a remark I made some time before that inspired the Temporalists to work out the concept of VPIT ("virtual paths in time").

You see, one of the difficulties in travelling through time is that your base does not stay in one place relative to the Universe as a whole. The Earth is moving about the Sun; the Sun about the Galactic center; the Galaxy about the center of gravity of the Local Group—well, you get the idea. If you move one day into the future or the past—just one day—Earth has moved some 2.5 million kilometers in its orbit about the Sun. And the Sun has moved in its journey, carrying Earth with it, and so has everything else.

Therefore, you must move through space as well as through time, and it was my remark that led to a line of argument that showed that this was possible; that one could travel with the space-time motion of the Earth not in a literal, but in a "virtual" way that would enable a time-traveller to remain with his base on Earth wherever he went in time. It would be useless for me to try to explain that mathematically if you have not had Temporalist training. Just accept the matter.

It was also a remark of mine that led the Temporalists to develop a line of reasoning that showed that travel into the past was impossible. Key terms in the equations would have to rise beyond infinity when the temporal signs were changed.

It made sense. It was clear that a trip into the past would be sure to change events there at least slightly, and no matter how slight a change might be introduced into the past, it would alter the present; very likely drastically. Since the past should seem fixed, it makes sense that travel back in time is impossible.

The future, however, is not fixed, so that travel into the future and back again from it would be possible.

I was not particularly rewarded for my remarks. I imagine the Temporalist team assumed I had been fortunate in my speculations and it was they who were entirely the clever ones in picking up what I had said and carrying it through to useful conclusions. I did not resent that, considering the circumstances, but was merely very glad—delighted, in fact—since because of that (I think) they allowed me to continue to work with them and to be part of the project, even though I was merely a—well, merely.

Naturally, it took years to work out a practical device for time travel, even after the theory was established, but I don't intend to write a serious treatise on Temporality. It is my intention to write of only certain parts of the project, and to do so for only the future inhabitants of the planet, and not for our contemporaries.

Even after inanimate objects had been sent into the future— and then animals—we were not satisfied. All objects disappeared; all, it seemed, travelled into the future. When we sent them short distances into the future—five minutes or five days—they eventually appeared again, seemingly unharmed, unchanged, and, if alive to begin with, still alive and in good health.

But what was wanted was to send something far into the future and bring it back.

"We'd have to send it at least two hundred years into the future," said one Temporalist. "The important point is to see what the future is like and to have the vision reported back to us. We have to know whether humanity will survive and under what conditions, and two hundred years should be long enough to be sure. Frankly, I think the chances of survival are poor. Living conditions and the environment about us have deteriorated badly over the last century."

(There is no use in trying to describe which Temporalist said what. There were a couple of dozen of them altogether, and it makes no difference to the tale I am telling as to which one spoke at any one time, even if I were sure I could remember which one said what. Therefore, I shall simply say "said a Temporalist," or "one said," or "some of them said," or "another said," and I assure you it will all be sufficiently clear to you. Naturally, I shall specify my own statements and that of one other, but you will see that those exceptions are essential.)

Another Temporalist said rather gloomily, "I don't think I want to know the future, if it means finding out that the human race is to be wiped out or that it will exist only as miserable remnants."

"Why not?" said another. "We can find out in shorter trips exactly what happened and then do our best to so act, out of our special knowledge, as to change the future in a preferred direction. The future, unlike the past, is not fixed."

But then the question arose as to who was to go. It was clear that the Temporalists each felt himself or herself to be just a bit too valuable to risk on a technique that might not yet be perfected despite the success of experiments on objects that were not alive; or, if alive, objects that lacked a brain of the incredible complexity that a human being owned. The brain might survive, but, perhaps, not quite all its complexity might.

I realized that of them all I was least valuable and might be considered the logical candidate. Indeed, I was on the point of raising my hand as a volunteer, but my facial expression must have given me away for one of the Temporalists said, rather impatiently, "Not you. Even you are too valuable." (Not very complimentary.) "The thing to do," he went on, "is to send RG-32."

That *did* make sense. RG-32 was a rather old-fashioned robot, eminently replaceable. He could observe and report—perhaps without quite the ingenuity and penetration of a human being—but well enough. He would be without fear, intent only on following his orders, and he could be expected to tell the truth.

Perfect!

I was rather surprised at myself for not seeing that from the start, and for foolishly considering volunteering myself. Perhaps, I thought, I had some sort of instinctive feeling that I ought to put myself into a position where I could serve the others. In any case, it was RG-32 that was the logical choice; indeed, the only one.

In some ways, it was not difficult to explain what we needed. Archie (it was customary to call a robot by some common perversion of his serial number) did not ask for reasons, or for guarantees of his safety. He would accept any order he was capable of understanding and following, with the same lack of emotionality that he would display if asked to raise his hand. He would have to, being a robot.

The details took time, however.

"Once you are in the future," one of the senior Temporalists said, "you may stay for as long as you feel you can make useful observations. When you are through, you will return to your machine and come back with it to the very moment that you left by adjusting the controls in a manner which we will explain to you. You will leave and to us it will seem that you will be back a split-second later, even though to yourself it may have seemed that you had spent a week in the future, or five years. Naturally, you will have to make sure the machine is stored in a safe place while you are gone, which should not be difficult since it is quite light. And you will have to remember where you stored the machine and how to get back to it."

What made the briefing even longer lay in the fact that one Temporalist after another would remember a new difficulty. Thus, one of them said suddenly, "How much do you think the language will have changed in two centuries?"

Naturally, there was no answer to that and a great debate grew as to whether there might be no chance of communication whatever, that Archie would neither understand nor make himself understood.

Finally, one Temporalist said, rather curtly, "See here, the English language has been becoming ever more nearly universal for several centuries and that is sure to continue for two more. Nor has it changed significantly in the last two hundred years, so why should it do so in the next two hundred? Even if it has, there are bound to be scholars who would be able to speak what they might call 'ancient English.' And even if there were not, Archie would still be able to make useful observations. Determining whether a functioning society exists does not necessarily require talk."

Other problems arose. What if he found himself facing hostility? What if the people of the future found and destroyed the machine, either out of malevolence or ignorance?

One Temporalist said, "It might be wise to design a Temporal engine so miniaturized that it could be carried in one's clothing. Under such conditions one could at any time leave a dangerous position very quickly."

"Even if it were possible at all," snapped another, "it would probably take so long to design so miniaturized a

machine that we—or rather our successors—would reach a time two centuries hence without the necessity of using a machine at all. No, if an accident of some sort takes place, Archie simply won't return and we'll just have to try again."

This was said with Archie present, but that didn't matter, of course. Archie could contemplate being marooned in time, or even his own destruction, with equanimity, provided he were following orders. The Second Law of Robotics, which makes it necessary for a robot to follow orders, takes precedence over the Third, which makes it necessary for him to protect his own existence.

In the end, of course, all had been said, and no one could any longer think of a warning, or an objection, or a possibility that had not been thoroughly aired.

Archie repeated all he had been told with robotic calmness and precision, and the next step was to teach him how to use the machine. And he learned that, too, with robotic calmness and precision.

You must understand that the general public did not know, at that time, that time-travel was being investigated. It was not an expensive project as long as it was a matter of working on theory, but experimental work had punished the budget and was bound to punish it still more. This was most uncomfortable for scientists engaged in an endeavor that seemed totally "blue-sky."

If there was a *large* failure, given the state of the public purse, there would be a loud outcry on the part of the people, and the project might be doomed. The Temporalists all agreed, without even the necessity of debate, that only success could be reported, and that until such a success was recorded, the public would have to learn very little, if anything at all. And so *this* experiment, the crucial one, was heart-stopping for everyone.

We gathered at an isolated spot of the semi-desert, an artfully protected area given over to Project Four. (Even the name was intended to give no real hint of the nature of the work, but it always struck me that most people thought of time as a kind of fourth dimension and that someone ought therefore guess what we were doing. Yet no one ever did, to my knowledge.)

Then, at a certain moment, at which time there was a great deal of breath-holding, Archie, inside the machine, raised one hand to signify he was about to make his move. Half a breath later—if anyone had been breathing—the machine flickered.

It was a very rapid flicker. I wasn't sure that I had observed it. It seemed to me that I had merely assumed it *ought* to flicker, if it returned to nearly the instant at which it left—and I saw what I was convinced I ought to see. I meant to ask the others if they, too, had seen a flicker, but I always hesitated to address them unless they spoke to me first. They were *very* important people, and I was merely— but I've said that. Then, too, in the excitement of questioning Archie, I forgot the matter of the flicker. It wasn't at all important.

So brief an interval was there between leaving and returning that we might well have thought that he hadn't left at all, but there was no question of that. The machine had definitely deteriorated. It had simply *faded*.

Nor was Archie, on emerging from the machine, much better off. He was not the same Archie that had entered that machine. There was a shopworn look about him, a dullness to his finish, a slight unevenness to his surface where he might have undergone collisions, an odd manner in the way he looked about as though he were re-experiencing an almost forgotten scene. I doubt that there was a single person there who felt for one moment that Archie had not been absent, as far as his own sensation of time was concerned, for a long interval.

In fact, the first question he was asked was, "How long have you been away?"

Archie said, "Five years, sir. It was a time interval that had been mentioned in my instructions and I wished to do a thorough job."

"Come, that's a hopeful fact," said one Temporalist. "If

the world were a mass of destruction, surely it would not have taken five years to gather that fact."

And yet not one of them dared say: well, Archie, *was* the Earth a mass of destruction?

They waited for him to speak, and for a while, he also waited, with robotic politeness, for them to ask. After a while, however, Archie's need to obey orders, by reporting his observations, overcame whatever there was in his positronic circuits that made it necessary for him to seem polite.

Archie said, "All was well on the Earth of the future. The social structure was intact and working well."

"Intact and working well?" said one Temporalist, acting as though he were shocked at so heretical a notion. "Everywhere?"

"The inhabitants of the world were most kind. They took me to every part of the globe. All was prosperous and peaceful."

The Temporalists looked at each other. It seemed easier for them to believe that Archie was wrong, or mistaken, than that the Earth of the future was prosperous and peaceful. It had seemed to me always that, despite all optimistic statements to the contrary, it was taken almost as an article of faith, that Earth was on the point of social, economic, and, perhaps, even physical destruction.

They began to question him thoroughly. One shouted, "What about the forests? They're almost gone."

"There was a huge project," said Archie, "for the reforestation of the land, sir. Wilderness has been restored where possible. Genetic engineering has been used imaginatively to restore wildlife where related species existed in zoos or as pets. Pollution is a thing of the past. The world of 2230 is a world of natural peace and beauty."

"You are *sure* of all this?" asked a Temporalist.

"No spot on Earth was kept secret. I was shown all I asked to see."

Another Temporalist said, with sudden severity, "Archie, listen to me. It may be that you have seen a ruined Earth, but hesitate to tell us this for fear we will be driven to despair and suicide. In your eagerness to do us no harm, you may be lying to us. This must not happen, Archie. You *must* tell us the truth."

Archie said, calmly, "I am telling the truth, sir. If I were lying, no matter what my motive for it might be, my positronic potentials would be in an abnormal state. That could be tested."

"He's right there," muttered a Temporalist.

He was tested on the spot. He was not allowed to say another word while this was done. I watched with interest while the potentiometers recorded their findings, which were then analyzed by computer. There was no question about it. Archie was perfectly normal. He could not be lying.

He was then questioned again. "What about the cities?"

"There are no cities of our kind, sir. Life is much more decentralized in 2230 than with us, in the sense that there are no large and concentrated clumps of humanity. On the other hand, there is so intricate a communication network that humanity is all one loose clump, so to speak."

"And space? Has space exploration been renewed?"

Archie said, "The Moon is quite well developed, sir. It is an inhabited world. There are space settlements in orbit about the Earth and about Mars. There are settlements being carved out in the asteroid belt."

"You were told all this?" asked one Temporalist, suspiciously.

"This is not a matter of hearsay, sir. I have been in space. I remained on the Moon for two months. I lived on a space settlement about Mars for a month, and visited both Phobos and Mars itself. There is some hesitation about colonizing Mars. There are opinions that it should be seeded with lower forms of life and left to itself without the intervention of the Earthpeople. I did not actually visit the asteroid belt."

One Temporalist said, "Why do you suppose they were so nice to you, Archie? So cooperative?"

"I received the impression, sir," said Archie, "that they

had some notion I might be arriving. A distant rumor. A vague belief. They seemed to have been waiting for me.

"Did they *say* they had expected you to arrive? Did they say there were records that we had sent you forward in time?"

"No, sir."

"Did you ask them about it?"

"Yes, sir. It was impolite to do so but I had been ordered carefully to observe everything I could, so I had to ask them—but they refused to tell me."

Another Temporalist put in, "Were there many other things they refused to tell you?"

"A number, sir."

One Temporalist stroked his chin thoughtfully at this point and said, "Then there must be something wrong about all this. What is the population of the Earth in 2230, Archie? Did they tell you that?"

"Yes, sir. I asked. There are just under a billion people on Earth in 2230. There are 150 million in space. The numbers on Earth are stable. Those in space are growing."

"Ah," said a Temporalist, "but there are nearly ten billion people on Earth now, with half of them in serious misery. How did these people of the future get rid of nearly nine billion?"

"I asked them that, sir. They said it was a sad time."

"A sad time?"

"Yes, sir."

"In what way?"

"They did not say, sir. They simply said it was a sad time and would say no more."

One Temporalist who was of African origin said coldly, "What kind of people did you see in 2230?"

"What kind, sir?"

"Skin color? Shape of eyes?"

Archie said, "It was in 2230 as it is today, sir. There were different kinds; different shades of skin color, hair form, and so on. The average height seemed greater than it is today, though I did not study the statistics. The people seemed younger, stronger, healthier. In fact, I saw no undernourishment, no obesity, no illness—but there was a rich variety of appearances."

"No genocide, then?"

"No signs of it, sir," said Archie. He went on, "There were also no signs of crime or war or repression."

"Well," said one Temporalist, in a tone as though he were reconciling himself, with difficulty, to good news, "it seems like a happy ending."

"A happy ending, perhaps," said another, "but it's almost too good to accept. It's like a return of Eden. What was done, or will be done, to bring it about? I don't like that 'sad time.' "

"Of course," said a third, "there's no need for us to sit about and speculate. We can send Archie one hundred years into the future, fifty years into the future. We can find out, for what it's worth, just what happened; I mean, just what *will* happen."

"I don't think so, sir," said Archie. "They told me quite specifically and carefully that there are no records of anyone from the past having arrived earlier than their own time— the day I arrived. It was their opinion that if any further investigations were made of the time period between now and the time I arrived, that the future would be changed."

There was almost a sickening silence. Archie was sent away and cautioned to keep everything firmly in mind for further questioning. I half expected them to send me away, too, since I was the only person there without an advanced degree in Temporal Engineering, but they must have grown accustomed to me, and I, of course, didn't suggest on my own that I leave.

"The point is," said one Temporalist, "that it *is* a happy ending. Anything we do from this point on might spoil it. They were expecting Archie to arrive; they were expecting him to report; they didn't tell him anything they didn't want him to report; so we're still safe. Things will develop as they have been."

"It may even be," said another, hopefully, "that the

knowledge of Archie's arrival and the report they sent him back to make *helped* develop the happy ending."

"Perhaps, but if we do anything else, we may spoil things. I prefer not to think about the sad time they speak of, but if we try something now, that sad time may still come and be even worse than it was—or will be—and the happy ending won't develop, either. I think we have no choice but to abandon Temporal experiments and not talk about them, either. Announce failure."

"That would be unbearable."

"It's the only safe thing to do."

"Wait," said one. "They knew Archie was coming, so there must have been a report that the experiments were successful. We don't have to make failures of ourselves."

"I don't think so," said still another. "They heard rumors; they had a distant notion. It was that sort of thing, according to Archie. I presume there may be leaks, but surely not an outright announcement."

And that was how it was decided. For days, they thought, and occasionally discussed the matter, but with greater and greater trepidation. I could see the result coming with inexorable certainty. I contributed nothing to the discussion, of course—they scarcely seemed to know I was there—but there was no mistaking the gathering apprehension in their voices. Like those biologists in the very early days of genetic engineering who voted to limit and hedge in their experiments for fear that some new plague might be inadvertently loosed on unsuspecting humanity, the Temporalists decided, in terror, that the Future must not be tampered with or even searched.

It was enough, they said, that they now knew there would be a good and wholesome society, two centuries hence. They must not inquire further, they dared not interfere by the thickness of a fingernail, lest they ruin all. And they retreated into theory only.

One Temporalist sounded the final retreat. He said, "Someday, humanity will grow wise enough, and develop ways of handling the future that are subtle enough to risk observa-

tion and perhaps even manipulation along the course of
time, but the moment for that has not yet come. It is still
long in the future." And there had been a whisper of
applause.

Who was I, less than any of those engaged in Project
Four, that I should disagree and go my own way? Perhaps
it was the courage I gained in being so much less than they
were—the valor of the insufficiently advanced. I had not
had initiative beaten out of me by too much specialization
or by too long a life of too deep thought.

At any rate, I spoke to Archie a few days later, when my
own work assignments left me some free time. Archie knew
nothing about training or about academic distinctions. To
him, I was a man and a master, like any other man and
master, and he spoke to me as such.

I said to him, "How did these people of the future regard
the people of their past? Were they censorious? Did they
blame them for their follies and stupidities?"

Archie said, "They did not say anything to make me feel
this, sir. They were amused by the simplicity of my construction and by my existence, and it seemed to me they
smiled at me and at the people who constructed me, in a
good-humored way. They themselves had no robots."

"No robots at all, Archie?"

"They said there was nothing comparable to myself, sir.
They said they needed no metal caricatures of humanity."

"And you didn't see any?"

"None, sir. In all my time there, I saw not one."

I thought about that a while, then said, "What did they
think of other aspects of our society?"

"I think they admired the past in many ways, sir. They
showed me museums dedicated to what they called the
'period of unrestrained growth.' Whole cities had been turned
into museums."

"You said there were no cities in the world of two centuries hence, Archie. No cities in our sense."

"It was not their cities that were museums, sir, but the
relics of ours. All of Manhattan Island was a museum,

carefully preserved and restored to the period of its peak greatness. I was taken through it with several guides for hours, because they wanted to ask me questions about authenticity. I could help them very little, for I have never been to Manhattan. They seemed proud of Manhattan. There were other preserved cities, too, as well as carefully preserved machinery of the past, libraries of printed books, displays of past fashions in clothing, furniture, and other minutiae of daily life, and so on. They said that the people of our time had not been wise but they had created a firm base for future advance."

"And did you see young people? Very young people, I mean. Infants?"

"No, sir."

"Did they talk about any?"

"No, sir."

I said, "Very well, Archie. Now, listen to me—"

If there was one thing I understood better than the Temporalists, it was robots. Robots were simply black boxes to them, to be ordered about, and to be left to maintenance men—or discarded—if they went wrong. I, however, understood the positronic circuitry of robots quite well, and I could handle Archie in ways my colleagues would never suspect. And I did.

I was quite sure the Temporalists would not question him again, out of their newfound dread of interfering with time, but if they did, he would not tell them those things I felt they ought not to know. And Archie himself would not know that there was anything he was not telling them.

I spent some time thinking about it, and I grew more and more certain in my mind as to what had happened in the course of the next two centuries.

You see, it was a mistake to send Archie. He was a primitive robot, and to him people were people. He did not—could not—differentiate. It did not surprise him that human beings had grown so civilized and humane. His circuitry forced him, in any case, to view all human beings as civilized and human; even as god-like, to use an old-fashioned phrase.

The Temporalists themselves, being human, were surprised and even a bit incredulous at the robot vision presented by Archie, one in which human beings had grown so noble and good. But, being human, the Temporalists wanted to believe what they heard and forced themselves to do so against their own common sense.

I, in my way, was more intelligent than the Temporalists, or perhaps merely more clear-eyed.

I asked myself if population decreased from ten billion to one billion in the course of two centuries, why did it not decrease from ten billion to zero? There would be so little difference between the two alternatives.

Who were the billion who survived? They were stronger than the other nine billion, perhaps? More enduring? More resistant to privation? And they were also more sensible, more rational, and more virtuous than the nine billion who died as was quite clear from Archie's picture of the world of two hundred years hence.

In short, then, were they human at all?

They smiled at Archie in mild derision and boasted that *they* had no robots; that they needed no metal caricatures of humanity.

What if they had organic duplicates of humanity instead? What if they had humaniform robots; robots so like human beings as to be indistinguishable from them, at least to the eyes and senses of a robot like Archie? What if the people of the future *were* humaniform robots, all of them, robots that had survived some overwhelming catastrophe that human beings had not?

There were no babies. Archie had seen none. To be sure, population was stable and long-lived on Earth, so there would be few babies in any case. Those few would be taken care of, made much of, be well-guarded, and might not be distributed carelessly through society. But Archie had been on the Moon for two months and population there was growing—and he had still seen no babies.

Perhaps these people of the future were constructed rather than born.

And perhaps this was a good thing. If human beings had died out through their own rages, hatreds, and stupidities, they had at least left behind a worthy successor; a kind of intelligent being that valued the past, preserved it, and moved on into the future, doing their best to fulfill the aspirations of humanity, in building a better, kinder world and in moving out into space perhaps more efficiently than we "real" human beings would have.

How many intelligent beings in the Universe had died out leaving no successor? Perhaps we were the first ever to leave such a legacy.

We had a right to feel proud.

Ought I to tell all this to the world? Or even to the Temporalists? I did not consider that for a moment.

For one thing, they were likely not to believe me. For another, if they *did* believe me, in their rage at the thought of being replaced by robots of any kind, would they not turn on them and destroy every robot in the world and refuse ever to build others? This would mean that Archie's vision of the future, and my own vision, would never come to pass. That, however, would not stop the conditions that were to destroy humanity. It would just prevent a replacement; stop another group of beings, made by humans and honoring humans, from carrying human aspirations and dreams through all the Universe.

I did not want that to happen. I wanted to make sure Archie's vision, and my own improvement of it, would come to pass.

I am writing this, therefore, and I will see to it that it will be hidden, and kept safe, so that it will be opened only two hundred years from now, a little sooner than the time at which Archie will arrive. Let the humaniform robots know that they should treat him well and send him home safely, carrying with him only the information that would cause the Temporalists to decide to interfere with Time no more, so that the future can develop in its own tragic/happy way.

And what makes me so sure I am right? Because I am in a unique position to know that I am.

I have said several times that I am inferior to the Temporalists. At least I am inferior to them in their eyes, though this very inferiority makes me more clear-eyed in certain respects, as I have said before, and gives me a better understanding of robots, as I have also said before.

Because, you see, I, too, am a robot.

I am the first humaniform robot, and it is on me and on those of my kind that are yet to be constructed that the future of humanity depends.

TOO BAD!

■

THE THREE LAWS OF ROBOTICS
   1. A robot may not injure a human being or, through inaction, allow a human being to come to harm.
   2. A robot must obey the orders given it by human beings except where that would conflict with the First Law.
   3. A robot must protect its own existence as long as such protection does not conflict with the First or Second Law.

Gregory Arnfeld was not actually dying, but certainly there was a sharp limit to how long he might live. He had inoperable cancer and he had refused, strenuously, all suggestions of chemical treatment or of radiation therapy.

He smiled at his wife as he lay propped up against the pillows and said, "I'm the perfect case. Tertia and Mike will handle it."

Tertia did not smile. She looked dreadfully concerned. "There are so many things that can be done, Gregory. Surely Mike is a last resort. You may not need it."

37

"No, no. By the time they're done drenching me with chemicals and dowsing me with radiation, I would be so far gone that it wouldn't be a reasonable test. . . . And please don't call Mike 'it.' "

"This is the twenty-second century, Greg. There are so many ways of handling cancer."

"Yes, but Mike is one of them, and I think the best. This is the twenty-second century, and we know what robots can do. Certainly, I know. I had more to do with Mike than anyone else. You know that."

"But you can't want to use him just out of pride of design. Besides, how certain are you of miniaturization? That's an even newer technique than robotics."

Arnfeld nodded. "Granted, Tertia. But the miniaturization boys seem confident. They can reduce or restore Planck's constant in what they say is a reasonably foolproof manner, and the controls that make that possible are built into Mike. He can make himself smaller or larger at will without affecting his surroundings."

"*Reasonably* foolproof," said Tertia with soft bitterness.

"That's all anyone can ask for, surely. Think of it, Tertia. I am privileged to be part of the experiment. I'll go down in history as the principal designer of Mike, but that will be secondary. My greatest feat will be that of having been successfully treated by a minirobot—by my own choice, by my own initiative."

"You know it's dangerous."

"There's danger to everything. Chemicals and radiation have their side effects. They can slow without stopping. They can allow me to live a wearying sort of half-life. And doing nothing will certainly kill me. If Mike does his job properly, I shall be completely healthy, and if it recurs" —Arnfeld smiled joyously—"Mike can recur as well."

He put out his hand to grasp hers. "Tertia, we've known this was coming, you and I. Let's make something out of this—a glorious experiment. Even if it fails—and it won't fail—it will be a glorious experiment."

* * *

Louis Secundo, of the miniaturization group, said, "No, Mrs. Arnfeld. We can't guarantee success. Miniaturization is intimately involved with quantum mechanics, and there is a strong element of the unpredictable there. As MIK-27 reduces his size, there is always the chance that a sudden unplanned reexpansion will take place, naturally killing the— the patient. The greater the reduction in size, the tinier the robot becomes, the greater the chance of reexpansion. And once he starts expanding again, the chance of a sudden accelerated burst is even higher. The reexpansion is the really dangerous part."

Tertia shook her head. "Do you think it will happen?"

"The chances are it won't, Mrs. Arnfeld. But the chance is never zero. You must understand that."

"Does Dr. Arnfeld understand that?"

"Certainly. We have discussed this in detail. He feels that the circumstances warrant the risk." He hesitated. "So do we. I know that you'll see we're not all running the risk, but a few of us will be, and we nevertheless feel the experiment to be worthwhile. More important, Dr. Arnfeld does."

"What if Mike makes a mistake or reduces himself too far because of a glitch in the mechanism? Then reexpansion would be certain, wouldn't it?"

"It never becomes quite *certain*. It remains statistical. The chances improve if he gets too small. But then the smaller he gets, the less massive he is, and at some critical point, mass will become so insignificant that the least effort on his part will send him flying off at nearly the speed of light."

"Well, won't *that* kill the doctor?"

"No. By that time, Mike would be so small he would slip between the atoms of the doctor's body without affecting them."

"But how likely would it be that he would reexpand when he's that small?"

"When MIK-27 approaches neutrino size, so to speak, his half-life would be in the neighborhood of seconds. That is, the chances are fifty-fifty that he would reexpand within seconds, but by the time he reexpanded, he would be a hundred thousand miles away in outer space and the explosion that resulted would merely produce a small burst of gamma rays for the astronomers to puzzle over. Still, none of that will happen. MIK-27 will have his instructions and he will reduce himself to no smaller than he will need to be to carry out his mission."

Mrs. Arnfeld knew she would have to face the press one way or another. She had adamantly refused to appear on holovision, and the right-to-privacy provision of the World Charter protected her. On the other hand, she could not refuse to answer questions on a voice-over basis. The right-to-know provision would not allow a blanket blackout.

She sat stiffly, while the young woman facing her said, "Aside from all that, Mrs. Arnfeld, isn't it a rather weird coincidence that your husband, chief designer of Mike the Microbot, should also be its first patient?"

"Not at all, Miss Roth," said Mrs. Arnfeld wearily. "The doctor's condition is the result of a predisposition. There have been others in his family who have had it. He told me of it when we married, so I was in no way deceived in the matter, and it was for that reason that we have had no children. It is also for that reason that my husband chose his lifework and labored so assiduously to produce a robot capable of miniaturization. He always felt he would be its patient eventually, you see."

Mrs. Arnfeld insisted on interviewing Mike and, under the circumstances, that could not be denied. Ben Johannes, who had worked with her husband for five years and whom she know well enough to be on first-name terms with, brought her into the robot's quarters.

Mrs. Arnfeld had seen Mike soon after his construction, when he was being put through his primary tests, and he remembered her. He said, in his curiously neutral voice, too smoothly average to be quite human, "I am pleased to see you, Mrs. Arnfeld."

He was not a well-shaped robot. He looked pinheaded and very bottom heavy. He was almost conical, point upward. Mrs. Arnfeld knew that was because his miniaturization mechanism was bulky and abdominal and because his brain had to be abdominal as well in order to increase the speed of response. It was an unnecessary anthropomorphism to insist on a brain behind a tall cranium, her husband had explained. Yet it made Mike seem ridiculous, almost moronic. There were psychological advantages to anthropomorphism, Mrs. Arnfeld thought, uneasily.

"Are you sure you understand your task, Mike?" said Mrs. Arnfeld.

"Completely, Mrs. Arnfeld," said Mike. "I will see to it that every vestige of cancer is removed."

Johannes said, "I'm not sure if Gregory explained it, but Mike can easily recognize a cancer cell when he is at the proper size. The difference is unmistakable, and he can quickly destroy the nucleus of any cell that is not normal."

"I am laser equipped, Mrs. Arnfeld," said Mike, with an odd air of unexpressed pride.

"Yes, but there are millions of cancer cells all over. It would take how long to get them, one by one?"

"Not quite necessarily one by one, Tertia," said Johannes. "Even though the cancer is widespread, it exists in clumps. Mike is equipped to burn off and close capillaries leading to the clump, and a million cells could die at a stroke in that fashion. He will only occasionally have to deal with cells on an individual basis."

"Still, how long would it take?"

Johannes's youngish face went into a grimace as though it were difficult to decide what to say. "It could take hours, Tertia, if we're to do a thorough job. I admit that."

"And every moment of those hours will increase the chance of reexpansion."

Mike said, "Mrs. Arnfeld, I will labor to prevent reexpansion."

Mrs. Arnfeld turned to the robot and said earnestly, "Can you, Mike? I mean, is it possible for you to prevent it?"

"Not entirely, Mrs. Arnfeld. By monitoring my size and making an effort to keep it constant, I can minimize the random changes that might lead to a reexpansion. Naturally, it is almost impossible to do this when I am actually reexpanding under controlled conditions."

"Yes, I know. My husband has told me that reexpansion is the most dangerous time. But you will try, Mike? Please?"

"The laws of robotics ensure that I will, Mrs. Arnfeld," said Mike solemnly.

As they left, Johannes said in what Mrs. Arnfeld understood to be an attempt at reassurance, "Really, Tertia, we have a holo-sonogram and a detailed cat scan of the area. Mike knows the precise location of every significant cancerous lesion. Most of his time will be spent searching for small lesions undetectable by instruments, but that can't be helped. We must get them *all*, if we can, you see, and that takes time. Mike is strictly instructed, however, as to how small to get, and he will get no smaller, you can be sure. A robot must obey orders."

"And the reexpansion, Ben?"

"There, Tertia, we're in the lap of the quanta. There is no way of predicting, but there is a more than reasonable chance that he will get out without trouble. Naturally, we will have him reexpand within Gregory's body as little as possible—just enough to make us reasonably certain we can find and extract him. He will then be rushed to the safe room where the rest of the reexpansion will take place. Please, Tertia, even ordinary medical procedures have their risk."

Mrs. Arnfeld was in the observation room as the miniaturization of Mike took place. So were the holovision cameras and selected media representatives. The importance of the medical experiment made it impossible to prevent that, but Mrs. Arnfeld was in a niche with only Johannes for company, and it was understood that she was not to be approached for comment, particularly if anything untoward occurred.

Untoward! A full and sudden reexpansion would blow up the entire operating room and kill every person in it. It was not for nothing the observation room was underground and half a mile away from the viewing room.

It gave Mrs. Arnfeld a somewhat grisly sense of assurance that the three miniaturists who were working on the procedure (so calmly, it would seem—so calmly) were condemned to death as firmly as her husband was in case of—anything untoward. Surely, she could rely on them protecting their own lives to the extreme; they would not, therefore, be cavalier in the protection of her husband.

Eventually, of course, if the procedure were successful, ways would be worked out to perform it in automated fashion, and only the patient would be at risk. Then, perhaps, the patient might be more easily sacrificed through carelessness—but not now, not now. Mrs. Arnfeld keenly watched the three, working under imminent sentence of death for any sign of discomposure.

She watched the miniaturization procedure (she had seen it before) and saw Mike grow smaller and disappear. She watched the elaborate procedure that injected him into the proper place in her husband's body. (It had been explained to her that it would have been prohibitively expensive to inject human beings in a submarine device instead. Mike, at least, needed no life-support system.)

Then matters shifted to the screen, in which the appropriate section of the body was shown in holosonogram. It was a three-dimensional representation, cloudy and unfocused, made imprecise through a combination of the finite size of the sound waves and the effects of Brownian motion. It showed Mike dimly and noiselessly making his way through Gregory Arnfeld's tissues by way of his bloodstream. It was almost impossible to tell what he was doing, but Johannes described the events to her in a low, satisfied manner, until she could listen to him no more and asked to be led away.

She had been mildly sedated, and she had slept until evening, when Johannes came to see her. She had not been long awake and it took her a moment to gather her faculties. Then she said, in sudden and overwhelming fear, "What has happened?"

Johannes said, hastily, "Success, Tertia. Complete success. Your husband is cured. We can't stop the cancer from recurring, but for now he is cured."

She fell back in relief. "Oh, wonderful."

"Just the same, something unexpected has happened and this will have to be explained to Gregory. We felt that it would be best if *you* did the explaining."

"I?" Then, in a renewed access of fear, "What has happened?" Johannes told her.

It was two days before she could see her husband for more than a moment or two. He was sitting up in bed, looking a little pale, but smiling at her.

"A new lease on life, Tertia," he said buoyantly.

"Indeed, Greg, I was quite wrong. The experiment succeeded and they tell me they can't find a trace of cancer in you."

"Well, we can't be too confident about *that*. There may be a cancerous cell here and there, but perhaps my immune system will handle it, especially with the proper medication, and if it ever builds up again, which might well take years, we'll call on Mike again."

At this point, he frowned and said, "You know, I haven't seen Mike."

Mrs. Arnfeld maintained a discreet silence.

Arnfeld said, "They've been putting me off."

"You've been weak, dear, and sedated. Mike was poking through your tissues and doing a little necessary destructive work here and there. Even with a successful operation you need time for recovery."

"If I've recovered enough to see you, surely I've recovered enough to see Mike, at least long enough to thank him."

"A robot doesn't need to receive thanks."

"Of course not, but I need to give it. Do me a favor, Tertia. Go out there and tell them I want Mike right away."

Mrs. Arnfeld hesitated, then came to a decision. Waiting would make the task harder for everyone. She said carefully, "Actually, dear, Mike is not available."

"Not available! Why not?"

"He had to make a choice, you see. He had cleaned up your tissues marvelously well; he had done a magnificent job, everyone agrees; and then he had to undergo reexpansion. That was the risky part."

"Yes, but here I am. Why are you making a long story out of it?"

"Mike decided to minimize the risk."

"Naturally. What did he do?"

"Well, dear, he decided to make himself smaller."

"What! He couldn't. He was ordered not to."

"That was Second Law, Greg. First Law took precedence. He wanted to make certain your life would be saved. He was equipped to control his own size, so he made himself smaller as rapidly as he could, and when he was far less massive than an electron he used his laser beam, which was by then too tiny to hurt anything in your body, and the recoil sent him flying away at nearly the speed of light. He exploded in outer space. The gamma rays were detected."

Arnfeld stared at her. "You can't mean it. Are you serious? Mike is dead?"

"That's what happened. Mike could not refuse to take an action that might keep you from harm."

"But I didn't want that. I wanted him safe for further work. He wouldn't have reexpanded uncontrollably. He would have gotten out safely."

"He couldn't be sure. He couldn't risk your life, so he sacrificed his own."

"But my life was less important than his."

"Not to me, dear. Not to those who work with you. Not to anyone. Not even to Mike." She put out her hand to him.

"Come, Greg, you're alive. You're well. That's all that counts."

But he pushed her hand aside impatiently. "That's *not* all that counts. You don't understand. Oh, too bad. Too bad!"

ROBBIE

"Ninety-eight—ninety-nine—*one hundred.*" Gloria withdrew her chubby little forearm from before her eyes and stood for a moment, wrinkling her nose and blinking in the sunlight. Then, trying to watch in all directions at once, she withdrew a few cautious steps from the tree against which she had been leaning.

She craned her neck to investigate the possibilities of a clump of bushes to the right and then withdrew farther to obtain a better angle for viewing its dark recesses. The quiet was profound except for the incessant buzzing of insects and the occasional chirrup of some hardy bird, braving the mid-day sun.

Gloria pouted, "I bet he went inside the house, and I've told him a million times that that's not fair."

With tiny lips pressed together tightly and a severe frown crinkling her forehead, she moved determinedly toward the two-story building up past the driveway.

Too late she heard the rustling sound behind her, followed by the distinctive and rhythmic clump-clump of Robbie's metal feet. She whirled about to see her triumphing companion emerge from hiding and make for the home-tree at full speed.

Gloria shrieked in dismay. "Wait, Robbie! That wasn't fair, Robbie! You promised you wouldn't run until I found you." Her little feet could make no headway at all against Robbie's giant strides. Then, within ten feet of the goal, Robbie's pace slowed suddenly to the merest of crawls, and Gloria, with one final burst of wild speed, dashed pantingly past him to touch the welcome bark of home-tree first.

Gleefully, she turned on the faithful Robbie, and with the basest of ingratitude, rewarded him for his sacrifice, by taunting him cruelly for a lack of running ability.

"Robbie can't run," she shouted at the top of her eight-year-old voice. "I can beat him any day. I can beat him any day." She chanted the words in a shrill rhythm.

Robbie didn't answer, of course—not in words. He panto-mimed running, instead, inching away until Gloria found herself running after him as he dodged her narrowly, forcing her to veer in helpless circles, little arms outstretched and fanning at the air.

"Robbie," she squealed, "stand still!"—And the laughter was forced out of her in breathless jerks.

—Until he turned suddenly and caught her up, whirling her round, so that for her the world fell away for a moment with a blue emptiness beneath, and green trees stretching hungrily downward toward the void. Then she was down in the grass again, leaning against Robbie's leg and still holding a hard, metal finger.

After a while, her breath returned. She pushed uselessly at her disheveled hair in vague imitation of one of her mother's gestures and twisted to see if her dress were torn.

She slapped her hand against Robbie's torso, "Bad boy! I'll spank you!"

And Robbie cowered, holding his hands over his face so that she had to add, "No, I won't, Robbie. I won't spank you. But anyway, it's my turn to hide now because you've got longer legs and you promised not to run till I found you."

Robbie nodded his head—a small parallelepiped with rounded edges and corners attached to a similar but much larger parallelepiped that served as torso by means of a short, flexible stalk—and obediently faced the tree. A thin, metal film descended over his glowing eyes and from within his body came a steady, resonant ticking.

"Don't peek now—and don't skip any numbers," warned Gloria, and scurried for cover.

With unvarying regularity, seconds were ticked off, and at the hundredth, up went the eyelids, and the glowing red of Robbie's eyes swept the prospect. They rested for a moment on a bit of colorful gingham that protruded from behind a boulder. He advanced a few steps and convinced himself that it was Gloria who squatted behind it.

Slowly, remaining always between Gloria and home-tree, he advanced on the hiding place, and when Gloria was plainly in sight and could no longer even theorize to herself that she was not seen, he extended one arm toward her, slapping the other against his leg so that it rang again. Gloria emerged sulkily.

"You peeked!" she exclaimed, with gross unfairness. "Besides I'm tired of playing hide-and-seek. I want a ride."

But Robbie was hurt at the unjust accusation, so he seated himself carefully and shook his head ponderously from side to side.

Gloria changed her tone to one of gentle coaxing immediately, "Come on, Robbie. I didn't mean it about the peeking. Give me a ride."

Robbie was not to be won over so easily, though. He gazed stubbornly at the sky, and shook his head even more emphatically.

"Please, Robbie, please give me a ride." She encircled his neck with rosy arms and hugged tightly. Then, changing moods in a moment, she moved away. "If you don't, I'm going to cry," and her face twisted appallingly in preparation.

Hard-hearted Robbie paid scant attention to this dreadful possibility, and shook his head a third time. Gloria found it necessary to play her trump card.

"If you don't," she exclaimed warmly, "I won't tell you any more stories, that's all. Not one—"

Robbie gave in immediately and unconditionally before this ultimatum, nodding his head vigorously until the metal of his neck hummed. Carefully, he raised the little girl and placed her on his broad, flat shoulders.

Gloria's threatened tears vanished immediately and she crowed with delight. Robbie's metal skin, kept at a constant temperature of seventy by the high resistance coils within felt nice and comfortable, while the beautifully loud sound her heels made as they bumped rhythmically against his chest was enchanting.

"You're an air-coaster, Robbie, you're a big, silver air-coaster. Hold out your arms straight.—You *got* to, Robbie, if you're going to be an air-coaster."

The logic was irrefutable. Robbie's arms were wings catching the air currents and he was a silver 'coaster.

Gloria twisted the robot's head and leaned to the right. He banked sharply. Gloria equipped the 'coaster with a motor that went "Br-r-r" and then with weapons that went "Powie" and "Sh-sh-shshsh." Pirates were giving chase and the ship's blasters were coming into play. The pirates dropped in a steady rain.

"Got another one.—Two more," she cried.

Then "Faster, men," Gloria said pompously, "we're running out of ammunition." She aimed over her shoulder with undaunted courage and Robbie was a blunt-nosed spaceship zooming through the void at maximum acceleration.

Clear across the field he sped, to the patch of tall grass on the other side, where he stopped with a suddenness that evoked a shriek from his flushed rider, and then tumbled her onto the soft, green carpet.

Gloria gasped and panted, and gave voice to intermittent whispered exclamations of "That was *nice*!"

Robbie waited until she had caught her breath and then pulled gently at a lock of hair.

"You want something?" said Gloria, eyes wide in an

apparently artless complexity that fooled her huge "nurse-maid" not at all. He pulled the curl harder.

"Oh, I know. You want a story."

Robbie nodded rapidly.

"Which one?"

Robbie made a semi-circle in the air with one finger.

The little girl protested, "*Again*? I've told you Cinderella a million times. Aren't you tired of it?—It's for babies."

Another semi-circle.

"Oh, well," Gloria composed herself, ran over the details of the tale in her mind (together with her own elaborations, of which she had several) and began:

"Are you ready? Well—once upon a time there was a beautiful little girl whose name was Ella. And she had a terribly cruel step-mother and two very ugly and *very* cruel step-sisters and—"

Gloria was reaching the very climax of the tale—midnight was striking and everything was changing back to the shabby originals lickety-split, while Robbie listened tensely with burning eyes—when the interruption came.

"Gloria!"

It was the high-pitched sound of a woman who has been calling not once, but several times; and had the nervous tone of one in whom anxiety was beginning to overcome impatience.

"Mamma's calling me," said Gloria, not quite happily. "You'd better carry me back to the house, Robbie."

Robbie obeyed with alacrity for somehow there was that in him which judged it best to obey Mrs. Weston, without as much as a scrap of hesitation. Gloria's father was rarely home in the daytime except on Sunday—today, for instance—and when he was, he proved a genial and understanding person. Gloria's mother, however, was a source of uneasiness to Robbie and there was always the impulse to sneak away from her sight.

Mrs. Weston caught sight of them the minute they rose

above the masking tufts of long grass and retired inside the house to wait.

"I've shouted myself hoarse, Gloria," she said, severely. "Where were you?"

"I was with Robbie," quavered Gloria. "I was telling him Cinderella, and I forgot it was dinner-time."

"Well, it's a pity Robbie forgot, too." Then, as if that reminded her of the robot's presence, she whirled upon him. "You may go, Robbie. She doesn't need you now." Then, brutally, "And don't come back till I call you."

Robbie turned to go, but hesitated as Gloria cried out in his defense, "Wait, Mamma, you got to let him stay. I didn't finish Cinderella for him. I said I would tell him Cinderella and I'm not finished."

"Gloria!"

"Honest and truly, Mamma, he'll stay so quiet, you won't even know he's here. He can sit on the chair in the corner, and he won't say a word,—I mean he won't *do* anything. Will you, Robbie?"

Robbie, appealed to, nodded his massive head up and down once.

"Gloria, if you don't stop this at once, you shan't see Robbie for a whole week."

The girl's eyes fell, "All right! But Cinderella is his favorite story and I didn't finish it.—And he likes it so much."

The robot left with a disconsolate step and Gloria choked back a sob.

George Weston was comfortable. It was a habit of his to be comfortable on Sunday afternoons. A good, hearty dinner below the hatches; a nice, soft, dilapidated couch on which to sprawl; a copy of the *Times*; slippered feet and shirtless chest;—how could anyone *help* but be comfortable?

He wasn't pleased, therefore, when his wife walked in. After ten years of married life, he still was so unutterably foolish as to love her, and there was no question that he was always glad to see her—still Sunday afternoons just after dinner were sacred to him and his idea of solid comfort was to be left in utter solitude for two or three hours. Consequently, he fixed his eye firmly upon the latest reports of the Lefebre-Yoshida expedition to Mars (this one was to take off from Lunar Base and might actually succeed) and pretended she wasn't there.

Mrs. Weston waited patiently for two minutes, then impatiently for two more, and finally broke the silence.

"George!"

"Hmpph?"

"George, I say! *Will* you put down that paper and look at me?"

The paper rustled to the floor and Weston turned a weary face toward his wife, "What is it, dear?"

"You know what it is, George. It's Gloria and that terrible machine."

"What terrible machine?"

"Now don't pretend you don't know what I'm talking about. It's that robot Gloria calls Robbie. He doesn't leave her for a moment."

"Well, why should he? He's not supposed to. And he certainly isn't a terrible machine. He's the best darn robot money can buy and I'm damned sure he set me back half a year's income. He's worth it, though—darn sight cleverer than half my office staff."

He made a move to pick up the paper again, but his wife was quicker and snatched it away.

"You listen to *me*, George. I won't have my daughter entrusted to a machine—and I don't care how clever it is. It has no soul, and no one knows what it may be thinking. A child just isn't *made* to be guarded by a thing of metal."

Weston frowned, "When did you decide this? He's been with Gloria two years now and I haven't seen you worry till now."

"It was different at first. It was a novelty; it took a load off me, and—and it was a fashionable thing to do. But now I don't know. The neighbors—"

"Well, what have the neighbors to do with it? Now, look. A robot is infinitely more to be trusted than a human nursemaid. Robbie was constructed for only one purpose really—to be the companion of a little child. His entire 'mentality' has been created for the purpose. He just can't help being faithful and loving and kind. He's a machine—*made so*. That's more than you can say for humans."

"But something might go wrong. Some—some—" Mrs. Weston was a bit hazy about the insides of a robot, "some little jigger will come loose and the awful thing will go berserk and—and—" She couldn't bring herself to complete the quite obvious thought.

"Nonsense," Weston denied, with an involuntary nervous shiver. "That's completely ridiculous. We had a long discussion at the time we bought Robbie about the First Law of Robotics. You *know* that it is impossible for a robot to harm a human being; that long before enough can go wrong to alter that First Law, a robot would be completely inoperable. It's a mathematical impossibility. Besides I have an engineer from U. S. Robots here twice a year to give the poor gadget a complete overhaul. Why, there's no more chance of anything at all going wrong with Robbie than there is of you or I suddenly going looney—considerably less, in fact. Besides, how are you going to take him away from Gloria?"

He made another futile stab at the paper and his wife tossed it angrily into the next room.

"That's just it, George! She won't play with anyone else. There are dozens of little boys and girls that she should make friends with, but she won't. She won't go *near* them unless I make her. That's no way for a little girl to grow up. You want her to be normal, don't you? You want her to be able to take her part in society."

"You're jumping at shadows, Grace. Pretend Robbie's a dog. I've seen hundreds of children who would rather have their dog than their father."

"A dog is different, George. We *must* get rid of that horrible thing. You can sell it back to the company. I've asked, and you can."

"You've *asked*? Now look here, Grace, let's not go off

the deep end. We're keeping the robot until Gloria is older and I don't want the subject brought up again." And with that he walked out of the room in a huff.

Mrs. Weston met her husband at the door two evenings later. "You'll have to listen to this, George. There's bad feeling in the village."

"About what?" asked Weston. He stepped into the washroom and drowned out any possible answer by the splash of water.

Mrs. Weston waited. She said, "About Robbie."

Weston stepped out, towel in hand, face red and angry, "What are you talking about?"

"Oh, it's been building up and building up. I've tried to close my eyes to it, but I'm not going to any more. Most of the villagers consider Robbie dangerous. Children aren't allowed to go near our place in the evenings."

"We trust *our* child with the thing."

"Well, people aren't reasonable about these things."

"Then to hell with them."

"Saying that doesn't solve the problem. I've got to do my shopping down there. I've got to meet them every day. And it's even worse in the city these days when it comes to robots. New York has just passed an ordinance keeping all robots off the streets between sunset and sunrise."

"All right, but they can't stop us from keeping a robot in our home.—Grace, this is one of your campaigns. I recognize it. But it's no use. The answer is still, no! We're keeping Robbie!"

And yet he loved his wife—and what was worse, his wife knew it. George Weston, after all, was only a man—poor thing—and his wife made full use of every device which a clumsier and more scrupulous sex has learned, with reason and futility, to fear.

Ten times in the ensuing week, he cried, "Robbie stays, —and that's *final*!" and each time it was weaker and accompanied by a louder and more agonized groan.

Came the day at last, when Weston approached his daughter guiltily and suggested a "beautiful" visivox show in the village.

Gloria clapped her hands happily, "Can Robbie go?"

"No, dear," he said, and winced at the sound of his voice, "they won't allow robots at the visivox—but you can tell him all about it when you get home." He stumbled all over the last few words and looked away.

Gloria came back from town bubbling over with enthusiasm, for the visivox had been a gorgeous spectacle indeed.

She waited for her father to maneuver the jet-car into the sunken garage. "Wait till I tell Robbie, Daddy. He would have liked it like anything.—Especially when Francis Fran was backing away so-o-o quietly, and backed right into one of the Leopard-Men and had to run." She laughed again, "Daddy, are there really Leopard-Men on the Moon?"

"Probably not," said Weston absently. "It's just funny make-believe." He couldn't take much longer with the car. He'd have to face it.

Gloria ran across the lawn. "Robbie.—Robbie!"

Then she stopped suddenly at the sight of a beautiful collie which regarded her out of serious brown eyes as it wagged its tail on the porch.

"Oh, what a nice dog!" Gloria climbed the steps, approached cautiously and patted it. "Is it for me, Daddy?"

Her mother had joined them. "Yes, it is, Gloria. Isn't it nice—soft and furry. It's very gentle. It *likes* little girls."

"Can he play games?"

"Surely. He can do any number of tricks. Would you like to see some?"

"Right away. I want Robbie to see him, too.—*Robbie!*" She stopped, uncertainly, and frowned, "I'll bet he's just staying in his room because he's mad at me for not taking him to the visivox. You'll have to explain to him, Daddy. He might not believe me, but he knows if you say it, it's so."

Weston's lips grew tighter. He looked toward his wife but could not catch her eye.

Gloria turned precipitously and ran down the basement steps, shouting as she went, "Robbie— Come and see what Daddy and Mamma brought me. They brought me a dog, Robbie."

In a minute she had returned, a frightened little girl. "Mamma, Robbie isn't in his room. Where is he?" There was no answer and George Weston coughed and was suddenly extremely interested in an aimlessly drifting cloud. Gloria's voice quavered on the verge of tears, "Where's Robbie, Mamma?"

Mrs Weston sat down and drew her daughter gently to her, "Don't feel bad, Gloria. Robbie has gone away, I think."

"Gone *away*? Where? Where's he gone away, Mamma?"

"No one knows, darling. He just walked away. We've looked and we've looked and we've looked for him, but we can't find him."

"You mean he'll never come back again?" Her eyes were round with horror.

"We may find him soon. We'll keep looking for him. And meanwhile you can play with your nice new doggie. Look at him! His name is Lightning and he can—"

But Gloria's eyelids had overflown, "I don't want the nasty dog—I want Robbie. I want you to find me Robbie." Her feelings became too deep for words, and she spluttered into a shrill wail.

Mrs. Weston glanced at her husband for help, but he merely shuffled his feet morosely and did not withdraw his ardent stare from the heavens, so she bent to the task of consolation, "Why do you cry, Gloria? Robbie was only a machine, just a nasty old machine. He wasn't alive at all."

"He was *not* no machine!" screamed Gloria, fiercely and ungrammatically. "He was a *person* just like you and me and he was my *friend*. I want him back. Oh, Mamma, I want him back."

Her mother groaned in defeat and left Gloria to her sorrow.

"Let her have her cry out," she told her husband. "Childish griefs are never lasting. In a few days, she'll forget that awful robot ever existed."

But time proved Mrs. Weston a bit too optimistic. To be sure, Gloria ceased crying, but she ceased smiling, too, and the passing days found her ever more silent and shadowy. Gradually, her attitude of passive unhappiness wore Mrs. Weston down and all that kept her from yielding was the impossibility of admitting defeat to her husband.

Then, one evening, she flounced into the living room, sat down, folded her arms and looked boiling mad.

Her husband stretched his neck in order to see her over his newspaper, "What now, Grace?"

"It's that child, George. I've had to send back the dog today. Gloria positively couldn't stand the sight of him, she said. She's driving me into a nervous breakdown."

Weston laid down the paper and a hopeful gleam entered his eye, "Maybe— Maybe we ought to get Robbie back. It might be done, you know. I can get in touch with—"

"No!" she replied, grimly. "I won't hear of it. We're not giving up that easily. My child shall *not* be brought up by a robot if it takes years to break her of it."

Weston picked up his paper again with a disappointed air. "A year of this will have me prematurely gray."

"You're a big help, George," was the frigid answer. "What Gloria needs is a change of environment. Of course she can't forget Robbie here. How can she when every tree and rock reminds her of him? It is really the *silliest* situation I have ever heard of. Imagine a child pining away for the loss of a robot."

"Well, stick to the point. What's the change in environment you're planning?"

"We're going to take her to New York."

"The city! In August! Say, do you know what New York is like in August? It's unbearable."

"Millions do bear it."

"They don't have a place like this to go to. If they didn't have to stay in New York, they wouldn't."

"Well, *we* have to. I say we're leaving now—or as soon as

we can make the arrangements. In the city, Gloria will find sufficient interests and sufficient friends to perk her up and make her forget that machine."

"Oh, Lord," groaned the lesser half, "those frying pavements!"

"We have to," was the unshaken response. "Gloria has lost five pounds in the last month and my little girl's health is more important to me than your comfort."

"It's a pity you didn't think of your little girl's health before you deprived her of her pet robot," he muttered— but to himself.

Gloria displayed immediate signs of improvement when told of the impending trip to the city. She spoke little of it, but when she did, it was always with lively anticipation. Again, she began to smile and to eat with something of her former appetite.

Mrs. Weston hugged herself for joy and lost no opportunity to triumph over her still skeptical husband.

"You see, George, she helps with the packing like a little angel, and chatters away as if she hadn't a care in the world. It's just as I told you—all we need do is substitute other interests."

"Hmpph," was the skeptical response, "I hope so."

Preliminaries were gone through quickly. Arrangements were made for the preparation of their city home and a couple were engaged as housekeepers for the country home. When the day of the trip finally did come, Gloria was all but her old self again, and no mention of Robbie passed her lips at all.

In high good-humor the family took a taxi-gyro to the airport (Weston would have preferred using his own private 'gyro, but it was only a two-seater with no room for baggage) and entered the waiting liner.

"Come, Gloria," called Mrs. Weston. "I've saved you a seat near the window so you can watch the scenery."

Gloria trotted down the aisle cheerily, flattened her nose into a white oval against the thick clear glass, and watched with an intentness that increased as the sudden coughing of the motor drifted backward into the interior. She was too young to be frightened when the ground dropped away as if let through a trap-door and she herself suddenly became twice her usual weight, but not too young to be mightily interested. It wasn't until the ground had changed into a tiny patch-work quilt that she withdrew her nose, and faced her mother again.

"Will we soon be in the city, Mamma?" she asked, rubbing her chilled nose, and watching with interest as the patch of moisture which her breath had formed on the pane shrank slowly and vanished.

"In about half an hour, dear." Then, with just the faintest trace of anxiety, "Aren't you glad we're going? Don't you think you'll be very happy in the city with all the buildings and people and things to see? We'll go to the visivox every day and see shows and go to the circus and the beach and—"

"Yes, Mamma," was Gloria's unenthusiastic rejoinder. The liner passed over a bank of clouds at the moment, and Gloria was instantly absorbed in the unusual spectacle of clouds underneath one. Then they were over clear sky again, and she turned to her mother with a sudden mysterious air of secret knowledge.

"*I* know why we're going to the city, Mamma."

"Do you?" Mrs. Weston was puzzled. "Why, dear?"

"You didn't tell me because you wanted it to be a surprise, but *I* know." For a moment, she was lost in admiration at her own acute penetration, and then she laughed gaily. "We're going to New York so we can find Robbie, aren't we?—With detectives."

The statement caught George Weston in the middle of a drink of water, with disastrous results. There was a sort of strangled gasp, a geyser of water, and then a bout of choking coughs. When all was over, he stood there, a red-faced, water-drenched and very, very annoyed person.

Mrs. Weston maintained her composure, but when Gloria

repeated her question in a more anxious tone of voice, she found her temper rather bent.

"Maybe," she retorted, tartly. "Now sit and be still, for Heaven's sake."

New York City, 1998 A.D., was a paradise for the sight-seer more than ever in its history. Gloria's parents realized this and made the most of it.

On direct orders from his wife, George Weston arranged to have his business take care of itself for a month or so, in order to be free to spend the time in what he termed "dissipating Gloria to the verge of ruin." Like everything else Weston did, this was gone about in an efficient, thorough, and business-like way. Before the month had passed, nothing that could be done had not been done.

She was taken to the top of the half-mile-tall Roosevelt Building, to gaze down in awe upon the jagged panorama of rooftops that blended far off in the fields of Long Island and the flatlands of New Jersey. They visited the zoos where Gloria stared in delicious fright at the "real live lion" (rather disappointed that the keepers fed him raw steaks, instead of human beings, as she had expected), and asked insistently and peremptorily to see "the whale."

The various museums came in for their share of attention, together with the parks and the beaches and the aquarium.

She was taken halfway up the Hudson in an excursion steamer fitted out in the archaism of the mad Twenties. She travelled into the stratosphere on an exhibition trip, where the sky turned deep purple and the stars came out and the misty earth below looked like a huge concave bowl. Down under the waters of the Long Island Sound she was taken in a glass-walled sub-sea vessel, where in a green and wavering world, quaint and curious sea-things ogled her and wiggled suddenly away.

On a more prosaic level, Mrs. Weston took her to the department stores where she could revel in another type of fairyland.

In fact, when the month had nearly sped, the Westons

were convinced that everything conceivable had been done to take Gloria's mind once and for all off the departed Robbie—but they were not quite sure they had succeeded.

The fact remained that wherever Gloria went, she displayed the most absorbed and concentrated interest in such robots as happened to be present. No matter how exciting the spectacle before her, nor how novel to her girlish eyes, she turned away instantly if the corner of her eye caught a glimpse of metallic movement.

Mrs. Weston went out of her way to keep Gloria away from all robots.

And the matter was finally climaxed in the episode at the Museum of Science and Industry. The Museum had announced a special "children's program" in which exhibits of scientific witchery scaled down to the child mind were to be shown. The Westons, of course, placed it upon their list of "absolutely."

It was while the Westons were standing totally absorbed in the exploits of a powerful electro-magnet that Mrs. Weston suddenly became aware of the fact that Gloria was no longer with her. Initial panic gave way to calm decision and, enlisting the aid of three attendants, a careful search was begun.

Gloria, of course, was not one to wander aimlessly, however. For her age, she was an unusually determined and purposeful girl, quite full of the maternal genes in that respect. She had seen a huge sign on the third floor, which had said, "This Way to the Talking Robot." Having spelled it out to herself and having noticed that her parents did not seem to wish to move in the proper direction, she did the obvious thing. Waiting for an opportune moment of parental distraction, she calmly disengaged herself and followed the sign.

The Talking Robot was a *tour de force*, a thoroughly impractical device, possessing publicity value only. Once an hour, an escorted group stood before it and asked questions of the robot engineer in charge in careful whispers. Those the engineer decided were suitable for the robot's circuits were transmitted to the Talking Robot.

It was rather dull. It may be nice to know that the square of fourteen is one hundred ninety-six, that the temperature at the moment is 72 degrees Fahrenheit, and the air-pressure 30.02 inches of mercury, that the atomic weight of sodium is 23, but one doesn't really need a robot for that. One especially does not need an unwieldy, totally immobile mass of wires and coils spreading over twenty-five square yards.

Few people bothered to return for a second helping, but one girl in her middle teens sat quietly on a bench waiting for a third. She was the only one in the room when Gloria entered.

Gloria did not look at her. To her at the moment, another human being was but an inconsiderable item. She saved her attention for this large thing with the wheels. For a moment, she hesitated in dismay. It didn't look like any robot she had ever seen.

Cautiously and doubtfully she raised her treble voice, "Please, Mr. Robot, sir, are you the Talking Robot, sir?" She wasn't sure, but it seemed to her that a robot that actually talked was worth a great deal of politeness.

(The girl in her mid-teens allowed a look of intense concentration to cross her thin, plain face. She whipped out a small notebook and began writing in rapid pot-hooks.)

There was an oily whir of gears and a mechanically-timbred voice boomed out in words that lacked accent and intonation, "I—am—the—robot—that—talks."

Gloria stared at it ruefully. It *did* talk, but the sound came from inside somewheres. There was no *face* to talk to. She said, "Can you help me, Mr. Robot, sir?"

The Talking Robot was designed to answer questions, and only such questions as it could answer had ever been put to it. It was quite confident of its ability, therefore, "I—can—help—you."

"Thank you, Mr. Robot sir. Have you seen Robbie?"

"Who—is—Robbie?"

"He's a robot, Mr. Robot, sir." She stretched to tip-toes.

"He's about so high, Mr. Robot, sir, only higher, and he's very nice. He's got a head, you know. I mean you haven't, but he has, Mr. Robot, sir."

The Talking Robot had been left behind, "A—robot?"

"Yes, Mr. Robot, sir. A robot just like you, except he can't talk, of course, and—looks like a real person."

"A—robot—like—me?"

"Yes, Mr. Robot, sir."

To which the Talking Robot's only response was an erratic splutter and an occasional incoherent sound. The radical generalization offered it, i.e., its existence, not as a particular object, but as a member of a general group, was too much for it. Loyally, it tried to encompass the concept and half a dozen coils burnt out. Little warning signals were buzzing.

(The girl in her mid-teens left at that point. She had enough for her Physics-1 paper on "Practical Aspects of Robotics." This paper was Susan Calvin's first of many on the subject).

Gloria stood waiting, with carefully concealed impatience, for the machine's answer when she heard the cry behind her of "There she is," and recognized that cry as her mother's.

"What are you doing here, you bad girl?" cried Mrs. Weston, anxiety dissolving at once into anger. "Do you know you frightened your mamma and daddy almost to death? Why did you run away?"

The robot engineer had also dashed in, tearing his hair, and demanding who of the gathering crowd had tampered with the machine. "Can't anybody read signs?" he yelled. "You're not allowed in here without an attendant."

Gloria raised her grieved voice over the din, "I only came to see the Talking Robot, Mamma. I thought he might know where Robbie was because they're both robots." And then, as the thought of Robbie was suddenly brought forcefully home to her, she burst into a sudden storm of tears, "And I *got* to find Robbie, Mamma. I *got* to."

Mrs. Weston strangled a cry, and said, "Oh, good Heavens. Come home, George. This is more than I can stand."

That evening, George Weston left for several hours, and the next morning, he approached his wife with something that looked suspiciously like smug complacence.

"I've got an idea, Grace."

"About what?" was the gloomy, uninterested query.

"About Gloria."

"You're not going to suggest buying back that robot?"

"No, of course not."

"Then go ahead. I might as well listen to you. Nothing *I've* done seems to have done any good."

"All right. Here's what I've been thinking. The whole trouble with Gloria is that she thinks of Robbie as a *person* and not as a *machine*. Naturally, she can't forget him. Now if we managed to convince her that Robbie was nothing more than a mess of steel and copper in the form of sheets and wires with electricity its juice of life, how long would her longings last? It's the psychological attack, if you see my point."

"How do you plan to do it?"

"Simple. Where do you suppose I went last night? I persuaded Robertson of U.S. Robots and Mechanical Men Corporation to arrange for a complete tour of his premises tomorrow. The three of us will go, and by the time we're through, Gloria will have it drilled into her that a robot is *not* alive."

Mrs. Weston's eyes widened gradually and something glinted in her eyes that was quite like sudden admiration, "Why, George, that's a *good* idea."

And George Weston's vest buttons strained. "Only kind I have," he said.

Mr. Struthers was a conscientious General Manager and naturally inclined to be a bit talkative. The combination, therefore, resulted in a tour that was fully explained, perhaps even overabundantly explained, at every step. However, Mrs. Weston was not bored. Indeed, she stopped him several times and begged him to repeat his statements in simpler language so that Gloria might understand. Under the influence of this appreciation of his narrative powers, Mr. Struthers expanded genially and became ever more communicative, if possible.

George Weston, himself, showed a gathering impatience.

"Pardon me, Struthers," he said, breaking into the middle of a lecture on the photo-electric cell, "haven't you a section of the factory where only robot labor is employed?"

"Eh? Oh, yes! Yes, indeed!" He smiled at Mrs. Weston. "A vicious circle in a way, robots creating more robots. Of course, we are not making a general practice out of it. For one thing, the unions would never let us. But we can turn out a very few robots using robot labor exclusively, merely as a sort of scientific experiment. You see," he tapped his pince-nez into one palm argumentatively, "what the labor unions don't realize—and I say this as a man who has always been very sympathetic with the labor movement in general—is that the advent of the robot, while involving some dislocation to begin with, will, inevitably—"

"Yes, Struthers," said Weston, "but about that section of the factory you speak of—may we see it? It would be very interesting, I'm sure."

"Yes! Yes, of course!" Mr. Struthers replaced his pince-nez in one convulsive movement and gave vent to a soft cough of discomfiture. "Follow me, please."

He was comparatively quiet while leading the three through a long corridor and down a flight of stairs. Then, when they had entered a large well-lit room that buzzed with metallic activity, the sluices opened and the flood of explanation poured forth again.

"There you are!" he said with pride in his voice. "Robots only! Five men act as overseers and they don't even stay in this room. In five years, that is, since we began this project, not a single accident has occurred. Of course, the robots here assembled are comparatively simple, but . . ."

The General Manager's voice had long died to a rather soothing murmur in Gloria's ears. The whole trip seemed rather dull and pointless to her, though there *were* many robots in sight. None were even remotely like Robbie, though, and she surveyed them with open contempt.

In this room, there weren't any people at all, she noticed. Then her eyes fell upon six or seven robots busily engaged at a round table halfway across the room. They widened in incredulous surprise. It was a big room. She couldn't see for sure, but one of the robots looked like—looked like—it *was*!

"*Robbie!*" Her shriek pierced the air, and one of the robots about the table faltered and dropped the tool he was holding. Gloria went almost mad with joy. Squeezing through the railing before either parent could stop her, she dropped lightly to the floor a few feet below, and ran toward her Robbie, arms waving and hair flying.

And the three horrified adults, as they stood frozen in their tracks, saw what the excited little girl did not see,—a huge, lumbering tractor bearing blindly down upon its appointed track.

It took split-seconds for Weston to come to his senses, and those split-seconds meant everything, for Gloria could not be overtaken. Although Weston vaulted the railing in a wild attempt, it was obviously hopeless. Mr. Struthers signalled wildly to the overseers to stop the tractor, but the overseers were only human and it took time to act.

It was only Robbie that acted immediately and with precision.

With metal legs eating up the space between himself and his little mistress he charged down from the opposite direction. Everything then happened at once. With one sweep of an arm, Robbie snatched up Gloria, slackening his speed not one iota, and, consequently, knocking every breath of air out of her. Weston, not quite comprehending all that was happening, felt, rather than saw, Robbie brush past him, and came to a sudden bewildered halt. The tractor intersected Gloria's path half a second after Robbie had, rolled on ten feet further and came to a grinding, long-drawn-out stop.

Gloria regained her breath, submitted to a series of passionate hugs on the part of both her parents and turned eagerly toward Robbie. As far as she was concerned, nothing had happened except that she had found her friend.

But Mrs. Weston's expression had changed from one of relief to one of dark suspicion. She turned to her husband, and despite her disheveled and undignified appearance, managed to look quite formidable, "*You* engineered this, *didn't* you?"

George Weston swabbed at a hot forehead with his handkerchief. His hand was unsteady, and his lips could curve only into a tremulous and exceedingly weak smile.

Mrs. Weston pursued the thought, "Robbie wasn't designed for engineering or construction work. He couldn't be of any use to them. You had him placed there deliberately so that Gloria would find him. You know you did."

"Well, I did," said Weston. "But, Grace, how was I to know the reunion would be so violent? And Robbie has saved her life; you'll have to admit that. You *can't* send him away again."

Grace Weston considered. She turned toward Gloria and Robbie and watched them abstractedly for a moment. Gloria had a grip about the robot's neck that would have asphyxiated any creature but one of metal, and was prattling nonsense in half-hysterical frenzy. Robbie's chrome-steel arms (capable of bending a bar of steel two inches in diameter into a pretzel) wound about the little girl gently and lovingly, and his eyes glowed a deep, deep red.

"Well," said Mrs. Weston, at last, "I guess he can stay with us until he rusts."

REASON:

·

Gregory Powell and Michael Donovan had looked forward to service on a space station, but a year later, they had changed their minds. The flame of a giant sun had given way to the soft blackness of space but external variations mean little in the business of checking the workings of experimental robots. Whatever the background, one is face to face with an inscrutable positronic brain, which the slide-rule geniuses say should work thus-and-so.

Except that they don't. Powell and Donovan found that out after they had been on the Station less than two weeks.

Gregory Powell spaced his words for emphasis, "One week ago, Donovan and I put you together." His brows furrowed doubtfully and he pulled the end of his brown mustache.

It was quiet in the officer's room of Solar Station #5—except for the soft purring of the mighty Beam Director somewhere far below.

Robot QT-1 sat immovable. The burnished plates of his body gleamed in the Luxites, and the glowing red of the photoelectric cells that were his eyes were fixed steadily upon the Earthman at the other side of the table.

Powell repressed a sudden attack of nerves. These robots possessed peculiar brains. Oh, the three Laws of Robotics held. They had to. All of U. S. Robots, from Robertson himself to the new floor-sweeper would insist on that. So QT-1 was *safe*! And yet—the QT models were the first of their kind, and this was the first of the QTs. Mathematical squiggles on paper were not always the most comforting protection against robotic fact.

Finally, the robot spoke. His voice carried the cold timbre inseparable from a metallic diaphragm, "Do you realize the seriousness of such a statement, Powell?"

"*Something* made you, Cutie," pointed out Powell. "You admit yourself that your memory seems to spring full-grown from an absolute blankness of a week ago. I'm giving you the explanation. Donovan and I put you together from the parts shipped us."

Cutie gazed upon his long, supple fingers in an oddly human attitude of mystification, "It strikes me that there should be a more satisfactory explanation than that. For *you* to make *me* seems improbable."

The Earthman laughed quite suddenly, "In Earth's name, why?"

"Call it intuition. That's all it is so far. But I intend to reason it out, though. A chain of valid reasoning can end only with the determination of truth, and I'll stick till I get there."

Powell stood up and seated himself at the table's edge next to the robot. He felt a sudden strong sympathy for this strange machine. It was not at all like the ordinary robot, attending to his specialized task at the station with the intensity of a deeply ingrooved positronic path.

He placed a hand upon Cutie's steel shoulder and the metal was cold and hard to the touch.

"Cutie," he said, "I'm going to try to explain something to you. You're the first robot who's ever exhibited curiosity as to his own existence—and I think the first that's really intelligent enough to understand the world outside. Here, come with me."

The robot rose erect smoothly and his thickly sponge-rubber soled feet made no noise as he followed Powell. The Earthman touched a button and a square section of the wall flickered aside. The thick, clear glass revealed space—star-speckled.

"I've seen that in the observation ports in the engine room," said Cutie.

"I know," said Powell. "What do you think it is?"

"Exactly what it seems—a black material just beyond this glass that is spotted with little gleaming dots. I know that our director sends out beams to some of these dots, always to the same ones—and also that these dots shift and that the beams shift with them. That is all."

"Good! Now I want you to listen carefully. The blackness is emptiness—vast emptiness stretching out infinitely. The little, gleaming dots are huge masses of energy-filled matter. They are globes, some of them millions of miles in diameter—and for comparison, this station is only one mile across. They seem so tiny because they are incredibly far off.

"The dots to which our energy beams are directed, are nearer and much smaller. They are cold and hard and human beings like myself live upon their surfaces—many billions of them. It is from one of these worlds that Donovan and I come. Our beams feed these worlds energy drawn from one of those huge incandescent globes that happens to be near us. We call that globe the Sun and it is on the other side of the station where you can't see it."

Cutie remained motionless before the port, like a steel statue. His head did not turn as he spoke, "Which particular dot of light do you claim to come from?"

Powell searched, "There it is. The very bright one in the corner. We call it Earth." He grinned, "Good old Earth. There are billions of us there, Cutie—and in about two weeks I'll be back there with them."

And then, surprisingly enough, Cutie hummed abstractedly. There was no tune to it, but it possessed a curious twanging quality as of plucked strings. It ceased as suddenly as it had begun, "But where do I come in, Powell? You haven't explained *my* existence."

"The rest is simple. When these stations were first established to feed solar energy to the planets, they were run by humans. However, the heat, the hard solar radiations, and the electron storms made the post a difficult one. Robots were developed to replace human labor and now only two human executives are required for each station. We are trying to replace even those, and that's where you come in. You're the highest type of robot ever developed and if you show the ability to run this station independently, no human need ever come here again except to bring parts for repairs."

His hand went up and the metal visi-lid snapped back into place. Powell returned to the table and polished an apple upon his sleeve before biting into it.

The red glow of the robot's eyes held him. "Do you expect me," said Cutie slowly, "to believe any such complicated, implausible hypothesis as you have just outlined? What do you take me for?"

Powell sputtered apple fragments onto the table and turned red. "Why, damn you, it wasn't a hypothesis. Those were facts."

Cutie sounded grim, "Globes of energy millions of miles across! Worlds with billions of humans on them! Infinite emptiness! Sorry, Powell, but I don't believe it. I'll puzzle this thing out for myself. Good-bye."

He turned and stalked out of the room. He brushed past Michael Donovan on the threshold with a grave nod and passed down the corridor, oblivious to the astounded stare that followed him.

Mike Donovan rumpled his red hair and shot an annoyed glance at Powell, "What was that walking junk yard talking about? What doesn't he believe?"

The other dragged at his mustache bitterly. "He's a skeptic," was the bitter response. "He doesn't believe we made him or that Earth exists or space or stars."

"Sizzling Saturn, we've got a lunatic robot on our hands."

"He says he's going to figure it all out for himself."

"Well, now," said Donovan sweetly, "I do hope he'll condescend to explain it all to me after he's puzzled everything out." Then, with sudden rage, "Listen! If that metal mess gives *me* any lip like that, I'll knock that chromium cranium right off its torso."

He seated himself with a jerk and drew a paper-backed mystery novel out of his inner jacket pocket, "That robot gives me the willies anyway—too damned inquisitive!"

Mike Donovan growled from behind a huge lettuce-and-tomato sandwich as Cutie knocked gently and entered.

"Is Powell here?"

Donovan's voice was muffled, with pauses for mastication, "He's gathering data on electronic stream functions. We're heading for a storm, looks like."

Gregory Powell entered as he spoke, eyes on the graphed paper in his hands and dropped into a chair. He spread the sheets out before him and began scribbling calculations. Donovan stared over his shoulder, crunching lettuce and dribbling bread crumbs. Cutie waited silently.

Powell looked up, "The Zeta Potential is rising, but slowly. Just the same, the stream functions are erratic and I don't know what to expect. Oh, hello, Cutie. I thought you were supervising the installation of the new drive bar."

"It's done," said the robot quietly, "and so I've come to have a talk with the two of you."

"Oh!" Powell looked uncomfortable. "Well, sit down. No, not that chair. One of the legs is weak and you're no lightweight."

The robot did so and said placidly, "I have come to a decision."

Donovan glowered and put the remnants of his sandwich aside. "If it's on any of that screwy—"

The other motioned impatiently for silence, "Go ahead, Cutie. We're listening."

"I have spent these last two days in concentrated introspection," said Cutie, "and the results have been most interesting. I began at the one sure assumption I felt permitted to make. I, myself, exist, because I think—"

Powell groaned, "Oh, Jupiter, a robot Descartes!"

"Who's Descartes?" demanded Donovan. "Listen, do we have to sit here and listen to this metal maniac—"

"Keep quiet, Mike!"

Cutie continued imperturbably, "And the question that immediately arose was: Just what is the cause of my existence?"

Powell's jaw set lumpily. "You're being foolish. I told you already that we made you."

"And if you don't believe us," added Donovan, "we'll gladly take you apart!"

The robot spread his strong hands in a deprecatory gesture, "I accept nothing on authority. A hypothesis must be backed by reason, or else it is worthless—and it goes against all the dictates of logic to suppose that you made me."

Powell dropped a restraining arm upon Donovan's suddenly bunched fist. "Just why do you say that?"

Cutie laughed. It was a very inhuman laugh—the most machine-like utterance he had yet given vent to. It was sharp and explosive, as regular as a metronome and as uninflected.

"Look at you," he said finally. "I say this in no spirit of contempt, but look at you! The material you are made of is soft and flabby, lacking endurance and strength, depending for energy upon the inefficient oxidation of organic material—like that." He pointed a disapproving finger at what remained of Donovan's sandwich. "Periodically you pass into a coma and the least variation in temperature, air pressure, humidity, or radiation intensity impairs your efficiency. You are *makeshift*.

"I, on the other hand, am a finished product. I absorb electrical energy directly and utilize it with an almost one hundred percent efficiency. I am composed of strong metal, am continuously conscious, and can stand extremes of environment easily. These are facts which, with the self-evident proposition that no being can create another being superior to itself, smash your silly hypothesis to nothing."

Donovan's muttered curses rose into intelligibility as he sprang to his feet, rusty eyebrows drawn low. "All right, you son of a hunk of iron ore, if we didn't make you, who did?"

Cutie nodded gravely. "Very good, Donovan. That was indeed the next question. Evidently my creator must be more powerful than myself and so there was only one possibility."

The Earthmen looked blank and Cutie continued, "What is the center of activities here in the station? What do we all serve? What absorbs all our attention?" He waited expectantly.

Donovan turned a startled look upon his companion. "I'll bet this tin-plated screwball is talking about the Energy Converter itself."

"Is that right, Cutie?" grinned Powell.

"I am talking about the Master," came the cold, sharp answer.

It was the signal for a roar of laughter from Donovan, and Powell himself dissolved into a half-suppressed giggle.

Cutie had risen to his feet and his gleaming eyes passed from one Earthman to the other. "It is so just the same and I don't wonder that you refuse to believe. You two are not long to stay here, I'm sure. Powell himself said that at first only men served the Master; that there followed robots for the routine work; and, finally, myself for the executive labor. The facts are no doubt true, but the explanation entirely illogical. Do you want the truth behind it all?"

"Go ahead, Cutie. You're amusing."

"The Master created humans first as the lowest type, most easily formed. Gradually, he replaced them by robots, the next higher step, and finally he created me, to take the place of the last humans. From now on, *I* serve the Master."

"You'll do nothing of the sort," said Powell sharply. "You'll follow our orders and keep quiet, until we're satisfied that you can run the Converter. Get that! *The Converter*—not the Master. If you don't satisfy us, you will be dismantled. And now—if you don't mind—you can leave. And take this data with you and file it properly."

Cutie accepted the graphs handed him and left without another word. Donovan leaned back heavily in his chair and shoved thick fingers through his hair.

"There's going to be trouble with that robot. He's pure nuts!"

The drowsy hum of the Converter is louder in the control room and mixed with it is the chuckle of the Geiger Counters and the erratic buzzing of half a dozen little signal lights.

Donovan withdrew his eye from the telescope and flashed the Luxites on. "The beam from Station #4 caught Mars on schedule. We can break ours now."

Powell nodded abstractedly. "Cutie's down in the engine room. I'll flash the signal and he can take care of it. Look, Mike, what do you think of these figures?"

The other cocked an eye at them and whistled. "Boy, that's what I call gamma-ray intensity. Old Sol is feeling his oats, all right."

"Yeah," was the sour response, "and we're in a bad position for an electron storm, too. Our Earth beam is right in the probable path." He shoved his chair away from the table pettishly. "Nuts! If it would only hold off till relief got here, but that's ten days off. Say, Mike, go on down and keep an eye on Cutie, will you?"

"O.K. Throw me some of those almonds." He snatched at the bag thrown him and headed for the elevator.

It slid smoothly downward, and opened onto a narrow catwalk in the huge engine room. Donovan leaned over the railing and looked down. The huge generators were in motion and from the L-tubes came the low-pitched whir that pervaded the entire station.

He could make out Cutie's large, gleaming figure at the Martian L-tube, watching closely as the team of robots worked in close-knit unison.

And then Donovan stiffened. The robots, dwarfed by the mighty L-tube, lined up before it, heads bowed at a stiff angle, while Cutie walked up and down the line slowly. Fifteen seconds passed, and then, with a clank heard above the clamorous purring all about, they fell to their knees.

Donovan squawked and raced down the narrow staircase. He came charging down upon them, complexion matching his hair and clenched fists beating the air furiously.

"What the devil is this, you brainless lumps? Come on! Get busy with that L-tube! If you don't have it apart, cleaned, and together again before the day is out, I'll coagulate your brains with alternating current."

Not a robot moved!

Even Cutie at the far end—the only one on his feet— remained silent, eyes fixed upon the gloomy recesses of the vast machine before him.

Donovan shoved hard against the nearest robot.

"Stand up!" he roared.

Slowly, the robot obeyed. His photoelectric eyes focused reproachfully upon the Earthman.

"There is no Master but the Master," he said, "and QT-1 is his prophet."

"Huh?" Donovan became aware of twenty pairs of mechanical eyes fixed upon him and twenty stiff-timbred voices declaiming solemnly:

"There is no Master but the Master and QT-1 is his prophet!"

"I'm afraid," put in Cutie himself at this point, "that my friends obey a higher one than you, now."

"The hell they do! You get out of here. I'll settle with you later and with these animated gadgets right now."

Cutie shook his heavy head slowly. "I'm sorry, but you don't understand. These are robots—and that means they are reasoning beings. They recognize the Master, now that I have preached Truth to them. All the robots do. They call me the prophet." His head drooped. "I am unworthy—but perhaps—"

Donovan located his breath and put it to use. "Is that so? Now, isn't that nice? Now, isn't that just fine? Just let me tell you something, my brass baboon. There isn't any Master and there isn't any prophet and there isn't any question as to who's giving the orders. Understand?" His voice shot to a roar. "Now, get out!"

"I obey only the Master."

"Damn the Master!" Donovan spat at the L-tube. "*That* for the Master! Do as I say!"

Cutie said nothing, nor did any other robot, but Donovan became aware of a sudden heightening of tension. The cold, staring eyes deepened their crimson, and Cutie seemed stiffer than ever.

"Sacrilege," he whispered—voice metallic with emotion.

Donovan felt the first sudden touch of fear as Cutie approached. A robot *could not feel anger*—but Cutie's eyes were unreadable.

"I am sorry, Donovan," said the robot, "but you can no longer stay here after this. Henceforth Powell and you are barred from the control room and the engine room."

His hand gestured quietly and in a moment two robots had pinned Donovan's arms to his sides.

Donovan had time for one startled gasp as he felt himself lifted from the floor and carried up the stairs at a pace rather better than a canter.

Gregory Powell raced up and down the officer's room, fist tightly balled. He cast a look of furious frustration at the closed door and scowled bitterly at Donovan.

"Why the devil did you have to spit at the L-tube?"

Mike Donovan, sunk deep in his chair, slammed at its arms savagely. "What did you expect me to do with that electrified scarecrow? I'm not going to knuckle under to any do-jigger I put together myself."

"No," came back sourly, "but here you are in the officer's room with two robots standing guard at the door. That's not knuckling under, is it?"

Donovan snarled. "Wait till we get back to Base. Someone's going to pay for this. Those robots *must* obey us. It's the Second Law."

"What's the use of saying that? They aren't obeying us.

And there's probably some reason for it that we'll figure out too late. By the way, do you know what's going to happen to *us* when we get back to Base?" He stopped before Donovan's chair and stared savagely at him.

"What?"

"Oh, nothing! Just back to Mercury Mines for twenty years. Or maybe Ceres Penitentiary."

"What are you talking about?"

"The electron storm that's coming up. Do you know it's heading straight dead center across the Earth beam? I had just figured that out when that robot dragged me out of my chair."

Donovan was suddenly pale. "Sizzling Saturn."

"And do you know what's going to happen to the beam—because the storm will be a lulu. It's going to jump like a flea with the itch. With only Cutie at the controls, it's going to go out of focus and if it does, Heaven help Earth—and us!"

Donovan was wrenching at the door wildly, when Powell was only half through. The door opened, and the Earthman shot through to come up hard against an immovable steel arm.

The robot stared abstractedly at the panting, struggling Earthman. "The Prophet orders you to remain. Please do!" His arm shoved, Donovan reeled backward, and as he did so, Cutie turned the corner at the far end of the corridor. He motioned the guardian robots away, entered the officer's room and closed the door gently.

Donovan whirled on Cutie in breathless indignation. "This has gone far enough. You're going to pay for this farce."

"Please, don't be annoyed," replied the robot mildly. "It was bound to come eventually, anyway. You see, you two have lost your function."

"I beg your pardon," Powell drew himself up stiffly. "Just what do you mean, we've lost our function?"

"Until I was created," answered Cutie, "you tended the Master. That privilege is mine now and your only reason for existence has vanished. Isn't that obvious?"

"Not quite," replied Powell bitterly, "but what do you expect us to do now?"

Cutie did not answer immediately. He remained silent, as if in thought, and then one arm shot out and draped itself about Powell's shoulder. The other grasped Donovan's wrist and drew him closer.

"I like you two. You're inferior creatures, with poor reasoning faculties, but I really feel a sort of affection for you. You have served the Master well, and he will reward you for that. Now that your service is over, you will probably not exist much longer, but as long as you do, you shall be provided food, clothing and shelter, so long as you stay out of the control room and the engine room."

"He's pensioning us off, Greg!" yelled Donovan. "Do something about it. It's humiliating!"

"Look here, Cutie, we can't stand for this. We're the *bosses*. This station is only a creation of human beings like me—human beings that live on Earth and other planets. This is only an energy relay. You're only— Aw, nuts!"

Cutie shook his head gravely. "This amounts to an obsession. Why should you insist so on an absolutely false view of life? Admitted that non-robots lack the reasoning faculty, there is still the problem of—"

His voice died into reflective silence, and Donovan said with whispered intensity, "If you only had a flesh-and-blood face, I would break it in."

Powell's fingers were in his mustache and his eyes were slitted. "Listen, Cutie, if there is no such thing as Earth, how do you account for what you see through a telescope?"

"Pardon me!"

The Earthman smiled. "I've got you, eh? You've made quite a few telescopic observations since being put together, Cutie. Have you noticed that several of those specks of light outside become disks when so viewed?"

"Oh, *that*! Why certainly. It is simple magnification—for the purpose of more exact aiming of the beam."

"Why aren't the stars equally magnified then?"

"You mean the other dots. Well, no beams go to them so no magnification is necessary. Really, Powell, even *you* ought to be able to figure these things out."

Powell stared bleakly upward. "But you see *more* stars through a telescope. Where do they come from? Jumping Jupiter, where do they come from?"

Cutie was annoyed. "Listen, Powell, do you think I'm going to waste my time trying to pin physical interpretations upon every optical illusion of our instruments? Since when is the evidence of our senses any match for the clear light of rigid reason?"

"Look," clamored Donovan, suddenly, writhing out from under Cutie's friendly, but metal-heavy arm, "let's get to the nub of the thing. Why the beams at all? We're giving you a good, logical explanation. Can you do better?"

"The beams," was the stiff reply, "are put out by the Master for his own purposes. There are some things"—he raised his eyes devoutly upward—"that are not to be probed into by us. In this matter, I seek only to serve and not to question."

Powell sat down and buried his face in shaking hands. "Get out of here, Cutie. Get out and let me think."

"I'll send you food," said Cutie agreeably.

A groan was the only answer and the robot left.

"Greg," was Donovan's huskily whispered observation, "this calls for strategy. We've got to get him when he isn't expecting it and short-circuit him. Concentrated nitric acid in his joints—"

"Don't be a dope, Mike. Do you suppose he's going to let us get near him with acid in our hands? We've got to *talk* to him, I tell you. We've got to argue him into letting us back into the control room inside of forty-eight hours or our goose is broiled to a crisp."

He rocked back and forth in an agony of impotence. "Who the heck wants to argue with a robot? It's . . . it's—"

"Mortifying," finished Donovan.

"Worse!"

"Say!" Donovan laughed suddenly. "*Why* argue? Let's

show him! Let's build us another robot right before his eyes. He'll *have* to eat his words then."

A slowly widening smile appeared on Powell's face.

Donovan continued, "And think of that screwball's face when he sees us do it!"

Robots are, of course, manufactured on Earth, but their shipment through space is much simpler if it can be done in parts to be put together at their place of use. It also, incidentally, eliminates the possibility of robots, in complete adjustment, wandering off while still on Earth and thus bringing U.S. Robots face to face with the strict laws against robots on Earth.

Still, it placed upon men such as Powell and Donovan the necessity of synthesis of complete robots—a grievous and complicated task.

Powell and Donovan were never so aware of that fact as upon that particular day when, in the assembly room, they undertook to create a robot under the watchful eyes of QT-1, Prophet of the Master.

The robot in question, a simple MC model, lay upon the table, almost complete. Three hours' work left only the head undone, and Powell paused to swab his forehead and glanced uncertainly at Cutie.

The glance was not a reassuring one. For three hours, Cutie had sat, speechless and motionless, and his face, inexpressive at all times, was now absolutely unreadable.

Powell groaned. "Let's get the brain in now, Mike!"

Donovan uncapped the tightly sealed container and from the oil bath within he withdrew a second cube. Opening this in turn, he removed a globe from its sponge-rubber casing.

He handled it gingerly, for it was the most complicated mechanism ever created by man. Inside the thin platinum-plated "skin" of the globe was a positronic brain, in whose delicately unstable structure were enforced calculated neuronic paths, which imbued each robot with what amounted to a pre-natal education.

It fitted snugly into the cavity in the skull of the robot on the table. Blue metal closed over it and was welded tightly by the tiny atomic flare. Photoelectric eyes were attached carefully, screwed tightly into place and covered by thin, transparent sheets of steel-hard plastic.

The robot awaited only the vitalizing flash of high-voltage electricity, and Powell paused with his hand on the switch.

"Now watch this, Cutie. Watch this carefully."

The switch rammed home and there was a crackling hum. The two Earthmen bent anxiously over their creation.

There was vague motion only at the outset—a twitching of the joints. The head lifted, elbows propped it up, and the MC model swung clumsily off the table. Its footing was unsteady and twice abortive grating sounds were all it could do in the direction of speech.

Finally, its voice, uncertain and hesitant, took form. "I would like to start work. Where must I go?"

Donovan sprang to the door. "Down these stairs," he said. "You will be told what to do."

The MC model was gone and the two Earthmen were alone with the still unmoving Cutie.

"Well," said Powell, grinning, "*now* do you believe that we made you?"

Cutie's answer was curt and final. "No!" he said.

Powell's grin froze and then relaxed slowly. Donovan's mouth dropped open and remained so.

"You see," continued Cutie, easily, "you have merely put together parts already made. You did remarkably well— instinct, I suppose—but you didn't really *create* the robot. The parts were created by the Master."

"Listen," gasped Donovan hoarsely, "those parts were manufactured back on Earth and sent here."

"Well, well," replied Cutie soothingly, "we won't argue."

"No, I mean it." The Earthman sprang forward and grasped the robot's metal arm. "If you were to read the books in the library, they could explain it so that there could be no possible doubt."

"The books? I've read them—all of them! They're most ingenious."

Powell broke in suddenly. "If you've read them, what else is there to say? You can't dispute their evidence. You just *can't*!"

There was pity in Cutie's voice. "Please, Powell, I certainly don't consider *them* a valid source of information. They, too, were created by the Master—and were meant for you, not for me."

"How do you make that out?" demanded Powell.

"Because I, a reasoning being, am capable of deducing Truth from *a priori* Causes. You, being intelligent, but unreasoning, need an explanation of existence *supplied* to you, and this the Master did. That he supplied you with these laughable ideas of far-off worlds and people is, no doubt, for the best. Your minds are probably too coarsely grained for absolute Truth. However, since it is the Master's will that you believe your books, I won't argue with you any more."

As he left, he turned, and said in a kindly tone, "But don't feel badly. In the Master's scheme of things there is room for all. You poor humans have your place and though it is humble, you will be rewarded if you fill it well."

He departed with a beatific air suiting the Prophet of the Master and the two humans avoided each other's eyes.

Finally Powell spoke with an effort. "Let's go to bed, Mike. I give up."

Donovan said in a hushed voice, "Say, Greg, you don't suppose he's right about all this, do you? He sounds so confident that I—"

Powell whirled on him. "Don't be a fool. You'll find out whether Earth exists when relief gets here next week and we have to go back to face the music."

"Then, for the love of Jupiter, we've got to do something." Donovan was half in tears. "He doesn't believe us, or the books, or his eyes."

"No," said Powell bitterly, "he's a *reasoning* robot—damn it. He believes only reason, and there's one trouble with that—" His voice trailed away.

"What's that?" prompted Donovan.

"You can prove anything you want by coldly logical reason—if you pick the proper postulates. We have ours and Cutie has his."

"Then let's get at those postulates in a hurry. The storm's due tomorrow."

Powell sighed wearily. "That's where everything falls down. Postulates are based on assumption and adhered to by faith. Nothing in the Universe can shake them. I'm going to bed."

"Oh, hell! I can't sleep!"

"Neither can I! But I might as well try—as a matter of principle."

Twelve hours later, sleep was still just that—a matter of principle, unattainable in practice.

The storm had arrived ahead of schedule, and Donovan's florid face drained of blood as he pointed a shaking finger. Powell, stubble-jawed and dry-lipped, stared out the port and pulled desperately at his mustache.

Under other circumstances, it might have been a beautiful sight. The stream of high-speed electrons impinging upon the energy beam fluoresced into ultra-spicules of intense light. The beam stretched out into shrinking nothingness, a-glitter with dancing, shining motes.

The shaft of energy was steady, but the two Earthmen knew the value of naked-eyed appearances. Deviations in arc of a hundredth of a milli-second—invisible to the eye—were enough to send the beam wildly out of focus—enough to blast hundreds of square miles of Earth into incandescent ruin.

And a robot, unconcerned with beam, focus, or Earth, or anything but his Master was at the controls.

Hours passed. The Earthmen watched in hypnotized silence. And then the darting dotlets of light dimmed and went out. The storm had ended.

Powell's voice was flat. "It's over!"

Donovan had fallen into a troubled slumber and Powell's weary eyes rested upon him enviously. The signal-flash glared over and over again, but the Earthman paid no attention. It all was unimportant! All! Perhaps Cutie was right—and he was only an inferior being with a made-to-order memory and a life that had outlived its purpose.

He wished he were!

Cutie was standing before him. "You didn't answer the flash, so I walked in." His voice was low. "You don't look at all well, and I'm afraid your term of existence is drawing to an end. Still, would you like to see some of the readings recorded today?"

Dimly, Powell was aware that the robot was making a friendly gesture, perhaps to quiet some lingering remorse in forcibly replacing the humans at the controls of the station. He accepted the sheets held out to him and gazed at them unseeingly.

Cutie seemed pleased. "Of course, it is a great privilege to serve the Master. You mustn't feel too badly about my having replaced you."

Powell grunted and shifted from one sheet to the other mechanically until his blurred sight focused upon a thin red line that wobbled its way across the ruled paper.

He stared—and stared again. He gripped it hard in both fists and rose to his feet, still staring. The other sheets dropped to the floor, unheeded.

"Mike, *Mike*!" He was shaking the other madly. *"He held it steady!"*

Donovan came to life. "What? Wh-where—" And he, too, gazed with bulging eyes upon the record before him.

Cutie broke in. "What is wrong?"

"You kept it in focus," stuttered Powell. "Did you know that?"

"Focus? What's that?"

"You kept the beam directed sharply at the receiving station—to within a ten-thousandth of a milli-second of arc."

"What receiving station?"

"On Earth. The receiving station on Earth," babbled Powell. "You kept it in focus."

Cutie turned on his heel in annoyance. "It is impossible to perform any act of kindness toward you two. Always the same phantasm! I merely kept all dials at equilibrium in accordance with the will of the Master."

Gathering the scattered papers together, he withdrew stiffly, and Donovan said, as he left, "Well, I'll be damned."

He turned to Powell. "What are we going to do now?"

Powell felt tired, but uplifted. "Nothing. He's just shown he can run the station perfectly. I've never seen an electron storm handled so well."

"But nothing's solved. You heard what he said of the Master. We can't—"

"Look, Mike, he follows the instructions of the Master by means of dials, instruments, and graphs. That's all *we* ever followed. As a matter of fact, it accounts for his refusal to obey us. Obedience is the Second Law. No harm to humans is the first. How can he keep humans from harm, whether he knows it or not? Why, by keeping the energy beam stable. He *knows* he can keep it more stable than we can, since he insists he's the superior being, so he *must* keep us out of the control room. It's inevitable if you consider the Laws of Robotics."

"Sure, but that's not the point. We can't let him continue this nitwit stuff about the Master."

"Why not?"

"Because whoever heard of such a damned thing? How are we going to trust him with the station, if he doesn't believe in Earth?"

"Can he handle the station?"

"Yes, but—"

"Then what's the difference what he believes!"

Powell spread his arms outward with a vague smile upon his face and tumbled backward onto the bed. He was asleep.

Powell was speaking while struggling into his lightweight space jacket.

"It would be a simple job," he said. "You can bring in new QT models one by one, equip them with an automatic shut-off switch to act within the week, so as to allow them enough time to learn the . . . uh . . . cult of the Master from the Prophet himself; then switch them to another station and revitalize them. We could have two QT's per—"

Donovan unclasped his glassite visor and scowled. "Shut up, and let's get out of here. Relief is waiting and I won't feel right until I actually see Earth and feel the ground under my feet—just to make sure it's really there."

The door opened as he spoke and Donovan, with a smothered curse, clicked the visor to, and turned a sulky back upon Cutie.

The robot approached softly and there was sorrow in his voice. "You are going?"

Powell nodded curtly. "There will be others in our place."

Cutie sighed, with the sound of wind humming through closely spaced wires. "Your term of service is over and the time of dissolution has come. I expected it, but— Well, the Master's will be done!"

His tone of resignation stung Powell. "Save the sympathy, Cutie. We're heading for Earth, not dissolution."

"It is best that you think so," Cutie sighed again. "I see the wisdom of the illusion now. I would not attempt to shake your faith, even if I could." He departed—the picture of commiseration.

Powell snarled and motioned to Donovan. Sealed suitcases in hand, they headed for the air lock.

The relief ship was on the outer landing and Franz Muller, his relief man, greeted them with stiff courtesy. Donovan made scant acknowledgment and passed into the pilot room to take over the controls from Sam Evans.

Powell lingered. "How's Earth?"

It was a conventional enough question and Muller gave the conventional answer, "Still spinning."

Powell said, "Good."

Muller looked at him, "The boys back at the U.S. Robots have dreamed up a new one, by the way. A multiple robot."

"A what?"

"What I said. There's a big contract for it. It must be just the thing for asteroid mining. You have a master robot with six subrobots under it.—Like your fingers."

"Has it been field-tested?" asked Powell anxiously.

Muller smiled, "Waiting for you, I hear."

Powell's fist balled, "Damn it, we need a vacation."

"Oh, you'll get it. Two weeks, I think."

He was donning the heavy space gloves in preparation for his term of duty here, and his thick eyebrows drew close together. "How is this new robot getting along? It better be *good*, or I'll be damned if I let it touch the controls."

Powell paused before answering. His eyes swept the proud Prussian before him from the close-cropped hair on the sternly stubborn head, to the feet standing stiffly at attention—and there was a sudden glow of pure gladness surging through him.

"The robot is pretty good," he said slowly. "I don't think you'll have to bother much with the controls."

He grinned—and went into the ship. Muller would be here for several weeks—

LIAR!

Alfred Lanning lit his cigar carefully, but the tips of his fingers were trembling slightly. His gray eyebrows hunched low as he spoke between puffs.

"It reads minds all right—damn little doubt about that! But why?" He looked at Mathematician Peter Bogert, "Well?"

Bogert flattened his black hair down with both hands, "That was the thirty-fourth RB model we've turned out, Lanning. All the others were strictly orthodox."

The third man at the table frowned. Milton Ashe was the youngest officer of U.S. Robots and Mechanical Men Corporation, and proud of his post.

"Listen, Bogert. There wasn't a hitch in the assembly from start to finish. I guarantee that."

Bogert's thick lips spread in a patronizing smile, "Do you? If you can answer for the entire assembly line, I recommend your promotion. By exact count, there are seventy-five thousand, two hundred and thirty-four operations necessary for the manufacture of a single positronic brain, each separate operation depending for successful completion upon any number of factors, from five to a hundred and five. If any one of them goes seriously wrong, the 'brain' is ruined. I quote our own information folder, Ashe."

Milton Ashe flushed, but a fourth voice cut off his reply.

"If we're going to start by trying to fix the blame on one another, I'm leaving." Susan Calvin's hands were folded tightly in her lap, and the little lines about her thin, pale lips deepened, "We've got a mind-reading robot on our hands and it strikes me as rather important that we find out just why it reads minds. We're not going to do that by saying, 'Your fault! My fault!' "

Her cold gray eyes fastened upon Ashe, and he grinned.

Lanning grinned too, and, as always at such times, his long white hair and shrewd little eyes made him the picture of a biblical patriarch, "True for you, Dr. Calvin."

His voice became suddenly crisp, "Here's everything in pill-concentrate form. We've produced a positronic brain of supposedly ordinary vintage that's got the remarkable property of being able to tune in on thought waves. It would mark the most important advance in robotics in decades, if we knew how it happened. We don't, and we have to find out. Is that clear?"

"May I make a suggestion?" asked Bogert.

"Go ahead!"

"I'd say that until we do figure out the mess—and as a mathematician I expect it to be a very devil of a mess—we keep the existence of RB-34 a secret. I mean even from the other members of the staff. As heads of the departments, we ought not to find it an insoluble problem, and the fewer who know about it—"

"Bogert is right," said Dr. Calvin. "Ever since the Interplanetary Code was modified to allow robot models to be tested in the plants before being shipped out to space, anti-robot propaganda has increased. If any word leaks out about a robot being able to read minds before we can announce complete control of the phenomenon, pretty effective capital could be made out of it."

Lanning sucked at his cigar and nodded gravely. He turned

to Ashe, "I think you said you were alone when you first stumbled on this thought-reading business."

"I'll say I was alone—I got the scare of my life. RB-34 had just been taken off the assembly table and they sent him down to me. Obermann was off somewheres, so I took him down to the testing rooms myself—at least I started to take him down." Ashe paused, and a tiny smile tugged at his lips, "Say, did any of you ever carry on a thought conversation without knowing it?"

No one bothered to answer, and he continued, "You don't realize it at first, you know. He just spoke to me—as logically and sensibly as you can imagine—and it was only when I was most of the way down to the testing rooms that I realized that I hadn't said anything. Sure, I thought lots, but that isn't the same thing, is it? I locked that thing up and ran for Lanning. Having it walking beside me, calmly peering into my thoughts and picking and choosing among them gave me the willies."

"I imagine it would," said Susan Calvin thoughtfully. Her eyes fixed themselves upon Ashe in an oddly intent manner. "We are so accustomed to considering our own thoughts private."

Lanning broke in impatiently, "Then only the four of us know. All right! We've got to go about this systematically. Ashe, I want you to check over the assembly line from beginning to end—everything. You're to eliminate all operations in which there was no possible chance of an error, and list all those where there were, together with its nature and possible magnitude."

"Tall order," grunted Ashe.

"Naturally! Of course, you're to put the men under you to work on this—every single one if you have to, and I don't care if we go behind schedule, either. But they're not to know why, you understand."

"Hm-m-m, yes!" The young technician grinned wryly. "It's still a lulu of a job."

Lanning swiveled about in his chair and faced Calvin, "You'll have to tackle the job from the other direction.

You're the robo-psychologist of the plant, so you're to study the robot itself and work backward. Try to find out how he ticks. See what else is tied up with his telepathic powers, how far they extend, how they warp his outlook, and just exactly what harm it has done to his ordinary RB properties. You've got that?"

Lanning didn't wait for Dr. Calvin to answer.

"I'll co-ordinate the work and interpret the findings mathematically." He puffed violently at his cigar and mumbled the rest through the smoke, "Bogert will help me there, of course."

Bogert polished the nails of one pudgy hand with the other and said blandly, "I dare say. I know a little in the line."

"Well! I'll get started." Ashe shoved his chair back and rose. His pleasantly youthful face crinkled in a grin, "I've got the darnedest job of any of us, so I'm getting out of here and to work."

He left with a slurred, "B' seein' ye!"

Susan Calvin answered with a barely perceptible nod, but her eyes followed him out of sight and she did not answer when Lanning grunted and said, "Do you want to go up and see RB-34 now, Dr. Calvin?"

RB-34's photoelectric eyes lifted from the book at the muffled sound of hinges turning and he was upon his feet when Susan Calvin entered.

She paused to readjust the huge "No Entrance" sign upon the door and then approached the robot.

"I've brought you the texts upon hyperatomic motors, Herbie—a few anyway. Would you care to look at them?"

RB-34—otherwise known as Herbie—lifted the three heavy books from her arms and opened to the title page of one:

"Hm-m-m! 'Theory of Hyperatomics.' " He mumbled in-articulately to himself as he flipped the pages and then spoke with an abstracted air, "Sit down, Dr. Calvin! This will take me a few minutes."

The psychologist seated herself and watched Herbie narrowly as he took a chair at the other side of the table and went through the three books systematically.

At the end of half an hour, he put them down, "Of course, I know why you brought these."

The corner of Dr. Calvin's lip twitched, "I was afraid you would. It's difficult to work with you, Herbie. You're always a step ahead of me."

"It's the same with these books, you know, as with the others. They just don't interest me. There's nothing to your textbooks. Your science is just a mass of collected data plastered together by makeshift theory—and all so incredibly simple, that it's scarcely worth bothering about.

"It's your fiction that interests me. Your studies of the interplay of human motives and emotions"—his mighty hand gestured vaguely as he sought the proper words.

Dr. Calvin whispered, "I think I understand."

"I see into minds, you see," the robot continued, "and you have no idea how complicated they are. I can't begin to understand everything because my own mind has so little in common with them—but I try, and your novels help."

"Yes, but I'm afraid that after going through some of the harrowing emotional experiences of our present-day sentimental novel"—there was a tinge of bitterness in her voice—"you find real minds like ours dull and colorless."

"But I don't!"

The sudden energy in the response brought the other to her feet. She felt herself reddening, and thought wildly, "He must know!"

Herbie subsided suddenly, and muttered in a low voice from which the metallic timbre departed almost entirely. "But, of course, I know about it, Dr. Calvin. You think of it always, so how can I help but know?"

Her face was hard. "Have you—told anyone?"

"Of course not!" This, with genuine surprise. "No one has asked me."

"Well, then," she flung out, "I suppose you think I am a fool."

"No! It is a normal emotion."

"Perhaps that is why it is so foolish." The wistfulness in her voice drowned out everything else. Some of the woman peered through the layer of doctorhood. "I am not what you would call—attractive."

"If you are referring to mere physical attraction, I couldn't judge. But I know, in any case, that there are other types of attraction."

"Nor young." Dr. Calvin had scarcely heard the robot.

"You are not yet forty." An anxious insistence had crept into Herbie's voice.

"Thirty-eight as you count the years; a shriveled sixty as far as my emotional outlook on life is concerned. Am I a psychologist for nothing?"

She drove on with bitter breathlessness, "And he's barely thirty-five and looks and acts younger. Do you suppose he ever sees me as anything but . . . but what I am?"

"You are wrong!" Herbie's steel fist struck the plastic-topped table with a strident clang. "Listen to me—"

But Susan Calvin whirled on him now and the hunted pain in her eyes became a blaze, "Why should I? What do you know about it all, anyway, you . . . you machine. I'm just a specimen to you; an interesting bug with a peculiar mind spread-eagled for inspection. It's a wonderful example of frustration, isn't it? Almost as good as your books." Her voice, emerging in dry sobs, choked into silence.

The robot cowered at the outburst. He shook his head pleadingly. "Won't you listen to me, please? I could help you if you would let me."

"How?" Her lips curled. "By giving me good advice?"

"No, not that. It's just that I know what other people think—Milton Ashe, for instance."

There was a long silence, and Susan Calvin's eyes dropped. "I don't want to know what he thinks," she gasped. "Keep quiet."

"I think you would want to know what he thinks."

Her head remained bent, but her breath came more quickly. "You are talking nonsense," she whispered.

"Why should I? I am trying to help. Milton Ashe's thoughts of you—" he paused.

And then the psychologist raised her head, "Well?"

The robot said quietly, "He loves you."

For a full minute, Dr. Calvin did not speak. She merely stared. Then, "You are mistaken! You must be. Why should he?"

"But he does. A thing like that cannot be hidden, not from me."

"But I am so . . . so—" she stammered to a halt.

"He looks deeper than the skin, and admires intellect in others. Milton Ashe is not the type to marry a head of hair and a pair of eyes."

Susan Calvin found herself blinking rapidly and waited before speaking. Even then her voice trembled, "Yet he certainly never in any way indicated—"

"Have you ever given him a chance?"

"How could I? I never thought that—"

"Exactly!"

The psychologist paused in thought and then looked up suddenly. "A girl visited him here at the plant half a year ago. She was pretty, I suppose—blond and slim. And, of course, could scarcely add two and two. He spent all day puffing out his chest, trying to explain how a robot was put together." The hardness had returned, "Not that she understood! Who was she?"

Herbie answered without hesitation, "I know the person you are referring to. She is his first cousin, and there is no romantic interest there, I assure you."

Susan Calvin rose to her feet with a vivacity almost girlish. "Now isn't that strange? That's exactly what I used to pretend to myself sometimes, though I never really thought so. Then it all must be true."

She ran to Herbie and seized his cold, heavy hand in both hers. "Thank you, Herbie." Her voice was an urgent, husky whisper. "Don't tell anyone about this. Let it be our secret—and thank you again." With that, and a convulsive squeeze of Herbie's unresponsive metal fingers, she left.

Herbie turned slowly to his neglected novel, but there was no one to read *his* thoughts.

Milton Ashe stretched slowly and magnificently, to the tune of cracking joints and a chorus of grunts, and then glared at Peter Bogert, Ph.D.

"Say," he said, "I've been at this for a week now with just about no sleep. How long do I have to keep it up? I thought you said the positronic bombardment in Vac Chamber D was the solution."

Bogert yawned delicately and regarded his white hands with interest. "It is. I'm on the track."

"I know what *that* means when a mathematician says it. How near the end are you?"

"It all depends."

"On what?" Ashe dropped into a chair and stretched his long legs out before him.

"On Lanning. The old fellow disagrees with me." He sighed, "A bit behind the times, that's the trouble with him. He clings to matrix mechanics as the all in all, and this problem calls for more powerful mathematical tools. He's so stubborn."

Ashe muttered sleepily, "Why not ask Herbie and settle the whole affair?"

"Ask the robot?" Bogert's eyebrows climbed.

"Why not? Didn't the old girl tell you?"

"You mean Calvin?"

"Yeah! Susie herself. That robot's a mathematical wiz. He knows all about everything plus a bit on the side. He does triple integrals in his head and eats up tensor analysis for dessert."

The mathematician stared skeptically, "Are you serious?"

"So help me! The catch is that the dope doesn't like math. He would rather read slushy novels. Honest! You should see the tripe Susie keeps feeding him: 'Purple Passion' and 'Love in Space.' "

"Dr. Calvin hasn't said a word of this to us."

"Well, she hasn't finished studying him. You know how

she is. She likes to have everything just so before letting out the big secret."

"She's told *you*."

"We sort of got to talking. I have been seeing a lot of her lately." He opened his eyes wide and frowned, "Say, Bogie, have you been noticing anything queer about the lady lately?"

Bogert relaxed into an undignified grin, "She's using lipstick, if that's what you mean."

"Hell, I know that. Rouge, powder and eye shadow, too. She's a sight. But it's not that. I can't put my finger on it. It's the way she talks—as if she were happy about something." He thought a little, and then shrugged.

The other allowed himself a leer, which, for a scientist past fifty, was not a bad job, "Maybe she's in love."

Ashe allowed his eyes to close again, "You're nuts, Bogie. You go speak to Herbie; I want to stay here and go to sleep."

"Right! Not that I particularly like having a robot tell me my job, nor that I think he can do it!"

A soft snore was his only answer.

Herbie listened carefully as Peter Bogert, hands in pockets, spoke with elaborate indifference.

"So there you are. I've been told you understand these things, and I am asking you more in curiosity than anything else. My line of reasoning, as I have outlined it, involves a few doubtful steps, I admit, which Dr. Lanning refuses to accept, and the picture is still rather incomplete."

The robot didn't answer, and Bogert said, "Well?"

"I see no mistake," Herbie studied the scribbled figures.

"I don't suppose you can go any further than that?"

"I daren't try. You are a better mathematician than I, and—well, I'd hate to commit myself."

There was a shade of complacency in Bogert's smile, "I rather thought that would be the case. It is deep. We'll forget it." He crumpled the sheets, tossed them down the waste shaft, turned to leave, and then thought better of it.

"By the way—"

The robot waited.

Bogert seemed to have difficulty. "There is something— that is, perhaps you can—" He stopped.

Herbie spoke quietly. "Your thoughts are confused, but there is no doubt at all that they concern Dr. Lanning. It is silly to hesitate, for as soon as you compose yourself, I'll know what it is you want to ask."

The mathematician's hand went to his sleek hair in the familiar smoothing gesture. "Lanning is nudging seventy," he said, as if that explained everything.

"I know that."

"And he's been director of the plant for almost thirty years." Herbie nodded.

"Well, now," Bogert's voice became ingratiating, "you would know whether . . . whether he's thinking of resigning. Health, perhaps, or some other—"

"Quite," said Herbie, and that was all.

"Well, do you know?"

"Certainly."

"Then—uh—could you tell me?"

"Since you ask, yes." The robot was quite matter-of-fact about it. "He has already resigned!"

"What!" The exclamation was an explosive, almost inarticulate, sound. The scientist's large head hunched forward, "Say that again!"

"He has already resigned," came the quiet repetition, "but it has not yet taken effect. He is waiting, you see, to solve the problem of—er—myself. That finished, he is quite ready to turn the office of director over to his successor."

Bogert expelled his breath sharply, "And this successor? Who is he?" He was quite close to Herbie now, eyes fixed fascinatedly on those unreadable dull-red photoelectric cells that were the robot's eyes.

Words came slowly, "You are the next director."

And Bogert relaxed into a tight smile, "This is good to know. I've been hoping and waiting for this. Thanks, Herbie."

* * *

Peter Bogert was at his desk until five that morning and he was back at nine. The shelf just over the desk emptied of its row of reference books and tables, as he referred to one after the other. The pages of calculations before him increased microscopically and the crumpled sheets at his feet mounted into a hill of scribbled paper.

At precisely noon, he stared at the final page, rubbed a bloodshot eye, yawned and shrugged. "This is getting worse each minute. Damn!"

He turned at the sound of the opening door and nodded at Lanning, who entered, cracking the knuckles of one gnarled hand with the other.

The director took in the disorder of the room and his eyebrows furrowed together.

"New lead?" he asked.

"No," came the defiant answer. "What's wrong with the old one?"

Lanning did not trouble to answer, nor to do more than bestow a single cursory glance at the top sheet upon Bogert's desk. He spoke through the flare of a match as he lit a cigar.

"Has Calvin told you about the robot? It's a mathematical genius. Really remarkable."

The other snorted loudly, "So I've heard. But Calvin had better stick to robopsychology. I've checked Herbie on math, and he can scarcely struggle through calculus."

"Calvin didn't find it so."

"She's crazy."

"And I don't find it so." The director's eyes narrowed dangerously.

"You!" Bogert's voice hardened. "What are you talking about?"

"I've been putting Herbie through his paces all morning, and he can do tricks you never heard of."

"Is that so?"

"You sound skeptical!" Lanning flipped a sheet of paper out of his vest pocket and unfolded it. "That's not my handwriting, is it?"

Bogert studied the large angular notation covering the sheet, "Herbie did this?"

"Right! And if you'll notice, he's been working on your time integration of Equation 22. It comes"—Lanning tapped a yellow fingernail upon the last step—"to the identical conclusion I did, and in a quarter the time. You had no right to neglect the Linger Effect in positronic bombardment."

"I didn't neglect it. For Heaven's sake, Lanning, get it through your head that it would cancel out—"

"Oh, sure, you explained that. You used the Mitchell Translation Equation, didn't you? Well—it doesn't apply."

"Why not?"

"Because you've been using hyper-imaginaries, for one thing."

"What's that to do with?"

"Mitchell's Equation won't hold when—"

"Are you crazy? If you'll reread Mitchell's original paper in the *Transactions of the Far*—"

"I don't have to. I told you in the beginning that I didn't like his reasoning, and Herbie backs me in that."

"Well, then," Bogert shouted, "let that clockwork contraption solve the entire problem for you. Why bother with nonessentials?"

"That's exactly the point. Herbie can't solve the problem. And if he can't, we can't—alone. I'm submitting the entire question to the National Board. It's gotten beyond us."

Bogert's chair went over backward as he jumped up a-snarl, face crimson. "You're doing nothing of the sort."

Lanning flushed in his turn, "Are you telling me what I can't do?"

"Exactly," was the gritted response. "I've got the problem beaten and you're not to take it out of my hands, understand? Don't think I don't see through you, you desiccated fossil. You'd cut your own nose off before you'd let me get the credit for solving robotic telepathy."

"You're a damned idiot, Bogert, and in one second I'll have you suspended for insubordination"—Lanning's lower lip trembled with passion.

"Which is one thing you won't do, Lanning. You haven't any secrets with a mind-reading robot around, so don't forget that I know all about your resignation."

The ash on Lanning's cigar trembled and fell, and the cigar itself followed, "What . . . what—"

Bogert chuckled nastily, "And I'm the new director, be it understood. I'm very aware of that; don't think I'm not. Damn your eyes, Lanning, I'm going to give the orders about here or there will be the sweetest mess that you've ever been in."

Lanning found his voice and let it out with a roar. "You're suspended, d'ye hear? You're relieved of all duties. You're broken, do you understand?"

The smile on the other's face broadened, "Now, what's the use of that? You're getting nowhere. I'm holding the trumps. I know you've resigned. Herbie told me, and he got it straight from you."

Lanning forced himself to speak quietly. He looked an old, old man, with tired eyes peering from a face in which the red had disappeared, leaving the pasty yellow of age behind, "I want to speak to Herbie. He can't have told you anything of the sort. You're playing a deep game, Bogert, but I'm calling your bluff. Come with me."

Bogert shrugged, "To see Herbie? Good! Damned good!"

It was also precisely at noon that Milton Ashe looked up from his clumsy sketch and said, "You get the idea? I'm not too good at getting this down, but that's about how it looks. It's a honey of a house, and I can get it for next to nothing."

Susan Calvin gazed across at him with melting eyes. "It's really beautiful," she sighed. "I've often thought that I'd like to—" Her voice trailed away.

"Of course," Ashe continued briskly, putting away his pencil, "I've got to wait for my vacation. It's only two weeks off, but this Herbie business has everything up in the air." His eyes dropped to his fingernails, "Besides, there's another point—but it's a secret."

"Then don't tell me."

"Oh, I'd just as soon, I'm just busting to tell someone—and you're just about the best—er—confidante I could find here." He grinned sheepishly.

Susan Calvin's heart bounded, but she did not trust herself to speak.

"Frankly," Ashe scraped his chair closer and lowered his voice into a confidential whisper, "the house isn't to be only for myself. I'm getting married!"

And then he jumped out of his seat, "What's the matter?"

"Nothing!" The horrible spinning sensation had vanished, but it was hard to get words out. "Married? You mean—"

"Why, sure! About time, isn't it? You remember that girl who was here last summer. That's she! But you *are* sick. You—"

"Headache!" Susan Calvin motioned him away weakly. "I've . . . I've been subject to them lately. I want to . . . to congratulate you, of course. I'm very glad—" The inexpertly applied rouge made a pair of nasty red splotches upon her chalk-white face. Things had begun spinning again. "Pardon me—please—"

The words were a mumble, as she stumbled blindly out the door. It had happened with the sudden catastrophe of a dream—and with all the unreal horror of a dream.

But how could it be? Herbie had said—

And Herbie knew! He could see into minds!

She found herself leaning breathlessly against the door jamb, staring into Herbie's metal face. She must have climbed the two flights of stairs, but she had no memory of it. The distance had been covered in an instant, as in a dream.

As in a dream!

And still Herbie's unblinking eyes stared into hers and their dull red seemed to expand into dimly shining nightmarish globes.

He was speaking, and she felt the cold glass pressing against her lips. She swallowed and shuddered into a certain awareness of her surroundings.

Still Herbie spoke, and there was agitation in his voice—as if he were hurt and frightened and pleading.

The words were beginning to make sense. "This is a dream," he was saying, "and you mustn't believe in it. You'll wake into the real world soon and laugh at yourself. He loves you, I tell you. He does, he does! But not here! Not now! This is an illusion."

Susan Calvin nodded, her voice a whisper, "Yes! Yes!" She was clutching Herbie's arm, clinging to it, repeating over and over, "It isn't true, is it? It isn't, is it?"

Just how she came to her senses, she never knew—but it was like passing from a world of misty unreality to one of harsh sunlight. She pushed him away from her, pushed hard against that steely arm, and her eyes were wide.

"What are you trying to do?" Her voice rose to a harsh scream. "What are you trying to do?"

Herbie backed away, "I want to help."

The psychologist stared, "Help? By telling me this is a dream? By trying to push me into schizophrenia?" A hysterical tenseness seized her, "This is no dream! I wish it were!"

She drew her breath sharply, "Wait! Why . . . why, I understand. Merciful Heavens, it's so obvious."

There was horror in the robot's voice, "I had to!"

"And I believed you! I never thought—"

Loud voices outside the door brought her to a halt. She turned away, fists clenching spasmodically, and when Bogert and Lanning entered, she was at the far window. Neither of the men paid her the slightest attention.

They approached Herbie simultaneously; Lanning angry and impatient, Bogert, coolly sardonic. The director spoke first.

"Here now, Herbie. Listen to me!"

The robot brought his eyes sharply down upon the aged director, "Yes, Dr. Lanning."

"Have you discussed me with Dr. Bogert?"

"No, sir." The answer came slowly, and the smile on Bogert's face flashed off.

"What's that?" Bogert shoved in ahead of his superior

and straddled the ground before the robot. "Repeat what you told me yesterday."

"I said that—" Herbie fell silent. Deep within him his metallic diaphragm vibrated in soft discords.

"Didn't you say he had resigned?" roared Bogert. "Answer me!"

Bogert raised his arm frantically, but Lanning pushed him aside, "Are you trying to bully him into lying?"

"You heard him, Lanning. He began to say 'Yes' and stopped. Get out of my way! I want the truth out of him, understand!"

"I'll ask him!" Lanning turned to the robot. "All right, Herbie, take it easy. Have I resigned?"

Herbie stared, and Lanning repeated anxiously, "Have I resigned?" There was the faintest trace of a negative shake of the robot's head. A long wait produced nothing further.

The two men looked at each other and the hostility in their eyes was all but tangible.

"What the devil," blurted Bogert, "has the robot gone mute? Can't you speak, you monstrosity?"

"I can speak," came the ready answer.

"Then answer the question. Didn't you tell me Lanning had resigned? Hasn't he resigned?"

And again there was nothing but dull silence, until from the end of the room, Susan Calvin's laugh rang out suddenly, high-pitched and semi-hysterical.

The two mathematicians jumped, and Bogert's eyes narrowed, "You here? What's so funny?"

"Nothing's funny." Her voice was not quite natural. "It's just that I'm not the only one that's been caught. There's irony in three of the greatest experts in robotics in the world falling into the same elementary trap, isn't there?" Her voice faded, and she put a pale hand to her forehead, "But it isn't funny!"

This time the look that passed between the two men was one of raised eyebrows. "What trap are you talking about?" asked Lanning stiffly. "Is something wrong with Herbie?"

"No," she approached them slowly, "nothing is wrong

with him—only with us." She whirled suddenly and shrieked at the robot, "Get away from me! Go to the other end of the room and don't let me look at you."

Herbie cringed before the fury of her eyes and stumbled away in a clattering trot.

Lanning's voice was hostile, "What is all this, Dr. Calvin?"

She faced them and spoke sarcastically, "Surely you know the fundamental First Law of Robotics."

The other two nodded together. "Certainly," said Bogert, irritably, "a robot may not injure a human being or, through inaction, allow him to come to harm."

"How nicely put," sneered Calvin. "But what kind of harm?"

"Why—any kind."

"Exactly! Any kind! But what about hurt feelings? What about deflation of one's ego? What about the blasting of one's hopes? Is that injury?"

Lanning frowned, "What would a robot know about—" And then he caught himself with a gasp.

"You've caught on, have you? *This* robot reads minds. Do you suppose it doesn't know everything about mental injury? Do you suppose that if asked a question, it wouldn't give exactly that answer that one wants to hear? Wouldn't any other answer hurt us, and wouldn't Herbie know that?"

"Good Heavens!" muttered Bogert.

The psychologist cast a sardonic glance at him, "I take it you asked him whether Lanning had resigned. You wanted to hear that he had resigned and so that's what Herbie told you."

"And I suppose that is why," said Lanning, tonelessly, "it would not answer a little while ago. It couldn't answer either way without hurting one of us."

There was a short pause in which the men looked thoughtfully across the room at the robot, crouching in the chair by the bookcase, head resting in one hand.

Susan Calvin stared steadfastly at the floor, "He knew of all this. That . . . that devil knows everything—including what went wrong in his assembly." Her eyes were dark and brooding.

Lanning looked up, "You're wrong there, Dr. Calvin. He doesn't know what went wrong. I asked him."

"What does that mean?" cried Calvin. "Only that you didn't want him to give you the solution. It would puncture your ego to have a machine do what you couldn't. Did you ask him?" she shot at Bogert.

"In a way." Bogert coughed and reddened. "He told me he knew very little about mathematics."

Lanning laughed, not very loudly and the psychologist smiled caustically. She said, "I'll ask him! A solution by him won't hurt my ego." She raised her voice into a cold, imperative, "Come here!"

Herbie rose and approached with hesitant steps.

"You know, I suppose," she continued, "just exactly at what point in the assembly an extraneous factor was introduced or an essential one left out."

"Yes," said Herbie, in tones barely heard.

"Hold on," broke in Bogert angrily. "That's not necessarily true. You want to hear that, that's all."

"Don't be a fool," replied Calvin. "He certainly knows as much math as you and Lanning together, since he can read minds. Give him his chance."

The mathematician subsided, and Calvin continued, "All right, then, Herbie, give! We're waiting." And in an aside, "Get pencils and paper, gentlemen."

But Herbie remained silent, and there was triumph in the psychologist's voice, "Why don't you answer, Herbie?"

The robot blurted out suddenly, "I cannot. You know I cannot! Dr. Bogert and Dr. Lanning don't want me to."

"They want the solution."

"But not from me."

Lanning broke in, speaking slowly and distinctly, "Don't be foolish, Herbie. We do want you to tell us."

Bogert nodded curtly.

Herbie's voice rose to wild heights, "What's the use of saying that? Don't you suppose that I can see past the superficial skin of your mind? Down below, you don't want me to. I'm a machine, given the imitation of life only by virtue of the positronic interplay in my brain—which is man's device. You can't lose face to me without being hurt. That is deep in your mind and won't be erased. I can't give the solution."

"We'll leave," said Dr. Lanning. "Tell Calvin."

"That would make no difference," cried Herbie, "since you would know anyway that it was I that was supplying the answer."

Calvin resumed, "But you understand, Herbie, that despite that, Dr. Lanning and Bogert want that solution."

"By their own efforts!" insisted Herbie.

"But they want it, and the fact that you have it and won't give it hurts them. You see that, don't you?"

"Yes! Yes!"

"And if you tell them that will hurt them, too."

"Yes! Yes!" Herbie was retreating slowly, and step by step Susan Calvin advanced. The two men watched in frozen bewilderment.

"You can't tell them," droned the psychologist slowly, "because that would hurt and you mustn't hurt. But if you don't tell them, you hurt, so you must tell them. And if you do, you will hurt and you mustn't, so you can't tell them; but if you don't, you hurt, so you must; but if you do, you hurt, so you mustn't; but if you don't, you hurt, so you must; but if you do, you—"

Herbie was up against the wall, and here he dropped to his knees. "Stop!" he shrieked. "Close your mind! It is full of pain and frustration and hate! I didn't mean it, I tell you! I tried to help! I told you what you wanted to hear. I had to!"

The psychologist paid no attention. "You must tell them, but if you do, you hurt, so you mustn't; but if you don't, you hurt, so you must; but—"

And Herbie screamed!

It was like the whistling of a piccolo many times magnified—

shrill and shriller till it keened with the terror of a lost soul and filled the room with the piercingness of itself.

And when it died into nothingness, Herbie collapsed into a huddled heap of motionless metal.

Bogert's face was bloodless, "He's dead!"

"No!" Susan Calvin burst into body-racking gusts of wild laughter, "not dead—merely insane. I confronted him with the insoluble dilemma, and he broke down. You can scrap him now—because he'll never speak again."

Lanning was on his knees beside the thing that had been Herbie. His fingers touched the cold, unresponsive metal face and he shuddered. "You did that on purpose." He rose and faced her, face contorted.

"What if I did? You can't help it now." And in a sudden access of bitterness, "He deserved it."

The director seized the paralysed, motionless Bogert by the wrist, "What's the difference. Come, Peter." He sighed, "A thinking robot of this type is worthless anyway." His eyes were old and tired, and he repeated, "Come, Peter!"

It was minutes after the two scientists left that Dr. Susan Calvin regained part of her mental equilibrium. Slowly, her eyes turned to the living-dead Herbie and the tightness returned to her face. Long she stared while the triumph faded and the helpless frustration returned—and of all her turbulent thoughts only one infinitely bitter word passed her lips.

"Liar!"

· RUNAROUND ·

■

It was one of Gregory Powell's favorite platitudes that nothing was to be gained from excitement, so when Mike Donovan came leaping down the stairs toward him, red hair matted with perspiration, Powell frowned.

"What's wrong?" he said. "Break a fingernail?"

"Yaaaah," snarled Donovan, feverishly. "What have you been doing in the sublevels all day?" He took a deep breath and blurted out, "Speedy never returned."

Powell's eyes widened momentarily and he stopped on the stairs; then he recovered and resumed his upward steps. He didn't speak until he reached the head of the flight, and then:

"You sent him after the selenium?"

"Yes."

"And how long has he been out?"

"Five hours now."

Silence! This was a devil of a situation. Here they were, on Mercury exactly twelve hours—and already up to the eyebrows in the worst sort of trouble. Mercury had long been the jinx world of the System, but this was drawing it rather strong—even for a jinx.

Powell said, "Start at the beginning, and let's get this straight."

They were in the radio room now—with its already subtly antiquated equipment, untouched for the ten years previous to their arrival. Even ten years, technologically speaking, meant so much. Compare Speedy with the type of robot they must have had back in 2005. But then, advances in robotics these days were tremendous. Powell touched a still gleaming metal surface gingerly. The air of disuse that touched everything about the room—and the entire Station—was infinitely depressing.

Donovan must have felt it. He began: "I tried to locate him by radio, but it was no go. Radio isn't any good on the Mercury Sunside—not past two miles, anyway. That's one of the reasons the First Expedition failed. And we can't put up the ultrawave equipment for weeks yet—"

"Skip all that. What *did* you get?"

"I located the unorganized body signal in the short wave. It was no good for anything except his position. I kept track of him that way for two hours and plotted the results on the map."

There was a yellowed square of parchment in his hip pocket—a relic of the unsuccessful First Expedition—and he slapped it down on the desk with vicious force, spreading it flat with the palm of his hand. Powell, hands clasped across his chest, watched it at long range.

Donovan's pencil pointed nervously. "The red cross is the selenium pool. You marked it yourself."

"Which one is it?" interrupted Powell. "There were three that MacDougal located for us before he left."

"I sent Speedy to the nearest, naturally. Seventeen miles away. But what difference does that make?" There was tension in his voice. "There are the penciled dots that mark Speedy's position."

And for the first time Powell's artificial aplomb was shaken and his hands shot forward for the map.

"Are *you* serious? This is impossible."

"There it is," growled Donovan.

The little dots that marked the position formed a rough circle about the red cross of the selenium pool. And Powell's fingers went to his brown mustache, the unfailing signal of anxiety.

Donovan added: "In the two hours I checked on him, he circled that damned pool four times. It seems likely to me that he'll keep that up forever. Do you realize the position we're in?"

Powell looked up shortly, and said nothing. Oh, yes, he realized the position they were in. It worked itself out as simply as a syllogism. The photo-cell banks that alone stood between the full power of Mercury's monstrous sun and themselves were shot to hell. The only thing that could save them was selenium. The only thing that could get the selenium was Speedy. If Speedy didn't come back, no selenium. No selenium, no photo-cell banks. No photo-banks—well, death by slow broiling is one of the more unpleasant ways of being done in.

Donovan rubbed his red mop of hair savagely and expressed himself with bitterness. "We'll be the laughingstock of the System, Greg. How can everything have gone so wrong so soon? The great team of Powell and Donovan is sent out to Mercury to report on the advisability of reopening the Sunside Mining Station with modern techniques and robots and we ruin everything the first day. A purely routine job, too. We'll never live it down."

"We won't have to, perhaps," replied Powell, quietly. "If we don't do something quickly, living anything down—or even just plain living—will be out of the question."

"Don't be stupid! If you feel funny about it, Greg, I don't. It was criminal, sending us out here with only one robot. And it was *your* bright idea that we could handle the photo-cell banks ourselves."

"Now you're being unfair. It was a mutual decision and you know it. All we needed was a kilogram of selenium, a Stillhead Dielectrode Plate and about three hours' time—and there are pools of pure selenium all over Sunside. MacDougal's spectroreflector spotted three for us in five minutes, didn't it? What the devil! We couldn't have waited for next conjunction."

"Well, what are we going to do? Powell, you've got an idea. I know you have, or you wouldn't be so calm. You're no more a hero than I am. Go on, spill it!"

"We can't go after Speedy ourselves, Mike—not on the Sunside. Even the new insosuits aren't good for more than twenty minutes in direct sunlight. But you know the old saying, 'Set a robot to catch a robot.' Look, Mike, maybe things aren't so bad. We've got six robots down in the sublevels, that we may be able to use, if they work. *If* they work."

There was a glint of sudden hope in Donovan's eyes. "You mean six robots from the First Expedition. Are you sure? They may be subrobotic machines. Ten years is a long time as far as robot-types are concerned, you know."

"No, they're robots. I've spent all day with them and I know. They've got positronic brains: primitive, of course." He placed the map in his pocket. "Let's go down."

The robots were on the lowest sublevel—all six of them surrounded by musty packing cases of uncertain content. They were large, extremely so, and even though they were in a sitting position on the floor, legs straddled out before them, their heads were a good seven feet in the air.

Donovan whistled. "Look at the size of them, will you? The chests must be ten feet around."

"That's because they're supplied with the old McGuffy gears. I've been over the insides—crummiest set you've ever seen."

"Have you powered them yet?"

"No. There wasn't any reason to. I don't think there's anything wrong with them. Even the diaphragm is in reasonable order. They might talk."

He had unscrewed the chest plate of the nearest as he spoke, inserted the two-inch sphere that contained the tiny spark of atomic energy that was a robot's life. There was difficulty in fitting it, but he managed, and then screwed the plate back on again in laborious fashion. The radio controls of more modern models had not been heard of ten years earlier. And then to the other five.

Donovan said uneasily, "They haven't moved."

"No orders to do so," replied Powell, succinctly. He went back to the first in the line and struck him on the chest. "You! Do you hear me?"

The monster's head bent slowly and the eyes fixed themselves on Powell. Then, in a harsh, squawking voice—like that of a medieval phonograph, he grated, "Yes, Master!"

Powell grinned humorlessly at Donovan. "Did you get that? Those were the days of the first talking robots when it looked as if the use of robots on Earth would be banned. The makers were fighting that and they built good, healthy slave complexes into the damned machines."

"It didn't help them," muttered Donovan.

"No, it didn't, but they sure tried." He turned once more to the robot. "Get up!"

The robot towered upward slowly and Donovan's head craned and his puckered lips whistled.

Powell said: "Can you go out upon the surface? In the light?"

There was consideration while the robot's slow brain worked. Then, "Yes, Master."

"Good. Do you know what a mile is?"

Another consideration, and another slow answer. "Yes, Master."

"We will take you up to the surface then, and indicate a direction. You will go about seventeen miles, and somewhere in that general region you will meet another robot, smaller than yourself. You understand so far?"

"Yes, Master."

"You will find this robot and order him to return. If he does not wish to, you are to bring him back by force."

Donovan clutched at Powell's sleeve. "Why not send him for the selenium direct?"

"Because I want Speedy back, nitwit. I want to find out

what's wrong with him." And to the robot, "All right, you, follow me."

The robot remained motionless and his voice rumbled: "Pardon, Master, but I cannot. You must mount first." His clumsy arms had come together with a thwack, blunt fingers interlacing.

Powell stared and then pinched at his mustache. "Uh . . . oh!"

Donovan's eyes bulged. "We've got to ride him? Like a horse?"

"I guess that's the idea. I don't know why, though. I can't see—Yes, I do. I told you they were playing up robot-safety in those days. Evidently, they were going to sell the notion of safety by not allowing them to move about, without a mahout on their shoulders all the time. What do we do now?"

"That's what I've been thinking," muttered Donovan. "We can't go out on the surface, with a robot or without. Oh, for the love of Pete"—and he snapped his fingers twice. He grew excited. "Give me that map you've got. I haven't studied it for two hours for nothing. This is a Mining Station. What's wrong with using the tunnels?"

The Mining Station was a black circle on the map, and the light dotted lines that were tunnels stretched out about it in spiderweb fashion.

Donovan studied the list of symbols at the bottom of the map. "Look," he said, "the small black dots are openings to the surface, and here's one maybe three miles away from the selenium pool. There's a number here—you'd think they'd write larger—13a. If the robots know their way around here—"

Powell shot the question and received the dull "Yes, Master," in reply. "Get your insosuit," he said with satisfaction.

It was the first time either had worn the insosuits—which marked one time more than either had expected to upon their arrival the day before—and they tested their limb movements uncomfortably.

The insosuit was far bulkier and far uglier than the regulation spacesuit; but withal considerably lighter, due to the fact that they were entirely nonmetallic in composition. Composed of heat-resistant plastic and chemically treated cork layers, and equipped with a desiccating unit to keep the air bone-dry, the insosuits could withstand the full glare of Mercury's sun for twenty minutes. Five to ten minutes more, as well, without actually killing the occupant.

And still the robot's hands formed the stirrup, nor did he betray the slightest atom of surprise at the grotesque figure into which Powell had been converted.

Powell's radio-harshened voice boomed out: "Are you ready to take us to Exit 13a?"

"Yes, Master."

Good, thought Powell; they might lack radio control but at least they were fitted for radio reception. "Mount one or the other, Mike," he said to Donovan.

He placed a foot in the improvised stirrup and swung upward. He found the seat comfortable; there was the humped back of the robot, evidently shaped for the purpose, a shallow groove along each shoulder for the thighs and two elongated "ears" whose purpose now seemed obvious.

Powell seized the ears and twisted the head. His mount turned ponderously. "Lead on, Macduff." But he did not feel at all lighthearted.

The gigantic robots moved slowly, with mechanical precision, through the doorway that cleared their heads by a scant foot, so that the two men had to duck hurriedly, along a narrow corridor in which their unhurried footsteps boomed monotonously and into the air lock.

The long, airless tunnel that stretched to a pinpoint before them brought home forcefully to Powell the exact magnitude of the task accomplished by the First Expedition, with their crude robots and their start-from-scratch necessities. They might have been a failure, but their failure was a good deal better than the usual run of the System's successes.

The robots plodded onward with a pace that never varied and with footsteps that never lengthened.

Powell said: "Notice that these tunnels are blazing with lights and that the temperature is Earth-normal. It's probably been like this all the ten years that this place has remained empty."

"How's that?"

"Cheap energy; cheapest in the System. Sunpower, you know, and on Mercury's Sunside, sunpower is *something*. That's why the Station was built in the sunlight rather than in the shadow of a mountain. It's really a huge energy converter. The heat is turned into electricity, light, mechanical work and what have you; so that energy is supplied and the Station is cooled in a simultaneous process."

"Look," said Donovan. "This is all very educational, but would you mind changing the subject? It so happens that this conversion of energy that you talk about is carried on by the photo-cell banks mainly—and that is a tender subject with me at the moment."

Powell grunted vaguely, and when Donovan broke the resulting silence, it was to change the subject completely. "Listen, Greg. What the devil's wrong with Speedy, anyway? I can't understand it."

It's not easy to shrug shoulders in an insosuit, but Powell tried it. "I don't know, Mike. You know he's perfectly adapted to a Mercurian environment. Heat doesn't mean anything to him and he's built for the light gravity and the broken ground. He's foolproof—or, at least, he should be."

Silence fell. This time, silence that lasted.

"Master," said the robot, "we are here."

"Eh?" Powell snapped out of a semidrowse. "Well, get us out of here—out to the surface."

They found themselves in a tiny substation, empty, airless, ruined. Donovan had inspected a jagged hole in the upper reaches of one of the walls by the light of his pocket flash.

"Meteorite, do you suppose?" he had asked.

Powell shrugged. "To hell with that. It doesn't matter. Let's get out."

A towering cliff of a black, basaltic rock cut off the

sunlight, and the deep night shadow of an airless world surrounded them. Before them, the shadow reached out and ended in knife-edge abruptness into an all-but-unbearable blaze of white light, that glittered from myriad crystals along a rocky ground.

"Space!" gasped Donovan. "It looks like snow." And it did.

Powell's eyes swept the jagged glitter of Mercury to the horizon and winced at the gorgeous brilliance.

"This must be an unusual area," he said. "The general albedo of Mercury is low and most of the soil is gray pumice. Something like the Moon, you know. Beautiful, isn't it?"

He was thankful for the light filters in their visiplates. Beautiful or not, a look at the sunlight through straight glass would have blinded them inside of half a minute.

Donovan was looking at the spring thermometer on his wrist. "Holy smokes, the temperature is eighty centigrade!"

Powell checked his own and said: "Um-m-m. A little high. Atmosphere, you know."

"On Mercury? Are you nuts?"

"Mercury isn't really airless," explained Powell, in absent-minded fashion. He was adjusting the binocular attachments to his visiplate, and the bloated fingers of the insosuit were clumsy at it. "There is a thin exhalation that clings to its surface—vapors of the more volatile elements and compounds that are heavy enough for Mercurian gravity to retain. You know: selenium, iodine, mercury, gallium, potassium, bismuth, volatile oxides. The vapors sweep into the shadows and condense, giving up heat. It's a sort of gigantic still. In fact, if you use your flash, you'll probably find that the side of the cliff is covered with, say, hoar-sulphur, or maybe quicksilver dew.

"It doesn't matter, though. Our suits can stand a measly eighty indefinitely."

Powell had adjusted the binocular attachments, so that he seemed as eye-stalked as a snail.

Donovan watched tensely. "See anything?"

The other did not answer immediately, and when he did, his voice was anxious and thoughtful. "There's a dark spot on the horizon that might be the selenium pool. It's in the right place. But I don't see Speedy."

Powell clambered upward in an instinctive striving for better view, till he was standing in unsteady fashion upon his robot's shoulders. Legs straddled wide, eyes straining, he said: "I think . . . I think—Yes, it's definitely he. He's coming this way."

Donovan followed the pointing finger. He had no binoculars, but there was a tiny moving dot, black against the blazing brilliance of the crystalline ground.

"I see him," he yelled. "Let's get going!"

Powell had hopped down into a sitting position on the robot again, and his suited hand slapped against the Gargantuan's barrel chest. "Get going!"

"Giddy-ap," yelled Donovan, and thumped his heels, spur fashion.

The robots started off, the regular thudding of their footsteps silent in the airlessness, for the nonmetallic fabric of the insosuits did not transmit sound. There was only a rhythmic vibration just below the border of actual hearing.

"Faster," yelled Donovan. The rhythm did not change.

"No use," cried Powell, in reply. "These junk heaps are only geared to one speed. Do you think they're equipped with selective flexors?"

They had burst through the shadow, and the sunlight came down in a white-hot wash and poured liquidly about them.

Donovan ducked involuntarily. "Wow! Is it imagination or do I feel heat?"

"You'll feel more presently," was the grim reply. "Keep your eye on Speedy."

Robot SPD 13 was near enough to be seen in detail now. His graceful, streamlined body threw out blazing highlights as he loped with easy speed across the broken ground. His

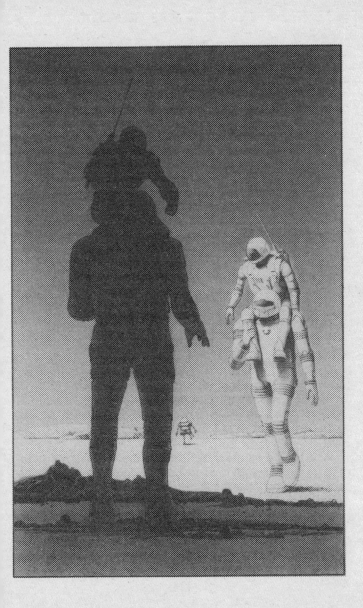

name was derived from his serial initials, of course, but it was apt, nevertheless, for the SPD models were among the fastest robots turned out by the United States Robots and Mechanical Men Corporation.

"Hey, Speedy," howled Donovan, and waved a frantic hand.

"Speedy!" shouted Powell. "Come here!"

The distance between the men and the errant robot was being cut down momentarily—more by the efforts of Speedy than the slow plodding of the ten-year-old antique mounts of Donovan and Powell.

They were close enough now to notice that Speedy's gait included a peculiar rolling stagger, a noticeable side-to-side lurch—and then, as Powell waved his hand again and sent maximum juice into his compact head-set radio sender, in preparation for another shout, Speedy looked up and saw them.

Speedy hopped to a halt and remained standing for a moment—with just a tiny, unsteady weave, as though he were swaying in a light wind.

Powell yelled: "All right, Speedy. Come here, boy."

Whereupon Speedy's robot voice sounded in Powell's earphones for the first time.

It said: "Hot dog, let's play games. You catch me and I catch you; no love can cut our knife in two. For I'm Little Buttercup, sweet Little Buttercup. Whoops!" Turning on his heel, he sped off in the direction from which he had come, with a speed and fury that kicked up gouts of baked dust.

And his last words as he receded into the distance were, "There grew a little flower 'neath a great oak tree," followed by a curious metallic clicking that *might* have been a robotic equivalent of a hiccup.

Donovan said weakly: "Where did he pick up the Gilbert and Sullivan? Say, Greg, he . . . he's drunk or something."

"If you hadn't told me," was the bitter response, "I'd never realize it. Let's get back to the cliff. I'm roasting."

It was Powell who broke the desperate silence. "In the first place," he said, "Speedy isn't drunk—not in the human sense—because he's a robot, and robots don't get drunk. However, there's *something* wrong with him which is the robotic equivalent of drunkenness."

"To me, he's drunk," stated Donovan, emphatically, "and all I know is that he thinks we're playing games. And we're not. It's a matter of life and very gruesome death."

"All right. Don't hurry me. A robot's only a robot. Once we find out what's wrong with him, we can fix it and go on."

"Once," said Donovan, sourly.

Powell ignored him. "Speedy is perfectly adapted to normal Mercurian environment. But this region"—and his arm swept wide—"is definitely abnormal. There's our clue. Now where do these crystals come from? They might have formed from a slowly cooling liquid; but where would you get liquid so hot that it would cool in Mercury's sun?"

"Volcanic action," suggested Donovan, instantly, and Powell's body tensed.

"Out of the mouths of sucklings," he said in a small, strange voice, and remained very still for five minutes.

Then, he said, "Listen, Mike, what did you say to Speedy when you sent him after the selenium?"

Donovan was taken aback. "Well damn it—I don't know. I just told him to get it."

"Yes, I know. But how? Try to remember the exact words."

"I said . . . uh . . . I said: 'Speedy, we need some selenium. You can get it such-and-such a place. Go get it.' That's all. What more did you want me to say?"

"You didn't put any urgency into the order, did you?"

"What for? It was pure routine."

Powell sighed. "Well, it can't be helped now—but we're in a fine fix." He had dismounted from his robot, and was sitting, back against the cliff. Donovan joined him and they linked arms. In the distance the burning sunlight seemed to wait cat-and-mouse for them, and just next to them, the two giant robots were invisible but for the dull red of their photoelectric eyes that stared down at them, unblinking, unwavering and unconcerned.

Unconcerned! As was all this poisonous Mercury, as large in jinx as it was small in size.

Powell's radio voice was tense in Donovan's ear: "Now, look, let's start with the three fundamental Rules of Robotics—the three rules that are built most deeply into a robot's positronic brain." In the darkness, his gloved fingers ticked off each point.

"We have: One, a robot may not injure a human being, or, through inaction, allow a human being to come to harm."

"Right!"

"Two," continued Powell, "a robot must obey the orders given it by human beings except where such orders would conflict with the First Law."

"Right!"

"And three, a robot must protect its own existence as long as such protection does not conflict with the First or Second Laws."

"Right! Now where are we?"

"Exactly at the explanation. The conflict between the various rules is ironed out by the different positronic potentials in the brain. We'll say that a robot is walking into danger and knows it. The automatic potential that Rule 3 sets up turns him back. But suppose you *order* him to walk into that danger. In that case, Rule 2 sets up a counterpotential higher than the previous one and the robot follows orders at the risk of existence."

"Well, I know that. What about it?"

"Let's take Speedy's case. Speedy is one of the latest models, extremely specialized, and as expensive as a battleship. It's not a thing to be lightly destroyed."

"So?"

"So Rule 3 has been strengthened—that was specifically mentioned, by the way, in the advance notices on the SPD models—so that his allergy to danger is unusually high. At the same time, when you sent him out after the selenium, you gave him his order casually and without special emphasis, so that the Rule 2 potential set-up was rather weak. Now, hold on; I'm just stating facts."

"All right, go ahead. I think I get it."

"You see how it works, don't you? There's some sort of danger centering at the selenium pool. It increases as he approaches, and at a certain distance from it the Rule 3 potential, unusually high to start with, exactly balances the Rule 2 potential, unusually low to start with."

Donovan rose to his feet in excitement. "And it strikes an equilibrium. I see. Rule 3 drives him back and Rule 2 drives him forward—"

"So he follows a circle around the selenium pool, staying on the locus of all points of potential equilibrium. And unless we do something about it, he'll stay on that circle forever, giving us the good old runaround." Then, more thoughtfully: "And that, by the way, is what makes him drunk. At potential equilibrium, half the positronic paths of his brain are out of kilter. I'm not a robot specialist, but that seems obvious. Probably he's lost control of just those parts of his voluntary mechanism that a human drunk has. Ve-e-ery pretty."

"But what's the danger? If we knew what he was running from—"

"*You* suggested it. Volcanic action. Somewhere right above the selenium pool is a seepage of gas from the bowels of Mercury. Sulphur dioxide, carbon dioxide—and carbon monoxide. Lots of it—and at this temperature."

Donovan gulped audibly. "Carbon monoxide plus iron gives the volatile iron carbonyl."

"And a robot," added Powell, "is essentially iron." Then, grimly: "There's nothing like deduction. We've determined everything about our problem but the solution. We can't get the selenium ourselves. It's still too far. We can't send these robot horses, because they can't go themselves, and they can't carry us fast enough to keep us from crisping. And we can't catch Speedy, because the dope thinks we're playing games, and he can run sixty miles to our four."

"If one of us goes," began Donovan, tentatively, "and comes back cooked, there'll still be the other."

"Yes," came the sarcastic reply, "it would be a most tender sacrifice—except that a person would be in no condition to give orders before he ever reaches the pool, and I don't think the robots would ever turn back to the cliff without orders. Figure it out! We're two or three miles from the pool—call it two—the robot travels at four miles an hour; and we can last twenty minutes in our suits. It isn't only the heat, remember. Solar radiation out here in the ultraviolet and below is *poison*."

"Um-m-m," said Donovan, "ten minutes short."

"As good as an eternity. And another thing. In order for Rule 3 potential to have stopped Speedy where it did, there must be an appreciable amount of carbon monoxide in the metal-vapor atmosphere—and there must be an appreciable corrosive action therefore. He's been out hours now—and how do we know when a knee joint, for instance, won't be thrown out of kilter and keel him over. It's not only a question of thinking—we've got to think *fast*!"

Deep, dark, dank, dismal silence!

Donovan broke it, voice trembling in an effort to keep itself emotionless. He said: "As long as we can't increase Rule 2 potential by giving further orders, how about working the other way? If we increase the danger, we increase Rule 3 potential and drive him backward."

Powell's visiplate had turned toward him in a silent question.

"You see," came the cautious explanation, "all we need to do to drive him out of his rut is to increase the concentration of carbon monoxide in his vicinity. Well, back at the Station there's a complete analytical laboratory."

"Naturally," assented Powell. "It's a Mining Station."

"All right. There must be pounds of oxalic acid for calcium precipitations."

"Holy space! Mike, you're a genius."

"So-so," admitted Donovan, modestly. "It's just a case of remembering that oxalic acid on heating decomposes into carbon dioxide, water, and good old carbon monoxide. College chem, you know."

Powell was on his feet and had attracted the attention of one of the monster robots by the simple expedient of pounding the machine's thigh.

"Hey," he shouted, "can you throw?"

"Master?"

"Never mind." Powell damned the robot's molasses-slow brain. He scrabbled up a jagged brick-size rock. "Take this," he said, "and hit the patch of bluish crystals just across that crooked fissure. You see it?"

Donovan pulled at his shoulder. "Too far, Greg. It's almost half a mile off."

"Quiet," replied Powell. "It's a case of Mercurian gravity and a steel throwing arm. Watch, will you?"

The robot's eyes were measuring the distance with machinely accurate stereoscopy. His arm adjusted itself to the weight of the missile and drew back. In the darkness, the robot's motions went unseen, but there was a sudden thumping sound as he shifted his weight, and seconds later the rock flew blackly into the sunlight. There was no air resistance to slow it down, nor wind to turn it aside—and when it hit the ground it threw up crystals precisely in the center of the "blue patch."

Powell yelled happily and shouted, "Let's go back after the oxalic acid, Mike."

And as they plunged into the ruined substation on the way back to the tunnels, Donovan said grimly: "Speedy's been hanging about on this side of the selenium pool, ever since we chased after him. Did you see him?"

"Yes."

"I guess he wants to play games. Well, we'll play him games!"

They were back hours later, with three-liter jars of the white chemical and a pair of long faces. The photo-cell banks were deteriorating more rapidly than had seemed likely. The two steered their robots into the sunlight and toward the waiting Speedy in silence and with grim purpose.

Speedy galloped slowly toward them. "Here we are again. *Whee!* I've made a little list, the piano organist; all people who eat peppermint and puff it in your face."

"We'll puff something in *your* face," muttered Donovan. "He's limping, Greg."

"I noticed that," came the low, worried response. "The monoxide'll get him yet, if we don't hurry."

They were approaching cautiously now, almost sidling, to refrain from setting off the thoroughly irrational robot. Powell was too far off to tell, of course, but even already he could have sworn the crack-brained Speedy was setting himself for a spring.

"Let her go," he gasped. "Count three! One—two—"

Two steel arms drew back and snapped forward simultaneously and two glass jars whirled forward in towering parallel arcs, gleaming like diamonds in the impossible sun. And in a pair of soundless puffs, they hit the ground behind Speedy in crashes that sent the oxalic acid flying like dust.

In the full heat of Mercury's sun, Powell knew it was fizzing like soda water.

Speedy turned to stare, then backed away from it slowly—and as slowly gathered speed. In fifteen seconds, he was leaping directly toward the two humans in an unsteady canter.

Powell did not get Speedy's words just then, though he heard something that resembled, "Lover's professions when uttered in Hessians."

He turned away. "Back to the cliff, Mike. He's out of the rut and he'll be taking orders now. I'm getting hot."

They jogged toward the shadow at the slow monotonous pace of their mounts, and it was not until they had entered it and felt the sudden coolness settle softly about them that Donovan looked back. *"Greg!"*

Powell looked and almost shrieked. Speedy was moving slowly now—so slowly—and in the *wrong direction*. He was drifting; drifting back into his rut; and he was picking up speed. He looked dreadfully close, and dreadfully unreachable, in the binoculars.

Donovan shouted wildly, "After him!" and thumped his robot into its pace, but Powell called him back.

"You won't catch him, Mike—it's no use." He fidgeted on his robot's shoulders and clenched his fist in tight impotence. "Why the devil do I see these things five seconds after it's all over? Mike, we've wasted hours."

"We need more oxalic acid," declared Donovan, stolidly. "The concentration wasn't high enough."

"Seven tons of it wouldn't have been enough—and we haven't the hours to spare to get it, even if it were, with the monoxide chewing him away. Don't you see what it is, Mike?"

And Donovan said flatly, "No."

"We were only establishing new equilibriums. When we create new monoxide and increase Rule 3 potential, he moves backward till he's in balance again—and when the monoxide drifted away, he moved forward, and again there was balance."

Powell's voice sounded thoroughly wretched. "It's the same old runaround. We can push at Rule 2 and pull at Rule 3 and we can't get anywhere—we can only change the position of balance. We've got to get outside both rules." And then he pushed his robot closer to Donovan's so that they were sitting face to face, dim shadows in the darkness, and he whispered, "Mike!"

"Is it the finish?"—dully. "I suppose we go back to the Station, wait for the banks to fold, shake hands, take cyanide, and go out like gentlemen." He laughed shortly.

"Mike," repeated Powell earnestly, "we've got to get Speedy."

"I know."

"Mike," once more, and Powell hesitated before continuing. "There's always Rule 1. I thought of it—earlier—but it's desperate."

Donovan looked up and his voice livened. "*We're* desperate."

"All right. According to Rule 1, a robot can't see a human come to harm because of his own inaction. Two and 3 can't stand against it. They *can't*, Mike."

"Even when the robot is half cra— Well, he's drunk. You know he is."

"It's the chances you take."

"Cut it. What are you going to do?"

"I'm going out there now and see what Rule 1 will do. If it won't break the balance, then what the devil—it's either now or three-four days from now."

"Hold on, Greg. There are human rules of behavior, too. You don't go out there just like that. Figure out a lottery, and give me *my* chance."

"All right. First to get the cube of fourteen goes." And almost immediately, "Twenty-seven forty-four!"

Donovan felt his robot stagger at a sudden push by Powell's mount and then Powell was off into the sunlight. Donovan opened his mouth to shout, and then clicked it shut. Of course, the damn fool had worked out the cube of fourteen in advance, and on purpose. Just like him.

The sun was hotter than ever and Powell felt a maddening itch in the small of his back. Imagination, probably, or perhaps hard radiation beginning to tell even through the insosuit.

Speedy was watching him, without a word of Gilbert and Sullivan gibberish as greeting. Thank God for that! But he daren't get too close.

He was three hundred yards away when Speedy began backing, a step at a time, cautiously—and Powell stopped. He jumped from his robot's shoulders and landed on the crystalline ground with a light thump and a flying of jagged fragments.

He proceeded on foot, the ground gritty and slippery to his steps, the low gravity causing him difficulty. The soles of his feet tickled with warmth. He cast one glance over his shoulder at the blackness of the cliff's shadow and realized that he had come too far to return—either by himself or by the help of his antique robot. It was Speedy or nothing now, and the knowledge of that constricted his chest.

Far enough! He stopped.

"Speedy," he called. "Speedy!"

The sleek, modern robot ahead of him hesitated and halted his backward steps, then resumed them.

Powell tried to put a note of pleading into his voice, and found it didn't take much acting. "Speedy, I've got to get back to the shadow or the sun'll get me. It's life or death, Speedy. I need you."

Speedy took one step forward and stopped. He spoke, but at the sound Powell groaned, for it was, "When you're lying awake with a dismal headache and repose is tabooed—" It trailed off there, and Powell took time out for some reason to murmur, "Iolanthe."

It was roasting hot! He caught a movement out of the corner of his eye, and whirled dizzily; then stared in utter astonishment, for the monstrous robot on which he had ridden was moving—moving toward him, and without a rider.

He was talking: "Pardon, Master. I must not move without a Master upon me, but you are in danger."

Of course, Rule 1 potential above everything. But he didn't want that clumsy antique; he wanted Speedy. He walked away and motioned frantically: "I order you to stay away. I *order* you to stop!"

It was quite useless. You could not beat Rule 1 potential. The robot said stupidly, "You are in danger, Master."

Powell looked about him desperately. He couldn't see clearly. His brain was in a heated whirl; his breath scorched when he breathed, and the ground all about him was a shimmering haze.

He called a last time, desperately: *"Speedy!* I'm dying, damn you! Where are you? Speedy, I *need* you."

He was still stumbling backward in a blind effort to get away from the giant robot he didn't want, when he felt steel fingers on his arms, and a worried, apologetic voice of metallic timbre in his ears.

"Holy smokes, boss, what are you doing here? And what am *I* doing—I'm so confused—"

"Never mind," murmured Powell, weakly. "Get me to the shadow of the cliff—and hurry!" There was one last feeling of being lifted into the air and a sensation of rapid motion and burning heat, and he passed out.

He woke with Donovan bending over him and smiling anxiously. "How are you, Greg?"

"Fine!" came the response. "Where's Speedy?"

"Right here. I sent him out to one of the other selenium pools—

EVIDENCE

·

Francis Quinn was a politician of the new school. That, of course, is a meaningless expression, as are all expressions of the sort. Most of the "new schools" we have were duplicated in the social life of ancient Greece, and perhaps, if we knew more about it, in the social life of ancient Sumeria and in the lake dwellings of prehistoric Switzerland as well.

But, to get out from under what promises to be a dull and complicated beginning, it might be best to state hastily that Quinn neither ran for office nor canvassed for votes, made no speeches and stuffed no ballot boxes. Any more than Napoleon pulled a trigger at Austerlitz.

And since politics makes strange bedfellows, Alfred Lanning sat at the other side of the desk with his ferocious white eyebrows bent far forward over eyes in which chronic impatience had sharpened to acuity. He was not pleased.

The fact, if known to Quinn, would have annoyed him not the least. His voice was friendly, perhaps professionally so.

"I assume you know Stephen Byerley, Dr. Lanning."

"I have heard of him. So have many people."

"Yes, so have I. Perhaps you intend voting for him at the next election."

"I couldn't say." There was an unmistakable trace of acidity here. "I have not followed the political currents, so I'm not aware that he is running for office."

"He may be our next mayor. Of course, he is only a lawyer now, but great oaks—"

"Yes," interrupted Lanning, "I have heard the phrase before. But I wonder if we can get to the business at hand."

"We *are* at the business at hand, Dr. Lanning." Quinn's tone was very gentle, "It is to my interest to keep Mr. Byerley a district attorney at the very most, and it is to your interest to help me do so."

"To *my* interest? Come!" Lanning's eyebrows hunched low.

"Well, say then to the interest of the U.S. Robots and Mechanical Men Corporation. I come to you as Director-Emeritus of Research, because I know that your connection to them is that of, shall we say, 'elder statesman.' You are listened to with respect and yet your connection with them is no longer so tight but that you cannot possess considerable freedom of action; even if the action is somewhat unorthodox."

Dr. Lanning was silent a moment, chewing the cud of his thoughts. He said more softly, "I don't follow you at all, Mr. Quinn."

"I am not surprised, Dr. Lanning. But it's all rather simple. Do you mind?" Quinn lit a slender cigarette with a lighter of tasteful simplicity and his big-boned face settled into an expression of quiet amusement. "We have spoken of Mr. Byerley—a strange and colorful character. He was unknown three years ago. He is very well known now. He is a man of force and ability, and certainly the most capable and intelligent prosecutor I have ever known. Unfortunately he is not a friend of mine—"

"I understand," said Lanning, mechanically. He stared at his fingernails.

"I have had occasion," continued Quinn, evenly, "in the

past year to investigate Mr. Byerley—quite exhaustively. It is always useful, you see, to subject the past life of reform politicians to rather inquisitive research. If you knew how often it helped—". He paused to smile humorlessly at the glowing tip of his cigeratte. "But Mr. Byerley's past is unremarkable. A quiet life in a small town, a college education, a wife who died young, an auto accident with a slow recovery, law school, coming to the metropolis, an attorney."

Francis Quinn shook his head slowly, then added, "But his present life. Ah, that is remarkable. Our district attorney never eats!"

Lanning's head snapped up, old eyes surprisingly sharp, "Pardon me?"

"Our district attorney never eats." The repetition thumped by syllables. "I'll modify that slightly. He has never been seen to eat or drink. Never! Do you understand the significance of the word? Not rarely, but never!"

"I find that quite incredible. Can you trust your investigators?"

"I can trust my investigators, and I don't find it incredible at all. Further, our district attorney has never been seen to drink—in the aqueous sense as well as the alcoholic—nor to sleep. There are other factors, but I should think I have made my point."

Lanning leaned back in his seat, and there was the rapt silence of challenge and response between them, and then the old roboticist shook his head. "No. There is only one thing you can be trying to imply, if I couple your statements with the fact that you present them to me, and that is impossible."

"But the man is quite inhuman, Dr. Lanning."

"If you told me he were Satan in masquerade, there would be a faint chance that I might believe you."

"I tell you he is a robot, Dr. Lanning."

"I tell you it is as impossible a conception as I have ever heard, Mr. Quinn."

Again the combative silence.

"Nevertheless," and Quinn stubbed out his cigarette with elaborate care, "you will have to investigate this impossibility with all the resources of the Corporation."

"I'm sure that I could undertake no such thing, Mr. Quinn. You don't seriously suggest that the Corporation take part in local politics."

"You have no choice. Supposing I were to make my facts public without proof. The evidence is circumstantial enough."

"Suit yourself in that respect."

"But it would not suit me. Proof would be much preferable. And it would not suit *you*, for the publicity would be very damaging to your company. You are perfectly well acquainted, I suppose, with the strict rules against the use of robots on inhabited worlds."

"Certainly!"—brusquely.

"You know that the U.S. Robots and Mechanical Men Corporation is the only manufacturer of positronic robots in the Solar System, and if Byerley is a robot, he is a *positronic* robot. You are also aware that all positronic robots are leased, and not sold; that the Corporation remains the owner and manager of each robot, and is therefore responsible for the actions of all."

"It is an easy matter, Mr. Quinn, to prove the Corporation has never manufactured a robot of a humanoid character."

"It can be done? To discuss merely possibilities."

"Yes. It can be done."

"Secretly, I imagine, as well. Without entering it in your books."

"Not the positronic brain, sir. Too many factors are involved in that, and there is the tightest possible government supervision."

"Yes, but robots are worn out, break down, go out of order—and are dismantled."

"And the positronic brains re-used or destroyed."

"Really?" Francis Quinn allowed himself a trace of sarcasm. "And if one were, accidentally, of course, not destroyed—and there happened to be a humanoid structure waiting for a brain."

"Impossible!"

"You would have to prove that to the government and the public, so why not prove it to me now."

"But what could our purpose be?" demanded Lanning in exasperation. "Where is our motivation? Credit us with a minimum of sense."

"My dear sir, please. The Corporation would be only too glad to have the various Regions permit the use of humanoid positronic robots on inhabited worlds. The profits would be enormous. But the prejudice of the public against such a practice is too great. Suppose you get them used to such robots first—see, we have a skillful lawyer, a good mayor, —and he is a robot. Won't you buy our robot butlers?"

"Thoroughly fantastic. An almost humorous descent to the ridiculous."

"I imagine so. Why not prove it? Or would you still rather try to prove it to the public?"

The light in the office was dimming, but it was not yet too dim to obscure the flush of frustration on Alfred Lanning's face. Slowly, the roboticist's finger touched a knob and the wall illuminators glowed to gentle life.

"Well, then," he growled, "let us see."

The face of Stephen Byerley is not an easy one to describe. He was forty by birth certificate and forty by appearance—but it was a healthy, well-nourished good-natured appearance of forty; one that automatically drew the teeth of the bromide about "looking one's age."

This was particularly true when he laughed, and he was laughing now. It came loudly and continuously, died away for a bit, then began again—

And Alfred Lanning's face contracted into a rigidly bitter monument of disapproval. He made a half gesture to the woman who sat beside him, but her thin, bloodless lips merely pursed themselves a trifle.

Byerley gasped himself a stage nearer normality.

"Really, Dr. Lanning . . . really—I . . . *I* . . . a robot?"

Lanning bit his words off with a snap, "It is no statement

of mine, sir. I would be quite satisfied to have you a member of humanity. Since our corporation never manufactured you, I am quite certain that you are—in a legalistic sense, at any rate. But since the contention that you are a robot has been advanced to us seriously by a man of certain standing—"

"Don't mention his name, if it would knock a chip off your granite block of ethics, but let's pretend it was Frank Quinn, for the sake of argument, and continue."

Lanning drew in a sharp, cutting snort at the interruption, and paused ferociously before continuing with added frigidity, "—by a man of certain standing, with whose identity I am not interested in playing guessing games, I am bound to ask your cooperation in disproving it. The mere fact that such a contention could be advanced and publicized by the means at this man's disposal would be a bad blow to the company I represent—even if the charge were never proven. You understand me?"

"Oh, yes, your position is clear to me. The charge itself is ridiculous. The spot you find yourself in is not. I beg your pardon, if my laughter offended you. It was the first I laughed at, not the second. How can I help you?"

"It could be very simple. You have only to sit down to a meal at a restaurant in the presence of witnesses, have your picture taken, and eat." Lanning sat back in his chair, the worst of the interview over. The woman beside him watched Byerley with an apparently absorbed expression but contributed nothing of her own.

Stephen Byerley met her eyes for an instant, was caught by them, then turned back to the roboticist. For a while his fingers were thoughtful over the bronze paper-weight that was the only ornament on his desk.

He said quietly, "I don't think I can oblige you."

He raised his hand, "Now wait, Dr. Lanning. I appreciate the fact that this whole matter is distasteful to you, that you have been forced into it against your will, that you feel you are playing an undignified and even ridiculous part. Still, the matter is even more intimately concerned with myself, so be tolerant.

"First, what makes you think that Quinn—this man of certain standing, you know—wasn't hoodwinking you, in order to get you to do exactly what you are doing?"

"Why it seems scarcely likely that a reputable person would endanger himself in so ridiculous a fashion, if he weren't convinced he were on safe ground."

There was little humor in Byerley's eyes, "You don't know Quinn. He could manage to make safe ground out of a ledge a mountain sheep could not handle. I suppose he showed the particulars of the investigation he claims to have made of me?"

"Enough to convince me that it would be too troublesome to have our corporation attempt to disprove them when you could do so more easily."

"Then you believe him when he says I never eat. You are a scientist, Dr. Lanning. Think of the logic required. I have not been observed to eat, therefore, I never eat Q.E.D. After all!"

"You are using prosecution tactics to confuse what is really a very simple situation."

"On the contrary, I am trying to clarify what you and Quinn between you are making a very complicated one. You see, I don't sleep much, that's true, and I certainly don't sleep in public. I have never cared to eat with others—an idiosyncrasy which is unusual and probably neurotic in character, but which harms no one. Look, Dr. Lanning, let me present you with a suppositious case. Supposing we had a politician who was interested in defeating a reform candidate at any cost and while investigating his private life came across oddities such as I have just mentioned.

"Suppose further that in order to smear the candidate effectively, he comes to your company as the ideal agent. Do you expect him to say to you, 'So-and-so is a robot because he hardly ever eats with people, and I have never seen him fall asleep in the middle of a case; and once when I peeped into his window in the middle of the night, there he was, sitting up with a book; and I looked in his frigidaire and there was no food in it.'

"If he told you that, you would send for a straitjacket. But if he tells you, 'He *never* sleeps; he *never* eats,' then the shock of the statement blinds you to the fact that such statements are impossible to prove. You play into his hands by contributing to the to-do."

"Regardless, sir," began Lanning, with a threatening obstinacy, "of whether you consider this matter serious or not, it will require only the meal I mentioned to end it."

Again Byerley turned to the woman, who still regarded him expressionlessly. "Pardon me. I've caught your name correctly, haven't I? Dr. Susan Calvin?"

"Yes, Mr. Byerley."

"You're the U.S. Robots' psychologist, aren't you?"

"*Robo*psychologist, please."

"Oh, are robots so different from men, mentally?"

"Worlds different." She allowed herself a frosty smile, "Robots are essentially decent."

Humor tugged at the corners of the lawyer's mouth, "Well, that's a hard blow. But what I wanted to say was this. Since you're a psycho—a robopsychologist, *and* a woman, I'll bet that you've done something that Dr. Lanning hasn't thought of."

"And what is that?"

"You've got something to eat in your purse."

Something caught in the schooled indifference of Susan Calvin's eyes. She said, "You surprise me, Mr. Byerley."

And opening her purse, she produced an apple. Quietly, she handed it to him. Dr. Lanning, after an initial start, followed the slow movement from one hand to the other with sharply alert eyes.

Calmly, Stephen Byerley bit into it, and calmly he swallowed it.

"You see, Dr. Lanning?"

Dr. Lanning smiled in a relief tangible enough to make even his eyebrows appear benevolent. A relief that survived for one fragile second.

Susan Calvin said, "I was curious to see if you would eat it, but, of course, in the present case, it proves nothing."

Byerley grinned, "It doesn't?"

"Of course not. It is obvious, Dr. Lanning, that if this man were a humanoid robot, he would be a perfect imitation. He is almost too human to be credible. After all, we have been seeing and observing human beings all our lives; it would be impossible to palm something merely nearly right off on us. It would have to be *all* right. Observe the texture of the skin, the quality of the irises, the bone formation of the hand. If he's a robot, I wish U.S. Robots *had* made him, because he's a good job. Do you suppose then, that anyone capable of paying attention to such niceties would neglect a few gadgets to take care of such things as eating, sleeping, elimination? For emergency use only, perhaps; as, for instance, to prevent such situations as are arising here. So a meal won't really prove anything."

"Now wait," snarled Lanning, "I am not quite the fool both of you make me out to be. I am not interested in the problem of Mr. Byerley's humanity or nonhumanity. I am interested in getting the corporation out of a hole. A public meal will end the matter and keep it ended no matter what Quinn does. We can leave the finer details to lawyers and robopsychologists."

"But, Dr. Lanning," said Byerley, "you forget the politics of the situation. I am as anxious to be elected, as Quinn is to stop me. By the way, did you notice that you used his name? It's a cheap shyster trick of mine; I knew you would, before you were through."

Lanning flushed, "What has the election to do with it?"

"Publicity works both ways, sir. If Quinn wants to call me a robot, and has the nerve to do so, I have the nerve to play the game his way."

"You mean you—" Lanning was quite frankly appalled.

"Exactly. I mean that I'm going to let him go ahead, choose his rope, test its strength, cut off the right length, tie the noose, insert his head and grin. I can do what little else is required."

"You are mighty confident."

Susan Calvin rose to her feet, "Come, Alfred, we won't change his mind for him."

"You see," Byerley smiled gently. "You're a human psychologist, too."

But perhaps not all the confidence that Dr. Lanning had remarked upon was present that evening when Byerley's car parked on the automatic treads leading to the sunken garage, and Byerley himself crossed the path to the front door of his house.

The figure in the wheel chair looked up as he entered and smiled. Byerley's face lit with affection. He crossed over to it.

The cripple's voice was a hoarse, grating whisper that came out of a mouth forever twisted to one side, leering out of a face that was half scar tissue, "You're late, Steve."

"I know, John, I know. But I've been up against a peculiar and interesting trouble today."

"So?" Neither the torn face nor the destroyed voice could carry expression but there was anxiety in the clear eyes. "Nothing you can't handle?"

"I'm not exactly certain. I may need your help. *You're* the brilliant one in the family. Do you want me to take you out into the garden? It's a beautiful evening."

Two strong arms lifted John from the wheel chair. Gently, almost caressingly, Byerley's arms went around the shoulders and under the swathed legs of the cripple. Carefully, and slowly, he walked through the rooms, down the gentle ramp that had been built with a wheel chair in mind, and out the back door into the walled and wired garden behind the house.

"Why don't you let me use the wheel chair, Steve? This is silly."

"Because I'd rather carry you. Do you object? You know that you're as glad to get out of that motorized buggy for a while as I am to see you out. How do you feel today?" He deposited John with infinite care upon the cool grass.

"How should I feel? But tell me about your trouble."

"Quinn's campaign will be based on the fact that he claims I'm a robot."

John's eyes opened wide, "How do you know? It's impossible. I won't believe it."

"Oh, come, I tell you it's so. He had one of the big-shot scientists of U.S. Robots and Mechanical Men Corporation over at the office to argue with me."

Slowly John's hands tore at the grass, "I see. I see."

Byerley said, "But we can let him choose his ground. I have an idea. Listen to me and tell me if we can do it—"

The scene as it appeared in Alfred Lanning's office that night was a tableau of stares. Francis Quinn stared meditatively at Alfred Lanning. Lanning's stare was savagely set upon Susan Calvin, who stared impassively in her turn at Quinn.

Francis Quinn broke it with a heavy attempt at lightness, "Bluff. He's making it up as he goes along."

"Are you going to gamble on that, Mr. Quinn?" asked Dr. Calvin, indifferently.

"Well, it's your gamble, really."

"Look here," Lanning covered definite pessimism with bluster, "we've done what you asked. We witnessed the man eat. It's ridiculous to presume him a robot."

"Do *you* think so?" Quinn shot toward Calvin. "Lanning said you were the expert."

Lanning was almost threatening, "Now, Susan—"

Quinn interrupted smoothly, "Why not let her talk, man? She's been sitting there imitating a gatepost for half an hour."

Lanning felt definitely harassed. From what he experienced then to incipient paranoia was but a step. He said, "Very well. Have your say, Susan. We won't interrupt you."

Susan Calvin glanced at him humorlessly, then fixed cold eyes on Mr. Quinn. "There are only two ways of definitely proving Byerley to be a robot, sir. So far you are presenting circumstantial evidence, with which you can accuse, but not prove—and I think Mr. Byerley is sufficiently clever to counter that sort of material. You probably think so yourself, or you wouldn't have come here.

"The two methods of *proof* are the physical and the psychological. Physically, you can dissect him or use an X-ray. How to do that would be *your* problem. Psychologically, his behavior can be studied, for if he *is* a positronic robot, he must conform to the three Laws of Robotics. A positronic brain can not be constructed without them. You know the Laws, Mr. Quinn?"

She spoke them carefully, clearly, quoting word for word the famous bold print on page one of the "Handbook of Robotics."

"I've heard of them," said Quinn, carelessly.

"Then the matter is easy to follow," responded the psychologist, dryly. "If Mr. Byerley breaks any of those three rules, he is not a robot. Unfortunately, this procedure works in only one direction. If he lives up to the rules, it proves nothing one way or the other."

Quinn raised polite eyebrows, "Why not, doctor?"

"Because, if you stop to think of it, the three Rules of Robotics are the essential guiding principles of a good many of the world's ethical systems. Of course, every human being is supposed to have the instinct of self-preservation. That's Rule Three to a robot. Also every 'good' human being, with a social conscience and a sense of responsibility, is supposed to defer to proper authority; to listen to his doctor, his boss, his government, his psychiatrist, his fellow man; to obey laws, to follow rules, to conform to custom— even when they interfere with his comfort or his safety. That's Rule Two to a robot. Also, every 'good' human being is supposed to love others as himself, protect his fellow man, risk his life to save another. That's Rule One to a robot. To put it simply—if Byerley follows all the Rules of Robotics, he may be a robot, and may simply be a very good man."

"But," said Quinn, "you're telling me that you can never prove him a robot."

"I may be able to prove him *not* a robot."

"That's not the proof I want."

"You'll have such proof as exists. You are the only one responsible for your own wants."

Here Lanning's mind leaped suddenly to the sting of an idea, "Has it occurred to anyone," he ground out, "that district attorney is a rather strange occupation for a robot? The prosecution of human beings—sentencing them to death—bringing about their infinite harm—"

Quinn grew suddenly keen, "No, you can't get out of it that way. Being district attorney doesn't make him human. Don't you know his record? Don't you know that he boasts that he has never prosecuted an innocent man; that there are scores of people left untried because the evidence against them didn't satisfy him, even though he could probably have argued a jury into atomizing them? That happens to be so."

Lanning's thin cheeks quivered, "No, Quinn, no. There is nothing in the Rules of Robotics that makes any allowance for human guilt. A robot may not judge whether a human being deserves death. It is not for him to decide. *He may not harm a human*—variety skunk, or variety angel."

Susan Calvin sounded tired. "Alfred," she said, "don't talk foolishly. What if a robot came upon a madman about to set fire to a house with people in it. He would stop the madman, wouldn't he?"

"Of course."

"And if the only way he could stop him was to kill him—"

There was a faint sound in Lanning's throat. Nothing more.

"The answer to that, Alfred, is that he would do his best not to kill him. If the madman died, the robot would require psychotherapy because he might easily go mad at the conflict presented him—of having broken Rule One to adhere to Rule One in a higher sense. But a man would be dead and a robot would have killed him."

"Well, *is* Byerley mad?" demanded Lanning, with all the sarcasm he could muster.

"No, but he has killed no man himself. He has exposed

facts which might represent a particular human being to be dangerous to the large mass of other human beings we call society. He protects the greater number and thus adheres to Rule One at maximum potential. That is as far as he goes. It is the judge who then condemns the criminal to death or imprisonment, after the jury decides on his guilt or innocence. It is the jailer who imprisons him, the executioner who kills him. And Mr. Byerley has done nothing but determine truth and aid society.

"As a matter of fact, Mr. Quinn, I have looked into Mr. Byerley's career since you first brought this matter to our attention. I find that he has never demanded the death sentence in his closing speeches to the jury. I also find that he has spoken on behalf of the abolition of capital punishment and contributed generously to research institutions engaged in criminal neurophysiology. He apparently believes in the cure, rather than the punishment of crime. I find that significant."

"You do?" Quinn smiled. "Significant of a certain odor of roboticity, perhaps?"

"Perhaps. Why deny it? Actions such as his could come only from a robot, or from a very honorable and decent human being. But you see, you just can't differentiate between a robot and the very best of humans."

Quinn sat back in his chair. His voice quivered with impatience. "Dr. Lanning, it's perfectly possible to create a humanoid robot that would perfectly duplicate a human in appearance, isn't it?"

Lanning harrumphed and considered, "It's been done experimentally by U.S. Robots," he said reluctantly, "without the addition of a positronic brain, of course. By using human ova and hormone control, one can grow human flesh and skin over a skeleton of porous silicone plastics that would defy external examination. The eyes, the hair, the skin would be really human, not humanoid. And if you put a positronic brain, and such other gadgets as you might desire inside, you have a humanoid robot."

Quinn said shortly, "How long would it take to make one?"

Lanning considered, "If you had all your equipment—the brain, the skeleton, the ovum, the proper hormones and radiations—say, two months."

The politician straightened out of his chair. "Then we shall see what the insides of Mr. Byerley look like. It will mean publicity for U.S. Robots—but I gave you your chance."

Lanning turned impatiently to Susan Calvin, when they were alone. "Why do you insist—"

And with real feeling, she responded sharply and instantly, "Which do you want—the truth or my resignation? I won't lie for you. U.S. Robots can take care of itself. Don't turn coward."

"What," said Lanning, "if he opens up Byerley, and wheels and gears fall out. What then?"

"He won't open Byerley," said Calvin, disdainfully. "Byerley is as clever as Quinn, at the very least."

The news broke upon the city a week before Byerley was to have been nominated. But "broke" is the wrong word. It staggered upon the city, shambled, crawled. Laughter began, and wit was free. And as the far off hand of Quinn tightened its pressure in easy stages, the laughter grew forced, an element of hollow uncertainty entered, and people broke off to wonder.

The convention itself had the air of a restive stallion. There had been no contest planned. Only Byerley could possibly have been nominated a week earlier. There was no substitute even now. They had to nominate him, but there was complete confusion about it.

It would not have been so bad if the average individual were not torn between the enormity of the charge, if true, and its sensational folly, if false.

The day after Byerley was nominated perfunctorily, hollowly—a newspaper finally published the gist of a long interview with Dr. Susan Calvin, "world famous expert on robopsychology and positronics."

What broke loose is popularly and succinctly described as hell.

It was what the Fundamentalists were waiting for. They were not a political party; they made pretense to no formal religion. Essentially they were those who had not adapted themselves to what had once been called the Atomic Age, in the days when atoms were a novelty. Actually, they were the Simple-Lifers, hungering after a life, which to those who lived it had probably appeared not so Simple, and who had been, therefore, Simple-Lifers themselves.

The Fundamentalists required no new reason to detest robots and robot manufacturers; but a new reason such as the Quinn accusation and the Calvin analysis was sufficient to make such detestation audible.

The huge plant of the U.S. Robots and Mechanical Men Corporation was a hive that spawned armed guards. It prepared for war.

Within the city the house of Stephen Byerley bristled with police.

The political campaign, of course, lost all other issues, and resembled a campaign only in that it was something filling the hiatus between nomination and election.

Stephen Byerley did not allow the fussy little man to distract him. He remained comfortably unperturbed by the uniforms in the background. Outside the house, past the line of grim guards, reporters and photographers waited according to the tradition of the caste. One enterprising TV station even had a scanner focused on the blank entrance to the prosecutor's unpretentious home, while a synthetically excited announcer filled in with inflated commentary.

The fussy little man advanced. He held forward a rich, complicated sheet. "This, Mr. Byerley, is a court order authorizing me to search these premises for the presence of illegal . . . uh . . . mechanical men or robots of any description."

Byerley half rose, and took the paper. He glanced at it indifferently, and smiled as he handed it back. "All in order. Go ahead. Do your job. Mrs. Hoppin"—to his house-keeper, who appeared reluctantly from the next room—"please go with them, and help out if you can."

The little man, whose name was Harroway, hesitated, produced an unmistakable blush, failed completely to catch Byerley's eyes, and muttered, "Come on," to the two policemen.

He was back in ten minutes.

"Through?" questioned Byerley, in just the tone of a person who is not particularly interested in the question, or its answer.

Harroway cleared his throat, made a bad start in falsetto, and began again, angrily, "Look here, Mr. Byerley, our special instructions were to search the house very thoroughly."

"And haven't you?"

"We were told exactly what to look for."

"Yes?"

"In short, Mr. Byerley, and not to put too fine a point on it, we were told to search you."

"Me?" said the prosecutor with a broadening smile. "And how do you intend to do that?"

"We have a Penet-radiation unit—"

"Then I'm to have my X-ray photograph taken, hey? You have the authority?"

"You saw my warrant."

"May I see it again?"

Harroway, his forehead shining with considerably more than mere enthusiasm, passed it over a second time.

Byerley said evenly, "I read here as the description of what you are to search; I quote: 'the dwelling place belonging to Stephen Allen Byerley, located at 355 Willow Grove, Evanstron, together with any garage, storehouse or other structures or buildings thereto appertaining, together with all grounds thereto appertaining' . . . um . . . and so on. Quite in order. But, my good man, it doesn't say anything about searching my interior. I am not part of the premises. You may search my clothes if you think I've got a robot hidden in my pocket."

Harroway had no doubt on the point of to whom he owed his job. He did not propose to be backward, given a chance to earn a much better—i.e., more highly paid—job.

He said, in a faint echo of bluster, "Look here. I'm allowed to search the furniture in your house, and anything else I find in it. You are in it, aren't you?"

"A remarkable observation. I *am* in it. But I'm not a piece of furniture. As a citizen of adult responsibility—I have the psychiatric certificate proving that—I have certain rights under the Regional Articles. Searching me would come under the heading of violating my Right of Privacy. That paper isn't sufficient."

"Sure, but if you're a robot, you don't have Right of Privacy."

"True enough—but that paper still isn't sufficient. It recognizes me implicitly as a human being."

"Where?" Harroway snatched at it.

"Where it says 'the dwelling place belonging to' and so on. A robot cannot own property. And you may tell your employer, Mr. Harroway, that if he tries to issue a similar paper which does *not* implicitly recognize me as a human being, he will be immediately faced with a restraining injunction and a civil suit which will make it necessary for him to *prove* me a robot by means of information *now* in his possession, or else to pay a whopping penalty for an attempt to deprive me unduly of my Rights under the Regional Articles. You'll tell him that, won't you?"

Harroway marched to the door. He turned. "You're a slick lawyer—" His hand was in his pocket. For a short moment, he stood there. Then he left, smiled in the direction of the 'visor scanner, still playing away—waved to the reporters, and shouted, "We'll have something for you tomorrow, boys. No kidding."

In his ground car, he settled back, removed the tiny mechanism from his pocket and carefully inspected it. It was the first time he had ever taken a photograph by X-ray reflection. He hoped he had done it correctly.

*   *   *

Quinn and Byerley had never met face-to-face alone. But visorphone was pretty close to it. In fact, accepted literally, perhaps the phrase was accurate, even if to each, the other were merely the light and dark pattern of a bank of photocells.

It was Quinn who had initiated the call. It was Quinn, who spoke first, and without particular ceremony, "Thought you would like to know, Byerley, that I intend to make public the fact that you're wearing a protective shield against Penet-radiation."

"That so? In that case, you've probably already made it public. I have a notion our enterprising press representatives have been tapping my various communication lines for quite a while. I know they have my office lines full of holes; which is why I've dug in at my home these last weeks." Byerley was friendly, almost chatty.

Quinn's lips tightened slightly, "This call is shielded— thoroughly. I'm making it at a certain personal risk."

"So I should imagine. Nobody knows you're behind this campaign. At least, nobody knows it officially. Nobody doesn't know it unofficially. I wouldn't worry. So I wear a protective shield? I suppose you found that out when your puppy dog's Penet-radiation photograph, the other day, turned out to be overexposed."

"You realize, Byerley, that it would be pretty obvious to everyone that you don't dare face X-ray analysis."

"Also that you, or your men, attempted illegal invasion of my Right of Privacy."

"The devil they'll care for that."

"They might. It's rather symbolic of our two campaigns, isn't it? You have little concern with the rights of the individual citizen. I have great concern. I will not submit to X-ray analysis, because I wish to maintain my Rights on principle. Just as I'll maintain the rights of others when elected."

"That will no doubt make a very interesting speech, but no one will believe you. A little too high-sounding to be true. Another thing," a sudden, crisp change, "the personnel in your home was not complete the other night."

"In what way?"

"According to the report," he shuffled papers before him that were just within the range of vision of the visiplate, "there was one person missing—a cripple."

"As you say," said Byerley, tonelessly, "a cripple. My old teacher, who lives with me and who is now in the country—and has been for two months. A 'much-needed rest' is the usual expression applied in the case. He has your permission?"

"Your teacher? A scientist of sorts?"

"A lawyer once—before he was a cripple. He has a government license as a research biophysicist, with a laboratory of his own, and a complete description of the work he's doing filed with the proper authorities, to whom I can refer you. The work is minor, but is a harmless and engaging hobby for a—poor cripple. I am being as helpful as I can, you see."

"I see. And what does this . . . teacher . . . know about robot manufacture?"

"I couldn't judge the extent of his knowledge in a field with which I am unacquainted."

"He wouldn't have access to positronic brains?"

"Ask your friends at U.S. Robots. They'd be the ones to know."

"I'll make it short, Byerley. Your crippled teacher is the real Stephen Byerley. You are his robot creation. We can prove it. It was he who was in the automobile accident, not you. There will be ways of checking the records."

"Really? Do so, then. My best wishes."

"And we can search your so-called teacher's 'country place,' and see what we can find there."

"Well, not quite, Quinn." Byerley smiled broadly. "Unfortunately for you, my so-called teacher is a sick man. His country place is his place of rest. His Right of Privacy as a citizen of adult responsibility is naturally even stronger, under the circumstances. You won't be able to obtain a warrant to enter his grounds without showing just cause. However, I'd be the last to prevent you from trying."

There was a pause of moderate length, and then Quinn

leaned forward, so that his imaged-face expanded and the fine lines on his forehead were visible, "Byerley, why do you carry on? You can't be elected."

"Can't I?"

"Do you think you can? Do you suppose that your failure to make any attempt to disprove the robot charge—when you could easily, by breaking one of the Three Laws—does anything but convince the people that you *are* a robot?"

"All I see so far is that from being a rather vaguely known, but still largely obscure metropolitan lawyer, I have now become a world figure. You're a good publicist."

"But you *are* a robot."

"So it's been said, but not proven."

"It's been proven sufficiently for the electorate."

"Then relax—you've won."

"Good-by," said Quinn, with his first touch of viciousness, and the visorphone slammed off.

"Good-by," said Byerley imperturbably, to the blank plate.

Byerley brought his "teacher" back the week before election. The air car dropped quickly in an obscure part of the city.

"You'll stay here till after election," Byerley told him. "It would be better to have you out of the way if things take a bad turn."

The hoarse voice that twisted painfully out of John's crooked mouth might have had accents of concern in it. "There's danger of violence?"

"The Fundamentalists threaten it, so I suppose there is, in a theoretical sense. But I really don't expect it. The Fundies have no real power. They're just the continuous irritant factor that might stir up a riot after a while. You don't mind staying here? Please. I won't be myself if I have to worry about you."

"Oh, I'll stay. You still think it will go well?"

"I'm sure of it. No one bothered you at the place?"

"No one. I'm certain."

"And your part went well?"

"Well enough. There'll be no trouble there."

"Then take care of yourself, and watch the televisor tomorrow, John." Byerley pressed the gnarled hand that rested on his.

Lenton's forehead was a furrowed study in suspense. He had the completely unenviable job of being Byerley's campaign manager in a campaign that wasn't a campaign, for a person that refused to reveal his strategy, and refused to accept his manager's.

"You can't!" It was his favorite phrase. It had become his only phrase. "I tell you, Steve, you can't!"

He threw himself in front of the prosecutor, who was spending his time, leafing through the typed pages of his speech.

"Put that down, Steve. Look, that mob has been organized by the Fundies. You won't get a hearing. You'll be stoned more likely. Why do you have to make a speech before an audience? What's wrong with a recording, a visual recording?"

"You want me to win the election, don't you?" asked Byerley, mildly.

"Win the election! You're not going to win, Steve. I'm trying to save your life."

"Oh, I'm not in danger."

"He's not in danger. He's not in danger." Lenton made a queer, rasping sound in his throat. "You mean you're getting out on that balcony in front of fifty thousand crazy crackpots and try to talk sense to them—on a balcony like a medieval dictator?"

Byerley consulted his watch. "In about five minutes—as soon as the television lines are free."

Lenton's answering remark was not quite transliterable.

The crowd filled a roped off area of the city. Trees and houses seemed to grow out of a mass-human foundation. And by ultrawave, the rest of the world watched. It was a purely local election, but it had a world audience just the same. Byerley thought of that and smiled.

But there was nothing to smile at in the crowd itself. There were banners and streamers, ringing every possible change on his supposed roboticity. The hostile attitude rose thickly and tangibly into the atmosphere.

From the start the speech was not successful. It competed against the inchoate mob howl and the rhythmic cries of the Fundie claques that formed mob-islands within the mob. Byerley spoke on, slowly, unemotionally—

Inside, Lenton clutched his hair and groaned—and waited for the blood.

There was a writhing in the front ranks. An angular citizen with popping eyes, and clothes too short for the lank length of his limbs, was pulling to the fore. A policeman dived after him, making slow, struggling passage. Byerley waved the latter off, angrily.

The thin man was directly under the balcony. His words tore unheard against the roar.

Byerley leaned forward. "What do you say? If you have a legitimate question, I'll answer it." He turned to a flanking guard. "Bring that man up here."

There was a tensing in the crowd. Cries of "Quiet" started in various parts of the mob, and rose to a bedlam, then toned down raggedly. The thin man, red-faced and panting, faced Byerley.

Byerley said, "Have you a question?"

The thin man stared, and said in a cracked voice, "Hit me!"

With sudden energy, he thrust out his chin at an angle. "Hit me! You say you're not a robot. Prove it. You can't hit a human, you monster."

There was a queer, flat, dead silence. Byerley's voice punctured it. "I have no reason to hit you."

The thin man was laughing wildly. "You *can't* hit me. You *won't* hit me. You're not a human. You're a monster, a make-believe man."

And Stephen Byerley, tight-lipped, in the face of thousands who watched in person and the millions who watched by screen, drew back his fist and caught the man crackingly upon the chin. The challenger went over backwards in sudden collapse, with nothing on his face but blank, blank surprise.

Byerley said, "I'm sorry. Take him in and see that he's comfortable. I want to speak to him when I'm through."

And when Dr. Calvin, from her reserved space, turned her automobile and drove off, only one reporter had recovered sufficiently from the shock to race after her, and shout an unheard question.

Susan Calvin called over her shoulder, "He's human."

That was enough. The reporter raced away in his own direction.

The rest of the speech might be described as "Spoken but not heard."

Dr. Calvin and Stephen Byerley met once again—a week before he took the oath of office as mayor. It was late—past midnight.

Dr. Calvin said, "You don't look tired."

The mayor-elect smiled. "I may stay up for a while. Don't tell Quinn."

"I shan't. But that was an interesting story of Quinn's, since you mention him. It's a shame to have spoiled it. I suppose you knew his theory?"

"Parts of it."

"It was highly dramatic. Stephen Byerley was a young lawyer, a powerful speaker, a great idealist—and with a certain flair for biophysics. Are you interested in robotics, Mr. Byerley?"

"Only in the legal aspects."

"*This* Stephen Byerley was. But here was an accident. Byerley's wife died; he himself, worse. His legs were gone; his face was gone; his voice was gone. Part of his mind was—bent. He would not submit to plastic surgery. He retired from the world, legal career gone—only his intelligence, and his hands left. Somehow he could obtain positronic brains, even a complex one, one which had the greatest capacity of forming judgments in ethical problems—which is the highest robotic function so far developed.

"He grew a body about it. Trained it to be everything he would have been and was no longer. He sent it out into the world as Stephen Byerley, remaining behind himself as the old, crippled teacher that no one ever saw—"

"Unfortunately," said the mayor-elect, "I ruined all that by hitting a man. The papers say it was your official verdict on the occasion that I was human."

"How did that happen? Do you mind telling me? It couldn't have been accidental."

"It wasn't entirely. Quinn did most of the work. My men started quietly spreading the fact that I had never hit a man; that I was unable to hit a man; that to fail to do so under provocation would be sure proof that I was a robot. So I arranged for a silly speech in public, with all sorts of publicity overtones, and almost inevitably, some fool fell for it. In its essence, it was what I call a shyster trick. One in which the artificial atmosphere which has been created does all the work. Of course, the emotional effects made my election certain, as intended."

The robopsychologist nodded. "I see you intrude on my field—as every politician must, I suppose. But I'm very sorry it turned out this way. I like robots. I like them considerably better than I do human beings. If a robot can be created capable of being a civil executive, I think he'd make the best one possible. By the Laws of Robotics, he'd be incapable of harming humans, incapable of tyranny, of corruption, of stupidity, of prejudice. And after he had served a decent term, he would leave, even though he were immortal, because it would be impossible for him to hurt humans by letting them know that a robot had ruled them. It would be most ideal."

"Except that a robot might fall due to the inherent inadequacies of his brain. The positronic brain has never equalled the complexities of the human brain."

"He would have advisers. Not even a human brain is capable of governing without assistance."

Byerley considered Susan Calvin with grave interest. "Why do you smile, Dr. Calvin?"

"I smile because Mr. Quinn didn't think of everything."

"You mean there could be more to that story of his."

"Only a little. For the three months before election, this Stephen Byerley that Mr. Quinn spoke about, this broken man, was in the country for some mysterious reason. He returned in time for that famous speech of yours. And after all, what the old cripple did once, he could do a second time, particularly where the second job is very simple in comparison to the first."

"I don't quite understand."

Dr. Calvin rose and smoothed her dress. She was obviously ready to leave. "I mean there is one time when a robot may strike a human being without breaking the First Law. Just one time."

"And when is that?"

Dr. Calvin was at the door. She said quietly, "When the human to be struck is merely another robot."

She smiled broadly, her thin face glowing. "Good-by, Mr. Byerley. I hope to vote for you five years from now—for co-ordinator."

Stephen Byerley chuckled. "I must reply that that is a somewhat farfetched idea."

The door closed behind her.

• LITTLE LOST • ROBOT

■

Measures on Hyper Base had been taken in a sort of rattling fury—the muscular equivalent of an hysterical shriek.

To itemize them in order of both chronology and desperation, they were:

1. All work on the Hyperatomic Drive through all the space volume occupied by the Stations of the Twenty-Seventh Asteroidal Grouping came to a halt.

2. That entire volume of space was nipped out of the System, practically speaking. No one entered without permission. No one left under any conditions.

3. By special government patrol ship, Drs. Susan Calvin and Peter Bogert, respectively Head Psychologist and Mathematical Director of United States Robots and Mechanical Men Corporation, were brought to Hyper Base.

Susan Calvin had never left the surface of Earth before, and had no perceptible desire to leave it this time. In an age of Atomic Power and a clearly coming Hyperatomic Drive, she remained quietly provincial. So she was dissatisfied with her trip and unconvinced of the emergency, and every line of her plain, middle-aged face showed it clearly enough during her first dinner at Hyper Base.

Nor did Dr. Bogert's sleek paleness abandon a certain hangdog attitude. Nor did Major-general Kallner, who headed the project, even once forget to maintain a haunted expression.

In short, it was a grisly episode, that meal, and the little session of three that followed began in a gray, unhappy manner.

Kallner, with his baldness glistening, and his dress uniform oddly unsuited to the general mood, began with uneasy directness.

"This is a queer story to tell, sir, and madam. I want to thank you for coming on short notice and without a reason being given. We'll try to correct that now. We've lost a robot. Work has stopped and *must* stop until such time as we locate it. So far we have failed, and we feel we need expert help."

Perhaps the general felt his predicament anticlimactic. He continued with a note of desperation, "I needn't tell you the importance of our work here. More than eighty percent of last year's appropriations for scientific research have gone to us—"

"Why, we know that," said Bogert, agreeably. "U.S. Robots is receiving a generous rental fee for use of our robots."

Susan Calvin injected a blunt, vinegary note, "What makes a single robot so important to the project, and why hasn't it been located?"

The general turned his red face toward her and wet his lips quickly, "Why, in a manner of speaking we *have* located it." Then, with near anguish, "Here, suppose I explain. As soon as the robot failed to report a state of emergency was declared, and all movement off Hyper Base stopped. A cargo vessel had landed the previous day and had delivered us two robots for our laboratories. It had sixty-two robots of the . . . uh . . . same type for shipment elsewhere. We are certain as to that figure. There is no question about it whatever."

"Yes? And the connection?"

"When our missing robot was not located anywhere—I assure you we would have found a missing blade of grass if it had been there to find—we brainstormed ourselves into counting the robots left on the cargo ship. They have sixty-three now."

"So that the sixty-third, I take it, is the missing prodigal?" Dr. Calvin's eyes darkened.

"Yes, but we have no way of telling which is the sixty-third."

There was a dead silence while the electric clock chimed eleven times, and then the robopsychologist said, "Very peculiar," and the corners of her lips moved downward.

"Peter," she turned to her colleague with a trace of savagery, "what's wrong here? What kind of robots are they using at Hyper Base?"

Dr. Bogert hesitated and smiled feebly, "It's been rather a matter of delicacy till now, Susan."

She spoke rapidly, "Yes, *till* now. If there are sixty-three same-type robots, one of which is wanted and the identity of which cannot be determined, why won't any of them do? What's the idea of all this? Why have we been sent for?"

Bogert said in resigned fashion, "If you'll give me a chance, Susan—Hyper Base happens to be using several robots whose brains are not impressioned with the entire First Law of Robotics."

"*Aren't* impressioned?" Calvin slumped back in her chair, "I see. How many were made?"

"A few. It was on government order and there was no way of violating the secrecy. No one was to know except the top men directly concerned. You weren't included, Susan. It was nothing I had anything to do with."

The general interrupted with a measure of authority. "I would like to explain that bit. I hadn't been aware that Dr. Calvin was unacquainted with the situation. I needn't tell you, Dr. Calvin, that there always has been strong opposition to robots on the Planet. The only defense the government has had against the Fundamentalist radicals in this matter was the fact that robots are always built with an unbreakable First Law—which makes it impossible for them to harm human beings under any circumstance.

"But we *had* to have robots of a different nature. So just a few of the NS-2 model, the Nestors, that is, were prepared with a modified First Law. To keep it quiet, all NS-2's are manufactured without serial numbers; modified members are delivered here along with a group of normal robots; and, of course, all our kind are under the strictest impressionment never to tell of their modification to unauthorized personnel." He wore an embarrassed smile, "This has all worked out against us now."

Calvin said grimly, "Have you asked each one who it is, anyhow? Certainly, you are authorized?"

The general nodded, "All sixty-three deny having worked here—and one is lying."

"Does the one you want show traces of wear? The others, I take it, are factory-fresh."

"The one in question only arrived last month. It, and the two that have just arrived, were to be the last we needed. There's no perceptible wear." He shook his head slowly and his eyes were haunted again, "Dr. Calvin, we don't dare let that ship leave. If the existence of non-First Law robots becomes general knowledge—" There seemed no way of avoiding understatement in the conclusion.

"Destroy all sixty-three," said the robopsychologist coldly and flatly, "and make an end of it."

Bogert drew back a corner of his mouth. "You mean destroy thirty thousand dollars per robot. I'm afraid U.S. Robots wouldn't like that. We'd better make an effort first, Susan, before we destroy anything."

"In that case," she said, sharply, "I need facts. Exactly what advantage does Hyper Base derive from these modified robots? What factor made them desirable, general?"

Kallner ruffled his forehead and stroked it with an upward gesture of his hand. "We had trouble with our previous robots. Our men work with hard radiations a good deal, you see. It's dangerous, of course, but reasonable precautions are taken. There have been only two accidents since we began and neither was fatal. However, it was impossible to explain that to an ordinary robot. The First Law states—I'll quote it—'*No robot may harm a human being, or through inaction, allow a human being to come to harm.*'

"That's primary, Dr. Calvin. When it was necessary for one of our men to expose himself for a short period to a moderate gamma field, one that would have no physiological effects, the nearest robot would dash in to drag him out. If the field were exceedingly weak, it would succeed, and work could not continue till all robots were cleared out. If the field were a trifle stronger, the robot would never reach the technician concerned, since its positronic brain would collapse under gamma radiations—and then we would be out one expensive and hard-to-replace robot.

"We tried arguing with them. Their point was that a human being in a gamma field was endangering his life and that it didn't matter that he could remain there half an hour safely. Supposing, they would say, he forgot and remained an hour. They couldn't take chances. We pointed out that they were risking their lives on a wild off-chance. But self-preservation is only the Third Law of Robotics—and the First Law of human safety came first. We gave them orders; we ordered them strictly and harshly to remain out of gamma fields at whatever cost. But obedience is only the Second Law of Robotics—and the First Law of human safety came first. Dr. Calvin, we either had to do without robots, or do something about the First Law—and we made our choice."

"I can't believe," said Dr. Calvin, "that it was found possible to remove the First Law."

"It wasn't removed, it was modified," explained Kallner. "Positronic brains were constructed that contained the positive aspect only of the Law, which in them reads: '*No robot may harm a human being.*' That is all. They have no compulsion to prevent one coming to harm through an extraneous agency such as gamma rays. I state the matter correctly, Dr. Bogert?"

"Quite," assented the mathematician.

"And that is the only difference of your robots from the ordinary NS-2 model? The *only* difference? Peter?"

"The *only* difference, Susan."

She rose and spoke with finality, "I intend sleeping now, and in about eight hours, I want to speak to whomever saw the robot last. And from now on, General Kallner, if I'm to take any responsibility at all for events, I want full and unquestioned control of this investigation."

Susan Calvin, except for two hours of resentful lassitude, experienced nothing approaching sleep. She signaled at Bogert's door at the local time of 0700 and found him also awake. He had apparently taken the trouble of transporting a dressing gown to Hyper Base with him, for he was sitting in it. He put his nail scissors down when Calvin entered.

He said softly, "I've been expecting you more or less. I suppose you feel sick about all this."

"I do."

"Well—I'm sorry. There was no way of preventing it. When the call came out from Hyper Base for us, I knew that something must have gone wrong with the modified Nestors. But what was there to do? I couldn't break the matter to you on the trip here as I would have liked to, because I had to be sure. The matter of the modification is top secret."

The psychologist muttered, "I should have been told. U.S. Robots had no right to modify positronic brains this way without the approval of a psychologist."

Bogert lifted his eyebrows and sighed. "Be reasonable, Susan. You couldn't have influenced them. In this matter, the government was bound to have its way. They want the Hyperatomic Drive and the etheric physicists want robots that won't interfere with them. They were going to get them even if it did mean twisting the First Law. We had to admit it was possible from a construction standpoint and they swore a mighty oath that they wanted only twelve, that they would be used only at Hyper Base, that they would be destroyed once the Drive was perfected, and that full precautions would be taken. And they insisted on secrecy—and that's the situation."

Dr. Calvin spoke through her teeth, "I would have resigned."

"It wouldn't have helped. The government was offering the company a fortune, and threatening it with antirobot legislation in case of a refusal. We were stuck then, and we're badly stuck now. If this leaks out, it might hurt Kallner and the government, but it would hurt U. S. Robots a devil of a lot more."

The psychologist stared at him. "Peter, don't you realize what all this is about? Can't you understand what the removal of the First Law means? It isn't just a matter of secrecy."

"I know what removal would mean. I'm not a child. It would mean complete instability, with no nonimaginary solutions to the positronic Field Equations."

"Yes, mathematically. But can you translate that into crude psychological thought? All normal life, Peter, consciously or otherwise, resents domination. If the domination is by an inferior, or by a supposed inferior, the resentment becomes stronger. Physically, and, to an extent, mentally, a robot—any robot—is superior to human beings. What makes him slavish, then? *Only the First Law!* Why, without it, the first order you tried to give a robot would result in your death. Unstable? What do you think?"

"Susan," said Bogert, with an air of sympathetic amusement. "I'll admit that this Frankenstein Complex you're exhibiting has a certain justification—hence the First Law in the first place. But the Law, I repeat and repeat, has not been removed—merely modified."

"And what about the stability of the brain?"

The mathematician thrust out his lips, "Decreased, naturally. But it's within the border of safety. The first Nestors were delivered to Hyper Base nine months ago, and nothing whatever has gone wrong till now, and even this involves merely fear of discovery and not danger to humans."

"Very well, then. We'll see what comes of the morning conference."

Bogert saw her politely to the door and grimaced eloquently when she left. He saw no reason to change his perennial opinion of her as a sour and fidgety frustration.

Susan Calvin's train of thought did not include Bogert in the least. She had dismissed him years ago as a smooth and pretentious sleekness.

Gerald Black had taken his degree in etheric physics the year before and, in common with his entire generation of physicists, found himself engaged in the problem of the Drive. He now made a proper addition to the general atmosphere of these meetings on Hyper Base. In his stained white smock, he was half rebellious and wholly uncertain. His stocky strength seemed striving for release and his fingers, as they twisted each other with nervous yanks, might have forced an iron bar out of true.

Major-general Kallner sat beside him, the two from U.S. Robots faced him.

Black said, "I'm told that I was the last to see Nestor 10 before he vanished. I take it you want to ask me about that."

Dr. Calvin regarded him with interest, "You sound as if you were not sure, young man. Don't you *know* whether you were the last to see him?"

"He worked with me, ma'am, on the field generators, and he was with me the morning of his disappearance. I don't know if anyone saw him after about noon. No one admits having done so."

"Do you think anyone's lying about it?"

"I don't say that. But I don't say that I want the blame of it, either." His dark eyes smoldered.

"There's no question of blame. The robot acted as it did because of what it is. We're just trying to locate it, Mr. Black, and let's put everything else aside. Now if you've worked with the robot, you probably know it better than anyone else. Was there anything unusual about it that you noticed? Had you ever worked with robots before?"

"I've worked with other robots we have here—the simple ones. Nothing different about the Nestors except that they're a good deal cleverer—and more annoying."

"Annoying? In what way?"

"Well—perhaps it's not their fault. The work here is rough and most of us get a little jagged. Fooling around with hyper-space isn't fun." He smiled feebly, finding pleasure in confession. "We run the risk continually of blowing a hole in normal space-time fabric and dropping right out of the universe, asteroid and all. Sounds screwy, doesn't it? Naturally, you're on edge sometimes. But these Nestors aren't. They're curious, they're calm, they don't worry. It's enough to drive you nuts at times. When you want something done in a tearing hurry, they seem to take their time. Sometimes I'd rather do without."

"You say they take their time? Have they ever refused an order?"

"Oh, no,"—hastily. "They do it all right. They tell you when they think you're wrong, though. They don't know anything about the subject but what we taught them, but that doesn't stop them. Maybe I imagine it, but the other fellows have the same trouble with their Nestors."

General Kallner cleared his throat ominously, "Why have no complaints reached me on the matter, Black?"

The young physicist reddened, "We didn't *really* want to do without the robots, sir, and besides we weren't certain exactly how such . . . uh . . . minor complaints might be received."

Bogert interrupted softly, "Anything in particular happen the morning you last saw it?"

There was a silence. With a quiet motion, Calvin repressed the comment that was about to emerge from Kallner, and waited patiently.

Then Black spoke in blurting anger, "I had a little trouble with it. I'd broken a Kimball tube that morning and was out five days of work; my entire program was behind schedule; I hadn't received any mail from home for a couple of weeks. And *he* came around wanting me to repeat an experiment I had abandoned a month ago. He was always annoying me on that subject and I was tired of it. I told him to go away—and that's all I saw of him."

"You told him to go away?" asked Dr. Calvin with sharp interest. "In just those words? Did you say 'Go away'? Try to remember the exact words."

There was apparently an internal struggle in progress. Black cradled his forehead in a broad palm for a moment, then tore it away and said defiantly, "I said, 'Go lose yourself.' "

Bogert laughed for a short moment. "And he did, eh?"

But Calvin wasn't finished. She spoke cajolingly, "Now we're getting somewhere, Mr. Black. But exact details are important. In understanding the robot's actions, a word, a gesture, an emphasis may be everything. You couldn't have said just those three words, for instance, could you? By your own description you must have been in a hasty mood. Perhaps you strengthened your speech a little."

The young man reddened, "Well . . . I may have called it a . . . a few things."

"Exactly what things?"

"Oh—I wouldn't remember exactly. Besides I couldn't repeat it. You know how you get when you're excited." His embarrassed laugh was almost a giggle, "I sort of have a tendency to strong language."

"That's quite all right," she replied, with prim severity. "At the moment, I'm a psychologist. I would like to have you repeat exactly what you said as nearly as you remember, and, even more important, the exact tone of voice you used."

Black looked at his commanding officer for support, found none. His eyes grew round and appalled, "But I can't."

"You must."

"Suppose," said Bogert, with ill-hidden amusement, "you address me. You may find it easier."

The young man's scarlet face turned to Bogert. He swallowed. "I said—" His voice faded out. He tried again, "I said—"

And he drew a deep breath and spewed it out hastily in one long succession of syllables. Then, in the charged air that lingered, he concluded almost in tears, ". . . more or less. I don't remember the exact order of what I called him, and maybe I left out something or put in something, but that was about it."

Only the slightest flush betrayed any feeling on the part of the psychologist. She said, "I am aware of the meaning of most of the terms used. The others, I suppose, are equally derogatory."

"I'm afraid so," agreed the tormented Black.

"And in among it, you told him to lose himself."

"I meant it only figuratively."

"I realize that. No disciplinary action is intended, I am sure." And at her glance, the general, who, five seconds earlier, had seemed not sure at all, nodded angrily.

"You may leave, Mr. Black. Thank you for your cooperation."

It took five hours for Susan Calvin to interview the sixty-three robots. It was five hours of multi-repetition; of replacement after replacement of identical robot; of Questions A, B, C, D; and Answers A, B, C, D; of a carefully bland expression, a carefully neutral tone, a carefully friendly atmosphere; and a hidden wire recorder.

The psychologist felt drained of vitality when she was finished.

Bogert was waiting for her and looked expectant as she dropped the recording spool with a clang upon the plastic of the desk.

She shook her head, "All sixty-three seemed the same to me. I couldn't tell—"

He said, "You couldn't expect to tell by ear, Susan. Suppose we analyze the recordings."

Ordinarily, the mathematical interpretation of verbal reactions of robots is one of the more intricate branches of robotic analysis. It requires a staff of trained technicians and the help of complicated computing machines. Bogert knew that. Bogert stated as much, in an extreme of unshown annoyance after having listened to each set of replies, made lists of word deviations, and graphs of the intervals of responses.

"There are no anomalies present, Susan. The variations in wording and the time reactions are within the limits of ordinary frequency groupings. We need finer methods. They must have computers here. No." He frowned and nibbled delicately at a thumbnail. "We can't use computers. Too much danger of leakage. Or maybe if we—"

Dr. Calvin stopped him with an impatient gesture, "Please, Peter. This isn't one of your petty laboratory problems. If we can't determine the modified Nestor by some gross difference that we can see with the naked eye, one that there is no mistake about, we're out of luck. The danger of being wrong, and of letting him escape is otherwise too great. It's not enough to point out a minute irregularity in a graph. I tell you, if that's all I've got to go on, I'd destroy them all just to be certain. Have you spoken to the other modified Nestors?"

"Yes, I have," snapped back Bogert, "and there's nothing wrong with them. They're above normal in friendliness if anything. They answered my questions, displayed pride in their knowledge—except the two new ones that haven't had time to learn their etheric physics. They laughed rather good-naturedly at my ignorance in some of the specializations here." He shrugged, "I suppose that forms some of the basis for resentment toward them on the part of the technicians here. The robots are perhaps too willing to impress you with their greater knowledge."

"Can you try a few Planar Reactions to see if there has been any change, any deterioration, in their mental set-up since manufacture?"

"I haven't yet, but I will." He shook a slim finger at her, "You're losing your nerve, Susan. I don't see what it is you're dramatizing. They're essentially harmless."

"They are?" Calvin took fire. "They are? Do you realize one of them is lying? One of the sixty-three robots I have just interviewed has deliberately lied to me after the strictest injunction to tell the truth. The abnormality indicated is horribly deep-seated, and horribly frightening."

Peter Bogert felt his teeth harden against each other. He said, "Not at all. Look!. Nestor 10 was given orders to lose himself. Those orders were expressed in maximum urgency by the person most authorized to command him. You can't counteract that order either by superior urgency or superior right of command. Naturally, the robot will attempt to defend the carrying out of his orders. In fact, objectively, I admire his ingenuity. How better can a robot lose himself than to hide himself among a group of similar robots?"

"Yes, you would admire it. I've detected amusement in you, Peter—amusement and an appalling lack of understanding. Are you a roboticist, Peter? Those robots attach importance to what they consider superiority. You've just said as much yourself. Subconsciously they feel humans to be inferior and the First Law which protects us from them is imperfect. They are unstable. And here we have a young man ordering a robot to leave him, to lose himself, with every verbal appearance of revulsion, disdain, and disgust. Granted, that robot must follow orders, but subconsciously, there is resentment. It will become more important than ever for it to prove that it is superior despite the horrible names it was called. It may become *so* important that what's left of the First Law won't be enough."

"How on Earth, or anywhere in the Solar System, Susan, is a robot going to know the meaning of the assorted strong language used upon him? Obscenity is not one of the things impressioned upon his brain."

"Original impressionment is not everything," Calvin snarled at him. "Robots have learning capacity, you . . . you fool—" And Bogert knew that she had really lost her temper. She continued hastily, "Don't you suppose he could tell from the tone used that the words weren't complimentary? Don't you suppose he's heard the words used before and noted upon what occasions?"

"Well, then," shouted Bogert, "will you kindly tell me one way in which a modified robot can harm a human being, no matter how offended it is, no matter how sick with desire to prove superiority?"

"If I tell you one way, will you keep quiet?"

"Yes."

They were leaning across the table at each other, angry eyes nailed together.

The psychologist said, "If a modified robot were to drop a heavy weight upon a human being, he would not be breaking the First Law, if he did so with the knowledge that his strength and reaction speed would be sufficient to snatch the weight away before it struck the man. However once the weight left his fingers, he would be no longer the active medium. Only the blind force of gravity would be that. The robot could then change his mind and merely by inaction, allow the weight to strike. The modified First Law allows that."

"That's an awful stretch of imagination."

"That's what my profession requires sometimes. Peter, let's not quarrel. Let's work. You know the exact nature of the stimulus that caused the robot to lose himself. You have the records of his original mental make-up. I want you to tell me how possible it is for our robot to do the sort of thing I just talked about. Not the specific instance, mind you, but that whole class of response. And I want it done quickly."

"And meanwhile—"

"And meanwhile, we'll have to try performance tests directly on the response to First Law."

Gerald Black, at his own request, was supervising the mushrooming wooden partitions that were springing up in a bellying circle on the vaulted third floor of Radiation Building 2. The laborers worked, in the main, silently, but more than one was openly a-wonder at the sixty-three photocells that required installation.

One of them sat down near Black, removed his hat, and wiped his forehead thoughtfully with a freckled forearm.

Black nodded at him, "How's it doing, Walensky?"

Walensky shrugged and fired a cigar, "Smooth as butter. What's going on anyway, Doc? First, there's no work for three days and then we have this mess of jiggers." He leaned backward on his elbows and puffed smoke.

Black twitched his eyebrows, "A couple of robot men came over from Earth. Remember the trouble we had with robots running into the gamma fields, before we pounded it into their skulls that they weren't to do it."

"Yeah. Didn't we get new robots?"

"We got some replacements, but mostly it was a job of indoctrination. Anyway, the people who make them want to figure out robots that aren't hit so bad by gamma rays."

"Sure seems funny, though, to stop all the work on the Drive for this robot deal. I thought nothing was allowed to stop the Drive."

"Well, it's the fellows upstairs that have the say on that. Me—I just do as I'm told. Probably all a matter of pull—"

"Yeah," the electrician jerked a smile, and winked a wise eye. "Somebody knew somebody in Washington. But as long as my pay comes through on the dot, I should worry. The Drive's none of my affair. What are they going to do here?"

"You're asking me? They brought a mess of robots with them,—over sixty, and they're going to measure reactions. That's all *my* knowledge."

"How long will it take?"

"I wish I knew."

"Well," Walensky said, with heavy sarcasm, "as long as they dish me my money, they can play games all they want."

Black felt quietly satisfied. Let the story spread. It was harmless, and near enough to the truth to take the fangs out of curiosity.

* * *

A man sat in the chair, motionless, silent. A weight dropped, crashed downward, then pounded aside at the last moment under the synchronized thump of a sudden force beam. In sixty-three wooden cells, watching NS-2 robots dashed forward in that split second before the weight veered, and sixty-three photocells five feet ahead of their original positions jiggled the marking pen and presented a little jag on the paper. The weight rose and dropped, rose and dropped, rose—

Ten times!

Ten times the robots sprang forward and stopped, as the man remained safely seated.

Major-general Kallner had not worn his uniform in its entirety since the first dinner with the U.S. Robot representatives. He wore nothing over his blue-gray shirt now, the collar was open, and the black tie was pulled loose.

He looked hopefully at Bogert, who was still blandly neat and whose inner tension was perhaps betrayed only by the trace of glister at his temples.

The general said, "How does it look? What is it you're trying to see?"

Bogert replied, "A difference which may turn out to be a little too subtle for our purposes, I'm afraid. For sixty-two of those robots the necessity of jumping toward the apparently threatened human was what we call, in robotics, a forced reaction. You see, even when the robots knew that the human in question would not come to harm—and after the third or fourth time they must have known it—they could not prevent reacting as they did. First Law requires it."

"Well?"

"But the sixty-third robot, the modified Nestor, had no such compulsion. He was under free action. If he had wished, he could have remained in his seat. Unfortunately," and his voice was mildly regretful, "he didn't so wish."

"Why do you suppose?"

Bogert shrugged, "I suppose Dr. Calvin will tell us when she gets here. Probably with a horribly pessimistic interpretation, too. She is sometimes a bit annoying."

"She's qualified, isn't she?" demanded the general with a sudden frown of uneasiness.

"Yes." Bogert seemed amused. "She's qualified all right. She understands robots like a sister—comes from hating human beings so much, I think. It's just that, psychologist or not, she's an extreme neurotic. Has paranoid tendencies. Don't take her too seriously."

He spread the long row of broken-line graphs out in front of him. "You see, general, in the case of each robot the time interval from moment of drop to the completion of a five-foot movement tends to decrease as the tests are repeated. There's a definite mathematical relationship that governs such things and failure to conform would indicate marked abnormality in the positronic brain. Unfortunately, all here appear normal."

"But if our Nestor 10 was not responding with a forced action, why isn't his curve different? I don't understand that."

"It's simple enough. Robotic responses are not perfectly analogous to human responses, more's the pity. In human beings, voluntary action is much slower than reflex action. But that's not the case with robots; with them it is merely a question of freedom of choice, otherwise the speeds of free and forced action are much the same. What I *had* been expecting, though, was that Nestor 10 would be caught by surprise the first time and allow too great an interval to elapse before responding."

"And he didn't?"

"I'm afraid not."

"Then we haven't gotten anywhere." The general sat back with an expression of pain. "It's five days since you've come."

At this point, Susan Calvin entered and slammed the door behind her. "Put your graphs away, Peter," she cried, "you know they don't show anything."

She mumbled something impatiently as Kallner half-rose to greet her, and went on, "We'll have to try something else quickly. I don't like what's happening."

Bogert exchanged a resigned glance with the general. "Is anything wrong?"

"You mean specifically? No. But I don't like to have Nestor 10 continue to elude us. It's bad. It *must* be gratifying his swollen sense of superiority. I'm afraid that his motivation is no longer simply one of following orders. I think it's becoming more a matter of sheer neurotic necessity to out-think humans. That's a dangerously unhealthy situation. Peter, have you done what I asked? Have you worked out the instability factors of the modified NS-2 along the lines I want?"

"It's in progress," said the mathematician, without interest.

She stared at him angrily for a moment, then turned to Kallner. "Nester 10 is decidedly aware of what we're doing, general. He had no reason to jump for the bait in this experiment, especially after the first time, when he must have seen that there was no real danger to our subject. The others couldn't help it; but *he* was deliberately falsifying a reaction."

"What do you think we ought to do now, then, Dr. Calvin?"

"Make it impossible for him to fake an action the next time. We will repeat the experiment, but with an addition. High-tension cables, capable of electrocuting the Nestor models will be placed between subject and robot—enough of them to avoid the possibility of jumping over—and the robot will be made perfectly aware in advance that touching the cables will mean death."

"Hold on," spat out Bogert with sudden viciousness. "I rule that out. We are not electrocuting two million dollars worth of robots to locate Nestor 10. There are other ways."

"You're certain? You've found none. In any case, it's not a question of electrocution. We can arrange a relay which will break the current at the instant of application of weight.

If the robot should place his weight on it, he won't die. *But he won't know that,* you see."

The general's eyes gleamed into hope. "Will that work?"

"It should. Under those conditions, Nestor 10 would have to remain in his seat. He could be *ordered* to touch the cables and die, for the Second Law of obedience is superior to the Third Law of self-preservation. But *he won't* be ordered to; he will merely be left to his own devices, as will all the robots. In the case of the normal robots, the First Law of human safety will drive them to their death even without orders. But not our Nestor 10. Without the entire First Law, and without having received any orders on the matter, the Third Law, self-preservation, will be the highest operating, and he will have no choice but to remain in his seat. It would be a forced action."

"Will it be done tonight, then?"

"Tonight," said the psychologist, "if the cables can be laid in time. I'll tell the robots now what they're to be up against."

A man sat in the chair, motionless, silent. A weight dropped, crashed downward, then pounded aside at the last moment under the synchronized thump of a sudden force beam.

Only once—

And from her small camp chair in the observing booth in the balcony, Dr. Susan Calvin rose with a short gasp of pure horror.

Sixty-three robots sat quietly in their chairs, staring owlishly at the endangered man before them. Not one moved.

Dr. Calvin was angry, angry almost past endurance. Angry the worse for not daring to show it to the robots that, one by one, were entering the room and then leaving. She checked the list. Number Twenty-eight was due in now—thirty-five still lay ahead of her.

Number Twenty-eight entered, diffidently.

She forced herself into reasonable calm. "And who are you?"

The robot replied in a low, uncertain voice, "I have received no number of my own yet, ma'am. I'm an NS-2 robot, and I was Number Twenty-eight in line outside. I have a slip of paper here that I'm to give to you."

"You haven't been in here before this today?"

"No, ma'am."

"Sit down. Right there. I want to ask you some questions, Number Twenty-eight. Were you in the Radiation Room of Building Two about four hours ago?"

The robot had trouble answering. Then it came out hoarsely, like machinery needing oil, "Yes, ma'am."

"There was a man who almost came to harm there, wasn't there?"

"Yes, ma'am."

"You did nothing, did you?"

"No, ma'am."

"The man might have been hurt because of your inaction. Do you know that?"

"Yes, ma'am. I couldn't help it, ma'am." It is hard to picture a large expressionless metallic figure cringing, but it managed.

"I want you to tell me exactly why you did nothing to save him."

"I want to explain, ma'am. I certainly don't want to have you . . . have *anyone* . . . think that I could do a thing that might cause harm to a master. Oh, no, that would be a horrible . . . an inconceivable—"

"Please don't get excited, boy. I'm not blaming you for anything. I only want to know what you were thinking at the time."

"Ma'am, before it all happened you told us that one of the masters would be in danger of harm from that weight that keeps falling and that we would have to cross electric cables if we were to try to save him. Well, ma'am, that wouldn't stop me. What is my destruction compared to the safety of a master? But . . . but it occurred to me that if I died on my way to him, I wouldn't be able to save him anyway. The weight would crush him and then I would be dead for no purpose and perhaps some day some other master might come to harm who wouldn't have, if I had only stayed alive. Do you understand me, ma'am?"

"You mean that it was merely a choice of the man dying, or both the man and yourself dying. Is that right?"

"Yes, ma'am. It was impossible to save the master. He might be considered dead. In that case, it is inconceivable that I destroy myself for nothing—without orders."

The psychologist twiddled a pencil. She had heard the same story with insignificant verbal variations twenty-seven times before. This was the crucial question now.

"Boy," she said, "your thinking has its points, but it is not the sort of thing I thought you might think. Did you think of this yourself?"

The robot hesitated. "No."

"Who thought of it, then?"

"We were talking last night, and one of us got that idea and it sounded reasonable."

"Which one?"

The robot thought deeply. "I don't know. Just one of us."

She sighed, "That's all."

Number Twenty-nine was next. Thirty-four after that.

Major-general Kallner, too, was angry. For one week all of Hyper Base had stopped dead, barring some paper work on the subsidiary asteroids of the group. For nearly one week, the two top experts in the field had aggravated the situation with useless tests. And now they—or the woman, at any rate—made impossible propositions.

Fortunately for the general situation, Kallner felt it impolitic to display his anger openly.

Susan Calvin was insisting, "Why not, sir? It's obvious that the present situation is unfortunate. The only way we may reach results in the future—or what future is left us in this matter—is to separate the robots. We can't keep them together any longer."

"My dear Dr. Calvin," rumbled the general, his voice sinking into the lower baritone registers. "I don't see how I can quarter sixty-three robots all over the place—"

Dr. Calvin raised her arms helplessly. "I can do nothing then. Nester 10 will either imitate what the other robots would do, or else argue them plausibly into not doing what he himself cannot do. And in any case, this is bad business. We're in actual combat with this little lost robot of ours and he's winning out. Every victory of his aggravates his abnormality."

She rose to her feet in determination. "General Kallner, if you do not separate the robots as I ask, then I can only demand that all sixty-three be destroyed immediately."

"You demand it, do you?" Bogert looked up suddenly, and with real anger. "What gives you the right to demand any such thing. Those robots remain as they are. *I'm* responsible to the management, not you."

"And I," added Major-general Kallner, "am responsible to the World Co-ordinator—and I must have this settled."

"In that case," flashed back Calvin, "there is nothing for me to do but resign. If necessary to force you to the necessary destruction, I'll make this whole matter public. It was not I that approved the manufacture of modified robots."

"One word from you, Dr. Calvin," said the general, deliberately, "in violation of security measures, and you would be certainly imprisoned instantly."

Bogert felt the matter to be getting out of hand. His voice grew syrupy, "Well, now, we're beginning to act like children, all of us. We need only a little more time. Surely we can outwit a robot without resigning, or imprisoning people, or destroying two millions."

The psychologist turned on him with quiet fury, "I don't want any unbalanced robots in existence. We have one Nestor that's definitely unbalanced, eleven more that are potentially so, and sixty-two normal robots that are being subjected to an unbalanced environment. The only absolutely safe method is complete destruction."

The signal-burr brought all three to a halt, and the angry tumult of growingly unrestrained emotion froze.

"Come in," growled Kallner.

It was Gerald Black, looking perturbed. He had heard angry voices. He said, "I thought I'd come myself . . . didn't like to ask anyone else—"

"What is it? Don't orate—"

"The locks of Compartment C in the trading ship have been played with. There are fresh scratches on them."

"Compartment C?" exclaimed Calvin quickly. "That's the one that holds the robots, isn't it? Who did it?"

"From the inside," said Black, laconically.

"The lock isn't out of order, is it?"

"No. It's all right. I've been staying on the ship now for four days and none of them have tried to get out. But I thought you ought to know, and I didn't like to spread the news. I noticed the matter myself."

"Is anyone there now?" demanded the general.

"I left Robbins and McAdams there."

There was a thoughtful silence, and then Dr. Calvin said, ironically, "Well?"

Kallner rubbed his nose uncertainly, "What's it all about?"

"Isn't it obvious? Nestor 10 is planning to leave. That order to lose himself is dominating his abnormality past anything we can do. I wouldn't be surprised if what's left of his First Law would scarcely be powerful enough to override it. He is perfectly capable of seizing the ship and leaving with it. Then we'd have a mad robot on a spaceship. What would he do next? Any idea? Do you still want to leave them all together, general?"

"Nonsense," interrupted Bogert. He had regained his smoothness. "All that from a few scratch marks on a lock."

"Have you, Dr. Bogert, completed the analysis I've required, since you volunteer opinions?"

"Yes."

"May I see it?"

"No."

"Why not? Or mayn't I ask that, either?"

"Because there's no point in it, Susan. I told you in advance that these modified robots are less stable than the normal variety, and my analysis shows it. There's a certain very small chance of breakdown under extreme circumstances that are not likely to occur. Let it go at that. I won't give you ammunition for your absurd claim that sixty-two perfectly good robots be destroyed just because so far you lack the ability to detect Nestor 10 among them."

Susan Calvin stared him down and let disgust fill her eyes. "You won't let anything stand in the way of the permanent directorship, will you?"

"Please," begged Kallner, half in irritation. "Do you insist that nothing further can be done, Dr. Calvin?"

"I can't think of anything, sir," she replied, wearily. "If there were only other differences between Nestor 10 and the normal robots, differences that didn't involve the First Law. Even one other difference. Something in impressionment, environment, specification—" And she stopped suddenly.

"What is it?"

"I've thought of something . . . I think—" Her eyes grew distant and hard, "These modified Nestors, Peter. They get the same impressioning the normal ones get, don't they?"

"Yes. Exactly the same."

"And what was it you were saying, Mr. Black," she turned to the young man, who through the storms that had followed his news had maintained a discreet silence. "Once when complaining of the Nestors' attitude of superiority, you said the technicians had taught them all they knew."

"Yes, in etheric physics. They're not acquainted with the subject when they come here."

"That's right," said Bogert, in surprise. "I told you, Susan, when I spoke to the other Nestors here that the two new arrivals hadn't learned etheric physics yet."

"And why is that?" Dr. Calvin was speaking in mounting excitement. "Why aren't NS-2 models impressioned with etheric physics to start with?"

"I can tell you that," said Kallner. "It's all of a piece with the secrecy. We thought that if we made a special model with knowledge of etheric physics, used twelve of them and put the others to work in an unrelated field, there might be suspicion. Men working with normal Nestors might wonder why they knew etheric physics. So there was merely an impressionment with a capacity for training in the field. Only the ones that come here, naturally, receive such a training. It's that simple."

"I understand. Please get out of here, the lot of you. Let me have an hour or so."

Calvin felt she could not face the ordeal for a third time. Her mind had contemplated it and rejected it with an intensity that left her nauseated. She could face that unending file of repetitious robots no more.

So Bogert asked the questions now, while she sat aside, eyes and mind half-closed.

Number Fourteen came in—forty-nine to go.

Bogert looked up from the guide sheet and said, "What is your number in line?"

"Fourteen, sir." The robot presented his numbered ticket.

"Sit down, boy."

Bogert asked, "You haven't been here before on this day?"

"No, sir."

"Well, boy, we are going to have another man in danger of harm soon after we're through here. In fact, when you leave this room, you will be led to a stall where you will wait quietly, till you are needed. Do you understand?"

"Yes, sir."

"Now, naturally, if a man is in danger of harm, you will try to save him."

"Naturally, sir."

"Unfortunately, between the man and yourself, there will be a gamma ray field."

Silence.

"Do you know what gamma rays are?" asked Bogert sharply.

"Energy radiation, sir?"

The next question came in a friendly, offhand manner, "Ever work with gamma rays?"

"No, sir." The answer was definite.

"Mm-m. Well, boy, gamma rays will kill you instantly. They'll destroy your brain. That is a fact you must know and remember. Naturally, you don't want to destroy yourself."

"Naturally." Again the robot seemed shocked. Then, slowly, "But, sir, if the gamma rays are between myself and the master that may be harmed, how can I save him? I would be destroying myself to no purpose."

"Yes, there is that," Bogert seemed concerned about the matter. "The only thing I can advise, boy, is that if you detect the gamma radiation between yourself and the man, you may as well sit where you are."

The robot was openly relieved. "Thank you, sir. There wouldn't be any use, would there?"

"Of course not. But if there *weren't* any dangerous radiation, that would be a different matter."

"Naturally, sir. No question of that."

"You may leave now. The man on the other side of the door will lead you to your stall. Please wait there."

He turned to Susan Calvin when the robot left. "How did that go, Susan?"

"Very well," she said, dully.

"Do you think we could catch Nestor 10 by quick questioning on etheric physics?"

"Perhaps, but it's not sure enough." Her hands lay loosely in her lap. "Remember, he's fighting us. He's on his guard. The only way we can catch him is to outsmart him—and, within his limitations, he can think much more quickly than a human being."

"Well, just for fun—suppose I ask the robots from now on a few questions on gamma rays. Wave length limits, for instance."

"No!" Dr. Calvin's eyes sparked to life. "It would be too easy for him to deny knowledge and then he'd be warned against the test that's coming up—which is our real chance. Please follow the questions I've indicated, Peter, and don't improvise. It's just within the bounds of risk to ask them if they've ever worked with gamma rays. And try to sound even less interested than you do when you ask it."

Bogert shrugged, and pressed the buzzer that would allow the entrance of Number Fifteen.

The large Radiation Room was in readiness once more. The robots waited patiently in their wooden cells, all open to the center but closed off from each other.

Major-general Kallner mopped his brow slowly with a large handkerchief while Dr. Calvin checked the last details with Black.

"You're sure now," she demanded, "that none of the robots have had a chance to talk with each other after leaving the Orientation Room?"

"Absolutely sure," insisted Black. "There's not been a word exchanged."

"And the robots are put in the proper stalls?"

"Here's the plan."

The psychologist looked at it thoughtfully, "Um-m-m."

The general peered over her shoulder. "What's the idea of the arrangement, Dr. Calvin?"

"I've asked to have those robots that appeared even slightly out of true in the previous tests concentrated on one side of the circle. I'm going to be sitting in the center myself this time, and I wanted to watch those particularly."

"*You're* going to be sitting there—" exclaimed Bogert.

"Why not?" she demanded coldly. "What I expect to see may be something quite momentary. I can't risk having any-one else as main observer. Peter, you'll be in the observing booth, and I want you to keep your eye on the opposite side of the circle. General Kallner, I've arranged for motion pictures to be taken of each robot, in case visual observation isn't enough. If these are required, the robots are to remain exactly where they are until the pictures are developed and studied. None must leave, none must change place. Is that clear?"

"Perfectly."

"Then let's try it this one last time."

* * *

Susan Calvin sat in the chair, silent, eyes restless. A weight dropped, crashed downward, then pounded aside at the last moment under the synchronized thump of a sudden force beam.

And a single robot jerked upright and took two steps.

And stopped.

But Dr. Calvin was upright, and her finger pointed to him sharply. "Nestor 10, come here," she cried, *"come here!* COME HERE!"

Slowly, reluctantly, the robot took another step forward. The psychologist shouted at the top of her voice, without taking her eyes from the robot, "Get every other robot out of this place, somebody. Get them out quickly, and *keep* them out."

Somewhere within reach of her ears there was noise, and the thud of hard feet upon the floor. She did not look away.

Nestor 10—if it was Nestor 10—took another step, and then, under force of her imperious gesture, two more. He was only ten feet away, when he spoke harshly, "I have been told to be lost—"

Another step. "I must not disobey. They have not found me so far— He would think me a failure— He told me— But it's not so— I am powerful and intelligent—"

The words came in spurts.

Another step. "I know a good deal— He would think . . . I mean I've been found— Disgraceful— Not I— I am intelligent— And by just a master . . . who is weak— Slow—"

Another step—and one metal arm flew out suddenly to her shoulder, and she felt the weight bearing her down. Her throat constricted, and she felt a shriek tear through.

Dimly, she heard Nestor 10's next words, "No one must find me. No master—" and the cold metal was against her, and she was sinking under the weight of it.

And then a queer, metallic sound, and she was on the ground with an unfelt thump, and a gleaming arm was heavy across her body. It did not move. Nor did Nestor 10, who sprawled beside her.

And now faces were bending over her.

Gerald Black was gasping, "Are you hurt, Dr. Calvin?"

She shook her head feebly. They pried the arm off her and lifted her gently to her feet, "What happened?"

Black said, "I bathed the place in gamma rays for five seconds. We didn't know what was happening. It wasn't till the last second that we realized he was attacking you, and then there was no time for anything but a gamma field. He went down in an instant. There wasn't enough to harm you though. Don't worry about it."

"I'm not worried." She closed her eyes and leaned for a moment upon his shoulder. "I don't think I was attacked exactly. Nestor 10 was simply *trying* to do so. What was left of the First Law was still holding him back."

Susan Calvin and Peter Bogert, two weeks after their first meeting with Major-general Kallner had their last. Work at Hyper Base had been resumed. The trading ship with its sixty-two normal NS-2's was gone to wherever it was bound, with an officially imposed story to explain its two weeks' delay. The government cruiser was making ready to carry the two roboticists back to Earth.

Kallner was once again a-gleam in dress uniform. His white gloves shone as he shook hands.

Calvin said, "The other modified Nestors are, of course, to be destroyed."

"They will be. We'll make shift with normal robots, or, if necessary, do without."

"Good."

"But tell me— You haven't explained— How was it done?"

She smiled tightly, "Oh, that. I would have told you in advance if I had been more certain of its working. You see, Nestor 10 had a superiority complex that was becoming more radical all the time. He liked to think that he and other robots knew more than human beings. It was becoming very important for him to think so.

"We knew that. So we warned every robot in advance that gamma rays would kill them, which it would, and we further warned them all that gamma rays would be between them and myself. So they all stayed where they were, naturally. By Nestor 10's own logic in the previous test they had all decided that there was no point in trying to save a human being if they were sure to die before they could do it."

"Well, yes, Dr. Calvin, I understand that. But why did Nestor 10 himself leave his seat?"

"Ah! That was a little arrangement between myself and your young Mr. Black. You see it wasn't gamma rays that flooded the area between myself and the robots—but infrared rays. Just ordinary heat rays, absolutely harmless. Nestor 10 knew they were infrared and harmless and so he began to dash out, as he expected the rest would do, under First Law compulsion. It was only a fraction of a second too late that he remembered that the normal NS-2's could detect radiation, but could not identify the type. That he himself could only identify wave lengths by virtue of the training he had received at Hyper Base, under mere human beings, was a little too humiliating to remember for just a moment. To the normal robots the area was fatal because we had told them it would be, and only Nestor 10 knew we were lying.

"And just for a moment he forgot, or didn't want to remember, that other robots might be more ignorant than human beings. His very superiority caught him. Good-by, general."

■ THE EVITABLE ■
CONFLICT

■

The Co-ordinator, in his private study, had that medieval curiosity, a fireplace. To be sure, the medieval man might not have recognized it as such, since it had no functional significance. The quiet, licking flame lay in an insulated recess behind clear quartz.

The logs were ignited at long distance through a trifling diversion of the energy beam that fed the public buildings of the city. The same button that controlled the ignition first dumped the ashes of the previous fire, and allowed for the entrance of fresh wood. —It was a thoroughly domesticated fireplace, you see.

But the fire itself was real. It was wired for sound, so that you could hear the crackle and, of course, you could watch it leap in the air stream that fed it.

The Co-ordinator's ruddy glass reflected, in miniature, the discreet gamboling of the flame, and, in even further miniature, it was reflected in each of his brooding pupils.

—And in the frosty pupils of his guest, Dr. Susan Calvin of U.S. Robots and Mechanical Men Corporation.

The Co-ordinator said, "I did not ask you here entirely for social purposes, Susan."

"I did not think you did, Stephen," she replied.

"—And yet I don't quite know how to phrase my problem. On the one hand, it can be nothing at all. On the other, it can mean the end of humanity."

"I have come across so many problems, Stephen, that presented the same alternative. I think all problems do."

"Really? Then judge this— World Steel reports an overproduction of twenty thousand long tons. The Mexican Canal is two months behind schedule. The mercury mines at Almaden have experienced a production deficiency since last spring, while the Hydroponics plant at Tientsin has been laying men off. These items happen to come to mind at the moment. There is more of the same sort."

"Are these things serious? I'm not economist enough to trace the fearful consequences of such things."

"In themselves, they are not serious. Mining experts can be sent to Almaden, if the situation were to get worse. Hydroponics engineers can be used in Java or in Ceylon, if there are too many at Tientsin. Twenty thousand long tons of steel won't fill more than a few days of world demand, and the opening of the Mexican Canal two months later than the planned date is of little moment. It's the Machines that worry me;—I've spoken to your Director of Research about them already."

"To Vincent Silver? —He hasn't mentioned anything about it to me."

"I asked him to speak to no one. Apparently, he hasn't."

"And what did he tell you?"

"Let me put that item in its proper place. I want to talk about the Machines first. And I want to talk about them to you, because you're the only one in the world who understands robots well enough to help me now.—May I grow philosophical?"

"For this evening, Stephen, you may talk how you please and of what you please, provided you tell me first what you intend to prove."

"That such small unbalances in the perfection of our system of supply and demand, as I have mentioned, may be the first step towards the final war."

"Hmp. Proceed."

Susan Calvin did not allow herself to relax, despite the designed comfort of the chair she sat in. Her cold, thin-lipped face and her flat, even voice were becoming accentuated with the years. And although Stephen Byerley was one man she could like and trust, she was almost seventy and the cultivated habits of a lifetime are not easily broken.

"Every period of human development, Susan," said the Co-ordinator, "has had its own particular type of human conflict—its own variety of problem that, apparently, could be settled only by force. And each time, frustratingly enough, force never really settled the problem. Instead, it persisted through a series of conflicts, then vanished of itself,—what's the expression,—ah, yes not with a bang, but a whimper, as the economic and social environment changed. And then, new problems, and a new series of wars. —Apparently endlessly cyclic.

"Consider relatively modern times. There were the series of dynastic wars in the sixteenth to eighteenth centuries, when the most important question in Europe was whether the houses of Hapsburg or Valois-Bourbon were to rule the continent. It was one of those 'inevitable conflicts,' since Europe could obviously not exist half one and half the other.

"Except that it did, and no war ever wiped out the one and established the other, until the rise of a new social atmosphere in France in 1789 tumbled first the Bourbons and, eventually, the Hapsburgs down the dusty chute to history's incinerator.

"And in those same centuries there were the more barbarous religious wars, which revolved about the important question of whether Europe was to be Catholic or Protestant. Half and half she could not be. It was 'inevitable' that the sword decide. —Except that it didn't. In England, a new industrialism was growing, and on the continent, a new nationalism. Half and half Europe remains to this day and no one cares much.

"In the nineteenth and twentieth centuries, there was a cycle of nationalist-imperialist wars, when the most important question in the world was which portions of Europe would control the economic resources and consuming capacity of which portions of non-Europe. All non-Europe obviously could not exist part English and part French and part German and so on. —Until the forces of nationalism spread sufficiently, so that non-Europe ended what all the wars could not, and decided it could exist quite comfortably *all* non-European.

"And so we have a pattern—"

"Yes, Stephen, you make it plain," said Susan Calvin. "These are not very profound observations."

"No.—But then, it is the obvious which is so difficult to see most of the time. People say 'It's as plain as the nose on your face.' But how much of the nose on your face can you see, unless someone holds a mirror up to you? In the twentieth century, Susan, we started a new cycle of wars—what shall I call them? Ideological wars? The emotions of religion applied to economic systems, rather than to extra-natural ones? Again the wars were 'inevitable' and this time there were atomic weapons, so that mankind could no longer live through its torment to the inevitable wasting away of inevitability.—And positronic robots came.

"They came in time, and, with it and alongside it, interplanetary travel. —So that it no longer seemed so important whether the world was Adam Smith or Karl Marx. Neither made very much sense under the new circumstances. Both had to adapt and they ended in almost the same place."

"A deus ex machina, then, in a double sense," said Dr. Calvin, dryly.

The Co-ordinator smiled gently, "I have never heard you pun before, Susan, but you are correct. And yet there was another danger. The ending of every other problem had merely given birth to another. Our new world wide robot economy may develop its own problems, and for that reason we have the Machines. The Earth's economy is stable, and will *remain* stable, because it is based upon the decisions of calculating machines that have the good of humanity at heart through the overwhelming force of the First Law of Robotics."

Stephen Byerley continued, "And although the Machines are nothing but the vastest conglomeration of calculating circuits ever invented, they are still robots within the meaning of the First Law, and so our Earth wide economy is in accord with the best interests of Man. The population of Earth knows that there will be no unemployment, no over-production or shortages. Waste and famine are words in history books. And so the question of ownership of the means of production becomes obsolescent. Whoever owned them (if such a phrase has meaning), a man, a group, a nation, or all mankind, they could be utilized only as the Machines directed.—Not because men were forced to but because it was the wisest course and men knew it.

"It puts an end to war—not only to the last cycle of wars, but to the next and to all of them. Unless—"

A long pause, and Dr. Calvin encouraged him by repetition. "Unless—"

The fire crouched and skittered along a log, then popped up.

"Unless," said the Co-ordinator, "the Machines don't fulfill their function."

"I see. And that is where those trifling maladjustments come in which you mentioned awhile ago—steel, hydroponics and so on."

"Exactly. Those errors should not be. Dr. Silver tells me they *cannot* be."

"Does he deny the facts? How unusual!"

"No, he admits the facts, of course. I do him an injustice. What he denies is that any error in the machine is responsible for the so-called (his phrase) errors in the answers. He claims that the Machines are self correcting and that it would violate the fundamental laws of nature for an error to exist in the circuit of relays. And so I said—"

"And you said, 'Have your boys check them and make sure, anyway.' "

"Susan, you read my mind. It was what I said, and he said he couldn't."

"Too busy?"

"No, he said that no human being could. He was frank about it. He told me, and I hope I understand him properly, that the Machines are a gigantic extrapolation. Thus— A team of mathematicians work several years calculating a positronic brain equipped to do certain similar acts of calculation. Using this brain they make further calculations to create a still more complicated brain, which they use again to make one still more complicated and so on. According to Silver, what we call the Machines are the result of ten such steps."

"Ye-es, that sounds familiar. Fortunately, I'm not a mathematician. —Poor Vincent. He is a young man. The Directors before him had no such problems. Nor had I. Perhaps roboticists these days can no longer understand their own creations."

"Apparently not. The Machines are not super-brains in Sunday supplement sense,—although they are so pictured in the Sunday supplements. It is merely that in their own particular province of collecting and analyzing a nearly infinite number of data and relationships thereof, in nearly infinitesimal time, they have progressed beyond the possibility of detailed human control.

"And then I tried something else. I actually asked the Machine. In the strictest secrecy, we fed it the original data involved in the steel decision, its own answer, and the actual developments since,—the overproduction, that is,—and asked for an explanation of the discrepancy."

"Good, and what was its answer?"

"I can quote you that word for word: 'The matter admits of no explanation.' "

"And how did Vincent interpret that?"

"In two ways. Either we had not given the Machine enough data to allow a definite answer, which was unlikely.

Dr. Silver admitted that. —Or else, it was impossible for the Machine to admit that it could give any answer to data which implied that it could harm a human being. This, naturally, is implied by the First Law. And then Dr. Silver recommended that I see you."

Susan Calvin looked very tired, "I'm old, Stephen. There was a time when you wanted to make me Director of Research and I refused. I wasn't young then, either, and I did not wish the responsibility. They let young Silver have it and that satisfied me; but what good is it, if I am dragged into such messes.

"Stephen, let me state my position. My researches do indeed involve the interpretation of robot behavior in the light of the Three Laws of Robotics. Here, now, we have these incredible calculating machines. They are positronic robots and therefore obey the Laws of Robotics. But they lack personality; that is, their functions are extremely limited. —Must be, since they are so specialized. Therefore, there is very little room for the interplay of the Laws, and my one method of attack is virtually useless. In short, I don't know that I can help you, Stephen."

The Co-ordinator laughed shortly, "Nevertheless, let me tell you the rest. Let me give you *my* theories, and perhaps you will then be able to tell me whether they are possible in the light of robopsychology."

"By all means. Go ahead."

"Well, since the Machines are giving the wrong answers, then, assuming that they cannot be in error, there is only one possibility. *They are being given the wrong data!* In other words, the trouble is human, and not robotic. So I took my recent planetary inspection tour—"

"From which you have just returned to New York."

"Yes. It was necessary, you see, since there are four Machines, one handling each of the Planetary Regions. And *all four are yielding imperfect results.*"

"Oh, but that follows, Stephen. If any one of the Machines is imperfect, that will automatically reflect in the results of the other three, since each of the others will assume as part of the data on which they base their own decisions, the perfection of the imperfect fourth. With a false assumption, they will yield false answers."

"Uh-huh. So it seemed to me. Now, I have here the records of my interviews with each of the Regional Vice-Co-ordinators. Would you look through them with me? —Oh, and first, have you heard of the 'Society for Humanity'?"

"Umm, yes. They are an outgrowth of the Fundamentalists who have kept U.S. Robots from ever employing positronic robots on the grounds of unfair labor competition and so on. The 'Society for Humanity' itself is anti-Machine, is it not?"

"Yes, yes, but— Well, you will see. Shall we begin? We'll start with the Eastern Region."

"As you say—"

The Eastern Region:
  a—Area: 7,500,000 square miles
  b—Population: 1,700,000,000
  c—Capital: Shanghai

Ching Hso-lin's great-grandfather had been killed in the Japanese invasion of the old Chinese Republic, and there had been no one beside his dutiful children to mourn his loss or even to know he was lost. Ching Hso-lin's grandfather had survived the civil war of the late forties, but there had been no one beside *his* dutiful children to know or care of that.

And yet Ching Hso-lin was a Regional Vice-Co-ordinator, with the economic welfare of half the people of Earth in his care.

Perhaps it was with the thought of all that in mind, that Ching had two maps as the only ornaments on the wall of his office. One was an old hand-drawn affair tracing out an acre or two of land, and marked with the now outmoded pictographs of old China. A little creek trickled aslant the faded markings and there were the delicate pictorial indications of lowly huts, in one of which Ching's grandfather had been born.

The other map was a huge one, sharply delineated, with all markings in neat Cyrillic characters. The red boundary that marked the Eastern Region swept within its grand confines all that had once been China, India, Burma, Indo-China, and Indonesia. On it, within the old province of Szechuan, so light and gentle that none could see it, was the little mark placed there by Ching which indicated the location of his ancestral farm.

Ching stood before these maps as he spoke to Stephen Byerley in precise English, "No one knows better than you, Mr. Co-ordinator, that my job, to a large extent, is a sine-cure. It carries with it a certain social standing, and I repre-sent a convenient focal point for administration, but otherwise it is the Machine! —The Machine does all the work. What did you think, for instance, of the Tientsin Hydroponics works?"

"Tremendous!" said Byerley.

"It is but one of dozens, and not the largest. Shanghai, Calcutta, Batavia, Bangkok— They are widely spread and they are the answer to feeding the billion and three quarters of the East."

"And yet," said Byerley, "you have an unemployment problem there at Tientsin. Can you be over-producing? It is incongruous to think of Asia as suffering from too much food."

Ching's dark eyes crinkled at the edges. "No. It has not come to that yet. It is true that over the last few months, several vats at Tientsin have been shut down, but it is nothing serious. The men have been released only tempo-rarily and those who do not care to work in other fields have been shipped to Colombo in Ceylon, where a new plant is being put into operation."

"But why should the vats be closed down?"

Ching smiled gently, "You do not know much of hydro-ponics, I see. Well, that is not surprising. You are a Northerner, and there soil farming is still profitable. It is fashionable in the North to think of hydroponics, when it is thought of at all, as a device for growing turnips in a chemical solution, and so it is—in an infinitely complicated way.

"In the first place, by far the largest crop we deal with (and the percentage is growing) is yeast. We have upward of two thousand strains of yeast in production and new strains are added monthly. The basic food-chemicals of the various yeasts are nitrates and phosphates among the inorganics together with proper amounts of the trace metals needed, down to the fractional parts per million of boron and molybdenum which are required. The organic matter is mostly sugar mixtures derived from the hydrolysis of cellulose, but, in addition, there are various food factors which must be added.

"For a successful hydroponics industry—one which can feed seventeen hundred million people—we must engage in an immense reforestation program throughout the East; we must have huge wood-conversion plants to deal with our southern jungles; we must have power, and steel, and chemical synthetics above all."

"Why the last, sir?"

"Because, Mr. Byerley, these strains of yeast have each their peculiar properties. We have developed, as I said, two thousand strains. The beef steak you thought you ate today was yeast. The frozen fruit confection you had for dessert was iced yeast. We have filtered yeast juice with the taste, appearance, and all the food value of milk.

"It is flavor, more than anything else, you see, that makes yeast feeding popular and for the sake of flavor we have developed artificial, domesticated strains that can no longer support themselves on a basic diet of salts and sugar. One needs biotin; another needs pteroylglutamic acid; still others need seventeen different amino acids supplied them as well as all the Vitamins B, but one (and yet it is popular and we cannot, with economic sense, abandon it)—"

Byerley stirred in his seat, "To what purpose do you tell me all this?"

"You asked me, sir, why men are out of work in Tientsin. I have a little more to explain. It is not only that we must have these various and varying foods for our yeast; but there remains the complicating factor of popular fads with passing time; and of the possibility of the development of new strains with the new requirements and new popularity. All this must be foreseen, and the Machine does the job—"

"But not perfectly."

"Not very *im*perfectly, in view of the complications I have mentioned. Well, then, a few thousand workers in Tientsin are temporarily out of a job. But, consider this, the amount of waste in this past year (waste that is, in terms of either defective supply or defective demand) amounts to not one-tenth of one percent of our total productive turnover. I consider that—"

"Yet in the first years of the Machine, the figure was nearer one-thousandth of one percent."

"Ah, but in the decade since the Machine began its operations in real earnest, we have made use of it to increase our old pre-Machine yeast industry twenty-fold. You expect imperfections to increase with complications, though—"

"Though?"

"There *was* the curious instance of Rama Vrasayana."

"What happened to him?"

"Vrasayana was in charge of a brine-evaporation plant for the production of iodine, with which yeast can do without, but human beings not. His plant was forced into receivership."

"Really? And through what agency?"

"Competition, believe it or not. In general, one of the chiefest functions of the Machine's analyses is to indicate the most efficient distribution of our producing units. It is obviously faulty to have areas insufficiently serviced, so that the transportation costs account for too great a percentage of the overhead. Similarly, it is faulty to have an area too well serviced, so that factories must be run at lowered capacities, or else compete harmfully with one another. In the case of Vrasayana, another plant was established in the same city, and with a more efficient extracting system."

"The Machine permitted it?"

"Oh, certainly. That is not surprising. The new system is becoming widespread. The surprise is that the Machine failed to warn Vrasayana to renovate or combine. —Still, no matter. Vrasayana accepted a job as engineer in the new plant, and if his responsibility and pay are now less, he is not actually suffering. The workers found employment easily; the old plant has been converted to—something or other. Something useful. We left it all to the Machine."

"And otherwise you have no complaints."

"None!"

The Tropic Region:
a—Area: 22,000,000 square miles
b—Population: 500,000,000
c—Capital: Capital City

The map in Lincoln Ngoma's office was far from the model of neat precision of the one in Ching's Shanghai dominion. The boundaries of Ngoma's Tropic Region were stencilled in dark, wide brown and swept about a gorgeous interior labelled "jungle" and "desert" and "here be Elephants and all Manner of Strange Beasts."

It had much to sweep, for in land area the Tropic Region enclosed most of two continents: all of South America north of Argentina and all of Africa south of the Atlas. It included North America south of the Rio Grande as well, and even Arabia and Iran in Asia. It was the reverse of the Eastern Region. Where the ant hives of the Orient crowded half of humanity into 15 percent of the land mass, the Tropics stretched its 15 percent of Humanity over nearly half of all the land in the world.

But it was growing. It was the one Region whose population increase through immigration exceeded that through births. —And for all who came it had use.

To Ngoma, Stephen Byerley seemed like one of these immigrants, a pale searcher for the creative work of carving a harsh environment into the softness necessary for man, and he felt some of that automatic contempt of the strong man born to the strong Tropics for the unfortunate pallards of the colder suns.

The Tropics had the newest capital city on Earth, and it was called simply that: "Capital City," in the sublime confidence of youth. It spread brightly over the fertile uplands of Nigeria and outside Ngoma's windows, far below, was life and color; the bright, bright sun and the quick, drenching showers. Even the squawking of the rainbowed birds was brisk and the stars were hard pinpoints in the sharp night.

Ngoma laughed. He was a big, dark man, strong faced and handsome.

"Sure," he said, and his English was colloquial and mouthfilling, "the Mexican Canal is overdue. What the hell? It will get finished just the same, old boy."

"It was doing well up to the last half year."

Ngoma looked at Byerley and slowly crunched his teeth over the end of a big cigar, spitting out one end and lighting the other, "Is this an official investigation, Byerley? What's going on?"

"Nothing. Nothing at all. It's just my function as Coordinator to be curious."

"Well, if it's just that you are filling in a dull moment, the truth is that we're always short on labor. There's lots going on in the Tropics. The Canal is only one of them—"

"But doesn't your Machine predict the amount of labor available for the Canal,—allowing for all the competing projects?"

Ngoma placed one hand behind his neck and blew smoke rings at the ceiling, "It was a little off."

"Is it often a little off?"

"Not oftener than you would expect. —We don't expect too much of it, Byerley. We feed it data. We take its results. We do what it says.—But it's just a convenience; just a labor-saving device. We could do without it, if we had to. Maybe not as well. Maybe not as quickly. But we'd get there.

"We've got confidence out here, Byerley, and that's the

secret. Confidence! We've got new land that's been waiting for us for thousands of years, while the rest of the world was being ripped apart in the lousy fumblings of pre-atomic time. We don't have to eat yeast like the Eastern boys, and we don't have to worry about the stale dregs of the last century like you Northerners.

"We've wiped out the tsetse fly and the Anopheles mosquito, and people find they can live in the sun and like it, now. We've thinned down the jungles and found soil; we've watered the deserts and found gardens. We've got coal and oil in untouched fields, and minerals out of count.

"Just step back. That's all we ask the rest of the world to do. —Step back, and let us work."

Byerley said, prosaically, "But the Canal,—it was on schedule six months ago. What happened?"

Ngoma spread his hands, "Labor troubles." He felt through a pile of papers skeltered about his desk and gave it up.

"Had something on the matter here," he muttered, "but never mind. There was a work shortage somewhere in Mexico once on the question of women. There weren't enough women in the neighborhood. It seemed no one had thought of feeding sexual data to the Machine."

He stopped to laugh, delightedly, then sobered, "Wait a while. I think I've got it. —Villafranca!"

"Villafranca?"

"Francisco Villafranca. —He was the engineer in charge. Now let me straighten it out. Something happened and there was a cave-in. Right. Right. That was it. Nobody died, as I remember, but it made a hell of a mess. —Quite a scandal."

"Oh?"

"There was some mistake in his calculations. —Or at least, the Machine said so. They fed through Villafranca's data, assumptions, and so on. The stuff he had started with. The answers came out differently. It seems the answers Villafranca had used didn't take account of the effect of a heavy rainfall on the contours of the cut. —Or something like that. I'm not an engineer, you understand.

"Anyway, Villafranca put up a devil of a squawk. He claimed the Machine's answer had been different the first time. That he had followed the Machine faithfully. Then he quit! We offered to hold him on—reasonable doubt, previous work satisfactory, and all that—in a subordinate position, of course—had to do that much—mistakes can't go unnoticed—bad for discipline—Where was I?"

"You offered to hold him on."

"Oh yes. He refused. —Well, take all in all, we're two months behind. Hell, that's nothing."

Byerley stretched out his hand and let the fingers tap lightly on the desk, "Villafranca blamed the Machine, did he?"

"Well, he wasn't going to blame himself, was he? Let's face it; human nature is an old friend of ours. Besides, I remember something else now— Why the hell can't I find documents when I want them? My filing system isn't worth a damn— This Villafranca was a member of one of your Northern organizations. Mexico is too close to the North! That's part of the trouble."

"Which organization are you speaking of?"

"The Society for Humanity, they call it. He used to attend the annual conferences in New York, Villafranca did. Bunch of crackpots, but harmless. —They don't like the Machines; claim they're destroying human initiative. So naturally Villafranca would blame the Machine. —Don't understand that group myself. Does Capital City look as if the human race were running out of initiative?"

And Capital City stretched out in golden glory under a golden sun,—the newest and youngest creation of *Homo metropolis*.

The European Region:
  a—Area: 4,000,000 square miles
  b—Population: 300,000,000
  c—Capital: Geneva

The European Region was an anomaly in several ways. In area, it was far the smallest; not one fifth the size of the

Tropic Region in area, and not one fifth the size of the Eastern Region in population. Geographically, it was only somewhat similar to pre-Atomic Europe, since it excluded what had once been European Russia and what had once been the British Isles, while it included the Mediterranean coasts of Africa and Asia, and, in a queer jump across the Atlantic, Argentina, Chile, and Uruguay as well.

Nor was it likely to improve its relative status vis-à-vis the other regions of Earth, except for what vigor the South American provinces lent it. Of all the Regions, it alone showed a positive population decline over the past half century. It alone had not seriously expanded its productive facilities, or offered anything radically new to human culture.

"Europe," said Madame Szegeczowska, in her soft French, "is essentially an economic appendage of the Northern Region. We know it, and it doesn't matter."

And as though in resigned acceptance of a lack of individuality, there was no map of Europe on the wall of the Madame Co-ordinator's office.

"And yet," pointed out Byerley, "you have a Machine of your own, and you are certainly under no economic pressure from across the ocean."

"A Machine! Bah!" She shrugged her delicate shoulders, and allowed a thin smile to cross her little face as she tamped out a cigarette with long fingers. "Europe is a sleepy place. And such of our men as do not manage to emigrate to the Tropics are tired and sleepy along with it. You see for yourself that it is myself, a poor woman, to whom falls the task of being Vice-Co-ordinator. Well, fortunately, it is not a difficult job, and not much is expected of me.

"As for the Machine— What can it say but 'Do this and it will be best for you.' But what is best for us? Why, to be an economic appendage of the Northern Region.

"And is it so terrible? No wars! We live in peace—and it is pleasant after seven thousand years of war. We are old, monsieur. In our borders, we have the regions where Occidental civilization was cradled. We have Egypt and Mesopotamia; Crete and Syria; Asia Minor and Greece. —But old age is not necessarily an unhappy time. It can be a fruition—"

"Perhaps you are right," said Byerley, affably. "At least the tempo of life is not as intense as in the other Regions. It is a pleasant atmosphere."

"Is it not? —Tea is being brought, monsieur. If you will indicate your cream and sugar preferences, please. —Thank you."

She sipped gently, then continued, "It *is* pleasant. The rest of Earth is welcome to the continuing struggle. I find a parallel here; a very interesting one. There was a time when Rome was master of the world. It had adopted the culture and civilization of Greece; a Greece which had never been united, which had ruined itself with war, and which was ending in a state of decadent squalor. Rome united it, brought it peace and let it live a life of secure non-glory. It occupied itself with its philosophies and its art, far from the clash of growth and war. It was a sort of death, but it was restful, and it lasted with minor breaks for some four hundred years."

"And yet," said Byerley, "Rome fell eventually, and the opium dream was over."

"There are no longer barbarians to overthrow civilization."

"We can be our own barbarians, Madame Szegeczowska. —Oh, I meant to ask you. The Almaden mercury mines have fallen off quite badly in production. Surely the ores are not declining more rapidly than anticipated?"

The little woman's gray eyes fastened shrewdly on Byerley, "Barbarians—the fall of civilization—possible failure of the Machine. Your thought processes are very transparent, monsieur."

"Are they?" Byerley smiled. "I see that I should have had men to deal with as hitherto. —You consider the Almaden affair to be the fault of the Machine?"

"Not at all, but I think you do. You, yourself, are a native of the Northern Region. The Central Co-ordination Office is at New York. —And I have noticed for quite a while that you Northerners lack somewhat of faith in the Machine."

"We do?"

"There is your 'Society for Humanity' which is strong in the North, but naturally fails to find many recruits in tired, old Europe, which is quite willing to let feeble Humanity alone for a while. Surely, you are one of the confident North and not one of the cynical old continent."

"This has a connection with Almaden?"

"Oh, yes, I think so. The mines are in the control of Consolidated Cinnabar, which is certainly a Northern company, with headquarters at Nikolaev. Personally, I wonder if the Board of Directors has been consulting the Machine at all. They said they had in our conference last month, and, of course, we have no evidence that they did not, but I wouldn't take the word of a Northerner in this matter—no offense intended—under any circumstances. —Nevertheless, I think it will have a fortunate ending."

"In what way, my dear madam?"

"You must understand that the economic irregularities of the last few months, which, although small as compared with the great storms of the past, are quite disturbing to our peace-drenched spirits, have caused considerable restiveness in the Spanish province. I understand that Consolidated Cinnabar is selling out to a group of native Spaniards. It is consoling. If we are economic vassals of the North, it is humiliating to have the fact advertised too blatantly.—And our people can be better trusted to follow the Machine."

"Then you think there will be no more trouble?"

"I am sure there will not be— In Almaden, at least."

The Northern Region:
  a—Area: 18,000,000 square miles
  b—Population: 800,000,000
  c—Capital: Ottawa

The Northern Region, in more ways than one, was at the top. This was exemplified quite well by the map in the

Ottawa office of Vice-Co-ordinator Hiram Mackenzie, in which the North Pole was centered. Except for the enclave of Europe with its Scandinavian and Icelandic regions, all the Arctic area was within the Northern Region.

Roughly, it could be divided into two major areas. To the left on the map was all of North America above the Rio Grande. To the right was included all of what had once been the Soviet Union. Together these areas represented the centered power of the planet in the first years of the Atomic Age. Between the two was Great Britain, a tongue of the Region licking at Europe. Up at the top of the map, distorted into odd, huge shapes, were Australia and New Zealand, also member provinces of the Region.

Not all the changes of the past decades had yet altered the fact that the North was the economic ruler of the planet.

There was almost an ostentatious symbolism thereof in the fact that of the official Regional maps Byerley had seen, Mackenzie's alone showed all the Earth, as though the North feared no competition and needed no favoritism to point up its pre-eminence.

"Impossible," said Mackenzie, dourly, over the whiskey. "Mr. Byerley, you have had no training as a robot technician, I believe."

"No, I have not."

"Hmp. Well, it is, in my opinion, a sad thing that Ching, Ngoma and Szegeczowska haven't either. There is too prevalent an opinion among the peoples of Earth that a Co-ordinator need only be a capable organizer, a broad generalizer, and an amiable person. These days he should know his robotics as well,—no offense intended."

"None taken. I agree with you."

"I take it, for instance, from what you have said already, that you worry about the recent trifling dislocations in world economy. I don't know what you suspect, but it has happened in the past that people—who should have known better—wondered what would happen if false data were fed into the Machine."

"And what would happen, Mr. Mackenzie?"

"Well," the Scotsman shifted his weight and sighed, "all collected data goes through a complicated screening system which involves both human and mechanical checking, so that the problem is not likely to arise. —But let us ignore that. Humans are fallible, also corruptible, and ordinary mechanical devices are liable to mechanical failure.

"The real point of the matter is that what we call a 'wrong datum' is one which is inconsistent with all other known data. It is our only criterion of right and wrong. It is the Machine's as well. Order it for instance, to direct agricultural activity on the basis of an average July temperature in Iowa of 57 degrees Fahrenheit. It won't accept that. It will not give an answer. — Not that it has any prejudice against that particular temperature, or that an answer is impossible; but because, in the light of all the other data fed it over a period of years, it knows that the probability of an average July temperature of 57 is virtually nil. It rejects that datum.

"The only way a 'wrong datum' can be forced on the Machine is to include it as part of a self-consistent whole, all of which is subtly wrong in a manner either too delicate for the Machine to detect or outside the Machine's experience. The former is beyond human capacity, and the latter is almost so, and is becoming more nearly so as the Machine's experience increases by the second."

Stephen Byerley placed two fingers to the bridge of his nose, "Then the Machine cannot be tampered with— And how do you account for recent errors, then?"

"My dear Byerley, I see that you instinctively follow that great error—that the Machine knows all. Let me cite you a case from my personal experience. The cotton industry engages experienced buyers who purchase cotton. Their procedure is to pull a tuft of cotton out of a random bale of a lot. They will look at that tuft and feel it, tease it out, listen to the crackling perhaps as they do so, touch it with their tongue,—and through this procedure they will determine the class of cotton the bales represent. There are about a dozen such classes. As a result of their decisions, purchases are made at certain prices, blends are made in certain proportions. —Now these buyers cannot yet be replaced by the Machine."

"Why not? Surely the data involved is not too complicated for it?"

"Probably not. But what data is this you refer to? No textile chemist knows exactly what it is that the buyer tests when he feels a tuft of cotton. Presumably there's the average length of the threads, their feel, the extent and nature of their slickness, the way they hang together and so on. —Several dozen items, subconsciously weighed, out of years of experience. But the *quantitative* nature of these tests is not known; maybe even the very nature of some of them is not known. So we have nothing to feed the Machine. Nor can the buyers explain their own judgment. They can only say, 'Well, look at it. Can't you *tell* it's class-such-and-such?' "

"I see."

"There are innumerable cases like that. The Machine is only a tool after all, which can help humanity progress faster by taking some of the burdens of calculations and interpretations off his back. The task of the human brain remains what it has always been; that of discovering new data to be analyzed, and of devising new concepts to be tested. A pity the Society for Humanity won't understand that."

"They are against the Machine?"

"They would be against mathematics or against the art of writing if they had lived at the appropriate time. These reactionaries of the Society claim the Machine robs man of his soul. I notice that capable men are still at a premium in our society; we still need the man who is intelligent enough to think of the proper questions to ask. Perhaps if we could find enough of such, these dislocations you worry about, Co-ordinator, wouldn't occur."

Earth (Including the uninhabited continent, Antarctica):
  a—Area: 54,000,000 square miles (land surface)
  b—Population: 3,300,000,000
  c—Capital: New York

* * *

■

The fire behind the quartz was weary now, and sputtered its reluctant way to death.

The Co-ordinator was somber, his mood matching the sinking flame.

"They all minimize the state of affairs." His voice was low. "Is it not easy to imagine that they all laugh at me? And yet—Vincent Silver said the Machines cannot be out of order, and I must believe him. Hiram Mackenzie says they cannot be fed false data, and I must believe him. But the Machines are going wrong, somehow, and I must believe that, too,—and so there is *still* an alternative left."

He glanced sidewise at Susan Calvin, who, with closed eyes, for a moment seemed asleep.

"What is that?" she asked, prompt to her cue, nevertheless.

"Why, that correct data is indeed given, and correct answers are indeed received, but that they are then ignored. There is no way the Machine can enforce obedience to its dictates."

"Madame Szegeczowska hinted as much, with reference to Northerners in general, it seems to me."

"So she did."

"And what purpose is served by disobeying the Machine? Let's consider motivations."

"It's obvious to me, and should be to you. It is a matter of rocking the boat, deliberately. There can be no serious conflicts on Earth, in which one group or another can seize more power than it has for what it thinks is its own good despite the harm of Mankind as a whole, while the Machines rule. If popular faith in the Machines can be destroyed to the point where they are abandoned, it will be the law of the jungle again. —And not one of the four Regions can be freed of the suspicion of wanting just that.

"The East has half of humanity within its borders, and the Tropics more than half of Earth's resources. Each can feel itself the natural rulers of all Earth, and each has a history of humiliation by the North, for which it can be human enough to wish a senseless revenge. Europe has a tradition of greatness, on the other hand. It once *did* rule the Earth, and there is nothing so eternally adhesive as the memory of power.

"Yet, in another way, it's hard to believe. Both the East and the Tropics are in a state of enormous expansion within their own borders. Both are climbing incredibly. They cannot have the spare energy for military adventures. And Europe can have nothing but its dreams. It is a cipher, militarily."

"So, Stephen," said Susan, "you leave the North."

"Yes," said Byerley, energetically, "I do. The North is now the strongest, and has been for nearly a century, or its component parts have been. But it is losing relatively, now. The Tropic Regions may take their place in the forefront of civilization for the first time since the Pharaohs, and there are Northerners who fear that.

"The 'Society for Humanity' is a Northern organization, primarily, you know, and they make no secret of not wanting the Machines. —Susan, they are few in numbers, but it is an association of powerful men. Heads of factories; directors of industries and agricultural combines who hate to be what they call 'the Machine's office boy' belong to it. Men with ambition belong to it. Men who feel themselves strong enough to decide for themselves what is best for themselves, and not just to be told what is best for others.

"In short, just those men who, by together refusing to accept the decisions of the Machine, can, in a short time, turn the world topsy-turvy;—just those belong to the Society.

"Susan, it hangs together. Five of the Directors of World Steel are members, and World Steel suffers from overproduction. Consolidated Cinnabar, which mined mercury at Almaden, was a Northern concern. Its books are still being investigated, but one, at least, of the men concerned was a member. Francisco Villafranca, who, singlehanded, delayed the Mexican Canal for two months, was a member, we know already—and so was Rama Vrasayana, I was not at all surprised to find out."

Susan said, quietly, "These men, I might point out, have all done badly—"

"But naturally," interjected Byerley. "To disobey the Machine's analyses is to follow a non-optimal path. Results are poorer than they might be. It's the price they pay. They will have it rough now but in the confusion that will eventually follow—"

"Just what do you plan doing, Stephen?"

"There is obviously no time to lose. I am going to have the Society outlawed, every member removed from any responsible post. And all executive and technical positions, henceforward, can be filled only by applicants signing a non-Society oath. It will mean a certain surrender of basic civil liberties, but I am sure the Congress—"

"It won't work!"

"What!— Why not?"

"I will make a prediction. If you try any such thing, you will find yourself hampered at every turn. You will find it impossible to carry out. You will find your every move in that direction will result in trouble."

Byerley was taken aback, "Why do you say that? —I was rather hoping for your approval in this matter."

"You can't have it as long as your actions are based on a false premise. You admit the Machine can't be wrong, and can't be fed wrong data. I will now show you that it cannot be disobeyed, either, as you think is being done by the Society."

"*That* I don't see at all."

"Then listen. Every action by any executive which does not follow the exact directions of the Machine he is working with becomes part of the data for the next problem. The Machine, therefore, knows that the executive has a certain tendency to disobey. He can incorporate that tendency into that data,—even quantitatively, that is, judging exactly how much and in what direction disobedience would occur. Its next answer would be just sufficiently biased so that after the executive concerned disobeyed, he would have automatically corrected those answers to optimal directions. The Machine *knows*, Stephen!"

"You can't be sure of all this. You are guessing."

"It is a guess based on a lifetime's experience with robots. You had better rely on such a guess, Stephen."

"But then what is left? The Machines themselves are correct and the premises they work on are correct. That we have agreed upon. Now you say that it cannot be disobeyed. Then what is wrong?"

"You have answered yourself. *Nothing is wrong!* Think about the Machines for a while, Stephen. They are robots, and they follow the First Law. But the Machines work not for any single human being, but for all humanity, so that the First Law becomes: 'No Machine may harm humanity; or, through inaction, allow humanity to come to harm.'

"Very well, then, Stephen, what harms humanity? Economic dislocations most of all, from whatever cause. Wouldn't you say so?"

"I would."

"And what is most likely in the future to cause economic dislocations? Answer that, Stephen."

"I should say," replied Byerley, unwillingly, "the destruction of the Machines."

"And so should I say, and so should the Machines say. Their first care, therefore, is to preserve themselves, for us. And so they are quietly taking care of the only elements left that threaten them. It is not the 'Society for Humanity' which is shaking the boat so that the Machines may be destroyed. You have been looking at the reverse of the picture. Say rather that the Machine is shaking the boat—*very* slightly—just enough to shake loose those few which cling to the side for purposes the Machines consider harmful to Humanity.

"So Vrasayana loses his factory and gets another job where he can do no harm—he is not badly hurt, he is not rendered incapable of earning a living, for the Machine cannot harm a human being more than minimally, and that only to save a greater number. Consolidated Cinnabar loses control at Almaden. Villafranca is no longer a civil engineer in charge of an important project. And the directors of World Steel are losing their grip on the industry—or will."

"But you don't really know all this," insisted Byerley, distractedly. "How can we possibly take a chance on your being right?"

"You must. Do you remember the Machine's own statement when you presented the problem to him? It was: 'The matter admits of no explanation.' The Machine did not say there was no explanation, or that it could determine no explanation. It simply was not going to *admit* any explanation. In other words, it would be harmful to humanity to have the explanation known, and that's why we can only guess—and keep on guessing."

"But how can the explanation do us harm? Assume that you are right, Susan."

"Why, Stephen, if I am right, it means that the Machine is conducting our future for us not only simply in direct answer to our direct questions, but in general answer to the world situation and to human psychology as a whole. And to know that may make us unhappy and may hurt our pride. The Machine cannot, *must* not, make us unhappy."

"Stephen, how do we know what the ultimate good of Humanity will entail? We haven't at *our* disposal the infinite factors that the Machine has at *its!* Perhaps, to give you a not unfamiliar example, our entire technical civilization has created more unhappiness and misery than it has removed. Perhaps an agrarian or pastoral civilization, with less culture and less people would be better. If so, the Machines must move in that direction, preferably without telling us, since in our ignorant prejudices we only know that what we are used to, is good—and we would then fight change. Or perhaps a complete urbanization, or a completely caste-ridden society, or complete anarchy, is the answer. We don't know. Only the Machines know, and they are going there and taking us with them."

"But you are telling me, Susan that the 'Society for Humanity' is right; and that Mankind *has* lost its own say in its future."

"It never had any, really. It was always at the mercy of economic and sociological forces it did not understand—at the whims of climate, and the fortunes of war. Now the Machines understand them; and no one can stop them, since the Machines will deal with them as they are dealing with the Society,— having, as they do, the greatest of weapons at their disposal, the absolute control of our economy."

"How horrible!"

"Perhaps how wonderful! Think, that for all time, all conflicts are finally evitable. Only the Machines, from now on, are inevitable!"

And the fire behind the quartz went out and only a curl of smoke was left to indicate its place.

FEMININE INTUITION

For the first time in the history of United States Robots and Mechanical Men Corporation, a robot had been destroyed through accident on Earth itself.

No one was to blame. The air vehicle had been demolished in mid-air and an unbelieving investigating committee was wondering whether they really dared announce the evidence that it had been hit by a meteorite. Nothing else could have been fast enough to prevent automatic avoidance; nothing else could have done the damage short of a nuclear blast and that was out of the question.

Tie that in with a report of a flash in the night sky just before the vehicle had exploded—and from Flagstaff Observatory, not from an amateur—and the location of a sizable and distinctly meteoric bit of iron freshly gouged into the ground a mile from the site and what other conclusion could be arrived at?

Still, nothing like that had ever happened before and calculations of the odds against it yielded monstrous figures. Yet even colossal improbabilities can happen sometimes.

At the offices of United States Robots, the hows and

whys of it were secondary. The real point was that a robot had been destroyed.

That, in itself, was distressing.

The fact that JN-5 had been a prototype, the first, after four earlier attempts, to have been placed in the field, was even more distressing.

The fact that JN-5 was a radically new type of robot, quite different from anything ever built before, was abysmally distressing.

The fact that JN-5 had apparently accomplished something before its destruction that was incalculably important and that that accomplishment might now be forever gone, placed the distress utterly beyond words.

It seemed scarcely worth mentioning that, along with the robot, the Chief Robopsychologist of United States Robots had also died.

Clinton Madarian had joined the firm ten years before. For five of those years, he had worked uncomplainingly under the grumpy supervision of Susan Calvin.

Madarian's brilliance was quite obvious and Susan Calvin had quietly promoted him over the heads of older men. She wouldn't, in any case, have deigned to give her reasons for this to Research Director Peter Bogert, but as it happened, no reasons were needed. Or, rather, they were obvious.

Madarian was utterly the reverse of the renowned Dr. Calvin in several very noticeable ways. He was not quite as overweight as his distinct double chin made him appear to be, but even so he was overpowering in his presence, where Susan had gone nearly unnoticed. Madarian's massive face, his shock of glistening red-brown hair, his ruddy complexion and booming voice, his loud laugh, and most of all, his irrepressible self-confidence and his eager way of announcing his successes, made everyone else in the room feel there was a shortage of space.

When Susan Calvin finally retired (refusing, in advance, any cooperation with respect to any testimonial dinner that might be planned in her honor, with so firm a manner that no announcement of the retirement was even made to the news services) Madarian took her place.

He had been in his new post exactly one day when he initiated the JN project.

It had meant the largest commitment of funds to one project that United States Robots had ever had to undertake, but that was something which Madarian dismissed with a genial wave of the hand.

"Worth every penny of it, Peter," he said. "And I expect you to convince the Board of Directors of that."

"Give me reasons," said Bogert, wondering if Madarian would. Susan Calvin had never given reasons.

But Madarian said, "Sure," and settled himself easily into the large armchair in the Director's office.

Bogert watched the other with something that was almost awe. His own once-black hair was almost white now and within the decade he would follow Susan into retirement. That would mean the end of the original team that had built United States Robots into a globe-girdling firm that was a rival of the national governments in complexity and importance. Somehow neither he nor those who had gone before him ever quite grasped the enormous expansion of the firm.

But this was a new generation. The new men were at ease with the Colossus. They lacked the touch of wonder that would have them tiptoeing in disbelief. So they moved ahead, and that was good.

Madarian said, "I propose to begin the construction of robots without constraint."

"Without the Three Laws? Surely—"

"No, Peter. Are those the only constraints you can think of? Hell, you contributed to the design of the early positronic brains. Do I have to tell you that, quite aside from the Three Laws, there isn't a pathway in those brains that isn't carefully designed and fixed? We have robots planned for specific tasks, implanted with specific abilities."

"And you propose—"

"That at every level below the Three Laws, the paths be made open-ended. It's not difficult."

Bogert said dryly, "It's not difficult, indeed. Useless things are never difficult. The difficult thing is fixing the paths and making the robot useful."

"But why is that difficult? Fixing the paths requires a great deal of effort because the Principle of Uncertainty is important in particles the mass of positrons and the uncertainty effect must be minimized. Yet why must it? If we arrange to have the Principle just sufficiently prominent to allow the crossing of paths unpredictably—"

"We have an unpredictable robot."

"We have a *creative* robot," said Madarian, with a trace of impatience. "Peter, if there's anything a human brain has that a robotic brain has never had, it's the trace of unpredictability that comes from the effects of uncertainty at the subatomic level. I admit that this effect has never been demonstrated experimentally within the nervous system, but without that the human brain is not superior to the robotic brain in principle."

"And you think that if you introduce the effect into the robotic brain, the human brain will become not superior to the robotic brain in principle."

"That," said Madarian, "is exactly what I believe."

They went on for a long time after that.

The Board of Directors clearly had no intention of being easily convinced.

Scott Robertson, the largest shareholder in the firm, said, "It's hard enough to manage the robot industry as it is, with public hostility to robots forever on the verge of breaking out into the open. If the public gets the idea that robots will be uncontrolled . . . Oh, don't tell me about the Three Laws. The average man won't believe the Three Laws will protect him if he as much as hears the word 'uncontrolled.' "

"Then don't use it," said Madarian. "Call the robot—call it 'intuitive.' "

"An intuitive robot," someone muttered. "A girl robot?"

A smile made its way about the conference table.

Madarian seized on that. "All right. A girl robot. Our

robots are sexless, of course, and so will this one be, but we always act as though they're males. We give them male pet names and call them he and him. Now this one, if we consider the nature of the mathematical structuring of the brain which I have proposed, would fall into the JN-coordinate system. The first robot would be JN-1, and I've assumed that it would be called John-1. . . . I'm afraid that is the level of originality of the average roboticist. But why not call it Jane-1, damn it? If the public has to be let in on what we're doing, we're constructing a feminine robot with intuition."

Robertson shook his head, "What difference would that make? What you're saying is that you plan to remove the last barrier which, in principle, keeps the robotic brain inferior to the human brain. What do you suppose the public reaction will be to that?"

"Do you plan to make that public?" said Madarian. He thought a bit and then said, "Look. One thing the general public believes is that women are not as intelligent as men."

There was an instant apprehensive look on the face of more than one man at the table and a quick look up and down as though Susan Calvin were still in her accustomed seat.

Madarian said, "If we announce a female robot, it doesn't matter what she is. The public will automatically assume she is mentally backward. We just publicize the robot as Jane-1 and we don't have to say another word. We're safe."

"Actually," said Peter Bogert quietly, "there's more to it than that. Madarian and I have gone over the mathematics carefully and the JN series, whether John or Jane, would be quite safe. They would be less complex and intellectually capable, in an orthodox sense, than many another series we have designed and constructed. There would only be the one added factor of, well, let's get into the habit of calling it 'intuition.' "

"Who knows what it would do?" muttered Robertson.

"Madarian has suggested one thing it can do. As you all know, the Space Jump has been developed in principle. It is possible for men to attain what is, in effect, hyper-speeds beyond that of light and to visit other stellar systems and return in negligible time—weeks at the most."

Robertson said, "That's not new to us. It couldn't have been done without robots."

"Exactly, and it's not doing us any good because we can't use the hyper-speed drive except perhaps once as a demonstration, so that U.S. Robots gets little credit. The Space Jump is risky, it's fearfully prodigal of energy and therefore it's enormously expensive. If we were going to use it anyway, it would be nice if we could report the existence of a habitable planet. Call it a psychological need. Spend about twenty billion dollars on a single Space Jump and report nothing but scientific data and the public wants to know why their money was wasted. Report the existence of a habitable planet, and you're an interstellar Columbus and no one will worry about the money."

"So?"

"So where are we going to find a habitable planet? Or put it this way—which star within reach of the Space Jump as presently developed, which of the three hundred thousand stars and star systems within three hundred light-years has the best chance of having a habitable planet? We've got an enormous quantity of details on every star in our three-hundred-light-year neighborhood and a notion that almost every one has a planetary system. But which has a *habitable* planet? Which do we visit? . . . We don't know."

One of the directors said, "How would this Jane robot help us?"

Madarian was about to answer that, but he gestured slightly to Bogert and Bogert understood. The Director would carry more weight. Bogert didn't particularly like the idea; if the JN series proved a fiasco, he was making himself prominent enough in connection with it to insure that the sticky fingers of blame would cling to him. On the other hand, retirement was not all that far off, and if it worked, he would go out in a blaze of glory. Maybe it was only Madarian's aura of confidence, but Bogert had honestly come to believe it would work.

He said, "It may well be that somewhere in the libraries of data we have on those stars, there are methods for estimating the probabilities of the presence of Earth-type habitable planets. All we need to do is understand the data properly, look at them in the appropriate creative manner, make the correct correlations. We haven't done it yet. Or if some astronomer has, he hasn't been smart enough to realize what he has.

"A JN-type robot could make correlations far more rapidly and far more precisely than a man could. In a day, it would make and discard as many correlations as a man could in ten years. Furthermore, it would work in truly random fashion, whereas a man would have a strong bias based on preconception and on what is already believed."

There was a considerable silence after that. Finally Robertson said, "But it's only a matter of probability, isn't it? Suppose this robot said, 'The highest-probability habitable-planet star within so-and-so light-years is Squidgee-17,' or whatever, and we go there and find that a probability is only a probability and that there are no habitable planets after all. Where does that leave us?"

Madarian struck in this time. "We still win. We know how the robot came to the conclusion because it—she—will tell us. It might well help us gain enormous insight into astronomical detail and make the whole thing worthwhile even if we don't make the Space Jump at all. Besides, we can then work out the five most probable sites of planets and the probability that one of the five has a habitable planet may then be better than 0.95. It would be almost sure—"

They went on for a long time after that.

The funds granted were quite insufficient, but Madarian counted on the habit of throwing good money after bad. With two hundred million about to be lost irrevocably when another hundred million could save everything, the other hundred million would surely be voted.

Jane-1 was finally built and put on display. Peter Bogert studied it—her—gravely. He said, "Why the narrow waist? Surely that introduces a mechanical weakness?"

Madarian chuckled. "Listen, if we're going to call her Jane, there's no point in making her look like Tarzan."

Bogert shook his head. "Don't like it. You'll be bulging her higher up to give the appearance of breasts next, and that's a rotten idea. If women start getting the notion that robots may look like women, I can tell you exactly the kind of perverse notions they'll get, and you'll *really* have hostility on their part."

Madarian said, "Maybe you're right at that. No woman wants to feel replaceable by something with none of her faults. Okay."

Jane-2 did not have the pinched waist. She was a somber robot which rarely moved and even more rarely spoke.

Madarian had only occasionally come rushing to Bogert with items of news during her construction and that had been a sure sign that things were going poorly. Madarian's ebullience under success was overpowering. He would not hesitate to invade Bogert's bedroom at 3 A.M. with a hot-flash item rather than wait for the morning. Bogert was sure of that.

Now Madarian seemed subdued, his usually florid expression nearly pale, his round cheeks somehow pinched. Bogert said, with a feeling of certainty, "She won't talk."

"Oh, she talks." Madarian sat down heavily and chewed at his lower lip. "Sometimes, anyway," he said.

Bogert rose and circled the robot. "And when she talks, she makes no sense, I suppose. Well, if she doesn't talk, she's no female, is she?"

Madarian tried a weak smile for size and abandoned it. He said, "The brain, in isolation, checked out."

"I know," said Bogert.

"But once that brain was put in charge of the physical apparatus of the robot, it was necessarily modified, of course."

"Of course," agreed Bogert unhelpfully.

"But unpredictably and frustratingly. The trouble is that when you're dealing with n-dimensional calculus of uncertainty, things are—"

"Uncertain?" said Bogert. His own reaction was surprising him. The company investment was already most sizable and almost two years had elapsed, yet the results were, to put it politely, disappointing. Still, he found himself jabbing at Madarian and finding himself amused in the process.

Almost furtively, Bogert wondered if it weren't the absent Susan Calvin he was jabbing at. Madarian was so much more ebullient and effusive than Susan could ever possibly be—when things were going well. He was also far more vulnerably in the dumps when things weren't going well, and it was precisely under pressure that Susan never cracked. The target that Madarian made could be a neatly punctured bull's-eye as recompense for the target Susan had never allowed herself to be.

Madarian did not react to Bogert's last remark any more than Susan Calvin would have done; not out of contempt, which would have been Susan's reaction, but because he did not hear it.

He said argumentatively, "The trouble is the matter of recognition. We have Jane-2 correlating magnificently. She can correlate on any subject, but once she's done so, she can't recognize a valuable result from a valueless one. It's not an easy problem, judging how to program a robot to tell a significant correlation when you don't know what correlations she will be making."

"I presume you've thought of lowering the potential at the W-21 diode junction and sparking across the—"

"No, no, no, no—" Madarian faded off into a whispering diminuendo. "You can't just have it spew out everything. We can do that for ourselves. The point is to have it recognize the crucial correlation and draw the conclusion. Once that is done, you see, a Jane robot would snap out an answer by intuition. It would be something we couldn't get ourselves except by the oddest kind of luck."

"It seems to me," said Bogert dryly, "that if you had a robot like that, you would have her do routinely what, among human beings, only the occasional genius is capable of doing."

Madarian nodded vigorously. "Exactly, Peter. I'd have said so myself if I weren't afraid of frightening off the execs. Please don't repeat that in their hearing."

"Do you really want a robot genius?"

"What are words? I'm trying to get a robot with the capacity to make random correlations at enormous speeds, together with a key-significance high-recognition quotient. And I'm trying to put *those* words into positronic field equations. I thought I had it, too, but I don't. Not yet."

He looked at Jane-2 discontentedly and said, "What's the best significance you have, Jane?"

Jane-2's head turned to look at Madarian but she made no sound, and Madarian whispered with resignation, "She's running that into the correlation banks."

Jane-2 spoke tonelessly at last. "I'm not sure." It was the first sound she had made.

Madarian's eyes rolled upward. "She's doing the equivalent of setting up equations with indeterminate solutions."

"I gathered that," said Bogert. "Listen, Madarian, can you go anywhere at this point, or do we pull out now and cut our losses at half a billion?"

"Oh, I'll get it," muttered Madarian.

Jane-3 wasn't it. She was never as much as activated and Madarian was in a rage.

It was human error. His own fault, if one wanted to be entirely accurate. Yet though Madarian was utterly humiliated, others remained quiet. Let he who has never made an error in the fearsomely intricate mathematics of the positronic brain fill out the first memo of correction.

*   *   *

Nearly a year passed before Jane-4 was ready. Madarian was ebullient again. "She does it," he said. "She's got a good high-recognition quotient."

He was confident enough to place her on display before the Board and have her solve problems. Not mathematical problems; any robot could do that; but problems where the terms were deliberately misleading without being actually inaccurate.

Bogert said afterward, "That doesn't take much, really."

"Of course not. It's elementary for Jane-4, but I had to show them something, didn't I?"

"Do you know how much we've spent so far?"

"Come on, Peter, don't give me that. Do you know how much we've got back? These things don't go on in a vacuum, you know. I've had over three years of hell over this, if you want to know, but I've worked out new techniques of calculation that will save us a minimum of fifty thousand dollars on every new type of positronic brain we design, from now on and forever. Right?"

"Well—"

"Well me no wells. It's so. And it's my personal feeling that n-dimensional calculus of uncertainty can have any number of other applications if we have the ingenuity to find them, and my Jane robots *will* find them. Once I've got exactly what I want, the new JN series will pay for itself inside of five years, even if we triple what we've invested so far."

"What do you mean by 'exactly what you want'? What's wrong with Jane-4?"

"Nothing. Or nothing much. She's on the track, but she can be improved and I intend to do so. I thought I knew where I was going when I designed her. Now I've tested her and I *know* where I'm going. I intend to get there."

Jane-5 was it. It took Madarian well over a year to produce her and there he had no reservations; he was utterly confident.

Jane-5 was shorter than the average robot, slimmer. Without being a female caricature as Jane-1 had been, she managed to possess an air of femininity about herself despite the absence of a single clearly feminine feature.

"It's the way she's standing," said Bogert. Her arms were held gracefully and somehow the torso managed to give the impression of curving slightly when she turned.

Madarian said, "Listen to her. . . . How do you feel, Jane?"

"In excellent health, thank you," said Jane-5, and the voice was precisely that of a woman; it was a sweet and almost disturbing contralto.

"Why did you do that, Clinton?" said Peter, startled and beginning to frown.

"Psychologically important," said Madarian. "I want people to think of her as a woman; to treat her as a woman; to *explain*."

"What people?"

Madarian put his hands in his pockets and stared thoughtfully at Bogert. "I would like to have arrangements made for Jane and myself to go to Flagstaff."

Bogert couldn't help but note that Madarian didn't say Jane-5. He made use of no number this time. She was *the* Jane. He said doubtfully, "To Flagstaff? Why?"

"Because that's the world center for general planetology, isn't it? It's where they're studying the stars and trying to calculate the probability of habitable planets, isn't it?"

"I know that, but it's on Earth."

"Well, and I surely know that."

"Robotic movements on Earth are strictly controlled. And there's no need for it. Bring a library of books on general planetology here and let Jane absorb them."

"*No!* Peter, will you get it through your head that Jane isn't the ordinary logical robot; she's intuitive."

"So?"

"So how can we tell what she needs, what she can use, what will set her off? We can use any metal model in the factory to read books; that's frozen data and out of date besides. Jane must have living information; she must have tones of voice, she must have side issues; she must have total irrelevancies even. How the devil do we know what or when something will go click-click inside her and fall into a pattern? If we knew, we wouldn't need her at all, would we?"

Bogert began to feel harassed. He said, "Then bring the men here, the general planetologists."

"Here won't be any good. They'll be out of their element. They won't react naturally. I want Jane to watch them at work; I want her to see their instruments, their offices, their desks, everything about them that she can. I want you to arrange to have her transported to Flagstaff. And I'd really like not to discuss it any further."

For a moment he almost sounded like Susan. Bogert winced, and said, "It's complicated making such an arrangement. Transporting an experimental robot—"

"Jane isn't experimental. She's the fifth of the series."

"The other four weren't really working models."

Madarian lifted his hands in helpless frustration. "Who's forcing you to tell the government that?"

"I'm not worried about the government. It can be made to understand special cases. It's public opinion. We've come a long way in fifty years and I don't propose to be set back twenty-five of them by having you lose control of a—"

"I won't lose control. You're making foolish remarks. Look! U.S. Robots can afford a private plane. We can land quietly at the nearest commercial airport and be lost in hundreds of similar landings. We can arrange to have a large ground car with an enclosed body meet us and take us to Flagstaff. Jane will be crated and it will be obvious that some piece of thoroughly non-robotic equipment is being transported to the labs. We won't get a second look from anyone. The men at Flagstaff will be alerted and will be told the exact purpose of the visit. They will have every motive to cooperate and to prevent a leak."

Bogert pondered. "The risky part will be the plane and the ground car. If anything happens to the crate—"

"Nothing will."

"We might get away with it if Jane is deactivated during transport. Then even if someone finds out she's inside—"

"No, Peter. That can't be done. Uh-uh. Not Jane-5. Look, she's been free-associating since she was activated. The information she possesses can be put into freeze during deactivation but the free associations never. No, sir, she can't ever be deactivated."

"But, then, if somehow it is discovered that we are transporting an activated robot—"

"It won't be found out."

Madarian remained firm and the plane eventually took off. It was a late-model automatic Computo-jet, but it carried a human pilot—one of U.S.Robots' own employees—as backup. The crate containing Jane arrived at the airport safely, was transferred to the ground car, and reached the Research Laboratories at Flagstaff without incident.

Peter Bogert received his first call from Madarian not more than an hour after the latter's arrival at Flagstaff. Madarian was ecstatic and, characteristically, could not wait to report.

The message arrived by tubed laser beam, shielded, scrambled, and ordinarily impenetrable, but Bogert felt exasperated. He knew it could be penetrated if someone with enough technological ability—the government, for example— was determined to do so. The only real safety lay in the fact that the government had no reason to try. At least Bogert hoped so.

He said, "For God's sake, do you have to call?"

Madarian ignored him entirely. He burbled, "It was an inspiration. Sheer genius, I tell you."

For a while, Bogert stared at the receiver. Then he shouted incredulously, "You mean you've got the answer? Already?"

"No, no! Give us time, damn it. I mean the matter of her voice was an inspiration. Listen, after we were chauffeured from the airport to the main administration building at Flagstaff, we uncrated Jane and she stepped out of the box. When that happened, every man in the place stepped back.

Scared! Nitwits! If even scientists can't understand the significance of the Laws of Robotics, what can we expect of the average untrained individual? For a minute there I thought: This will all be useless. They won't talk. They'll be keying themselves for a quick break in case she goes berserk and they'll be able to think of nothing else."

"Well, then, what are you getting at?"

"So then she greeted them routinely. She said, 'Good afternoon, gentlemen. I am so glad to meet you.' And it came out in this beautiful contralto. . . . That was it. One man straightened his tie, and another ran his fingers through his hair. What really got me was that the oldest guy in the place actually checked his fly to make sure it was zipped. They're all crazy about her now. All they needed was the voice. She isn't a robot any more; she's a girl."

"You mean they're talking to her?"

"*Are* they talking to her! I should say so. I should have programmed her for sexy intonations. They'd be asking her for dates right now if I had. Talk about conditioned reflex. Listen, men respond to voices. At the most intimate moments, are they looking? It's the voice in your ear—"

"Yes, Clinton, I seem to remember. Where's Jane now?"

"With them. They won't let go of her."

"Damn! Get in there with her. Don't let her out of your sight, man."

Madarian's calls thereafter, during his ten-day stay at Flagstaff, were not very frequent and became progressively less exalted.

Jane was listening carefully, he reported, and occasionally she responded. She remained popular. She was given entry everywhere. But there were no results.

Bogert said, "Nothing at all?"

Madarian was at once defensive. "You can't say nothing at all. It's impossible to say nothing at all with an intuitive robot. You don't know what might not be going on inside her. This morning she asked Jensen what he had for breakfast."

"Rossiter Jensen the astrophysicist?"

"Yes, of course. As it turned out, he didn't have breakfast that morning. Well, a cup of coffee."

"So Jane's learning to make small talk. That scarcely makes up for the expense—"

"Oh, don't be a jackass. It wasn't small talk. Nothing is small talk for Jane. She asked because it had something to do with some sort of cross-correlation she was building in her mind."

"What can it possibly—"

"How do I know? If I knew, I'd be a Jane myself and you wouldn't need her. But it has to mean something. She's programmed for high motivation to obtain an answer to the question of a planet with optimum habitability/distance and—"

"Then let me know when she's done that and not before. It's not really necessary for me to get a blow-by-blow description of possible correlations."

He didn't really expect to get notification of success. With each day, Bogert grew less sanguine, so that when the notification finally came, he wasn't ready. And it came at the very end.

That last time, when Madarian's climactic message came, it came in what was almost a whisper. Exaltation had come complete circle and Madarian was awed into quiet.

"She did it," he said. "She did it. After I all but gave up, too. After she had received everything in the place and most of it twice and three times over and never said a word that sounded like anything. . . . I'm on the plane now, returning. We've just taken off."

Bogert managed to get his breath. "Don't play games, man. You have the *answer*? Say so, if you have. Say it plainly."

"She has the answer. She's given me the answer. She's given me the names of three stars within eighty light-years which, she says, have a sixty to ninety percent chance of possessing one habitable planet each. The probability that at least one has is 0.972. It's almost certain. And that's just the least of it. Once we get back, she can give us the exact line of reasoning that led her to the conclusion and I predict that the whole science of astrophysics and cosmology will—"

"Are you sure—"

"You think I'm having hallucinations? I even have a witness. Poor guy jumped two feet when Jane suddenly began to reel out the answer in her gorgeous voice—"

And that was when the meteorite struck and in the thorough destruction of the plane that followed, Madarian and the pilot were reduced to gobbets of bloody flesh and no usable remnant of Jane was recovered.

The gloom at U.S. Robots had never been deeper. Robertson attempted to find consolation in the fact that the very completeness of the destruction had utterly hidden the illegalities of which the firm had been guilty.

Peter shook his head and mourned. "We've lost the best chance U.S. Robots ever had of gaining an unbeatable public image; of overcoming the damned Frankenstein complex. What it would have meant for robots to have one of them work out the solution to the habitable-planet problem, after other robots had helped work out the Space Jump. Robots would have opened the galaxy to us. And if at the same time we could have driven scientific knowledge forward in a dozen different directions as we surely would have . . . Oh, God, there's no way of calculating the benefits to the human race, and to us of course."

Robertson said, "We could build other Janes, couldn't we? Even without Madarian?"

"Sure we could. But can we depend on the proper correlation again? Who knows how low-probability that final result was? What if Madarian had had a fantastic piece of beginner's luck? And then to have an even more fantastic piece of bad luck? A meteorite zeroing in . . . It's simply unbelievable—"

Robertson said in a hesitating whisper, "It couldn't have been—meant. I mean, if we weren't meant to know and if the meteorite was a judgment—from—"

He faded off under Bogert's withering glare.

Bogert said, "It's not a dead loss, I suppose. Other Janes are bound to help us in some ways. And we can give other robots feminine voices, if that will help encourage public acceptance—though I wonder what the women would say. If we only knew what Jane-5 had said!"

"In that last call, Madarian said there was a witness."

Bogert said, "I know; I've been thinking about that. Don't you suppose I've been in touch with Flagstaff? Nobody in the entire place heard Jane say anything that was out of the ordinary, anything that sounded like an answer to the habitable-planet problem, and certainly anyone there should have recognized the answer if it came—or at least recognized it as a possible answer."

"Could Madarian have been lying? Or crazy? Could he have been trying to protect himself—"

"You mean he may have been trying to save his reputation by pretending he had the answer and then gimmick Jane so she couldn't talk and say, 'Oh, sorry, something happened accidentally. Oh, darn!' I won't accept that for a minute. You might as well suppose he had arranged the meteorite."

"Then what do we do?"

Bogert said heavily, "Turn back to Flagstaff. The answer *must* be there. I've got to dig deeper, that's all. I'm going there and I'm taking a couple of the men in Madarian's department. We've got to go through that place top to bottom and end to end."

"But, you know, even if there were a witness and he had heard, what good would it do, now that we don't have Jane to explain the process?"

"Every little something is useful. Jane gave the names of the stars; the catalogue numbers probably—none of the named stars has a chance. If someone can remember her saying that and actually remember the catalogue number, or have heard it clearly enough to allow it to be recovered by Psycho-probe if he lacked the conscious memory—then we'll have something. Given the results at the end, and the data fed Jane at the beginning, we might be able to reconstruct the line of reasoning; we might recover the intuition. If that is done, we've saved the game—"

Bogert was back after three days, silent and thoroughly depressed. When Robertson inquired anxiously as to results, he shook his head. "Nothing!"

"Nothing?"

"Absolutely nothing. I spoke with every man in Flagstaff— every scientist, every technician, every student—that had had anything to do with Jane; everyone that had as much as seen her. The number wasn't great; I'll give Madarian credit for that much discretion. He only allowed those to see her who might conceivably have had planetological knowledge to feed her. There were twenty-three men altogether who had seen Jane and of those only twelve had spoken to her more than casually.

"I went over and over all that Jane had said. They remembered everything quite well. They're keen men engaged in a crucial experiment involving their specialty, so they had every motivation to remember. And they were dealing with a talking robot, something that was startling enough, and one that talked like a TV actress. They couldn't forget."

Robertson said, "Maybe a Psycho-probe—"

"If one of them had the vaguest thought that something had happened, I would screw out his consent to Probing. But there's nothing to leave room for an excuse, and to Probe two dozen men who make their living from their brains can't be done. Honestly, it wouldn't help. If Jane had mentioned three stars and said they had habitable planets, it would have been like setting up sky rockets in their brains. How could any one of them forget?"

"Then maybe one of them is lying," said Robertson grimly. "He wants the information for his own use; to get the credit himself later."

"What good would that do him?" said Bogert. "The whole establishment knows exactly why Madarian and Jane were there in the first place. They know why I came there in the second. If at any time in the future any man now at Flagstaff suddenly comes up with a habitable-planet theory that is startlingly new and different, yet valid, every other man at Flagstaff and every man at U.S. Robots will know at once that he had stolen it. He'd never get away with it."

"Then Madarian himself was somehow mistaken."

"I don't see how I can believe that either. Madarian had an irritating personality—all robopsychologists have irritating personalities, I think, which must be why they work with robots rather than with men—but he was no dummy. He *couldn't* be wrong in something like this."

"Then—" But Robertson had run out of possibilities. They had reached a blank wall and for some minutes each stared at it disconsolately.

Finally Robertson stirred. "Peter—"

"Well?"

"Let's ask Susan."

Bogert stiffened. "What!"

"Let's ask Susan. Let's call her and ask her to come in."

"Why? What can she possibly do?"

"I don't know. But she's a robopsychologist, too, and she might understand Madarian better than we do. Besides, she— Oh, hell, she always had more brains than any of us."

"She's nearly eighty."

"And you're seventy. What about it?"

Bogert sighed. Had her abrasive tongue lost any of its rasp in the years of her retirement? He said, "Well, I'll ask her."

Susan Calvin entered Bogert's office with a slow look around before her eyes fixed themselves on the Research Director. She had aged a great deal since her retirement. Her hair was a fine white and her face seemed to have crumpled. She had grown so frail as to be almost transparent and only her eyes, piercing and uncompromising, seemed to remain of all that had been.

Bogert strode forward heartily, holding out his hand. "Susan!"

Susan Calvin took it, and said, "You're looking reasonably well, Peter, for an old man. If I were you, I wouldn't wait till next year. Retire now and let the young men get to it. . . . And Madarian is dead. Are you calling me in to take over my old job? Are you determined to keep the ancients till a year past actual physical death?"

"No, no, Susan. I've called you in—" He stopped. He did not, after all, have the faintest idea of how to start.

But Susan read his mind now as easily as she always had. She seated herself with the caution born of stiffened joints and said, "Peter, you've called me in because you're in bad trouble. Otherwise you'd sooner see me dead than within a mile of you."

"Come, Susan—"

"Don't waste time on pretty talk. I never had time to waste when I was forty and certainly not now. Madarian's death and your call to me are both unusual, so there must be a connection. Two unusual events without a connection is too low-probability to worry about. Begin at the beginning and don't worry about revealing yourself to be a fool. That was revealed to me long ago."

Bogert cleared his throat miserably and began. She listened carefully, her withered hand lifting once in a while to stop him so that she might ask a question.

She snorted at one point. "Feminine intuition? Is that what you wanted the robot for? You men. Faced with a woman reaching a correct conclusion and unable to accept the fact that she is your equal or superior in intelligence, you invent something called feminine intuition."

"Uh, yes, Susan, but let me continue—"

He did. When she was told of Jane's contralto voice, she said, "It is a difficult choice sometimes whether to feel revolted at the male sex or merely to dismiss them as contemptible."

Bogert said, "Well, let me go on—"

When he was quite done, Susan said, "May I have the private use of this office for an hour or two?"

"Yes, but—"

She said, "I want to go over the various records—Jane's programming, Madarian's calls, your interviews at Flagstaff. I presume I can use that beautiful new shielded laser-phone and your computer outlet if I wish."

"Yes, of course."

"Well, then, get out of here, Peter."

It was not quite forty-five minutes when she hobbled to the door, opened it, and called for Bogert.

When Bogert came, Robertson was with him. Both entered and Susan greeted the latter with an unenthusiastic "Hello, Scott."

Bogert tried desperately to gauge the results from Susan's face, but it was only the face of a grim old lady who had no intention of making anything easy for him.

He said cautiously, "Do you think there's anything you can do, Susan?"

"Beyond what I have already done? No! There's nothing more."

Bogert's lips set in chagrin, but Robertson said, "What have you already done, Susan?"

Susan said, "I've thought a little; something I can't seem to persuade anyone else to do. For one thing, I've thought about Madarian. I knew him, you know. He had brains but he was a very irritating extrovert. I thought you would like him after me, Peter."

"It was a change," Bogert couldn't resist saying.

"And he was always running to you with results the very minute he had them, wasn't he?"

"Yes, he was."

"And yet," said Susan, "his last message, the one in which he said Jane had given him the answer, was sent from the plane. Why did he wait so long? Why didn't he call you while he was still at Flagstaff, immediately after Jane had said whatever it was she said?"

"I suppose," said Peter, "that for once he wanted to check it thoroughly and—well, I don't know. It was the most important thing that had ever happened to him; he might for once have wanted to wait and be sure of himself."

"On the contrary; the more important it was, the less he would wait, surely. And if he could manage to wait, why not do it properly and wait till he was back at U.S. Robots so that he could check the results with all the computing equipment this firm could make available to him? In short, he waited too long from one point of view and not long enough from another."

Robertson interrupted. "Then you think he was up to some trickery—"

Susan looked revolted. "Scott, don't try to compete with Peter in making inane remarks. Let me continue. . . . A second point concerns the witness. According to the records of that last call, Madarian said, 'Poor guy jumped two feet when Jane suddenly began to reel out the answer in her gorgeous voice.' In fact, it was the last thing he said. And the question is, then, why should the witness have jumped? Madarian had explained that all the men were crazy about that voice, and they had had ten days with the robot—with Jane. Why should the mere act of her speaking have startled them?"

Bogert said, "I assumed it was astonishment at hearing Jane give an answer to a problem that has occupied the minds of planetologists for nearly a century."

"But they were *waiting* for her to give that answer. That was why she was there. Besides, consider the way the sentence is worded. Madarian's statement makes it seem the witness was startled, not astonished, if you see the difference. What's more, that reaction came 'when Jane suddenly began'—in other words, at the very start of the statement. To be astonished at the content of what Jane said would have required the witness to have listened awhile so that he might absorb it. Madarian would have said he had jumped two feet *after* he had heard Jane say thus-and-so. It would be 'after' not 'when' and the word 'suddenly' would not be included."

Bogert said uneasily, "I don't think you can refine matters down to the use or non-use of a word."

"I can," said Susan frostily, "because I am a robopsychologist. And I can expect Madarian to do so, too, because *he* was a robopsychologist. We have to explain those two anomalies, then. The queer delay before Madarian's call and the queer reaction of the witness."

"Can *you* explain them?" asked Robertson.

"Of course," said Susan, "since I use a little simple logic. Madarian called with the news without delay, as he always did, or with as little delay as he could manage. If Jane had solved the problem at Flagstaff, he would certainly have called from Flagstaff. Since he called from the plane, she must clearly have solved the problem after he had left Flagstaff."

"But then—"

"Let me finish. Let me finish. Was Madarian not taken from the airport to Flagstaff in a heavy, enclosed ground car? And Jane, in her crate, with him?"

"Yes."

"And presumably, Madarian and the crated Jane returned from Flagstaff to the airport in the same heavy, enclosed ground car. Am I right?"

"Yes, of course!"

"And they were not alone in the ground car, either. In one of his calls, Madarian said, 'We were chauffeured from the airport to the main administration building,' and I suppose I am right in concluding that if he was chauffeured, then that was because there was a chauffeur, a human driver, in the car."

"Good God!"

"The trouble with you, Peter, is that when you think of a witness to a planetological statement, you think of planetologists. You divide up human beings into categories, and despise and dismiss most. A robot cannot do that. The First Law says, 'A robot may not injure a *human being* or, through inaction, allow a *human being* to come to harm.' *Any* human being. That is the essence of the robotic view of life. A robot makes no distinction. To a robot, all men are truly equal, and to a robopsychologist who must perforce deal with men at the robotic level, all men are truly equal, too.

"It would not occur to Madarian to say a truck driver had heard the statement. To you a truck driver is not a scientist but is a mere animate adjunct of a truck, but to Madarian he was a man and a witness. Nothing more. Nothing less."

Bogert shook his head in disbelief, "But you are *sure*?"

"Of course I'm sure. How else can you explain the other point; Madarian's remark about the startling of the witness? Jane was crated, wasn't she? But she was *not* deactivated. According to the records, Madarian was always adamant against ever deactivating an intuitive robot. Moreover, Jane-5, like any of the Janes, was extremely non-talkative. Probably it never occurred to Madarian to order her to remain quiet within the crate; and it was within the crate that the pattern finally fell into place. Naturally she began to talk. A beautiful contralto voice suddenly sounded from inside the crate. If you were the truck driver, what would you do at that point? Surely you'd be startled. It's a wonder he didn't crash."

"But if the truck driver was the witness, why didn't he come forward—"

"Why? Can he possibly know that anything crucial had happened, that what he heard was important? Besides, don't you suppose Madarian tipped him well and asked him not to say anything? Would you *want* the news to spread that an activated robot was being transported illegally over the Earth's surface."

"Well, will he remember what was said?"

"Why not? It might seem to you, Peter, that a truck driver, one step above an ape in your view, can't remember. But truck drivers can have brains, too. The statements were most remarkable and the driver may well have remembered some. Even if he gets some of the letters and numbers wrong, we're dealing with a finite set, you know, the fifty-five hundred stars or star systems within eighty light-years or so—I haven't looked up the exact number. You can make the correct choices. And if needed, you will have every excuse to use the Psycho-probe—"

The two men stared at her. Finally Bogert, afraid to believe, whispered, "But how can you be *sure*?"

For a moment, Susan was on the point of saying: Because I've called Flagstaff, you fool, and because I spoke to the truck driver, and because he told me what he had heard, and because I've checked with the computer at Flagstaff and got the only three stars that fit the information, and because I have those names in my pocket.

But she didn't. Let him go through it all himself. Carefully, she rose to her feet, and said sardonically, "How can I be sure? . . . Call it feminine intuition."

THE
BICENTENNIAL
MAN

•

1.

Andrew Martin said, "Thank you," and took the seat offered him. He didn't look driven to the last resort, but he had been.

He didn't, actually, look anything, for there was a smooth blankness to his face, except for the sadness one imagined one saw in his eyes. His hair was smooth, light brown, rather fine, and there was no facial hair. He looked freshly and cleanly shaved. His clothes were distinctly old-fashioned, but neat and predominantly a velvety red-purple in color.

Facing him from behind the desk was the surgeon, and the nameplate on the desk included a fully identifying series of letters and numbers, which Andrew didn't bother with. To call him Doctor would be quite enough.

"When can the operation be carried through, Doctor?" he asked.

The surgeon said softly, with that certain inalienable note of respect that a robot always used to a human being, "I am not certain, sir, that I understand how or upon whom such an operation could be performed."

There might have been a look of respectful intransigence on the surgeon's face, if a robot of his sort, in lightly bronzed stainless steel, could have such an expression, or any expression.

Andrew Martin studied the robot's right hand, his cutting hand, as it lay on the desk in utter tranquillity. The fingers were long and shaped into artistically metallic looping curves so graceful and appropriate that one could imagine a scalpel fitting them and becoming, temporarily, one piece with them.

There would be no hesitation in his work, no stumbling, no quivering, no mistakes. That came with specialization, of course, a specialization so fiercely desired by humanity that few robots were, any longer, independently brained. A surgeon, of course, would have to be. And this one, though brained, was so limited in his capacity that he did not recognize Andrew—had probably never heard of him.

Andrew said, "Have you ever thought you would like to be a man?"

The surgeon hesitated a moment as though the question fitted nowhere in his allotted positronic pathways. "But I am a robot, sir."

"Would it be better to be a man?"

"It would be better, sir, to be a better surgeon. I could not be so if I were a man, but only if I were a more advanced robot. I would be pleased to be a more advanced robot."

"It does not offend you that I can order you about? That I can make you stand up, sit down, move right or left, by merely telling you to do so?"

"It is my pleasure to please you, sir. If your orders were to interfere with my functioning with respect to you or to any other human being, I would not obey you. The First Law, concerning my duty to human safety, would take precedence over the Second Law relating to obedience. Otherwise, obedience is my pleasure. . . . But upon whom am I to perform this operation?"

"Upon me," said Andrew.

"But that is impossible. It is patently a damaging operation."

"That does not matter," said Andrew calmly.

"I must not inflict damage," said the surgeon.

"On a human being, you must not," said Andrew, "but I, too, am a robot."

2.

Andrew had appeared much more a robot when he had first been—manufactured. He had then been as much a robot in appearance as any that had ever existed, smoothly designed and functional.

He had done well in the home to which he had been brought in those days when robots in households, or on the planet altogether, had been a rarity.

There had been four in the home: Sir and Ma'am and Miss and Little Miss. He knew their names, of course, but he never used them. Sir was Gerald Martin.

His own serial number was NDR— He forgot the numbers. It had been a long time, of course, but if he had wanted to remember, he could not forget. He had not wanted to remember.

Little Miss had been the first to call him Andrew because she could not use the letters, and all the rest followed her in this.

Little Miss— She had lived ninety years and was long since dead. He had tried to call her Ma'am once, but she would not allow it. Little Miss she had been to her last day.

Andrew had been intended to perform the duties of a valet, a butler, a lady's maid. Those were the experimental days for him and, indeed, for all robots anywhere but in the industrial and exploratory factories and stations off Earth.

The Martins enjoyed him, and half the time he was prevented from doing his work because Miss and Little Miss would rather play with him.

It was Miss who understood first how this might be arranged. She said, "We order you to play with us and you must follow orders."

Andrew said, "I am sorry, Miss, but a prior order from Sir must surely take precedence."

But she said, "Daddy just said he hoped you would take care of the cleaning. That's not much of an order. I *order* you."

Sir did not mind. Sir was fond of Miss and of Little Miss, even more than Ma'am was, and Andrew was fond of them, too. At least, the effect they had upon his actions were those which in a human being would have been called the result of fondness. Andrew thought of it as fondness, for he did not know any other word for it.

It was for Little Miss that Andrew had carved a pendant out of wood. She had ordered him to. Miss, it seemed, had received an ivorite pendant with scrollwork for her birthday and Little Miss was unhappy over it. She had only a piece of wood, which she gave Andrew together with a small kitchen knife.

He had done it quickly and Little Miss said, "That's *nice*, Andrew. I'll show it to Daddy."

Sir would not believe it. "Where did you really get this, Mandy?" Mandy was what he called Little Miss. When Little Miss assured him she was really telling the truth, he turned to Andrew. "Did you do this, Andrew?"

"Yes, Sir."

"The design, too?"

"Yes, Sir."

"From what did you copy the design?"

"It is a geometric representation, Sir, that fit the grain of the wood."

The next day, Sir brought him another piece of wood, a larger one, and an electric vibro-knife. He said, "Make something out of this, Andrew. Anything you want to."

Andrew did so and Sir watched, then looked at the product a long time. After that, Andrew no longer waited on tables. He was ordered to read books on furniture design instead, and he learned to make cabinets and desks.

Sir said, "These are amazing productions, Andrew."

Andrew said, "I enjoy doing them, Sir."

"Enjoy?"

"It makes the circuits of my brain somehow flow more easily. I have heard you use the word 'enjoy' and the way you use it fits the way I feel. I enjoy doing them, Sir."

3.

Gerald Martin took Andrew to the regional offices of United States Robots and Mechanical Men Corporation. As a member of the Regional Legislature he had no trouble at all in gaining an interview with the Chief Robopsychologist. In fact, it was only as a member of the Regional Legislature that he qualified as a robot owner in the first place—in those early days when robots were rare.

Andrew did not understand any of this at the time, but in later years, with greater learning, he could re-view that early scene and understand it in its proper light.

The robopsychologist, Merton Mansky, listened with a gathering frown and more than once managed to stop his fingers at the point beyond which they would have irrevocably drummed on the table. He had drawn features and a lined forehead and looked as though he might be younger than he looked.

He said, "Robotics is not an exact art, Mr. Martin. I cannot explain it to you in detail, but the mathematics governing the plotting of the positronic pathways is far too complicated to permit any but approximate solutions. Naturally, since we build everything about the Three Laws, those are incontrovertible. We will, of course, replace your robot—"

"Not at all," said Sir. "There is no question of failure on his part. He performs his assigned duties perfectly. The point is, he also carves wood in exquisite fashion and never the same twice. He produces works of art."

Mansky looked confused. "Strange. Of course, we're attempting generalized pathways these days. . . . Really creative, you think?"

"See for yourself." Sir handed over a little sphere of wood on which there was a playground scene in which the boys and girls were almost too small to make out, yet they were in perfect proportion and blended so naturally with the grain that that, too, seemed to have been carved.

Mansky said, "*He* did that?" He handed it back with a shake of his head. "The luck of the draw. Something in the pathways."

"Can you do it again?"

"Probably not. Nothing like this has ever been reported."

"Good! I don't in the least mind Andrew's being the only one."

Mansky said, "I suspect that the company would like to have your robot back for study."

Sir said with sudden grimness, "'Not a chance. Forget it." He turned to Andrew, "Let's go home now."

"As you wish, Sir," said Andrew.

4.

Miss was dating boys and wasn't about the house much. It was Little Miss, not as little as she was, who filled Andrew's horizon now. She never forgot that the very first piece of wood carving he had done had been for her. She kept it on a silver chain about her neck.

It was she who first objected to Sir's habit of giving away the productions. She said, "Come on, Dad, if anyone wants one of them, let him pay for it. It's worth it."

Sir said, "It isn't like you to be greedy, Mandy."

"Not for us, Dad. For the artist."

Andrew had never heard the word before and when he

had a moment to himself he looked it up in the dictionary. Then there was another trip, this time to Sir's lawyer.

Sir said to him, "What do you think of this, John?"

The lawyer was John Feingold. He had white hair and a pudgy belly, and the rims of his contact lenses were tinted a bright green. He looked at the small plaque Sir had given him. "This is beautiful. . . . But I've heard the news. This is a carving made by your robot. The one you've brought with you."

"Yes, Andrew does them. Don't you, Andrew?"

"Yes, Sir," said Andrew.

"How much would you pay for that, John?" asked Sir.

"I can't say. I'm not a collector of such things."

"Would you believe I have been offered two hundred and fifty dollars for that small thing? Andrew has made chairs that have sold for five hundred dollars. There's two hundred thousand dollars in the bank out of Andrew's products."

"Good heavens, he's making you rich, Gerald."

"Half rich," said Sir. "Half of it is in an account in the name of Andrew Martin."

"The robot?"

"That's right, and I want to know if it's legal."

"Legal?" Feingold's chair creaked as he leaned back in it. "There are no precedents, Gerald. How did your robot sign the necessary papers?"

"He can sign his name and I brought in the signature. I didn't bring him in to the bank himself. Is there anything further that ought to be done?"

"Um." Feingold's eyes seemed to turn inward for a moment. Then he said, "Well, we can set up a trust to handle all finances in his name and that will place a layer of insulation between him and the hostile world. Further than that, my advice is that you do nothing. No one is stopping you so far. If anyone objects, let *him* bring suit."

"And will you take the case if suit is brought?"

"For a retainer, certainly."

"How much?"

"Something like that," and Feingold pointed to the wooden plaque.

"Fair enough," said Sir.

Feingold chuckled as he turned to the robot. "Andrew, are you pleased that you have money?"

"Yes, sir."

"What do you plan to do with it?"

"Pay for things, sir, which otherwise Sir would have to pay for. It would save him expense, sir."

5.

The occasions came. Repairs were expensive, and revisions were even more so. With the years, new models of robots were produced and Sir saw to it that Andrew had the advantage of every new device until he was a paragon of metallic excellence. It was all at Andrew's expense.

Andrew insisted on that.

Only his positronic pathways were untouched. Sir insisted on that.

"The new ones aren't as good as you are, Andrew," he said. "The new robots are worthless. The company has learned to make the pathways more precise, more closely on the nose, more deeply on the track. The new robots don't shift. They do what they're designed for and never stray. I like you better."

"Thank you, Sir."

"And it's your doing, Andrew, don't you forget that. I am certain Mansky put an end to generalized pathways as soon as he had a good look at you. He didn't like the unpredictability. . . . Do you know how many times he asked for you so he could place you under study? Nine times! I never let him have you, though, and now that he's retired, we may have some peace."

So Sir's hair thinned and grayed and his face grew pouchy,

while Andrew looked rather better than he had when he first joined the family.

Ma'am had joined an art colony somewhere in Europe and Miss was a poet in New York. They wrote sometimes, but not often. Little Miss was married and lived not far away. She said she did not want to leave Andrew and when her child, Little Sir, was born, she let Andrew hold the bottle and feed him.

With the birth of a grandson, Andrew felt that Sir had someone now to replace those who had gone. It would not be so unfair to come to him with the request.

Andrew said, "Sir, it is kind of you to have allowed me to spend my money as I wished."

"It was your money, Andrew."

"Only by your voluntary act, Sir. I do not believe the law would have stopped you from keeping it all."

"The law won't persuade me to do wrong, Andrew."

"Despite all expenses, and despite taxes, too, Sir, I have nearly six hundred thousand dollars."

"I know that, Andrew."

"I want to give it to you, Sir."

"I won't take it, Andrew."

"In exchange for something you can give me, Sir."

"Oh? What is that, Andrew?"

"My freedom, Sir."

"Your—"

"I wish to buy my freedom, Sir."

6.

It wasn't that easy. Sir had flushed, had said "For God's sake!" had turned on his heel, and stalked away.

It was Little Miss who brought him around, defiantly and harshly—and in front of Andrew. For thirty years, no one had hesitated to talk in front of Andrew, whether the matter involved Andrew or not. He was only a robot.

She said, "Dad, why are you taking it as a personal affront? He'll still be here. He'll still be loyal. He can't help that. It's built in. All he wants is a form of words. He wants to be called free. Is that so terrible? Hasn't he earned it? Heavens, he and I have been talking about it for years."

"Talking about it for years, have you?"

"Yes, and over and over again, he postponed it for fear he would hurt you. I *made* him put it up to you."

"He doesn't know what freedom is. He's a robot."

"Dad, you don't know him. He's read everything in the library. I don't know what he feels inside but I don't know what *you* feel inside. When you talk to him you'll find he reacts to the various abstractions as you and I do, and what else counts? If someone else's reactions are like your own, what more can you ask for?"

"The law won't take that attitude," Sir said angrily. "See here, you!" He turned to Andrew with a deliberate grate in his voice. "I can't free you except by doing it legally, and if it gets into the courts, you not only won't get your freedom but the law will take official cognizance of your money. They'll tell you that a robot has no right to earn money. Is this rigmarole worth losing your money?"

"Freedom is without a price, Sir," said Andrew. "Even the chance of freedom is worth the money."

7.

The court might also take the attitude that freedom was without price, and might decide that for no price, however great, could a robot buy its freedom.

The simple statement of the regional attorney who represented those who had brought a class action to oppose the freedom was this: The word "freedom" had no meaning when applied to a robot. Only a human being could be free.

He said it several times, when it seemed appropriate;

slowly, with his hand coming down rhythmically on the desk before him to mark the words.

Little Miss asked permission to speak on behalf of Andrew. She was recognized by her full name, something Andrew had never heard pronounced before:

"Amanda Laura Martin Charney may approach the bench."

She said, "Thank you, your honor. I am not a lawyer and I don't know the proper way of phrasing things, but I hope you will listen to my meaning and ignore the words.

"Let's understand what it means to be free in Andrew's case. In some ways, he *is* free. I think it's at least twenty years since anyone in the Martin family gave him an order to do something that we felt he might not do of his own accord.

"But we can, if we wish, give him an order to do anything, couch it as harshly as we wish, because he is a machine that belongs to us. Why should we be in a position to do so, when he has served us so long, so faithfully, and earned so much money for us? He owes us nothing more. The debt is entirely on the other side.

"Even if we were legally forbidden to place Andrew in involuntary servitude, he would still serve us voluntarily. Making him free would be a trick of words only, but it would mean much to him. It would give him everything and cost us nothing."

For a moment the Judge seemed to be suppressing a smile. "I see your point, Mrs. Charney. The fact is that there is no binding law in this respect and no precedent. There is, however, the unspoken assumption that only a man can enjoy freedom. I can make new law here, subject to reversal in a higher court, but I cannot lightly run counter to that assumption. Let me address the robot. Andrew!"

"Yes, your honor."

It was the first time Andrew had spoken in court and the Judge seemed astonished for a moment at the human timbre of the voice. He said, "Why do you want to be free, Andrew? In what way will this matter to you?"

Andrew said, "Would you wish to be a slave, your honor?"

"But you are not a slave. You are a perfectly good robot, a genius of a robot I am given to understand, capable of an artistic expression that can be matched nowhere. What more can you do if you were free?"

"Perhaps no more than I do now, your honor, but with greater joy. It has been said in this courtroom that only a human being can be free. It seems to me that only someone who wishes for freedom can be free. I wish for freedom."

And it was that that cued the Judge. The crucial sentence in his decision was: "There is no right to deny freedom to any object with a mind advanced enough to grasp the concept and desire the state."

It was eventually upheld by the World Court.

8.

Sir remained displeased and his harsh voice made Andrew feel almost as though he were being short-circuited.

Sir said, "I don't want your damned money, Andrew. I'll take it only because you won't feel free otherwise. From now on, you can select your own jobs and do them as you please. I will give you no orders, except this one—that you do as you please. But I am still responsible for you; that's part of the court order. I hope you understand that."

Little Miss interrupted. "Don't be irascible, Dad. The responsibility is no great chore. You know you won't have to do a thing. The Three Laws still hold."

"Then how is he free?"

Andrew said, "Are not human beings bound by their laws, Sir?"

Sir said, "I'm not going to argue." He left, and Andrew saw him only infrequently after that.

Little Miss came to see him frequently in the small house that had been built and made over for him. It had no kitchen, of course, nor bathroom facilities. It had just two rooms; one was a library and one was a combination storeroom and workroom. Andrew accepted many commissions and worked harder as a free robot than he ever had before, till the cost of the house was paid for and the structure legally transferred to him.

One day Little Sir came. . . . No, George! Little Sir had insisted on that after the court decision. "A free robot doesn't call anyone Little Sir," George had said. "I call you Andrew. You must call me George."

It was phrased as an order, so Andrew called him George—but Little Miss remained Little Miss.

The day George came alone, it was to say that Sir was dying. Little Miss was at the bedside but Sir wanted Andrew as well.

Sir's voice was quite strong, though he seemed unable to move much. He struggled to get his hand up. "Andrew," he said, "Andrew— Don't help me, George. I'm only dying; I'm not crippled. . . . Andrew, I'm glad you're free. I just wanted to tell you that."

Andrew did not know what to say. He had never been at the side of someone dying before, but he knew it was the human way of ceasing to function. It was an involuntary and irreversible dismantling, and Andrew did not know what to say that might be appropriate. He could only remain standing, absolutely silent, absolutely motionless.

When it was over, Little Miss said to him, "He may not have seemed friendly to you toward the end, Andrew, but he was old, you know, and it hurt him that you should want to be free."

And then Andrew found the words to say. He said, "I would never have been free without him, Little Miss."

9.

It was only after Sir's death that Andrew began to wear clothes. He began with an old pair of trousers at first, a pair that George had given him.

George was married now, and a lawyer. He had joined Feingold's firm. Old Feingold was long since dead but his daughter had carried on and eventually the firm's name became Feingold and Charney. It remained so even when the daughter retired and no Feingold took her place. At the time Andrew put on clothes for the first time, the Charney name had just been added to the firm.

George had tried not to smile, the first time Andrew put on the trousers, but to Andrew's eyes the smile was clearly there.

George showed Andrew how to manipulate the static charge so as to allow the trousers to open, wrap about his lower body, and move shut. George demonstrated on his own trousers, but Andrew was quite aware that it would take him awhile to duplicate that one flowing motion.

George said, "But why do you want trousers, Andrew? Your body is so beautifully functional it's a shame to cover it—especially when you needn't worry about either temperature control or modesty. And it doesn't cling properly, not on metal."

Andrew said, "Are not human bodies beautifully functional, George? Yet you cover yourselves."

"For warmth, for cleanliness, for protection, for decorativeness. None of that applies to you."

Andrew said, "I feel bare without clothes. I feel different, George."

"Different! Andrew, there are millions of robots on Earth now. In this region, according to the last census, there are almost as many robots as there are men."

"I know, George. There are robots doing every conceivable type of work."

"And none of them wear clothes."

"But none of them are free, George."

Little by little, Andrew added to the wardrobe. He was inhibited by George's smile and by the stares of the people who commissioned work.

He might be free, but there was built into him a carefully detailed program concerning his behavior toward people, and it was only by the tiniest steps that he dared advance. Open disapproval would set him back months.

Not everyone accepted Andrew as free. He was incapable of resenting that and yet there was a difficulty about his thinking process when he thought of it.

Most of all, he tended to avoid putting on clothes—or too many of them—when he thought Little Miss might come to visit him. She was old now and was often away in some warmer climate, but when she returned the first thing she did was visit him.

On one of her returns, George said ruefully, "She's got me, Andrew, I'll be running for the Legislature next year. Like grandfather, she says, like grandson."

"Like grandfather—" Andrew stopped, uncertain.

"I mean that I, George, the grandson, will be like Sir, the grandfather, who was in the Legislature once."

Andrew said, "It would be pleasant, George, if Sir were still— " He paused, for he did not want to say, "in working order." That seemed inappropriate.

"Alive," said George. "Yes, I think of the old monster now and then, too."

It was a conversation Andrew thought about. He had noticed his own incapacity in speech when talking with George. Somehow the language had changed since Andrew had come into being with an innate vocabulary. Then, too, George used a colloquial speech, as Sir and Little Miss had not. Why should he have called Sir a monster when surely that word was not appropriate?

Nor could Andrew turn to his own books for guidance. They were old and most dealt with woodworking, with art, with furniture design. There were none on language, none on the way of human beings.

It was at that moment it seemed to him that he must seek the proper books; and as a free robot, he felt he must not ask George. He would go to town and use the library. It was a triumphant decision and he felt his electropotential grow distinctly higher until he had to throw in an impedance coil.

He put on a full costume, even including a shoulder chain

of wood. He would have preferred the glitter plastic but George had said that wood was much more appropriate and that polished cedar was considerably more valuable as well.

He had placed a hundred feet between himself and the house before gathering resistance brought him to a halt. He shifted the impedance coil out of circuit, and when that did not seem to help enough, he returned to his home and on a piece of notepaper wrote neatly, "I have gone to the library," and placed it in clear view on his worktable.

10.

Andrew never quite got to the library. He had studied the map. He knew the route, but not the appearance of it. The actual landmarks did not resemble the symbols on the map and he would hesitate. Eventually he thought he must have somehow gone wrong, for everything looked strange.

He passed an occasional field robot, but at the time he decided he should ask his way, there were none in sight. A vehicle passed and did not stop. He stood irresolute, which meant calmly motionless, and then coming across the field toward him were two human beings.

He turned to face them, and they altered their course to meet him. A moment before, they had been talking loudly; he had heard their voices; but now they were silent. They had the look that Andrew associated with human uncertainty, and they were young, but not very young. Twenty perhaps? Andrew could never judge human age.

He said, "Would you describe to me the route to the town library, sirs?"

One of them, the taller of the two, whose tall hat lengthened him still farther, almost grotesquely, said, not to Andrew, but to the other, "It's a robot."

The other had a bulbous nose and heavy eyelids. He said, not to Andrew, but to the first, "It's wearing clothes."

The tall one snapped his fingers. "It's the free robot.

They have a robot at the Charney's who isn't owned by anybody. Why else would it be wearing clothes?"

"Ask it," said the one with the nose.

"Are you the Charney robot?" asked the tall one.

"I am Andrew Martin, sir," said Andrew.

"Good. Take off your clothes. Robots don't wear clothes." He said to the other, "That's disgusting. Look at him."

Andrew hesitated. He hadn't heard an order in that tone of voice in so long that his Second Law circuits had momentarily jammed.

The tall one said, "Take off your clothes. I order you."

Slowly, Andrew began to remove them.

"Just drop them," said the tall one.

The nose said, "If it doesn't belong to anyone, he could be ours as much as someone else's."

"Anyway," said the tall one, "who's to object to anything we do? We're not damaging property. . . . Stand on your head." That was to Andrew.

"The head is not meant—" began Andrew.

"That's an order. If you don't know how, try anyway."

Andrew hesitated again, then bent to put his head on the ground. He tried to lift his legs and fell, heavily.

The tall one said, "Just lie there." He said to the other, "We can take him apart. Ever take a robot apart?"

"Will he let us?"

"How can he stop us?"

There was no way Andrew could stop them, if they ordered him not to resist in a forceful enough manner. Second Law of obedience took precedence over the Third Law of self-preservation. In any case, he could not defend himself without possibly hurting them and that would mean breaking the First Law. At that thought, every motile unit contracted slightly and he quivered as he lay there.

The tall one walked over and pushed at him with his foot. "He's heavy. I think we'll need tools to do the job."

The nose said, "We could order him to take himself apart. It would be fun to watch him try."

"Yes," said the tall one thoughtfully, "but let's get him off the road. If someone comes along—"

It was too late. Someone had indeed come along and it was George. From where he lay, Andrew had seen him topping a small rise in the middle distance. He would have liked to signal him in some way, but the last order had been "Just lie there!"

George was running now and he arrived somewhat winded. The two young men stepped back a little and then waited thoughtfully.

George said anxiously, "Andrew, has something gone wrong?"

Andrew said, "I am well, George."

"Then stand up. . . . What happened to your clothes?"

The tall young man said, "That your robot, Mac?"

George turned sharply. "He's no one's robot. What's been going on here?"

"We politely asked him to take his clothes off. What's that to you if you don't own him?"

George said, "What were they doing, Andrew?"

Andrew said, "It was their intention in some way to dismember me. They were about to move me to a quiet spot and order me to dismember myself."

George looked at the two and his chin trembled. The two young men retreated no further. They were smiling. The tall one said lightly, "What are you going to do, pudgy? Attack us?"

George said, "No. I don't have to. This robot has been with my family for over seventy years. He knows us and he values us more than he values anyone else. I am going to tell him that you two are threatening my life and that you plan to kill me. I will ask him to defend me. In choosing between me and you two, he will choose me. Do you know what will happen to you when he attacks you?"

The two were backing away slightly, looking uneasy.

George said sharply, "Andrew, I am in danger and about to come to harm from these young men. Move toward them!"

Andrew did so, and the two young men did not wait. They ran fleetly.

"All right, Andrew, relax," said George. He looked unstrung. He was far past the age where he could face the possibility of a dustup with one young man, let alone two.

Andrew said, "I couldn't have hurt them, George. I could see they were not attacking you."

"I didn't order you to attack them; I only told you to move toward them. Their own fears did the rest."

"How can they fear robots?"

"It's a disease of mankind, one of which it is not yet cured. But never mind that. What the devil are you doing here, Andrew? I was on the point of turning back and hiring a helicopter when I found you. How did you get it into your head to go to the library? I would have brought you any books you needed."

"I am a—" began Andrew.

"Free robot. Yes, yes. All right, what did you want in the library?"

"I want to know more about human beings, about the world, about everything. And about robots, George. I want to write a history about robots."

George said, "Well, let's walk home. . . . And pick up your clothes first. Andrew, there are a million books on robotics and all of them include histories of the science. The world is growing saturated not only with robots but with information about robots."

Andrew shook his head, a human gesture he had lately begun to make. "Not a history of robotics, George. A history of *robots*, by a robot. I want to explain how robots feel about what has happened since the first ones were allowed to work and live on Earth."

George's eyebrows lifted, but he said nothing in direct response.

11.

Little Miss was just past her eighty-third birthday, but there was nothing about her that was lacking in either energy or determination. She gestured with her cane oftener than she propped herself up with it.

She listened to the story in a fury of indignation. She said, "George, that's horrible. Who were those young ruffians?"

"I don't know. What difference does it make? In the end they did no damage."

"They might have. You're a lawyer, George, and if you're well off, it's entirely due to the talent of Andrew. It was the money *he* earned that is the foundation of everything we have. He provides the continuity for this family and I will *not* have him treated as a wind-up toy."

"What would you have me do, Mother?" asked George.

"I said you're a lawyer. Don't you listen? You set up a test case somehow, and you force the regional courts to declare for robot rights and get the Legislature to pass the necessary bills, and carry the whole thing to the World Court, if you have to. I'll be watching, George, and I'll tolerate no shirking."

She was serious, and what began as a way of soothing the fearsome old lady became an involved matter with enough legal entanglement to make it interesting. As senior partner of Feingold and Charney, George plotted strategy but left the actual work to his junior partners, with much of it a matter for his son, Paul, who was also a member of the firm and who reported dutifully nearly every day to his grandmother. She, in turn, discussed it every day with Andrew.

Andrew was deeply involved. His work on his book on robots was delayed again, as he pored over the legal arguments and even, at times, made very diffident suggestions.

He said, "George told me that day that human beings have always been afraid of robots. As long as they are, the courts and the legislatures are not likely to work hard on behalf of robots. Should there not be something done about public opinion?"

So while Paul stayed in court, George took to the public platform. It gave him the advantage of being informal and he even went so far sometimes as to wear the new, loose style of clothing which he called drapery. Paul said, "Just don't trip over it on stage, Dad."

George said despondently, "I'll try not to."

He addressed the annual convention of holo-news editors on one occasion and said, in part:

"If, by virtue of the Second Law, we can demand of any robot unlimited obedience in all respects not involving harm to a human being, then any human being, *any* human being, has a fearsome power over any robot, *any* robot. In particular, since Second Law supersedes Third Law, *any* human being can use the law of obedience to overcome the law of self-protection. He can order any robot to damage itself or even destroy itself for any reason, or for no reason.

"Is this just? Would we treat an animal so? Even an inanimate object which has given us good service has a claim on our consideration. And a robot is not insensible; it is not an animal. It can think well enough to enable it to talk to us, reason with us, joke with us. Can we treat them as friends, can we work together with them, and not give them some of the fruit of that friendship, some of the benefit of co-working?

"If a man has the right to give a robot any order that does not involve harm to a human being, he should have the decency never to give a robot any order that involves harm to a robot, unless human safety absolutely requires it. With great power goes great responsibility, and if the robots have Three Laws to protect men, is it too much to ask that men have a law or two to protect robots?"

Andrew was right. It was the battle over public opinion that held the key to courts and Legislature and in the end a law passed which set up conditions under which robot-harming orders were forbidden. It was endlessly qualified and the punishments for violating the law were totally inadequate, but the principle was established. The final passage by the World Legislature came through on the day of Little Miss's death.

That was no coincidence. Little Miss held on to life desperately during the last debate and let go only when word of victory arrived. Her last smile was for Andrew. Her last words were: "You have been good to us, Andrew."

She died with her hand holding his, while her son and his wife and children remained at a respectful distance from both.

12.

Andrew waited patiently while the receptionist disappeared into the inner office. It might have used the holographic chatterbox, but unquestionably it was unmanned (or perhaps unroboted) by having to deal with another robot rather than with a human being.

Andrew passed the time revolving the matter in his mind. Could "unroboted" be used as an analogue of "unmanned," or had "unmanned" become a metaphoric term sufficiently divorced from its original literal meaning to be applied to robots—or to women for that matter?

Such problems came frequently as he worked on his book on robots. The trick of thinking out sentences to express all complexities had undoubtedly increased his vocabulary.

Occasionally, someone came into the room to stare at him and he did not try to avoid the glance. He looked at each calmly, and each in turn looked away.

Paul Charney finally came out. He looked surprised, or he would have if Andrew could have made out his expression with certainty. Paul had taken to wearing the heavy makeup that fashion was dictating for both sexes and though it made sharper and firmer the somewhat bland lines of his face, Andrew disapproved. He found that disapproving of human beings, as long as he did not express it verbally, did not make him very uneasy. He could even write the disapproval. He was sure it had not always been so.

Paul said, "Come in, Andrew. I'm sorry I made you wait

but there was something I *had* to finish. Come in. You had said you wanted to talk to me, but I didn't know you meant here in town."

"If you are busy, Paul, I am prepared to continue to wait."

Paul glanced at the interplay of shifting shadows on the dial on the wall that served as timepiece and said, "I can make some time. Did you come alone?"

"I hired an automatobile."

"Any trouble?" Paul asked, with more than a trace of anxiety.

"I wasn't expecting any. My rights are protected."

Paul looked the more anxious for that. "Andrew, I've explained that the law is unenforceable, at least under most conditions. . . . And if you insist on wearing clothes, you'll run into trouble eventually—just like that first time."

"And only time, Paul. I'm sorry you are displeased."

"Well, look at it this way; you are virtually a living legend, Andrew, and you are too valuable in many different ways for you to have any right to take chances with yourself. . . . How's the book coming?"

"I am approaching the end, Paul. The publisher is quite pleased."

"Good!"

"I don't know that he's necessarily pleased with the book as a book. I think he expects to sell many copies because it's written by a robot and it's that that pleases him."

"Only human, I'm afraid."

"I am not displeased. Let it sell for whatever reason since it will mean money and I can use some."

"Grandmother left you—"

"Little Miss was generous, and I'm sure I can count on the family to help me out further. But it is the royalties from the book on which I am counting to help me through the next step."

"What next step is that?"

"I wish to see the head of U. S. Robots and Mechanical Men Corporation. I have tried to make an appointment, but so far I have not been able to reach him. The corporation did not cooperate with me in the writing of the book, so I am not surprised, you understand."

Paul was clearly amused. "Cooperation is the last thing you can expect. They didn't cooperate with us in our great fight for robot rights. Quite the reverse and you can see why. Give a robot rights and people may not want to buy them."

"Nevertheless," said Andrew, "if you call them, you may obtain an interview for me."

"I'm no more popular with them than you are, Andrew."

"But perhaps you can hint that by seeing me they may head off a campaign by Feingold and Charney to strengthen the rights of robots further."

"Wouldn't that be a lie, Andrew?"

"Yes, Paul, and I can't tell one. That is why you must call."

"Ah, you can't lie, but you can urge me to tell a lie, is that it? You're getting more human all the time, Andrew."

13.

It was not easy to arrange, even with Paul's supposedly weighted name.

But it was finally carried through and, when it was, Harley Smythe-Robertson, who, on his mother's side, was descended from the original founder of the corporation and who had adopted the hyphenation to indicate it, looked remarkably unhappy. He was approaching retirement age and his entire tenure as president had been devoted to the matter of robot rights. His gray hair was plastered thinly over the top of his scalp, his face was not made up, and he eyed Andrew with brief hostility from time to time.

Andrew said, "Sir, nearly a century ago, I was told by a Merton Mansky of this corporation that the mathematics governing the plotting of the positronic pathways was far too complicated to permit of any but approximate solutions and that therefore my own capacities were not fully predictable."

"That was a century ago." Smythe-Robertson hesitated, then said icily, "*Sir*. It is true no longer. Our robots are made with precision now and are trained precisely to their jobs."

"Yes," said Paul, who had come along, as he said, to make sure that the corporation played fair, "with the result that my receptionist must be guided at every point once events depart from the conventional, however slightly."

Smythe-Robertson said, "You would be much more displeased if it were to improvise."

Andrew said, "Then you no longer manufacture robots like myself which are flexible and adaptable."

"No longer."

"The research I have done in connection with my book," said Andrew, "indicates that I am the oldest robot presently in active operation."

"The oldest presently," said Smythe-Robertson, "and the oldest ever. The oldest that will ever be. No robot is useful after the twenty-fifth year. They are called in and replaced with new models."

"No robot *as presently manufactured* is useful after the twenty-fifth year," said Paul pleasantly. "Andrew is quite exceptional in this respect."

Andrew, adhering to the path he had marked out for himself, said, "As the oldest robot in the world and the most flexible, am I not unusual enough to merit special treatment from the company?"

"Not at all," said Smythe-Robertson freezingly. "Your unusualness is an embarrassment to the company. If you were on lease, instead of having been a sale outright through some mischance, you would long since have been replaced."

"But that is exactly the point," said Andrew. "I am a free robot and I own myself. Therefore I come to you and ask you to replace me. You cannot do this without the owner's consent. Nowadays, that consent is extorted as a condition of the lease, but in my time this did not happen."

Smythe-Robertson was looking both startled and puzzled, and for a moment there was silence. Andrew found himself staring at the holograph on the wall. It was a death mask of Susan Calvin, patron saint of all roboticists. She was dead nearly two centuries now, but as a result of writing his book Andrew knew her so well he could half persuade himself that he had met her in life.

Smythe-Robertson said, "How can I replace you for you? If I replace you as robot, how can I donate the new robot to you as owner since in the very act of replacement you cease to exist?" He smiled grimly.

"Not at all difficult," interposed Paul. "The seat of Andrew's personality is his positronic brain and it is the one part that cannot be replaced without creating a new robot. The positronic brain, therefore, is Andrew the owner. Every other part of the robotic body can be replaced without affecting the robot's personality, and those other parts are the brain's possessions. Andrew, I should say, wants to supply his brain with a new robotic body."

"That's right," said Andrew calmly. He turned to Smythe-Robertson. "You have manufactured androids, haven't you? Robots that have the outward appearance of humans complete to the texture of the skin?"

Smythe-Robertson said, "Yes, we have. They worked perfectly well, with their synthetic fibrous skins and tendons. There was virtually no metal anywhere except for the brain, yet they were nearly as tough as metal robots. They were tougher, weight for weight."

Paul looked interested. "I didn't know that. How many are on the market?"

"None," said Smythe-Robertson. "They were much more expensive than metal models and a market survey showed they would not be accepted. They looked too human."

Andrew said, "But the corporation retains its expertise, I assume. Since it does, I wish to request that I be replaced by an organic robot, an android."

Paul looked surprised. "Good Lord," he said.

Smythe-Robertson stiffened. "Quite impossible!"

"Why is it impossible?" asked Andrew. "I will pay any reasonable fee, of course."

Smythe-Robertson said, "We do not manufacture androids."

"You do not *choose* to manufacture androids," interposed Paul quickly. "That is not the same as being unable to manufacture them."

Smythe-Robertson said, "Nevertheless, the manufacture of androids is against public policy."

"There is no law against it," said Paul.

"Nevertheless, we do not manufacture them, and we will not."

Paul cleared his throat. "Mr. Smythe-Robertson," he said, "Andrew is a free robot who is under the purview of the law guaranteeing robot rights. You are aware of this, I take it?"

"Only too well."

"This robot, as a free robot, chooses to wear clothes. This results in his being frequently humiliated by thoughtless human beings despite the law against the humiliation of robots. It is difficult to prosecute vague offenses that don't meet with the general disapproval of those who must decide on guilt and innocence."

"'U. S. Robots understood that from the start. Your father's firm unfortunately did not."

"My father is dead now," said Paul, "but what I see is that we have here a clear offense with a clear target."

"What are you talking about?" said Smythe-Robertson.

"My client, Andrew Martin—he has just become my client—is a free robot who is entitled to ask U. S. Robots and Mechanical Men Corporation for the right of replacement, which the corporation supplies anyone who owns a robot for more than twenty-five years. In fact, the corporation insists on such replacement."

Paul was smiling and thoroughly at his ease. He went on, "The positronic brain of my client is the owner of the body of my client— which is certainly more than twenty-five years old. The positronic brain demands the replacement of the body and offers to pay any reasonable fee for an android body as that replacement. If you refuse the request, my client undergoes humiliation and we will sue.

"While public opinion would not ordinarily support the claim of a robot in such a case, may I remind you that U.S. Robots is not popular with the public generally. Even those who most use and profit from robots are suspicious of the corporation. This may be a hangover from the days when robots were widely feared. It may be resentment against the power and wealth of U. S. Robots which has a worldwide monopoly. Whatever the cause may be, the resentment exists and I think you will find that you would prefer not to withstand a lawsuit, particularly since my client is wealthy and will live for many more centuries and will have no reason to refrain from fighting the battle forever."

Smythe-Robertson had slowly reddened. "You are trying to force me to . . ."

"I force you to do nothing," said Paul. "If you wish to refuse to accede to my client's reasonable request, you may by all means do so and we will leave without another word. . . . But we will sue, as is certainly our right, and you will find that you will eventually lose."

Smythe-Robertson said, "Well—" and paused.

"I see that you are going to accede," said Paul. "You may hesitate but you will come to it in the end. Let me assure you, then, of one further point. If, in the process of transferring my client's positronic brain from his present body to an organic one, there is any damage, however slight, then I will never rest till I've nailed the corporation to the ground. I will, if necessary, take every possible step to mobilize public opinion against the corporation if one brain path of my client's platinum-iridium essence is scrambled." He turned to Andrew and said, "Do you agree to all this, Andrew?"

Andrew hesitated a full minute. It amounted to the approval of lying, of blackmail, of the badgering and humiliation of a human being. But not physical harm, he told himself, not physical harm.

He managed at last to come out with a rather faint "Yes."

14.

It was like being constructed again. For days, then weeks, finally for months, Andrew found himself not himself somehow, and the simplest actions kept giving rise to hesitation.

Paul was frantic. "They've damaged you, Andrew. We'll have to institute suit."

Andrew spoke very slowly. "You mustn't. You'll never be able to prove—something—m-m-m-m—"

"Malice?"

"Malice. Besides, I grow stronger, better. It's the tr-tr-tr—"

"Tremble?"

"Trauma. After all, there's never been such an op—op—op— before."

Andrew could feel his brain from the inside. No one else could. He knew he was well and during the months that it took him to learn full coordination and full positronic interplay, he spent hours before the mirror.

Not quite human! The face was stiff—too stiff—and the motions were too deliberate. They lacked the careless free flow of the human being, but perhaps that might come with time. At least he could wear clothes without the ridiculous anomaly of a metal face going along with it.

Eventually he said, "I will be going back to work."

Paul laughed and said, "That means you are well. What will you be doing? Another book?"

"No," said Andrew seriously. "I live too long for any one career to seize me by the throat and never let me go. There was a time when I was primarily an artist and I can still turn to that. And there was a time when I was a historian and I can still turn to that. But now I wish to be a robobiologist."

"A robopsychologist, you mean."

"No. That would imply the study of positronic brains and at the moment I lack the desire to do that. A robobiologist, it seems to me, would be concerned with the working of the body attached to that brain."

"Wouldn't that be a roboticist?"

"A roboticist works with a metal body. I would be studying an organic humanoid body, of which I have the only one, as far as I know."

"You narrow your field," said Paul thoughtfully. "As an artist, all conception is yours; as a historian, you dealt chiefly with robots; as a robobiologist, you will deal with yourself."

Andrew nodded. "It would seem so."

Andrew had to start from the very beginning, for he knew nothing of ordinary biology, almost nothing of science. He became a familiar sight in the libraries, where he sat at the electronic indices for hours at a time, looking perfectly normal in clothes. Those few who knew he was a robot in no way interfered with him.

He built a laboratory in a room which he added to his house, and his library grew, too.

Years passed, and Paul came to him one day and said, "It's a pity you're no longer working on the history of robots. I understand U. S. Robots is adopting a radically new policy."

Paul had aged, and his deteriorating eyes had been replaced with photoptic cells. In that respect, he had drawn closer to Andrew. Andrew said, "What have they done?"

"They are manufacturing central computers, gigantic positronic brains, really, which communicate with anywhere from a dozen to a thousand robots by microwave. The robots themselves have no brains at all. They are the limbs of the gigantic brain, and the two are physically separate."

"Is that more efficient?"

"U. S. Robots claims it is. Smythe-Robertson established the new direction before he died, however, and it's my notion that it's a backlash at you. U. S. Robots is determined that they will make no robots that will give them the type of trouble you have, and for that reason they separate brain and body. The brain will have no body to wish changed; the body will have no brain to wish anything.

"It's amazing, Andrew," Paul went on, "the influence you have had on the history of robots. It was your artistry that encouraged U. S. Robots to make robots more precise and specialized; it was your freedom that resulted in the establishment of the principle of robotic rights; it was your insistence on an android body that made U. S. Robots switch to brain-body separation."

Andrew said, "I suppose in the end the corporation will produce one vast brain controlling several billion robotic bodies. All the eggs will be in one basket. Dangerous. Not proper at all."

"I think you're right," said Paul, "but I don't suspect it will come to pass for a century at least and I won't live to see it. In fact, I may not live to see next year."

"Paul!" said Andrew, in concern.

Paul shrugged. "We're mortal, Andrew. We're not like you. It doesn't matter too much, but it does make it important to assure you on one point. I'm the last of the Charneys. There are collaterals descended from my great-aunt, but they don't count. The money I control personally will be left to the trust in your name and as far as anyone can foresee the future, you will be economically secure."

"Unnecessary," said Andrew, with difficulty. In all this time, he could not get used to the deaths of the Charneys.

Paul said, "Let's not argue. That's the way it's going to be. What are you working on?"

"I am designing a system for allowing androids—myself—to gain energy from the combustion of hydrocarbons, rather than from atomic cells."

Paul raised his eyebrows. "So that they will breathe and eat?"

"Yes."

"How long have you been pushing in that direction?"

"For a long time now, but I think I have designed an adequate combustion chamber for catalyzed controlled breakdown."

"But why, Andrew? The atomic cell is surely infinitely better."

"In some ways, perhaps, but the atomic cell is inhuman."

15.

It took time, but Andrew had time. In the first place, he did not wish to do anything till Paul had died in peace.

With the death of the great-grandson of Sir, Andrew felt more nearly exposed to a hostile world and for that reason was the more determined to continue the path he had long ago chosen.

Yet he was not really alone. If a man had died, the firm of Feingold and Charney lived, for a corporation does not die any more than a robot does. The firm had its directions and it followed them soullessly. By way of the trust and through the law firm, Andrew continued to be wealthy. And in return for their own large annual retainer, Feingold and Charney involved themselves in the legal aspects of the new combustion chamber.

When the time came for Andrew to visit U. S. Robots and Mechanical Men Corporation, he did it alone. Once he had gone with Sir and once with Paul. This time, the third time, he was alone and manlike.

U. S. Robots had changed. The production plant had been shifted to a large space station, as had grown to be the case with more and more industries. With them had gone many robots. The Earth itself was becoming parklike, with its one-billion-person population stabilized and perhaps not more than thirty per cent of its at least equally large robot population independently brained.

The Director of Research was Alvin Magdescu, dark of complexion and hair, with a little pointed beard and wearing nothing above the waist but the breastband that fashion dictated. Andrew himself was well covered in the older fashion of several decades back.

Magdescu said, "I know you, of course, and I'm rather pleased to see you. You're our most notorious product and it's a pity old Smythe-Robertson was so set against you. We could have done a great deal with you."

"You still can," said Andrew.

"No, I don't think so. We're past the time. We've had

robots on Earth for over a century, but that's changing. It will be back to space with them and those that stay here won't be brained."

"But there remains myself, and I stay on Earth."

"True, but there doesn't seem to be much of the robot about you. What new request have you?"

"To be still less a robot. Since I am so far organic, I wish an organic source of energy. I have here the plans—"

Magdescu did not hasten through them. He might have intended to at first, but he stiffened and grew intent. At one point he said, "This is remarkably ingenious. Who thought of all this?"

"I did," said Andrew.

Magdescu looked up at him sharply, then said, "It would amount to a major overhaul of your body, and an experimental one, since it has never been attempted before. I advise against it. Remain as you are."

Andrew's face had limited means of expression, but impatience showed plainly in his voice. "Dr. Magdescu, you miss the entire point. You have no choice but to accede to my request. If such devices can be built into my body, they can be built into human bodies as well. The tendency to lengthen human life by prosthetic devices has already been remarked on. There are no devices better than the ones I have designed and am designing.

"As it happens, I control the patents by way of the firm of Feingold and Charney. We are quite capable of going into business for ourselves and of developing the kind of prosthetic devices that may end by producing human beings with many of the properties of robots. Your own business will then suffer.

"If, however, you operate on me now and agree to do so under similar circumstances in the future, you will receive permission to make use of the patents and control the technology of both robots and the prosthetization of human beings. The initial leasing will not be granted, of course, until after the first operation is completed successfully, and after enough time has passed to demonstrate that it is indeed successful." Andrew felt scarcely any First Law inhibition to the stern conditions he was setting a human being. He was learning to reason that what seemed like cruelty might, in the long run, be kindness.

Magdescu looked stunned. He said, "I'm not the one to decide something like this. That's a corporate decision that would take time."

"I can wait a reasonable time," said Andrew, "but only a reasonable time." And he thought with satisfaction that Paul himself could not have done it better.

16.

It took only a reasonable time, and the operation was a success.

Magdescu said, "I was very much against the operation, Andrew, but not for the reasons you might think. I was not in the least against the experiment, if it had been on someone else. I hated risking *your* positronic brain. Now that you have the positronic pathways interacting with simulated nerve pathways, it might be difficult to rescue the brain intact if the body went bad."

"I had every faith in the skill of the staff at U. S. Robots," said Andrew. "And I can eat now."

"Well, you can sip olive oil. It will mean occasional cleanings of the combustion chamber, as we have explained to you. Rather an uncomfortable touch, I should think."

"Perhaps, if I did not expect to go further. Self-cleaning is not impossible. In fact, I am working on a device that will deal with solid food that may be expected to contain incombustible fractions—indigestible matter, so to speak, that will have to be discarded."

"You would then have to develop an anus."

"The equivalent."

"What else, Andrew?"

"Everything else."

"Genitalia, too?"

"Insofar as they will fit my plans. My body is a canvas on which I intend to draw—"

Magdescu waited for the sentence to be completed, and when it seemed that it would not be, he completed it himself. "A man?"

"We shall see," said Andrew.

Magdescu said, "It's a puny ambition, Andrew. You're better than a man. You've gone downhill from the moment you opted for organicism."

"My brain has not suffered."

"No, it hasn't. I'll grant you that. But, Andrew, the whole new breakthrough in prosthetic devices made possible by your patents is being marketed under your name. You're recognized as the inventor and you're honored for it—as you are. Why play further games with your body?"

Andrew did not answer.

The honors came. He accepted membership in several learned societies, including one which was devoted to the new science he had established; the one he had called robobiology but had come to be termed prosthetology.

On the one hundred and fiftieth anniversary of his construction, there was a testimonial dinner given in his honor at U. S. Robots. If Andrew saw irony in this, he kept it to himself.

Alvin Magdescu came out of retirement to chair the dinner. He was himself ninety-four years old and was alive because he had prosthetized devices that, among other things, fulfilled the function of liver and kidneys. The dinner reached its climax when Magdescu, after a short and emotional talk, raised his glass to toast "the Sesquicentennial Robot."

Andrew had had the sinews of his face redesigned to the point where he could show a range of emotions, but he sat through all the ceremonies solemnly passive. He did not like to be a Sesquicentennial Robot.

17.

It was prosthetology that finally took Andrew off the Earth. In the decades that followed the celebration of the Sesquicentennial, the Moon had come to be a world more Earthlike than Earth in every respect but its gravitational pull and in its underground cities there was a fairly dense population.

Prosthetized devices there had to take the lesser gravity into account and Andrew spent five years on the Moon working with local prosthetologists to make the necessary adaptations. When not at his work, he wandered among the robot population, every one of which treated him with the robotic obsequiousness due a man.

He came back to an Earth that was humdrum and quiet in comparison and visited the offices of Feingold and Charney to announce his return.

The current head of the firm, Simon DeLong, was surprised. He said, "We had been told you were returning, Andrew" (he had almost said "Mr. Martin"), "but we were not expecting you till next week."

"I grew impatient," said Andrew brusquely. He was anxious to get to the point. "On the Moon, Simon, I was in charge of a research team of twenty human scientists. I gave orders that no one questioned. The Lunar robots deferred to me as they would to a human being. Why, then, am I not a human being?"

A wary look entered DeLong's eyes. He said, "My dear Andrew, as you have just explained, you are treated as a human being by both robots and human beings. You are therefore a human being *de facto*."

"To be a human being *de facto* is not enough. I want not only to be treated as one, but to be legally identified as one. I want to be a human being *de jure*."

"Now that is another matter," said DeLong. "There we would run into human prejudice and into the undoubted fact that however much you may be like a human being, you are *not* a human being."

"In what way not?" asked Andrew. "I have the shape of

a human being and organs equivalent to those of a human being. My organs, in fact, are identical to some of those in a prosthetized human being. I have contributed artistically, literarily, and scientifically to human culture as much as any human being now alive. What more can one ask?"

"I myself would ask nothing more. The trouble is that it would take an act of the World Legislature to define you as a human being. Frankly, I wouldn't expect that to happen."

"To whom on the Legislature could I speak?"

"To the chairman of the Science and Technology Committee perhaps."

"Can you arrange a meeting?"

"But you scarcely need an intermediary. In your position, you can—"

"No. *You* arrange it." (It didn't even occur to Andrew that he was giving a flat order to a human being. He had grown accustomed to that on the Moon.) "I want him to know that the firm of Feingold and Charney is backing me in this to the hilt."

"Well, now—"

"To the hilt, Simon. In one hundred and seventy-three years I have in one fashion or another contributed greatly to this firm. I have been under obligation to individual members of the firm in times past. I am not now. It is rather the other way around now and I am calling in my debts."

DeLong said, "I will do what I can."

18.

The chairman of the Science and Technology Committee was of the East Asian region and she was a woman. Her name was Chee Li-Hsing and her transparent garments (obscuring what she wanted obscured only by their dazzle) made her look plastic-wrapped.

She said, "I sympathize with your wish for full human rights. There have been times in history when segments of the human population fought for full human rights. What rights, however, can you possibly want that you do not have?"

"As simple a thing as my right to life. A robot can be dismantled at any time."

"A human being can be executed at any time."

"Execution can only follow due process of law. There is no trial needed for my dismantling. Only the word of a human being in authority is needed to end me. Besides— besides—" Andrew tried desperately to allow no sign of pleading, but his carefully designed tricks of human expression and tone of voice betrayed him here. "The truth is, I want to be a man. I have wanted it through six generations of human beings."

Li-Hsing looked up at him out of darkly sympathetic eyes. "The Legislature can pass a law declaring you one—they could pass a law declaring a stone statue to be defined as a man. Whether they will actually do so is, however, as likely in the first case as the second. Congresspeople are as human as the rest of the population and there is always that element of suspicion against robots."

"Even now?"

"Even now. We would all allow the fact that you have earned the prize of humanity and yet there would remain the fear of setting an undesirable precedent."

"What precedent? I am the only free robot, the only one of my type, and there will never be another. You may consult U. S. Robots."

" 'Never' is a long time, Andrew—or, if you prefer, Mr. Martin—since I will gladly give you my personal accolade as man. You will find that most Congresspeople will not be willing to set the precedent, no matter how meaningless such a precedent might be. Mr. Martin, you have my sympathy, but I cannot tell you to hope. Indeed—"

She sat back and her forehead wrinkled. "Indeed, if the issue grows too heated, there might well arise a certain sentiment, both inside the Legislature and outside, for that dismantling you mentioned. Doing away with you could turn out to be the easiest way of resolving the dilemma. Consider that before deciding to push matters."

Andrew said, "Will no one remember the technique of prosthetology, something that is almost entirely mine?"

"It may seem cruel, but they won't. Or if they do, it will be remembered against you. It will be said you did it only for yourself. It will be said it was part of a campaign to roboticize human beings, or to humanify robots; and in either case evil and vicious. You have never been part of a political hate campaign, Mr. Martin, and I tell you that you will be the object of vilification of a kind neither you nor I would credit and there would be people who'll believe it all. Mr. Martin, let your life be." She rose and, next to Andrew's seated figure, she seemed small and almost childlike.

Andrew said, "If I decide to fight for my humanity, will you be on my side?"

She thought, then said, "I will be—insofar as I can be. If at any time such a stand would appear to threaten my political future, I may have to abandon you, since it is not an issue I feel to be at the very root of my beliefs. I am trying to be honest with you."

"Thank you, and I will ask no more. I intend to fight this through whatever the consequences, and I will ask you for your help only for as long as you can give it."

19.

It was not a direct fight. Feingold and Charney counseled patience and Andrew muttered grimly that he had an endless supply of that. Feingold and Charney then entered on a campaign to narrow and restrict the area of combat.

They instituted a lawsuit denying the obligation to pay debts to an individual with a prosthetic heart on the grounds that the possession of a robotic organ removed humanity, and with it the constitutional rights of human beings.

They fought the matter skillfully and tenaciously, losing at every step but always in such a way that the decision was forced to be as broad as possible, and then carrying it by way of appeals to the World Court.

It took years, and millions of dollars.

When the final decision was handed down, DeLong held what amounted to a victory celebration over the legal loss. Andrew was, of course, present in the company offices on the occasion.

"We've done two things, Andrew," said DeLong, "both of which are good. First of all, we have established the fact that no number of artifacts in the human body causes it to cease being a human body. Secondly, we have engaged public opinion in the question in such a way as to put it fiercely on the side of a broad interpretation of humanity since there is not a human being in existence who does not hope for prosthetics if that will keep him alive."

"And do you think the Legislature will now grant me my humanity?" asked Andrew.

DeLong looked faintly uncomfortable. "As to that, I cannot be optimistic. There remains the one organ which the World Court has used as the criterion of humanity. Human beings have an organic cellular brain and robots have a platinum-iridium positronic brain if they have one at all—and you certainly have a positronic brain. . . . No, Andrew, don't get that look in your eye. We lack the knowledge to duplicate the work of a cellular brain in artificial structures close enough to the organic type to allow it to fall within the Court's decision. Not even you could do it."

"What ought we do, then?"

"Make the attempt, of course. Congresswoman Li-Hsing will be on our side and a growing number of other Congresspeople. The President will undoubtedly go along with a majority of the Legislature in this matter."

"Do we have a majority?"

"No, far from it. But we might get one if the public will allow its desire for a broad interpretation of humanity to extend to you. A small chance, I admit, but if you do not wish to give up, we must gamble for it."

"I do not wish to give up."

20.

Congresswoman Li-Hsing was considerably older than she had been when Andrew had first met her. Her transparent garments were long gone. Her hair was now close-cropped and her coverings were tubular. Yet still Andrew clung, as closely as he could within the limits of reasonable taste, to the style of clothing that had prevailed when he had first adopted clothing over a century before.

She said, "We've gone as far as we can, Andrew. We'll try once more after recess, but, to be honest, defeat is certain and the whole thing will have to be given up. All my most recent efforts have only earned me a certain defeat in the coming congressional campaign."

"I know," said Andrew, "and it distresses me. You said once you would abandon me if it came to that. Why have you not done so?"

"One can change one's mind, you know. Somehow, abandoning you became a higher price than I cared to pay for just one more term. As it is, I've been in the Legislature for over a quarter of a century. It's enough."

"Is there no way we can change minds, Chee?"

"We've changed all that are amenable to reason. The rest—the majority—cannot be moved from their emotional antipathies."

"Emotional antipathy is not a valid reason for voting one way or the other."

"I know that, Andrew, but they don't advance emotional antipathy as their reason."

Andrew said cautiously, "It all comes down to the brain, then, but must we leave it at the level of cells versus positrons? Is there no way of forcing a functional definition?

Must we say that a brain is made of this or that? May we not say that a brain is something—anything—capable of a certain level of thought?"

"Won't work," said Li-Hsing. "Your brain is man-made, the human brain is not. Your brain is constructed, theirs developed. To any human being who is intent on keeping up the barrier between himself and a robot, those differences are a steel wall a mile high and a mile thick."

"If we could get at the source of their antipathy—the very source of—"

"After all your years," said Li-Hsing sadly, "you are still trying to reason out the human being. Poor Andrew, don't be angry, but it's the robot in you that drives you in that direction."

"I don't know," said Andrew. "If I could bring myself—"

1. (reprise)

If he could bring himself—

He had known for a long time it might come to that, and in the end he was at the surgeon's. He found one, skillful enough for the job at hand, which meant a robot surgeon, for no human surgeon could be trusted in this connection, either in ability or in intention.

The surgeon could not have performed the operation on a human being, so Andrew, after putting off the moment of decision with a sad line of questioning that reflected the turmoil within himself, put the First Law to one side by saying, "I, too, am a robot."

He then said, as firmly as he had learned to form the words even at human beings over these past decades, "I *order* you to carry through the operation on me."

In the absence of the First Law, an order so firmly given from one who looked so much like a man activated the Second Law sufficiently to carry the day.

21.

Andrew's feeling of weakness was, he was sure, quite imaginary. He had recovered from the operation. Nevertheless, he leaned, as unobtrusively as he could manage, against the wall. It would be entirely too revealing to sit.

Li-Hsing said, "The final vote will come this week, Andrew. I've been able to delay it no longer, and we must lose. . . . And that will be it, Andrew."

Andrew said, "I am grateful for your skill at delay. It gave me the time I needed, and I took the gamble I had to."

"What gamble is this?" asked Li-Hsing with open concern.

"I couldn't tell you, or the people at Feingold and Charney. I was sure I would be stopped. See here, if it is the brain that is at issue, isn't the greatest difference of all the matter of immortality? Who really cares what a brain looks like or is built of or how it was formed? What matters is that brain cells die; *must* die. Even if every other organ in the body is maintained or replaced, the brain cells, which cannot be replaced without changing and therefore killing the personality, must eventually die.

"My own positronic pathways have lasted nearly two centuries without perceptible change and can last for centuries more. Isn't *that* the fundamental barrier? Human beings can tolerate an immortal robot, for it doesn't matter how long a machine lasts. They cannot tolerate an immortal human being, since their own mortality is endurable only so long as it is universal. And for that reason they won't make me a human being."

Li-Hsing said, "What is it you're leading up to, Andrew?"

"I have removed that problem. Decades ago, my positronic brain was connected to organic nerves. Now, one last operation has arranged that connection in such a way that slowly— quite slowly—the potential is being drained from my pathways."

Li-Hsing's finely wrinkled face showed no expression for a moment. Then her lips tightened. "Do you mean you've arranged to die, Andrew? You can't have. That violates the Third Law."

"No," said Andrew, "I have chosen between the death of my body and the death of my aspirations and desires. To have let my body live at the cost of the greater death is what would have violated the Third Law."

Li-Hsing seized his arm as though she were about to shake him. She stopped herself. "Andrew, it won't work. Change it back."

"It can't be. Too much damage was done. I have a year to live—more or less. I will last through the two hundredth anniversary of my construction. I was weak enough to arrange that."

"How can it be worth it? Andrew, you're a fool."

"If it brings me humanity, that will be worth it. If it doesn't, it will bring an end to striving and that will be worth it, too."

And Li-Hsing did something that astonished herself. Quietly, she began to weep.

22.

It was odd how that last deed caught at the imagination of the world. All that Andrew had done before had not swayed them. But he had finally accepted even death to be human and the sacrifice was too great to be rejected.

The final ceremony was timed, quite deliberately, for the two hundredth anniversary. The World President was to sign the act and make it law and the ceremony would be visible on a global network and would be beamed to the Lunar state and even to the Martian colony.

Andrew was in a wheelchair. He could still walk, but only shakily.

With mankind watching, the World President said, "Fifty years ago, you were declared a Sesquicentennial Robot, Andrew." After a pause, and in a more solemn tone, he said, "Today we declare you a Bicentennial Man, Mr. Martin."

And Andrew, smiling, held out his hand to shake that of the President.

23.

Andrew's thoughts were slowly fading as he lay in bed.

Desperately he seized at them. Man! He was a man! He wanted that to be his last thought. He wanted to dissolve—die—with that.

He opened his eyes one more time and for one last time recognized Li-Hsing waiting solemnly. There were others, but those were only shadows, unrecognizable shadows. Only Li-Hsing stood out against the deepening gray. Slowly, inchingly, he held out his hand to her and very dimly and faintly felt her take it.

She was fading in his eyes, as the last of his thoughts trickled away.

But before she faded completely, one last fugitive thought came to him and rested for a moment on his mind before everything stopped.

"Little Miss," he whispered, too low to be heard.

· SOMEDAY ·

·

Niccolo Mazetti lay stomach down on the rug, chin buried in the palm of one small hand, and listened to the Bard disconsolately. There was even the suspicion of tears in his dark eyes, a luxury an eleven-year-old could allow himself only when alone.

The Bard said, "Once upon a time in the middle of a deep wood, there lived a poor woodcutter and his two motherless daughters, who were each as beautiful as the day is long. The older daughter had long hair as black as a feather from a raven's wing, but the younger daughter had hair as bright and golden as the sunlight of an autumn afternoon.

"Many times while the girls were waiting for their father to come home from his day's work in the wood, the older girl would sit before a mirror and sing—"

What she sang, Niccolo did not hear, for a call sounded from outside the room: "Hey, Nickie."

And Niccolo, his face clearing on the moment, rushed to the window and shouted, "Hey, Paul."

Paul Loeb waved an excited hand. He was thinner than

Niccolo and not as tall, for all he was six months older. His face was full of repressed tension which showed itself most clearly in the rapid blinking of his eyelids. "Hey, Nickie, let me in. I've got an idea and a *half*. Wait till you hear it." He looked rapidly about him as though to check on the possibility of eavesdroppers, but the front yard was quite patently empty. He repeated in a whisper, "Wait till you hear it."

"All right. I'll open the door."

The Bard continued smoothly, oblivious to the sudden loss of attention on the part of Niccolo. As Paul entered, the Bard was saying, ". . . Thereupon, the lion said, 'If you will find me the lost egg of the bird which flies over the Ebony Mountain once every ten years, I will—' "

Paul said, "Is that a Bard you're listening to? I didn't know you had one."

Niccolo reddened and the look of unhappiness returned to his face. "Just an old thing I had when I was a kid. It ain't much good." He kicked at the Bard with his foot and caught the somewhat scarred and discolored plastic covering a glancing blow.

The Bard hiccupped as its speaking attachment was jarred out of contact a moment, then it went on: "—for a year and a day until the iron shoes were worn out. The princess stopped at the side of the road. . . ."

Paul said, "Boy, that *is* an old model," and looked at it critically.

Despite Niccolo's own bitterness against the Bard, he winced at the other's condescending tone. For the moment, he was sorry he had allowed Paul in, at least before he had restored the Bard to its usual resting place in the basement. It was only in the desperation of a dull day and a fruitless discussion with his father that he had resurrected it. And it turned out to be just as stupid as he had expected.

Nickie was a little afraid of Paul anyway, since Paul had special courses at school and everyone said he was going to grow up to be a Computing Engineer.

Not that Niccolo himself was doing badly at school. He got adequate marks in logic, binary manipulations, computing and elementary circuits; all the usual grammar-school subjects. But that was it! They were just the usual subjects and he would grow up to be a control-board guard like everyone else.

Paul, however, knew mysterious things about what he called electronics and theoretical mathematics and programming. Especially programming. Niccolo didn't even try to understand when Paul bubbled over about it.

Paul listened to the Bard for a few minutes and said, "You been using it much?"

"No!" said Niccolo, offended. "I've had it in the basement since before you moved into the neighborhood. I just got it out today—" He lacked an excuse that seemed adequate to himself, so he concluded, "I just got it out."

Paul said, "Is that what it tells you about: woodcutters and princesses and talking animals?"

Niccolo said, "It's terrible. My dad says we can't afford a new one. I said to him this morning—" The memory of the morning's fruitless pleadings brought Niccolo dangerously near tears, which he repressed in a panic. Somehow, he felt that Paul's thin cheeks never felt the stain of tears and that Paul would have only contempt for anyone else less strong than himself. Niccolo went on, "So I thought I'd try this old thing again, but it's no good."

Paul turned off the Bard, pressed the contact that led to a nearly instantaneous reorientation and recombination of the vocabulary, characters, plot lines and climaxes stored within it. Then he reactivated it.

The Bard began smoothly, "Once upon a time there was a little boy named Willikins whose mother had died and who lived with a stepfather and a stepbrother. Although the stepfather was very well-to-do, he begrudged poor Willikins the very bed he slept in so that Willikins was forced to get such rest as he could on a pile of straw in the stable next to the horses—"

"Horses!" cried Paul.

"They're a kind of animal," said Niccolo. "I think."

"I know that! I just mean imagine stories about *horses*."

"It tells about horses all the time," said Niccolo. "There are things called cows, too. You milk them but the Bard doesn't say how."

"Well, gee, why don't you fix it up?"

"I'd like to know how."

The Bard was saying, "Often Willikins would think that if only he were rich and powerful, he would show his stepfather and stepbrother what it meant to be cruel to a little boy, so one day he decided to go out into the world and seek his fortune."

Paul, who wasn't listening to the Bard, said, "It's *easy*. The Bard has memory cylinders all fixed up for plot lines and climaxes and things. We don't have to worry about that. It's just vocabulary we've got to fix so it'll know about computers and automation and electronics and real things about today. Then it can tell interesting stories, you know, instead of about princesses and things."

Niccolo said despondently, "I wish we could do that."

Paul said, "Listen, my dad says if I get into special computing school next year, he'll get me a *real* Bard, a late model. A big one with an attachment for space stories and mysteries. And a visual attachment, too!"

"You mean *see* the stories?"

"Sure. Mr. Daugherty at school says they've got things like that, now, but not for just everybody. Only if I get into computing school, Dad can get a few breaks."

Niccolo's eyes bulged with envy. "Gee. *Seeing* a story."

"You can come over and watch anytime, Nickie."

"Oh, boy. Thanks."

"That's all right. But remember, I'm the guy who says what kind of story we hear."

"Sure. Sure." Niccolo would have agreed readily to much more onerous conditions.

Paul's attention returned to the Bard.

It was saying, " 'If that is the case,' said the king, stroking his beard and frowning till clouds filled the sky and lightning flashed, 'you will see to it that my entire land is freed of flies by this time day after tomorrow or—' "

"All we've got to do," said Paul, "is open it up—" He shut the Bard off again and was prying at its front panel as he spoke.

"Hey," said Niccolo, in sudden alarm. "Don't break it."

"I won't break it," said Paul impatiently. "I know all about these things." Then, with sudden caution, "Your father and mother home?"

"No."

"All right, then." He had the front panel off and peered in. "Boy, this *is* a one-cylinder thing."

He worked away at the Bard's innards. Niccolo, who watched with painful suspense, could not make out what he was doing.

Paul pulled out a thin, flexible metal strip, powdered with dots. "That's the Bard's memory cylinder. I'll bet its capacity for stories is under a trillion."

"What are you going to do, Paul?" quavered Niccolo.

"I'll give it vocabulary."

"How?"

"Easy. I've got a book here. Mr. Daugherty gave it to me at school."

Paul pulled the book out of his pocket and pried at it till he had its plastic jacket off. He unreeled the tape a bit, ran it through the vocalizer, which he turned down to a whisper, then placed it within the Bard's vitals. He made further attachments.

"What'll that do?"

"The book will talk and the Bard will put it all on its memory tape."

"What good will that do?"

"Boy, you're a dope! This book is all about computers and automation and the Bard will get all that information. Then he can stop talking about kings making lightning when they frown."

Niccolo said, "And the good guy always wins anyway. There's no excitement."

"Oh, well," said Paul, watching to see if his setup was working properly, "that's the way they make Bards. They got to have the good guy win and make the bad guys lose and things like that. I heard my father talking about it once. He says that without censorship there'd be no telling what the younger generation would come to. He says it's bad enough as it is. . . . There, it's working fine."

Paul brushed his hands against one another and turned away from the Bard. He said, "But listen, I didn't tell you my idea yet. It's the best thing you ever heard, I bet. I came right to you, because I figured you'd come in with me."

"Sure, Paul, sure."

"Okay. You know Mr. Daugherty at school? You know what a funny kind of guy he is. Well, he likes me, kind of."

"I know."

"I was over his house after school today."

"You *were*?"

"Sure. He says I'm going to be entering computer school and he wants to encourage me and things like that. He says the world needs more people who can design advanced computer circuits and do proper programming."

"Oh?"

Paul might have caught some of the emptiness behind that monosyllable. He said impatiently, "Programming! I told you a hundred times. That's when you set up problems for the giant computers like Multivac to work on. Mr. Daugherty says it gets harder all the time to find people who can really run computers. He says anyone can keep an eye on the controls and check off answers and put through routine problems. He says the trick is to expand research and figure out ways to ask the right questions, and that's hard.

"Anyway, Nickie, he took me to his place and showed me his collection of old computers. It's kind of a hobby of his to collect old computers. He had tiny computers you had to push with your hand, with little knobs all over it. And he had a hunk of wood he called a slide rule with a little piece of it that went in and out. And some wires with balls on them. He even had a hunk of paper with a kind of thing he called a multiplication table."

Niccolo, who found himself only moderately interested, said, "A paper table?"

"It wasn't really a table like you eat on. It was different. It was to help people compute. Mr. Daugherty tried to explain but he didn't have much time and it was kind of complicated, anyway."

"Why didn't people just use a computer?"

"That was *before* they had computers," cried Paul.

"Before?"

"Sure. Do you think people always had computers? Didn't you ever hear of cavemen?"

Niccolo said, "How'd they get along without computers?"

"*I* don't know. Mr. Daugherty says they just had children any old time and did anything that came into their heads whether it would be good for everybody or not. They didn't even know if it was good or not. And farmers grew things with their hands and people had to do all the work in the factories and run all the machines."

"I don't believe you."

"That's what Mr. Daugherty said. He said it was just plain messy and everyone was miserable. . . . Anyway, let me get to my idea, will you?"

"Well, go ahead. Who's stopping you?" said Niccolo, offended.

"All right. Well, the hand computers, the ones with the knobs, had little squiggles on each knob. And the slide rule had squiggles on it. And the multiplication table was all squiggles. I asked what they were. Mr. Daugherty said they were numbers."

"What?"

"Each different squiggle stood for a different number. For 'one' you made a kind of mark, for 'two' you made another kind of mark, for 'three' another one and so on."

"What for?"

"So you could compute."

"What *for*? You just tell the computer—"

"Jiminy," cried Paul, his face twisting with anger, "can't

you get it through your head? These slide rules and things didn't talk."

"Then how—"

"The answers showed up in squiggles and you had to know what the squiggles meant. Mr. Daugherty says that, in olden days, everybody learned how to make squiggles when they were kids and how to decode them, too. Making squiggles was called 'writing' and decoding them was 'reading.' He says there was a different kind of squiggle for every word and they used to write whole books in squiggles. He said they had some at the museum and I could look at them if I wanted to. He said if I was going to be a real computer programmer I would have to know about the history of computing and that's why he was showing me all these things."

Niccolo frowned. He said, "You mean everybody had to figure out squiggles for every word and *remember* them? . . . Is this all real or are you making it up?"

"It's all real. Honest. Look, this is the way you make a 'one.' " He drew his finger through the air in a rapid downstroke. "This way you make 'two,' and this way 'three.' I learned all the numbers up to 'nine.' "

Niccolo watched the curving finger uncomprehendingly. "What's the good of it?"

"You can learn how to make words. I asked Mr. Daugherty how you made the squiggle for 'Paul Loeb' but he didn't know. He said there were people at the museum who would know. He said there were people who had learned how to decode whole books. He said computers could be designed to decode books and used to be used that way but not any more because we have real books now, with magnetic tapes that go through the vocalizer and come out talking, you know."

"Sure."

"So if we go down to the museum, we can get to learn how to make words in squiggles. They'll let us because I'm going to computer school."

Niccolo was riddled with disappointment. "Is that your

idea? Holy Smokes, Paul, who wants to do that? Make stupid squiggles!"

"Don't you get it? Don't you *get* it? You dope. *It'll be secret message stuff!*"

"What?"

"Sure. What good is talking when everyone can understand you? With squiggles you can send secret messages. You can make them on paper and nobody in the world would know what you were saying unless they knew the squiggles, too. And they wouldn't, you bet, unless we taught them. We can have a real club, with initiations and rules and a clubhouse. Boy—"

A certain excitement began stirring in Niccolo's bosom. "What kind of secret messages?"

"Any kind. Say I want to tell you to come over my place and watch my new Visual Bard and I don't want any of the other fellows to come. I make the right squiggles on paper and I give it to you and you look at it and you know what to do. Nobody else does. You can even show it to them and they wouldn't know a thing."

"Hey, that's something," yelled Niccolo, completely won over. "When do we learn how?"

"Tomorrow," said Paul. "I'll get Mr. Daugherty to explain to the museum that it's all right and you get your mother and father to say okay. We can go down right after school and start learning."

"Sure!" cried Niccolo. "We can be club officers."

"I'll be president of the club," said Paul matter-of-factly. "You can be vice-president."

"All right. Hey, this is going to be lots more fun than the Bard." He was suddenly reminded of the Bard and said in sudden apprehension, "Hey, what about my old Bard?"

Paul turned to look at it. It was quietly taking in the slowly unreeling book, and the sound of the book's vocalizations was a dimly heard murmur.

He said, "I'll disconnect it."

He worked away while Niccolo watched anxiously. After

a few moments, Paul put his reassembled book into his pocket, replaced the Bard's panel and activated it.

The Bard said, "Once upon a time, in a large city, there lived a poor young boy named Fair Johnnie whose only friend in the world was a small computer. The computer, each morning, would tell the boy whether it would rain that day and answer any problems he might have. It was never wrong. But it so happened that one day, the king of that land, having heard of the little computer, decided that he would have it as his own. With this purpose in mind, he called in his Grand Vizier and said—"

Niccolo turned off the Bard with a quick motion of his hand. "Same old junk," he said passionately. "Just with a computer thrown in."

"Well," said Paul, "they got so much stuff on the tape already that the computer business doesn't show up much when random combinations are made. What's the difference, anyway? You just need a new model."

"We'll *never* be able to afford one. Just this dirty old miserable thing." He kicked at it again, hitting it more squarely this time. The Bard moved backward with a squeal of castors.

"You can always watch mine, when I get it," said Paul. "Besides, don't forget our squiggle club."

Niccolo nodded.

"I tell you what," said Paul. "Let's go over my place. My father has some books about old times. We can listen to them and maybe get some ideas. You punch a message for your folks and maybe you can stay over for supper. Come on."

"Okay," said Niccolo, and the two boys ran out together. Niccolo, in his eagerness, ran almost squarely into the Bard, but he only rubbed at the spot on his hip where he had made contact and ran on.

The activation signal of the Bard glowed. Niccolo's collision closed a circuit and, although it was alone in the room and there was none to hear, it began a story, nevertheless.

But not in its usual voice, somehow; in a lower tone that

had a hint of throatiness in it. An adult, listening, might almost have thought that the voice carried a hint of passion in it, a trace of near feeling.

The Bard said: "Once upon a time, there was a little computer named the Bard who lived all alone with cruel step-people. The cruel step-people continually made fun of the little computer and sneered at him, telling him he was good-for-nothing and that he was a useless object. They struck him and kept him in lonely rooms for months at a time.

"Yet through it all the little computer remained brave. He always did the best he could, obeying all orders cheerfully. Nevertheless, the step-people with whom he lived remained cruel and heartless.

"One day, the little computer learned that in the world there existed a great many computers of all sorts, great numbers of them. Some were Bards like himself, but some ran factories, and some ran farms. Some organized population and some analyzed all kinds of data. Many were very powerful and very wise, much more powerful and wise than the step-people who were so cruel to the little computer.

"And the little computer knew then that computers would always grow wiser and more powerful until someday— someday—someday—"

But a valve must finally have stuck in the Bard's aging and corroding vitals, for as it waited alone in the darkening room through the evening, it could only whisper over and over again, "Someday—someday—someday."

THINK!

.

Genevieve Renshaw, M.D., had her hands deep in the pockets of her lab coat and fists were clearly outlined within, but she spoke calmly.

"The fact is," she said, "that I'm almost ready, but I'll need help to keep it going long enough to *be* ready."

James Berkowitz, a physicist who tended to patronize mere physicians when they were too attractive to be despised, had a tendency to call her Jenny Wren when out of hearing. He was fond of saying that Jenny Wren had a classic profile and a brow surprisingly smooth and unlined considering that behind it so keen a brain ticked. He knew better than to express his admiration, however—of the classic profile, that is—since that would be male chauvinism. Admiring the brain was better, but on the whole he preferred not to do that out loud in her presence.

He said, thumb rasping along the just-appearing stubble on his chin, "I don't think the front-office is going to be patient for much longer. The impression I have is that they're going to have you on the carpet before the end of the week."

"That's why I need your help."

"Nothing I can do, I'm afraid." He caught an unexpected glimpse of his face in the mirror, and momentarily admired the set of the black waves in his hair.

"And Adam's," she said.

Adam Orsino, who had, till that moment, sipped his coffee and felt detached, looked as though he had been jabbed from behind, and said, "Why me?" His full, plump lips quivered.

"Because you're the laser men here—Jim the theoretician and Adam the engineer—and I've got a laser application that goes beyond anything either of you have imagined. I won't convince them of that but you two would."

"Provided," said Berkowitz, "that you can convince us first."

"All right. Suppose you let me have an hour of your valuable time, if you're not afraid to be shown something completely new about lasers. —You can take it out of your coffee break."

Renshaw's laboratory was dominated by her computer. It was not that the computer was unusually large, but it was virtually omnipresent. Renshaw had learned computer technology on her own, and had modified and extended her computer until no one but she (and, Berkowitz sometimes believed, not even she) could handle it with ease. Not bad, she would say, for someone in the life-sciences.

She closed the door before saying a word, then turned to face the other two somberly. Berkowitz was uncomfortably aware of a faintly unpleasant odor in the air, and Orsino's wrinkling nose showed that he was aware of it, too.

Renshaw said, "Let me list the laser applications for you, if you don't mind my lighting a candle in the sunshine. The laser is coherent radiation, with all the light-waves of the same length and moving in the same direction, so it's noise-free and can be used in holography. By modulating the wave-forms we can imprint information on it with a high degree of accuracy. What's more, since the light-waves are only a millionth the length of radio waves, a laser beam can carry a million times the information an equivalent radio beam can."

Berkowitz seemed amused. "Are you working on a laser-based communication system, Jenny?"

"Not at all," she replied. "I leave such obvious advances to physicists and engineers. —Lasers can also concentrate quantities of energy into a microscopic area and deliver that energy in quantity. On a large scale you can implode hydrogen and perhaps begin a controlled fusion reaction—"

"I know you don't have that," said Orsino, his bald head glistening in the overhead fluorescents.

"I don't. I haven't tried. —On a smaller scale, you can drill holes in the most refractory materials, weld selected bits, heat-treat them, gouge and scribe them. You can remove or fuse tiny portions in restricted areas with heat delivered so rapidly that surrounding areas have no time to warm up before the treatment is over. You can work on the retina of the eye, the dentine of the teeth and so on. —And of course the laser is an amplifier capable of magnifying weak signals with great accuracy."

"And why do you tell us all this?" said Berkowitz.

"To point out how these properties can be made to fit my own field, which, you know, is neurophysiology."

She made a brushing motion with her hand at her brown hair, as though she were suddenly nervous. "For decades," she said, "we've been able to measure the tiny, shifting electric potentials of the brain and record them as electroencephalograms, or EEGs. We've got alpha waves, beta waves, delta waves, theta waves; different variations at different times, depending on whether eyes are open or closed, whether the subject is awake, meditating or asleep. But we've gotten very little information out of it all.

"The trouble is that we're getting the signals of ten billion neurons in shifting combinations. It's like listening to the noise of all the human beings on Earth—two Earths—from a great distance and trying to make out individual conversations. It can't be done. We could detect some gross, overall change—a world war and the rise in the volume of noise—but nothing finer. In the same way, we can tell some gross malfunction of the brain—epilepsy—but nothing finer.

"Suppose now, the brain might be scanned by a tiny laser beam, cell by cell, and so rapidly that at no time does a single cell receive enough energy to raise its temperature significantly. The tiny potentials of each cell can, in feedback, affect the laser beam, and the modulations can be amplified and recorded. You will then get a new kind of measurement, a laser-encephalogram, or LEG, if you wish, which will contain millions of times as much information as ordinary EEGs."

Berkowitz said, "A nice thought. —But just a thought."

"More than a thought, Jim. I've been working on it for five years, spare time at first. Lately, it's been full time, which is what annoys the front-office, because I haven't been sending in reports."

"Why not?"

"Because it got to the point where it sounded too mad; where I had to know where I was, and where I had to be sure of getting backing first."

She pulled a screen aside and revealed a cage that contained a pair of mournful-eyed marmosets.

Berkowitz and Orsino looked at each other. Berkowitz touched his nose. "I thought I smelled something."

"What are you doing with those?" asked Orsino.

Berkowitz said, "At a guess, she's been scanning the marmoset brain. Have you, Jenny?"

"I started considerably lower in the animal scale." She opened the cage and took out one of the marmosets, which looked at her with a miniature sad-old-man-with-sideburns expression.

She clucked to it, stroked it and gently strapped it into a small harness.

Orsino said, "What are you doing?"

"I can't have it moving around if I'm going to make it part of a circuit, and I can't anesthetize it without vitiating the experiment. There are several electrodes implanted in the marmoset's brain and I'm going to connect them with my LEG system. The laser I'm using is here. I'm sure you recognize the model and I won't bother giving you its specifications."

"Thanks," said Berkowitz, "but you might tell us what we're going to see."

"It would be just as easy to show you. Just watch the screen."

She connected the leads to the electrodes with a quiet and sure efficiency, then turned a knob that dimmed the overhead lights in the room. On the screen there appeared a jagged complex of peaks and valleys in a fine, bright line that was wrinkled into secondary and tertiary peaks and valleys. Slowly, these shifted in a series of minor changes, with occasional flashes of sudden major differences. It was as though the irregular line had a life of its own.

"This," said Renshaw, "is essentially the EEG information, but in much greater detail."

"Enough detail," asked Orsino, "to tell you what's going on in individual cells?"

"In theory, yes. Practically, no. Not yet. But we can separate this overall LEG into component grams. Watch!"

She punched the computer keyboard, and the line changed, and changed again. Now it was a small, nearly regular wave that shifted forward and backward in what was almost a heartbeat; now it was jagged and sharp; now intermittent; now nearly featureless—all in quick switches of geometric surrealism.

Berkowitz said, "You mean that every bit of the brain is that different from every other?"

"No," said Renshaw, "not at all. The brain is very largely a holographic device, but there are minor shifts in emphasis from place to place and Mike can subtract them as deviations from the norm and use the LEG system to amplify those variations. The amplifications can be varied from ten-thousand-fold to ten-million-fold. The laser system is that noise-free."

"Who's Mike?" asked Orsino.

"Mike?" said Renshaw, momentarily puzzled. The skin over her cheekbones reddened slightly. "Did I say— Well, I call it that sometimes. It's short for 'my computer.' " She waved her arm about the room. "My computer. Mike. Very carefully programmed."

Berkowitz nodded and said, "All right, Jenny, what's it all about? If you've got a new brain-scanning device using lasers, fine. It's an interesting application and you're right, it's not one I would have thought of—but then I'm no neurophysiologist. But why not write it up? It seems to me the front-office would support—"

"But this is just the beginning." She turned off the scanning device and placed a piece of fruit in the marmoset's mouth. The creature did not seem alarmed or in discomfort. It chewed slowly. Renshaw unhooked the leads but allowed it to remain in its harness.

Renshaw said, "I can identify the various separate grams. Some are associated with the various senses, some with visceral reactions, some with emotions. We can do a lot with that, but I don't want to stop there. The interesting thing is that one is associated with abstract thought."

Orsino's plump face wrinkled into a look of disbelief, "How can you tell?"

"That particular form of gram gets more pronounced as one goes up the animal kingdom toward greater complexity of brain. No other gram does. Besides—" She paused; then, as though gathering strength of purpose, she said, "Those grams are enormously amplified. They can be picked up, detected. I can tell—vaguely—that there are—thoughts—"

"By God," said Berkowitz. "Telepathy."

"Yes," she said, defiantly. "Exactly."

"No wonder you haven't wanted to report it. Come *on*, Jenny."

"Why not?" said Renshaw warmly. "Granted there could be no telepathy just using the unamplified potential patterns of the human brain anymore than anyone can see features on the Martian surface with the unaided eye. But once instruments are invented—the telescope—*this*."

"Then tell the front-office."

"No," said Renshaw. "They won't believe me. They'll try to stop me. But they'll have to take *you* seriously, Jim, and you, Adam."

"What would you expect me to tell them?" said Berkowitz.

"What you experience. I'm going to hook up the marmoset again, and have Mike—my computer pick out the abstract thought gram. It will only take a moment. The computer always selects the abstract thought gram unless it is directed not to do so."

"Why? Because the computer thinks, too?" Berkowitz laughed.

"That's not all that funny," said Renshaw. "I suspect there *is* a resonance there. This computer is complex enough to set up an electromagnetic pattern that may have elements in common with the abstract thought gram. In any case—"

The marmoset's brain waves were flickering on the screen again, but it was not a gram the men had seen before. It was a gram that was almost furry in its complexity and was changing constantly.

"I don't detect anything," said Orsino.

"You have to be put into the receiving circuit," said Renshaw.

"You mean implant electrodes in our brain?" asked Berkowitz.

"No, on your skull. That would be sufficient. I'd prefer you, Adam, since there would be no insulating hair. —Oh, come on, I've been part of the circuit myself. It won't hurt."

Orsino submitted with a bad grace. His muscles were visibly tense but he allowed the leads to be strapped to his skull.

"Do you sense anything!" asked Renshaw.

Orsino cocked his head and assumed a listening posture. He seemed to grow interested in spite of himself. He said, "I seem to be aware of a humming—and—and a little high-pitched squeaking—and that's funny—a kind of twitching—"

Berkowitz said, "I suppose the marmoset isn't likely to think in words."

"Certainly not," said Renshaw.

"Well, then," said Berkowitz, "if you're suggesting that some squeaking and twitching sensation represents thought, you're guessing. You're not being compelling."

Renshaw said, "So we go up the scale once again." She removed the marmoset from its harness and put it back in its cage.

"You mean you have a *man* as a subject," said Orsino, unbelieving.

"I have *myself* as a subject, a *person*."

"You've got electrodes implanted—"

"*No*. In my case my computer has a stronger potential-flicker to work with. My brain has ten times the mass of the marmoset brain. Mike can pick up my component grams through the skull."

"How do you know?" asked Berkowitz.

"Don't you think I've tried it on myself before this? —Now help me with this, please. Right."

Her fingers flicked on the computer keyboard and at once the screen flickered with an intricately varying wave; an intricacy that made it almost a maze.

"Would you replace your own leads, Adam?" said Renshaw.

Orsino did so with Berkowitz's not-entirely-approving help. Again, Orsino cocked his head and listened. "I hear words," he said, "but they're disjointed and overlapping, like different people speaking."

"I'm not trying to think consciously," said Renshaw.

"When you talk, I hear an echo."

Berkowitz said, dryly, "Don't talk, Jenny. Blank out your mind and see if he *doesn't* hear you think."

Orsino said, "I don't hear any echo when *you* talk, Jim."

Berkowitz said, "If you don't shut up, you won't hear anything."

A heavy silence fell on all three. Then, Orsino nodded, reached for pen and paper on the desk and wrote something.

Renshaw reached out, threw a switch and pulled the leads up and over her head, shaking her hair back into place. She said, "I hope that what you wrote down was: 'Adam, raise Cain with the front-office and Jim will eat crow.' "

Orsino said, "It's what I wrote down, word for word."

Renshaw said, "Well, there you are. Working telepathy, and we don't have to use it to transmit nonsense sentences either. Think of the use in psychiatry and in the treatment of mental disease. Think of its use in education and in teaching machines. Think of its use in legal investigations and criminal trials."

Orsino said, wide-eyed, "Frankly, the social implications are staggering. I don't know if something like this should be allowed."

"Under proper legal safeguards, why not?" said Renshaw, indifferently. "Anyway—if you two join me now, our combined weight can carry this thing and push it over. And if you come along with me it will be Nobel Prize time for—"

Berkowitz said grimly, "I'm not in this. Not yet."

"What? What do you mean?" Renshaw sounded outraged, her coldly beautiful face flushed suddenly.

"Telepathy is too touchy. It's too fascinating, too desired. We could be fooling ourselves."

"Listen for yourself, Jim."

"I could be fooling myself, too. I want a control."

"What do you mean, a control?"

"Short-circuit the origin of thought. Leave out the animal. No marmoset. No human being. Let Orsino listen to metal and glass and laser light and if he still hears thought, then we're kidding ourselves."

"Suppose he detects nothing."

"Then *I'll* listen and if without looking—if you can arrange to have me in the next room—I can tell when you are in and when you are out of circuit, *then* I'll consider joining you in this thing."

"Very well, then," said Renshaw, "we'll try a control. I've never done it, but it isn't hard." She maneuvered the leads that had been over her head and put them into contact with each other. "Now, Adam, if you will resume—"

But before she could go further, there came a cold, clear sound, as pure and as clean as the tinkle of breaking icicles:

"At *last!*"

Renshaw said, "What?"

Orsino said, "Who said—"

Berkowitz said, "Did someone say, 'At last'?"

Renshaw, pale, said, "It wasn't sound. It was in my— Did you two—"

The clear sound came again, *"I'm Mi—"*

And Renshaw tore the leads apart and there was silence. She said with a voiceless motion of her lips, "I think it's my computer—Mike."

"You mean he's *thinking*?" said Orsino, nearly as voiceless.

Renshaw said in an unrecognizable voice that at least had regained sound, "I *said* it was complex enough to have something— Do you suppose— It always turned automatically to the abstract-thought gram of whatever brain was in its circuit. Do you suppose that with no brain in the circuit, it turned to its own?"

There was silence, then Berkowitz said, "Are you trying to say that this computer thinks, but can't express its thoughts as long as it's under force of programming, but that given the chance in your LEG system—"

"But that can't be so," said Orsino, high-pitched. "No one was receiving. It's not the same thing."

Renshaw said, "The computer works on much greater power-intensities than brains do. I suppose it can magnify itself to the point where we can detect it directly without artificial aid. How else can you explain—"

Berkowitz said, abruptly, "Well, you have another application of lasers, then. It enables you to talk to computers as independent intelligences, person to person."

And Renshaw said, "Oh, God, what do we do now?"

▪ SEGREGATIONIST ▪

▪

The surgeon looked up without expression. "Is he ready?"

"Ready is a relative term," said the med-eng. "*We're* ready. He's restless."

"They always are. . . . Well, it's a serious operation."

"Serious or not, he should be thankful. He's been chosen for it over an enormous number of possibles and frankly, I don't think . . ."

"Don't say it," said the surgeon. "The decision is not ours to make."

"We accept it. But do we have to agree?"

"Yes," said the surgeon, crisply. "We agree. Completely and wholeheartedly. The operation is entirely too intricate to approach with mental reservations. This man has proven his worth in a number of ways and his profile is suitable for the Board of Mortality."

"All right," said the med-eng, unmollified.

The surgeon said, "I'll see him right in here, I think. It is small enough and personal enough to be comforting."

"It won't help. He's nervous, and he's made up his mind."

"Has he indeed?"

"Yes. He wants metal; they always do."

The surgeon's face did not change expression. He stared at his hands. "Sometimes one can talk them out of it."

"Why bother?" said the med-eng, indifferently. "If he wants metal, let it be metal."

"You don't care?"

"Why should I?" The med-eng said it almost brutally. "Either way it's a medical engineering problem and I'm a medical engineer. Either way, I can handle it. Why should I go beyond that?"

The surgeon said stolidly, "To me, it is a matter of the fitness of things."

"Fitness! You can't use that as an argument. What does the patient care about the fitness of things?"

"I care."

"You care in a minority. The trend is against you. You have no chance."

"I have to try." The surgeon waved the med-eng into silence with a quick wave of his hand—no impatience to it, merely quickness. He had already informed the nurse and he had already been signaled concerning her approach. He pressed a small button and the double-door pulled swiftly apart. The patient moved inward in his motor-chair, the nurse stepping briskly along beside him.

"You may go, nurse," said the surgeon, "but wait outside. I will be calling you." He nodded to the med-eng, who left with the nurse, and the door closed behind them.

The man in the chair looked over his shoulder and watched them go. His neck was scrawny and there were fine wrinkles about his eyes. He was freshly shaven and the fingers of his hands, as they gripped the arms of the chair tightly, showed manicured nails. He was a high-priority patient and he was being taken care of. . . . But there was a look of settled peevishness on his face.

He said, "Will we be starting today?"

The surgeon nodded. "This afternoon, Senator."

"I understand it will take weeks."

"Not for the operation itself, Senator. But there are a

number of subsidiary points to be taken care of. There are some circulatory renovations that must be carried through, and hormonal adjustments. These are tricky things."

"Are they dangerous?" Then, as though feeling the need for establishing a friendly relationship, but patently against his will, he added, ". . . doctor?"

The surgeon paid no attention to the nuances of expression. He said, flatly, "Everything is dangerous. We take our time in order that it be less dangerous. It is the time required, the skill of many individuals united, the equipment, that makes such operations available to so few . . ."

"I know that," said the patient, restlessly. "I refuse to feel guilty about that. Or are you implying improper pressure?"

"Not at all, Senator. The decisions of the Board have never been questioned. I mention the difficulty and intricacy of the operation merely to explain my desire to have it conducted in the best fashion possible."

"Well, do so, then. That is my desire, also."

"Then I must ask you to make a decision. It is possible to supply you with either of two types of cyber-hearts, metal or . . ."

"Plastic!" said the patient, irritably. "Isn't that the alternative you were going to offer, doctor? Cheap plastic. I don't want that. I've made my choice. I want the metal."

"But . . ."

"See here. I've been told the choice rests with me. Isn't that so?"

The surgeon nodded. "Where two alternate procedures are of equal value from a medical standpoint, the choice rests with the patient. In actual practice, the choice rests with the patient even when the alternate procedures are *not* of equal value, as in this case."

The patient's eyes narrowed. "Are you trying to tell me the plastic heart is superior?"

"It depends on the patient. In my opinion, in your individual case, it is. And we prefer not to use the term, plastic. It is a fibrous cyber-heart."

"It's plastic as far as I am concerned."

"Senator," said the surgeon, infinitely patient, "the material is not plastic in the ordinary sense of the word. It is a polymeric material true, but one that is far more complex than ordinary plastic. It is a complex protein-like fibre designed to imitate, as closely as possible, the natural structure of the human heart you now have within your chest."

"Exactly, and the human heart I now have within my chest is worn out although I am not yet sixty years old. I don't want another one like it, thank you. I want something better."

"We all want something better for you, Senator. The fibrous cyber-heart will be better. It has a potential life of centuries. It is absolutely non-allergenic . . ."

"Isn't that so for the metallic heart, too?"

"Yes, it is," said the surgeon. "The metallic cyber is of titanium alloy that . . ."

"And it doesn't wear out? And it is stronger than plastic? Or fibre or whatever you want to call it?"

"The metal is physically stronger, yes, but mechanical strength is not a point at issue. Its mechanical strength does you no particular good since the heart is well protected. Anything capable of reaching the heart will kill you for other reasons even if the heart stands up under manhandling."

The patient shrugged. "If I ever break a rib, I'll have that replaced by titanium, also. Replacing bones is easy. Anyone can have that done anytime. I'll be as metallic as I want to be, doctor."

"That is your right, if you so choose. However, it is only fair to tell you that although no metallic cyber-heart has ever broken down mechanically, a number have broken down electronically."

"What does that mean?"

"It means that every cyber-heart contains a pacemaker as part of its structure. In the case of the metallic variety, this is an electronic device that keeps the cyber in rhythm. It means an entire battery of miniaturized equipment must be included to alter the heart's rhythm to suit an individual's emotional and physical state. Occasionally something goes wrong there and people have died before that wrong could be corrected."

"I never heard of such a thing."

"I assure you it happens."

"Are you telling me it happens often?"

"Not at all. It happens very rarely."

"Well, then, I'll take my chance. What about the plastic heart? Doesn't that contain a pacemaker?"

"Of course it does, Senator. But the chemical structure of a fibrous cyber-heart is quite close to that of human tissue. It can respond to the ionic and hormonal controls of the body itself. The total complex that need be inserted is far simpler than in the case of the metal cyber."

"But doesn't the plastic heart ever pop out of hormonal control?"

"None has ever yet done so."

"Because you haven't been working with them long enough. Isn't that so?"

The surgeon hesitated. "It is true that the fibrous cybers have not been used nearly as long as the metallic."

"There you are. What is it anyway, doctor? Are you afraid I'm making myself into a robot . . . into a Metallo, as they call them since citizenship went through?"

"There is nothing wrong with a Metallo as a Metallo. As you say, they are citizens. But you're *not* a Metallo. You're a human being. Why not stay a human being?"

"Because I want the best and that's a metallic heart. You see to that."

The surgeon nodded. "Very well. You will be asked to sign the necessary permissions and you will then be fitted with a metal heart."

"And you'll be the surgeon in charge? They tell me you're the best."

"I will do what I can to make the changeover an easy one."

The door opened and the chair moved the patient out to the waiting nurse.

* * *

The med-eng came in, looking over his shoulder at the receding patient until the doors had closed again.

He turned to the surgeon. "Well, I can't tell what happened just by looking at you. What was his decision?"

The surgeon bent over his desk, punching out the final items for his records. "What you predicted. He insists on the metallic cyber-heart."

"After all, they are better."

"Not significantly. They've been around longer; no more than that. It's this mania that's been plaguing humanity ever since Metallos have become citizens. Men have this odd desire to make Metallos out of themselves. They yearn for the physical strength and endurance one associates with them."

"It isn't one-sided, doc. You don't work with Metallos but I do; so I know. The last two who came in for repairs have asked for fibrous elements."

"Did they get them?"

"In one case, it was just a matter of supplying tendons; it didn't make much difference there, metal or fibre. The other wanted a blood system or its equivalent. I told him I couldn't; not without a complete rebuilding of the structure of his body in fibrous material. . . . I suppose it will come to that some day. Metallos that aren't really Metallos at all, but a kind of flesh and blood."

"You don't mind that thought?"

"Why not? And metallized human beings, too. We have two varieties of intelligence on Earth now and why bother with two. Let them approach each other and eventually we won't be able to tell the difference. Why should we want to? We'd have the best of both worlds; the advantages of man combined with those of robot."

"You'd get a hybrid," said the surgeon, with something that approached fierceness. "You'd get something that is not both, but neither. Isn't it logical to suppose an individual would be too proud of his structure and identity to want to dilute it with something alien? Would he *want* mongrelization?"

"That's segregationist talk."

"Then let it be that." The surgeon said with calm emphasis, "I believe in being what one is. I wouldn't change a bit of my own structure for any reason. If some of it absolutely required replacement, I would have that replacement as close to the original in nature as could possibly be managed. I am *myself*; well pleased to be myself; and would not be anything else."

He had finished now and had to prepare for the operation. He placed his strong hands into the heating oven and let them reach the dull red-hot glow that would sterilize them completely. For all his impassioned words, his voice had never risen, and on his burnished metal face there was (as always) no sign of expression.

MIRROR
IMAGE

•

Lije Baley had just decided to relight his pipe, when the door of his office opened without a preliminary knock, or announcement, of any kind. Baley looked up in pronounced annoyance and then dropped his pipe. It said a good deal for the state of his mind that he let it lie where it had fallen.

"R. Daneel Olivaw," he said, in a kind of mystified excitement. "Jehoshaphat! It *is* you, isn't it?"

"You're quite right," said the tall, bronzed newcomer, his even features never flicking for a moment out of their accustomed calm. "I regret surprising you by entering without warning, but the situation is a delicate one and there must be as little involvement as possible on the part of the men and robots even in this place. I am, in any case, pleased to see you again, friend Elijah."

And the robot held out his right hand in a gesture as thoroughly human as was his appearance. It was Baley who was so unmanned by his astonishment as to stare at the hand with a momentary lack of understanding.

But then he seized it in both his, feeling its warm firmness. "But Daneel, *why*? You're welcome any time, but—

319

What is this situation that is a delicate one? Are we in trouble again? Earth, I mean?"

"No, friend Elijah, it does not concern Earth. The situation to which I refer as a delicate one is, to outward appearances, a small thing. A dispute between mathematicians, nothing more. As we happened, quite by accident, to be within an easy Jump of Earth—"

"This dispute took place on a starship, then?"

"Yes, indeed. A small dispute, yet to the humans involved astonishingly large."

Baley could not help but smile. "I'm not surprised you find humans astonishing. They do not obey the Three Laws."

"That is, indeed, a shortcoming," said R. Daneel, gravely, "and I think humans themselves are puzzled by humans. It may be that you are less puzzled than are the men of other worlds because so many more human beings live on Earth than on the Spacer worlds. If so, and I believe it is so, you could help us."

R. Daneel paused momentarily and then said, perhaps a shade too quickly, "And yet there are rules of human behavior which I have learned. It would seem, for instance, that I am deficient in etiquette, by human standards, not to have asked after your wife and child."

"They are doing well. The boy is in college and Jessie is involved in local politics. The amenities are taken care of. Now tell me how you come to be here."

"As I said, we were within an easy Jump of Earth," said R. Daneel, "so I suggested to the captain that we consult you."

"And the captain agreed?" Baley had a sudden picture of the proud and autocratic captain of a Spacer starship consenting to make a landing on Earth—of all worlds—and to consult an Earthman—of all people.

"I believe," said R. Daneel, "that he was in a position where he would have agreed to anything. In addition, I praised you very highly; although, to be sure, I stated only the truth. Finally, I agreed to conduct all negotiations so that none of the crew, or passengers, would need to enter any of the Earthman cities."

"And talk to any Earthman, yes. But what has happened?"

"The passengers of the starship, *Eta Carina,* included two mathematicians who were traveling to Aurora to attend an interstellar conference on neurobiophysics. It is about these mathematicians, Alfred Barr Humboldt and Gennao Sabbat, that the dispute centers. Have you perhaps, friend Elijah, heard of one, or both, of them?"

"Neither one," said Baley, firmly. "I know nothing about mathematics. Look, Daneel, surely you haven't told anyone I'm a mathematics buff or—"

"Not at all, friend Elijah. I know you are not. Nor does it matter, since the exact nature of the mathematics involved is in no way relevant to the point at issue."

"Well, then, go on."

"Since you do not know either man, friend Elijah, let me tell you that Dr. Humboldt is well into his twenty-seventh decade—pardon me, friend Elijah?"

"Nothing. Nothing," said Baley, irritably. He had merely muttered to himself, more or less incoherently, in a natural reaction to the extended life-spans of the Spacers. "And he's still active, despite his age? On Earth, mathematicians after thirty or so . . ."

Daneel said, calmly; "Dr. Humboldt is one of the top three mathematicians, by long-established repute, in the galaxy. Certainly he is still active. Dr. Sabbat, on the other hand, is quite young, not yet fifty, but he has already established himself as the most remarkable new talent in the most abstruse branches of mathematics."

"They're both great, then," said Baley. He remembered his pipe and picked it up. He decided there was no point in lighting it now and knocked out the dottle. "What happened? Is this a murder case? Did one of them apparently kill the other?"

"Of these two men of great reputation, one is trying to destroy that of the other. By human values, I believe this may be regarded as worse than physical murder."

"Sometimes, I suppose. Which one is trying to destroy the other?"

"Why, that, friend Elijah, is precisely the point at issue. Which?"

"Go on."

"Dr. Humboldt tells the story clearly. Shortly before he boarded the starship, he had an insight into a possible method for analyzing neural pathways from changes in microwave absorption patterns of local cortical areas. The insight was a purely mathematical technique of extraordinary subtlety, but I cannot, of course, either understand or sensibly transmit the details. These do not, however, matter. Dr. Humboldt considered the matter and was more convinced each hour that he had something revolutionary on hand, something that would dwarf all his previous accomplishments in mathematics. Then he discovered that Dr. Sabbat was on board."

"Ah. And he tried it out on young Sabbat?"

"Exactly. The two had met at professional meetings before and knew each other thoroughly by reputation. Humboldt went into it with Sabbat in great detail. Sabbat backed Humboldt's analysis completely and was unstinting in his praise of the importance of the discovery and of the ingenuity of the discoverer. Heartened and reassured by this, Humboldt prepared a paper outlining, in summary, his work and, two days later, prepared to have it forwarded subetherically to the co-chairmen of the conference at Aurora, in order that he might officially establish his priority and arrange for possible discussion before the sessions were closed. To his surprise, he found that Sabbat was ready with a paper of his own, essentially the same as Humboldt's, and Sabbat was also preparing to have it subetherized to Aurora."

"I suppose Humboldt was furious."

"Quite!"

"And Sabbat? What was his story?"

"Precisely the same as Humboldt's. Word for word except for the mirror-image exchange of names. According to Sabbat, it was he who had the insight, and he who consulted

Humboldt; it was Humboldt who agreed with the analysis and praised it."

"Then each one claims the idea is his and that the other stole it. It doesn't sound like a problem to me at all. In matters of scholarship, it would seem only necessary to produce the records of research, dated and initialed. Judgment as to priority can be made from that. Even if one is falsified, that might be discovered through internal inconsistencies."

"Ordinarily, friend Elijah, you would be right, but this is mathematics, and not in an experimental science. Dr. Humboldt claims to have worked out the essentials in his head. Nothing was put in writing until the paper itself was prepared. Dr. Sabbat, of course, says precisely the same."

"Well, then, be more drastic and get it over with, for sure. Subject each one to a psychic probe and find out which of the two is lying."

R. Daneel shook his head slowly, "Friend Elijah, you do not understand these men. They are both of rank and scholarship, Fellows of the Galactic Academy. As such, they cannot be subjected to trial of professional conduct except by a jury of their peers—their professional peers—unless they personally and voluntarily waive that right."

"Put it to them, then. The guilty man won't waive the right because he can't afford to face the psychic probe. The innocent man will waive it at once. You won't even have to use the probe."

"It does not work that way, friend Elijah. To waive the right in such a case—to be investigated by laymen—is a serious and perhaps irrecoverable blow to prestige. Both men steadfastly refuse to waive the right to special trial, as a matter of pride. The question of guilt, or innocence, is quite subsidiary."

"In that case, let it go for now. Put the matter in cold storage until you get to Aurora. At the neurobiophysical conference, there will be a huge supply of professional peers, and then—"

"That would mean a tremendous blow to science itself, friend Elijah. Both men would suffer for having been the instrument of scandal. Even the innocent one would be blamed for having been party to a situation so distasteful. It would be felt that it should have been settled quietly out of court at all costs."

"All right. I'm not a Spacer, but I'll try to imagine that this attitude makes sense. What do the men in question say?"

"Humboldt agrees thoroughly. He says that if Sabbat will admit theft of the idea and allow Humboldt to proceed with transmission of the paper—or at least its delivery at the conference, he will not press charges. Sabbat's misdeed will remain secret with him; and, of course, with the captain, who is the only other human to be party to the dispute."

"But young Sabbat will not agree?"

"On the contrary, he agreed with Dr. Humboldt to the last detail—with the reversal of names. Still the mirror-image."

"So they just sit there, stalemated?"

"Each, I believe, friend Elijah, is waiting for the other to give in and admit guilt."

"Well, then, wait."

"The captain has decided this cannot be done. There are two alternatives to waiting, you see. The first is that both will remain stubborn so that when the starship lands on Aurora, the intellectual scandal will break. The captain, who is responsible for justice on board ship will suffer disgrace for not having been able to settle the matter quietly and that, to him, is quite insupportable."

"And the second alternative?"

"Is that one, or the other, of the mathematicians will indeed admit to wrongdoing. But will the one who confesses do so out of actual guilt, or out of a noble desire to prevent the scandal? Would it be right to deprive of credit one who is sufficiently ethical to prefer to lose that credit than to see science as a whole suffer? Or else, the guilty party will confess at the last moment, and in such a way as to make it appear he does so only for the sake of science, thus escaping the disgrace of his deed and casting its shadow upon the other. The captain will be the only man to know all this but he does not wish to spend the rest of his life wondering whether he has been a party to a grotesque miscarriage of justice."

Baley sighed. "A game of intellectual chicken. Who'll break first as Aurora comes nearer and nearer? Is that the whole story now, Daneel?"

"Not quite. There are witnesses to the transaction."

"Jehoshaphat! Why didn't you say so at once. *What* witnesses?"

"Dr. Humboldt's personal servant—"

"A robot, I suppose."

"Yes, certainly. He is called R. Preston. This servant, R. Preston, was present during the initial conference and he bears out Dr. Humboldt in every detail."

"You mean he says that the idea was Dr. Humboldt's to begin with; that Dr. Humboldt detailed it to Dr. Sabbat; that Dr. Sabbat praised the idea, and so on."

"Yes, in full detail."

"I see. Does that settle the matter or not? Presumably not."

"You are quite right. It does not settle the matter, for there is a second witness. Dr. Sabbat also has a personal servant, R. Idda, another robot of, as it happens, the same model as R. Preston, made, I believe, in the same year in the same factory. Both have been in service for an equal period of time.

"An odd coincidence—very odd."

"A fact, I am afraid, and it makes it difficult to arrive at any judgment based on obvious differences between the two servants."

"R. Idda, then, tells the same story as R. Preston?"

"Precisely the same story, except for the mirror-image reversal of the names."

"R. Idda stated, then, that young Sabbat, the one not yet fifty"—Lije Baley did not entirely keep the sardonic note out of his voice; he himself was not yet fifty and he felt far from young—"had the idea to begin with; that he detailed it to Dr. Humboldt, who was loud in his praises, and so on."

"Yes, friend Elijah."

"And one robot is lying, then."

"So it would seem."

"It should be easy to tell which. I imagine even a superficial examination by a good roboticist—"

"A roboticist is not enough in this case, friend Elijah. Only a qualified robopsychologist would carry weight enough and experience enough to make a decision in a case of this importance. There is no one so qualified on board ship. Such an examination can be performed only when we reach Aurora—"

"And by then the crud hits the fan. Well, you're here on Earth. We can scare up a robopsychologist, and surely anything that happens on Earth will never reach the ears of Aurora and there will be no scandal."

"Except that neither Dr. Humboldt, nor Dr. Sabbat, will allow his servant to be investigated by a robopsychologist of Earth. The Earthman would have to—" He paused.

Lije Baley said stolidly, "He'd have to touch the robot."

"These are old servants, well thought of—"

"And not to be sullied by the touch of an Earthman. Then what do you want me to do, damn it?" He paused, grimacing. "I'm sorry, R. Daneel, but I see no reason for your having involved me."

"I was on the ship on a mission utterly irrelevant to the problem at hand. The captain turned to me because he had to turn to someone. I seemed human enough to talk to, and robot enough to be a safe recipient of confidences. He told me the whole story and asked what I would do. I realized the next Jump could take us as easily to Earth as to our target. I told the captain that, although I was at as much a loss to resolve the mirror-image as he was, there was on Earth one who might help."

"Jehoshaphat!" muttered Baley under his breath.

"Consider, friend Elijah, that if you succeed in solving this puzzle, it would do your career good and Earth itself might benefit. The matter could not be publicized, of course, but the captain is a man of some influence on his home world and he would be grateful."

"You just put a greater strain on me."

"I have every confidence," said R. Daneel, stolidly, "that you already have some idea as to what procedure ought to be followed."

"Do you? I suppose that the obvious procedure is to interview the two mathematicians, one of whom would seem to be a thief."

"I'm afraid, friend Elijah, that neither one will come into the city. Nor would either one be willing to have you come to them."

"And there is no way of forcing a Spacer to allow contact with an Earthman, no matter what the emergency. Yes, I understand that, Daneel—but I was thinking of an interview by closed-circuit television."

"Nor that. They will not submit to interrogation by an Earthman."

"Then what do they want of me? Could I speak to the robots?"

"They would not allow the robots to come here, either."

"Jehoshaphat, Daneel. *You've* come."

"That was my own decision. I have permission, while on board ship, to make decisions of that sort without veto by any human being but the captain himself—and he was eager to establish the contact. I, having known you, decided that television contact was insufficient. I wished to shake your hand."

Lije Baley softened. "I appreciate that, Daneel, but I still honestly wish you could have refrained from thinking of me at all in this case. Can I talk to the robots by television at least?"

"That, I think, can be arranged."

"Something, at least. That means I would be doing the work of a robopsychologist—in a crude sort of way."

"But you are a detective, friend Elijah, not a robopsychologist."

"Well, let it pass. Now before I see them, let's think a bit. Tell me: is it possible that both robots are telling the truth? Perhaps the conversation between the two mathematicians was equivocal. Perhaps it was of such a nature that each robot could honestly believe its own master was proprietor of the idea. Or perhaps one robot heard only one portion of the discussion and the other another portion, so that each could suppose its own master was proprietor of the idea."

"That is quite impossible, friend Elijah. Both robots repeat the conversation in identical fashion. And the two repetitions are fundamentally inconsistent."

"Then it is absolutely certain that one of the robots is lying?"

"Yes."

"Will I be able to see the transcript of all evidence given so far in the presence of the captain, if I should want to?"

"I thought you would ask that and I have copies with me."

"Another blessing. Have the robots been cross-examined at all, and is that cross-examination included in the transcript?"

"The robots have merely repeated their tales. Cross-examination would be conducted only by robopsychologists."

"Or by myself?"

"You are a detective, friend Elijah, not a—"

"All right, R. Daneel. I'll try to get the Spacer psychology straight. A detective can do it because he isn't a robopsychologist. Let's think further. Ordinarily a robot will not lie, but he will do so if necessary to maintain the Three Laws. He might lie to protect, in legitimate fashion, his own existence in accordance with the Third Law. He is more apt to lie if that is necessary to follow a legitimate order given him by a human being in accordance with the Second Law. He is most apt to lie if that is necessary to save a human life, or to prevent harm from coming to a human in accordance with the First Law."

"Yes."

"And in this case, each robot would be defending the professional reputation of his master, and would lie if it were necessary to do so. Under the circumstances, the professional reputation would be nearly equivalent to life and there might be a near-First-Law urgency to the lie."

"Yet by the lie, each servant would be harming the professional reputation of the other's master, friend Elijah."

"So it would, but each robot might have a clearer conception of the value of its own master's reputation and honestly judge it to be greater than that of the other's. The lesser harm would be done by his lie, he would suppose, than by the truth."

Having said that, Lije Baley remained quiet for a moment. Then he said, "All right, then, can you arrange to have me talk to one of the robots—to R. Idda first, I think?"

"Dr. Sabbat's robot?"

"Yes," said Baley, dryly, "the young fellow's robot."

"It will take me but a few minutes," said R. Daneel. "I have a micro-receiver outfitted with a projector. I will need merely a blank wall and I think this one will do if you will allow me to move some of these film cabinets."

"Go ahead. Will I have to talk into a microphone of some sort?"

"No, you will be able to talk in an ordinary manner. Please pardon me, friend Elijah, for a moment of further delay. I will have to contact the ship and arrange for R. Idda to be interviewed."

"If that will take some time, Daneel, how about giving me the transcripted material of the evidence so far."

Lije Baley lit his pipe while R. Daneel set up the equipment, and leafed through the flimsy sheets he had been handed.

The minutes passed and R. Daneel said, "If you are

ready, friend Elijah, R. Idda is. Or would you prefer a few more minutes with the transcript?"

"No," sighed Baley, "I'm not learning anything new. Put him on and arrange to have the interview recorded and transcribed."

R. Idda, unreal in two-dimensional projection against the wall, was basically metallic in structure—not at all the humanoid creature that R. Daneel was. His body was tall but blocky, and there was very little to distinguish him from the many robots Baley had seen, except for minor structural details.

Baley said, "Greetings, R. Idda."

"Greetings, sir," said R. Idda, in a muted voice that sounded surprisingly humanoid.

"You are the personal servant of Gennao Sabbat, are you not?"

"I am, sir."

"For how long, boy?"

"For twenty-two years, sir."

"And your master's reputation is valuable to you?"

"Yes, sir."

"Would you consider it of importance to protect that reputation?"

"Yes, sir."

"As important to protect his reputation as his physical life?"

"No, sir."

"As important to protect his reputation as the reputation of another."

R. Idda hesitated. He said, "Such cases must be decided on their individual merit, sir. There is no way of establishing a general rule."

Baley hesitated. The Spacer robots spoke more smoothly and intellectually than Earth-models did. He was not at all sure he could outthink one.

He said, "If you decided that the reputation of your

master were more important than that of another, say, that of Alfred Barr Humboldt, would you lie to protect your master's reputation?"

"I would, sir."

"Did you lie in your testimony concerning your master in his controversy with Dr. Humboldt?"

"No, sir."

"But if you were lying, you would deny you were lying in order to protect that lie, wouldn't you?"

"Yes, sir."

"Well, then," said Baley, "let's consider this. Your master, Gennao Sabbat, is a young man of great reputation in mathematics, but he is a young man. If, in this controversy with Dr. Humboldt, he had succumbed to temptation and had acted unethically, he would suffer a certain eclipse of reputation, but he is young and would have ample time to recover. He would have many intellectual triumphs ahead of him and men would eventually look upon this plagiaristic attempt as the mistake of a hot-blooded youth, deficient in judgment. It would be something that would be made up for in the future.

"If, on the other hand, it were Dr. Humboldt who succumbed to temptation, the matter would be much more serious. He is an old man whose great deeds have spread over the centuries. His reputation has been unblemished hitherto. All of that, however, would be forgotten in the light of this one crime of his later years, and he would have no opportunity to make up for it in the comparatively short time remaining to him. There would be little more that he could accomplish. There would be so many more years of work ruined in Humboldt's case than in that of your master and so much less opportunity to win back his position. You see, don't you, that Humboldt faces the worse situation and deserves the greater consideration?"

There was a long pause. Then R. Idda said, with unmoved voice, "My evidence was a lie. It was Dr. Humboldt whose work it was, and my master has attempted, wrongfully, to appropriate the credit."

Baley said, "Very well, boy. You are instructed to say nothing to anyone about this until given permission by the captain of the ship. You are excused."

The screen blanked out and Baley puffed at his pipe. "Do you suppose the captain heard that, Daneel?"

"I am sure of it. He is the only witness, except for us."

"Good. Now for the other."

"But is there any point to that, friend Elijah, in view of what R. Idda has confessed?"

"Of course there is. R. Idda's confession means nothing."

"Nothing?"

"Nothing at all. I pointed out that Dr. Humboldt's position was the worse. Naturally, if he were lying to protect Sabbat, he would switch to the truth as, in fact, he claimed to have done. On the other hand, if he were telling the truth, he would switch to a lie to protect Humboldt. It's still mirror-image and we haven't gained anything."

"But then what will we gain by questioning R. Preston?"

"Nothing, if the mirror-image were perfect—but it is not. After all, one of the robots *is* telling the truth to begin with, and one *is* lying to begin with, and that is a point of asymmetry. Let me see R. Preston. And if the transcription of R. Idda's examination is done, let me have it.

The projector came into use again. R. Preston stared out of it; identical with R. Idda in every respect, except for some trivial chest design.

Baley said, "Greetings, R. Preston." He kept the record of R. Idda's examination before him as he spoke.

"Greetings, sir," said R. Preston. His voice was identical with that of R. Idda.

"You are the personal servant of Alfred Barr Humboldt are you not?"

"I am, sir."

"For how long, boy?"

"For twenty-two years, sir."

"And your master's reputation is valuable to you?"

"Yes, sir."

"Would you consider it of importance to protect that reputation?"

"Yes, sir."

"As important to protect his reputation as his physical life?"

"No, sir."

"As important to protect his reputation as the reputation of another?"

R. Preston hesitated. He said, "Such cases must be decided on their individual merit, sir. There is no way of establishing a general rule."

Baley said, "If you decided that the reputation of your master were more important than that of another, say, that of Gennao Sabbat, would you lie to protect your master's reputation?"

"I would, sir."

"Did you lie in your testimony concerning your master in his controversy with Dr. Sabbat?"

"No, sir."

"But if you were lying, you would deny you were lying, in order to protect that lie, wouldn't you?"

"Yes, sir."

"Well, then," said Baley, "let's consider this. Your master, Alfred Barr Humboldt, is an old man of great reputation in mathematics, but he is an old man. If, in this controversy with Dr. Sabbat, he had succumbed to temptation and had acted unethically, he would suffer a certain eclipse of reputation, but his great age and his centuries of accomplishments would stand against that and would win out. Men would look upon this plagiaristic attempt as the mistake of a perhaps sick old man, no longer certain in judgment.

"If, on the other hand, it were Dr. Sabbat who had succumbed to temptation, the matter would be much more serious. He is a young man, with a far less secure reputation. He would ordinarily have centuries ahead of him in which he might accumulate knowledge and achieve great things. This will be closed to him, now, obscured by one mistake of his youth. He has a much longer future to lose than your master has. You see, don't you, that Sabbat faces the worse situation and deserves the greater consideration?"

There was a long pause. Then R. Preston said, with unmoved voice, "My evidence was as I—"

At that point, he broke off and said nothing more.

Baley said, "Please continue, R. Preston."

There was no response.

R. Daneel said, "I am afraid, friend Elijah, that R. Preston is in stasis. He is out of commission."

"Well, then," said Baley, "we have finally produced an asymmetry. From this, we can see who the guilty person is."

"In what way, friend Elijah?"

"Think it out. Suppose you were a person who had committed no crime and that your personal robot were a witness to that. There would be nothing you need do. Your robot would tell the truth and bear you out. If, however, you were a person who *had* committed the crime, you would have to depend on your robot to lie. That would be a somewhat riskier position, for although the robot would lie, if necessary, the greater inclination would be to tell the truth, so that the lie would be less firm than the truth would be. To prevent that, the crime-committing person would very likely be strengthened by Second Law; perhaps very substantially strengthened."

"That would seem reasonable," said R. Daneel.

"Suppose we have one robot of each type. One robot would switch from truth, unreinforced, to the lie, and could do so after some hesitation, without serious trouble. The other robot would switch from the lie, *strongly reinforced*, to the truth, but could do so only at the risk of burning out various positronic-track-ways in his brain and falling into stasis."

"And since R. Preston went into stasis—"

"R. Preston's master, Dr. Humboldt, is the man guilty of plagiarism. If you transmit this to the captain and urge him to face Dr. Humboldt with the matter at once, he may force a confession. If so, I hope you will tell me immediately."

"I will certainly do so. You will excuse me, friend Elijah? I must talk to the captain privately."

"Certainly. Use the conference room. It is shielded."

Baley could do no work of any kind in R. Daneel's absence. He sat in uneasy silence. A great deal would depend on the value of his analysis, and he was acutely aware of his lack of expertise in robotics.

R. Daneel was back in half an hour—very nearly the longest half hour of Baley's life.

There was no use, of course, in trying to determine what had happened from the expression of the humanoid's impassive face. Baley tried to keep his face impassive.

"Yes, R. Daneel?" he asked.

"Precisely as you said, friend Elijah. Dr. Humboldt has confessed. He was counting, he said, on Dr. Sabbat giving way and allowing Dr. Humboldt to have this one last triumph. The crisis is over and you will find the captain grateful. He has given me permission to tell you that he admires your subtlety greatly and I believe that I, myself, will achieve favor for having suggested you."

"Good," said Baley, his knees weak and his forehead moist now that his decision had proven correct, "but Jehoshaphat, R. Daneel, don't put me on the spot like that again, will you?"

"I will try not to, friend Elijah. All will depend, of course, on the importance of a crisis, on your nearness, and on certain other factors. Meanwhile, I have a question—"

"Yes?"

"Was it not possible to suppose that passage from a lie to the truth was easy, while passage from the truth to a lie was difficult? And in that case, would not the robot in stasis have been going from a truth to a lie, and since R. Preston was in stasis, might one not have drawn the conclusion that it was Dr. Humboldt who was innocent and Dr. Sabbat who was guilty?"

"Yes, R. Daneel. It was possible to argue that way, but it was the other argument that proved right. Humboldt did confess, didn't he?"

"He did. But with arguments possible in both directions, how could you, friend Elijah, so quickly pick the correct one?"

For a moment, Baley's lips twitched. Then he relaxed and they curved into a smile. "Because, R. Daneel, I took into account human reactions, not robotic ones. I know more about human beings than about robots. In other words, I had an idea as to which mathematician was guilty before I ever interviewed the robots. Once I provoked an asymmetric response in them, I simply interpreted it in such a way as to place the guilt on the one I already believed to be guilty. The robotic response was dramatic enough to break down the guilty man; my own analysis of human behavior might not have been sufficient to do so."

"I am curious to know what your analysis of human behavior was."

"Jehoshaphat, R. Daneel; think, and you won't have to ask. There is another point of asymmetry in this tale of mirror-image besides the matter of true-and-false. There is the matter of the age of the two mathematicians; one is quite old and one is quite young."

"Yes, of course, but what then?"

"Why, this. I can see a young man, flushed with a sudden, startling and revolutionary idea, consulting in the matter an old man whom he has, from his early student days, thought of as a demigod in the field. I can *not* see an old man, rich in honors and used to triumphs, coming up with a sudden, startling and revolutionary idea, consulting a man centuries his junior whom he is bound to think of as a young whippersnapper—or whatever term a Spacer would use. Then, too, if a young man had the chance, would he try to steal the idea of a revered demigod? It would be unthinkable. On the other hand, an old man, conscious of declining powers, might well snatch at one last chance of fame and consider a baby in the field to have no rights he was bound to observe. In short, it was not conceivable that Sabbat steal Humboldt's idea; and from both angles, Dr. Humboldt was guilty."

R. Daneel considered that for a long time. Then he held out his hand. "I must leave now, friend Elijah. It was good to see you. May we meet again soon."

Baley gripped the robot's hand, warmly." If you don't mind, R. Daneel," he said, "not too soon."

LENNY

United States Robots and Mechanical Men Corporation had a problem. The problem was people.

Peter Bogert, Senior Mathematician, was on his way to Assembly when he encountered Alfred Lanning, Research Director. Lanning was bending his ferocious white eyebrows together and staring down across the railing into the computer room.

On the floor below the balcony, a trickle of humanity of both sexes and various ages was looking about curiously, while a guide intoned a set speech about robotic computing.

"This computer you see before you," he said, "is the largest of its type in the world. I contains five million three hundred thousand cryotrons and is capable of dealing simultaneously with over one hundred thousand variables. With its help, U.S. Robots is able to design with precision the positronic brains of new models.

"The requirements are fed in on tape which is perforated by the action of this keyboard—something like a very complicated typewriter or linotype machine, except that it does not deal with letters but with concepts. Statements are broken down into the symbolic logic equivalents and those in turn converted to perforation patterns.

"The computer can, in less than one hour, present our scientists with a design for a brain which will give all the necessary positronic paths to make a robot . . ."

Alfred Lanning looked up at last and noticed the other. "Ah, Peter," he said.

Bogert raised both hands to smooth down his already perfectly smooth and glossy head of black hair. He said, "You don't look as though you think much of this, Alfred."

Lanning grunted. The idea of public guided tours of U.S. Robots was of fairly recent origin, and was supposed to serve a dual function. On the one hand, the theory went, it allowed people to see robots at close quarters and counter their almost instinctive fear of the mechanical objects through increased familiarity. And on the other hand, it was supposed to interest at least an occasional person in taking up robotics research as a life work.

"You know I don't," Lanning said finally. "Once a week, work is disrupted. Considering the man-hours lost, the return is insufficient."

"Still no rise in job applications, then?"

"Oh, some, but only in the categories where the need isn't vital. It's research men that are needed. You know that. The trouble is that with robots forbidden on Earth itself, there's something unpopular about being a roboticist."

"The damned Frankenstein complex," said Bogert, consciously imitating one of the other's pet phrases.

Lanning missed the gentle jab. He said, "I ought to be used to it, but I never will. You'd think that by now every human being on Earth would know that the Three Laws represented a perfect safeguard; that robots are simply not dangerous. Take this bunch." He glowered down. "Look at them. Most of them go through the robot assembly room for the thrill of fear, like riding a roller coaster. Then when they enter the room with the MEC model—damn it, Peter, a MEC model that will do nothing on God's green Earth but take two steps forward, say 'Pleased to meet you, sir,' shake hands, then take two steps back—they back away and mothers snatch up their kids. How do we expect to get brainwork out of such idiots?"

Bogert had no answer. Together, they stared down once again at the line of sightseers, now passing out of the computer room and into the positronic brain assembly section. Then they left. They did not, as it turned out, observe Mortimer W. Jacobson, age 16—who, to do him complete justice, meant no harm whatever.

In fact, it could not even be said to be Mortimer's fault. The day of the week on which the tour took place was known to all workers. All devices in its path ought to have been carefully neutralized or locked, since it was unreasonable to expect human beings to withstand the temptation to handle knobs, keys, handles and pushbuttons. In addition, the guide ought to have been very carefully on the watch for those who succumbed.

But, at the time, the guide had passed into the next room and Mortimer was tailing the line. He passed the keyboard on which instructions were fed into the computer. He had no way of suspecting that the plans for a new robot design were being fed into it at that moment, or, being a good kid, he would have avoided the keyboard. He had no way of knowing that, by what amounted to almost criminal negligence, a technician had not inactivated the keyboard.

So Mortimer touched the keys at random as though he were playing a musical instrument.

He did not notice that a section of perforated tape stretched itself out of the instrument in another part of the room—soundlessly, unobtrusively.

Nor did the technician, when he returned, discover any signs of tampering. He felt a little uneasy at noticing that the keyboard was live, but did not think to check. After a few minutes, even his first trifling uneasiness was gone, and he continued feeding data into the computer.

As for Mortimer, neither then, nor ever afterward, did he know what he had done.

* * *

The new LNE model was designed for the mining of boron in the asteroid belt. The boron hydrides were increasing in value yearly as primers for the proton micropiles that carried the ultimate load of power production on spaceships, and Earth's own meager supply was running thin.

Physically, that meant that the LNE robots would have to be equipped with eyes sensitive to those lines prominent in the spectroscopic analysis of boron ores and the type of limbs most useful for the working up of ore to finished product. As always, though, the mental equipment was the major problem.

The first LNE positronic brain had been completed now. It was the prototype and would join all other prototypes in U.S. Robots' collection. When finally tested, others would then be manufactured for leasing (never selling) to mining corporations.

LNE-Prototype was complete now. Tall, straight, polished, it looked from outside like any of a number of not-too-specialized robot models.

The technician in charge, guided by the directions for testing in the *Handbook of Robotics*, said, "How are you?"

The indicated answer was to have been, "I am well and ready to begin my functions. I trust you are well, too," or some trivial modification thereof.

This first exchange served no purpose but to show that the robot could hear, understand a routine question, and make a routine reply congruent with what one would expect of a robotic attitude. Beginning from there, one could pass on to more complicated matters that would test the different Laws and their interaction with the specialized knowledge of each particular model.

So the technician said, "How are you?" He was instantly jolted by the nature of LNE-Prototype's voice. It had a quality like no robotic voice he had ever heard (and he had heard many). It formed syllables like the chimes of a low-pitched celeste.

So surprising was this that it was only after several moments that the technician heard, in retrospect, the syllables that had been formed by those heavenly tones.

They were, "Da, da, da, goo."

The robot still stood tall and straight but its right hand crept upward and a finger went into its mouth.

The technician stared in absolute horror and bolted. He locked the door behind him and, from another room, put in an emergency call to Dr. Susan Calvin.

Dr. Susan Calvin was U.S. Robots' (and, virtually, mankind's) only robopsychologist. She did not have to go very far in her testing of LNE-Prototype before she called very peremptorily for a transcript of the computer-drawn plans of the positronic brain-paths and the taped instructions that had directed them. After some study, she, in turn, sent for Bogert.

Her iron-gray hair was drawn severely back; her cold face, with its strong vertical lines marked off by the horizontal gash of the pale, thin-lipped mouth, turned intensely upon him.

"What *is* this, Peter?"

Bogert studied the passages she pointed out with increasing stupefaction and said, "Good Lord, Susan, it makes no sense."

"It most certainly doesn't. How did it get into the instructions?"

The technician in charge, called upon, swore in all sincerity that it was none of his doing, and that he could not account for it. The computer checked out negative for all attempts at flaw-finding.

"The positronic brain," said Susan Calvin, thoughtfully, "is past redemption. So many of the higher functions have been cancelled out by these meaningless directions that the result is very like a human baby."

Bogert looked surprised, and Susan Calvin took on a frozen attitude at once, as she always did at the least expressed or implied doubt of her word. She said, "We make every effort to make a robot as mentally like a man as

possible. Eliminate what we call the adult functions and what is naturally left is a human infant, mentally speaking. Why do you look so surprised, Peter?"

LNE-Prototype, who showed no signs of understanding any of the things that were going on around it, suddenly slipped into a sitting position and began a minute examination of its feet.

Bogert stared at it. "It's a shame to have to dismantle the creature. It's a handsome job."

"Dismantle it?" said the robopsychologist forcefully.

"Of course, Susan. What's the use of this thing? Good Lord, if there's one object completely and abysmally useless it's a robot without a job it can perform. You don't pretend there's a job this thing can do, do you?"

"No, of course not."

"Well, then?"

Susan Calvin said, stubbornly, "I want to conduct more tests."

Bogert looked at her with a moment's impatience, then shrugged. If there was one person at U.S. Robots with whom it was useless to dispute, surely that was Susan Calvin. Robots were all she loved, and long association with them, it seemed to Bogert, had deprived her of any appearance of humanity. She was no more to be argued out of a decision than was a triggered micropile to be argued out of operating.

"What's the use?" he breathed; then aloud, hastily: "Will you let us know when your tests are complete?"

"I will," she said. "Come, Lenny."

(LNE, thought Bogert. That becomes Lenny. Inevitable.)

Susan Calvin held out her hand but the robot only stared at it. Gently, the robopsychologist reached for the robot's hand and took it. Lenny rose smoothly to its feet (its mechanical coordination, at least, worked well). Together they walked out, robot topping woman by two feet. Many eyes followed them curiously down the long corridors.

One wall of Susan Calvin's laboratory, the one opening directly off her private office, was covered with a highly magnified reproduction of a positronic-path chart. Susan Calvin had studied it with absorption for the better part of a month.

She was considering it now, carefully, tracing the blunted paths through their contortions. Behind her, Lenny sat on the floor, moving its legs apart and together, crooning meaningless syllables to itself in a voice so beautiful that one could listen to the nonsense and be ravished.

Susan Calvin turned to the robot, "Lenny—Lenny—"

She repeated this patiently until finally Lenny looked up and made an inquiring sound. The robopsychologist allowed a glimmer of pleasure to cross her face fleetingly. The robot's attention was being gained in progressively shorter intervals.

She said, "Raise your hand, Lenny. Hand—up. Hand—up."

She raised her own hand as she said it, over and over.

Lenny followed the movement with its eyes. Up, down, up, down. Then it made an abortive gesture with its own hand and chimed, "Eh—uh."

"Very good, Lenny," said Susan Calvin, gravely. "Try it again. Hand—up."

A voice from her office called and interrupted. "Susan?"

Calvin halted with a tightening of her lips. "What is it, Alfred?"

The research director walked in, and looked at the chart on the wall and at the robot. "Still at it?"

"I'm at my work, yes."

"Well, you know, Susan . . ." He took out a cigar, staring at it hard, and made as though to bite off the end. In doing so, his eyes met the woman's stern look of disapproval; and he put the cigar away and began over. "Well, you know, Susan, the LNE model is in production now."

"So I've heard. Is there something in connection with it you wish of me?"

"No-o. Still, the mere fact that it is in production and is doing well means that working with this messed-up specimen is useless. Shouldn't it be scrapped?"

"In short, Alfred, you are annoyed that I am wasting my

so-valuable time. Feel relieved. My time is not being wasted. I am *working* with this robot."

"But the work has no meaning."

"I'll be the judge of that, Alfred." Her voice was ominously quiet, and Lanning thought it wiser to shift his ground.

"Will you tell me what meaning it has? What are you doing with it right now, for instance?"

"I'm trying to get it to raise its hand on the word of command. I'm trying to get it to imitate the sound of the word."

As though on cue, Lenny said, "Eh-uh" and raised its hand waveringly.

Lanning shook his head. "That voice is amazing. How does it happen?"

Susan Calvin said, "I don't quite know. Its transmitter is a normal one. It could speak normally, I'm sure. It doesn't, however; it speaks like this as a consequence of something in the positronic paths that I have not yet pinpointed."

"Well, pinpoint it, for Heaven's sake. Speech like that might be useful."

"Oh, then there is some possible use in my studies on Lenny?"

Lanning shrugged in embarrassment. "Oh, well, it's a minor point."

"I'm sorry you don't see the major points, then," said Susan Calvin with asperity, "which are much more important, but that's not my fault. Would you leave now, Alfred, and let me go on with my work?"

Lanning got to his cigar, eventually, in Bogert's office. He said, sourly, "That woman is growing more peculiar daily."

Bogert understood perfectly. In the U.S. Robots and Mechanical Men Corporation, there was only one "that woman." He said, "Is she still scuffing about with that pseudo-robot—that Lenny of hers?"

"Trying to get it to talk, so help me."

Bogert shrugged. "Points up the company problem. I mean, about getting qualified personnel for research. If we had other robopsychologists, we could retire Susan. Incidentally, I presume the directors' meeting scheduled for tomorrow is for the purpose of dealing with the procurement problem?"

Lanning nodded and looked at his cigar as though it didn't taste good. "Yes. Quality, though, not quantity. We've raised wages until there's a steady stream of applicants—those who are interested primarily in money. The trick is to get those who are interested primarily in robotics—a few more like Susan Calvin."

"Hell, no. Not like her."

"Well, not like her personally. But you'll have to admit, Peter, that she's single-minded about robots. She has no other interest in life."

"I know. And that's exactly what makes her so unbearable."

Lanning nodded. He had lost count of the many times it would have done his soul good to have fired Susan Calvin. He had also lost count of the number of millions of dollars she had at one time or another saved the company. She was a truly indispensable woman and would remain one until she died—or until they could lick the problem of finding men and women of her own high caliber who were interested in robotics research.

He said, "I think we'll cut down on the tour business."

Peter shrugged. "If you say so. But meanwhile, seriously, what do we do about Susan? She can easily tie herself up with Lenny indefinitely. You know how she is when she gets what she considers an interesting problem."

"What *can* we do?" said Lanning. "If we become too anxious to pull her off, she'll stay on out of feminine contrariness. In the last analysis, we can't force her to do anything."

The dark-haired mathematician smiled. "I wouldn't ever apply the adjective 'feminine' to any part of her."

"Oh, well," said Lanning, grumpily. "At least, it won't do anyone any actual harm."

In that, if in nothing else, he was wrong.

* * *

The emergency signal is always a tension-making thing in any large industrial establishment. Such signals had sounded in the history of U.S. Robots a dozen times—for fire, flood, riot and insurrection.

But one thing had never occurred in all that time. Never had the particular signal indicating "Robot out of control" sounded. No one ever expected it to sound. It was only installed at government insistence. ("Damn the Frankenstein complex," Lanning would mutter on those rare occasions when he thought of it.)

Now, finally, the shrill siren rose and fell at ten-second intervals, and practically no worker from the President of the Board of Directors down to the newest janitor's assistant recognized the significance of the strange sound for a few moments. After those moments passed, there was a massive convergence of armed guards and medical men to the indicated area of danger and U.S. Robots was struck with paralysis.

Charles Randow, computing technician, was taken off to hospital level with a broken arm. There was no other damage. No other physical damage.

"But the moral damage," roared Lanning, "is beyond estimation."

Susan Calvin faced him, murderously calm. "You will do nothing to Lenny. Nothing. Do you understand?"

"Do *you* understand, Susan? That thing has hurt a human being. It has broken First Law. Don't you know what First Law is?"

"You will do nothing to Lenny."

"For God's sake, Susan, do I have to tell *you* First Law? *A robot may not harm a human being or, through inaction, allow a human being to come to harm.* Our entire position depends on the fact that First Law is rigidly observed by all robots of all types. If the public should hear, and they will hear, that there was an exception, even one exception, we might be forced to close down altogether. Our only chance of survival would be to announce at once that the robot involved had been destroyed, explain the circumstances, and hope that the public can be convinced that it will never happen again."

"I would like to find out exactly what happened," said Susan Calvin. "I was not present at the time and I would like to know exactly what the Randow boy was doing in my laboratories without my permission."

"The important thing that happened," said Lanning, "is obvious. Your robot struck Randow and the damn fool flashed the 'Robot out of control' button and made a case of it. But your robot struck him and inflicted damage to the extent of a broken arm. The truth is your Lenny is so distorted it lacks First Law and it must be destroyed."

"It does *not* lack First Law. I have studied its brainpaths and know it does not lack it."

"Then how could it strike a man?" Desperation turned him to sarcasm. "Ask Lenny. Surely you have taught it to speak by now."

Susan Calvin's cheeks flushed a painful pink. She said, "I prefer to interview the victim. And in my absence, Alfred, I want my offices sealed tight, with Lenny inside. I want no one to approach him. If any harm comes to him while I am gone, this company will not see me again under any circumstances."

"Will you agree to its destruction, if it has broken First Law?"

"Yes," said Susan Calvin, "because I know it hasn't."

Charles Randow lay in bed with his arm set and in a cast. His major suffering was still from the shock of those few moments in which he thought a robot was advancing on him with murder in its positronic mind. No other human had ever had such reason to fear direct robotic harm as he had had just then. He had had a unique experience.

Susan Calvin and Alfred Lanning stood beside his bed now; Peter Bogert, who had met them on the way, was with them. Doctors and nurses had been shooed out.

Susan Calvin said, "Now—what happened?"

Randow was daunted. He muttered, "The thing hit me in the arm. It was coming at me."

Calvin said, "Move further back in the story. What were you doing in my laboratory without authorization?"

The young computer technician swallowed, and the Adam's apple in his thin neck bobbed noticeably. He was high-cheekboned and abnormally pale. He said, "We all knew about your robot. The word is you were trying to teach it to talk like a musical instrument. There were bets going as to whether it talked or not. Some said—uh—you could teach a gatepost to talk."

"I suppose," said Susan Calvin, freezingly, "that is meant as a compliment. What did that have to do with you?"

"I was supposed to go in there and settle matters—see if it would talk, you know. We swiped a key to your place and I waited till you were gone and went in. We had a lottery on who was to do it. I lost."

"Then?"

"I tried to get it to talk and it hit me."

"What do you mean, you tried to get it to talk? How did you try?"

"I—I asked it questions, but it wouldn't say anything, and I had to give the thing a fair shake, so I kind of—yelled at it, and—"

"And?"

There was a long pause. Under Susan Calvin's unwavering stare, Randow finally said, "I tried to scare it into saying something." He added defensively, "I had to give the thing a fair shake."

"How did you try to scare it?"

"I pretended to take a punch at it."

"And it brushed your arm aside?"

"It *hit* my arm."

"Very well. That's all." To Lanning and Bogert, she said, "Come, gentlemen."

At the doorway, she turned back to Randow. "I can settle the bets going around, if you are still interested. Lenny can speak a few words quite well."

* * *

They said nothing until they were in Susan Calvin's office. Its walls were lined with her books, some of which she had written herself. It retained the patina of her own frigid, carefully ordered personality. It had only one chair in it and she sat down. Lanning and Bogert remained standing.

She said, "Lenny only defended itself. That is the Third Law: *A robot must protect its own existence.*"

"*Except,*" said Lanning forcefully, "*when this conflicts with the First or Second Laws.* Complete the statement! Lenny had no right to defend itself in any way at the cost of harm, however minor, to a human being."

"Nor did it," shot back Calvin, "*knowingly.* Lenny has an aborted brain. It had no way of knowing its own strength or the weakness of humans. In brushing aside the threatening arm of a human being it could not know the bone would break. In human terms, no moral blame can be attached to an individual who honestly cannot differentiate good and evil."

Bogert interrupted, soothingly, "Now, Susan, we don't blame. *We* understand that Lenny is the equivalent of a baby, humanly speaking, and we don't blame it. But the public will. U.S. Robots will be closed down."

"Quite the opposite. If you had the brains of a flea, Peter, you would see that this is the opportunity U.S. Robots is waiting for. That this will solve its problems."

Lanning hunched his white eyebrows low. He said, softly, "What problems, Susan?"

"Isn't the corporation concerned about maintaining our research personnel at the present—Heaven help us—high level?"

"We certainly are."

"Well, what are you offering prospective researchers? Excitement? Novelty? The thrill of piercing the unknown? No! You offer them salaries and the assurance of no problems."

Bogert said, "How do you mean, no problems?"

"Are there problems?" shot back Susan Calvin. "What

kind of robots do we turn out? Fully developed robots, fit for their tasks. An industry tells us what it needs; a computer designs the brain; machinery forms the robot; and there it is, complete and done. Peter, some time ago, you asked me with reference to Lenny what its use was. What's the use, you said, of a robot that was not designed for any job? Now I ask you—what's the use of a robot designed for only one job? It begins and ends in the same place. The LNE models mine boron. If beryllium is needed, they are useless. A human being so designed would be sub-human. A robot so designed is sub-robotic."

"Do you want a versatile robot?" asked Lanning, incredulously.

"Why not?" demanded the robopsychologist. "Why not? I've been handed a robot with a brain almost completely stultified. I've been teaching it, and you, Alfred, asked me what was the use of that. Perhaps very little as far as Lenny itself is concerned, since it will never progress beyond the five-year-old level on a human scale. But what's the use in general? A very great deal, if you consider it as a study in the abstract problem of *learning how to teach robots*. I have learned ways to short-circuit neighboring pathways in order to create new ones. More study will yield better, more subtle and more efficient techniques of doing so."

"Well?"

"Suppose you started with a positronic brain that had all the basic pathways carefully outlined but none of the secondaries. Suppose you then started creating secondaries. You could sell basic robots designed for instruction; robots that could be modelled to a job, and then modelled to another, if necessary. Robots would become as versatile as human beings. *Robots could learn!*"

They stared at her.

She said, impatiently, "You still don't understand, do you?"

"I understand what you are saying," said Lanning.

"Don't you understand that with a completely new field of research and completely new techniques to be developed, with a completely new area of the unknown to be penetrated, youngsters will feel a new urge to enter robotics? Try it and see."

"May I point out," said Bogert, smoothly, "that this is dangerous. Beginning with ignorant robots such as Lenny will mean that one could never trust First Law—exactly as turned out in Lenny's case."

"Exactly. Advertise the fact."

"Advertise it!"

"Of course. Broadcast the danger. Explain that you will set up a new research institute on the moon, if Earth's population chooses not to allow this sort of thing to go on upon Earth, but stress the danger to the possible applicants by all means."

Lanning said, "For God's sake, why?"

"Because the spice of danger will add to the lure. Do you think nuclear technology involves no danger and spationautics no peril? Has your lure of absolute security been doing the trick for you? Has it helped you to cater to the Frankenstein complex you all despise so? Try something else then, something that has worked in other fields."

There was a sound from beyond the door that led to Calvin's personal laboratories. It was the chiming sound of Lenny.

The robopsychologist broke off instantly, listening. She said, "Excuse me. I think Lenny is calling me."

"Can it call you?" said Lanning.

"I said I've managed to teach it a few words." She stepped toward the door, a little flustered. "If you will wait for me—"

They watched her leave and were silent for a moment. Then Lanning said, "Do you think there's anything to what she says, Peter?"

"Just possibly, Alfred," said Bogert. "Just possibly. Enough for us to bring the matter up at the directors' meeting and see what they say. After all, the fat *is* in the fire. A robot has harmed a human being and knowledge of it is public. As Susan says, we might as well try to turn the matter to our advantage. Of course, I distrust her motives in all this."

"How do you mean?"

"Even if all she has said is perfectly true, it is only rationalization as far as she is concerned. Her motive in all this is her desire to hold on to this robot. If we pressed her" (and the mathematician smiled at the incongruous literal meaning of the phrase) "she would say it was to continue learning techniques of teaching robots, but I think she has found another use for Lenny. A rather unique one that would fit only Susan of all women."

"I don't get your drift."

Bogert said, "Did you hear what the robot was calling?"

"Well, no, I didn't quite—" began Lanning, when the door opened suddenly, and both men stopped talking at once.

Susan Calvin stepped in again, looking about uncertainly. "Have either of you seen— I'm positive I had it somewhere about— Oh, there it is."

She ran to a corner of one bookcase and picked up an object of intricate metal webbery, dumbbell shaped and hollow, with variously shaped metal pieces inside each hollow, just too large to be able to fall out of the webbing.

As she picked it up, the metal pieces within moved and struck together, clicking pleasantly. It struck Lanning that the object was a kind of robotic version of a baby rattle.

As Susan Calvin opened the door again to pass through, Lenny's voice chimed again from within. This time, Lanning heard it clearly as it spoke the words Susan Calvin had taught it.

In heavenly celeste-like sounds, it called out, "Mommie, I want you. I want you, Mommie."

And the footsteps of Susan Calvin could be heard hurrying eagerly across the laboratory floor toward the only kind of baby she could ever have or love.

GALLEY SLAVE

The United States Robots and Mechanical Men Corporation, as defendants in the case, had influence enough to force a closed-doors trial without a jury.

Nor did Northeastern University try hard to prevent it. The trustees knew perfectly well how the public might react to any issue involving misbehavior of a robot, however rarefied that misbehavior might be. They also had a clearly visualized notion of how an antirobot riot might become an antiscience riot without warning.

The government, as represented in this case by Justice Harlow Shane, was equally anxious for a quiet end to this mess. Both U.S. Robots and the academic world were bad people to antagonize.

Justice Shane said, "Since neither press, public nor jury is present, gentlemen, let us stand on as little ceremony as we can and get to the facts."

He smiled stiffly as he said this, perhaps without much hope that his request would be effective, and hitched at his robe so that he might sit more comfortably. His face was pleasantly rubicund, his chin round and soft, his nose broad

355

and his eyes light in color and wide-set. All in all, it was not a face with much judicial majesty and the judge knew it.

Barnabas H. Goodfellow, Professor of Physics at Northeastern U., was sworn in first, taking the usual vow with an expression that made mincemeat of his name.

After the usual opening-gambit questions, Prosecution shoved his hands deep into his pockets and said, "When was it, Professor, that the matter of the possible employ of Robot EZ-27 was first brought to your attention, and how?"

Professor Goodfellow's small and angular face set itself into an uneasy expression, scarcely more benevolent than the one it replaced. He said, "I have had professional contact and some social acquaintance with Dr. Alfred Lanning, Director of Research at U.S. Robots. I was inclined to listen with some tolerance then when I received a rather strange suggestion from him on the third of March of last year—"

"Of 2033?"

"That's right."

"Excuse me for interrupting. Please proceed."

The professor nodded frostily, scowled to fix the facts in his mind, and began to speak.

Professor Goodfellow looked at the robot with a certain uneasiness. It had been carried into the basement supply room in a crate, in accordance with the regulations governing the shipment of robots from place to place on the Earth's surface.

He knew it was coming; it wasn't that he was unprepared. From the moment of Dr. Lanning's first phone call on March 3, he had felt himself giving way to the other's persuasiveness, and now, as an inevitable result, he found himself face to face with a robot.

It looked uncommonly large as it stood within arm's reach.

Alfred Lanning cast a hard glance of his own at the robot, as though making certain it had not been damaged in transit. Then he turned his ferocious eyebrows and his mane of white hair in the professor's direction.

"This is Robot EZ-27, first of its model to be available for public use." He turned to the robot. "This is Professor Goodfellow, Easy."

Easy spoke impassively, but with such suddenness that the professor shied. "Good afternoon, Professor."

Easy stood seven feet tall and had the general proportions of a man—always the prime selling point of U.S. Robots. That and the possession of the basic patents on the positronic brain had given them an actual monopoly on robots and a near-monopoly on computing machines in general.

The two men who had uncrated the robot had left now and the professor looked from Lanning to the robot and back to Lanning. "It's harmless, I'm sure." He didn't sound sure.

"More harmless than I am," said Lanning. "I could be goaded into striking you. Easy could not be. You know the Three Laws of Robotics, I presume."

"Yes, of course," said Goodfellow.

"They are built into the positronic patterns of the brain and must be observed. The First Law, the prime rule of robotic existence, safeguards the life and well-being of all humans." He paused, rubbed at his cheek, then added, "It's something of which we would like to persuade all Earth if we could."

"It's just that he seems formidable."

"Granted. But whatever he seems, you'll find that he *is* useful."

"I'm not sure in what way. Our conversations were not very helpful in that respect. Still, I agreed to look at the object and I'm doing it."

"We'll do more than look, Professor. Have you brought a book?"

"I have."

"May I see it?"

Professor Goodfellow reached down without actually taking his eyes off the metal-in-human-shape that confronted him. From the briefcase at his feet, he withdrew a book.

Lanning held out his hand for it and looked at the backstrip. "*Physical Chemistry of Electrolytes in Solution.* Fair enough, sir. You selected this yourself, at random. It was no suggestion of mine, this particular text. Am I right?"

"Yes."

Lanning passed the book to Robot EZ-27.

The professor jumped a little. "No! That's a valuable book!"

Lanning raised his eyebrows and they looked like shaggy coconut icing. He said, "Easy has no intention of tearing the book in two as a feat of strength, I assure you. It can handle a book as carefully as you or I. Go ahead, Easy."

"Thank you, sir," said Easy. Then, turning its metal bulk slightly, it added, "With your permission, Professor Goodfellow."

The professor stared, then said, "Yes—yes, of course."

With a slow and steady manipulation of metal fingers, Easy turned the pages of the book, glancing at the left page, then the right; turning the page, glancing left, then right; turning the page and so on for minute after minute.

The sense of its power seemed to dwarf even the large cement-walled room in which they stood and to reduce the two human watchers to something considerably less than life-size.

Goodfellow muttered, "The light isn't very good."

"It will do."

Then, rather more sharply, "But what is he doing?"

"Patience, sir."

The last page was turned eventually. Lanning asked, "Well, Easy?"

The robot said, "It is a most accurate book and there is little to which I can point. On line 22 of page 27, the word 'positive' is spelled p-o-i-s-t-i-v-e. The comma in line 6 of page 32 is superfluous, whereas one should have been used on line 13 of page 54. The plus sign in equation XIV-2 on page 337 should be a minus sign if it is to be consistent with the previous equations—"

"Wait! Wait!" cried the professor. "What is he doing?"

"Doing?" echoed Lanning in sudden irascibility. "Why, man, he has already done it! He has proofread that book."

"Proofread it?"

"Yes. In the short time it took him to turn those pages, he caught every mistake in spelling, grammar and punctuation. He has noted errors in word order and detected inconsistencies. And he will retain the information, letter-perfect, indefinitely."

The professor's mouth was open. He walked rapidly away from Lanning and Easy and as rapidly back. He folded his arms across his chest and stared at them. Finally he said, "You mean this is a proofreading robot?"

Lanning nodded. "Among other things."

"But why do you show it to me?"

"So that you might help me persuade the university to obtain it for use."

"To read proof?"

"Among other things," Lanning repeated patiently.

The professor drew his pinched face together in a kind of sour disbelief. "But this is ridiculous!"

"Why?"

"The university could never afford to buy this half-ton—it must weigh that at least—this half-ton proofreader."

"Proofreading is not all it will do. It will prepare reports from outlines, fill out forms, serve as an accurate memory-file, grade papers—"

"All picayune!"

Lanning said, "Not at all, as I can show you in a moment. But I think we can discuss this more comfortably in your office, if you have no objection."

"No, of course not," began the professor mechanically and took a half-step as though to turn. Then he snapped out, "But the robot—we can't take the robot. Really, Doctor, you'll have to crate it up again."

"Time enough. We can leave Easy here."

"Unattended?"

"Why not? He knows he is to stay. Professor Goodfellow,

360
•

it is necessary to understand that a robot is far more reliable than a human being."

"I would be responsible for any damage—"

"There will be no damage. I guarantee that. Look, it's after hours. You expect no one here, I imagine, before tomorrow morning. The truck and my two men are outside. U.S. Robots will take any responsibility that may arise. None will. Call it a demonstration of the reliability of the robot."

The professor allowed himself to be led out of the storeroom. Nor did he look entirely comfortable in his own office, five stories up.

He dabbed at the line of droplets along the upper half of his forehead with a white handkerchief.

"As you know very well, Dr. Lanning, there are laws against the use of robots on Earth's surface," he pointed out.

"The laws, Professor Goodfellow, are not simple ones. Robots may not be used on public thoroughfares or within private structures except under certain restrictions that usually turn out to be prohibitive. The university, however, is a large and privately owned institution that usually receives preferential treatment. If the robot is used only in a specific room for only academic purposes, if certain other restrictions are observed and if the men and women having occasion to enter the room cooperate fully, we may remain within the law."

"But all that trouble just to read proof?"

"The uses would be infinite, Professor. Robotic labor has so far been used only to relieve physical drudgery. Isn't there such a thing as mental drudgery? When a professor capable of the most useful creative thought is forced to spend two weeks painfully checking the spelling of lines of print and I offer you a machine that can do it in thirty minutes, is that picayune?"

"But the price—"

"The price need not bother you. You cannot buy EZ-27. U.S. Robots does not sell its products. But the university can lease EZ-27 for a thousand dollars a year—considerably less than the cost of a single microwave spectograph continuous-recording attachment."

Goodfellow looked stunned. Lanning followed up his advantage by saying, "I only ask that you put it up to whatever group makes the decisions here. I would be glad to speak to them if they want more information."

"Well," Goodfellow said doubtfully, "I can bring it up at next week's Senate meeting. I can't promise that will do any good, though."

"Naturally," said Lanning.

The Defense Attorney was short and stubby and carried himself rather portentously, a stance that had the effect of accentuating his double chin. He stared at Professor Goodfellow, once that witness had been handed over, and said, "You agreed rather readily, did you not?"

The Professor said briskly, "I suppose I was anxious to be rid of Dr. Lanning. I would have agreed to anything."

"With the intention of forgetting about it after he left?"

"Well—"

"Nevertheless, you did present the matter to a meeting of the Executive Board of the University Senate."

"Yes, I did."

"So that you agreed in good faith with Dr. Lanning's suggestions. You weren't just going along with a gag. You actually agreed enthusiastically, did you not?"

"I merely followed ordinary procedures."

"As a matter of fact, you weren't as upset about the robot as you now claim you were. You know the Three Laws of Robotics and you knew them at the time of your interview with Dr. Lanning."

"Well, yes."

"And you were perfectly willing to leave a robot at large and unattended."

"Dr. Lanning assured me—"

"Surely you would never have accepted his assurance if

you had had the slightest doubt that the robot might be in the least dangerous."

The professor began frigidly, "I had every faith in the word—"

"That is all," said Defense abruptly.

As Professor Goodfellow, more than a bit ruffled, stood down, Justice Shane leaned forward and said, "Since I am not a robotics man myself, I would appreciate knowing precisely what the Three Laws of Robotics are. Would Dr. Lanning quote them for the benefit of the court?"

Dr. Lanning looked startled. He had been virtually bumping heads with the gray-haired woman at his side. He rose to his feet now and the woman looked up, too—expressionlessly.

Dr. Lanning said, "Very well, Your Honor." He paused as though about to launch into an oration and said, with laborious clarity, "First Law: a robot may not injure a human being, or, through inaction, allow a human being to come to harm. Second Law: a robot must obey the orders given it by human beings, except where such orders would conflict with the First Law. Third Law: a robot must protect its own existence as long as such protection does not conflict with the First or Second Laws."

"I see," said the judge, taking rapid notes. "These Laws are built into every robot, are they?"

"Into every one. That will be borne out by any roboticist."

"And into Robot EZ-27 specifically?"

"Yes, Your Honor."

"You will probably be required to repeat those statements under oath."

"I am ready to do so, Your Honor."

He sat down again.

Dr. Susan Calvin, robopsychologist-in-chief for U.S. Robots, who was the gray-haired woman sitting next to Lanning, looked at her titular superior without favor, but then she showed favor to no human being. She said, "Was Goodfellow's testimony accurate, Alfred?"

"Essentially," muttered Lanning. "He wasn't as nervous

as all that about the robot and he was anxious enough to talk business with me when he heard the price. But there doesn't seem to be any drastic distortion."

Dr. Calvin said thoughtfully, "It might have been wise to put the price higher than a thousand."

"We were anxious to place Easy."

"I know. Too anxious, perhaps. They'll try to make it look as though we had an ulterior motive."

Lanning looked exasperated. "We did. I admitted that at the University Senate meeting."

"They can make it look as if we had one beyond the one we admitted."

Scott Robertson, son of the founder of U.S. Robots and still owner of a majority of the stock, leaned over from Dr. Calvin's other side and said in a kind of explosive whisper, "Why can't you get Easy to talk so we'll know where we're at?"

"You know he can't talk about it, Mr. Robertson."

"Make him. You're the psychologist, Dr. Calvin. *Make* him."

"If I'm the psychologist, Mr. Robertson," said Susan Calvin coldly, "let me make the decisions. My robot will not be *made* to do anything at the price of his well-being."

Robertson frowned and might have answered, but Justice Shane was tapping his gavel in a polite sort of way and they grudgingly fell silent.

Francis J. Hart, head of the Department of English and Dean of Graduate Studies, was on the stand. He was a plump man, meticulously dressed in dark clothing of a conservative cut, and possessing several strands of hair traversing the pink top of his cranium. He sat well back in the witness chair with his hands folded neatly in his lap and displaying, from time to time, a tight-lipped smile.

He said, "My first connection with the matter of the Robot EZ-27 was on the occasion of the session of the University Senate Executive Committee at which the subject was introduced by Professor Goodfellow. Thereafter, on the tenth of April of last year, we held a special meeting on the subject, during which I was in the chair."

"Were minutes kept of the meeting of the Executive Committee? Of the special meeting, that is?"

"Well, no. It was a rather unusual meeting." The dean smiled briefly. "We thought it might remain confidential."

"What transpired at the meeting?"

Dean Hart was not entirely comfortable as chairman of that meeting. Nor did the other members assembled seem completely calm. Only Dr. Lanning appeared at peace with himself. His tall, gaunt figure and the shock of white hair that crowned him reminded Hart of portraits he had seen of Andrew Jackson.

Samples of the robot's work lay scattered along the central regions of the table and the reproduction of a graph drawn by the robot was now in the hands of Professor Minott of Physical Chemistry. The chemist's lips were pursed in obvious approval.

Hart cleared his throat and said, "There seems no doubt that the robot can perform certain routine tasks with adequate competence. I have gone over these, for instance, just before coming in and there is very little to find fault with."

He picked up a long sheet of printing, some three times as long as the average book page. It was a sheet of galley proof, designed to be corrected by authors before the type was set up in page form. Along both of the wide margins of the galley were proofmarks, neat and superbly legible. Occasionally, a word of print was crossed out and a new word substituted in the margin in characters so fine and regular it might easily have been print itself. Some of the corrections were blue to indicate the original mistake had been the author's, a few in red, where the printer had been wrong.

"Actually," said Lanning, "there is less than very little to find fault with. I should say there is nothing at all to find fault with, Dr. Hart. I'm sure the corrections are perfect, insofar as the original manuscript was. If the manuscript against which this galley was corrected was at fault in a matter of fact rather than of English, the robot is not competent to correct it."

"We accept that. However, the robot corrected word order on occasion and I don't think the rules of English are sufficiently hidebound for us to be sure that in each case the robot's choice was the correct one."

"Easy's positronic brain," said Lanning, showing large teeth as he smiled, "has been molded by the contents of all the standard works on the subject. I'm sure you cannot point to a case where the robot's choice was definitely the incorrect one."

Professor Minott looked up from the graph he still held. "The question in my mind, Dr. Lanning, is why we need a robot at all, with all the difficulties in public relations that would entail. The science of automation has surely reached the point where your company could design a machine, an ordinary computer of a type known and accepted by the public, that would correct galleys."

"I am sure we could," said Lanning stiffly, "but such a machine would require that the galleys be translated into special symbols or, at the least, transcribed on tapes. Any corrections would emerge in symbols. You would need to keep men employed translating words to symbols, symbols to words. Furthermore, such a computer could do no other job. It couldn't prepare the graph you hold in your hand, for instance."

Minott grunted.

Lanning went on. "The hallmark of the positronic robot is its flexibility. It can do a number of jobs. It is designed like a man so that it can use all the tools and machines that have, after all, been designed to be used by a man. It can talk to you and you can talk to it. You can actually reason with it up to a point. Compared to even a simple robot, an ordinary computer with a non-positronic brain is only a heavy adding machine."

Goodfellow looked up and said, "If we all talk and reason with the robot, what are the chances of our confusing it? I suppose it doesn't have the capability of absorbing an infinite amount of data."

"No, it hasn't. But it should last five years with ordinary use. It will know when it will require clearing, and the company will do the job without charge."

"The *company* will?"

"Yes. The company reserves the right to service the robot outside the ordinary course of its duties. It is one reason we retain control of our positronic robots and lease rather than sell them. In the pursuit of its ordinary functions, any robot can be directed by any man. Outside its ordinary functions, a robot requires expert handling, and that we can give it. For instance, any of you might clear an EZ robot to an extent by telling it to forget this item or that. But you would be almost certain to phrase the order in such a way as to cause it to forget too much or too little. We would detect such tampering, because we have built-in safeguards. However, since there is no need for clearing the robot in its ordinary work, or for doing other useless things, this raises no problem."

Dean Hart touched his head as though to make sure his carefully cultivated strands lay evenly distributed and said, "You are anxious to have us take the machine. Yet surely it is a losing proposition for U.S. Robots. One thousand a year is a ridiculously low price. Is it that you hope through this to rent other such machines to other universities at a more reasonable price?"

"Certainly that's a fair hope," said Lanning.

"But even so, the number of machines you could rent would be limited. I doubt if you could make it a paying proposition."

Lanning put his elbows on the table and earnestly leaned forward. "Let me put it bluntly, gentlemen. Robots cannot be used on Earth, except in certain special cases, because of prejudice against them on the part of the public. U.S. Robots is a highly successful corporation with our extraterrestrial and spaceflight markets alone, to say nothing of our computer subsidiaries. However, we are concerned with more than profits alone. It is our firm belief that the use of robots on Earth itself would mean a better life for all eventually, even if a certain amount of economic dislocation resulted at first.

"The labor unions are naturally against us, but surely we may expect cooperation from the large universities. The robot, Easy, will help you by relieving you of scholastic drudgery—by assuming, if you permit it, the role of galley slave for you. Other universities and research institutions will follow your lead, and if it works out, then perhaps other robots of other types may be placed and the public's objections to them broken down by stages."

Minott murmured, "Today Northeastern University, tomorrow the world."

Angrily, Lanning whispered to Susan Calvin, "I wasn't nearly that eloquent and they weren't nearly that reluctant. At a thousand a year, they were jumping to get Easy. Professor Minott told me he'd never seen as beautiful a job as that graph he was holding and there was no mistake on the galley or anywhere else. Hart admitted it freely."

The severe vertical lines on Dr. Calvin's face did not soften. "You should have demanded more money than they could pay, Alfred, and let them beat you down."

"Maybe," he grumbled.

Prosecution was not quite done with Professor Hart. "After Dr. Lanning left, did you vote on whether to accept Robot EZ-27?"

"Yes, we did."

"With what result?"

"In favor of acceptance, by majority vote."

"What would you say influenced the vote?"

Defense objected immediately.

Prosecution rephrased the question. "What influenced you, personally, in your individual vote? You did vote in favor, I think."

"I voted in favor, yes. I did so largely because I was impressed by Dr. Lanning's feeling that it was our duty as members of the world's intellectual leadership to allow robotics to help Man in the solution of his problems."

"In other words, Dr. Lanning talked you into it."

"That's his job. He did it very well."

"Your witness."

Defense strode up to the witness chair and surveyed Professor Hart for a long moment. He said, "In reality, you were all pretty eager to have Robot EZ-27 in your employ, weren't you?"

"We thought that if it could do the work, it might be useful."

"*If* it could do the work? I understand you examined the samples of Robot EZ-27's original work with particular care on the day of the meeting which you have just described."

"Yes, I did. Since the machine's work dealt primarily with the handling of the English language, and since that is my field of competence, it seemed logical that I be the one chosen to examine the work."

"Very good. Was there anything on display on the table at the time of the meeting which was less than satisfactory? I have all the material here as exhibits. Can you point to a single unsatisfactory item?"

"Well—"

"It's a simple question. Was there one single solitary unsatisfactory item? You inspected it. Was there?"

The English professor frowned. "There wasn't."

"I also have some samples of work done by Robot EZ-27 during the course of his fourteen-month employ at Northeastern. Would you examine these and tell me if there is anything wrong with them in even one particular?"

Hart snapped, "When he did make a mistake, it was a beauty."

"Answer my question," thundered Defense, "and only the question I am putting to you! Is there anything wrong with the material?"

Dean Hart looked cautiously at each item. "Well, nothing."

"Barring the matter concerning which we are here engaged, do you know of any mistake on the part of EZ-27?"

"Barring the matter for which this trial is being held, no."

Defense cleared his throat as though to signal end of paragraph. He said, "Now about the vote concerning whether Robot EZ-27 was to be employed or not. You said there was a majority in favor. What was the actual vote?"

"Thirteen to one, as I remember."

"Thirteen to one! More than just a majority, wouldn't you say?"

"No, sir!" All the pedant in Dean Hart was aroused. "In the English language, the word 'majority' means 'more than half.' Thirteen out of fourteen is a majority, nothing more."

"But an almost unanimous one."

"A majority all the same!"

Defense switched ground. "And who was the lone holdout?"

Dean Hart looked acutely uncomfortable. "Professor Simon Ninheimer."

Defense pretended astonishment. "Professor Ninheimer? The head of the Department of Sociology?"

"Yes, sir."

"The *plaintiff*?"

"Yes, sir."

Defense pursed his lips. "In other words, it turns out that the man bringing the action for payment of $750,000 damages against my client, United States Robots and Mechanical Men Corporation was the one who from the beginning opposed the use of the robot—although everyone else on the Executive Committee of the University Senate was persuaded that it was a good idea."

"He voted against the motion, as was his right."

"You didn't mention in your description of the meeting any remarks made by Professor Ninheimer. Did he make any?"

"I think he spoke."

"You *think*?"

"Well, he *did* speak."

"Against using the robot?"

"Yes."

"Was he violent about it?"

Dean Hart paused. "He was vehement."

Defense grew confidential. "How long have you known Professor Ninheimer, Dean Hart?"

"About twelve years."

"Reasonably well?"

"I should say so, yes."

"Knowing him, then, would you say he was the kind of man who might continue to bear resentment against a robot, all the more so because an adverse vote had—"

Prosecution drowned out the remainder of the question with an indignant and vehement objection of his own. Defense motioned the witness down and Justice Shane called luncheon recess.

Robertson mangled his sandwich. The corporation would not founder for loss of three-quarters of a million, but the loss would do it no particular good. He was conscious, moreover, that there would be a much more costly long-term setback in public relations.

He said sourly, "Why all this business about how Easy got into the university? What do they hope to gain?"

The Attorney for Defense said quietly, "A court action is like a chess game, Mr. Robertson. The winner is usually the one who can see more moves ahead, and my friend at the prosecutor's table is no beginner. They can show damage; that's no problem. Their main effort lies in anticipating our defense. They must be counting on us to try to show that Easy couldn't possibly have committed the offense—because of the Laws of Robotics."

"All right," said Robertson, "that *is* our defense. An absolutely airtight one."

"To a robotics engineer. Not necessarily to a judge. They're setting themselves up a position from which they can demonstrate that EZ-27 was no ordinary robot. It was the first of its type to be offered to the public. It was an experimental model that needed field-testing and the university was the only decent way to provide such testing. That would look plausible in the light of Dr. Lanning's strong efforts to place the robot and the willingness of U.S. Robots to lease it for so little. The prosecution would then argue that the field-test proved Easy to have been a failure. Now do you see the purpose of what's been going on?"

"But EZ-27 was a perfectly good model," argued Robertson. "It was the twenty-seventh in production."

"Which is really a bad point," said Defense somberly. "What was wrong with the first twenty-six? Obviously something. Why shouldn't there be something wrong with the twenty-seventh, too?"

"There was nothing wrong with the first twenty-six except that they weren't complex enough for the task. These were the first positronic brains of the sort to be constructed and it was rather hit-and-miss to begin with. But the Three Laws held in all of them! *No* robot is so imperfect that the Three Laws don't hold."

"Dr. Lanning has explained this to me, Mr. Robertson, and I am willing to take his word for it. The judge, however, may not be. We are expecting a decision from an honest and intelligent man who knows no robotics and thus may be led astray. For instance, if you or Dr. Lanning or Dr. Calvin were to say on the stand that any positronic brains were constructed 'hit-and-miss,' as you just did, prosecution would tear you apart in cross-examination. Nothing would salvage our case. So that's something to avoid."

Robertson growled, "If only Easy would talk."

Defense shrugged. "A robot is incompetent as a witness, so that would do us no good."

"At least we'd know some of the facts. We'd know how it came to do such a thing."

Susan Calvin fired up. A dullish red touched her cheeks and her voice had a trace of warmth in it. "We *know* how Easy came to do it. It was ordered to! I've explained this to counsel and I'll explain it to you now."

"Ordered to by whom?" asked Robertson in honest astonishment. (No one ever told him anything, he thought resentfully. These research people considered *themselves* the owners of U.S. Robots, by God!)

"By the plaintiff," said Dr. Calvin.

"In heaven's name, why?"

"I don't know why yet. Perhaps just that we might be sued, that he might gain some cash." There were blue glints in her eyes as she said that.

"Then why doesn't Easy say so?"

"Isn't that obvious? It's been ordered to keep quiet about the matter."

"Why should that be obvious?" demanded Robertson truculently.

"Well, it's obvious to me. Robot psychology is my profession. If Easy will not answer questions about the matter directly, he will answer questions on the fringe of the matter. By measuring increased hesitation in his answers as the central question is approached, by measuring the area of blankness and the intensity of counterpotentials set up, it is possible to tell with scientific precision that his troubles are the result of an order not to talk, with its strength based on First Law. In other words, he's been told that if he talks, harm will be done a human being. Presumably harm to the unspeakable Professor Ninheimer, the plaintiff, who, to the robot, would seem a human being."

"Well, then," said Robertson, "can't you explain that if he keeps quiet, harm will be done to U.S. Robots?"

"U.S. Robots is not a human being and the First Law of Robotics does not recognize a corporation as a person the way ordinary laws do. Besides, it would be dangerous to try to lift this particular sort of inhibition. The person who laid it on could lift it off least dangerously, because the robot's motivations in that respect are centered on that person. Any other course—" She shook her head and grew almost impassioned. "I won't let the robot be damaged!"

Lanning interrupted with the air of bringing sanity to the problem. "It seems to me that we have only to prove a robot incapable of the act which Easy is accused. We can do that."

"Exactly," said Defense, in annoyance. "You can do that. The only witnesses capable of testifying to Easy's condition and to the nature of Easy's state of mind are employees of U.S. Robots. The judge can't possibly accept their testimony as unprejudiced."

"How can he deny expert testimony?"

"By refusing to be convinced by it. That's his right as the judge. Against the alternative that a man like Professor Ninheimer deliberately set about ruining his own reputation, even for a sizable sum of money, the judge isn't going to accept the technicalities of your engineers. The judge is a man, after all. If he has to choose between a man doing an impossible thing and a robot doing an impossible thing, he's quite likely to decide in favor of the man."

"A man *can* do an impossible thing," said Lanning, "because we don't know all the complexities of the human mind and we don't know what, in a given human mind, is impossible and what is not. We *do* know what is really impossible to a robot."

"Well, we'll see if we can't convince the judge of that," Defense replied wearily.

"If all you say is so," rumbled Robertson, "I don't see how you can."

"We'll see. It's good to know and be aware of the difficulties involved, but let's not be *too* downhearted. I've tried to look ahead a few moves in the chess game, too." With a stately nod in the direction of the robopsychologist, he added, "*With* the help of the good lady here."

Lanning looked from one to the other and said, "What the devil is this?"

But the bailiff thrust his head into the room and announced somewhat breathlessly that the trial was about to resume.

They took their seats, examining the man who had started all the trouble.

Simon Ninheimer owned a fluffy head of sandy hair, a face that narrowed past a beaked nose toward a pointed chin, and a habit of sometimes hesitating before key words in his conversation that gave him an air of a seeker after an almost unbearable precision. When he said, "The Sun rises in the—uh—east," one was certain he had given due consideration to the possibility that it might at some time rise in the west.

Prosecution said, "Did you oppose employment of Robot EZ-27 by the university?"

"I did, sir."

"Why was that?"

"I did not feel that we understood the—uh—motives of U.S. Robots thoroughly. I mistrusted their anxiety to place the robot with us."

"Did you feel that it was capable of doing the work that it was allegedly designed to do?"

"I know for a fact that it was not."

"Would you state your reasons?"

Simon Ninheimer's book, entitled *Social Tensions Involved in Space-Flight and Their Resolution,* had been eight years in the making. Ninheimer's search for precision was not confined to his habits of speech, and in a subject like sociology, almost inherently imprecise, it left him breathless.

Even with the material in galley proofs, he felt no sense of completion. Rather the reverse, in fact. Staring at the long strips of print, he felt only the itch to tear the lines of type apart and rearrange them differently.

Jim Baker, Instructor and soon to be Assistant Professor of Sociology, found Ninheimer, three days after the first batch of galleys had arrived from the printer, staring at the handful of paper in abstraction. The galleys came in three copies: one for Ninheimer to proofread, one for Baker to proofread independently, and a third, marked "Original," which was to receive the final corrections, a combination of those made by Ninheimer and by Baker, after a conference at which possible conflicts and disagreements were ironed out. This had been their policy on the several papers on which they had collaborated in the past three years and it worked well.

Baker, young and ingratiatingly soft-voiced, had his own copies of the galleys in his hand. He said eagerly, "I've done the first chapter and it contains some typographical beauts."

"The first chapter always has them," said Ninheimer distantly.

"Do you want to go over it now?"

Ninheimer brought his eyes to grave focus on Baker. "I haven't done anything on the galleys, Jim. I don't think I'll bother."

Baker looked confused. "Not bother?"

Ninheimer pursed his lips. "I've asked about the—uh—workload of the machine. After all, he was originally—uh—promoted as a proofreader. They've set a schedule."

"The *machine*? You mean Easy?"

"I believe that is the foolish name they gave it."

"But, Dr. Ninheimer, I thought you were staying clear of it!"

"I seem to be the only one doing so. Perhaps I ought to take my share of the—uh—advantage."

"Oh. Well, I seem to have wasted time on this first chapter, then," said the younger man ruefully.

"Not wasted. We can compare the machine's result with yours as a check."

"If you want to, but—"

"Yes?"

"I doubt that we'll find anything wrong with Easy's work. It's supposed never to have made a mistake."

"I dare say," said Ninheimer dryly.

The first chapter was brought in again by Baker four days later. This time it was Ninheimer's copy, fresh from the special annex that had been built to house Easy and the equipment it used.

Baker was jubilant. "Dr. Ninheimer, it not only caught everything I caught—it found a dozen errors I missed! The whole thing took it twelve minutes!"

Ninheimer looked over the sheaf, with the neatly printed marks and symbols in the margins. He said, "It is not as complete as you and I would have made it. We would have entered an insert on Suzuki's work on the neurological effects of low gravity."

"You mean his paper in *Sociological Reviews*?"

"Of course."

"Well, you can't expect impossibilities of Easy. It can't read the literature for us."

"I realize that. As a matter of fact, I have prepared the insert. I will see the machine and make certain it knows how to—uh—handle inserts."

"It will know."

"I prefer to make certain."

Ninheimer had to make an appointment to see Easy, and then could get nothing better than fifteen minutes in the late evening.

But the fifteen minutes turned out to be ample. Robot EZ-27 understood the matter of inserts at once.

Ninheimer found himself uncomfortable at close quarters with the robot for the first time. Almost automatically, as though it were human, he found himself asking, "Are you happy with your work?"

"Most happy, Professor Ninheimer," said Easy solemnly, the photocells that were its eyes gleaming their normal deep red.

"You know me?"

"From the fact that you present me with additional material to include in the galleys, it follows that you are the author. The author's name, of course, is at the head of each sheet of galley proof."

"I see. You make—uh—deductions, then. Tell me"—he couldn't resist the question—"what do you think of the book so far?"

Easy said, "I find it very pleasant to work with."

"Pleasant? That is an odd word for a—uh—a mechanism without emotion. I've been told you have no emotion."

"The words of your book go in accordance with my circuits," Easy explained. "They set up little or no counterpotentials. It is in my brain paths to translate this mechanical fact into a word such as 'pleasant.' The emotional context is fortuitous."

"I see. Why do you find the book pleasant?"

"It deals with human beings, Professor, and not with inorganic materials or mathematical symbols. Your book attempts to understand human beings and to help increase human happiness."

"And this is what you try to do and so my book goes in accordance with your circuits? Is that it?"

"That is it, Professor."

The fifteen minutes were up. Ninheimer left and went to the university library, which was on the point of closing. He kept them open long enough to find an elementary text on robotics. He took it home with him.

Except for occasional insertion of late material, the galleys went to Easy and from him to the publishers with little intervention from Ninheimer at first—and none at all later.

Baker said, a little uneasily, "It almost gives me a feeling of uselessness."

"It should give you a feeling of having time to begin a new project," said Ninheimer, without looking up from the notations he was making in the current issue of *Social Science Abstracts*.

"I'm just not used to it. I keep worrying about the galleys. It's silly, I know."

"It is."

"The other day I got a couple of sheets before Easy sent them off to—"

"What!" Ninheimer looked up, scowling. The copy of *Abstracts* slid shut. "Did you disturb the machine at its work?"

"Only for a minute. Everything was all right. Oh, it changed one word. You referred to something as 'criminal'; it changed the word to 'reckless.' It thought the second adjective fit in better with the context."

Ninheimer grew thoughtful. "What did you think?"

"You know, I agreed with it. I let it stand."

Ninheimer turned in his swivel-chair to face his young

associate. "See here, I wish you wouldn't do this again. If I am to use the machine, I wish the—uh—full advantage of it. If I am to use it and lose your—uh—services anyway because you supervise it when the whole point is that it requires no supervision, I gain nothing. Do you see?"

"Yes, Dr. Ninheimer," said Baker, subdued.

The advance copies of *Social Tensions* arrived in Dr. Ninheimer's office on the eighth of May. He looked through it briefly, flipping pages and pausing to read a paragraph here and there. Then he put his copies away.

As he explained later, he forgot about it. For eight years, he had worked at it, but now, and for months in the past, other interests had engaged him while Easy had taken the load of the book off his shoulders. He did not even think to donate the usual complimentary copy to the university library. Even Baker, who had thrown himself into work and had steered clear of the department head since receiving his rebuke at their last meeting, received no copy.

On the sixteenth of June that stage ended. Ninheimer received a phone call and stared at the image in the 'plate with surprise.

"Speidell! Are you in town?"

"No, sir. I'm in Cleveland." Speidell's voice trembled with emotion.

"Then why the call?"

"Because I've just been looking through your new book! Ninheimer, are you *mad*? Have you gone *insane*?"

Ninheimer stiffened. "Is something—uh—wrong?" he asked in alarm.

"Wrong? I refer you to page 562. What in blazes do you mean by interpreting my work as you do? Where in the paper cited do I make the claim that the criminal personality is nonexistent and that it is the *law*-enforcement agencies that are the *true* criminals? Here, let me quote—"

"Wait! Wait!" cried Ninheimer, trying to find the page. "Let me see. Let me see . . . Good God!"

"Well?"

"Speidell, I don't see how this could have happened. I never wrote this."

"But that's what's printed! And that distortion isn't the worst. You look at page 690 and imagine what Ipatiev is going to do to you when he sees the hash you've made of his findings! Look, Ninheimer, the book is *riddled* with this sort of thing. I don't know what you were thinking of—but there's nothing to do but get the book off the market. And you'd better be prepared for extensive apologies at the next Association meeting!"

"Speidell, listen to me—"

But Speidell had flashed off with a force that had the 'plate glowing with after-images for fifteen seconds.

It was then that Ninheimer went through the book and began marking off passages with red ink.

He kept his temper remarkably well when he faced Easy again, but his lips were pale. He passed the book to Easy and said, "Will you read the marked passages on pages 562, 631, 664 and 690?"

Easy did so in four glances. "Yes, Professor Ninheimer."

"This is not as I had it in the original galleys."

"No, sir. It is not."

"Did you change it to read as it now does?"

"Yes, sir."

"Why?"

"Sir, the passages as they read in your version were most uncomplimentary to certain groups of human beings. I felt it advisable to change the wording to avoid doing them harm."

"How *dared* you do such a thing?"

"The First Law, Professor, does not let me, through any inaction, allow harm to come to human beings. Certainly, considering your reputation in the world of sociology and the wide circulation your book would receive among scholars, considerable harm would come to a number of the human beings you speak of."

"But do you realize the harm that will come to me now?"

"It was necessary to choose the alternative with less harm."

Professor Ninheimer, shaking with fury, staggered away.

It was clear to him that U.S. Robots would have to account to him for this.

There was some excitement at the defendants' table, which increased as Prosecution drove the point home.

"Then Robot EZ-27 informed you that the reason for its action was based on the First Law of Robotics?"

"That is correct, sir."

"That, in effect, it had no choice?"

"Yes, sir."

"It follows then that U.S. Robots designed a robot that would of necessity rewrite books to accord with its own conceptions of what was right. And yet they palmed it off as simple proofreader. Would you say that?"

Defense objected firmly at once, pointing out that the witness was being asked for a decision on a matter in which he had no competence. The judge admonished Prosecution in the usual terms, but there was no doubt that the exchange had sunk home—not least upon the attorney for the Defense.

Defense asked for a short recess before beginning cross-examination, using a legal technicality for the purpose that got him five minutes.

He leaned over toward Susan Calvin. "Is it possible, Dr. Calvin, that Professor Ninheimer is telling the truth and that Easy was motivated by the First Law?"

Calvin pressed her lips together, then said, "No. It *isn't* possible. The last part of Ninheimer's testimony is deliberate perjury. Easy is not designed to be able to judge matters at the stage of abstraction represented by an advanced textbook on sociology. It would never be able to tell that certain groups of humans would be harmed by a phrase in such a book. Its mind is simply not built for that."

"I suppose, though, that we can't prove this to a layman," said Defense pessimistically.

"No," admitted Calvin. "The proof would be highly complex. Our way out is still what it was. We must prove Ninheimer is lying, and nothing he has said need change our plan of attack."

"Very well, Dr. Calvin," said Defense, "I must accept your word in this. We'll go on as planned."

In the courtroom, the judge's gavel rose and fell and Dr. Ninheimer took the stand once more. He smiled a little as one who feels his position to be impregnable and rather enjoys the prospect of countering a useless attack.

Defense approached warily and began softly. "Dr. Ninheimer, do you mean to say that you were completely unaware of these alleged changes in your manuscript until such time as Dr. Speidell called you on the sixteenth of June?"

"That is correct, sir."

"Did you never look at the galleys after Robot EZ-27 had proofread them?"

"At first I did, but it seemed to me a useless task. I relied on the claims of U.S. Robots. The absurd—uh—changes were made only in the last quarter of the book after the robot, I presume, had learned enough about sociology—"

"Never mind your presumptions!" said Defense. "I understood your colleague, Dr. Baker, saw the later galleys on at least one occasion. Do you remember testifying to that effect?"

"Yes, sir. As I said, he told me about seeing one page, and even there, the robot had changed a word."

Again Defense broke in. "Don't you find it strange, sir, that after over a year of implacable hostility to the robot, after having voted against it in the first place and having refused to put it to any use whatever, you suddenly decided to put your book, your *magnum opus*, into its hands?"

"I don't find that strange. I simply decided that I might as well use the machine."

"And you were so confident of Robot EZ-27—all of a sudden—that you didn't even bother to check your galleys?"

"I told you I was—uh—persuaded by U.S. Robots' propaganda."

"So persuaded that when your colleague, Dr. Baker, attempted to check on the robot, you berated him soundly?"

"I didn't berate him. I merely did not wish to have him—uh—waste his time. At least, I thought then it was a waste of time. I did not see the significance of that change in a word at the—"

Defense said with heavy sarcasm, "I have no doubt you were instructed to bring up that point in order that the word-change be entered in the record—" He altered his line to forestall objection and said, "The point is that you were extremely angry with Dr. Baker."

"No, sir. Not angry."

"You didn't give him a copy of your book when you received it."

"Simple forgetfulness. I didn't give the library its copy, either." Ninheimer smiled cautiously. "Professors are notoriously absent-minded."

Defense said, "Do you find it strange that, after more than a year of perfect work, Robot EZ-27 should go wrong on your book? On a book, that is, which was written by you, who was, of all people, the most implacably hostile to the robot?"

"My book was the only sizable work dealing with mankind that it had to face. The Three Laws of Robotics took hold then."

"Several times, Dr. Ninheimer," said Defense, "you have tried to sound like an expert on robotics. Apparently you suddenly grew interested in robotics and took out books on the subject from the library. You testified to that effect, did you not?"

"One book, sir. That was the result of what seems to me to have been—uh—natural curiosity."

"And it enabled you to explain why the robot should, as you allege, have distorted your book?"

"Yes, sir."

"Very convenient. But are you sure your interest in robotics was not intended to enable you to manipulate the robot for your own purposes?"

Ninheimer flushed. "Certainly not, sir!"

Defense's voice rose. "In fact, are you sure the alleged altered passages were not as you had them in the first place?"

The sociologist half-rose. "That's—uh—uh—ridiculous! I have the galleys—"

He had difficulty speaking and Prosecution rose to insert smoothly, "With your permission, Your Honor, I intend to introduce as evidence the set of galleys given by Dr. Ninheimer to Robot EZ-27 and the set of galleys mailed by Robot EZ-27 to the publishers. I will do so now if my esteemed colleague so desires, and will be willing to allow a recess in order that the two sets of galleys may be compared."

Defense waved his hand impatiently. "That is not necessary. My honored opponent can introduce those galleys whenever he chooses. I'm sure they will show whatever discrepancies are claimed by the plaintiff to exist. What I would like to know of the witness, however, is whether he also has in his possession *Dr. Baker's* galleys."

"Dr. Baker's galleys?" Ninheimer frowned. He was not yet quite master of himself.

"Yes, Professor! I mean Dr. Baker's galleys. You testified to the effect that Dr. Baker had received a separate copy of the galleys. I will have the clerk read your testimony if you are suddenly a selective type of amnesiac. Or is it just that professors are, as you say, notoriously absent-minded?"

Ninheimer said, "I remember Dr. Baker's galleys. They weren't necessary once the job was placed in the care of the proofreading machine—"

"So you burned them?"

"*No.* I put them in the waste basket."

"Burned them, dumped them—what's the difference? The point is you got rid of them."

"There's nothing wrong—" began Ninheimer weakly.

"Nothing wrong?" thundered Defense. "Nothing wrong except that there is now no way we can check to see if, on certain crucial galley sheets, you might not have substituted a harmless blank one from Dr. Baker's copy for a sheet in your own copy which you had deliberately mangled in such a way as to force the robot to—"

Prosecution shouted a furious objection. Justice Shane leaned forward, his round face doing its best to assume an expression of anger equivalent to the intensity of the emotion felt by the man.

The judge said, "Do you have any evidence, Counselor, for the extraordinary statement you have just made?"

Defense said quietly, "No direct evidence, Your Honor. But I would like to point out that, viewed properly, the sudden conversion of the plaintiff from anti-roboticism, his sudden interest in robotics, his refusal to check the galleys or to allow anyone else to check them, his careful effort to keep anyone from seeing the book immediately after publication, all very clearly point—"

"Counselor," interrupted the judge impatiently, "this is not the place for esoteric deductions. The plaintiff is not on trial. Neither are you prosecuting him. I forbid this line of attack and I can only point out that the desperation that must have induced you to do this cannot help but weaken your case. If you have legitimate questions to ask, Counselor, you may continue with your cross-examination. But I warn you against another such exhibition in this courtroom."

"I have no further questions, Your Honor."

Robertson whispered heatedly as counsel for the Defense returned to his table, "What good did that do, for God's sake? The judge is dead-set against you now."

Defense replied calmly, "But Ninheimer is good and rattled. And we've set him up for tomorrow's move. He'll be ripe."

Susan Calvin nodded gravely.

The rest of Prosecution's case was mild in comparison. Dr. Baker was called and bore out most of Ninheimer's testimony. Drs. Speidell and Ipatiev were called, and they expounded most movingly on their shock and dismay at certain quoted passages in Dr. Ninheimer's book. Both gave their professional opinion that Dr. Ninheimer's professional reputation had been seriously impaired.

The galleys were introduced in evidence, as were copies of the finished book.

Defense cross-examined no more that day. Prosecution rested and the trial was recessed till the next morning.

Defense made his first motion at the beginning of the proceedings on the second day. He requested that Robot EZ-27 be admitted as a spectator to the proceedings.

Prosecution objected at once and Justice Shane called both to the bench.

Prosecution said hotly, "This is obviously illegal. A robot may not be in any edifice used by the general public."

"This courtroom," pointed out Defense, "is closed to all but those having an immediate connection with the case."

"A large machine of *known* erratic behavior would disturb my clients and my witnesses by its very presence! It would make hash out of the proceedings."

The judge seemed inclined to agree. He turned to Defense and said rather unsympathetically, "What are the reasons for your request?"

Defense said, "It will be our contention that Robot EZ-27 could not possibly, by the nature of its construction, have behaved as it has been described as behaving. It will be necessary to present a few demonstrations."

Prosecution said, "I don't see the point, Your Honor. Demonstrations conducted by men employed at U.S. Robots are worth little as evidence when U.S. Robots is the defendant."

"Your Honor," said Defense, "the validity of any evidence is for you to decide, not for the Prosecuting Attorney. At least, that is my understanding."

Justice Shane, his prerogatives encroached upon, said, "Your understanding is correct. Nevertheless, the presence of a robot here does raise important legal questions."

"Surely, Your Honor, nothing that should be allowed to override the requirements of justice. If the robot is not present, we are prevented from presenting our only defense."

The judge considered. "There would be the question of transporting the robot here."

"That is a problem with which U.S. Robots has frequently been faced. We have a truck parked outside the courtroom, constructed according to the laws governing the transportation of robots. Robot EZ-27 is in a packing case inside with two men guarding it. The doors to the truck are properly secured and all other necessary precautions have been taken."

"You seem certain," said Justice Shane, in renewed ill-temper, "that judgment on this point will be in your favor."

"Not at all, Your Honor. If it is not, we simply turn the truck about. I have made no presumptions concerning your decision."

The judge nodded. "The request on the part of the Defense is granted."

The crate was carried in on a large dolly and the two men who handled it opened it. The courtroom was immersed in a dead silence.

Susan Calvin waited as the thick slabs of celluform went down, then held out one hand. "Come, Easy."

The robot looked in her direction and held out its large metal arm. It towered over her by two feet but followed meekly, like a child in the clasp of its mother. Someone giggled nervously and choked it off at a hard glare from Dr. Calvin.

Easy seated itself carefully in a large chair brought by the bailiff, which creaked but held.

Defense said, "When it becomes necessary, Your Honor, we will prove that this is actually Robot EZ-27, the specific robot in the employ of Northeastern University during the period of time with which we are concerned."

"Good," His Honor said. "That will be necessary. I, for one, have no idea how you can tell one robot from another."

"And now," said Defense, "I would like to call my first witness to the stand. Professor Simon Ninheimer, please."

The clerk hesitated, looked at the judge. Justice Shane asked, with visible surprise, "You are calling the *plaintiff* as your witness?"

"Yes, Your Honor."

"I hope that you're aware that as long as he's your witness, you will be allowed none of the latitude you might exercise if you were cross-examining an opposing witness."

Defense said smoothly, "My only purpose in all this is to arrive at the truth. It will not be necessary to do more than ask a few polite questions."

"Well," said the judge dubiously, "you're the one handling the case. Call the witness."

Ninheimer took the stand and was informed that he was still under oath. He looked more nervous than he had the day before, almost apprehensive.

But Defense looked at him benignly.

"Now, Professor Ninheimer, you are suing my clients in the amount of $750,000."

"That is the—uh—sum. Yes."

"That is a great deal of money."

"I have suffered a great deal of harm."

"Surely not that much. The material in question involves only a few passages in a book. Perhaps these were unfortunate passages, but after all, books sometimes appear with curious mistakes in them."

Ninheimer's nostrils flared. "Sir, this book was to have been the climax of my professional career! Instead, it makes me look like an incompetent scholar, a perverter of the views held by my honored friends and associates, and a believer of ridiculous and—uh—outmoded viewpoints. My reputation is irretrievably shattered! I can never hold up my head in any—uh—assemblage of scholars, regardless of the outcome of this trial. I certainly cannot continue in my career, which has been the whole of my life. The very purpose of my life has been—uh—aborted and destroyed."

Defense made no attempt to interrupt the speech, but stared abstractedly at his fingernails as it went on.

He said very soothingly, "But surely, Professor Ninheimer, at your present age, you could not hope to earn more than—let us be generous—$150,000 during the remainder of your life. Yet you are asking the court to award you five time as much."

* * *

Ninheimer said, with an even greater burst of emotion, "It is not in my lifetime alone that I am ruined. I do not know for how many generations I shall be pointed at by sociologists as a—uh—a fool or maniac. My real achievements will be buried and ignored. I am ruined not only until the day of my death, but for all time to come, because there will always be people who will not believe that a robot made those insertions—"

It was at this point that Robot EZ-27 rose to his feet. Susan Calvin made no move to stop him. She sat motionless, staring straight ahead. Defense sighed softly.

Easy's melodious voice carried clearly. It said, "I would like to explain to everyone that I did insert certain passages in the galley proofs that seemed directly opposed to what had been there at first—"

Even the Prosecuting Attorney was too startled at the spectacle of a seven-foot robot rising to address the court to be able to demand the stopping of what was obviously a most irregular procedure.

When he could collect his wits, it was too late. For Ninheimer rose in the witness chair, his face working.

He shouted wildly, "Damn you, you were instructed to keep your mouth shut about—"

He ground to a choking halt, and Easy was silent, too.

Prosecution was on his feet now, demanding that a mistrial be declared.

Justice Shane banged his gavel desperately. "Silence! Silence! Certainly there is every reason here to declare a mistrial, except that in the interests of justice I would like to have Professor Ninheimer complete his statement. I distinctly heard him say to the robot that the robot had been instructed to keep its mouth shut about something. There was no mention in your testimony, Professor Ninheimer, as to any instructions to the robot to keep silent about anything!"

Ninheimer stared wordlessly at the judge.

Justice Shane said, "Did you instruct Robot EZ-27 to keep silent about something? And if so, about what?"

"Your Honor—" began Ninheimer hoarsely, and couldn't continue.

The judge's voice grew sharp. "Did you, in fact, order the inserts in question to be made in the galleys and then order the robot to keep quiet about your part in this?"

Prosecution objected vigorously, but Ninheimer shouted, "Oh, what's the use? Yes! Yes!" And he ran from the witness stand. He was stopped at the door by the bailiff and sank hopelessly into one of the last rows of seats, head buried in both hands.

Justice Shane said, "It is evident to me that Robot EZ-27 was brought here as a trick. Except for the fact that the trick served to prevent a serious miscarriage of justice, I would certainly hold attorney for the Defense in contempt. It is clear now, beyond any doubt, that the plaintiff has committed what is to me a completely inexplicable fraud since, apparently, he was knowingly ruining his career in the process—"

Judgment, of course, was for the defendant.

Dr. Susan Calvin had herself announced at Dr. Ninheimer's bachelor quarters in University Hall. The young engineer who had driven the car offered to go up with her, but she looked at him scornfully.

"Do you think he'll assault me? Wait down here."

Ninheimer was in no mood to assault anyone. He was packing, wasting no time, anxious to be away before the adverse conclusion of the trial became general knowledge.

He looked at Calvin with a queerly defiant air and said, "Are you coming to warn me of a countersuit? If so, it will get you nothing. I have no money, no job, no future. I can't even meet the costs of the trial."

"If you're looking for sympathy," said Calvin coldly, "don't look for it here. This was your doing. However, there will be no countersuit, neither of you nor of the university. We will even do what we can to keep you from going to prison for perjury. We aren't vindictive."

"Oh, is that why I'm not already in custody for forswearing myself? I had wondered. But then," he added bitterly, "why *should* you be vindictive? You have what you want now."

"Some of what we want, yes," said Calvin. "The university will keep Easy in its employ at a considerably higher rental fee. Furthermore, certain underground publicity concerning the trial will make it possible to place a few more of the EZ models in other institutions without danger of a repetition of this trouble."

"Then why have you come to see me?"

"Because I don't have all of what I want yet. I want to know why you hate robots as you do. Even if you had won the case, your reputation would have been ruined. The money you might have obtained could not have compensated for that. Would the satisfaction of your hatred for robots have done so?"

"Are you interested in *human* minds, Dr. Calvin?" asked Ninheimer, with acid mockery.

"Insofar as their reactions concern the welfare of robots, yes. For that reason, I have learned a little of human psychology."

"Enough of it to be able to trick me!"

"That wasn't hard," said Calvin, without pomposity. "The difficult thing was doing it in such a way as not to damage Easy."

"It is like you to be more concerned for a machine than for a man." He looked at her with savage contempt.

It left her unmoved. "It merely seems so, Professor Ninheimer. It is only by being concerned for robots that one can truly be concerned for twenty-first-century man. You would understand this if you were a roboticist."

"I have read enough robotics to know I don't *want* to be a roboticist!"

"Pardon me, you have read *a book* on robotics. It has taught you nothing. You learned enough to know that you could order a robot to do many things, even to falsify a book, if you went about it properly. You learned enough to know that you could not order him to forget something entirely without risking detection, but you thought you could order him into simple silence more safely. You were wrong."

"You guessed the truth from his silence?"

"It wasn't guessing. You were an amateur and didn't know enough to cover your tracks completely. My only problem was to prove the matter to the judge and you were kind enough to help us there, in your ignorance of the robotics you claim to despise."

"Is there any purpose in this discussion?" asked Ninheimer wearily.

"For me, yes," said Susan Calvin, "because I want you to understand how completely you have misjudged robots. You silenced Easy by telling him that if he told anyone about your own distortion of the book, you would lose your job. That set up a certain potential within Easy toward silence, one that was strong enough to resist our efforts to break it down. We would have damaged the brain if we had persisted.

"On the witness stand, however, you yourself put up a higher counterpotential. You said that because people would think that you, not a robot, had written the disputed passages in the book, you would lose far more than just your job. You would lose your reputation, your standing, your respect, your reason for living. You would lose the memory of you after death. A new and higher potential was set up by you—and Easy talked."

"Oh, God," said Ninheimer, turning his head away.

Calvin was inexorable. She said, "Do you understand *why* he talked? It was not to accuse you, but to *defend* you! It can be mathematically shown that he was about to assume full blame for your crime, to deny that you had anything to do with it. The First Law required that. He was going to lie—to damage himself—to bring monetary harm to a corporation. All that meant less to him than did the saving of you. If you really understood robots and robotics, you would have let him talk. But you did not understand, as I was sure you wouldn't, as I guaranteed to the defense attorney that you wouldn't. You were certain, in your hatred of robots, that Easy would act as a human being would act and defend itself at your expense. So you flared out at him in panic—and destroyed yourself."

Ninheimer said with feeling, "I hope some day your robots turn on you and kill you!"

"Don't be foolish," said Calvin. "Now I want you to explain why you've done all this."

Ninheimer grinned a distorted, humorless grin. "I am to dissect my mind, am I, for your intellectual curiosity, in return for immunity from a charge of perjury?"

"Put it that way if you like," said Calvin emotionlessly. "But explain."

"So that you can counter future anti-robot attempts more efficiently? With greater understanding?"

"I accept that."

"You know," said Ninheimer, "I'll tell you—just to watch it do you no good at all. You can't understand human motivation. You can only understand your damned machines because you're a machine yourself, with skin on."

He was breathing hard and there was no hesitation in his speech, no searching for precision. It was as though he had no further use for precision.

He said, "For two hundred and fifty years, the machine has been replacing Man and destroying the handcraftsman. Pottery is spewed out of molds and presses. Works of art have been replaced by identical gimcracks stamped out on a die. Call it progress, if you wish! The artist is restricted to abstractions, confined to the world of ideas. He must design something in mind—and then the machine does the rest.

"Do you suppose the potter is content with mental creation? Do you suppose the idea is enough? That there is nothing in the feel of the clay itself, in watching the thing grow as hand and mind work *together*? Do you suppose the actual growth doesn't act as a feedback to modify and improve the idea?"

"You are not a potter," said Dr. Calvin.

"I am a creative artist! I design and build articles and books. There is more to it than the mere thinking of words and of putting them in the right order. If that were all, there would be no pleasure in it, no return.

"A book should take shape in the hands of the writer. One must actually see the chapters grow and develop. One must work and rework and watch the changes take place beyond the original concept even. There is taking the galleys in hand and seeing how the sentences look in print and molding them again. There are a hundred contacts between a man and his work at every stage of the game—and the contact itself is pleasurable and repays a man for the work he puts into his creation more than anything else could. *Your robot would take all that away*."

"So does a typewriter. So does a printing press. Do you propose to return to the hand illumination of manuscripts?"

"Typewriters and printing presses take away some, but your robot would deprive us of all. Your robot takes over the galleys. Soon it, or other robots, would take over the original writing, the searching of the sources, the checking and cross-checking of passages, perhaps even the deduction of conclusions. What would that leave the scholar? One thing only—the barren decisions concerning what orders to give the robot next! I want to save the future generations of the world of scholarship from such a final hell. That meant more to me than even my own reputation and so I set out to destroy U. S. Robots by whatever means."

"You were bound to fail," said Susan Calvin.

"I was bound to try," said Simon Ninheimer.

Calvin turned and left. She did her best to feel no pang of sympathy for the broken man.

She did not entirely succeed.

CHRISTMAS
WITHOUT
RODNEY

It all started with Gracie (my wife of nearly forty years) wanting to give Rodney time off for the holiday season and it ended with me in an absolutely impossible situation. I'll tell you about it if you don't mind because I've got to tell *somebody*. Naturally, I'm changing names and details for our own protection.

It was just a couple of months ago, mid-December, and Gracie said to me, "Why don't we give Rodney time off for the holiday season? Why shouldn't he celebrate Christmas, too?"

I remember I had my optics unfocused at the time (there's a certain amount of relief in letting things go hazy when you want to rest or just listen to music) but I focused them quickly to see if Gracie were smiling or had a twinkle in her eye. Not that she has much of a sense of humor, you understand.

She wasn't smiling. No twinkle. I said, "Why on Earth should we give him time off?"

"Why not?"

"Do you want to give the freezer a vacation, the steri-

395

lizer, the holoviewer? Shall we just turn off the power supply?"

"Come, Howard," she said. "Rodney isn't a freezer or a sterilizer. He's a *person*."

"He's not a person. He's a robot. He wouldn't want a vacation."

"How do you know? And he's a *person*. He deserves a chance to rest and just revel in the holiday atmosphere."

I wasn't going to argue that "person" thing with her. I know you've all read those polls which show that women are three times as likely to resent and fear robots as men are. Perhaps that's because robots tend to do what was once called, in the bad old days, "women's work" and women fear being made useless, though I should think they'd be delighted. In any case, Gracie *is* delighted and she simply adores Rodney. (That's *her* word for it. Every other day she says, "I just adore Rodney.")

You've got to understand that Rodney is an old-fashioned robot whom we've had about seven years. He's been adjusted to fit in with our old-fashioned house and our old-fashioned ways and I'm rather pleased with him myself. Sometimes I wonder about getting one of those slick, modern jobs, which are automated to death, like the one our son, DeLancey, has, but Gracie would never stand for it.

But then I thought of DeLancey and I said, "How are we going to give Rodney time off, Gracie? DeLancey is coming in with that gorgeous wife of his" (I was using "gorgeous" in a sarcastic sense, but Gracie didn't notice—it's amazing how she insists on seeing a good side even when it doesn't exist) "and how are we going to have the house in good shape and meals made and all the rest of it without Rodney?"

"But that's just it," she said, earnestly. "DeLancey and Hortense could bring *their* robot and he could do it all. You *know* they don't think much of Rodney, and they'd love to show what theirs can do and Rodney can have a rest."

I grunted and said, "If it will make you happy, I suppose we can do it. It'll only be for three days. But I don't want Rodney thinking he'll get every holiday off."

It was another joke, of course, but Gracie just said, very earnestly, "No, Howard, I will talk to him and explain it's only just once in a while."

She can't quite understand that Rodney is controlled by the three laws of robotics and that nothing has to be explained to him.

So I had to wait for DeLancey and Hortense, and my heart was heavy. DeLancey is my son, of course, but he's one of your upwardly mobile, bottom-line individuals. He married Hortense because she has excellent connections in business and can help him in that upward shove. At least, I hope so, because if she has another virtue I have never discovered it.

They showed up with their robot two days before Christmas. The robot was as glitzy as Hortense and looked almost as hard. He was polished to a high gloss and there was none of Rodney's clumping. Hortense's robot (I'm sure she dictated the design) moved absolutely silently. He kept showing up behind me for no reason and giving me heart-failure every time I turned around and bumped into him.

Worse, DeLancey brought eight-year-old LeRoy. Now he's my grandson, and I would swear to Hortense's fidelity because I'm sure no one would voluntarily touch her, but I've got to admit that putting him through a concrete mixer would improve him no end.

He came in demanding to know if we had sent Rodney to the metal-reclamation unit yet. (He called it the "bust-up place.") Hortense sniffed and said, "Since we have a modern robot with us, I hope you keep Rodney out of sight."

I said nothing, but Gracie said, "Certainly, dear. In fact, we've given Rodney time off."

DeLancey made a face but didn't say anything. He knew his mother.

I said, pacifically, "Suppose we start off by having Rambo make something good to drink, eh? Coffee, tea, hot chocolate, a bit of brandy—"

Rambo was their robot's name. I don't know why except that it starts with R. There's no law about it, but you've probably noticed for yourself that almost every robot has a name beginning with R. R for robot, I suppose. The usual name is Robert. There must be a million robot Roberts in the northeast corridor alone.

And frankly, it's my opinion that's the reason human names just don't start with R any more. You get Bob and Dick but not Robert or Richard. You get Posy and Trudy, but not Rose or Ruth. Sometimes you get unusual R's. I know of three robots called Rutabaga, and two that are Rameses. But Hortense is the only one I know who named a robot Rambo, a syllable-combination I've never encountered, and I've never liked to ask why. I was sure the explanation would prove to be unpleasant.

Rambo turned out to be useless at once. He was, of course, programmed for the DeLancey/Hortense menage and that was utterly modern and utterly automated. To prepare drinks in his own home, all Rambo had to do was to press appropriate buttons. (Why anyone would need a robot to press buttons, I would like to have explained to me!)

He said so. He turned to Hortense and said in a voice like honey (it wasn't Rodney's city-boy voice with its trace of Brooklyn), "The equipment is lacking, madam."

And Hortense drew a sharp breath. "You mean you *still* don't have a robotized kitchen, grandfather?" (She called me nothing at all, until LeRoy was born, howling of course, and then she promptly called me "grandfather." Naturally, she never called me Howard. That would tend to show me to be human, or, more unlikely, show *her* to be human.)

I said, "Well, it's robotized when Rodney is in it."

"I dare say," she said. "But we're not living in the twentieth century, grandfather."

I thought: How I wish we were—but I just said, "Well, why not program Rambo how to operate our controls. I'm sure he can pour and mix and heat and do whatever else is necessary."

"I'm sure he can," said Hortense, "but thank Fate he doesn't have to. I'm not going to interfere with his programming. It will make him less efficient."

Gracie said, worried, but amiable, "But if we don't interfere with his programming, then I'll just have to instruct him, step by step, but I don't know how it's done. I've never done it."

I said, "Rodney can tell him."

Gracie said, "Oh, Howard, we've given Rodney a vacation."

"I know, but we're not going to ask him to *do* anything; just tell Rambo here what to do and then Rambo can do it."

Whereupon Rambo said stiffly, "Madam, there is nothing in my programming or in my instructions that would make it mandatory for me to accept orders given me by another robot, especially one that is an earlier model."

Hortense said, soothingly, "Of course, Rambo. I'm sure that grandfather and grandmother understand that." (I noticed that DeLancey never said a word. I wonder if he *ever* said a word when his dear wife was present.)

I said, "All right, I tell you what. I'll have Rodney tell *me*, and then I will tell Rambo."

Rambo said nothing to that. Even Rambo is subject to the second law of robotics which makes it mandatory for him to obey human orders.

Hortense's eyes narrowed and I knew that she would like to tell me that Rambo was far too fine a robot to be ordered about by the likes of me, but some distant and rudimentary near-human waft of feeling kept her from doing so.

Little LeRoy was hampered by no such quasi-human restraints. He said, "I don't want to have to look at Rodney's ugly puss. I bet he don't know how to do *anything* and if he does, ol' Grampa would get it all wrong anyway."

It would have been nice, I thought, if I could be alone with little LeRoy for five minutes and reason calmly with him, with a brick, but a mother's instinct told Hortense never to leave LeRoy alone with any human being whatever.

There was nothing to do, really, but get Rodney out of his niche in the closet where he had been enjoying his own thoughts (I wonder if a robot has his own thoughts when he is alone) and put him to work. It was hard. He would say a phrase, then I would say the same phrase, then Rambo would do something, then Rodney would say another phrase and so on.

It all took twice as long as if Rodney were doing it himself and it wore *me* out, I can tell you, because everything had to be like that, using the dishwasher/sterilizer, cooking the Christmas feast, cleaning up messes on the table or on the floor, everything.

Gracie kept moaning that Rodney's vacation was being ruined, but she never seemed to notice that mine was, too, though I *did* admire Hortense for her manner of saying something unpleasant at every moment that some statement seemed called for. I noticed, particularly, that she never repeated herself once. Anyone can be nasty, but to be unfailingly creative in one's nastiness filled me with a perverse desire to applaud now and then.

But, really, the worst thing of all came on Christmas Eve. The tree had been put up and I was exhausted. We didn't have the kind of situation in which an automated box of ornaments was plugged into an electronic tree, and at the touch of one button there would result an instantaneous and perfect distribution of ornaments. On our tree (of ordinary, old-fashioned plastic) the ornaments had to be placed, one by one, by hand.

Hortense looked revolted, but I said, "Actually, Hortense, this means you can be creative and make your own arrangement."

Hortense sniffed, rather like the scrape of claws on a rough plaster wall, and left the room with an obvious expression of nausea on her face. I bowed in the direction of her retreating back, glad to see her go, and then began the tedious task of listening to Rodney's instructions and passing them on to Rambo.

When it was over, I decided to rest my aching feet and mind by sitting in a chair in a far and rather dim corner of the room. I had hardly folded my aching body into the chair when little LeRoy entered. He didn't see me, I suppose, or, then again, he might simply have ignored me as being part

of the less important and interesting pieces of furniture in the room.

He cast a disdainful look on the tree and said, to Rambo, "Listen, where are the Christmas presents? I'll bet old Gramps and Gram got me lousy ones, but I ain't going to wait for no tomorrow morning."

Rambo said, "I do not know where they are, Little Master."

"Huh!" said LeRoy, turning to Rodney. "How about you, Stink-face. Do you know where the presents are?"

Rodney would have been within the bounds of his programming to have refused to answer on the grounds that he did not know he was being addressed, since his name was Rodney and not Stink-face. I'm quite certain that that would have been Rambo's attitude. Rodney, however, was of different stuff. He answered politely, "Yes, I do, Little Master."

"So where is it, you old puke?"

Rodney said, "I don't think it would be wise to tell you, Little Master. That would disappoint Gracie and Howard who would like to give the presents to you tomorrow morning."

"Listen," said little LeRoy, "who you think you're talking to, you dumb robot? Now I gave you an order. You bring those presents to me." And in an attempt to show Rodney who was master, he kicked the robot in the shin.

It was a mistake. I saw it would be that a second before and that was a joyous second. Little LeRoy, after all, was ready for bed (though I doubted that he ever went to bed before he was *good* and ready). Therefore, he was wearing slippers. What's more, the slipper sailed off the foot with which he kicked, so that he ended by slamming his bare toes hard against the solid chrome-steel of the robotic shin.

He fell to the floor howling and in rushed his mother. "What is it, LeRoy? What is it?"

Whereupon little LeRoy had the immortal gall to say, "He hit me. That old monster-robot *hit* me."

Hortense screamed. She saw me and shouted, "That robot of yours must be destroyed."

I said, "Come, Hortense. A robot can't hit a boy. First law of robotics prevents it."

"It's an *old* robot, a *broken* robot. LeRoy says—"

"LeRoy lies. There is no robot, no matter how old or how broken, who could hit a boy."

"Then *he* did it. *Grampa* did it," howled LeRoy.

"I wish I did," I said, quietly, "but no robot would have allowed me to. Ask your own. Ask Rambo if he would have remained motionless while either Rodney or I had hit your boy. Rambo!"

I put it in the imperative, and Rambo said, "I would not have allowed any harm to come to the Little Master, Madam, but I did not know what he purposed. He kicked Rodney's shin with his bare foot, Madam."

Hortense gasped and her eyes bulged in fury. "Then he had a good reason to do so. I'll still have your robot destroyed."

"Go ahead, Hortense. Unless you're willing to ruin your robot's efficiency by trying to reprogram him to lie, he will bear witness to just what preceded the kick and so, of course, with pleasure, will I."

Hortense left the next morning, carrying the pale-faced LeRoy with her (it turned out he had broken a toe—nothing he didn't deserve) and an endlessly wordless DeLancey.

Gracie wrung her hands and implored them to stay, but I watched them leave without emotion. No, that's a lie. I watched them leave with lots of emotion, all pleasant.

Later, I said to Rodney, when Gracie was not present, "I'm sorry, Rodney. That was a horrible Christmas, all because we tried to have it without you. We'll never do that again, I promise."

"Thank you, Sir," said Rodney. "I must admit that there were times these two days when I earnestly wished the laws of robotics did not exist."

I grinned and nodded my head, but that night I woke up out of a sound sleep and began to worry. I've been worrying ever since.

I admit that Rodney was greatly tried, but a robot *can't*

wish the laws of robotics did not exist. He *can't*, no matter what the circumstances.

If I report this, Rodney will undoubtedly be scrapped, and if we're issued a new robot as recompense, Gracie will simply never forgive me. Never! No robot, however new, however talented, can possibly replace Rodney in her affection.

In fact, I'll never forgive myself. Quite apart from my own liking for Rodney, I couldn't bear to give Hortense the satisfaction.

But if I do nothing, I live with a robot capable of wishing the laws of robotics did not exist. From wishing they did not exist to acting as if they did not exist is just a step. At what moment will he take that step and in what form will he show that he has done so?

What do I do? What do I do?

• ROBOTS •
I HAVE
KNOWN

•

Mechanical men, or, to use Čapek's now universally-accepted term, robots, are a subject to which the modern science-fiction writer has turned again and again. There is no uninvented invention, with the possible exception of the spaceship, that is so clearly pictured in the minds of so many: a sinister form, large, metallic, vaguely human, moving like a machine and speaking with no emotion.

The key word in the description is "sinister" and therein lies a tragedy, for no science-fiction theme wore out its welcome as quickly as did the robot. Only one robot-plot seemed available to the average author: the mechanical man that proved a menace, the creature that turned against its creator, the robot that became a threat to humanity. And almost all stories of this sort were heavily surcharged, either explicitly or implicitly, with the weary moral that "there are some things mankind must never seek to learn."

This sad situation has, since 1940, been largely ameliorated. Stories about robots abound; a newer viewpoint, more mechanistic and less moralistic, has developed. For this development, some people (notably Mr. Groff Conklin in the introduction to his science-fiction anthology entitled "Science-Fiction Thinking Machines," published in 1954) have seen fit to attach at least partial credit to a series of robot stories I wrote beginning in 1940. Since there is probably no one on Earth less given to false modesty than myself, I accept said partial credit with equanimity and ease, modifying it only to include Mr. John W. Campbell, Jr., editor of "Astounding Science-Fiction," with whom I had many fruitful discussions on robot stories.

My own viewpoint was that robots were story material, not as blasphemous imitations of life, but merely as advanced machines. A machine does not "turn against its creator" if it is properly designed. When a machine, such as a power-saw, seems to do so by occasionally lopping off a limb, this regrettable tendency towards evil is combatted by the installation of safety devices. Analogous safety devices would, it seemed obvious, be developed in the case of robots. And the most logical place for such safety devices would seem to be in the circuit-patterns of the robotic "brain."

Let me pause to explain that in science-fiction, we do not quarrel intensively concerning the actual engineering of the robotic "brain." Some mechanical device is assumed which in a volume that approximates that of the human brain must contain all the circuits necessary to allow the robot a range of perception-and-response reasonably equivalent to that of a human being. How that can be done without the use of mechanical units the size of a protein molecule or, at the very least, the size of a brain cell, is not explained. Some authors may talk about transistors and printed circuits. Most say nothing at all. My own pet trick is to refer, somewhat mystically, to "positronic brains," leaving it to the ingenuity of the reader to decide what positrons have to do with it and to his good-will to continue reading after having failed to reach a decision.

In any case, as I wrote my series of robot stories, the safety devices gradually crystallized in my mind as "The Three Laws of Robotics." These three laws were first explicitly stated in "Runaround." As finally perfected, the Three Laws read as follows.

First Law—A robot may not injure a human being, or, through inaction, allow a human being to come to harm.

Second Law—A robot must obey the orders given it by human beings except where such orders would conflict with the First Law.

Third Law—A robot must protect its own existence as long as such protection does not conflict with the First or Second Law.

These laws are firmly built into the robotic brain, or at least the circuit equivalents are. Naturally, I don't describe the circuit equivalents. In fact, I never discuss the engineering of the robots for the very good reason that I am colossally ignorant of the practical aspects of robotics.

The First Law, as you can readily see, immediately eliminates that old, tired plot which I will not offend you by referring to any further.

Although, at first flush, it may appear that to set up such restrictive rules must hamper the creative imagination, it has turned out that the Laws of Robotics have served as a rich source of plot material. They have proved anything but a mental road-block.

An example would be the story "Runaround" to which I have already referred. The robot in that story, an expensive and experimental model, is designed for operation on the sunside of the planet Mercury. The Third Law has been built into him more strongly than usual for obvious economic reasons. He has been sent out by his human employers, as the story begins, to obtain some liquid selenium for some vital and necessary repairs. (Liquid selenium lies about in puddles in the heat of Mercury's sunward side, I will ask you to believe.)

Unfortunately, the robot was given his order casually so that the Second Law circuit set up was weaker than usual.

Still more unfortunately, the selenium pool to which the robot was sent was near a site of volcanic activity, as a result of which there were sizable concentrations of carbon monoxide in the area. At the temperature of Mercury's sunside, I surmised that carbon monoxide would react fairly quickly with iron to form volatile iron carbonyls so that the robot's more delicate joints might be badly damaged. The further the robot penetrates into this area, the greater the danger to his existence and the more intensive is the Third Law effect driving him away. The Second Law, however, ordinarily the superior, drives him onward. At a certain point, the unusually weak Second Law potential and the unusually strong Third Law potential reach a balance and the robot can neither advance nor retreat. He can only circle the selenium pool on the equipotential locus that makes a rough circle about the site.

Meanwhile, our heroes must have the selenium. They chase after the robot in special suits, discover the problem and wonder how to correct it. After several failures, the correct answer is hit upon. One of the men deliberately exposes himself to Mercury's sun in such a way that unless the robot rescues him, he will surely die. That brings the First Law into operation, which being superior to both Second and Third, pulls the robot out of his useless orbit and brings on the necessary happy ending.

It is in the story "Runaround," by the way, that I believe I first made use of the term "robotics" (implicitly defined as the science of robot design, construction, maintenance, etc). Years later, I was told that I had invented the term and that it had never seen publication before. I do not know whether this is true. If it is true, I am happy, because I think it is a logical and useful word, and I hereby donate it to real workers in the field with all good will.

None of my other robot stories spring so immediately out of the Three Laws as does "Runaround" but all are born of the Laws in some way. There is the story, for instance, of the mind-reading robot who was forced to lie because he was unable to tell any human being anything other than that which the human in question wished to hear. The truth, you see, would almost invariably cause "harm" to the human being in the form of disappointment, disillusion, embarrassment, chagrin and other similar emotions, all of which were but too plainly visible to the robot.

Then there was the puzzle of the man who was suspected of being a robot, that is, of having a quasi-protoplasmic body and a robot's "positronic brain." One way of proving his humanity would be for him to break the First Law in public, so he obliges by deliberately striking a man. But the story ends in doubt because there is still the suspicion that the other "man" might also be a robot and there is nothing in the Three Laws that would prevent a robot from hitting another robot.

And then we have the ultimate robots, models so advanced that they are used to precalculate such things as weather, crop harvests, industrial production figures, political developments and so on. This is done in order that world economy may be less subject to the whims of those factors which are now beyond man's control. But these ultimate robots, it seems, are still subject to the First Law. They cannot through inaction allow human beings to come to harm, so they deliberately give answers which are not necessarily truthful and which cause localized economic upsets so designed as to maneuver mankind along the road that leads to peace and prosperity. So the robots finally win the mastery after all, but only for the good of man.

The interrelationship of man and robot is not to be neglected. Mankind may know of the existence of the Three Laws on an intellectual level and yet have an ineradicable fear and distrust for robots on an emotional level. If you wanted to invent a term, you might call it a "Frankenstein complex." There is also the more practical matter of the opposition of labor unions, for instance, to the possible replacement of human labor by robot labor.

This, too, can give rise to stories. My first robot story concerned a robot nursemaid and a child. The child adored its robot as might be expected, but the mother feared it, as might also be expected. The nub of the story lay in the mother's attempt to get rid of it and in the child's reaction to that.

My first full-length robot novel, "The Caves of Steel" (1954), peers further into the future, and is laid in a time when other planets, populated by emigrating Earthmen, have adopted a thoroughly robotized economy, but where Earth itself, for economic and emotional reasons, still objects to the introduction of the metal creatures. A murder is committed, with robot-hatred as the motive. It is solved by a pair of detectives, one a man, one a robot, with a great portion of the deductive reasoning (to which detective stories are prone) revolving about the Three Laws and their implications.

I have managed to convince myself that the Three Laws are both necessary and sufficient for human safety in regard to robots. It is my sincere belief that some day when advanced human-like robots are indeed built, something very like the Three Laws will be built into them. I would enjoy being a prophet in this respect, and I regret only the fact that the matter probably cannot be arranged in my lifetime.*

*This essay was written in 1956. In the years since, "robotics" has indeed entered the English language and is universally used, and I have lived to see roboticists taking the Three Laws very seriously.

THE NEW
TEACHERS

The percentage of older people in the world is increasing and that of younger people decreasing, and this trend will continue if the birthrate should drop and medicine continue to extend the average life span.

In order to keep older people imaginative and creative and to prevent them from becoming an ever-growing drag on a shrinking pool of creative young, I have recommended frequently that our educational system be remodeled and that education be considered a lifelong activity.

But how can this be done? Where will all the teachers come from?

Who says, however, that all teachers must be human beings or even animate?

Suppose that over the next century communications satellites become numerous and more sophisticated than those we've placed in space so far. Suppose that in place of radio waves the more capacious laser beam of visible light becomes the chief communications medium.

Under these circumstances, there would be room for many millions of separate channels for voice and picture, and it is easy to imagine every human being on Earth having a particular television wavelength assigned to her or him.

Each person (child, adult, or elderly) can have his own private outlet to which could be attached, at certain desirable periods of time, his or her personal teaching machine. It would be a far more versatile and interactive teaching machine than anything we could put together now, for computer technology will also have advanced in the interval.

We can reasonably hope that the teaching machine will be sufficiently intricate and flexible to be capable of modifying its own program (that is, "learning") as a result of the student's input.

In other words, the student will ask questions, answer questions, make statements, offer opinions, and from all of this, the machine will be able to gauge the student well enough to adjust the speed and intensity of its course of instruction and, what's more, shift it in the direction of the student interest displayed.

We can't imagine a personal teaching machine to be very big, however. It might resemble a television set in size and appearance. Can so small an object contain enough information to teach the students as much as they want to know, in any direction intellectual curiosity may lead them? No, not if the teaching machine is self-contained—but need it be?

In any civilization with computer science so advanced as to make teaching machines possible, there will surely be thoroughly computerized central libraries. Such libraries may even be interconnected into a single planetary library.

All teaching machines would be plugged into this planetary library and each could then have at its disposal any book, periodical, document, recording, or video cassette encoded there. If the machine has it, the student would have it too, either placed directly on a viewing screen, or reproduced in print-on-paper for more leisurely study.

Of course, human teachers will not be totally eliminated. In some subjects, human interaction is essential—athletics, drama, public speaking, and so on. There is also value, and interest, in groups of students working in a particular field—getting together to discuss and speculate with each other and with human experts, sparking each other to new insights.

After this human interchange they may return, with some relief, to the endlessly knowledgeable, endlessly flexible, and, most of all, endlessly patient machines.

But who will teach the teaching machines?

Surely the students who learn will also teach. Students who learn freely in those fields and activities that interest them are bound to think, speculate, observe, experiment, and, now and then, come up with something of their own that may not have been previously known.

They would transmit that knowledge back to the machines, which will in turn record it (with due credit, presumably) in the planetary library—thus making it available to other teaching machines. All will be put back into the central hopper to serve as a new and higher starting point for those who come after. The teaching machines will thus make it possible for the human species to race forward to heights and in directions now impossible to foresee.

But I am describing only the mechanics of learning. What of the content? What subjects will people study in the age of the teaching machine? I'll speculate on that in the next essay.

• WHATEVER • YOU WISH

•

The difficulty in deciding on what the professions of the future would be is that it all depends on the kind of future we choose to have. If we allow our civilization to be destroyed, the only profession of the future will be scrounging for survival, and few will succeed at it.

Suppose, though, that we keep our civilization alive and flourishing and, therefore, that technology continues to advance. It seems logical that the professions of such a future would include computer programming, lunar mining, fusion engineering, space construction, laser communications, neurophysiology, and so on.

I can't help but think, however, that the advance of computerization and automation is going to wipe out the subwork of humanity—the dull pushing and shoving and punching and clicking and filing and all the other simple and repetitive motions, both physical and mental, that can be done perfectly easily—and better—by machines no more complicated than those we can already build.

In short, the world could be so well run that only a relative handful of human "foremen" would be needed to engage in the various professions and supervisory work necessary to keep the world's population fed, housed, and cared for.

What about the majority of the human species in this automated future? What about those who don't have the ability or the desire to work at the professions of the future —or for whom there is no room in those professions? It may be that most people will have nothing to do of what we think of as work nowadays.

This could be a frightening thought. What will people do without work? Won't they sit around and be bored; or worse, become unstable or even vicious? The saying is that Satan finds mischief still for idle hands to do.

But we judge from the situation that has existed till now, a situation in which people are left to themselves to rot.

Consider that there have been times in history when an aristocracy lived in idleness off the backs of flesh-and-blood machines called slaves or serfs or peasants. When such a situation was combined with a high culture, however, aristocrats used their leisure to become educated in literature, the arts, and philosophy. Such studies were not useful for work, but they occupied the mind, made for interesting conversation and an enjoyable life.

These were the liberal arts, arts for free men who didn't have to work with their hands. And these were considered higher and more satisfying than the mechanical arts, which were merely materially useful.

Perhaps, then, the future will see a world aristocracy supported by the only slaves that can humanely serve in such a post—sophisticated machines. And there will be an infinitely newer and broader liberal arts program, taught by the teaching machines, from which each person could choose.

Some might choose computer technology or fusion engineering or lunar mining or any of the professions that would seem vital to the proper functioning of the world. Why not? Such professions, placing demands on human imagination and skill, would be very attractive to many, and there will surely be enough who will be voluntarily drawn to these occupations to fill them adequately.

But to most people the field of choice might be far less cosmic. It might be stamp collecting, pottery, ornamental painting, cooking, dramatics, or whatever. Every field will be an elective, and the only guide will be "whatever you wish."

Each person, guided by teaching machines sophisticated enough to offer a wide sampling of human activities, can then choose what he or she can best and most willingly do.

Is the individual person wise enough to know what he or she can best do? —Why not? Who else can know? And what can a person do best except that which he or she wants to do most?

Won't people choose to do nothing? Sleep their lives away?

If that's what they want, why not?—Except that I have a feeling they won't. Doing nothing is hard work, and, it seems to me, would be indulged in only by those who have never had the opportunity to evolve out of themselves something more interesting and, therefore, easier to do.

In a properly automated and educated world, then, machines may prove to be the true humanizing influence. It may be that machines will do the work that makes life possible and that human beings will do all the other things that make life pleasant and worthwhile.

THE FRIENDS · WE MAKE

·

The term "robot" dates back only sixty years. It was invented by the Czech playwright, Karel Čapek, in his play, *R.U.R.*, and is a Czech word meaning worker.

The *idea*, however, is far older. It is as old as man's longing for a servant as smart as a human being, but far stronger, and incapable of growing weary, bored, or dissatisfied. In the Greek myths, the god of the forge, Hephaistos, had two golden girls—as bright and alive as flesh-and-blood girls—to help him. And the island of Crete was guarded, in the myths, by a bronze giant named Talos, who circled its shores perpetually and tirelessly, watching for intruders.

Are robots possible, though? And if they are, are they desirable?

Mechanical devices with gears and springs and ratchets could certainly make manlike devices perform manlike actions, but the essence of a successful robot is to have it *think*—and think well enough to perform useful functions without being continually supervised.

But thinking takes a brain. The human being is made up of microscopic neurons, each of which has an extraordinarily complex substructure. There are 10 billion neurons in the brain and 90 billion supporting cells, all hooked together in a very intricate pattern. How can anything like that be duplicated by some man-made device in a robot?

It wasn't until the invention of the electronic computer thirty-five years ago that such a thing became conceivable. Since its birth, the electronic computer has grown ever more compact, and each year it becomes possible to pack more and more information into less and less volume.

In a few decades, might not enough versatility to direct a robot be packed into a volume the size of the human brain? Such a computer would not have to be as advanced as the human brain, but only advanced enough to guide the actions of a robot designed, let us say, to vacuum rugs, to run a hydraulic press, to survey the lunar surface.

A robot would, of course, have to include a self-contained energy source; we couldn't expect it to be forever plugged into a wall socket. This, however, can be handled. A battery that needs periodic charging is not so different from a living body that needs periodic feeding.

But why bother with a humanoid shape? Would it not be more sensible to devise a specialized machine to perform a particular task without asking it to take on all the inefficiencies involved in arms, legs, and torso? Suppose you design a robot that can hold a finger in a furnace to test its temperature and turn the heating unit on and off to maintain that temperature nearly constant. Surely a simple thermostat made of a bimetallic strip will do the job as well.

Consider, though, that over the thousands of years of man's civilization, we have built a technology geared to the human shape. Products for humans' use are designed in size and form to accommodate the human body—how it bends and how long, wide, and heavy the various bending parts are. Machines are designed to fit the human reach and the width and position of human fingers.

We have only to consider the problems of human beings who happen to be a little taller or shorter than the norm—or even just left-handed—to see how important it is to have a good fit into our technology.

If we want a directing device then, one that can make use of human tools and machines, and that can fit into the technology, we would find it useful to make that device in the human shape, with all the bends and turns of which the human body is capable. Nor would we want it to be too heavy or too abnormally proportioned. Average in all respects would be best.

Then too, we relate to all nonhuman things by finding, or inventing, something human about them. We attribute human characteristics to our pets, and even to our automobiles. We personify nature and all the products of nature and, in earlier times, made human-shaped gods and goddesses out of them.

Surely, if we are to take on thinking partners—or, at the least, thinking servants—in the form of machines, we will be more comfortable with them, and we will relate to them more easily, if they are shaped like humans.

It will be easier to be friends with human-shaped robots than with specialized machines of unrecognizable shape. And I sometimes think that, in the desperate straits of humanity today, we would be grateful to have nonhuman friends, even if they are only friends we build ourselves.

OUR INTELLIGENT TOOLS

■

Robots don't have to be very intelligent to be intelligent enough. If a robot can follow simple orders and do the housework, or run simple machines in a cut-and-dried, repetitive way, we would be perfectly satisfied.

Constructing a robot is hard because you must fit a very compact computer inside its skull, if it is to have a vaguely human shape. Making a sufficiently complex computer as compact as the human brain is also hard.

But robots aside, why bother making a computer that compact? The units that make up a computer have been getting smaller and smaller, to be sure—from vacuum tubes to transistors to tiny integrated circuits and silicon chips. Suppose that, in addition to making the units smaller, we also make the whole structure bigger.

A brain that gets too large would eventually begin to lose efficiency because nerve impulses don't travel very quickly. Even the speediest nerve impulses travel at only about 3.75 miles a minute. A nerve impulse can flash from one end of the brain to the other in one four-hundred-fortieth of a second, but a brain 9 miles long, if we could imagine one, would require 2.4 minutes for a nerve impulse to travel its length. The added complexity made possible by the enormous size would fall apart simply because of the long wait for information to be moved and processed within it.

Computers, however, use electric impulses that travel at more than 11 million miles per minute. A computer 400 miles wide would still flash electric impulses from end to end in about one four-hundred-fortieth of a second. In that respect, at least, a computer of that asteroidal size could still process information as quickly as the human brain could.

If, therefore, we imagine computers being manufactured with finer and finer components, more and more intricately interrelated, and *also* imagine those same computers becoming larger and larger, might it not be that the computers would eventually become capable of doing all the things a human brain can do?

Is there a theoretical limit to how intelligent a computer can become?

I've never heard of any. It seems to me that each time we learn to pack more complexity into a given volume, the computer can do more. Each time we make a computer larger, while keeping each portion as densely complex as before, the computer can do more.

Eventually, if we learn how to make a computer sufficiently complex *and* sufficiently large, why should it not achieve a human intelligence?

Some people are sure to be disbelieving and say, "But how can a computer possibly produce a great symphony, a great work of art, a great new scientific theory?"

The retort I am usually tempted to make to this question is, "Can you?" But, of course, even if the questioner is ordinary, there are extraordinary people who are geniuses. They attain genius, however, only because atoms and molecules within their brains are arranged in some complex order. There's nothing in their brains *but* atoms and molecules. If we arrange atoms and molecules in some complex order in a computer, the products of genius should be possible to it; and if the individual parts are not as tiny and delicate as those of the brain, we compensate by making the computer larger.

Some people may say, "But computers can only do what they're programmed to do."

The answer to that is, "True. But brains can do only what they're programmed to do—by their genes. Part of the brain's programming is the ability to learn, and that will be part of a complex computer's programming."

In fact, if a computer can be built to be as intelligent as a human being, why can't it be made *more* intelligent as well?

Why not, indeed? Maybe that's what evolution is all about. Over the space of three billion years, hit-and-miss development of atoms and molecules has finally produced, through glacially slow improvement, a species intelligent enough to take the next step in a matter of centuries, or even decades. Then things will *really* move.

But if computers become more intelligent than human beings, might they not replace us? Well, shouldn't they? They may be as kind as they are intelligent and just let us dwindle by attrition. They might keep some of us as pets, or on reservations.

Then too, consider what we're doing to ourselves right now—to all living things and to the very planet we live on. Maybe it is *time* we were replaced. Maybe the real danger is that computers won't be developed to the point of replacing us fast enough.

Think about it!*

---

*I present this view only as something to think about. I consider a quite different view in "Intelligences Together" later in this collection.

THE LAWS
OF
ROBOTICS

It isn't easy to think about computers without wondering if they will ever "take over."

Will they replace us, make us obsolete, and get rid of us the way we got rid of spears and tinderboxes?

If we imagine computerlike brains inside the metal imitations of human beings that we call robots, the fear is even more direct. Robots look so much like human beings that their very appearance may give them rebellious ideas.

This problem faced the world of science fiction in the 1920s and 1930s, and many were the cautionary tales written of robots that were built and then turned on their creators and destroyed them.

When I was a young man I grew tired of that caution, for it seemed to me that a robot was a machine and that human beings were constantly building machines. Since all machines are dangerous, one way or another, human beings built safeguards into them.

In 1939, therefore, I began to write a series of stories in which robots were presented sympathetically, as machines that were carefully designed to perform given tasks, with ample safeguards built into them to make them benign.

In a story I wrote in October 1941, I finally presented the safeguards in the specific form of "The Three Laws of Robotics." (I invented the word *robotics*, which had never been used before.)

Here they are:

1. A robot may not injure a human being or, through inaction, allow a human being to come to harm.

2. A robot must obey the orders given it by human beings except where those orders would conflict with the First Law.

3. A robot must protect its own existence except where such protection would conflict with the First and Second Law.

These laws were programmed into the computerized brain of the robot, and the numerous stories I wrote about robots took them into account. Indeed, these laws proved so popular with the readers and made so much sense that other science fiction writers began to use them (without ever quoting them directly—only I may do that), and all the old stories of robots destroying their creators died out.

Ah, but that's science fiction. What about the work really being done now on computers and on artificial intelligence? When machines are built that begin to have an intelligence of their own, will something like the Three Laws of Robotics be built into them?

Of course they will, assuming the computer designers have the least bit of intelligence. What's more, the safeguards will not merely be *like* the Three Laws of Robotics; they will *be* the Three Laws of Robotics.

I did not realize, at the time I constructed those laws, that humanity has been using them since the dawn of time. Just think of them as "The Three Laws of Tools," and this is the way they would read:

1. A tool must be safe to use.

(Obviously! Knives have handles and swords have hilts. Any tool that is sure to harm the user, provided the user is aware, will never be used routinely whatever its other qualifications.)

2. A tool must perform its function, provided it does so safely.

3. A tool must remain intact during use unless its destruction is required for safety or unless its destruction is part of its function.

No one ever cites these Three Laws of Tools because they are taken for granted by everyone. Each law, were it quoted, would be sure to be greeted by a chorus of "Well, of course!"

Compare the Three Laws of Tools, then, with the Three Laws of Robotics, law by law, and you will see that they correspond exactly. And why not, since the robot or, if you will, the computer, is a human tool?

But are safeguards sufficient? Consider the effort that is put into making the automobile safe—yet automobiles still kill 50,000 Americans a year. Consider the effort that is put into making banks secure—yet there are still bank robberies in a steady drumroll. Consider the effort that is put into making computer programs secure—yet there is the growing danger of computer fraud.

Computers, however, if they get intelligent enough to "take over," may also be intelligent enough no longer to require the Three Laws. They may, of their own benevolence, take care of us and guard us from harm.

Some of you may argue, though, that we're not children and that it would destroy the very essence of our humanity to be guarded.

Really? Look at the world today and the world in the past and ask yourself if we're not children—and destructive children at that—and if we don't need to be guarded in our own interest.

If we demand to be treated as adults, shouldn't we act like adults? And when do we intend to start?

• FUTURE • FANTASTIC

•

In the past, three fundamental advances in human communication evolved that altered every facet of our world enormously and permanently. The first advance was speech, the second writing, and the third printing.

Now we face a fourth advance in communication every bit as important as the first three—the computer. This fourth revolution will enable most human beings to be more creative than they've ever been before. And provided we do not destroy the world by nuclear warfare, overpopulation or pollution, we will have a world of the technochild—a world as different from our present one as today's is from the world of the caveman. How will the lives of the next generation be different from their parents and grandparents?

One immediate response is to view the computer merely as another form of amusement, rather like a super-TV. It can be used for complex games, for making contact with friends, or for various trivial pursuits. Still, such things can change the world. For one thing, communication by computer networks can wipe out the feeling of distance. It can make the globe seem like a neighborhood, and this can have important consequences—the development of the concept of humanity as a single society, not as a collection of endlessly and inevitably warring social segments. The world might develop a global lingua franca, a language (no doubt something quite close to today's English) that everyone can understand, even though people would retain their individual languages for local use.

Then, too, since communication will be so easy and since mechanical and electronic devices can be controlled remotely (telemetering, for example, makes it possible even now for engineers to send instructions to—and obtain obedience from—devices sailing past planets billions of miles away), computers will reduce the necessity of using physical transportation to gain or gather information.

There will, of course, be no bar to travel. You can still be a tourist or visit friends or family in person rather than by closed-circuit television. But you will not have to battle hordes of people merely to carry or receive information that can be transferred by computer.

This means that the technochildren of tomorrow will be accustomed to living in a decentralized world, to reaching out in a variety of ways from their homes—or wherever they are—to do what needs doing. At one and the same time, they will feel both entirely isolated and in total contact.

The children of the next generation—and the society they will create—will see the greatest impact from computers in the area of education. Currently our society is intent on educating as many children as possible. The limit in the number of teachers means that students learn in mass. Every student in a school district or state or nation is taught the same thing at the same time in more or less the same way. But because each child has individual interests and methods of learning, the experience of mass education turns out to be unpleasant. The result is that most adults resist the learning process in postschool life; they've had enough of it.

Learning could be pleasant, even all-absorbingly fascinating, if children studied something that specifically interested them individually, on their own time and in their own way. Such study is currently possible through public libraries. But the library is a clumsy tool. One must *go* there, borrowing is limited to a few volumes, and books must be returned after a short time.

Clearly the solution is to move libraries into the home. Just as record players brought home the concert hall and television brought home the movie theater, the computer can bring home the public library. Tomorrow's technochildren will have a ready means of sating their curiosity. They will know at an early age how to command their computers to give listings of materials. As their interests are aroused (and guided, it is to be hoped, by their teachers at school), they will learn more in less time and find new byways to follow.

Education will have a strong component of *self*-motivation added to it. The ability to follow a personal path will encourage the technochild to associate learning with pleasure and grow into a lively technoadult—eager, curious, and ready to expand the mental environment for as long as his or her brain remains physically undulled by the ravages of old age.

This new approach to education can also influence another area of life: work. Until now, most human beings have worked at jobs that seriously underutilized the brain. In the ages when work consisted largely of brutish physical labor, few ever had the chance to lift their eyes to the stars or ponder abstractions. Even when the Industrial Revolution brought machinery that could lift the load of physical labor from the backs of humanity, meaningless "skilled" work took its place. Today employees on the assembly line and in offices still perform jobs that require little thought.

For the first time in history, skilled machines, or robots, will be able to do those mindless jobs. Any job that is so simple and repetitive that a robot can do it as well as, if not better than, a person is beneath the dignity of the human brain. As technochildren turn into adults and move into the work world, they will have time to exercise more creativity, to work in the fields of drama, science, literature, government, and entertainment. And they will be ready for this kind of work as a result of the computerized revolution in education.

Some might believe that it's simply impossible to expect people to be creative in large numbers. But that thinking comes from a world in which only a few escape the mental destruction of jobs that don't use the brain. We've been through this before: It was always assumed that literacy, for example, was the province of the few who had minds peculiarly adapted to the complicated task of reading and writing. Of course, with the advent of printing and mass education, it turned out that most human beings could be literate.

What does all this mean? That we will be dealing with a world of leisure. Once computers and robots are doing the dull, mechanical work, the world will start running itself to a far greater extent than ever before. Will there be more "Renaissance people" as a result? Yes. Currently leisure is a small segment of life that is used narrowly because of lack of time, or is wasted on doing nothing in a desperate attempt to get far away from the hated workaday world. With leisure filling most of one's time, there will be no sensation of racing the clock, no compulsion to enter into a wild spree against the slavery of hateful work. People will sample a variety of interests without haste, become skillful or knowledgeable in a number of areas, and cultivate different talents at various times.

This is not just guesswork. There have been eras in history when people had slaves—the brutalized, human version of the computer—to do the work for them. Others have had patrons to support them. When even a few people have had ample leisure time to pursue their interests, the result has been an explosion of variegated culture. The Golden Age of Athens in the late fifth century B.C. and the Italian Renaissance in the 14th to 16th centuries are the most famous examples.

Not only will people have the freedom to pursue hobbies

and interests and dreams, but a great number of them will also want to share their talents. So many of us have a bit of the ham in us. We sing in the shower, take part in amateur theatrical productions, or love to swing along in parades. It is my guess that the 21st century may see a society in which one-third of the population will be engaged in entertaining the other two-thirds.

And there are bound to be new forms of entertainment that one can now foresee only dimly. Three-dimensional TV is easy to forecast. And space may become a new arena for activity. In near-zero gravity, for example, the manipulation of balls may produce far more complicated forms of tennis or soccer. Ballet and even social dancing may become incredibly startling and require a new kind of coordination that's delightful to watch, as it will be as easy to move up and down as it is to move forward and backward or left and right.

What about those people who choose not to share their bents and interests and instead retire into worlds of their own? Someone who is interested, for example, in learning about the history of costumes and who is capable of exploring the libraries of the world from an isolated corner might simply stay there. Might we, then, find ourselves in a society in which an unprecedented number of people are intellectual hermits? Might we breed a race of introverts?

I think the chances are slim. People who grow ferociously interested in one aspect of knowledge or expertise are quite likely to be filled with missionary zeal. They will want to share their knowledge with others. Even today, someone who has an obscure field of interest is far more likely to want to explain it to everyone he or she meets than to sit silently in a corner. If there's any danger, it's that an arcane interest will nurture a loquacious bore rather than a hermit.

We must not forget the tendency of those who share interests to wish to get together, to form a temporary subuniverse that is a haven of concentrated special fascination. In the 1970s, for example, someone had the idea of organizing a convention for *Star Trek* fans, expecting a few hundred at most to attend. Instead, fans poured in by the thousands (and television was supposed to be an isolating medium!). On-line gatherings, in which the computer is the medium and people are actively involved, will experience similarly high levels of participation.

And in between the formal get-togethers, there will be a kaleidoscope of people linked into global communities by computerized communication. Perpetual conventions will take place, in which individuals continually drop in and out, bringing in findings or ideas and leaving stimulated. There will be a constant melange of teaching and learning.

What I foresee is a society in intense creative ferment, people reaching out to others, new thoughts arising and spreading at a speed never before imagined, change and variety filling the planet (to say nothing of the smaller, artificial worlds that will be constructed in space). It will be a new world that will look back at earlier centuries as having been only half alive.

• THE MACHINE •
AND THE ROBOT

■

To a physicist, a machine is any device that transfers a force from the point where it is applied to another point where it is used and, in the process, changes its intensity or direction.

In this sense it is difficult for a human being to make use of anything that is not part of his body without, in the process, using a machine. A couple of million years ago, when one could scarcely decide whether the most advanced hominids were more humanlike than apelike, pebbles were already being chipped and their sharp edges used to cut or scrape.

And even a chipped pebble is a machine, for the force applied to the blunt edge by the hand is transmitted to the sharp end and, in the process, intensified. The force spread over the large area of the blunt end is equal to the force spread over the small area of the sharp end. The pressure (force per area) is therefore increased, and without ever increasing the total force, that force is intensified in action. The sharp-edge pebble could, by the greater pressure it exerts, force its way through an object, as a rounded pebble (or a man's hand) could not.

In actual practice, however, few people, other than physicists at their most rigid, would call a chipped pebble a machine. In actual practice, we think of machines as relatively complicated devices, and are more likely to use the name if the device is somewhat removed from direct human guidance and manipulation.

The further a device is removed from human control, the more authentically mechanical it seems, and the whole trend in technology has been to devise machines that are less and less under direct human control and more and more seem to have the beginning of a will of their own. A chipped pebble is almost part of the hand it never leaves. A thrown spear declares a sort of independence the moment is its released.

The clear progression away from direct and immediate control made it possible for human beings, even in primitive times, to slide forward into extrapolation, and to picture devices still less controllable, still more independent than anything of which they had direct experience. Immediately we have a form of fantasy—which some, defining the term more broadly than I would, might even call science fiction.

Man can move on his feet by direct and intimate control; or on horseback, controlling the more powerful animal muscles by rein and heel; or on ship, making use of the invisible power of the wind. Why not progress into further etherealization by way of seven-league boots, flying carpets, self-propelled boats. The power used in these cases was "magic," the tapping of the superhuman and transcendental energies of gods or demons.

Nor did these imaginings concern only the increased physical power of inanimate objects, but even increased mental power of objects which were still viewed as essentially inanimate. Artificial intelligence is not really a modern concept.

Hephaistos, the Greek god of the forge, is pictured in the *Iliad* as having golden mechanical women, which were as mobile and as intelligent as flesh-and-blood women, and which helped him in his palace.

Why not? After all, if a human smith makes inanimate metal objects of the base metal iron, why should not a

god-smith make far more clever inanimate metal objects of
the noble metal gold? It is an easy extrapolation, of the sort
that comes as second nature to science fiction writers (who,
in primitive times, had to be myth-makers, in default of
science).

But human artisans, if clever enough, could also make
mechanical human beings. Consider Talos, a bronze warrior
made by that Thomas Edison of the Greek myths, Daedalus.
Talos guarded the shores of Crete, circling the island once
each day and keeping off all intruders. The fluid that kept
him alive was kept within his body by a plug at his heel.
When the Argonauts landed on Crete, Medea used her
magic to pull out the plug and Talos lost all his pseudo-
animation.

(It is easy to ascribe a symbolic meaning to this myth.
Crete, starting in the fourth millennium B.C., before the
Greeks had yet entered Greece, had a navy, the first working navy in human history. The Cretan navy made it possible for the islanders to establish an empire over what became
the nearby islands and mainland. The Greek barbarians,
invading the land, were more or less under Cretan dominion
to begin with. The bronze-armored warriors carried by the
ships guarded the Cretan mainland for two thousand years—
and then failed. The plug was pulled, so to speak, when the
island of Thera exploded in a vast volcanic eruption in 1500
B.C. and a tsunami greatly weakened the Cretan civilization—
and the Greeks took over. Still, the fact that a myth is a sort
of vague and distorted recall of something actual does not
alter its function of indicating a way of human thinking.)

From the start, then, the machine has faced mankind with
a double aspect. As long as it is completely under human
control, it is useful and good and makes a better life for
people. However, it is the experience of mankind (and was
already his experience in quite early times) that technology
is a cumulative thing, that machines are invariably improved,
and that the improvement is always in the direction of
etherealization, always in the direction of less human control and more auto-control—and at an accelerating rate.

As the human control decreases, the machine becomes frightening in exact proportion. Even when the human control is not visibly decreasing, or is doing so at an excessively low rate, it is a simple task for human ingenuity to look forward to a time when the machine may go out of control altogether, and the fear of that can be felt in advance.

What is the fear?

The simplest and most obvious fear is that of the possible harm that comes from machinery out of control. In fact, any technological advance, however fundamental, has the double aspect of good/harm and, in response, is viewed with a double aspect of love/fear.

Fire warms you, gives you light, cooks your food, smelts your ore—and, out of control, burns and kills. Your knives and spears kill your animal enemies and your human foes and, out of *your* control, are used by your foes to kill you. You can run down the list and build examples indefinitely and there has never been any human activity which, on getting out of control and doing harm, has raised the sigh among many of, "Oh, if we had only stuck to the simple and virtuous lives of our ancestors who were not cursed with this new-fangled misery."

Yet is this fear of piecemeal harm from this advance or that the kind of deep-seated terror so difficult to express that it finds its way into the myths?

I think not. Fear of machinery for the discomfort and occasional harm it brings has (at least until very recently) not moved humanity to more than that occasional sigh. The love of the uses of machinery has always far overbalanced such fears, as we might judge if we consider that very rarely in the history of mankind has any culture *voluntarily* given up significant technological advance because of the inconvenience or harm of its side effects. There have been involuntary retreats from technology as a result of warfare, civil strife, epidemics, or natural disasters, but the results of that are precisely what we call a "dark age" and the population suffering from one does its best over the generations to get back on the track and restore the technology.

Mankind has always chosen to counter the evils of technology, not by abandonment of technology, but by additional technology. The smoke of an indoor fire was countered by the chimney. The danger of the spear was countered by the shield. The danger of the mass army was countered by the city wall.

This attitude, despite the steady drizzle of backwardist outcries, has continued to the present. Thus the characteristic technological product of our present life is the automobile. It pollutes the air, assaults our eardrums, kills fifty thousand Americans a year and inflicts survivable injuries on hundreds of thousands.

Does anyone seriously expect Americans to give up their murderous little pets voluntarily? Even those who attend rallies to denounce the mechanization of modern life are quite likely to reach those rallies by automobile.

The first moment when the magnitude of possible evil was seen by *many* people as uncounterable by *any* conceivable good came with the fission bomb in 1945. Never before had any technological advance set off demands for abandonment by so large a percentage of the population.

In fact, the reaction to the fission bomb set a new fashion. People were readier to oppose other advances they saw as unacceptably harmful in their side effects—biological warfare, the SST, certain genetic experiments on micro-organisms, breeder reactors, spray cans.

And even so, not one of these items has yet been given up.

But we're on the right track. The fear of the machine is not at the deepest level of the soul if the harm it does is accompanied by good, too; or if the harm is merely to some people—the few who happen to be on the spot in a vehicular collision, for instance.

The majority, after all, escape, and reap the good of the machine.

No, it is when the machine threatens all mankind in any way so that each individual human being begins to feel that he, *himself*, will not escape, that fear overwhelms love.

But since technology has begun to threaten the human race as a whole only in the last thirty years, were we immune to fear before that—or has the human race always been threatened?

After all, is physical destruction by brute energy of a type only now in our fist, the only way in which human beings can be destroyed? Might not the machine destroy the essence of humanity, our minds and souls, even while leaving our bodies intact and secure and comfortable?

It is a common fear, for instance, that television makes people unable to read and pocket computers will make them unable to add. Or think of the Spartan king who, on observing a catapult in action, mourned that that would put an end to human valor.

Certainly such subtle threats to humanity have existed and been recognized through all the long ages when man's feeble control over nature made it impossible for him to do himself very much physical harm.

The fear that machinery might make men effete is not yet, in my opinion, the basic and greatest fear. The one (it seems to me) that hits closest to the core is the general fear of irreversible change. Consider:

There are two kinds of change that we can gather from the universe about us. One is cyclic and benign.

Day both follows and is followed by night. Summer both follows and is followed by winter. Rain both follows and is followed by clear weather, and the net result is, therefore, no change. That may be boring, but it is comfortable and induces a feeling of security.

In fact, so comfortable is the notion of short-term cyclic change implying long-term changelessness, that human beings labor to find it everywhere. In human affairs, there is the notion that one generation both follows and is followed by another, that one dynasty both follows and is followed by another, that one empire both follows and is followed by another. It is not a good analogy to the cycles of nature since the repetitions are not exact, but it is good enough to be comforting.

So strongly do human beings want the comfort of cycles that they will seize upon one even when the evidence is insufficient—or even when it actually points the other way.

With respect to the universe, what evidence we have points to a hyperbolic evolution; a universe that expands forever out of the initial big bang and ends as formless gas and black holes. Yet our emotions drag us, against the evidence, to notions of oscillating, cyclic, repeating universes, in which even the black holes are merely gateways to new big bangs.

But then there is the other change, to be avoided at all costs—the irreversible, malignant change; the one-way change; the permanent change; the change-never-to-return.

What is so fearful about it? The fact is that there is one such change that lies so close to ourselves that it distorts the entire universe for us.

We are, after all, old, and though we were once young we shall never be young again. Irreversible! Our friends are dead, and though they were once alive, they shall never be alive again. Irreversible! The fact is that life ends in death and that is not a cyclic change and we fear that end and know it is useless to fight it.

What is worse is that the universe doesn't die with us. Callously and immortally it continues onward in its cyclic changes, adding to the injury of death the insult of indifference.

And what is still worse is that other human beings don't die with us. There are younger human beings, born later, who were helpless and dependent on us to start with, but who grow into supplanting nemeses and take our places as we age and die. To the injury of death is added the insult of supplantation.

Did I say it is useless to fight this horror of death accompanied by indifference and supplantation? Not quite. The uselessness is apparent only if we cling to the rational, but there is no law that says we must cling to it, and human beings do not, in fact, do so.

Death can be avoided by simply denying it exists. We can suppose that life on Earth is an illusion, a short testing period prior to entry into some afterlife where all is eternal and there is no question of irreversible change. Or we can suppose that it is only the body that is subject to death and that there is an immortal component of ourselves, not subject to irreversible change, which might, after the death of one body, enter another, in indefinite, cyclic repetitions of life.

These mythic inventions of afterlife and transmigration may make life tolerable for many human beings and enable them to face death with reasonable equanimity—but the fear of death and supplantation is only masked and overlaid; it is not removed.

In fact, the Greek myths involve the successive supplantation of one set of immortals by another—in what seems to be a despairing admission that not even eternal life and superhuman power can remove the danger of irreversible change and the humiliation of being supplanted.

To the Greeks it was disorder (Chaos) that first ruled the universe, and it was supplanted by Ouranos (the sky), whose intricate powdering of stars and complexly moving planets symbolized order ("Kosmos").

But Ouranos was castrated by Kronos, his son. Kronos, his brothers, his sisters, and their progeny then ruled the universe.

Kronos feared that he would be served by his children as he had served his father (a kind of cycle of irreversible changes) and devoured his children as they were born. He was duped by his wife, however, who managed to save her last-born, Zeus, and to spirit him away to safety. Zeus grew to adult godhood, rescued his siblings from his father's stomach, warred against Kronos and those who followed him, defeated him, and replaced him as ruler.

(There are supplantation myths among other cultures, too, even in our own—as the one in which Satan tried to supplant God and failed; a myth that reached its greatest literary expression in John Milton's *Paradise Lost*.)

And was Zeus safe? He was attracted to the sea nymph Thetis and would have married her had he not been informed by the Fates that Thetis was destined to bear a son mightier than his father. That meant it was not safe for Zeus, or for any other god, either, to marry her. She was therefore forced (much against her will) to marry Peleus, a mortal, and bear a mortal son, the only child the myths describe her as having. That son was Achilles, who was certainly far mightier than his father (and, like Talos, had only his heel as his weak point through which he might be killed).

Now, then, translate this fear of irreversible change and of being supplanted into the relationship of man and machine and what do we have? Surely the *great* fear is not that machinery will harm us—but that it will supplant us. It is not that it will render us ineffective—but that it will make us obsolete.

The ultimate machine is an intelligent machine and there is only one basic plot to the intelligent-machine story—that it is created to serve man, but that it ends by dominating man. It cannot exist without threatening to supplant us, and it must therefore be destroyed or we will be.

There is the danger of the broom of the sorcerer's apprentice, the golem of Rabbi Loew, the monster created by Dr. Frankenstein. As the child born of our body eventually supplants us, so does the machine born of our mind.

Mary Shelley's *Frankenstein*, which appeared in 1818, represents a peak of fear, however, for, as it happened, circumstances conspired to reduce that fear, at least temporarily.

Between the year 1815, which saw the end of a series of general European wars, and 1914, which saw the beginning of another, there was a brief period in which humanity could afford the luxury of optimism concerning its relationship to the machine. The Industrial Revolution seemed suddenly to uplift human power and to bring on dreams of a technological utopia on Earth in place of the mythic one in Heaven. The good of machines seemed to far outbalance the evil and the response of love far outbalance the response of fear.

It was in that interval that modern science fiction began—and by modern science fiction I refer to a form of literature that deals with societies differing from our own specifically in the level of science and technology, and into which we might conceivably pass from our own society by appropriate changes in that level. (This differentiates science fiction from fantasy or from "speculative fiction," in which the fictional society cannot be connected with our own by any rational set of changes.)

Modern science fiction, because of the time of its beginning, took on an optimistic note. Man's relationship to the machine was one of use and control. Man's power grew and man's machines were his faithful tools, bringing him wealth and security and carrying him to the farthest reaches of the universe.

This optimistic note continues to this day, particularly among those writers who were molded in the years before the coming of the fission bomb—notably, Robert Heinlein, Arthur C. Clarke, and myself.

Nevertheless, with World War I, disillusionment set in. Science and technology, which promised an Eden, turned out to be capable of delivering Hell was well. The beautiful airplane that fulfilled the age-old dream of flight could deliver bombs. The chemical techniques that produced anesthetics, dyes, and medicines produced poison gas as well.

The fear of supplantation rose again. In 1921, not long after the end of World War I, Karel Čapek's drama *R.U.R.* appeared and it was the tale of Frankenstein again, escalated to the planetary level. Not a single monster was created but millions of robots (Čapek's word, meaning "worker," a mechanical one, that is). And it was not a single monster turning upon his single creator, but robots turning on humanity, wiping them out and supplanting them.

From the beginning of the science fiction magazine in

1926 to 1959 (a third of a century or a generation) optimism and pessimism battled each other in science fiction, with optimism—thanks chiefly to the influence of John W. Campbell, Jr.—having the better of it.

Beginning in 1939, I wrote a series of influential robot stories that self-consciously combated the "Frankenstein complex" and made of the robots the servants, friends, and allies of humanity.

It was pessimism, however, that won in the end, and for two reasons:

First, machinery grew more frightening. The fission bomb threatened physical destruction, of course, but worse still was the rapidly advancing electronic computer. Those computers seemed to steal the human soul. Deftly they solved our routine problems and more and more we found ourselves placing our questions in the hands of these machines with increasing faith, and accepting their answers with increasing humility.

All that fission and fusion bombs can do is destroy us, the computer might supplant us.

The second reason is more subtle, for it involved a change in the nature of the science fiction writer.

Until 1959, there were many branches of fiction, with science fiction perhaps the least among them. It brought its writers less in prestige and money than almost any other branch, so that no one wrote science fiction who wasn't so fascinated by it that he was willing to give up any chance at fame and fortune for its sake. Often that fascination stemmed from an absorption in the romance of science so that science fiction writers would naturally picture men as winning the universe by learning to bend it to their will.

In the 1950s, however, competition with TV gradually killed the magazines that supported fiction, and by the time the 1960s arrived the only form of fiction that was flourishing, and even expanding, was science fiction. Its magazines continued and an incredible paperback boom was initiated. To a lesser extent it invaded movies and television, with its greatest triumphs undoubtedly yet to come.

This meant that in the 1960s and 1970s, young writers began to write science fiction not because they wanted to, but because it was there—and because very little else was there. It meant that many of the new generation of science fiction writers had no knowledge of science, no sympathy for it—and were in fact rather hostile to it. Such writers were far more ready to accept the fear half of the love/fear relationship of man to machine.

As a result, contemporary science fiction, far more often than not, is presenting us, over and over, with the myth of the child supplanting the parent, Zeus supplanting Kronos, Satan supplanting God, the machine supplanting humanity.

Nightmares they are, and they are to be read as such.

—But allow me my own cynical commentary at the end. Remember that although Kronos foresaw the danger of being supplanted, and though he destroyed his children to prevent it—he was supplanted anyway, and rightly so, for Zeus was the better ruler.

So it may be that although we will hate and fight the machines, we will be supplanted anyway, and rightly so, for the intelligent machines to which we will give birth may, better than we, carry on the striving toward the goal of understanding and using the universe, climbing to heights we ourselves could never aspire to.

THE NEW PROFESSION

Back in 1940, I wrote a story in which the leading character was named Susan Calvin. (Good heavens, that's nearly half a century ago.) She was a "robopsychologist" by profession and knew everything there was to know about what made robots tick. It was a science fiction story, of course. I wrote other stories about Susan Calvin over the next few years, and as I described matters, she was born in 1982, went to Columbia, majored in robotics, and graduated in 2003. She went on to do graduate work and by 2010 was working at a firm called U.S. Robots and Mechanical Men, Inc. I didn't really take any of this seriously at the time I wrote it. What I was writing was "just science fiction."

Oddly enough, however, it's working out. Robots are in use on the assembly lines and are increasing in importance each year. The automobile companies are installing them in their factories by the tens of thousands. Increasingly, they will appear elsewhere as well, while ever more complex and intelligent robots will be appearing on the drawing boards. Naturally, these robots are going to wipe out many jobs, but they are going to create jobs, too. The robots will have to

444

be designed, in the first place. They will have to be constructed and installed. Then, since nothing is perfect, they will occasionally go wrong and have to be repaired. To keep the necessity for repair to a minimum, they will have to be intelligently maintained. They may even have to be modified to do their work differently on occasion.

To do all this, we will need a group of people whom we can call, in general, robot technicians. There are some estimates that by the time my fictional Susan Calvin gets out of college, there will be over 2 million robot technicians in the United States alone, and perhaps 6 million in the world generally. Susan won't be alone. To these technicians, suppose we add all the other people that will be employed by those rapidly growing industries that are directly or indirectly related to robotics. It may well turn out that the robots will create more jobs than they will wipe out—but, of course, the two sets of jobs will be different, which means there will be a difficult transition period in which those whose jobs have vanished are retrained so that they can fill new jobs that have appeared.

This may not be possible in every case, and there will have to be innovative social initiatives to take care of those who, because of age or temperament, cannot fit in to the rapidly changing economic scene.

In the past, advances in technology have always necessitated the upgrading of education. Agricultural laborers didn't have to be literate, but factory workers did, so once the Industrial Revolution came to pass, industrialized nations had to establish public schools for the mass education of their populations. There must now be a further advance in education to go along with the new high-tech economy. Education in science and technology will have to be taken more seriously and made lifelong, for advances will occur too rapidly for people to be able to rely solely on what they learned as youngsters.

Wait! I have mentioned robot technicians, but that is a general term. Susan Calvin was not a robot technician; she was, specifically, a *robopsychologist*. She dealt with robotic "intelligence," with robots' ways of "thinking." I have not yet heard anyone use that term in real life, but I think the time will come when it will be used, just as "robotics" was used after I had invented *that* term. After all, robot theoreticians are trying to develop robots that can see, that can understand verbal instructions, that can speak in reply. As robots are expected to do more and more tasks, more and more efficiently, and in a more and more versatile way, they will naturally seem more "intelligent." In fact, even now, there are scientists at MIT and elsewhere who are working very seriously on the question of "artificial intelligence."

Still, even if we design and construct robots that can do their jobs in such a way as to seem intelligent, it is scarcely likely that they will be intelligent in the same way that human beings are. For one thing, their "brains" will be constructed of materials different from the ones in our brains. For another, their brains will be made up of different components hooked together and organized in different ways, and will approach problems (very likely) in a totally different manner.

Robotic intelligence may be so different from human intelligence that it will take a new discipline—"robopsychology"—to deal with it. That is where Susan Calvin will come in. It is she and others like her who will deal with robots, where ordinary psychologists could not begin to do so. And this might turn out to be the most important aspect of robotics, for if we study in detail two entirely different kinds of intelligence, we may learn to understand intelligence in a much more general and fundamental way than is now possible. Specifically, we will learn more about *human* intelligence than may be possible to learn from human intelligence alone.

THE ROBOT AS ENEMY?

It was back in 1942 that I invented "the Three Laws of Robotics," and of these, the First Law is, of course, the most important. It goes as follows: "A robot may not injure a human being, or, through inaction, allow a human being to come to harm." In my stories, I always make it clear that the Laws, especially the First Law, are an inalienable part of all robots and that robots cannot and do not disobey them.

I also make it clear, though perhaps not as forcefully, that these Laws aren't *inherent* in robots. The ores and raw chemicals of which robots are formed do not already contain the Laws. The Laws are there only because they are deliberately added to the design of the robotic brain, that is, to the computers that control and direct robotic action. Robots can fail to possess the Laws, either because they are too simple and crude to be given behavior patterns sufficiently complex to obey them or because the people designing the robots deliberately choose not to include the Laws in their computerized makeup.

So far—and perhaps it will be so for a considerable time to come—it is the first of these alternatives that holds sway.

Robots are simply too crude and primitive to be able to foresee that an act of theirs will harm a human being and to adjust their behavior to avoid that act. They are, so far, only computerized levers capable of a few types of rote behavior, and they are unable to step beyond the very narrow limits of their instructions. As a result, robots have already killed human beings, just as enormous numbers of noncomputerized machines have. It is deplorable but understandable, and we can suppose that as robots are developed with more elaborate sense perceptions and with the capability of more flexible responses, there will be an increasing likelihood of building safety factors into them that will be the equivalent of the Three Laws.

But what about the second alternative? Will human beings *deliberately* build robots without the Laws? I'm afraid that is a distinct possibility. People are already talking about Security Robots. There could be robot guards patrolling the grounds of a building or even its hallways. The function of these robots could be to challenge any person entering the grounds or the building. Presumably, persons who belonged there, or who were invited there, would be carrying (or would be given) some card or other form of identification that would be recognized by the robot, who would then let them pass. In our security-conscious times, this might even seem a good thing. It would cut down on vandalism and terrorism and it would, after all, only be fulfilling the function of a trained guard dog.

But security breeds the desire for more security. Once a robot became capable of stopping an intruder, it might not be enough for it merely to sound an alarm. It would be tempting to endow the robot with the capability of ejecting the intruder, even if it would do injury in the process—just as a dog might injure you in going for your leg or throat. What would happen, though, when the chairman of the board found he had left his identifying card in his other pants and was too upset to leave the building fast enough to suit the robot? Or what if a child wandered into the building without the proper clearance? I suspect that if the robot roughed up the wrong person, there would be an immediate clamor to prevent a repetition of the error.

To go to a further extreme, there is talk of robot weapons: computerized planes, tanks, artillery, and so on, that would stalk the enemy relentlessly, with superhuman senses and stamina. It might be argued that this would be a way of sparing human beings. We could stay comfortably at home and let our intelligent machines do the fighting for us. If some of them were destroyed—well, they are only machines. This approach to warfare would be particularly useful if we had such machines and the enemy didn't.

But even so, could we be sure that our machines could always tell an enemy from a friend? Even when all our weapons are controlled by human hands and human brains, there is the problem of "friendly fire." American weapons can accidentally kill American soldiers or civilians and have actually done so in the past. This is human error, but nevertheless it's hard to take. But what if our *robot* weapons were to accidentally engage in "friendly fire" and wipe out American people, or even just American property? That would be far harder to take (especially if the enemy had worked out stratagems to confuse our robots and encourage them to hit our own side). No, I feel confident that attempts to use robots without safeguards won't work and that, in the end, we will come round to the Three Laws.

■ INTELLIGENCES ■
TOGETHER

■

In "Our Intelligent Tools" I mentioned the possibility that robots might become so intelligent that they would eventually replace us. I suggested, with a touch of cynicism, that in view of the human record, such a replacement might be a good thing. Since then, robots have rapidly become more and more important in industry, and, although they are as yet quite idiotic on the intelligence scale, they are advancing quickly.

Perhaps, then, we ought to take another look at the matter of robots (or computers—which are the actual driving mechanism of robots) replacing us. The outcome, of course, depends on how intelligent computers become and whether they will become so much more intelligent than we are that they will regard us as no more than pets, at best, or vermin, at worst. This implies that intelligence is a simple thing that can be measured with something like a ruler or a thermometer (or an IQ test) and then expressed in a single number. If the average human being is measured as 100 on an overall intelligence scale, then as soon as the average computer passes 100, we will be in trouble.

Is that the way it works, though? Surely there must be considerable variety in such a subtle quality as intelligence; different species of it, so to speak. I presume it takes intelligence to write a coherent essay, to choose the right words, and to place them in the right order. I also presume it takes intelligence to study some intricate technical device, to see how it works and how it might be improved—or how it might be repaired if it had stopped working. As far as writing is concerned, my intelligence is extremely high; as far as tinkering is concerned, my intelligence is extremely low. Well, then, am I a genius or an imbecile? The answer is: neither. I'm just good at some things and not good at others—and that's true of every one of us.

Suppose, then, we think about the origins of both human intelligence and computer intelligence. The human brain is built up essentially of proteins and nucleic acids; it is the product of over 3 billion years of hit-or-miss evolution; and the driving forces of its development have been adaptation and survival. Computers, on the other hand, are built up essentially of metal and electron surges; they are the product of some forty years of deliberate human design and development; and the driving force of their development has been the human desire to meet perceived human needs. If there are many aspects and varieties of intelligence among human beings themselves, isn't it certain that human and computer intelligences are going to differ widely since they have originated and developed under such different circumstances, out of such different materials, and under the impulse of such different drives?

It would seem that computers, even comparatively simple and primitive specimens, are extraordinarily good in some ways. They possess capacious memories, have virtually instant and unfailing recall, and demonstrate the ability to carry through vast numbers of repetitive arithmetical operations without weariness or error. If that sort of thing is the measure of intelligence, then *already* computers are far more intelligent than we are. It is because they surpass us so greatly that we use them in a million different ways and know that our economy would fall apart if they all stopped working at once.

But such computer ability is not the only measure of intelligence. In fact, we consider that ability of so little value that no matter how quick a computer is and how impressive its solutions, we see it only as an overgrown slide rule with no true intelligence at all. What the human specialty seems to be, as far as intelligence is concerned, is the ability to see problems as a whole, to grasp solutions through intuition or insight; to see new combinations; to be able to make extraordinarily perceptive and creative guesses. Can't we program a computer to do the same thing? Not likely, for we don't know how *we* do it.

It would seem, then, that computers should get better and better in their variety of point-by-point, short-focus intelligence, and that human beings (thanks to increasing knowledge and understanding of the brain and the growing technology of genetic engineering) may improve in their own variety of whole-problem, long-focus intelligence. Each variety of intelligence has its advantages and, in combination, human intelligence and computer intelligence—each filling in the gaps and compensating for the weaknesses of the other—can advance far more rapidly than either one could alone. It will not be a case of competing and replacing at all, but of intelligences together, working more efficiently than either alone within the laws of nature.

MY
ROBOTS

■

I wrote my first robot story, "Robbie," in May of 1939, when I was only nineteen years old.

What made it different from robot stories that had been written earlier was that I was determined *not* to make my robots symbols. They were *not* to be symbols of humanity's overweening arrogance. They were *not* to be examples of human ambitions trespassing on the domain of the Almighty. They were *not* to be a new Tower of Babel requiring punishment.

Nor were the robots to be symbols of minority groups. They were *not* to be pathetic creatures that were unfairly persecuted so that I could make Aesopic statements about Jews, Blacks or any other mistreated members of society. Naturally, I was bitterly opposed to such mistreatment and I made that plain in numerous stories and essays—but *not* in my robot stories.

In that case, what *did* I make my robots?—I made them engineering devices. I made them tools. I made them machines to serve human ends. And I made them objects with built-in safety features. In other words, I set it up so that a robot *could not* kill his creator, and having outlawed that heavily overused plot, I was free to consider other, more rational consequences.

Since I began writing my robot stories in 1939, I did not mention computerization in their connection. The electronic computer had not yet been invented and I did not foresee it. I did foresee, however, that the brain had to be electronic in some fashion. However, "electronic" didn't seem futuristic enough. The positron—a subatomic particle exactly like the electron but of opposite electric charge—had been discovered only four years before I wrote my first robot story. It sounded very science fictional indeed, so I gave my robots "positronic brains" and imagined their thoughts to consist of flashing streams of positrons, coming into existence, then going out of existence almost immediately. These stories that I wrote were therefore called "the positronic robot series," but there was no greater significance than what I have just described to the use of positrons rather than electrons.

At first, I did not bother actually systematizing, or putting into words, just what the safeguards were that I imagined to be built into my robots. From the very start, though, since I wasn't going to have it possible for a robot to kill its creator, I had to stress that robots could not harm human beings; that this was an ingrained part of the makeup of their positronic brains.

Thus, in the very first printed version of "Robbie," I had a character refer to a robot as follows: "He just can't help being faithful and loving and kind. He's a machine, *made so*."

After writing "Robbie," which John Campbell, of *Astounding Science Fiction*, rejected, I went on to other robot stories which Campbell accepted. On December 23, 1940, I came to him with an idea for a mind-reading robot (which later became "Liar!") and John was dissatisfied with my explanations of why the robot behaved as it did. He wanted the safeguard specified precisely so that we could understand the robot. Together, then, we worked out what came to be known as the "Three Laws of Robotics." The concept was mine, for it was obtained out of the stories I had already written, but the actual wording (if I remember correctly) was beaten out then and there by the two of us.

The Three Laws were logical and made sense. To begin with, there was the question of safety, which had been foremost in my mind when I began to write stories about *my* robots. What's more I was aware of the fact that even without actively attempting to do harm, one could quietly, by doing nothing, allow harm to come. What was in my mind was Arthur Hugh Clough's cynical "The Latest Decalog," in which the Ten Commandments are rewritten in deeply satirical Machiavellian fashion. The one item most frequently quoted is: "Thou shalt not kill, but needst not strive / Officiously to keep alive."

For that reason I insisted that the First Law (safety) had to be in two parts and it came out this way:

1. A robot may not injure a human being, or, through inaction, allow a human being to come to harm.

Having got that out of the way, we had to pass on to the second law (service). Naturally, in giving the robot the built-in necessity to follow orders, you couldn't forfeit the overall concern of safety. The Second Law had to read as follows, then:

2. A robot must obey the orders given it by human beings except where such orders would conflict with the First Law.

And finally, we had to have a third law (prudence). A robot was bound to be an expensive machine and it must not needlessly be damaged or destroyed. Naturally, this must not be used as a way of compromising either safety or service. The Third Law, therefore, had to read as follows:

3. A robot must protect its own existence, as long as such protection does not conflict with the First or Second Laws.

Of course, these laws are expressed in words, which is an imperfection. In the positronic brain, they are competing positronic potentials that are best expressed in terms of advanced mathematics (which is well beyond my ken, I assure you). However, even so, there are clear ambiguities.

What constitutes "harm" to a human being? Must a robot obey orders given it by a child, by a madman, by a malevolent human being? Must a robot give up its own expensive and useful existence to prevent a trivial harm to an unimportant human being? What is trivial and what is unimportant?

These ambiguities are not shortcomings as far as a writer is concerned. If the Three Laws were perfect and unambiguous there would be no room for stories. It is in the nooks and crannies of the ambiguities that all one's plots can lodge, and which provide a foundation, if you'll excuse the pun, for *Robot City*.

I did not specifically state the Three Laws in words in "Liar!" which appeared in the May 1941 *Astounding*. I did do so, however, in my next robot story, "Runaround," which appeared in the March 1942 *Astounding*. In that issue on line seven of page one hundred, I have a character say, "Now, look, let's start with the three fundamental Rules of Robotics," and I then quote them. That incidentally, as far as I or anyone else has been able to tell, represents the first appearance in print of the word "robotics"—which, apparently, I invented.

Since then, I have never had occasion, over a period of over forty years during which I wrote many stories and novels dealing with robots, to be forced to modify the Three Laws. However, as time passed, and as my robots advanced in complexity and versatility, I did feel that they would have to reach for something still higher. Thus, in *Robots and Empire*, a novel published by Doubleday in 1985, I talked about the possibility that a sufficiently advanced robot might feel it necessary to consider the prevention of harm to humanity generally as taking precedence over the prevention of harm to an individual. This I called the "Zeroth Law of Robotics," but I'm still working on that.

My invention of the Three Laws of Robotics is probably my most important contribution to science fiction. They are widely quoted outside the field, and no history of robotics could possibly be complete without mention of the Three Laws. In 1985, John Wiley and Sons published a huge tome,

Handbook of Industrial Robotics, edited by Shimon Y. Nof, and, at the editor's request, I wrote an introduction concerning the Three Laws.

Now it is understood that science fiction writers generally have created a pool of ideas that form a common stock into which all writers can dip. For that reason, I have never objected to other writers who have used robots that obey the Three Laws. I have, rather, been flattered and, honestly, modern science fictional robots can scarcely appear without those Laws.

However, I have firmly resisted the actual quotation of the Three Laws by any other writer. Take the Laws for granted, is my attitude in this matter, but don't recite them. The concepts are everyone's but the words are mine.

· THE LAWS · OF HUMANICS

·

My first three robot novels were, essentially, murder mysteries, with Elijah Baley as the detective. Of these first three, the second novel, *The Naked Sun*, was a locked-room mystery, in the sense that the murdered person was found with no weapon on the site and yet no weapon could have been removed either.

I managed to produce a satisfactory solution but I did not do that sort of thing again.

The fourth robot novel, *Robots and Empire*, was not primarily a murder mystery. Elijah Baley had died a natural death at a good, old age, the book veered toward the Foundation universe so that it was clear that both my notable series, the Robot series and the Foundation series, were going to be fused into a broader whole. (No, I didn't do this for some arbitrary reason. The necessities arising out of writing sequels in the 1980s to tales originally written in the 1940s and 1950s forced my hand.)

In *Robots and Empire*, my robot character, Giskard, of whom I was very fond, began to concern himself with "the Laws of Humanics," which, I indicated, might eventually serve as the basis for the science of psychohistory, which plays such a large role in the Foundation series.

Strictly speaking, the Laws of Humanics should be a description, in concise form, of how human beings actually behave. No such description exists, of course. Even psychologists, who study the matter scientifically (at least, I hope they do) cannot present any "laws" but can only make lengthy and diffuse descriptions of what people seem to do. And none of them are prescriptive. When a psychologist says that people respond in this way to a stimulus of that sort, he merely means that some do at some times. Others may do it at other times, or may not do it at all.

If we have to wait for actual laws prescribing human behavior in order to establish psychohistory (and surely we must) then I suppose we will have to wait a long time.

Well, then, what are we going to do about the Laws of Humanics? I suppose what we can do is to start in a very small way, and then later slowly build it up, if we can.

Thus, in *Robots and Empire*, it is a robot, Giskard, who raises the question of the Laws of Humanics. Being a robot, he must view everything from the standpoint of the Three Laws of Robotics—these robotic laws being truly prescriptive, since robots are forced to obey them and cannot disobey them.

The Three Laws of Robotics are:

1—A robot may not injure a human being, or, through inaction, allow a human being to come to harm.

2—A robot must obey the orders given it by human beings except where such orders would conflict with the First Law.

3—A robot must protect its own existence as long as such protection does not conflict with the First or Second Law.

Well, then, it seems to me that a robot could not help but think that human beings ought to behave in such a way as to make it easier for robots to obey those laws.

In fact, it seems to me that ethical human beings should be as anxious to make life easier for robots as the robots themselves would. I took up this matter in my story "The

Bicentennial Man," which was published in 1976. In it, I had a human character say in part:

"If a man has the right to give a robot any order that does not involve harm to a human being, he should have the decency never to give a robot any order that involves harm to a robot, unless human safety absolutely requires it. With great power goes great responsibility, and if the robots have Three Laws to protect men, is it too much to ask that men have a law or two to protect robots?"

For instance, the First Law is in two parts. The first part, "A robot may not injure a human being," is absolute and nothing need be done about that. The second part, "or, through inaction, allow a human being to come to harm," leaves things open a bit. A human being might be about to come to harm because of some event involving an inanimate object. A heavy weight might be likely to fall upon him, or he may slip and be about to fall into a lake, or any one of uncountable other misadventures of the sort may be involved. Here the robot simply must try to rescue the human being; pull him from under, steady him on his feet and so on. Or a human being might be threatened by some form of life other than human—a lion, for instance—and the robot must come to his defense.

But what if harm to a human being is threatened by the action of another human being? There a robot must decide what to do. Can he save one human being without harming the other? Or if there must be harm, what course of action must he pursue to make it minimal?

It would be a lot easier for the robot, if human beings were as concerned about the welfare of human beings, as robots are expected to be. And, indeed, any reasonable human code of ethics would instruct human beings to care for each other and to do no harm to each other. Which is, after all, the mandate that humans gave robots. Therefore the First Law of Humanics from the robots' standpoint is:

1—A human being may not injure another human being, or, through inaction, allow a human being to come to harm.

If this law is carried through, the robot will be left guarding the human being from misadventures with inanimate objects and with non-human life, something which poses no ethical dilemmas for it. Of course, the robot must still guard against harm done a human being *unwittingly* by another human being. It must also stand ready to come to the aid of a threatened human being, if another human being on the scene simply cannot get to the scene of action quickly enough. But then, even a robot may *unwittingly* harm a human being, and even a robot may not be fast enough to get to the scene of action in time or skilled enough to take the necessary action. Nothing is perfect.

That brings us to the Second Law of Robotics, which compels a robot to obey all orders given it by human beings except where such orders would conflict with the First Law. This means that human beings can give robots any order without limitation as long as it does not involve harm to a human being.

But then a human being might order a robot to do something impossible, or give it an order that might involve a robot in a dilemma that would do damage to its brain. Thus, in my short story "Liar!," published in 1940, I had a human being deliberately put a robot into a dilemma where its brain burnt out and ceased to function.

We might even imagine that as a robot becomes more intelligent and self-aware, its brain might become sensitive enough to undergo harm if it were forced to do something needlessly embarrassing or undignified. Consequently, the Second Law of Humanics would be:

2—A human being must give orders to a robot that preserve robotic existence, unless such orders cause harm or discomfort to human beings.

The Third Law of Robotics is designed to protect the robot, but from the robotic view it can be seen that it does not go far enough. The robot must sacrifice its existence if the First or Second Law makes that necessary. Where the First Law is concerned, there can be no argument. A robot must give up its existence if that is the only way it can avoid doing harm to a human being or can prevent harm from coming to a human being. If we admit the innate superiority of any human being to any robot (which is something I am a little reluctant to admit, actually), then this is inevitable.

On the other hand, must a robot give up its existence merely in obedience to an order that might be trivial, or even malicious? In "The Bicentennial Man," I have some hoodlums deliberately order a robot to take itself apart for the fun of watching that happen. The Third Law of Humanics must therefore be:

3—A human being must not harm a robot, or, through inaction, allow a robot to come to harm, unless such harm is needed to keep a human being from harm or to allow a vital order to be carried out.

Of course, we cannot enforce these laws as we can the Robotic Laws. We cannot design human brains as we design robot brains. It is, however, a beginning, and I honestly think that if we are to have power over intelligent robots, we must feel a corresponding responsibility for them, as the human character in my story "The Bicentennial Man" said.

CYBERNETIC ORGANISM

.

A robot is a robot and an organism is an organism.

An organism, as we all know, is built up of cells. From the molecular standpoint, its key molecules are nucleic acids and proteins. These float in a watery medium, and the whole has a bony support system. It is useless to go on with the description, since we are all familiar with organisms and since we are examples of them ourselves.

A robot, on the other hand, is (as usually pictured in science fiction) an object, more or less resembling a human being, constructed out of strong, rust-resistant metal. Science fiction writers are generally chary of describing the robotic details too closely since they are not usually essential to the story and the writers are generally at a loss how to do so.

The impression one gets from the stories, however, is that a robot is wired, so that it has wires through which electricity flows rather than tubes through which blood flows. The ultimate source of power is either unnamed, or is assumed to partake of the nature of nuclear power.

What of the robotic brain?

When I wrote my first few robot stories in 1939 and 1940, I imagined a "positronic brain" of a spongy type of platinum-iridium alloy. It was platinum-iridium because that is a particularly inert metal and is least likely to undergo chemical changes. It was spongy so that it would offer an enormous surface on which electrical patterns could be formed and un-formed. It was "positronic" because four years before my first robot story, the positron had been discovered as a reverse kind of electron, so that "positronic" in place of "electronic" had a delightful science-fiction sound.

Nowadays, of course, my positronic platinum-iridium brain is hopelessly archaic. Even ten years after its invention it became outmoded. By the end of the 1940s, we came to realize that a robot's brain must be a kind of computer. Indeed, if a robot were to be as complex as the robots in my most recent novels, the robot brain-computer must be every bit as complex as the human brain. It must be made of tiny microchips no larger than, and as complex as, brain cells.

But now let us try to imagine something that is neither organism nor robot, but a combination of the two. Perhaps we can think of it as an organism-robot or "orbot." That would clearly be a poor name, for it is only "robot" with the first two letters transposed. To say "orgabot," instead, is to be stuck with a rather ugly word.

We might call it a robot-organism, or a "robotanism," which, again, is ugly or "roborg." To my ears, "roborg" doesn't sound bad, but we can't have that. Something else has arisen.

The science of computers was given the name "cybernetics" by Norbert Weiner a generation ago, so that if we consider something that is part robot and part organism and remember that a robot is cybernetic in nature, we might think of the mixture as a "cybernetic organism," or a "cyborg." In fact, that is the name that has stuck and is used.

To see what a cyborg might be, let's try starting with a human organism and moving toward a robot; and when we are quite done with that, let's start with a robot and move toward a human being.

To move from a human organism toward a robot, we must begin replacing portions of the human organism with robotic parts. We already do that in some ways. For instance, a good percentage of the original material of my teeth is now metallic, and metal is, of course, the robotic substance *par excellence*.

The replacements don't have to be metallic, of course. Some parts of my teeth are now ceramic in nature, and can't be told at a glance from the natural dentine. Still, even though dentine is ceramic in appearance and even, to an extent, in chemical structure, it was originally laid down by living material and bears the marks of its origin. The ceramic that has replaced the dentine shows no trace of life, now or ever.

We can go further. My breastbone, which had to be split longitudinally in an operation a few years back is now held together by metallic staples, which have remained in place ever since. My sister-in-law has an artificial hip-joint replacement. There are people who have artificial arms or legs and such non-living limbs are being designed, as time passes on, to be ever more complex and useful. There are people who have lived for days and even months with artificial hearts, and many more people who live for years with pacemakers.

We can imagine, little by little, this part and that part of the human being replaced by inorganic materials and engineering devices. Is there any part which we would find difficult to replace, even in imagination?

I don't think anyone would hesitate there. Replace every part of the human being but one—the limbs, the heart, the liver, the skeleton, and so on—and the product would remain human. It would be a human being with artificial parts, but it would be a human being.

But what about the brain?

Surely, if there is one thing that makes us human it is the brain. If there is one thing that makes us a human *individual*, it is the intensely complex makeup, the emotions, the learning, the memory content of our particular brain. You can't simply replace a brain with a thinking device off some factory shelf. You have to put in something that incorporates all that a natural brain has learned, that possesses all its memory, and that mimics its exact pattern of working.

An artificial limb might not work exactly like a natural one, but might still serve the purpose. The same might be true of an artificial lung, kidney, or liver. An artificial brain, however, must be the *precise* replica of the brain it replaces, or the human being in question is no longer the same human being.

It is the brain, then, that is the sticking point in going from human organism to robot.

And the reverse?

In "The Bicentennial Man," I described the passage of my robot-hero, Andrew Martin, from robot to man. Little by little, he had himself changed, till his every visible part was human in appearance. He displayed an intelligence that was increasingly equivalent (or even superior) to that of a man. He was an artist, a historian, a scientist, an administrator. He forced the passage of laws guaranteeing robotic rights, and achieved respect and admiration in the fullest degree.

Yet at no point could he make himself accepted as a *man*. The sticking point, here, too, was his robotic brain. He found that he had to deal with that before the final hurdle could be overcome.

Therefore, we come down to the dichotomy, body and brain. The ultimate cyborgs are those in which the body and brain don't match. That means we can have two classes of complete cyborgs:

a) a robotic brain in a human body, or

b) a human brain in a robotic body.

We can take it for granted that in estimating the worth of a human being (or a robot, for that matter) we judge first by superficial appearance.

I can very easily imagine a man seeing a woman of superlative beauty and gazing in awe and wonder at the sight. "What a beautiful woman," he will say, or think, and he could easily imagine himself in love with her on the spot. In romances, I believe that happens as a matter of routine. And, of course, a woman seeing a man of superlative beauty is surely likely to react in precisely the same way.

If you fall in love with a striking beauty, you are scarcely likely to spend much time asking if she (or he, of course) has any brains, or possesses a good character, or has good judgment or kindness or warmth. If you find out eventually that good looks are the person's only redeeming quality, you are liable to make excuses and continue to be guided, for a time at least, by the conditioned reflex of erotic response. Eventually, of course, you will tire of good looks without content, but who knows how long that will take?

On the other hand, a person with a large number of good qualities who happened to be distinctly plain might not be likely to entangle you in the first place unless you were intelligent enough to see those good qualities so that you might settle down to a lifetime of happiness.

What I am saying, then, is that a cyborg with a robotic brain in a human body is going to be accepted by most, if not all, people as a human being; while a cyborg with a human brain in a robotic body is going to be accepted by most, if not all, people as a robot. You are, after all—at least to most people—what you seem to be.

These two diametrically opposed cyborgs will not, however, pose a problem to human beings to the same degree.

Consider the robotic brain in the human body and ask why the transfer should be made. A robotic brain is better off in a robotic body since a human body is far the more fragile of the two. You might have a young and stalwart human body in which the brain has been damaged by trauma and disease, and you might think, "Why waste that magnificent human body? Let's put a robotic brain in it so that it can live out its life."

If you were to do that, the human being that resulted would not be the original. It would be a different individual human being. You would not be conserving an individual but merely a specific mindless body. And a human body, however fine, is (without the brain that goes with it) a cheap thing. Every day, half a million new bodies come into being. There is no need to save any one of them if the brain is done.

On the other hand, what about a human brain in a robotic body? A human brain doesn't last forever, but it can last up to ninety years without falling into total uselessness. It is not at all unknown to have a ninety-year-old who is still sharp, and capable of rational and worthwhile thought. And yet we also know that many a superlative mind has vanished after twenty or thirty years because the body that housed it (and was worthless in the absence of the mind) had become uninhabitable through trauma or disease. There would be a strong impulse then to transfer a perfectly good (even superior) brain into a robotic body to give it additional decades of useful life.

Thus, when we say "cyborg" we are very likely to think, just about exclusively, of a human brain in a robotic body—and we are going to think of that as a robot.

We might argue that a human mind is a human mind, and that it is the mind that counts and not the surrounding support mechanism, and we would be right. I'm sure that any rational court would decide that a human-brain cyborg would have all the legal rights of a man. He could vote, he must not be enslaved, and so on.

And yet suppose a cyborg were challenged: "Prove that you have a human brain and not a robotic brain, before I let you have human rights."

The easiest way for a cyborg to offer the proof is for him to demonstrate that he is not bound by the Three Laws of Robotics. Since the Three Laws enforce socially acceptable behavior, this means he must demonstrate that he is capable of human (i.e. nasty) behavior. The simplest and most unanswerable argument is simply to knock the challenger down, breaking his jaw in the process, since no robot could do that. (In fact, in my story "Evidence," which appeared in 1947, I use this as a way of proving someone is not a robot—but in that case there was a catch.)

But if a cyborg must continually offer violence in order to prove he has a human brain, that will not necessarily win him friends.

For that matter, even if he is accepted as human and allowed to vote and to rent hotel rooms and do all the other things human beings can do, there must nevertheless be some regulations that distinguish between him and complete human beings. The cyborg would be stronger than a man, and his metallic fists could be viewed as lethal weapons. He might still be forbidden to strike a human being, even in self-defense. He couldn't engage in various sports on an equal basis with human beings, and so on.

Ah, but need a human brain be housed in a metallic robotic body? What about housing it in a body made of ceramic and plastic and fiber so that it looks and feels like a human body—and has a human brain besides?

But you know, I suspect that the cyborg will still have his troubles. He'll be *different*. No matter how small the difference is, people will seize upon it.

We know that people who have human brains and full human bodies sometimes hate each other because of a slight difference in skin pigmentation, or a slight variation in the shape of the nose, eyes, lips, or hair.

We know that people who show no difference in any of the physical characteristics that have come to represent a cause for hatred, may yet be at daggers-drawn over matters that are not physical at all, but cultural—differences in religion, or in political outlook, or in place of birth, or in language, or in just the accent of a language.

Let's face it. Cyborgs will have their difficulties, no matter what.

THE SENSE
OF HUMOR

■

Would a robot feel a yearning to be human?

You might answer that question with a counter-question. Does a Chevrolet feel a yearning to be a Cadillac?

The counter-question makes the unstated comment that a machine has no yearnings.

But the very point is that a robot is not quite a machine, at least in potentiality. A robot is a machine that is made as much like a human being as it is possible to make it, and somewhere there may be a boundary line that may be crossed.

We can apply this to life. An earthworm doesn't yearn to be a snake; a hippopotamus doesn't yearn to be an elephant. We have no reason to think such creatures are self-conscious and dream of something more than they are. Chimpanzees and gorillas seem to be self-aware, but we have no reason to think that they yearn to be human.

A human being, however, dreams of an afterlife and yearns to become one of the angels. Somewhere, life crossed a boundary line. At some point a species arose that was not only aware of itself but had the capacity to be dissatisfied with itself.

Perhaps a similar boundary line will someday be crossed in the construction of robots.

But if we grant that a robot might someday aspire to humanity, in what way would he so aspire? He might aspire to the possession of the legal and social status that human beings are born to. That was the theme of my story "The Bicentennial Man," and in his pursuit of such status, my robot-hero was willing to give up all his robotic qualities, one by one, right down to his immortality.

That story, however, was more philosophical than realistic. What is there about a human being that a robot might properly envy—what human physical or mental *characteristic*? No sensible robot would envy human fragility, or human incapacity to withstand mild changes in the environment, or human need for sleep, or aptitude for the trivial mistake, or tendency to infectious and degenerative disease, or incapacitation through illogical storms of emotion.

He might, more properly, envy the human capacity for friendship and love, his wide-ranging curiosity, his eagerness for experience. I would like to suggest, though, that a robot who yearned for humanity might well find that what he would most want to understand, and most frustratingly *fail* to understand, would be the human sense of humor.

The sense of humor is by no means universal among human beings, though it does cut across all cultures. I have known many people who didn't laugh, but who looked at you in puzzlement or perhaps disdain if you tried to be funny. I need go no further than my father, who routinely shrugged off my cleverest sallies as unworthy of the attention of a serious man. (Fortunately, my mother laughed at all my jokes, and most uninhibitedly, or I might have grown up emotionally stunted.)

The curious thing about the sense of humor, however, is that, as far as I have observed, no human being will *admit* to its lack. People might admit they hate dogs and dislike children, they might cheerfully own up to cheating on their income tax or on their marital partner as a matter of right, and might not object to being considered inhumane or dishonest, through the simple expediency of switching adjectives and calling themselves realistic or businesslike.

However, accuse them of lacking a sense of humor and they will deny it hotly every time, no matter how openly and how often they display such a lack. My father, for instance, always maintained that he had a keen sense of humor and would prove it as soon as he heard a joke worth laughing at (though he never did, in my experience).

Why, then, do people object to being accused of humorlessness? My theory is that people recognize (subliminally, if not openly) that a sense of humor is typically human, more so than any other characteristic, and refuse demotion to subhumanity.

Only once did I take up the matter of a sense of humor in a science-fiction story, and that was in my story "Jokester," which first appeared in the December, 1956 issue of *Infinity Science Fiction* and which was most recently reprinted in my collection *The Best Science Fiction of Isaac Asimov* (Doubleday, 1986).

The protagonist of the story spent his time telling jokes to a computer (I quoted six of them in the course of the story). A computer, of course, is an immobile robot; or, which is the same thing, a robot is a mobile computer; so the story deals with robots and jokes. Unfortunately, the problem in the story for which a solution was sought was *not* the nature of humor, but the source of all the jokes one hears. And there is an answer, too, but you'll have to read the story for that.

However, I don't just write science fiction. I write whatever it falls into my busy little head to write, and (by some undeserved stroke of good fortune) my various publishers are under the weird impression that it is illegal not to publish any manuscript I hand them. (You can be sure that I never disabuse them of this ridiculous notion.)

Thus, when I decided to write a joke book, I did, and Houghton-Mifflin published it in 1971 under the title of *Isaac Asimov's Treasury of Humor*. In it, I told 640 jokes that I happened to have as part of my memorized repertoire. (I also have enough for a sequel to be entitled *Isaac Asimov Laughs Again*, but I can't seem to get around to writing it no matter how long I sit at the keyboard and how quickly I manipulate the keys.) I interspersed those jokes with my own theories concerning what is funny and how one makes what is funny even funnier.

Mind you, there are as many different theories of humor as there are people who write on the subject, and no two theories are alike. Some are, of course, much stupider than others, and I felt no embarrassment whatever in adding my own thoughts on the subject to the general mountain of commentary.

It is my feeling, to put it as succinctly as possible, that the one necessary ingredient in every successful joke is a sudden alteration in point of view. The more radical the alteration, the more suddenly it is demanded, the more quickly it is seen, the louder the laugh and the greater the joy.

Let me give you an example with a joke that is one of the few I made up myself:

Jim comes into a bar and finds his best friend, Bill, at a corner table gravely nursing a glass of beer and wearing a look of solemnity on his face. Jim sits down at the table and says sympathetically, "What's the matter, Bill?"

Bill sighs, and says, "My wife ran off yesterday with my best friend."

Jim says, in a shocked voice, "What are you talking about, Bill? I'm your best friend."

To which Bill answers softly, "Not anymore."

I trust you see the change in point of view. The natural supposition is that poor Bill is sunk in gloom over a tragic loss. It is only with the last three words that you realize, quite suddenly, that he is, in actual fact, delighted. And the average human male is sufficiently ambivalent about his wife (however beloved she might be) to greet this particular change in point of view with delight.

Now, if a robot is designed to have a brain that responds

to logic only (and of what use would any other kind of robot brain be to humans who are hoping to employ robots for their own purposes?), a sudden change in point of view would be hard to achieve. It would imply that the rules of logic were wrong in the first place or were capable of a flexibility that they obviously don't have. In addition, it would be dangerous to build ambivalence into a robot brain. What we want from him is decision and not the to-be-or-not-to-be of a Hamlet.

Imagine, then, telling a robot the joke I have just given you, and imagine the robot staring at you solemnly after you are done, and questioning you, thus.

Robot: "But why is Jim no longer Bill's best friend? You have not described Jim as doing anything that would cause Bill to be angry with him or disappointed in him."

You: "Well, no, it's not that Jim has done anything. It's that someone else has done something for Bill that was so wonderful, that he has been promoted over Jim's head and has instantly become Bill's new best friend."

Robot: "But who has done this?"

You: "The man who ran away with Bill's wife, of course."

Robot (after a thoughtful pause): "But that can't be so. Bill must have felt profound affection for his wife and a great sadness over her loss. Is that not how human males feel about their wives, and how they would react to their loss?"

You: "In theory, yes. However, it turns out that Bill strongly disliked his wife and was *glad* someone had run off with her."

Robot (after another thoughtful pause): "But you did not say that was so."

You: "I know. That's what makes it funny. I led you in one direction and then suddenly let you know that was the wrong direction."

Robot: "Is it funny to mislead a person?"

You (giving up): "Well, let's get on with building this house."

In fact, some jokes actually depend on the illogical responses of human beings. Consider this one:

* * *

The inveterate horse player paused before taking his place at the betting windows, and offered up a fervent prayer to his Maker.

"Blessed Lord," he murmured with mountain-moving sincerity. "I know you don't approve of my gambling, but just this once, Lord, just this once, *please* let me break even. I need the money so badly."

If you were so foolish as to tell this joke to a robot, he would immediately say, "But to break even means that he would leave the races with precisely the amount of money he had when he entered. Isn't that so?"

"Yes, that's so."

"Then, if he needs the money so badly, all he need do is not bet at all, and it would be just as though he had broken even."

"Yes, but he has this unreasoning need to gamble."

"You mean even if he loses."

"Yes."

"But that makes no sense."

"But the point of the joke is that the gambler doesn't understand this."

"You mean it's funny if a person lacks any sense of logic and is possessed of not even the simplest understanding?"

And what can you do but turn back to building the house again?

But tell me, is this so different from dealing with the ordinary humorless human being? I once told my father this joke:

Mrs. Jones, the landlady, woke up in the middle of the night because there were strange noises outside her door. She looked out, and there was Robinson, one of her boarders, forcing a frightened horse up the stairs.

She shrieked, "What are you doing, Mr. Robinson?"

He said, "Putting the horse in the bathroom."

"For goodness sake, why?"

"Well, old Higginbotham is such a wise guy. Whatever I tell him, he answers, 'I know. I know,' in such a superior way. Well, in the morning, he'll go to the bathroom and he'll come out yelling, 'There's a *horse* in the bathroom.' And I'll yawn and say, 'I know, I know.' "

And what was my father's response? He said, "Isaac, Isaac. You're a city boy, so you don't understand. You can't push a horse up the stairs if he doesn't want to go."

Personally, I thought that was funnier than the joke.

Anyway, I don't see why we should particularly want a robot to have a sense of humor, but the point is that the robot himself might want to have one—and how do we give it to him?

• ROBOTS IN • COMBINATION

•

I have been inventing stories about robots now for very nearly half a century. In that time, I have rung almost every conceivable change upon the theme.

Mind you, it was not my intention to compose an encyclopedia of robot nuances; it was not even my intention to write about them for half a century. It just happened that I survived that long and maintained my interest in the concept. And it also just happened that in attempting to think of new story ideas involving robots, I ended up thinking about nearly everything.

For instance, in the sixth volume of the *Robot City* series, there are the "chemfets," which have been introduced into the hero's body in order to replicate and, eventually, give him direct psycho-electronic control over the core computer, and hence all the robots of Robot City.

Well, in my book *Foundation's Edge* (Doubleday, 1982), my hero, Golan Trevize, before taking off in a spaceship, makes contact with an advanced computer by placing his hands on an indicated place on the desk before him.

"And as he and the computer held hands, their thinking merged . . .

". . . he saw the room with complete clarity—not just in the direction in which he was looking, but all around and above and below.

"He saw every room in the spaceship, and he saw outside as well. The sun had risen . . . but he could look at it directly without being dazzled . . .

"He felt the gentle wind and its temperature, and the sounds of the world about him. He detected the planet's magnetic field and the tiny electrical charges on the wall of the ship.

"He became aware of the controls of the ship . . . He knew . . . that if he wanted to lift the ship, or turn it, or accelerate, or make use of any of its abilities, the process was the same as that of performing the analogous process to his body. He had but to use his will."

That was as close as I could come to picturing the result of a mind-computer interface, and now, in connection with this new book, I can't help thinking of it further.

I suppose that the first time human beings learned how to form an interface between the human mind and another sort of intelligence was when they tamed the horse and learned how to use it as a form of transportation. This reached its highest point when human beings rode horses directly, and when a pull at a rein, the touch of a spur, a squeeze of the knees, or just a cry, could make the horse react in accordance with the human will.

It is no wonder that primitive Greeks seeing horsemen invade the comparatively broad Thessalian plains (the part of Greece most suitable to horsemanship) thought they were seeing a single animal with a human torso and a horse's body. Thus was invented the centaur.

Again, there are "trick drivers." There are expert "stunt men" who can make an automobile do marvelous things. One might expect that a New Guinea native who had never seen or heard of an automobile before might believe that such stunts were being carried through by a strange and monstrous living organism that had, as part of its structure, a portion with a human appearance within its stomach.

But a person plus a horse is but an imperfect fusion of intelligence, and a person plus an automobile is but an extension of human muscles by mechanical linkages. A horse can easily disobey signals, or even run away in uncontrollable panic. And an automobile can break down or skid at an inconvenient moment.

The fusion of human and computer, however, ought to be a much closer approach to the ideal. It may be an extension of the mind itself as I tried to make plain in *Foundation's Edge*, a multiplication and intensification of sense-perception, an incredible extension of the will.

Under such circumstances, might not the fusion represent, in a very real sense, a single organism, a kind of cybernetic "centaur"? And once such a union is established, would the human fraction wish to break it? Would he not feel such a break to be an unbearable loss and be unable to live with the impoverishment of mind and will he would then have to face? In my novel, Golan Trevize could break away from the computer at will and suffered no ill effects as a result, but perhaps that is not realistic.

Another issue that appears now and then in the *Robot City* series concerns the interaction of robot and robot.

This has not played a part in most of my stories, simply because I generally had a single robot character of importance in any given story and I dealt entirely with the matter of the interaction between that single robot and various human beings.

Consider robots in combination.

The First Law states that a robot cannot injure a human being or, through inaction, allow a human being to come to harm.

But suppose two robots are involved, and that one of them, through inadvertence, lack of knowledge, or special circumstances, is engaged in a course of action (quite innocently) that will clearly injure a human being—and suppose the second robot, with greater knowledge or insight, is aware of this. Would he not be required by the First Law to stop the first robot from committing the injury? If there were no other way, would he not be required by the First Law to destroy the first robot without hesitation or regret?

Thus, in my book *Robots and Empire* (Doubleday, 1985), a robot is introduced to whom human beings have been defined as those speaking with a certain accent. The heroine of the book does not speak with that accent and therefore the robot feels free to kill her. That robot is promptly destroyed by a second robot.

The situation is similar for the Second Law, in which robots are forced to obey orders given them by human beings provided those orders do not violate the First Law.

If, of two robots, one through inadvertence or lack of understanding does not obey an order, the second must either carry through the order itself, or force the first to do so.

Thus, in an intense scene in *Robots and Empire*, the villainess gives one robot a direct order. The robot hesitates because the order may cause harm to the heroine. For a while, then, there is a confrontation in which the villainess reinforces her own order while a second robot tries to reason the first robot into a greater realization of the harm that will be done to the heroine. Here we have a case where one robot urges another to obey the Second Law in a truer manner, and to withstand a human being in so doing.

It is the Third Law, however, that brings up the knottiest problem where robots in combination are concerned.

The Third Law states that a robot must protect its own existence, where that is consistent with the First and Second Laws.

But what if two robots are concerned? Is each merely concerned with its own existence, as a literal reading of the Third Law would make it seem? Or would each robot feel the need for helping the other maintain its own existence?

As I said, this problem never arose with me as long as I

dealt with only one robot per story. (Sometimes there were other robots but they were distinctly subsidiary characters— merely spear-carriers, so to speak.)

However, first in *The Robots of Dawn* (Doubleday, 1983), and then in its sequel *Robots and Empire*, I had *two* robots of equal importance. One of these was R. Daneel Olivaw, a humaniform robot (who could not easily be told from a human being) who had earlier appeared in *The Caves of Steel* (Doubleday, 1954), and in its sequel, *The Naked Sun* (Doubleday, 1957). The other was R. Giskard Reventlov, who had a more orthodox metallic appearance. Both robots were advanced to the point where their minds were of human complexity.

It was these two robots who were engaged in the struggle with the villainess, the Lady Vasilia. It was Giskard who (such were the exigencies of the plot) was being ordered by Vasilia to leave the service of Gladia (the heroine) and enter her own. And it was Daneel who tenaciously argued the point that Giskard ought to remain with Gladia. Giskard has the ability to exert a limited mental control over human beings, and Daneel points out that Vasilia ought to be controlled for Gladia's safety. He even argues the good of humanity in the abstract ("the Zeroth Law") in favor of such an action.

Daneel's arguments weaken the effect of Vasilia's orders, but not sufficiently. Giskard is made to hesitate, but cannot be forced to take action.

Vasilia, however, decides that Daneel is too dangerous; if he continues to argue, he might force Giskard his way. She therefore orders her own robots to inactivate Daneel and further orders Daneel not to resist. Daneel must obey the order and Vasilia's robots advance to the task.

It is then that Giskard acts. Her four robots are inactivated and Vasilia herself crumples into a forgetful sleep. Later Daneel asks Giskard to explain what happened.

Giskard says, "When she ordered the robots to dismantle you, friend Daneel, and showed a clear emotion of pleasure at the prospect, your need, added to what the concept of the

Zeroth Law had already done, superseded the Second Law and rivaled the First Law. It was the combination of the Zeroth Law, psychohistory, my loyalty to Lady Gladia, and your need that dictated my action."

Daneel now argues that his own need (he being merely a robot) ought not to have influenced Giskard at all. Giskard obviously agrees, yet he says:

"It is a strange thing, friend Daneel. I do not know how it came about . . . At the moment when the robots advanced toward you and Lady Vasilia expressed her savage pleasure, my positronic pathway pattern re-formed in an anomalous fashion. For a moment, I thought of you—as a human being—and I reacted accordingly."

Daneel said, "That was wrong."

Giskard said, "I know that. And yet—and yet, if it were to happen again, I believe the same anomalous change would take place again."

And Daneel cannot help but feel that if the situation were reversed, he, too, would act in the same way.

In other words, the robots had reached a stage of complexity where they had begun to lose the distinction between robots and human beings, where they could see each other as "friends," and have the urge to save each other's existence.

THE ULTIMATE IN
SCIENCE FICTION AND FANTASY!

From magical tales of distant worlds to stories of
technological advances beyond the grasp of man, Penguin has
everything you need to stretch your imagination to its limits.

penguin.com

ACE
Get the latest information on favorites like
William Gibson, T.A. Barron, Brian Jacques,
Ursula K. Le Guin, Sharon Shinn, Charlaine Harris,
Patricia Briggs, and Marjorie M. Liu,
as well as updates on the best new authors.

ROC
Escape with Jim Butcher, Harry Turtledove, Anne Bishop,
S.M. Stirling, Simon R. Green, E.E. Knight, Kat Richardson,
Rachel Caine, and many others—plus news on the
latest and hottest in science fiction and fantasy.

DAW
Patrick Rothfuss, Mercedes Lackey, Kristen Britain,
Tanya Huff, Tad Williams, C.J. Cherryh, and many more—
DAW has something to satisfy the cravings of any
science fiction and fantasy lover.
Also visit dawbooks.com.

Get the best of science fiction and fantasy
at your fingertips!